ARU'S REALM

Aru's Realm by Harriet Arden Byrd
Bibliogoblin Publications
habyrd.com
© 2020 Harriet Arden Byrd

This story was completed a few years ago. Any similarities to people or events since 2016 is coincidental. Or perhaps slightly prophetic.

Cover: *Saltator Mundi* by Catherine Wesley
Illustrations by Catherine Wesley
Interior design by Keziah Wesley
ISBN: 978-1-7342084-1-2

ARU'S REALM

H. A. Byrd

Bibliogoblin

CONTENTS

I. TRAVEL

A SMELL of damp filled the cold hour before dawn—tree bark and moldering leaves, with a hint of mushrooms. Most of the ravens remained dormant on the cliffs, but a young female noticed movement under the fog below. Her launch and swoop woke several other birds, who followed her.

Hooves clomped on the road. Shadows passing beneath the dense pine branches took shape as a caravan of wagons. Living-wagons, these were. This was worth a look. One rarely saw wagons on this road, much less old-style traveling homes. Built up from between wooden wheels, their sides sloped slightly outward to meet the eaves of arched roofs. These vans were large, and well crafted. Judging by the state of the horses, they'd been traveling all night. Yet no lanterns shone.

The ravens' broad wings brought them down to circle and snoop as they so loved to do, and details were surrendered by the dim light. All the wagons were of bare weathered wood, grey somber things that creaked and swayed as the tall narrow wheels bumped over stones and roots. Shuttered windows were flanked by household items swinging from hooks: skillets and dustpans, twig brooms, musty garlic braids, chimney brushes, coal spades, and pitch-sealed buckets. The driver of the last wagon in the line pulled up the horse and cocked his head to listen for something behind.

"Don't tell me!" he growled. His voice sounded husky. He licked his lips. Gripping the porch bracket for leverage, he peered around the corner before he dropped the reins onto the footboard and rolled himself a cigarette. The wagon waited, horse blowing and pawing, while the others faded away into the mist along the track.

Noises from behind him on the road grew louder as someone approached. Swearing. Lots of cuss words. Strings of them. The source was a pale young woman in a brown silk traveling dress. She didn't look like much at the moment, rumpled and dirty and without a hat.

Aru puffed and panted through her tirade as she ran to catch up with the wagon. If those ravens hadn't alerted her she would have been left far behind. Twice she stumbled and nearly fell. Her knickers chafed, they'd gone all crooked, she tugged at them through her skirts as she hurried along. *Why can't the lead simply blow a whistle EVERYONE can hear?* she wondered. Her chest heaved, her side hurt. Once again they'd left her behind while she went to relieve herself! At last she reached the towering wagon, her lungs gasping for air as she looked up for a handhold.

The driver grinned. "No little adventures in the woods, Aru. Something might eat you."

Aru threw one last onslaught of teary curses at him and her feet barely touched the step-irons as he hoisted her aboard. She shoved him hard in the shoulder before squeezing behind him to disappear through the doorway. Nurphel chuckled. He finished his cigarette, sat for a moment, then grabbed the reins and clucked to the horse. The wagon lurched forward and they were off to catch up with the group.

The ravens followed for a few minutes, circling and playing in the wisp of smoke which trickled downward from the chimney pipe. Then they headed back to the roost.

Inside the shifting wagon a sleepy female voice murmured an indistinct question which contained Aru's name. The rattled young woman fumbled in the darkness to remove her boots, still sobbing a bit, and crawled into the lower bunk with all of her clothes still on. She didn't go right to sleep.

An hour later, an interruption of the relentless bounce and sway woke her up as the wagons stopped under some scraggly junipers by the side of the road. The company sat and ate together in the light drizzle. Aru was still ticked at Nurphel. He apologized, but it wasn't genuine. It didn't help that they all found the story funny. Aru dumped the scraps from her meal into the fire and was the first one back in the wagons and ready to go.

Only a dim grey light filled the wagon in which Aru rode, this despite sash windows and the raised crown with small side windows which ran the length of the roof. From her viewpoint on the floor, seated with her back against the door to the lower bunk, she could barely make out the designs on the curved matchboard of the ceiling.

Aru didn't need to be able to see well to identify her surroundings in the wagon. They'd been traveling for several weeks and by now she knew every crack and crevice in the narrow chamber. *It's so true what they say,* she thought. *The location of a home is the most important thing.* In this case the location certainly had a dreary impact. It was like night in this forest, no matter the time of day. Darkness crept its way to twilight and then did nothing more than return to darkness.

The cabinets towered over her, majestic and melancholy, tall narrow cupboards like spooky grandfathers from a distant era. As the caravan started to move forward again these elders began to creak and groan, complaining of their age and the passing of their glory. The wagon had been magnificent once, years ago. A cast iron stove, at one time the finest available, sat in an enameled alcove. A steel railing ran along the mantel.

The upholstery on the locker seats had worn through and only the valance remained of the original velvet bed curtains. The present curtains were of a dingy dark green wool. Aru recognized that the cabinetry was all of polished ebony, but for her the real magic lay in the chest of drawers.

She extended her hand to feel the familiar curves of the wood. Tarnished silver, the drawer pulls were wolf heads with flattened ears and fangs bared in challenge to any unauthorized person who might reach for them. Aru stood on the brink of adulthood, but she would busy herself like a young child in the shifting wagon exploring the contents of these drawers. She knew where each item was kept, but she'd open the drawers and handle them anyhow. On the left were pens and ink, a whetstone, a pocket knife, and a small tintype photograph of an old grey wolf. Other treasures included a typewriter ribbon tin filled with obsidian buttons, a pill box, old iron keys (which didn't fit anything Aru could find), and a mourning bracelet with charms made of jet. A coin purse of the tiniest onyx beads smelled like anise and was flexible and pleasing to manipulate with the fingers. A magnifying glass was usefully included in a drawer with several miniature books. Unfortunately, these books were printed in some strange language.

A noise came from behind the bed curtain, so Aru stood up and pushed it aside, peering into the duskiness. An old woman smiled up at her from under the heaps of bedding. Aru smiled back at her grandmother Auwu. She climbed up onto the edge of the bed and sat with her, not talking much because illness had taken over the frail body and the lady didn't have much energy to spare.

Aru sat with her grandmother for a long time, staring off into nothing, and eventually her gaze fell on a spider as it dangled in the corner of the window, just behind the curtain. She sat forward. "Here, I'll kill that spider for you," she said.

Auwu felt for her granddaughter's arm. "Why not leave him, Aru. He's been riding with us since we left home. Poor thing."

Aru leaned over her grandma to do it anyhow, but changed her mind. The old lady had started coughing. After helping Auwu wipe her lips with an old kerchief, Aru's thoughts returned to the spider. It really wasn't hurting anyone. Perhaps it might even eat a few of those horrid deer flies.

"Well," she said, "if it's going to ride with us, it probably should have a name."

"Yes, you're right," replied Grandmother Auwu, the effort making her cough a bit more. "But—what do you name a spider?"

"Do they make a sound?" Aru thought for a minute. "Kri-tikk. You know, the noise the big hairy ones make when scratching around in caves. Kritikk-kritikk-kritikk."

The grandmother smiled. "Kritikk he is, then." She fell back to sleep.

Aru watched her sleeping for a while, and then she put on her coat and went out. She jumped down to trot along beside the horse and exercise her restless legs until the company made camp.

The travelers' caravan consisted of several living-wagons, two small tilt carts, and an old hearse. The window glass of the hearse had been removed years ago. After its life as a funerary vehicle the thing had been used by several owners for the hauling of various cargoes. It was a heavy carriage, normally pulled by two horses. The family was now on the way up to the summer hunting camp and the hearse carried all the weighty oilskin tents, so an auxiliary cart horse was in harness.

The night's lengthy trek began to show both in the horses of the wagon train and in those who traveled beside them. Stumbles became more frequent. The fog had lifted a bit but it still obscured a view of any distance. These towering woods held scant forage for draft horses; often it would take hours to find a suitable camp. The horses were growing thin. Tempers also.

At last a shout from somewhere up front brought the wagons to a halt. In a matter of minutes the animals were unhitched, buckets were filled from the creek, and a couple of tents had been pitched in the shadows of the glade. Aru grabbed Pullka's lead rope as soon as the harness was off and found the best grazing spot she could. With the old mare staked out, her daughter and the other horses would stay around. Aru gave the mare water, and then slipped her some molasses bread she'd saved for her from her own meal. She knew how much the old girl loved molasses. Next, Aru gave all the horses grain. Her other chore was to make tea for everyone. She filled the great iron kettle and hung it on the tripod as soon as the fire had some coals.

The clan gathered for their simple tradition of fermented tea and some tough peppered jerky before turning in. The two elders present were furnished with chairs but the rest sat on logs or on coarse blankets spread on the ground. Only old Auwu and a sick child remained inside the wagons. The damp wood made a smoky fire, it couldn't be helped, and as the wind kept changing no way might be found to avoid the wandering smoke.

"At least we'll be well preserved!" grumbled the grey-haired woman crouching next to Aru. She blew on her steaming tea.

The conversation was formal, ritualized, and the speakers addressed each other as Brother and Sister. Most of them actually were brothers or sisters, or if not, then aunts or uncles. Vorffe sat across the fire from Aru, chewing tobacco. His wife was next to him, and a couple of their half-grown daughters. A big man, he didn't tolerate dissenters. Everyone feared him at least a little.

"Aru, fetch some more cups," he said.

While Aru looked for cups, poking around in the dusky interior of the wagon of the old tracker Yowffe, something spooked the horses. Aru froze. Someone was out there. She could hear strange voices.

Holding her breath, she crept over to the window and peeked with one eye between the curtains. A company of men had entered the camp. Messengers. Six of them. They were dressed splendidly, each in a black cloak of iridescent silk. They wore breeches and tight-fitted riding boots with pointed toes.

Invited to sit, the men declined. Instead they strutted about the camp while they talked, peering and poking at things as if it were their business. Most had shiny slicked-back hair, but one, younger and quite handsome, had a fashionable feathered haircut. Aru's attention was drawn to this one, but another man turned his face toward her wagon. He tilted his head and seemed to look right at her. Was that recognition in his sidelong glance? A swarthy, scary face he had, with a heavy hooked nose and piercing eyes. Aru ducked down. She backed away from the window.

The visitors spoke in harsh croaky voices, their tone insistent. An incident had occurred deep in the forest. A bull moose, a gigantic creature, had been injured by an arrow and fled south. The conversation didn't last long. A few minutes of directives and questions by both parties and then the strangers flew off in a great rush. After she was sure they were gone, Aru came out of the wagon with the cups. But no one worried about tea anymore. As he wiped the corner of his mouth with the cuff of his sleeve, Vorffe informed the others that all capable members of the group would join him in the search party immediately.

Most of the clan readied themselves. Goru, though, rose and began to clear up the dishes. "Well! Those shifty scavengers! They stole the rest of the bread!"

Nobody was particularly surprised.

For Aru, all this meant she'd be spending time in camp. It wasn't the first time this sort of thing had happened. She dreaded the waiting, alone with just the children and weaklings. She felt she should go on the hunt, but she knew Vorffe wouldn't agree. So that was that. Eyes down for several days of wasted time.

That evening she sat in the wagon with her grandmother Auwu, listening to the foreboding sounds of the forest around them. An owl called from a nearby tree. The noise of some unknown insect surrounded them, along with the chirping of what must have been several thousand crickets. Bats were out there, too. There were always bats around the wagon. Something about it seemed to attract gnats, which, in turn, attracted the bats. While Aru sat listening, and talking with Auwu, they heard the sound of wolves in the distance.

"Just sends a shiver up your spine to hear that, doesn't it," whispered the old grandmother.

"It's a beautiful sound, but so haunting,"

"They are going on and on," said Auwu. "I wouldn't want to be out there right now. Something's going to die soon."

"Well, not us, anyhow," said Aru. "We're safe as beetles in a bramble bush here in the wagon. And we'll be in Ysgarlad City before we know it. It's an easy journey from here. Painless."

Aru could not know how wrong she was.

The next evening, after a round of camp chores, Aru sat on the ground by the fusty old bender tent, helping Gruffa to keep an eye on the young ones who were playing chase and wrestling around under the wagons. Though stiff in the joints and almost blind, Gruffa never missed an errant little adventurer.

"The young have such a remarkable amount of energy," said Gruffa. "I wish you and I could borrow some of that, wouldn't that be nice?"

"Oh, yes! Oh yes it would." Aru tried to swallow her surprise. Her auntie had just spoken to her as an equal.

While she sat wondering about this, the half-grown Hirkah grew tired of holding her brother's head against the ground. She came, panting, to snuggle up against Aru. Her grey-green eyes looked up into Aru's face and then glanced at Gruffa before she blurted out her thoughts.

"How come you're a danger to us all?"

"What?" Aru stopped running her fingers through the girl's thick hair and stared down at her.

Meanwhile, Gruffa's "Shush!" quieted even the insects for a moment.

"Hirkah!" Aru exclaimed. "You can't be serious! Why would you say such a thing?"

But the elder growled a warning, and the young girl didn't dare open her mouth again. Aru knew better than to ask Gruffa about this, but she did question Hirkah later that night.

"One of the messengers said something about you," the girl whispered. "I don't know what."

"Me?"

Hirkah shrugged.

It started to rain in the wee hours. Around dawn it quieted into a light sprinkle. Aru wondered if the hunting party had made the kill, or if the ravens had been too late with their message. Moose meat could see the pack through the rest of the journey.

She felt so antsy she decided to go for a short walk up a nearby hill and see if she could find some morels or at least some inky caps. Frustrated by the shadowy half-light of the morning woods and the incessant mist that filled all the nooks, she didn't have much luck finding her mushrooms. The few she did find she gobbled up, so her sack remained empty. She sat down, feeling damp and sorry for herself, with her back against a tree. She stared at her grubby hands and then worked idly to flatten the wrinkles of the collection bag. The rain had stopped.

Aru sighed and gazed off through the trees. She couldn't imagine why the messengers would say she was a danger. *It's the way I look,* she thought. *That's what it is. Some backwoods villager we've passed, some witless bumpkin, must have started a rumor. Maybe they're right. I don't belong in this world. Maybe I'm not from here, hateful place.* She envisioned the planet, reeling and circling in the universe. Maybe it wasn't *her* planet. She started thinking about the great distances in space, the cold, the loneliness.

All at once, descending from nowhere, a sensation took hold of her.

"Oh, no. Not again," she pleaded. "Not again!"

Aru grabbed onto the exposed roots beside her and she held on tight, as if these handles could keep her from being sucked away. A wretched foreboding overwhelmed her. She stiffened and held her breath while all her sense of reality drained into nothingness.

Something wasn't right with her perception of depth; the three dimensions felt askew and the air around her seemed thick, strange, unstable somehow. All notion of who or even what she was fled away. She felt herself sliding into the void. Emptiness. There was nothing. Because nothing existed. She no longer understood what she was. What anything was.

Nameable yet unfamiliar objects surrounded her. Tree. Stone. Bush. She knew these words, but they were meaningless. Terror filled Aru. She plunged toward ceasing to exist entirely. No soul, nothing. Did anything exist at all? She didn't want the answer.

"Go away!" she screamed, to nothing there.

Then it was done. It was over.

As always, the torment left Aru as swiftly as it had come, leaving her with some shakiness, but she felt no fear at all now. After the absolute terror of a moment ago, life had gone back to normal. She headed back toward camp. She didn't know what to make of all this. She didn't understand it. It happened to her now and then, this horrible experience. That's all she knew.

Back at camp, Aru pitched in to help with the meal preparation. Strips of charred meat needed chopping, turtle beans needed mashing, and pepper pods must be opened. Aru was so busy in her work that she forgot all about her ordeal of fear. Supper came and went quickly with so few in camp. So did the cleanup. Aru and old Yowffe sat for a long time by the dying fire, sipping their tea.

Inside the wagon, Aru didn't mention anything about what had happened. Even so, only minutes went by before her grandmother asked her if she'd had one of those visions. Had she felt the Visyrn again? Aru said she had. Did it tell her anything?

"Nothing," said Aru.

Visyrn. In the old language, it meant something like "unseen" or "beyond one's grasp." She couldn't remember how she knew the name.

Grandmother Auwu had another fit of coughing. She'd been sleeping a lot these days and Aru began to worry about how much her condition might worsen before they made it to the city. Her skin tone seemed a bit dull. At least today in camp the bed lay still. No bouncing up and down. That would give her a rest.

Aru helped Auwu sit up against the pile of tapestry pillows on her bed. They talked for a while, Auwu speaking softly between small spoonfuls of prune duff. Aru didn't mention to her ailing grandma the things which the youngster had said to her, but she couldn't resist asking again why they must travel to Ysgarlad.

"I'm getting old, Aru," was her answer, "I won't be able to patch things up for you, not for much longer. Your mama got along well in the family, she knew her place. But you know you're not the way she was. You have a lot of me in you, Aru. You'll be happier in the city where there are all kinds of people. You'll see." Auwu smiled and said she was starting to feel sleepy. There wasn't room for any protest.

As Aru tucked her grandma under the covers the elder noticed something over the young woman's shoulder, in the window. She pointed.

"What is it, Grandmother?" Aru asked.

"Look, the fairy!"

As Aru turned to look, her eyes were drawn to something crawling up the off-side window. A sizeable lizard clung to the glass on the outside. With bulbous fingertips it gripped the pane. The shiny underbelly, pressed against the glass, had extraordinary hues.

"Oh my! Fairy?"

"Yes, Aru," said Grandma. "Those lizards are awfully peculiar." She paused to catch some breath. "They are charmed, somehow. Aren't they remarkable? This one spoke to me. It said it had been the pet of my niece. My sister's daughter. She lived in the east, remember? I never met her."

Aru thought Auwu must have been dreaming. She felt the old lady's forehead. Then, crossing to the window, she stroked the lizard through the glass with her finger, curious.

"Amazing." She studied the creature for a few minutes. "I saw one before, in the forest, when Mama and I were gathering blackberries. Eating spiders, if I remember. Oh—how's our friend Kritikk, I wonder?"

Aru climbed back up with her grandma and brushed the curtain of the big rear window aside to investigate. Hunting around in the shadows, she found nothing. Maybe Kritikk had finally departed. She felt a bit sad. After the preliminary visual inspection, she picked up a buttonhook and started poking it into the cracks of the window casing. She touched a dusty old cobweb and had quite a start when what looked like a dried up chunk of fly carcass suspended there unfolded into a spider, after all, and headed for the nearest crack.

"Well there you are, little stowaway," Aru whispered. She pulled the curtains closed to shut out the draft and went to bed.

A string of nightmares presented themselves. Mostly they involved being trapped somewhere in a hiding place or in her family's old cabin, and someone or a group of someones was trying to get in to kill her. All this took place between restless, wakeful periods of listening to her grandmother's labored breathing. When evening finally arrived she heard the noise of the camp being packed up. The others had returned.

A stranger was among the group now. The hunters, returning with full bellies and heavy quarters of meat, had encountered him on the road. He would be with them for a time. In these woods it proved safer to travel with a crowd, so it was customary to ask to join one.

Night fell as the caravan set out. Out of curiosity, and because she still felt restless, Aru decided that she would travel on foot rather than ride with her grandma as she ordinarily did. Her perverse interest in other people's business had her trotting just behind this old character as he waddled along. He managed to keep up with the procession despite the impressive weight of his fur coat. He wore a top hat, too, felted. Obviously, he owned land or something. It was revealed, after he had talked a while with the others, that he owned a large logging company and also had an interest in the new hydraulic power plants.

Eventually the gentleman looked around at Aru. He smiled and slowed his step so that she caught up to him. The man had a bit of a strange smell. He had friendly eyes, though, and when he said hello he told her she could call him by his nickname, Chip.

Chip gave a rather debonair impression despite his weight and his notably protruding and stained incisors. At first their conversation was mundane, but the hearse inspired the man to launch into the subject of vampires and he told a morbid tale involving missing coffins and dark ceremonies and a cavern filled with leeches. It ended with a secret revealed about a scary house on a hill. The story made Aru shiver and then she laughed. She liked this man. But he had a nervousness about him. He persisted in looking around at the other travelers as if worried about something and he continually wrung his hands or twiddled his thumbs. Aru found Chip's agitation to be somewhat contagious.

The next few nights found Aru traveling on foot. Auwu slept most of the time now and Aru needed someone to talk to. The twins also found the newcomer interesting, so the three of them would trot along with Chip or sometimes they'd all get up on the tilt cart tailgate behind the baggage. The brothers Orru and Orruhl were a couple of scoundrels, really, prone to aggression, but they could be civil when they wanted. They talked with their visitor about local woodland lore and hunting prospects, even the price of pelts. The man would invariably turn the conversation to more philosophical subjects and this is when Aru would join in. She grew to respect him and his knowledge. He certainly was brave to travel this way through the woods, old and alone as he was.

A few months previously, a terrible storm had blown through these woods and downed scores of the ancient trees. Now, in the deep of night, the wagons crossed the charred rubble of a great burn which resulted from the storm. All this time later, the sickening stench of the smoke filled one's nostrils. It clung in the throat, making breathing an effort. Everyone felt distressed from viewing the carnage but Chip was overwhelmed with grief. He didn't talk much. A darkness fell over him which calmed his nervous demeanor but left him sullen, unapproachable. The three youths kept him company anyhow. The little group took refuge up on the cart because of the ashes which, muddy and wet from the rain, stuck to their boots in great cakes of muck that made foot travel difficult.

The old man's mood sank lower as they passed miles of devastation which seemed unending. He began to mutter to himself and ramble when he spoke to the others. Aru prepared a special willow tea for him at the supper break, but he would not be cheered.

Dawn's light through heavy clouds did little to brighten the world. While the company packed up for the typical hour or so more of travel before they would sleep, Aru gathered dishes for washing. As she reached for Chip's bowl, he grabbed her arm.

His eyes were glazed over. The firm grip hurt her. His voice a strange whistle, he directed his speech right into her face. "Last of your family, Aru, you must beware. Watch for those who would govern your ways! Be mindful of who makes your choices. Doom is upon you."

He kept clutching her arm, kept staring at her, until she found her way out of the shock of the moment and pulled herself loose. "It comes for you. Doom is upon you. Doom manifest and real!" he moaned, "Mind carefully: none other than your own verities and the trickery of a jaybird will deliver you!"

She glared, then brushed herself off as if the creepiness could be shooed away like an insect that had landed on her. She walked away.

Nobody likes a dark prophecy. This new worry made Aru's burden too great. She couldn't shake the anxiety rising in her chest as she finished up her chores. What kind of madness was this? She seethed with frustration at the unfairness of the world. She banged things. She kicked things. When helping set Pullka back to harness, something distracted the horse and she wouldn't stand. Impatient with the animal's obstinance, Aru called her a rabid feist and gave her a cruel jab in the ribs. Nurphel ducked under Pullka's neck to stare at Aru with shock and tell her she was dismissed. After a small apologetic caress to the mare's soft muzzle, Aru turned and climbed blindly into the wagon.

Self-pity in full swing, she crawled up onto her grandma's bunk. Despite puffy, tearful eyes and trembling hands, Aru held back her cry so as not to wake the sleeping woman. After some time she calmed down, brooding in the half-light while smothered in her own darkness. She sat. For a while she languished in shame. There was no excuse for treating the horse in such a way. She picked a flea off the blanket and, absently, she killed it. Then, she noticed the odd sound of Auwu's breathing. Was something wrong? Those feelings of anguish that a moment ago were Aru's overwhelming reality seeped away as fear flowed in to replace them.

Aru reached for her grandmother's hand. She didn't know what to do. The breath was different, strained, something not right. Aru watched for a few minutes, listening. At last she couldn't stand it any more and she gave her grandma a gentle shove, calling her name. Auwu didn't wake. Again, Aru called her name. This time Auwu stirred, emerging from slumber into a confused state of awareness. After a moment of gathering her thoughts, Aru's grandma smiled to see her granddaughter. In the faint light her weak eyes kept her from noticing the girl's distress.

"I heard what your friend, that gentleman of industry, said to you," she told Aru.

"You heard him?"

"Mm, my darling, I suspect the whole pack heard him! A jaybird. A jaybird." Staring into the distance, she added, "Er, I wonder . . ." She grew silent. When she noticed Aru waiting, she said, "In any case, mind his words, Aru."

It took great maturity to refrain from further discussion, but Aru knew that Auwu needed peace and calm. Sometimes Aru still acted like a child, even at her age, but this was not one of those moments.

The wagons moved again. The familiar cadence of shaking and squeaking as they rolled along the road comforted Aru to some extent. She felt better with Auwu awake; things seemed all right once more. Hopefully the noisy breath, whatever that was, had passed. As the old lady drifted back to sleep, however, the disconcerting respirations returned. Aru stayed in her spot on the bed and kept careful watch.

Nervous fear made her vigilant for a while but other thoughts crept in, fuzzy memories of childhood with her grandmother and mother. These carried Aru far away, back to life in the bungalow at the edge of the wood. Shadowy memories of brighter circumstances, whispers and scattered images now, the fragrance of sarsaparilla and licorice root coming from the beer simmering in Mother's enormous kettle, the warmth from the coal in the cookstove filling the kitchen where Father showed her how to play—was it dominoes?—while Grandma sat busy at her loom. Now and then, Aru would drift back from these memories to notice the struggling breath and she'd focus on her worry again.

All at once she had a shock. Auwu's breathing had stopped. Aru's hands went to her mouth, her jaw dropped, and she stared at the silence in front of her. There. Another breath. Auwu began the heavy breathing again. Aru set her cheek against Auwu's forehead. No fever.

Sitting now like a watchful owl, the girl reached to pull the curtains shut and maintain a soft darkness to ease her grandma's sleep. She shifted the coverlet, which had started to slip off. Aru focused on each heave of breath as if she could will Auwu to be all right. While she sat listening and watching, the breathing stopped again. Aru held her own breath. After forever had passed, Auwu resumed breathing.

"Hauva!" Aru whispered as she jumped down from the bunk. "Hauva!" she called as she shoved apart the windows of the door.

Nurphel was up in front, at Pullka's head. He looked up, and when he caught Aru's expression he pulled up the horse.

"Help! Get Hauva! It's Grandma!" Aru cried.

Nurphel felt in his pocket for the whistle. When he found it he blew one long blast, causing all of the caravan up in front to halt. Aru turned back toward her grandmother. With the wagons at rest she could hear the man's boots in the sludge as he rushed forward to fetch Hauva.

In only a moment they arrived, Hauva and her young son. They both clambered up and entered in silence, leaving their ash-caked shoes on the board outside the door. The wagon train set to the road again. Vorffe would be starting to search for a campsite about now. Aru sat down on a storage bench in order to make room for Hauva to maneuver past her in the shifting van and see to her grandmother.

Instead of going straight to Auwu, the woman focused her attention on Aru. She brushed a stray lock out of the young woman's eyes and then touched her cheek.

"You look tired, Aru," she said. "You worry too much."

Unsure how to respond, Aru looked into Hauva's wistful round eyes, heavy with lampblack eyeliner. She glanced toward her grandmother.

Hauva gave a tight-lipped smile and turned to the old woman. Up on her toes, she reached to feel Auwu's temperature, then straightened the covers much as Aru had done. She leaned against the edge of the bunk, contemplating the situation. Auwu missed another breath, then another, but remained peacefully asleep despite her rough breathing.

Hauva's little boy had already curled in Aru's lap. Hauva sat down beside them on the locker. For a time she remained silent, gazing at her drowsy tyke, observing his fascination with a strand of Aru's strange sickly-looking hair.

"Tch, tch! Such a pale thing you are."

For once Aru wasn't defensive about her lack of an ordinary brown complexion.

"Aru, I must tell you something," said Hauva. Her hushed tone chilled the girl's very soul. She looked solemnly up at Aru's sleeping grandma and then back at Aru's face. Aru began to panic as she sensed what was about to be said. "Grandma won't be making the journey to Ysgarlad with us."

Aru closed her body like a gate and fended off the words.

"You've got to hear me, Aru."

"Are you saying," whispered Aru, "that my grandma is going to die?" She swallowed, looked around her, and sniffed. "You couldn't know."

Hauva took her time to reply.

"I've known for a brief while, Aru. Your grandmother is surrounded with the light scent of the chokecherry. It won't be long now. Hours, maybe days."

Aru replied, "No, you're wrong!" in such a shrill whisper she almost woke up Auwu.

The world changed for Aru in this moment. The scene of Hauva breaking the news to her would be revisited in her memory, joining the confused impressions of the loss of her parents.

The next two nights dragged by, yet Aru felt only half cognizant of what occurred around her. Hauva stayed in the wagon and helped with Auwu, leaving her young ones in the care of an older sibling. Others took over Aru's chores so she could remain at her dear grandmother's side. The wagons kept to their nightly course; their destination held a deadline. It seemed like Auwu faded more each hour, as if piece by piece the person she had been was vanishing. Occasionally wakefulness broke through the agitated sleep and during these times she appeared to be sinking. Aru felt a pang of dismay when Auwu turned away from the worsted stockings she'd been so keen to finish. Perhaps her eyes were tired. The photo album sat untouched. Distracted rather than disinterested, it seemed as if her focus was needed elsewhere.

Slowly, confusion set in. She started asking to go home . . . but seemed unclear about where home was. Several times she mistook Aru for Aru's mother Wuurue. She began to refuse food, to decline anything to drink. Aru and Hauva spoke tenderly with her, but eventually she lost the energy or ability to speak much at all.

Just when things looked terribly final, Auwu woke in the evening at mealtime and asked for caviar. With Hauva's help, Aru sat her up. She served her pumpernickel spread with lots of caviar and gave her a mug with a bit of cold tea. How could this be happening? As if to demonstrate a miracle, Auwu ate some of her caviar and had a sip of tea. She reached for Aru's hand. Aru climbed onto the bunk and hugged her grandmother. She told her how worried she'd been.

"I love you so much. I couldn't live without you!" she blurted.

Auwu held Aru's head to her shoulder. Her words came slow, but unfaltering. "You will, Aru. One day soon you will. It will be all right."

"No. I'm not ready, Grandma," said Aru.

"I need to know you'll be strong, girl," the frail woman replied. "You are my only legacy." She paused. "My reason for life."

Aru let these words sink in. She thought about her grandmother's life work, taking care of her family, the children of the clan. Old Auwu cared deeply for the young, but she had a special love for Aru, her one direct descendant. Then Aru realized that Auwu had another legacy. "You've forgotten about your weaving."

Aru's grandmother was known far and wide for her distinctive patterns, even though she herself had dressed in mourning all these years.

Auwu smiled at Aru. "You are my finest piece of handiwork," she said. Auwu's smile remained on her face while she drifted off to sleep. After a while, Aru fell asleep also. She slept lightly, feeling the labored breaths of her grandma as she kept her arms around her.

A few hours later Aru awoke, but Auwu slept on. When she did wake again it was as if the earlier events had never happened. Hauva helped move the old lady into a better position but her breath sounded worse than ever, pausing for agonizing moments which came more often now. She had a gurgly snoring noise at the base of her throat, a strange, rattling sound. Back to the confused stare she had before, Auwu had no more words. Her skin felt so cold to the touch.

Aru watched her grandmother decline. Eventually Auwu moved in and out of consciousness, never fully present. Hauva sang in a hushed voice, traditional songs which were well known to the three of them. Aru joined her some of the time. Incense smoldered.

Time slowed even more for Aru. Waiting for the inevitable was so hard. There could be no denial of Auwu's transition any more. Instances of discernable awareness were further and further apart. One moment Aru would tell herself that her grandma would pull through, that soon they would arrive in Ysgarlad and doctors would call at the great house, all would be well. The next moment she found herself wishing that the old lady would pass on, just get this over with. Then came the remorse for having such thoughts. Pain and uncertainty tore a gaping hole in Aru's core, creating a perfect doorway for guilt.

At some point Auwu stopped responding to any sort of stimulation. Time moved slowly along. As twilight approached, Hauva told Aru she should say goodbye. Without argument the girl gently placed one of Auwu's hands between her own and held it to her cheek.

"Grandma, I love you," she sobbed. "I always will. You've taught me so much, you've cared for me all these years. There's nobody like you. Nobody like you at all."

She returned Auwu's hand to the bed but kept it within her own.

"I love you," she said again. "I will remember you. I will remember Mama and Father, too."

Aru cried for a few minutes.

"Grandma, it's all right. You can go. You can go now."

A few moments later, Auwu gave a deep sigh.

Hauva sang about traveling beyond the woods and hills, a song the old people loved. Aru sang parts with her and cried during some of the rest. Auwu's eyes remained slightly open, but they looked glassy and her pupils were so large. Just near the end of the old ballad, Auwu took a couple of deep breaths. Her eyes flew wide open and she looked up to the ceiling beyond Hauva. "Mama!" she whispered.

Then she turned toward Aru with a smile. Her eyes narrowed. "Listen to me, Aru. The fairy lizard told of the coming of a rascal, a little scapegrace. An unnatural thing. Don't let the wretch sway you from your course." She placed her free hand on top of Aru's. "Your friend's prophecy—" She swallowed with effort. "Mind his words."

Her last breath seemed like a big yawn.

Aru could never be sure later on that she had seen it, but she thought a wisp of silvery grey smoke swirled up through the air. Aru must have had one foot in the spirit world herself, because somehow she failed to hear her grandmother's warning.

The old woman's form lay in solemn peace in the wagon. The burial would take place when they reached the low hills beyond the coal mining region. That was it. Life went on for the clan. None wasted time in remorse. Only Aru, who moved in a stupor. She sat through the night with her head in her hands. Hauva made a few efforts to console the girl but Aru was expected to move on with her life.

The following night Aru trotted behind the wagon, her head down, struggling with her abysmal grief. After a while, her worn-out spirit just couldn't carry her forward. She stopped. Her feet stood unmovable on the dusky road. Her mind went blank. She remained standing, weak and wobbly. What kept her upright was a mystery. Unnoticed, she stood there as the entourage continued on its way.

Aru stood alone, outside of time. Only the towering pines witnessed her misery. The broad charcoal scar of the burn had been left behind while Aru looked after her grandmother. Now the woods were thick and oppressive. The ominous darkness of the tall, silent trees enshrouded the world.

Her shivering body eventually brought Aru back to sensibility. There she stood, in the road. The wagons were long gone. She remained standing where she was. Somewhere inside her, it seemed like a borderline of sanity was crossed. She felt the bowels of the world pull her downward, down into the ground, like a shadow through the soil.

She ran. Through the trees she ran. Up a hill perhaps, maybe. It didn't matter. Blindly, bursting with emptiness, she plunged on. Wheezing and gasping, she was oblivious of any pressure in her chest as she went. She tripped and fell repeatedly. Her boot snagged on a root and she tumbled downhill. Only the closeness of the tree trunks saved her from rolling far. Aru lay still for several minutes and then made it to her feet. The urge to run was still with her but exhaustion slowed her now; she stumbled along the side the of the hill, allowing the topography to choose her course. The emptiness inside made her press on and on.

Something in her madness noticed an opening in the face of the hill, a gaping cavern, a truly horrible mouth of darkness. Fear should have gripped her heart, but there was nothing inside her to grab. Bats or bears or monsters, it didn't matter. She'd gone beyond fear. Only running, that was her focus.

Then, the blackberry. It caught her eye with the moon's reflected gleam, a lone berry, a late berry, dangling directly in front of her, just above. Such a small thing to capture her attention, yet she was strangely fascinated. Perfect confection, dark and bulging with ripe sweetness, it called to her. A cluster of tiny onyx jewels so plump and soft with the promise of juiciness. Pernicious berry, guarded by forbidding canes of bramble, sharp thorns, an open dare, the risk of scratches.

In that wild moment everything seemed clear. Aru reached up, onto her toes, straining, leaning hard into the stabbing vines to pluck that one berry.

She woke up in darkness. Dull confusion fogged her awareness. Aru wondered if she had met her death somehow. Blackness was everything, no difference with her eyes open or closed. Had she gone blind? In time, enough awareness came for her to realize, by the drool's path from her mouth, that she lay on her back. But where was she? She reached out with her hand, waving it in space. Was she confined in a tiny cell or exposed in an infinite emptiness—she had no way of knowing. Anything, anyone, could be right next to her. She lay completely at the mercy of the unknown.

Pain came then, letting her know that indeed she remained alive. Both disappointed and relieved, Aru let go of the perceived glimpse of an afterlife. For a moment she'd had a consciousness of the beyond; now she knew, as her mind kept clearing, no such thing had occurred. Memory came back: the departure of the wagons, reaching for the berry. Falling. She remembered falling, crashing downward—she was in a hole, a hole in the ground.

Something scurried up Aru's leg and across her thigh under her petticoats. She shrieked, jumped to her feet despite her injuries, and wildly shook out her skirts. The reflection of her sounds told her she was in a small space. She had no way to escape the spider or mouse or whatever it was. All she could do was stand there, sightless. She didn't notice that she continued to shriek. She felt outward with her hands, found the cold walls that encircled her, damp soil like the sides of a grave. But, graves—you can't stand up in a grave. It couldn't be a grave. She continued to rustle her skirt, an attempt to frighten away whatever crawled on her, because it was all she could do. She didn't know for sure if the creature had left her underclothes. Her voice became quiet. She didn't cry. She couldn't see.

If the fall had damaged her brain she could be blind. Or might there be a source of light that she could locate? Something made her think that if she could breathe she must be able to see. There must be light. She now stood rigid, her heart beating with overwhelming force. Desperate to see any faint glimmer, any outline of a shape, Aru swiveled her head around into every possible position, not to miss a speck of light which might be hiding. The deep blackness, the depth of starless space all around sank into her. It was no better with her eyes closed; she saw just as much horrible thick darkness with them shut. Her consciousness seemed centered in her head only, and her head felt like a rubber ball suspended in the pitch dark. Aru put her hands over her face. She found that tears were running down her cheeks.

If she fell, she must be in a hole. There had to be an opening above. Her blind eyes strained upwards, trying in such a panic to focus. She imagined, directly above her, a vague area which held less darkness. It began to seem she was looking up a tunnel. Aru felt nauseated. Perhaps the moon shifted from behind a cloud, because she truly could see a difference up there now. At the same time, it dawned on Aru that she stood deep in the ground, the opening so far away. She could never climb out. She would die in that hole, nobody around for miles. The terrible thought came: they'd never even find her body.

Aru begged for her life. She pleaded with the forces of nature. With her hands she felt the walls for a clue of some kind which might save her. She no longer concerned herself with what might crawl on her or grab her or bite her; nor did she focus on the sharp pain in her back and her ankle. She had to get out of this hole. The walls felt cold. Damp and smooth. No finger holds, no way. Even if there had been, she never could have climbed out.

An innate superstition had always led Aru to imagine that only others could die young, that somehow she was special. Now, in her shock, she found her connection to all of humanity. She sensed the shadowy vestiges of ones who had gone on before her in time; she could feel them in her body: her ancestors and others, as if they were standing right inside of her. The sense of individual and invulnerable existence was extinguished. Without it, more courage would be needed, but there was no point to bravery now. Aru's life was over. Nothing could she do; no choices to make.

Time faded to nothing. Aru stood, chest pounding, ears ringing. Only the sound of her short breaths came to her. Terror told her body to run but she couldn't do that. It said to hide, then, to freeze. And so she did, she remained motionless. Then, the scent of silk and flowers.

Aru reclined in a princess's boudoir, hung with dusky maroon lace and adorned with hellebore and lilies. Now in front of a mirror in the darkness, a kind but faceless woman combed Aru's hair. Her hair seemed thicker and longer, some of it piled in luxurious curls and braids on her head. Aru stared into the dark, empty mirror and noticed the darkness was water, first still and solid, then rushing behind the glass. Drips of condensation began to appear on the mirror, trickling, running down; streams came through, the glass was gone. Water poured through the opening, taking Aru and the furniture with it, a whirlpool circling down, down—but Aru had lost the ability to care.

Was she under the water or floating on it as she drained downward? It didn't matter, Aru had lost allegiance to any sentiment and felt no concern about her pain. She screamed with every fiber of her being.

Carrion goblins came and started scratching Aru with their long bony fingers. They squeezed her arm and sniggered and scratched at her and it hurt but it didn't matter. Pieces of her flesh were coming away, and somehow or another the water acted like acid, dissolving her tissue off of her bones. The goblins got her eyes and she couldn't see but then after that she could.

Softness. Aru wasn't quite awake yet, but she felt her aching body enveloped in softness. She lay in a bed, so fluffy, with blankets and eiderdown. Snuggled up against her were . . . puppies? No, small children, warm and snug. One reached its arms around her in an embrace. How could skin be so velvety smooth?

A sweet voice came from out of the mist near her elbow. "She's opened her eyes, Mama!"

Aru woke more, and noticed the smell of camphor. Twinges of pain jolted her body as she moved her wrist, or her ankle which had been bound. Every part of her hurt at least a little.

"Well!" A woman's face appeared over Aru's, squinting through thick glasses perched on an exceptionally pointy nose. "Welcome back to the world!" said a squeaky voice. "We thought we might lose you there for a while!" She put her hand on Aru's forehead, to check for fever.

Aru couldn't speak, but the woman went on: "You'll be all right now, dear, lots of bruising but nothing serious. You have a swollen ankle. I guess you were in a stupor, mostly. How you fell down there without killing yourself I'll never understand. Or how you managed to be that far out in the woods all alone! Such a fortune that you weren't eaten by a wild creature—tsk!"

Aru managed a smile. The room was poorly lit, but behind the woman she could see a dark fireplace with a cauldron, a china cabinet, a sideboard, and an enormous icebox. Her eyes asked the woman, "How did I get here?"

During the next while she found out that the woman's name was Molli. Her children's were Kret, Twrch, Gwadden, and Muul. The man who pulled Aru from the abandoned mine shaft was their uncle Talpa. She'd been screaming so hard he thought he felt the ground shake. He had pulled her out all by himself and carried her back to the mining village where she now found herself. She was in the children's bed, and they didn't mind. It was early evening. Before Aru found strength to reply to any of this or thank her rescuers she returned to sleep.

Aru felt much better when she awoke late the next morning. Molli and her young ones were seated around the table and when they noticed Aru awake they invited her to join them. They were having roast walnuts with sausage and it smelled wonderful. Aru had on a long nightgown and she found a flannel dressing gown laid out for her next to the bed. One of the youngsters, Gwadden, came to her and grabbed her arm and with shaky legs Aru made it to the dining table. Everyone wished Aru a good morning and she replied the same.

After introducing herself and answering a few questions about where she came from, Aru looked down to examine her hands. Her fingers were scraped and badly bruised and two were wrapped in bandages.

"You tried to scratch your way out of the pit," Molli told her. "You've done some frightful damage to your nails, but they'll grow back."

Aru's head was in a spin—thoughts of her grandmother mixed with images of the ordeal she'd been through—while she tried to get a real grasp on where she was and have polite conversation with these strangers who had so kindly cared for her.

They had a good feast. Not long after that, a lunch. Soon came tea time. Aru wondered if these people did anything but eat. They spent the day in cycles of cooking, eating, and washing up. Unfortunately for Aru, their meals largely consisted of foods she just couldn't bring herself to try. She recognized various invertebrates in the curry, and had to conceal her horror when Molli fried up a batch of large spiders.

Of course Aru had read about "these sorts" of people, but other than seeing them at the market in Meadowvale, she'd seldom encountered with them. Chatting with Molli and spending time with her family, she found much contrary to what she'd been taught. In fact, Aru learned these folks were perfectly happy working below the ground. Yes, they lived a humble life, but none ever went hungry, thanks to the village's benefit society. Aru was impressed by the freedom they enjoyed.

During tea, Molli mentioned that the next day she would take Aru down to the inn. She knew the innkeeper's sister well, an engineer who worked for the mining company. Molli used to do her gardening. The inn was an old lodge which catered mostly to tourists from Ysgarlad, and messengers often stopped there, making it the source of tidings for the greater community. Molli was certain the folks at the inn would be able to contact Aru's companions.

In the meantime, Aru did what she could to help out. She had enough strength to assist with taking down the washing. Although the clothes weren't quite dry, the clouds threatened rain and it needed to come in. Then, in spite of her sore fingers, she used the flatiron to press several of the dresses, including her own, and she folded up some of the children's clothes. All the while she chatted with Molli and her young ones. Kret would be starting at boarding school next year, something to which Molli looked forward with bittersweet anticipation.

The cottage would have been a gloomy, stuffy place but the gentle warmth of Molli and her children made it a comfortable home. At suppertime they showed Aru how to squeeze vermian sausage from the casing in order to make a savory pudding. Served with mashed turnips and potatoes it actually tasted pretty good. Aru had a new appreciation for the company of others, and despite her grief about her grandma's passing she found she enjoyed herself.

Behind the cottage sat a small brick kiln and an old coal shed which contained a broad table and shelves for drying and storing the crockery. The children showed Aru how to roll out coils of the dark grey clay and shape them into a dish. The youngest kept wanting to eat these worm-like coils and had to be dissuaded. Aru's lumpy bowl would never sell at the village market but still she felt a certain amount of pride as she set it on the shelf with the others.

At the children's bedtime Aru brushed Gwadden's short velvety hair. She thought it lovely: dark in color, but with nuances of a little taupe. The children burrowed under their blankets, cuddling together. Aru shared with them one of the stories that her grandmother had told her when she was small. Through the telling she felt animated, drawing vigour from the enthusiasm on the faces of the young. The story wanted to be known, and the characters came alive through Aru. Like old friends come to visit, they brought her back to her own childhood. She remembered sitting tucked up snug in her own bed, her head against her mother's bosom, and listening to Grandmother Auwu. She'd seen the forest animals as shadows on the wall, closed her eyes during the scary part, giggled at the ending. So long ago. That little girl was gone now. As the babes drifted off to sleep Aru's melancholy moment was interrupted by an invitation to sit and have tea with Molli.

The two talked for quite some time, mostly about Molli's life in the village and about Aru's remarkable blonde skin, her background, and her plans once she arrived in the great city of Ysgarlad. Aru wasn't sure what would happen now that her grandma was gone. Now that she would be alone in the world, she felt lost. She wished they hadn't left her home, the warm and comfortable cottage on the edge of the southern woods. She wished she had a lovely family, as Molli had.

"What made you come to leave home in the first place?" asked Molli.

"I don't know." Aru groaned softly. "I'd had thoughts of teaching at my old school, if, of course, the superiors granted permission to apply. Grandma believed I'd have a better life in the city."

"I'm sorry you don't get on well with your family."

"It's not that we don't get along. I've never fit in, you see. It's become obvious since leaving home. I don't feel like a member of the collective, merely a fellow traveler. I can't please them. Everything I do is wrong. They love me; I know they do. They don't understand me."

Aru went on to say her grandmother had arranged for the two of them to live in a certain manor in the city. It had been an exciting idea, but now she'd be alone, a stranger. Molli assured Aru it'd work out.

"I just don't know what to expect!" Aru complained.

"Don't expect anything. You have a situation waiting for you; do your job there and all will be well. Only make sure you've got meals to eat!" Molli said with a grin. "Don't carry so many worries, Aru."

"But what if I don't make the best choices? I want to live a life of purpose. I don't want to end up as a washerwoman." She paused. "Or a wretched doxy tramping the street."

It must have come as a bit of a shock to hear those words in her own home, but Molli answered kindly, nonetheless, "Funny freckle, you! How do you even know about things like that, at your age? You'll find people to guide you," she said. "In any case, there's no reason to fret about life's purpose. It very well may be that your entire purpose is to serve as a warning for others about what not to become!" Molli laughed but Aru didn't think this was so funny.

The next day Aru hugged Molli's little dears goodbye and the two of them headed off to the inn. It was another drizzly morning; the clouds were low. As they walked down the village lane Aru noticed how far apart the cottages were scattered. Many of the homes were secluded behind high walls or built back into the trees. She could only glimpse the greystone cottages as she passed by. Most had steep roofs and aging thatch. Each and every shutter appeared to be closed and yet smoke trickled from many of the chimneys.

In the cemetery behind a pointy wrought-iron fence, the monuments were small and simple, many made of ancient-looking wood. Aru noticed how high the soil was mounded over each resting place. No vegetation grew on the mounds but the lawn and shrubbery were carefully trimmed. Aru thought it looked odd, the smooth lawn with all those small brown hills of bare dirt. As she and Molli walked along, they encountered a tavern and a few shops all in a cluster, but these looked dark and still and there was no sign of life anywhere. Aru was reminded that the tunneling folk were private, solitary people.

The railway depot showed more activity; a train had arrived. Aru inhaled the pleasant smells of coal smoke and hot oil coming from the locomotive as it waited at the platform. A jet of smoke erupted noisily from the stack, a thick column rising in a dark plume. The coal loaders had just set to work with their square spades and a kid with grease smudged on her nose climbed under the engine with an oil can.

Two elderly ladies in mourning had disembarked the passenger car, and their trunk and carpet bags were presently being unloaded. The stationmaster wore glasses with tortoiseshell rims. He called, "Good morning!" to Aru and Molli as he hurried past them across the lane, his broad umbrella protecting his suit from the misty rain.

Molli led Aru down a narrow drive just beyond the station, passing under the arch of a sign which read *Willowbrook Lodge.*

They'd gone only a short way when they came to the edge of a gentle downward slope. Between the trees, Aru could see the inn below. Partially obscured by strands of mist, the main building took up the whole of a small island in a large pond. Several outbuildings stood right along the pond's shore, water sloshing against the walls. Only the stables were set back away from the water. Built almost entirely of thin hewn logs, the structures had a graceful country appeal.

A rugged hillside beyond the water was covered with leafless birches and tall grey hemlocks, except where shale cliffs broke through the shadows of the vegetation.

Willowbrook was a popular retreat for tourists in the summer, and was the host of important hockey tournaments in winter. Just now it was between seasons, explained Molli, and they had plenty of room to offer Aru a bed until she could be reunited with her companions.

As the two approached the buildings it became clear how massive they were. The lodge itself, accessible by a long wooden footbridge, was a fabulous piece of architecture. It appeared to have been built up over many years. The high steep roof had several small turrets and towers and four impressive river rock chimneys. Iron gargoyles, clinging beneath the scrolled brackets of the gables, glowered at visitors.

This time of year a short corduroy road of logs crossed the soggy area between the base of the slope and the bridge. The women stepped their way along this rugged path, and then as they approached the buildings a bestial and musky odor confronted them. Workers were busily applying creosote to preserve the log walls and shingled roofs.

In stark contrast to the mining village, the inn bustled with activity. A pair of rotund men in felted hats were busy oiling wide flat paddles of the type they used on the pond. Several folks worked eagerly at stripping logs. With the same eagerness, other workers stacked firewood in the lee of one of the outbuildings. Other than maintaining the lodge, Molli told Aru, these folks were mostly woodcutters. A sooty man with a top hat spotted the visitors and hurried over to give a cordial welcome. He ushered them along the walkway of the bridge and up to the front doors, where a doorkeeper dressed in a smart uniform greeted them. She directed them to wait in the large entry hall while the butler was summoned.

At the back of the hall a grand staircase climbed to the upper levels of the foyer. Broad and carpeted, the set of stairs divided, curved back on itself, and rejoined at the mezzanine. This impressiveness was enhanced by a carved balustrade, chiseled to the finest detail, painted a glossy black and painstakingly polished. Absolutely magnificent.

With Molli in tow, Aru went to peek through the nearest doorway. Heavy draperies drawn closed kept out the light, but they could see the furnishings of a quaint sitting room. Faces stared from a wall full of dusky old photographs. Popular tourists and celebrities, Molli supposed. There were a few cut-paper silhouettes framed in aging silver. Aru noticed a coffee table, graceful in style and inlaid with various woods and—

"Welcome to Willowbrook!" said a voice from behind them.

The butler had appeared. Aru turned to see a smiling man, a person much larger than his voice. He wore a monocle, and had impressive side-whiskers. His thick, luxurious hair was oiled and combed back. Although his large teeth were terribly cigar-stained, his smile seemed genuine and Aru liked him at once.

Molli introduced Aru, and the man said, "So pleased to make your acquaintance, young lady. I'm Kulks."

Kulks led them to the back of the foyer and through some doors. They went down a narrow stair and along a corridor. Smells of things baking and bubbling let Aru know they were headed to the kitchen.

He gestured them into a long, low-ceilinged, windowless room. A couple of oil lamps flickered. People labored at the table and sinks but the most dominant presence was the cook, a large woman with small laughing eyes. She had round eyeglasses. Aru and Molli were invited to take a seat. A bustle of genial efficiency, the cook didn't miss a stroke of her lightning-fast chopping while she welcomed and conversed with her visitors. She told them that the housekeeper, the head of all staff, had instructed her to look after Aru while she was there. She noted that Aru was a guest, but welcome to help out if she wanted to occupy herself. Aru said she would like that very much.

The time came for Molli to say goodbye; she and Aru parted after a hug and promises to look each other up one day. Aru felt it in the pit of her stomach. Another loss. Goodbye to a new friend she knew she'd never see again.

The cook's first idea was to have Aru join a young boy and girl who were learning to weave baskets right there in the kitchen. "This little shaver is Mert, our scullery boy. And this is Manna," she said.

The children said hello and set about to teach Aru to make willow baskets. They were terrible teachers. Their baskets were horrible too. But they were adorable children and time passed easily as Aru tried to figure out how to make a proper basket. She didn't have much success.

Most of the staff at the lodge, including Kulks, the cook, and the children, had similar features—a weak chin and large front teeth, with a big blocky upper jaw. From chatting with Manna and Mert Aru found out that the majority of the workers came from one extended family. Toward lunchtime a young woman about Aru's age came down to have her midday meal. She was clearly not a member of the family.

This girl was a parlor maid. She set her big feather duster right down on the kitchen table and Cook scolded her for it. The maid chuckled, and removed her duster to behind the coal scuttle. Her ebony hair had an iridescent shine. It had been pulled back into a rather messy bun and tied with a satin bow. She had the sharpest large nose Aru had ever seen on a human being. It was no surprise that she was, as it turned out, the daughter of a pair of messengers who frequented the inn. Not at all shy, she set about immediately to let Aru know that she already knew all about her. Messenger folk were privy to the bulk of everyone's business. She offered Aru condolences about her grandmother's passing. She informed the cook that Aru's companions would be coming to retrieve her the following evening. Getting herself a bowl of what smelled like rabbit stew she brought some for Aru also. The girl's name was Praahk. Her voice was loud and she talked up a storm. She and Aru quite took to one another and would spend the rest of Aru's time at Willowbrook in each other's company.

Praahk told Aru that she had seen Molli leaving, and she went on about what a nice lady Molli was. Then, a look of sincerity came to her eye. In her coarse voice she whispered, "Forget your sorrow, my friend, though other friends have flown before! Your Molli has brought you memories, although you'll see her nevermore."

Startled by the rhyming, Aru laughed.

Praahk laughed also, and went on to mention how unusual it was for one of the miners to be so outgoing; the villagers generally were so reclusive. That was just the nature of the tunneling folk, she said.

After lunch, with Cook's permission, Praahk invited Aru to come with her downstairs to the sewing room. Although still rather stiff from her fall, Aru tried her hand at working the treadle machine to hem tablecloths. She and Praahk talked about all sorts of things, and Aru found out about Praahk's plans to study ancient languages at university next year. In fact, during the next few hours Aru found out about the plans of everyone at the lodge, and learned just about everything that had ever happened to anyone in the entire district, or so it seemed.

That evening in the women's dorm their conversation continued. They had a bedchamber to themselves because of the season, and Praahk showed Aru the secret compartment in the bottom of her trunk where she'd stashed all manner of treats she had swiped from the kitchens. Aru noticed some shiny trinkets in there, too. At first she was shocked that her friend would behave in this way, but then, after all, this behavior corresponded to the type of person she was, relevant to her boisterous personality. Somehow that made it seem more acceptable. The two snacked and chatted. Praahk talked of the interesting business of people far and wide. They continued well into the night and this is how Aru came to know some of the details of her own family history. Praahk related the following story:

> Now, SOME years ago, in the southern reaches of our deep and ancient woods, there lived a fetching young man named Roore. This Roore was the pride of his clan. His feats of strength were overshadowed only by his deeds of bravery. While still a boy he had become known for driving off a band of robbers all on his own. Everyone admired him.

Roore was furiously in love with a girl named Reffa. These two made a marvelous pair. Exceptional trackers, both of them, they spent many of their hours roaming the forest together. It was assumed that they would marry and have a family.

Roore's dearest friend was a fellow named Arul. He wasn't robust like Roore, he was small and lean. It wasn't his brawn but his attitude and quick wit which made him chums with the champion. Arul was generally responsible for Roore's getting into or out of trouble. Arul had a sweetheart also, and the four were fast friends. All was well.

Then, little Arul's beloved was killed in a hunting accident. Roore's lady Reffa sought to comfort Arul and, sadly, those two subsequently fell in love. Intellectually, the young woman was more of a match with him than with Roore, and as much as her heart tried not to follow her mind it became set on Arul.

Painful times ensued. There were a lot of arguments. A lot of fights. Innumerable tears. The young men's friendship was torn apart as Arul and Reffa became a pair. One day they got in a fight that was so severe that Arul was nearly killed and Roore took a nasty blow to the head. After that they avoided one another.

It happened that a few months later they were stuck with each other's company. The two of them had been sent on a mission of trade by the leaders of their clan. They traveled all the way to the Gwyllt Mountains, the root of the western rivers, and on their successful return with the goods they found something which would change their lives. Out there, in the middle of the thickest wilds, lay a baby wrapped in a blanket. No one has ever determined where she came from. A tiny golden-haired thing with pinkish skin, her coloring was unlike anything else the people had seen. Some say she came from the stars. Others think she was left by foreign adventurers, or maybe by fairies.

Anyhow, on the journey home those two bonded with that little child. Unselfish love and mutual undertaking began, over time, to heal the relationship between them. For you see, along with Reffa they cared for the baby, as aunt and uncles, the three of them. They named the baby Auwu: that was, yes, your grandmother, Aru. Friendship between the three remained strained and confusing, but there was hope for happiness again.

Tragically, though, the next summer Roore died from complications of the earlier injury to his head.

Arul and Reffa eventually married, but she died birthing the second of a pair of twins; the baby was also lost. Arul raised the surviving twin Wruelle with your grandma. As children, the two girls were inseparable, but as time went on, because of their differences, they grew apart. Wruelle was the woman you knew of as your auntie, although you wouldn't remember her; she moved away long before you were born.

Sadly, Arul let the misfortunes of his past weigh on him. As the years went by, he fell into a downward spiral of drinking and disintegration. He slowly deteriorated until he was so bedraggled and infected with scabies that he was too weak to survive.

A short time before old Arul died, your grandma Auwu married your grandfather and had just one child, your mama.

"Aru, do you recall anything of this lady, your aunt Wruelle, at all?"

After a moment, Aru replied. "My memories are so distant. They're sepia-toned and dark around the edges. I can't remember any portraits or photographs of my auntie. I scarcely remember my father's face."

"He died when you were three years old."

"Yes, he died of illness that year, my father. Of the black pox."

"That must have been so awful," said Praahk.

"Yes."

"After that it was just you, your grandma, and your mother. Do you remember your mother well?"

"Fairly well."

"And do you recall what happened to her? Can you still remember?" Praahk seemed awfully curious about Aru's recollections, but this is the nature of her species.

"I do. It happened just before my fifth birthday. One of the summer's most glorious afternoons, and I was playing near the back of our cottage. Playing horsie or something. It was a dreamy day. The birds were singing, and I remember the air was full of summer smells."

"It was just after the solstice, wasn't it?"

"I think so," answered Aru. "I noticed my mother go and lie down in the grass and I scampered over to join her. I went to sleep curled up next to her, happy to share a quiet nap on such a pretty day. I didn't know. She'd suffered an obstruction of the coronaries. After that it was just my grandma and me."

A wave of panic swept over Aru as what she had just stated reached her own ears. She was alone in the world. It took her a minute to realize that Praahk had continued speaking. Aru hadn't heard a word. Praahk was undressing and about to put on her nightgown. She had extremely skinny and tubelike legs and wore dark stockings. Aru got ready for bed, too. It had been a long day.

"My grandma never told me the story, Praahk," she said as she lay back. "Why wouldn't she tell me where she came from? She must have known!"

"I was told she wanted you to feel like a true member of the clan." Praahk yawned and soon she started to snore.

The next morning was quiet. Most of the staff preferred to work late into the night and were asleep until midday. Praahk had some duties to perform, however. Aru helped her clean the grates of the dining room and the library fireplaces. It was a sooty, messy job but Praahk didn't seem to mind. She was as talkative as ever.

At lunchtime Praahk displayed a ravenous appetite. They had crabapple cakes smothered in maple syrup and she ate more than twice as much as Aru. Kulks came in for his lunch, along with a footman and one of the maids. He greeted Aru kindly and the bunch of them made pleasant conversation while they ate.

Toward the end of the meal, the footman rose and winked and pretended to be searching for something in the cupboard just behind Kulks. What he was actually doing was tying the butler's long coattails to the spindle bars underneath his chair seat. Kulks was a big man, and quite a bit broader at the hips than across the chest. When, a few minutes later, the footman suddenly slapped the table and yelled "BEARS!" the result was so spectacular that even Cook joined in the laughter, despite the destruction of a perfectly good chair.

Aru spent the afternoon helping Praahk with a few more tasks and eventually they ended up doing some dusting in the front office. Aru picked a photo up from the writing desk. In it a sizeable woman sat next to a stocky man with lengthy whiskers. He looked like a muskrat. She was about to ask if this was the doorkeeper and her husband when she heard someone in the foyer. A familiar voice? Taking a quick peek around the door, she had a happy surprise. It was Chip.

Two men in lavish fur coats had just entered the lodge and were shaking water out of their umbrellas. They had on galoshes. One was a young man, a really enormous person, a moose, who stood dumbly chewing his gum and looking around the hall. The other was the old fellow who had traveled along with Aru and her companions. He began rummaging in his pockets and muttering something about a key. He caught sight of the girl and smiled.

"Aru!" he exclaimed, "I heard you were here at Willowbrook. So glad that you are safe." Chip put out his hand for Aru to take.

It took a moment for the confounding flood of images to clear from Aru's mind enough that she could respond. When she found herself, she rushed over and greeted him. They talked for a few minutes. Chip apologized for having scared Aru so badly in the camp. He said he didn't know what had come over him. Chip invited her to meet him for tea in the rear parlor as soon as he had freshened up.

The parlor had no windows, but a couple of candles lit it well enough. Aru could see carved wood paneling on the walls and the cold fireplace behind a wrought iron screen. A piano stood in the shadows, silently marking time until after dinner when guests might come in. Aru entered and sat to wait for her friend. As she grew tired of looking around she began to play a little game with her eyes, closing them one at a time while she stared up at the grid of the low coffered ceiling. This made the crossbeams seem to jump up and down and Aru was trying to figure out just why this ought to occur, when Chip walked in.

Puffing on a pipe, with his short hair neatly combed back, he looked refreshed. He took a seat near Aru. He had a case which looked like a doctor's bag. This he set on the floor by his chair. "So, Aru," he said, "you must tell me about your adventures these past few days."

Just as he said this, an elderly and rather portly footman, whom Aru had seen below stairs, brought in a tray with their tea. He poured a lovely-smelling twig tea from an elegant pot made of hematite and jet.

"Thank you, Uncle," said Chip. He offered a cup to Aru. Then he opened a jar and spread something on a cracker which he presented to her. "Chasmal Sea smoked oyster pâté," he explained. "The best you will find anywhere. This hotel is run by my family, vegetarians all, but we are proud of the fare we offer our meat-eating guests."

Aru bit in and rolled her eyes because it tasted so good. "Exquisite!" she said. "But—you live here at Willowbrook? I had no idea!"

"Oh, no," he replied, "I live several hours east of here. This lodge belongs to my cousins." He took a sip of tea and a draw from his pipe. Then he added, "I've been traveling out rather often lately, in order to help manage the new hydroelectric apparatus in the old dam here at Willowbrook pond. But what about you, Aru? I heard only a snippet of what happened and I desire to know the whole story."

So Aru related the events since she became separated from the caravan, focusing on her experience in the mine pit.

Chip waited until she had finished her story and then he shuddered, saying, "How you survived all that I'll never know. There's nothing worse than being trapped. Nothing worse in the world." He shuddered again and pulled his suit jacket closed in front as if he were cold.

They talked a bit about fear and about how tough things come up in life which one must face. "It's funny, but what I fear most in those woods are the wolves," Chip said.

"Oh, I don't think that's peculiar at all," said Aru, "I have seen wolves do terrible things. Once when I was watching a wolf cross a field I saw a nice fat grouse poke her head out of the bushes. That grouse was gone in one gulp. A whole string of chicks was orphaned. The wolf had no concerns. That's what they are like. Very violent. Very practical. All that matters is the clan."

Praahk came to the parlor door. She excused herself and asked if it might be all right if she sat with them. She had flown right through the last bit of her chores and now she stood with her needlepoint in hand. Aru looked at Chip and he smiled. Of course she might.

Such a comically forward young woman, Praahk helped herself to some of Aru's oyster pâté. Chip asked about the welfare of her family these days and Praahk answered a couple of questions with her mouth a little fuller than was polite. This made the old fellow chuckle.

It was nice to see Chip at ease. He smiled more than he had while traveling, and didn't fidget so much, although he did twiddle his thumbs for a while and he did keep tamping and drawing on his pipe.

For several hours the three sat and talked. Chip shared another one of his ghoulish stories. A master at recounting these old fables, he wrought images Aru would never forget. In her mind she could clearly see the fish-stink zombie, crawling with flies, who rode the slobbering hellhound through the village on windy nights, tapping on windows with a spear made of charred bone.

Conversation, though, was dominated by Praahk. Aru got quite a bit said also. When the subject of her origins came up, Aru, feeling sentimental, decided to reveal a personal secret. She told her friends the truth. Although her heritage was clouded in mystery, she had an innate knowledge of who she truly was. Aru was a princess. She'd always known. Her grandmother had been orphaned while her high-born and genteel parents visited from a distant land. She simply knew this, somehow. She couldn't explain. But she was certain.

Praahk seemed surprised by this announcement and stared at Aru—first through her right eye and then the left, with her mouth open.

Aru went on to describe in detail what would take place when she arrived at the city Ysgarlad. The people there were educated. Someone would recognize her for who she was. She would receive royal treatment and be pampered until she was eventually reunited with her relatives at court.

Chip seemed amused by this.

Praahk responded by laughing, "Well if you're a princess, and just about to come into your own, you won't mind if I just have that last little bit of pâté there, will you?"

Aru grew silent.

After scraping the remainder of the smoked oyster pâté onto a cracker and pocketing the jar, Praahk asked Chip what was in his doctor's bag. In answer, Chip lifted it up onto the low table and opened it. Inside were a dozen or so stoppered glass jars, mostly full of herbs and powders. Aru noticed some of the labels—*Stinking Hellebore Blossoms, Dried,* and *Powdered Batflower.*

"Oh, what is this?" asked Praahk, grabbing a bundle of roots.

Chip reached for them and untied the string. "These," he whispered solemnly, "are water lily tubers." He winked. "A tasty snack."

While the three of them munched on the tubers Praahk continued to examine the bottles.

One had a bit of thick yellowish liquid. "Castoreum!" she exclaimed.

Chip grinned and handed her another jar, this one labeled *Mithridate*. Both of the girls wondered what this was.

Chip produced two tiny empty bottles. "This is an invaluable pharmaceutical. A draft of this mixture will remedy any poison." He poured a bit of the mithridate into each of the bottles, handing one to Aru and the other to Praahk. "Perhaps more importantly," he said as they peered at their bottles, "it's a phenomenal cure for acne."

Both Aru and Praahk thanked their friend sincerely and tucked the bottles away.

The footman returned and stood just inside the doorway. He looked slightly uncomfortable. "There is a rider here for you, miss, and, well, frankly, we'd prefer if he didn't come inside the lodge. Normal security precautions, you know. Nothing personal."

"That'll be one of your clan, Aru. To take you back to the caravan. I'll say goodbye here," Chip told her. "It's been fine to see you again." He packed up his things, gave her hand a cordial shake and, after a few more exchanges of courtesies, headed off toward the dining room.

Praahk accompanied Aru outside. They were directed to the stables. Orru was at the trough, watering the saddle horse before his return trip. At least, Aru thought it was Orru. It might have been Orruhl. When the twins weren't together she had trouble telling them apart. So, she didn't introduce him to Praahk. Instead she started up a barrage of chatter, hoping nobody would notice the lack of basic manners.

Aru learned that she had missed her grandmother's funeral. It had been a simple ceremony, as was typical of the forest clans. She'd been buried the previous evening in the woods, not far from the road. Praahks's questioning produced the information that the caravan had kept on and was probably about halfway between Willowbrook and Ysgarlad at this point. It would take hard riding all night to catch up. Orru, if that's who he was, showed clear signs of not being thrilled about having to come fetch Aru.

Praahk pulled Aru aside as if she was about to say something. Instead, she slipped a small locket into Aru's hand. The tarnished condition of the silver along with the melanite maple leaf made it obvious that this necklace rightfully belonged to someone in the family that operated the lodge. Praahk gave Aru a grin. Aru returned the smile, but shook her head. She grabbed her friend and hugged her.

Orru had tightened the cinch and was up in the saddle. He reached out for Aru's hand and she swung up behind him. They could still hear Praahk calling goodbye as they made the top of the hill.

By mid morning Orru and Aru came upon the wagon camp. They'd ridden all night with only the shortest of short breaks. Exhausted into a bleary insensibility, Aru could barely keep her seat on the horse. Riding double for long distances is a nightmare, and Aru's pride had kept her from holding on around Orru's waist. Her hands were killing her from gripping the cantle. By the time they met the caravan she was nearly delirious. The horse wasn't in any better shape. He was lathered and blowing, but he was a strong creature and he knew it.

Camp was just on the shoulder of the road. The wagons had pulled up into the shadows of the high walls of some ruins where crumbling blocks of shale and slate made a faint threat of imminent collapse. The fires were smoldering, nearly out, but Aru didn't care that she had missed the tea. While Orru led the horse on his cool-down Aru climbed up into the familiar wagon. Her exhaustion didn't keep her from feeling the emptiness inside. Nobody had moved into the space, but that wasn't surprising since most preferred to sleep on the forest floor. All the linens and bedding were gone, presumably for washing, but Aru climbed onto the bare mattress of her grandmother's bed and curled herself into a ball. She slept hard.

It was not acceptable for any person to go missing for any reason and thus cause concern for the clan. Aru knew she was fortunate that Vorffe didn't reprimand her beyond the punishment of confining her to the wagon for the remainder of her trip. Meals were brought to her by Hauva or one of the other aunties, who would stay and visit with Aru for a while, but most of her time was spent in the lonely gloom. She'd been active these past few days, distracted, and also numb in regard to the loss of her grandma. Now she had time to grieve.

At first she spent a lot of time curled on the bed, crying, but then she remembered that her grandma had taught her not to cry about anything too hard or for too long. She had told Aru that it was good to cry, to let things out, but after a few minutes one should stop. Aru couldn't think why. She glumly reflected on the fact that it would be up to her to carry on the teachings of her grandmother but she couldn't remember half of them.

A few days went by; Aru slept through them because it was easier than trying to sleep at night when the wagon was moving. She slept through many of the nighttime hours also. Captive in the wagon, too depressed to light a candle-lantern, her wakeful periods were spent in bleak moonlight filtered through the window curtains and skylights.

It would have been a productive time to compose some poetry. Aru's emotions were deep and her heart was bursting. But the depth of her feelings had her paralyzed, unable to endure her own thoughts. Breathing was enough. Just breathing. Existing.

Traveling along one evening, Aru laid her head back on the bolster. As she did so, a familiar feeling poured over her like tepid water. No—! She pulled her head forward in panic, but it was too late. Something about her was gone. Suddenly, nothing made sense. Fear pulsed through her. Items around her were recognizable, but that's where it ended. That was the bed curtain, this was the window. But it didn't mean anything.

Existence had no relevance. There was only her own terror that all she knew was a fading dream, headed toward nothingness. Terror. Nothingness! It seized her, it grew stronger, extreme. Once again, she didn't know what she was.

Outside of time. She felt the message before she heard it. The Visyrn spoke to Aru with silent words that came from nowhere. The voice was deep and clear.

The words were big. They filled up everything. *Realize. Remember.*

The grip on her lessened and Aru pulled herself back to life by focusing hard on a memory of her grandmother. Then she crawled off the bed. The cabinet. The cabinet . . . She couldn't think about the voice, it would draw her away. The cabinet was of wood. Ebony. Ebony is a tree. This is a drawer. What's inside?

After she felt better Aru slumped down onto the bench. She felt sorry for herself. She had no idea why this happened to her. And these strange words. What was the meaning?

She sat for a while, staring out the window into the foggy night. Nothing but grey shadows of tree trunks out there, passing by. The forest spread on and on, the road never ended. Aru felt suffocated by her confinement in the moving wagon and by the extensiveness of the forest. She had always lived by its edge but she had never known its depth. She didn't like it. She was tired.

Movement in the rear window caught her eye. Some little thing was wiggling. She stood up on the edge of the lower bunk, curious in spite of herself, and leaned over the bed to see. It was the spider. He was still there.

"Umm, umm—Skrittle! No, that's not it. Kritikk. That's it, Kritikk!" Aru felt like she'd encountered an old friend. "How are you, old boy?"

The rest of that night she spent on the locker seat, talking out loud now and then, comments directed toward Kritikk the spider. Kritikk didn't reply in any way. In fact, he didn't do much of anything. But he was surprisingly good company.

The following evening Aru sat on the locker seat again. She continued her conversations with Kritikk, although he was nowhere to be seen. She talked about her grandmother Auwu, and how much she regretted not demonstrating to her that she could be a competent member of the collective. Oh, and yet, how tired she was of getting snapped at by the aunties and uncles for doing things the wrong way. How crazy life can be. When Aru tired of talking she let herself enter a daze, waiting for time to pass.

Aru spotted a newspaper folded and tucked between the seat cushion and the wall of the stove's alcove. She pulled the paper out and unfolded the dingy pages, snapping them open and refolding so she could look at the front page. The main article was some boring thing about a businessman. Old news. The paper was from months ago.

Something interesting, though, below the fold. Police photographs of two hunched-over, grossly under-bathed old men. Same surname. They must've been brothers. Both had the same apathetic expression. Such hard, soulless eyes! One's bald head and skinny, sagging neck were covered with loose, bumpy skin. The lipless crack of the other's scowling mouth merged with a deep upward wrinkle in the concave cheek, creating what looked like a huge, insidious grin. Sparse, fuzzy grey hair poking out from their nasty, wrinkled scalps reminded Aru of plucked fowl. Aru wasn't one to judge others solely on their appearance, but these guys were obviously bad news.

Under the photo the headline read: *Grave Robbers Apprehended!* As she read on, she learned that these creeps had a history of ghastly crimes. Recently they had stolen a pit pony and some digging tools from one of the coal mines and had been caught ravaging graves in a village cemetery. Included in the article was a detailed list of items which were still missing at the time of the men's arrest and the paper's publication. These valuables were believed to have been sold through shady dealers up and down the coast. Rings and necklaces, mostly, not really that interesting to read about, although listed were several pieces of children's jewelry—that was sad. Oh, and apparently they had opened the tomb of a recently buried witch. Yipe! Not very smart! Still missing from that were a variety of objects: a knife, some rare books, a cingulum of fine silk, two silver goblets, and a prehistoric fertility doll carved of volcanic rock.

Aru looked at the photos again, shuddered, and put the paper down. At least she hadn't run across anyone like these two old vultures when she was alone in the woods.

Dozing off right on the bench, Aru spent the rest of the night in sporadic naps, propped up in the corner and laboring through her dreams. Awake she didn't feel rested; asleep she didn't feel any happier.

She was just finishing up a short nightmare which had undoubtedly been inspired by the newspaper article when she became aware of noises. In foggy sleep she realized the wagon had pulled up. And something was different.

Aru jerked awake and scrambled to her feet, startled by light streaming through the vermilion curtains and filling the interior of the wagon with a fiery glow. She eagerly parted the curtains and peered out the window. The glare stung her eyes. She staggered back, sheltering her face with her hand. They were out of the woods. They'd arrived!

II. FIERCE

LIBERATED from the confines of the wagon and freed from the shadow world of the forest, Aru stood and gaped. She'd forgotten about direct sunlight! The morning sun hit the iron-rich rock beneath her feet, causing the crimson and scarlet to glow as bright as a paper lantern. The landscape around her shone as a marvel, bathed in blazing colors. Aru held her palms upward and pointed her face eagerly toward the warmth of the sun. Through her closed eyelids came fiery orange light, mottled and wavering, and with wholehearted appreciation she felt the sun's radiance on her skin and circulating with her blood.

And here it was, Ysgarlad. The city by the sea! Daylight shone over the ocean. Coastal cliffs formed a great horseshoe around the city, cliffs striped thick with mineralized rust which echoed brilliantly the colors of a sunrise. Aru stood at the top, looking down on it all. Far below, the morning rays glanced off windows and polished copper roofs and turned the whole of legendary Ysgarlad into a jewel so bright that she really couldn't stare at it directly.

Aru's companions already had a fire crackling, built near the brink of the cliff so they all could enjoy the panorama while gorging on a hearty meal. The smell of spattery salt pork mixed with sea air. A checkered tablecloth spread on the ground held platters of leftover spareribs and a mountain of purple cabbage slaw with vinaigrette. Orruhl was spreading toast with jam. Aru trembled with excitement. Soon they'd take her down to introduce her to her new life in the city.

Even though she knew this would be her last real outdoor meal for a long while, Aru bolted her food and then got to her feet with her piece of toast in hand. She peered down toward the city, admiring those surrounding cliffs. Wholeheartedly she soaked up the hues. Vivid carmine and flushed papaya. Apricot. Centuries of erosion had wrinkled and pleated the cliff faces and carved pinnacles of fractured rock. The result was a colossal curving formation made of spectacular ferric bands of color. No textile mill could produce a more interesting pattern of thin and thick stripes. Aru felt she could stand and absorb all this forever. After a time, though, she heard her name called and turned to find Hauva patting the seat next to her, inviting Aru to come sit down and join her.

Hauva spoke for a few minutes about the beauty of the place and about what a strong young woman Aru had turned out to be, how well she would enjoy living in Ysgarlad. By the way her auntie's jaw quivered, Aru could tell that troubling news lurked behind these pleasantries. Hauva placed her hand on Aru's and continued, "Vorffe has decided you must go down to the city on your own. That lower route would cost us more time, and now with Auwu gone—"

Aru's mouth dropped open. "That was not the arrangement!" she protested. Her face flushed. The surge of astonishment tightened her throat. "Grandmother paid well for passage to Ysgarlad!" Then Aru looked daggers at Hauva. The injustice of it, and the fear of going on all alone, both of these enraged her. "You must take me down there—you just have to. Who will introduce me?"

Docile Hauva replied with her typical kindness, "You'll find it only a day's journey, Aru. If you start now you'll arrive before sunset. You remember the name of the house?"

"That terrible man!" Aru growled. "Horrible worthless curmudgeon! How could he!"

Hauva jumped up and set her hands on Aru's shoulders, as if to hold her down. "Calm yourself, girl. That language! Just you hope he doesn't hear." Hauva looked nervously over, but Vorffe was busy. A couple of boys had wrassled too near the embers of the fire, let alone the edge of the precipice.

Fury burned in Aru's chest. Hauva tried to remind her that the needs of the clan took precedence over her own concerns. All Aru knew was that she'd given of herself all her life, always tried to be an upstanding citizen in the community, and only to be cast out in the middle of nowhere. Like yesterday's roses. They'd never do this to one of the other family members.

"This is not the middle of nowhere, Aru," Hauva said softly. "Look, you can clearly see the city—you will be there before you know it.

Beyond this fork no descending road joins yours for the entire route to Ysgarlad. You cannot lose your way.

"Aru," she added, licking her lips, "do be cautious in your dealings once you arrive. Word is in on the wing that someone powerful, someone from the east, has an interest in your affairs."

"What? What do you mean, Hauva? You tell me this *now?*" Aru shook her head. The world had gone crazy. "Why? Why would some stranger be interested in me, of all people?"

Hauva lowered her brows and glanced at Vorffe, showing the whites of her eyes. "The clan has no involvement in this business of yours. That's all I know, Aru, what the messenger mentioned by chance. Gossip, frankly. A snippet of gossip that fell from undisciplined lips. That's all it was. Keep your wits about you, that's all. Be careful who you trust and stay downwind of trouble."

"Grandma always gave that advice when I was about to do anything new." Aru said this softly, brushing some crumbs from her dress and looking off again toward the city.

With help from Hauva, Aru packed her few belongings and a bit of food into her carpetbag. A beautiful thing, her bag, with delicate and fanciful roses on a deep plum ground. It had belonged to her mother.

After nothing more than brief goodbyes from her relatives, she set out to follow the road down to Ysgarlad. She'd known not to expect more of a fuss than these gruff farewells, but the lack of concern expressed for her made her miss her grandmother greatly.

I wish she was here, Aru thought. *Grandma cared about me. Unlike this self-serving pack of mongrels. She'd never let these louts abandon me in such a way.*

The track headed downhill along the face of the cliff. It had a steep decline, but it was wide and Aru kept to the inside so she felt secure despite the sheer drop-off on the left. Although angry and hurt to be forsaken by her own family, something in the back of Aru's mind made her thankful that she wasn't traveling down this cliffside in a wagon.

She grumbled as she went along, and chanted curses such as "barbarian shitty shitty shit-dogs" between clenched teeth. She kicked innocent little stones out of her way. Aru would have been ashamed if someone had heard her, but probably no one did.

Even worse what happened when she was out of sight of the others right around the first corner. Escalating her barrage of expletives, she grabbed a stick that lay by the roadside and took a swing at the rock cliff, meaning to pummel it. This stroke glanced off the rock and deflected back toward her head. The stick missed her, but barely. Like a slap in the face, this humiliation brought some sense to Aru. She stopped fuming, threw the stick aside, and headed on down the track.

After a hairpin turn, the descending road doubled back to where Aru was just about below the meal site. She couldn't see anyone up on the clifftop, but they'd had things pretty much cleaned up before she started out. Fine. She never wanted to see them again.

Aru turned to look at the great city. She had heard about Ysgarlad and its dazzling cliff shores all of her life, but the scene below was more brilliant and fascinating than she'd ever imagined. With the sun higher there was less glare and she could see everything. So much history lay spread out before her. Ysgarlad had easily two dozen sailing ships in the harbor. Busy canals radiated in from the bay, then meandered through the rocky terrain at the feet of the legendary seven hills of the city. A horrible fire in ancient times had taken almost everything, but the city had been rebuilt using brick and local stone. Only a few wooden relics remained. The roofs of the city were of terracotta tile, except for the many fine houses and city buildings roofed with hammered copper. From Aru's high viewpoint the lines of maples among these rooftops showed where winding roads crisscrossed the lowlands by the bay and where they climbed the steep hills.

Aru grabbed her carpetbag and set off again down the road. The bag, she decided, was too heavy to carry in hand. The next manzanita tree she passed lost a branch because Aru decided to lash her cumbersome bag on top of the foliage and pull it like a travois. This worked well on the smooth rock of the road. Unfortunately, it also acted like a broom, with the result that Aru was soon coated in ferruginous dust.

As she walked, wistful thoughts about her grandmother competed with Aru's resentment of the clan. Her bad feelings were still simmering but no longer likely to boil up as tears. She thought about how unfair Vorffe and the others could be. Her grandma had told her things would be different in the city; maybe that was true. Now and then on her way down the switchbacks Aru had a clear view of Ysgarlad. There were many absolutely palatial buildings. She wondered which might be the library, which the theaters.

As the morning went on, Aru needed to remove her jacket. She stopped briefly by a trickling brook to have a snack of blood sausage, which tasted all the better for being eaten in the warm sunshine. With her sense of adventure awakening, she rose and continued downhill, dragging her bag on the manzanita branch behind her.

In the afternoon the road straightened out a bit and followed a rusty creek along a canyon. There were no more views of the city, but the canyon rock had plenty of dramatic color. Hours went by. Aru found that walking through the bright sunlit scenery made her feel better. Irritation resurfaced, though, as she began to tire. When a glowing quality of the daylight signaled the sun's descent, Aru sat down to nurse a blister that was forming on her heel. Great. And she had no shoe grass. No soap. She soaked her foot in the cool water of the creek for a while and then pulled her stocking over the inflamed skin and put her shoe back on. She favored that foot as she walked along, trying to protect the heel from friction as much as she could.

A mile or two later she encountered a party coming up the road. Not many took this route. Aru hadn't expected to meet anyone. A man and several women, stately of airs and well dressed, yet they traveled on foot, accompanied by a donkey with a cart full of baggage. They stopped to greet Aru. The gentleman's unusual height was accentuated by his great velvet-covered hat, causing him to tower over Aru so much that she found it a bit frightening when he shook her hand. His breath smelled like sweetgrass and he carried a large bronze bugle over his shoulder. The women stood behind him, chewing something slowly and peering at Aru, too shy to come forward. Aru was sure they were staring because of her pale skin. Her limp, her dust cloud, and her manzanita travois may have had something to do with it, however.

Before the travelers continued their unenviable climb, they gave Aru the good news that she was nearly to Ysgarlad. Aru's descent soon brought her to a small adobe hut built up against the cliff. Nobody seemed home, but rosy-headed mud swallows were flitting about. Aru wondered if they were assessing her as a threat. Such darling birds.

A few more houses, larger ones, appeared here and there as she went, and then the canyon opened out to a broad vista and Aru found herself at the top of another cliff. A low cliff this time. The view was as if from a tall tower. Below her a busy street led into the city. Aru held her breath, captivated by the scene. While she sat herself down on the brink, her skirts and tired legs dangling over the edge, she kept her eyes on the dense crowd that bustled along the roadway. Aru was nearly down the mountain, but people still reminded her of insects from this height. How did they scurry along so quickly, passing among one another without colliding?

Several great barns and what looked like a foundry lay below, but this particular road led directly to a factory on a bare, dome-shaped hill. The long, swarming column of humanity was made up entirely of women. They looked identical in dresses of a dark cinnabar hue, belted tight around their tiny waists. Their hair, if they had any, was hidden under large turbans of the same color. The workers headed in the direction of the factory carried enormous packages on their shoulders. These grand industrial works were known for recruiting people who required order and routine in their lives. Hard workers, they got the job done. Aru couldn't imagine herself living in one of their colonies.

The hour was getting late and Aru wanted to reach her destination in the remaining daylight. She got to her feet, this time grabbing up her bag again and leaving her manzanita branch behind. Not far along from where she'd been sitting, she came upon some steps down to the avenue below. Carved from the rock, and lacking a handrail, these stairs went a long way down. It felt treacherous for someone with luggage, but Aru had been through so much and was so tired that somehow she made it down without too much worry.

Her feet reached the pavement and she stood for a moment. "I'm here, Grandma!" she whispered, "I'm here, I'm in Ysgarlad." She sighed and then smiled and walked on. Soon Aru was wending her way between the workers, who, strangely, didn't take much notice of her. In a while she reached the boundaries of the city itself. Finding the house should be easy, because it was near the top of the first big hill.

Only a short time later Aru stood panting, staring up at the house of Vulpeden. She felt like a mouse in front of its tall two stories and all its towers, the high peaked roof. Nonetheless, the house looked welcoming. Sunburst designs were beaten into the copper roofing. The stonework of the old walls, a dark blood color, was clearly formed of blocks quarried from the local cliffs. An early blush of pink came from azaleas surrounding the downstairs windows.

It was as if Aru remembered the place. She felt as though she had come home. Somehow she belonged here. The steadfast character of the mansion, with its dozen chimneys and all the balustrades and balconies, brought comfort to her. The grand entrance had an ogee-shaped gable above. Stately and sublime, Vulpeden represented to Aru the solid, secure home she required. This was all she had left of her family now: the security which her grandmother had arranged for her. She approached the front doors. She rang the bell.

After a moment the left door opened and a little weasel of a butler poked his head around it. With courtesy and well-starched dignity he allowed her in and then returned in a few minutes to guide her to the library. The lady of the house would receive her there.

The library smelled of aging rose-tanned leather books and wax-polished mahogany. Bookcases lined the walls and reached so high that Aru wondered how they ever got the volumes down. Vaulted ceilings and two stories of lattice windows in the room let in plenty of the early evening light, in addition to lit candelabras and the electric lamps which cast a warm glow through their tasseled crimson shades. A fireplace occupied the center of one wall, with a lusty blaze burning despite the pleasant weather. Curiously, on the mantel above stood a fine porcelain collection of what appeared to be beagle dogs of various sizes, mostly in leaping or howling positions, some with teeth bared.

Lady Akawu stood with her back toward Aru as she flipped through a thick ledger on a desk in the rear of the room. She was a slight woman, but stood erect, with her left hand on her hip. The Lady wore her bushy auburn hair pulled back into an exquisite braided chignon and she had on an expensive madder-dyed linen suit. The blazer, just a shade darker than her hair, had corset-style lacing in the back and a fashionable bustle below that. A black boot protruded from her skirts.

As she noticed Aru's footsteps she turned, and Aru could see her amber eyes. Those eyes, upturned toward the outer corners, had a shrewd, foxy look to them. The Lady smiled. Her nose was long and pointed, her face diamond-shaped, and her ears quite large. Her fine suit was complemented by a high-necked, ruffled white blouse and opera-length black gloves. While observing Aru, she reached to cap her elegant cranberry-glass inkwell. Then she drew her hands up before her bosom, the wrists bent. Lady Akawu was beautiful, and in a charismatic way.

When Aru approached, the Lady reached out her gloved hand, saying, "My dear, I believe I've made a faux pas. I should have realized you'd arrive today, and sent someone to the foot of the cliff to fetch you. But here you are. What a pleasure it is to meet you, Aru." They both sat down. "I was so distressed to hear the news of your Grandmother Auwu (may we cherish her memory)."

They chatted for a while, but the Lady could see that Aru was tired. Although she'd missed dinner, some food and her bag would be sent up to her apartment for her. In her soft, high-pitched voice, the Lady explained to Aru that they'd discuss the details of her contract at some other time and tomorrow she would meet the children because this was to be her employment. She would be the assistant to the Lady's oldest daughter, who acted as governess. Before sending Aru off to her new quarters, Lady Akawu again expressed condolences regarding the passing of Aru's grandmother. She had been fond of Auwu and regretted she'd not see her again.

Aru was hungry, but she was even more tired, so when she was brought to her room she gulped down the food, pulled off her clothes, and fell into bed. She didn't notice much of anything.

Late the next morning she woke warm and cozy to ruby-gold light coming through a handsome opalescent window. She was in a small but cheerful bedroom, and breakfast had been brought in while she slept. The maid had included a pad of lint and a roll of calico bandage for her blistered heel. She sighed. Things were going to be all right. A bunch of violets stood in a yellow vase on the nightstand.

Getting herself cleaned up and oriented took until lunchtime, but after that Aru was ready to meet the children. There were five of them. Five little imps with ruddy little cheeks and Aru fell in love immediately. A long, low room on the upper floor, the nursery had a view of the ocean over the sea of roofs that was Ysgarlad.

Lwynn, the Lady's eldest, the governess, seemed about Aru's age. She had hair like her mother's but she wore it down her back, brushed into a bushy sweep, loosely wrapped with ribbon. Oddly, she had on riding boots and jodhpurs. Aru had never seen a woman dressed this way, and she wasn't even out riding.

The children had good manners and Aru felt welcome. "Watch out especially for this little nipper over here," Lwynn told Aru, laughing. "His name is Gekker. He'll have you locked in a cupboard somewhere if you're not careful!" The boy smiled up at Aru, who smiled back and roughed up the hair on his head.

The wallpaper and soft wool carpet gave a sunny, peppermint-candy mood to the room. Peonies, cockscomb, and tiny poppies were in the wallpaper pattern and also embroidered in larger sizes on the window seat cushions.

The oldest girl showed Aru the favorite toy, a fire engine. It was a brightly painted steam pump, crafted in detail from wood and metal. A wooden horse in leather harness—with real mane and tail hair—was hitched to it; the other horse lay around the nursery somewhere.

Aru enjoyed her afternoon of getting to know Lwynn and the children and learning about her duties. The next day Lwynn took Aru with them to some of the local shops. It wasn't far to the shopping district so they all went down on foot. They made a fine sight with the children walking along in their new white bibs. The baby girl rode coddled in soft blankets of lush silk and linen damask in the fashionable wicker carriage. Aru had a child's hand in each of her own, but by the end of the day she'd wish she were an octopus.

They were still a short distance from the milliner's when they heard a cackling laugh from inside the shop. Lwynn gave Aru an odd smile.

"The hatter—" she explained softly, "Sadly, he was exposed to fumes of mercury for far too many years. However, you'll find he's harmless."

They entered the store to find no one there. After a moment, though, a head popped out to look at them from behind a pillar. The man had on a flashy felt cap of the brightest scarlet. His eyes were small and round and he had an angular face with chiseled features. His demeanor was affected by the severe tremors in his limbs which were a result of the mercury poisoning. He smiled a shy greeting.

The children thought Lwynn would look fine in the hat with the fuchsia and silver plumes. She told them that they were sillies and that it wouldn't go with her coloring. She did like the hair combs, because of the tiny garnets, but nothing truly tickled her fancy today. The proprietor observed them from behind the counter while they were shopping. Then he cocked his head to the side and said, "Excuse me a moment, won't you?" He fluttered clumsily into the other room.

A loud tapping sound came from the room where he'd gone. Rat-a-tat-tat! Rat-a-tat-tat!

"Is he banging his head on the wall?" asked Gekker, who was quickly shushed.

More rapping, and then the man returned, snacking on a plateful of something, to his position behind the counter. "I'm so sorry," he said between gulps, "it's just that we have carpenter ants."

"No, but of course . . ." said Lwynn politely. She wasn't quite sure what to say. They left the hat shop soon after.

The sweets shop—all jars and tins and pastel doilies—was popular with the whole group, because Lwynn gave Aru some coins to buy treats for everyone. Lwynn's friend was already in the store shopping, and with the two engaged in conversation it fell mostly to Aru to supervise the little ones. The talkative friend carried a basket she was filling with chocolate-dipped cherries and foiled chocolate ladybugs.

Some of the candies you could serve yourself; for some you had to ask the ladies behind the counter. There were paper cones of freshly spun fairy floss, sugar plums, peppermint sticks, and a barrel of spicy roasted pecans. In the window a big vase showed off rhubarb custard lollipops and candied roses. Strawberry creme truffles were Lwynn's favorite. Aru chose two pieces of pomegranate taffy for herself and several cranberry chocolate pastels. For the children she bought raspberry drops, strawberry watermelon sours, and cherry ropes. Gekker, predictably, wanted a candy apple and then bubblegum for later.

There was one more place the children wanted to visit. After they had enjoyed some of their candy on the bench outside the shop, they were ready to move along. Lwynn was still busy with her friend inside, so Aru went ahead and brought the kids to the next shop.

The sign above the door read *Sea Garden Curiosity Shop.* Once inside, Aru realized what a foolish mistake she'd made. This was not the sort of place to find yourself monitoring a group of sticky, sugar-infused children. The shop was so crowded with merchandise she'd had to leave the baby carriage outside, and holding the wakeful infant on one hip left her only one hand free to work with.

First of all, Gekker and Rommel had to be dissuaded from climbing on the giant rusty anchor. Then the children showed Aru a small box containing nothing but what looked like a kidney bean. They insisted she hold the bean on the palm of her hand. After a few minutes, the bean began to hop about on her palm. In their excitement, the children hopped up and down like jumping beans themselves, nearly knocking over a dozen different things. Aru laughed and suggested they each hold a bean. This kept them busy until Lwynn caught up with them.

While Lwynn and the little ones examined exotic corals and interesting jewelry made from beach glass, Aru, with the infant still on her hip, wandered toward the back of the store. An ancient scarlet-faced gentleman with glasses and a crackly voice was speaking loudly into a telephone handset. Aru wasn't accustomed to telephones, so she found herself listening to the strange one-sided conversation:

"What he said about me, it just about makes my blood boil.

"I say: 'It makes my blood boil!'

"Well, if I'm a bottom-dweller, then what is he?

"No, no, I don't think so.

"What? Don't you call me a crab! I may be old, but you oughtn't think of me as a crab.

"Well, anyway, I must go. That little vixen from Vulpeden is here with the youngsters."

The man hung up the phone and welcomed Aru to his store. She examined a plum pudding mold, turning it over in her hands. "You have a lot of copper items here," she observed. "I suppose most of this was mined locally; you seem to have an appreciation for it."

The man smiled. "Yes, it's true. I love it. My family has always dealt in it. I suppose I've copper in my blood." He scuttled right over and began showing her his finest copper items: a large polished kettle, a washbasin. He had a soup tureen decorated with a wonderful design of a gryphon and a tearful calf-head turtle. The old man had ruddy, weathered skin and large hands, one quite bigger than the other.

Lwynn decided to buy some dangly earrings made from coral carved into clusters of roses. While she did this, Aru called the children's attention to a fine collection of sunset seascapes and to a model ship which had somehow got inside a bottle. She also pointed out some candy-dipped insects. There was a small jar of fake blood. Gekker found some playing cards with romantically suggestive images in a beside-the-sea theme. Thankfully, Lwynn appeared at this moment and said it was time to go. The baby had fallen asleep and Aru was eager to set her in the carriage and head back to Vulpeden.

Although Aru had enjoyed her day she was amazed by how tired she felt. She went early to bed. When, the following day, the children were compelled to remain idle due to having caught a cold, Aru felt a bit guilty about taking pleasure in the situation. With drippy noses and a couple of slight fevers the little ones spent the day in the nursery with rubber hot water bottles and an extended naptime. Aru's spirit had a chance to catch up with her. She welcomed the time to relax a bit. She felt good about the way things were turning out for her. She would be happy living here.

Breakfast the next morning was kippers. Aru sat down with the Gentleman's valet, who had just finished his meal. He leaned back in his chair with his prized cherrywood pipe. Conversation, as often happened, turned to the unusual color of Aru's complexion. "You have such lovely skin," the man said. "As a younger fellow I traveled the world, but I've never seen a face like yours. How would you describe the color?"

Aru sighed. "A light rosy teacup cream with golden undertones."

"Hmmm," said the man. He was quiet for a moment. "I'd call it a pale shrimp bisque."

"Maybe so," said Aru. "At any rate, it does an excellent job."

"Of . . . ?"

"Keeping my innards from spilling all over the place." Aru was picking at her food.

"Hmmm," said the man. "I have heard of people who have skin like yours. But I've never seen it before. Those folk live far across the continent, somewhere in the northern mountains."

"I've heard of them, too. I believe those may be my people," said Aru. She paused, considering whether to suppress her impulse to continue. "I am a high princess. I mean to say that I'm fairly certain I am, but my family has hidden me away. However, I hope to soon rejoin my people." She startled, looked around, and added in a lower voice, "Please don't mention this to anyone."

"A princess, you say! So what's happened? You are in exile? What did you do, date the wrong sort?"

Aru was serious. "I really shouldn't have said anything. Please, let's change the subject."

They sat without speaking for a few minutes while the man smoked and Aru nibbled at her buckwheat toast.

"Why aren't you eating your fish?" asked the man.

"I don't like red herring."

"Well, there's a lot of it hereabouts, Princess," he said, "so if you want to remain here you're just going to have to put up with it."

After breakfast Aru was to go and speak with Lady Akawu in her second-floor office. She felt somewhat nervous, but it turned out that the purpose of the meeting was merely to check in with Aru and make sure that things were working out well for her. The Lady seemed pleased with Aru's performance so far. They were chatting pleasantly when a maid in a candy-striped apron rushed in, excused herself, and whispered something close to the Lady's ear.

The Lady asked Aru to kindly wait outside the office door for just a few minutes. The maid showed her to a comfortable alcove in the hallway, and as she seated herself on a velvet chaise lounge, the maid ushered a large and puffy bald man in a pink suit into the Lady's office. He had a little curly pigtail in the back. Aru watched the closed door for a while. She waited. It seemed longer than a few minutes. She stared at the carpet in front of her. A rich autumnal floral pattern. After a while, in the curlicues and designs, she began to see various creature faces. Or maybe they were transforms in their animal shapes. They looked just the same in a stylized design. That repeating crimson curl—she could see it as the head of a horse creature, or of a transforming horse, or even of a seahorse. She wondered what Lwynn and the children were doing at the moment. Slowly and purposefully, she pushed all her cuticles back with her thumbnail. She sat. She found a hole in her sleeve that she had never noticed before.

The big man came back out. He gave her a glance with friendly eyes as he passed, and a little grunt as a greeting, and hurried on his way. Looking after him Aru noticed a large heart-shaped birthmark behind his enormous left ear. She rose and let herself back into the office.

"Oh—Aru—" The Lady beckoned her to enter while she hurriedly brushed something from her mahogany desktop into a drawer and snapped it shut. Aru wasn't nosy, but it looked like a pile of fine glass gems or even rubies. Aru wanted to inquire but she didn't dare.

"Now, where were we?" asked the Lady. Her soft voice had gone to an even higher pitch than usual. "Yes, Aru, as I was saying before, I do regret to inform you that there has been a change of plan."

"Change of plan?"

"Indeed," she said.

She looked right at Aru, yet seemed to be looking past her, as if her mind was already on other things. "We won't be able to employ you here at Vulpeden, after all. However, I will personally arrange for your placement at another house. Now, you are a fine worker and a good girl, and I'm sure there won't be any trouble."

"But—"

"Don't interrupt, I'm a busy woman. There will be a coach engaged to pick you up tomorrow morning. Be ready at sunrise. Don't look that way now, girl—all this is quite in order with the arrangements made by your Grandmother Auwu (may we cherish her memory)."

Aru's shock prevented her from any rational response. The Lady brushed her out of the office just like she'd brushed the baubles from her desk. "Run along now, sweetheart," she said. "The children are feeling better, they'll probably be with Lwynn in the garden."

Aru went straight to her apartment. Why should she go to the garden, or go running about the house looking for the children? She'd already been let go. What was Akawu going to do, fire her again? She thought about running away, but to where? No, it would be best to wait and see what was in store for her. What sort of place would they send her to? Her mind raised a whirl of questions. What ever could have happened? She hadn't done anything wrong, she knew that. Had she?

This is how Aru's thinking went, all day long and through much of the night, as she remained in her room with intermittent periods of crying in exasperation and chagrin. That man with the big ears, did he say something to the Lady? Who was he? But no, what could he possibly have said? In the early hours of the morning she stood in front of the looking glass, holding the candle close to inspect her swollen puffy eyes. She critically observed a couple of bumps and some scarring on her cheek. At least the valet hadn't mentioned her acne when he evaluated her skin. She reached for the bottle her beaver friend had given her and applied some more mithridate. Aru turned her head to the side, keeping her eyes on the mirror. The elixir did seem to have made a difference already.

After stepping back to observe herself Aru took a long look into her own face and reflected on how much she looked like her mother. *I'm a princess,* she thought, *I will be fine.* She wondered if the new house might be even more impressive than this one.

As the sun peeked over the roofs of the city Aru stood with a footman in the street in front of the house of Vulpeden, waiting for the coach to arrive. In the glow of dawn the house again seemed so huge, and Aru felt so small. Such a comfortable, safe haven—and already she was an outsider once more. A passing cab pulled to the curb and the driver disembarked and opened the door for her. This was no coach! Just a battered, run-down cab with a scrawny, tired-looking sorrel horse. Aru climbed inside as the footman lifted her carpetbag for the driver and paid him. The door closed, the driver climbed up behind, and they were off. The cab turned and headed down the hill.

Through the window Aru had a last glimpse of the house. She'd been there such a short time, yet she knew she'd miss those babies. Still, she felt a tremble of excitement inside. On to another adventure! Maybe this new house would have a gramophone in the servants' quarters or a sunny arboretum she could visit. Or perhaps the lord of the manor would be an attractive young bachelor. Aru's thoughts headed in this direction as she peered at the early morning city going by.

The cab traveled a good distance across town but it all flashed past, a jumble of sights and smells. They arrived at a boulevard that ran right along the oceanfront. The cabby pulled up to let Aru off at the foot of one of several piers. There she stood. Alone in the midst of the great city. She didn't feel scared. Carrying her bag, she walked out to the end of the dock. A group of young girls were crabbing there, and several people stood gazing out to sea. For a while Aru stood inhaling the salt air. The smell of the ocean was invigorating, despite wafts of rotting corn and tomatoes from the canneries. The impressive brick buildings along the waterfront, the sailing ships, the red cliffs along the bay—all these things thrilled her. But eager curiosity now urged her to unfold a piece of paper the footman had given her. It read: *Mrs. Bukk Bukbagok, Rhedyn House, Number 14 Moab Seaboard Parkway.*

Aru headed back up to the street. None of the buildings seemed to have numbers. Anyway, these were all warehouses and the like. She must be on the wrong road. Aru stopped an old man who pushed a wheelbarrow brimming over with the remains of lobsters. He was sorry, he'd never heard of it. She asked a ragged apple-faced girl who was passing by. Number 14 Moab Seaboard Parkway—yes. That big building right over there. Mrs. Bukbagok would be around the back and up the stairs. Aru thanked her, feeling a little confused. However, the girl spoke as if she knew what she was talking about. If Aru had been more worldly, she'd have given the girl a copper coin. But Aru didn't know.

With pounding heart, Aru went to the back of the building. It smelled of stewed tomatoes. A narrow wooden stairway climbed the brick wall. This was obviously some sort of factory. This just made no sense whatsoever. She successfully ascended with her carpetbag to the precarious balcony high up on the upper floor. She found the door cracked open. She went in.

A short hallway, then a couple of cramped offices. Some boys stared from a doorway farther down. Everyone had on stodgy maroon uniforms. Mercifully, a man asked if he could be of help. He directed Aru into a large, sparsely furnished room. Here she'd find the matron, Mrs. Bukbagok, he told her.

Aru looked around the room and was about to wonder where Mrs. Bukbagok could be, when she had a shock: just over her right shoulder someone stood high up on a ladder! Aru's first sight of Mrs. Bukbagok was a view up her skirts, a view dominated by a pair of puffy reddish-brown bloomers with scrawny yellow-stockinged legs poking out of them. Aru turned her head, but it was too late. That image would be unalterably bound to her future memories of Mrs. Bukbagok.

Because Mrs. Bukbagok was involved in her work she didn't appear to notice Aru at first, but when she did acknowledge her presence she climbed down off her perch, set down her duster, and wiped her hands so she could greet the new arrival.

Mrs. Bukbagok had a loud voice of rather harsh timbre. Her dress and hair were both a rich mahogany, like her underpinnings. The hair, pulled into a topknot, was fastened with a large scarlet comb. Mouth fixed firmly into a frown as she talked, her round eyes were far apart and she wore far too much rouge. Her appearance was comical and yet quite frightening.

After welcoming Aru to Rhedyn House, Mrs. Bukbagok informed a worker who had just walked in that she was to take Aru to get a uniform and instruct her about her duties.

"Sorry, there's some mistake!" Aru exclaimed. "I'm to be working as a domestic, not in a factory. Is there a manor, Mrs. Bukbagok, that you oversee?"

Both of the women began to cackle in a terribly offensive way.

"No, my little chickabiddy, this place is quite enough to keep me busy. No, everything's in order, you were sent here to be in my employ. That's the arrangement. Unless you'd prefer to sleep in the street?" Mrs. Bukbagok gave a funny jerk to her head and peered at Aru. Then, while still assessing Aru with her eyes, she said to the worker, "You can skip the washing—she's quite clean. She just came down from Vulpeden, this one."

"Vulpeden! My!" The worker took Aru rather firmly by the arm and directed her along the passageway to another room. The smell of tomatoes filled the air. She sat Aru down on a bench in what amounted to a stuffy, glorified closet and returned in a few minutes with a folded uniform, some ugly shoes, and a sack.

"I think these will fit fine," she said. "Just change into these clothes and put your belongings in the bag. Your things will be kept for you."

Aru would have appreciated some privacy, but she didn't get it. The woman hovered over her while she reluctantly changed out of her dress and put on the pink cotton petticoat and shapeless maroon serge. Aru tied her shoes while the woman folded Aru's clothes and crammed them into the sack, shoving the carpetbag in after them.

"These will be cleaned," she said as she left the room.

"My bag? No—I don't want . . ." but the worker had disappeared.

Aru hugged herself while she sat staring at her lap. It was hot in the little room. Her skin felt damp. There was a big, sunny window, but looking up at it she could only see the brick of the building next door. She rubbed her sleeves and tugged at the fabric of the rough maroon smock. It smelled of starch. Aru leaned back against the wall. Where was that woman? Aru got up and paced the floor. She stood on the bench, but the window was too high. She sat back down. That aroma of tomatoes truly filled the air. A comforting smell, really. Aru remembered having tomato soup with her grandma; they made it from the garden tomatoes. She and Grandma would sit by the fire and sip spicy tomato soup out of their favorite mugs; Grandma would tell her stories about why the leaves turn color in the fall, or maybe she'd remember a good coming-of-age tale.

A high soprano voice startled Aru out of her thoughts. "Awke had an errand, so she sent me to come help you." A young woman, smallish, maybe slightly older than Aru, stood with her hands loosely clenched in front of her chest and peered at her with great big, soft, bulging eyes of the deepest brown. Aru got up from the bench, straightened her smock, and introduced herself.

"I'm Phfft-Psyfft," said the young lady, "It's good to make your acquaintance. Well, I suppose—I mean, I assume it is, I really don't know you yet. But you look like a nice person, don't you." She turned and led Aru through the doorway. What a beautiful color of rusty brown hair she had. It was hastily done up and all sticking out in tufts above her ears. "Come along," she said. Aru followed the girl down the hall the opposite way from where she'd entered the building and then they rounded a corner.

They were met with a blast of hot, humid air. They'd entered a huge room. "This is the peeling room. This is where you'll be working, but don't you worry about that right now. I'll show you around the plant. I'm in no rush to return to this particular crucible of drudgery."

In front of them were four tables, and several dozen uniformed workers, most of them standing on long, low platforms to avoid the juices and pulp which dribbled to the floor.

Near the center of the room were a couple of huge brick chimneys. Each of these had a great hole cut through the floorboards in front, with a block and tackle set over, and lots of steam rising from downstairs. Phfft-Psyfft explained that one allowed the scalded, unpeeled tomatoes up from below and the other was for the strained product to be lowered down. They went over to peer down through the holes. There were huge wooden tanks down there, and great copper cauldrons and lots of people rushing about.

"Let's go upstairs," said Aru's guide.

The upper floor was the dormitory. The two spent some time on the women's side, poking idly through people's things while Phfft-Psyfft chatted and gossiped about life at Rhedyn House and how much she hated tomato soup. Finally Aru asked where her own bed would be.

"Oh, you and I aren't in the dorm," said her new friend. "We're up here." She motioned for Aru to follow her as she crossed the room and climbed a narrow staircase which emerged into a sweltering garret under the eaves of the building. "It's a bit dark, but we have lamps.

It's too hot to stay up here right now, though. In the evening we open the dormers and it's not so bad. There's a bunch of us who sleep up here." As they descended the steep steps Phfft-Psyfft said they'd better be getting back to the workroom, anyway.

Aru followed obediently to peeling table number two, where she was introduced to Phfft-Psyfft's friends. These were two sisters, Tsik-Tsik and Churr, and their brother Piew. The third sister, Siew-Siew, worked downstairs as a cook. Phfft-Psyfft put on a headscarf to cover her hair, and handed one to Aru.

Peeling freshly-scalded tomatoes is a dreadful business. If coming to a new place or seeing the inside of a factory for the first time held even an element of fun for Aru, that was smashed now. By the time she had mangled her third tomato—"You'll be an expert soon enough," the others said—she was exasperated, and already tired of life in the Rhedyn cannery.

At any rate, there's been some sort of mistake, she thought. *Soon I'll hear from the house where I ought to have been delivered.* But she knew this wasn't so.

Aru could see immediately that the only way to make this job tolerable would be to enjoy socializing with the other people. She realized that, yes, she'd catch on to the peeling techniques, but she hadn't even learned them yet and she was bored with the job. She felt glad the workers were such a talkative lot. The chit-chat was incessant.

Besides the siblings and Phfft-Psyfft, there were three others at this table: an old woman named Wobwak, a fellow called Toktok, and his younger brother Piep, a child of only about eight years old. These three, as the day wore on, proved to be rather rude to Aru, if not downright unfriendly. At supper in the dining hall they were even worse. Not only that, there were others in the crowd that acted the same way toward Aru, insulting her, and Aru worried they might actually become violent. She realized that there was a reason Phfft-Psyfft had chosen to sit in the corner with their backs to the wall.

Up in the garret after supper the smelly oil lamps burned with a ruddy glow. As promised, gusts of sweet air came from the open windows.

Ready to fall into bed, Aru politely sat and talked with the others. None of those who had picked on Aru were with them in the attic, so she had an opportunity to ask about what might have caused this behavior.

"It's nothing personal," Phfft-Psyfft told her. "It's just their nature."

"Don't worry. They'll only be like this for a few days," said Churr.

"This is the way they act with any newcomer," added Siew-Siew.

Aru asked why there seemed to be only certain people in the attic. The girls laughed and one of them said the garret rooms were reserved for the real nutcases and those who were completely bats. They laughed again.

"Y'know," remarked Siew-Siew, "a few times I've seen mice up here."

"Mice?" shrieked a young woman Aru hadn't met. "I didn't know we had mice!"

"Indeed," said Siew-Siew, "we see them once in a while."

"That reminds me," said Phfft-Psyfft, and she rummaged in a crate at the end of her bed, producing something in a velvet bag which she presented to Aru.

"What's this?" asked Aru, and then she smelled it. "Tobacco?"

"Yes, you'll be needing that. Scatter it in a circle around your bed every night."

"Whatever for?"

Phfft-Psyfft's pretty copper-toned cheeks flushed. The other girls looked uncomfortable. There are some things that are just embarrassing to admit, no matter how fastidious you are about cleanliness.

"We've a tiny infestation of goblins," said Siew-Siew. "Hemogoblins."

"Are they dangerous?" asked Aru.

"They're after blood," Siew-Siew answered. "They make bumps on your skin. An itchy rash."

Phfft-Psyfft told Aru not to worry. "The ring of tobacco leaves will keep you safe; the hemogoblins hate the chemicals in the tobacco."

Despite the news about creepy-crawlies, Aru slept soundly and didn't wake until the morning bell at sunrise. Sorghum cereal for breakfast, and then they were back out on the floor. Aru spent another day fighting with the skins of tomatoes. A couple of times Mrs. Bukbagok checked in with Aru to see how she was doing. Workdays were sunrise to sundown, six days per week. On the free day, workers could come and go as they pleased, as long as they were ready for the workday next morning. Payday was the day before free day. Aru had no questions.

Days went by, one just like the other. Aru did indeed find that the workers who had been so nasty at first soon calmed down and accepted her. Old Wobwak, who had been especially foul with her comments, actually made a point of saying something nice. When the free day came, Aru didn't go anywhere. Exhausted from working in a suffocating environment all week, Aru chose to stay in the garret. They had opened up the windows for the day, and it wasn't too bad. She slept most of the time, covered only by a sheet to keep off the fruit flies. She didn't forget the protective tobacco.

All of the following week it was the same. Aru worked hard all day long and spent the evenings gossiping in the garret. She did become faster at peeling tomatoes. Joining in the conversations indeed helped the time to pass, but every morning she got up and got dressed with a dread of the day in her heart. She cried for her grandma. She missed Hauva and the others. How could her life have come to this?

Phfft-Psyfft knew Aru came from Vulpeden and she wanted to hear about that house. Aru told her how she had traveled up from her home with her ailing grandma and all that had happened along the way. One evening Phfft-Psyfft shared her own story with Aru.

Born in the Drey region of the southern quarter, Phfft-Psyfft was from a village among the orchards there. Her family grew chestnuts and filberts, along with a few apples. She had three brothers and a sister, and she was the second youngest, along with a twin brother. The area down that way was prosperous, and her parents were wealthy and conservative. Everything must be done in the traditional manner, following strict rules and rituals.

Life was easy in the orchards; for the soil was productive and the growing conditions ideal, and most of the families lived in a cradle of affluence. Although it wasn't truly required by their situation, people worked hard. The accumulation of a nice fat reserve of savings was of paramount importance. Always be ready for adversity, that was the age-old doctrine. They also spent a lot of time at play, though. People were physically active.

Phfft-Psyfft dabbed her eye with a lacey handkerchief embroidered with golden acorns, then smiled weakly and related the following:

"I grew up in a happy environment, cutting capers among the trees with my siblings and a couple of friends. One friend I have always been very close with, Olooka. She is my best friend, but I haven't seen her for ages. The two of us were constantly scolded by the elders because we'd want to do things differently. We didn't like nut picking. When we made cedar baskets we would add feathers and abalone just like the ladies from Eerie did. In our view, change is inherent in our traditions. But the elders weren't happy about what we were doing.

"One day Olooka found out that she must marry a certain fellow from another village. She and I had always assumed we'd marry in our own village. There was this one young man that we both thought most gorgeous. We'd have little fights, all in fun, about which of us would end up with him. When Olooka was sent away we were both devastated. She didn't know her husband at all.

"Then, some time later, my mother informed me that I would marry this boy called Phfft-Psyfft. Yes, the same name as me! This fellow was close friends with the very handsome boy. I had never particularly liked Phfft-Psyfft. He used to tease me when we were younger, he made fun of my rose madder dresses and he said I had fluffy hair. I never had fluffy hair.

"The wedding ceremony was grand but I was so indignant I don't remember much of it now. I cried a lot in those days and I missed Olooka terribly. My husband resented me as much as I him. We fought a lot. Once I bit him hard on the face. It drew blood. He had to walk around like that for days. I felt so ashamed. I truly was miserable. I still was attracted to the other boy, so I felt bad for every reason. Phfft-Psyfft and I—our marriage wasn't consummated for a long time.

"Slowly, though, I began to realize who he truly was and I began to have feelings for him. As my eyes opened I could see that the other fellow was nothing more than a pretty boy, flighty and without character. As I gained respect for Phfft-Psyfft, however, Phfft-Psyfft remained disparaging of me. So I hid my feelings—what else could I do?—and just tried to live my life as best I could.

"Time went on, and I was deeply in love, just a painful experience. I loved him, purely, fully, secretly. I so much wanted him to love me back. And still we never touched each other. Then we had a monstrous fight, the worst ever. I cried. Then he cried, because I was crying. I took his hand and he pulled me toward him. We kissed. Our passions poured forth into an amorous encounter. We weren't proficient . . . but it was nice. That was the only time. The only time ever.

"The next morning he was gone. It had seemed like he loved me, but he fled from me, went off by sea to look for his missing cousin, as I was told. That's when I ran away. That's how I ended up here. I didn't know I was with child. It's been four months and no one has heard anything of Phfft-Psyfft. It was a dangerous errand he pursued. They say he's been . . . They say he'll never be back."

"Oh, I wouldn't listen to that sort of talk!" said Aru. She did her best to encourage her friend, because—who knew?—maybe he loved her too, maybe he was alive out there somewhere. Maybe he'd find his maturity and then he'd find her. Aru hadn't had any idea that Phfft-Psyfft might be pregnant. Now she felt unsure how to feel.

Another week went by in the cannery. Aru did her best to comply, and to give the performance expected of her, but it was soul-squelching work. How could it be that the others didn't object to the discomfort and the mindless pace of the passing days? They seemed happy enough just doing their jobs and keeping company with one another. Aru wished she could foster that sort of attitude.

After Aru had become familiar with how things worked at Rhedyn House, her relationship with Phfft-Psyfft changed. When Aru had been new to the situation, Phfft-Psyfft looked out for her and helped her to adjust. Now Aru watched out for Phfft-Psyfft, her pregnant friend. Mrs. Bukbagok and her cronies among the workforce apparently enjoyed random picking and pecking at others. Phfft-Psyfft's current fruitfulness had recently become a favorite subject of gossip and Aru often found herself in a protective role.

As a result of one of these encounters with Mrs. Bukbagok and through the fault of Aru's defensive and uncensored tongue, Aru was sent to spend an afternoon at the soup kettles. If peeling could be called the worst job in the world, stirring fell a step below that. The look of shock on her co-workers' faces when she was told she'd be going downstairs was far from comforting.

On the first floor, aside from the huge wooden vats for scalding the tomatoes, there were four giant copper cauldrons. Three of these were for simmering the soup. Aru noticed Siew-Siew busy at a table, chopping something. She didn't recognize anyone else who she knew well. Directed to the first of the caldrons, Aru was made to climb up on a scaffold. The job was relatively simple: stir. Well, this couldn't be too hard—she saw an old lady stationed at the next kettle over. If an old lady could do it then certainly Aru could handle it. How soon Aru found the error of this observation! Saunas are refreshing and wonderful, but not when you have to spend the day in them. Upstairs had been sweltering and humid, but now Aru found herself directly in the steam. The task was to stir for a few minutes, rest for a few minutes, repeating without end. If she rested too long the soup would scorch. That would be trouble. So Aru stirred the soup.

After about an hour of this suffering, The Mister happened to come by. The Mister was, of course, the master, Mrs. Bukbagok's husband. He inquired as to how Aru was holding up. Then he continued on his way, sending young Mu up the scaffold to advise Aru about her stirring technique. Mu, like some of the other young men, had forsaken his uniform shirt in favor of a short-sleeved undershirt. A big, beefy boy with wistful eyes, he had a tattoo on his upper arm, a strange sort of rune that Aru couldn't interpret.

He gently took the paddle from Aru and showed her how to scrape the bottom of the kettle and how to use the shoulders and torso, not just the arms. "Lo, girl, your hands are looking mighty rough," he said.

Aru's hands were a mass of burns from peeling tomatoes, compounded now with blisters from stirring. She sighed. "I'm afraid I'll bleed into the tomato soup."

"You wouldn't be the first one." He laughed. "Don't worry, who's ever to know? A bit of extra protein will help the stock along." He did hand her a rag to use for gripping the paddle. Aru continued to stir and stir, on and on, endlessly.

The aching tiredness in Aru's arms from the repetative motion eventually morphed into veritable torture, and her breathing came with difficulty. No longer were her lungs pumping air in and out while she concerned herself with other things; now each moist breath took intent and Aru was compelled to squeeze the muscles of her diaphragm with the same type of effort it took to make a fist or move her legs. She knew her body would take over the effort if she could stop thinking about it. She couldn't stop thinking about it.

Thick bubbles in the swirling liquid rose and burst. Aru's eyes focused on them, internalizing the sensation as hot lava bubbling through her veins, flowing and burning through her lungs and furiously swollen heart. She felt she could vomit forth buckets and buckets of hot volcanic blood. Her body moved like a rag doll, mechanically circling into unreality, existing beyond the pain and beyond the punishment, beyond the tiredness.

A memory came, or else a fantasy, of floating inside the womb and all that orange-red light passing right through mother's flesh as if it were a parchment lampshade, filling the little world around her. But it wasn't mother she floated inside, after all, it was the sun. Searing, scorching, melting. Life had become a soup of wretched heat. Nothing really mattered, nothing really mattered at all . . .

"Here she comes."

Aru woke with an unhappy Mrs. Bukbagok, all in a flutter, leaning over her, fanning her and clucking away, "—give the girl some air . . . tsk-tsk . . . Such a thing! My stars!"

"Here she comes," repeated someone. "She's coming back to us."

"Take her up to her bed; it's been too long a day."

A pair of women helped her to her bed and out of her clothes. She drifted off to sleep

The following day was free day and there was no work. Aru was stiff and sore, but she did feel like going somewhere. Phfft-Psyfft and Aru, with the obligatory pearl-pink pinafores over their regular uniforms, took a streetcar up one of the higher hills to get a view of Ysgarlad.

They also planned to visit a little place that Phfft-Psyfft thought Aru ought to know about. They caught the smell of chili emanating from a busy restaurant as they approached, but the young women didn't have enough money to both eat and shop for trinkets, so they knew they'd be going hungry for lunch. They disembarked from the trolley and followed a winding lane uphill to reach the highest ground they could for the view. It was warm and sunny. A private estate sat on the crown of the hill, but just outside its walls a narrow alley led to an embankment shored up by brick.

As Aru climbed up the slope to reach the top of this wall she noticed an adorable fat little chickaree leaping from branch to branch in the madrona trees above. "What do you think of this gorgeous day, my squirrel friend?" she inquired with a smile. She sighed. "I'm so happy to be out here and away from that wretched cannery!"

After steeping herself in the glowing beauty of the scenery before her, Aru realized she'd lost track of Phfft-Psyfft. She couldn't see her, so she called out, "Phfft-Psyfft! I'm right here on the wall!"

Her friend answered from the lane just below Aru's feet.

"Oh, there you are!" exclaimed Aru. "I didn't see where you went."

Phfft-Psyfft scrambled up the steep hill to join Aru on top of the wall, her pregnant condition not slowing her down in the least. It felt good to sit on the sun-warmed brick and the cool dry air was a pleasant change. The two gazed out over all those clay roofs, they could see the entire bay and up the coast a way. There were several islands, all with high cliffs and rock formations like those along the shore.

The girls were quiet, having nothing they needed to say as their workdays were filled with chatting. It felt good to be doing nothing. Eventually, though, Phfft-Psyfft got tired of the silence. She asked Aru if she was feeling any better about yesterday's mishaps.

Aru kept staring off at the horizon. It took her a long time to say anything. "That day is one I don't care to repeat," she said, "but that's not really what's bothering me now." She continued her scan of the distant sea. "What's bothering me is: what about all of the days?"

Phfft-Psyfft didn't know what she meant.

"I just don't know what's the point," Aru said.

"The point?"

"Yes. Why do we get up in the morning, Phfft-Psyfft? It all seems so meaningless."

"I know what you mean," replied Phfft-Psyfft gently. Although, really, she didn't.

"I feel lost," whispered Aru. "It's as if I'm in the wrong universe. Blowing through this life like a leaf in the wind. Especially since my grandma died."

"You just need time. That's what I think," said Phfft-Psyfft. "You have to give yourself some time to heal, and to settle in. You'll feel better later on."

The shop's double doors were recessed between the front windows. As you walked up to these doors you could look through side windows to see many more items in an enticing display. It was a clever trap, this design of a storefront. By the time you were in the alcove surrounded by glass you were practically inside the shop; you may as well come all the way in.

Aru and Phfft-Psyfft poked through the merchandise and tried things on. Aru fell in love with a heart-shaped music box, sweet, but far too costly. There was also an apple doll, nicely crafted. The face had dried to look just like a cheery old woman, and she had a headscarf and calico dress. She quite resembled Aru's grandma, even though the skin was flushed and brown. She had rosy cheeks and bright little eyes. Unfortunately, Aru couldn't quite afford the doll, either. Reluctantly, she walked away. She did find something else, though: an old copy of *The Monster's Curse* for only a copper. She had never read it.

Aru didn't notice what happened the instant she'd turned away from the row of dolls. The eyes of a crudely carved figure popped wide open! An ugly doll she hadn't noticed, it was of a sausage shape with a hat like a cloven mushroom. Made from dark volcanic cinder, it had witches' marks scratched all along the side. This carving lay right beside the apple doll. The thing had a wicked smile.

While she continued to browse, something inside Aru pestered her until, returning with coins borrowed from Phfft-Psyfft, she reached for the apple doll. Neither she nor her friend, chattering away, observed the bloodshot eyes and wicked smile that transfered, appearing just for a moment, to Aru's new doll before she carried it to the register.

As they left the store to walk around window-shopping, Phfft-Psyfft handed Aru a bundle. "For you," she said with a smile. Inside the folded linen were a small embroidery hoop, a packet of needles, some tiny folding scissors, and embroidery floss in magenta, coral, and gold.

In response to Aru's bewilderment, Phfft-Psyfft explained that her great uncle had been quite talented at embroidery. His wife had suggested it as an occupation after he retired. He found it a wonderful meditation, and the family treasured his splendid embroidered chairs. Phfft-Psyfft thought it might be a nice activity for Aru.

Supper time approached, and the day was still quite warm. They boarded the trolley to head back down to the waterfront. Phfft-Psyfft felt tired, so after they disembarked she returned to Rhedyn House with most of their packages, but Aru followed the shoreline boulevard north until she came to an open area with a rocky beach below the cliff. A row of thick old cherry trees in full bloom ran along the rim, offering the perfect place to sit and watch the gorgeous sunset. She thought about her day with Phfft-Psyfft. The water in the bay was calm. The surface shimmered and dimpled beautifully, like hammered metal. The vivid colors of the sky reflected in it and also in the headlands beyond the bay. A windjammer with several tall masts of dark burgundy sails was leisurely drifting into port.

Aru sighed. The beauty, the warm sea breeze, it was soothing, but the loneliness in her heart felt compounded by the fact that this restful interlude ought to have made her at peace in her soul. And it didn't.

Aru opened up *The Monster's Curse* and leaned back against a tree. There should still be enough light to read for a while. A couple of cherry blossom petals fell on the page; she brushed them off. The story started out with a bang. A young man is involved in a horrible accident and as he lies prostrate on the forest highway an angry faceless form sweeps him up and carries him into the woods. His poor fiancée awakes, trapped under the overturned carriage, bleeding profusely, and—goodness, these cherry petals!

Aru read on, transfixed by the activity in the story, but the petals kept falling every moment or two and now even full blossoms were dropping. She began to get annoyed. Why so many petals falling, anyway? She looked up into the branches above. With a shriek she jumped to her feet. "Who—who are you? My thunder!" She stared. "You nearly stilled my heart!"

"Fairly obviously, I'm not an owl." This rude reply came from a gentleman who was casually sprawled on a limb of the tree above Aru's head. How had she not seen him?

"How long have you been there?" Aru covered her chest with her book while the other hand went to her temple.

Even in the course of this outlandish introduction, the young man's overwhelming attractiveness could not be overlooked. Observations flooded through Aru's mind: He had a perfect face. Kingly, she thought. His green eyes were those of a solitary soul, disenchanted and mistrusting, twice shy and full of young-man anger. She found this inexplicably attractive. Besides, those eyes had an intelligent depth that drew her in, somehow. She felt like she knew him. Aru found herself wanting to touch his face, to kiss him. Yes. To kiss him! This complete stranger!

He answered only with a smile, so Aru whispered, "What are you doing up there?"

Tossing another pair of cherry blossoms in her direction, he said, "I was enjoying the view of the ocean," then added, "but it wasn't ruined when you came along."

The young man had a quiet voice. Impeccably dressed, he wore a tailcoat of velvet the color of autumn rust. What kind of person would climb a tree dressed like that? "Are you going to climb down?"

In answer he rose up to crouch upon the branch and then he leapt all the way down to alight, gracefully, beside her. His thick hair was a dark ginger color. His breath smelled strongly of cloves or maybe cinnamon. Aru backed away. "I'm not going to bite you," he said.

Aru didn't know what to say.

"It's so warm this evening," she said. "Don't you think so?"

"What's that you're reading?" he asked. She showed him. He took the book and thumbed through it, returning it with a laugh. "I wouldn't want to read that, myself," he said. "I've enough demons in my life."

"I think it's the monsters in my own mind that make this kind of thing interesting," said Aru, smiling. "It's exciting. A crime story."

"Likely the poor monster's biggest crimes are its crimes against reality. Defying the laws of nature."

"Those aren't true crimes. They're not by choice."

"Nature's a heartless judge, though, isn't she."

"That's true enough," said Aru. "She can be."

"I'm reading something right now, an amusing novel. It concerns different perceptions of reality. Honestly, I'm starting to question the author's sanity."

"Oh, but that sounds interesting."

"Yes, it is. One has to pay attention; there are surprises and lots of things to notice. It's almost like a game. For instance, every chapter is a different color."

"What?"

"You'd have to read it."

He gave her the title and told her it was from the tiny library on Third and Bell. She could read it when he was finished, if she wanted.

The light was fading rapidly from the sky. "Look," the young man said, "You ought not be out here alone this time of the day. I live up by the public market. I'll walk you home." Anyone could tell by the uniform and smock that she belonged at Rhedyn.

"All right. Thank you." said Aru. And so they strolled back along the waterfront. He didn't talk much. She realized that his boots were making absolutely no sound on the pavement as they walked along. She felt a chill. For a moment she wondered if this fellow could be a ghost. No, what a silly idea!

Before Aru knew it, they had arrived at the cannery. He walked her to the foot of the stairs and waited politely until she reached the top. Then he bid her farewell. Before she shut the door she called out, "If you please, what is your name?"

"Nrouhw," he said.

"I'm Aru."

"Good night," said Nrouhw as he hurried off.

"Pleased to meet you, Nrouhw!" squeaked Aru as he disappeared down the alley. "Good night!"

After spending a few minutes just breathing, Aru floated down the hallway and then scurried upstairs to find her friends.

Over the next week, through the pressure and sticky heat of the days and the rosy-lit garret chatter in the evenings, Aru and Phfft-Psyfft relived Aru's encounter with the young gentleman countless times. When free day arrived the two stayed in, taking time to relax and rest. Phfft-Psyfft taught Aru simple embroidery stitches. Aru caught on quickly and created a rather pleasing dragonfly design. The magical process of seeing it in her mind's eye, then slowly appearing on the linen was a new experience for Aru. It didn't matter that the dragonfly looked little like the one she'd imagined. She was creating something. A little piece of herself, it would have its own journey through actuality. Aru found this comforting.

In the early evening Aru and Phfft-Psyfft headed off together down the waterfront boulevard, because they wanted to watch the sunset from the spot with the cherry trees. Unfortunately, no one else came along to enjoy the view except for an elderly man walking his dog.

The next thing Aru knew, she was back at the peeling table. It seemed like she always stood at the peeling table. If she wasn't there she carried dread of going there soon. The best part of Aru's week was the moment the bell rang to say the last work day was over. That was when there was the maximum time before she had to stand at the table again. Would this be her life? Growing old with scalded tomatoes and the commands of bells, as many of these people had done?

The work week went on. Chittering and chatting with the others brought some relief, but already Aru knew about as much as there was to know about most of her cannery friends, and some of their personalities were becoming tiresome. Aru didn't object to the friendly gossip, but the constant henpecking and backbiting wore her down.

On Thursday one of the cleaning girls stopped by the peeling table to say that Siew-Siew had told her that she overheard Wabwak say that the description of Aru's beau sounded like the fellow that took tickets at the SeaStar. Aru and Phfft-Psyfft looked at one another. "We're off to see a motion picture!" they cried in unison.

The SeaStar Theatre was a quick trolley ride away. On their next day off Phfft-Psyfft, Tsik-Tsik, Churr, and Siew-Siew, in their maroon uniforms dressed up with the pink smocks, went with Aru to the matinee. On their approach to the theatre they could see the young man in his ticket box. Yes, it definitely was him. Aru realized that she suddenly needed to go elsewhere, but her friends were having none of that. With quiet giggles and big smiles, they swept her along to the ticket window.

Nrouhw was even more gorgeous than Aru had recalled. Did he recognize her? He surely had a look of surprise on his face. This may have been evoked by the sight of Aru again, yes, but it also may have been caused by this group of young ladies who were apparently quite excited to see the film *Bare-Knuckle Blood*. With smiling faces they purchased their tickets. He didn't seem to recognize Aru, and the hearts of all the friends began to sink. Aru felt a numbness creeping in. She'd so hoped he'd remember her.

Just when they had thanked him and were about to turn from the box and enter the theater, the young man looked right at Aru and said, "It's so nice to see you again."

Caught by surprise, all Aru could do was blush and say, "The pleasure's mine," and try not to trip over her skirts as she walked away.

The motion picture was horrible. Why anyone would wish to spend their time watching boxers punch one another to pulp and then betray their closest friends, only to die violently of unrelated causes, was completely beyond the ken of Aru and her friends. Siew-Siew didn't seem to mind it, but the rest of them spent much of the hour with their hands over their eyes or looking down with their ears covered. The sound man's contribution may have been the worst part. Tsik-Tsik was brought to tears. Nobody suggested they leave early though, because no one wanted to embarrass Aru in front of her new boyfriend.

When the heavy velvet curtains were drawn and the girls made their way back out to the sunlight they were a bit disappointed that they didn't see the young man again. The group returned to Rhedyn for supper. That night there were some unpleasant dreams.

Luckily, the film the following week was a romantic adventure story. It had a tangible plot. Aru and Phfft-Psyfft enjoyed it, but more importantly the fellow named Nrouhw was there again at the ticket window. This time Aru came prepared and they had a bit of a conversation.

Tomato peeling at Rhedyn House went on, but it seemed more bearable to Aru now that she truly had something, or rather someone, to inspire her. Time didn't drag quite so much. To her great dismay however, everyone in the entire cannery seemed to know about her infatuation. Rumors multiplied. The culmination of this gossip arrived when that sweet old biddy from over in the filters section stopped by and congratulated Aru upon her engagement. Aru felt like climbing up onto the table and shouting, "Hold your tongues, everyone!" but what good would it even do?

That same afternoon Mrs. Bukbagok interrupted her inspection at the peeling table to give Aru a little lecture. Aru must be careful when going out on free day. She must be selective about to whom she speaks. Always there must be a chaperone. Aru must remember to protect her reputation. Then, as an afterthought, she added that the boy from the theater box office had a small art studio above that bakery by the market, did Aru know that? He made prints or something, she thought.

The next week's matinee featured the same pugilistic film as before. Aru felt certain the young man should suspect her attendance was more about seeing him than the picture. He appeared pleased to encounter her again, yet made no overtures whatsoever. Aru and Phfft-Psyfft went ahead and sat through some of the film's disturbing tripe but decided to leave early. Phfft-Psyfft had to keep getting up to use the toilet anyway, because her pregnant belly pushed on her bladder. She was getting so big her pregnancy showed through the shapeless uniform. As they walked up the aisle in the darkness Aru noticed that in the projection booth it was her friend Nrouhw running the film.

In the evenings, Aru continued to work on her stitchery. Phfft-Psyfft had guessed right, it did ease her mind. She finished the dragonfly. It came out quite well. She made the fabric into a small tasseled pocket which was such a joy to be able to give to little Churrie on her birthday.

The next project was a rather large one; a pillow with a border and a sizable ginger cat. Aru worked fast, and it wasn't long before Phfft-Psyfft took a look at Aru's progress and burst into laughter. Aru tried to suppress her indignance. It wasn't supposed to be comical. Was her needlework that bad?

"It's only the outline," said Aru. "It will look better filled in. I need to buy some more floss."

"Your design is lovely. That's not what's funny," said her friend. "What I'm laughing at is the cat's face."

"It's just a cat's face."

"Aru, look at it." Phfft-Psyfft handed the hoop back to her.

"There's nothing wrong. Two eyes, a nose . . . ?"

"Aru. It's *his* face. Clearly, it's *his* face!" Phfft-Psyfft had another volley of laughter. Cheeks flushing, Aru had to agree.

"We've got to get you over to that art studio," said Phfft-Psyfft.

Not long after this, the two friends were sitting in the café next to the bakery by the market. "What will you have for lunch?" asked Phfft-Psyfft.

Aru shuddered. "Anything that doesn't involve tomatoes!"

Café Ysgarlad had silk lampshades that looked like pink jellyfish. Knobbly cinnabar seahorses in the aging wall mural wore bridles with the reins floating in flourishes, and sea stars decorated the background. Intimate in size, the café had the comforting feel of a place where locals pass the time.

Much to Aru's well-anticipated delight, Nrouhw did come in before he left for his job at the theater. Unfortunately, although he noticed her and stopped to say hello, the conversation was brief and he soon departed with his cranberry muffin and a coffee in an old cracked cup.

Undeterred, Aru and Phfft-Psyfft returned the next week. This time fate smiled upon Aru. Her young gentleman had come in early enough for a leisurely midday meal; he was already seated when the girls arrived. They asked to join him.

Things went very well. The three of them had a nice time, during which it was gleaned that he had no romantic commitments and that he was twenty-six. He had such shiny hair. While they finished up their meal Phfft-Psyfft brought up the subject of Nrouhw's vocation and he told them that he only worked at the theater on Saturdays.

"Mainly," he said in his quiet voice, "I scratch out a living with etchings and other sorts of prints."

After a few sincere questions about his artwork, Aru asked, "May we come up and see your etchings?" There was a pause while Nrouhw looked at his pocket watch. Aru's circulatory system went full steam while he took time to consider his answer. He gave them a big grin and told them he'd be happy to show them his prints, as he had a few minutes before he must leave for his job.

Upstairs above the bakery, Nrouhw's studio was cluttered with art materials but bare of furnishings. It smelled of ink and sun-warmed beeswax. Where the two exposed brick walls met there sat a pile of big pillows which apparently served as his bed. The hardwood floor was well worn. There was no closet, but clothes were neatly hung on pegs. There was no spigot, only a basin which he must have been filling with a pitcher from downstairs.

He showed his visitors the small cherrywood etching press which had a large wheel on the side. It reminded Aru of a ship's steering wheel. Among the crates, copper plates, scattered bottles of liquid and other debris were his prints.

Nrouhw had been working on posters for a circus that would soon be in town. These had an exciting design with a carousel and tigers. He showed them fine landscapes. However, both girls most admired his elk. Though the walls of his studio were completely bare, a series of elk pictures, framed and unframed, was strewn amongst the mess. Aru's favorite had been sketched with a magenta crayon: a great bull rearing up onto his hind legs, and with the forest behind him.

It wasn't long before Nrouhw apologized and told them he must leave for the theater. He wondered if Aru and Phfft-Psyfft might be headed to the matinee, but they told him they wouldn't be able to attend the show that day. Just before parting in the street below, Phfft-Psyfft had a question. Nrouhw had mentioned that he would have the following Saturday off from work. Since they were so new to town, would he take her and Aru sightseeing in the downtown area?

That faint smile again. What did it mean? His eyes were so pensive, so distant, yet he looked right through a person. Nrouhw said he would be happy to give the young ladies a tour.

The weather grew hotter and cannery life even more sweaty and stifling. At night the garret girls would sleep without a cover over them and with a damp cloth on the forehead. The heat made it so miserable that even the hemogoblins left the attic. Aru had become accustomed to the scratching in the walls, so their departure strangely added to the difficulty of her sleeping. Anticipation of seeing Nrouhw on free day caused time to move slowly in some ways but quickly in others.

As planned, Aru and Phfft-Psyfft met Nrouhw at the café in the early afternoon. They looked forward to a fun experience because Nrouhw, as an artist, knew all the crazy and strange places surrounding the open-air Saturday market.

A short walk of only about six blocks brought them to the brick-paved market grounds, which overlooked the bay. Aru had never seen a market quite so huge. One could buy anything here. Nrouhw knew just where to go for the most delicious sticky buns, warm from the brick oven, and he bought some for the three of them. Aru made a few small purchases, placing them deep in her pink straw shopping bag. As she reached in to deposit a set of hair pins she'd bought for Siew-Siew, she thought she felt something wiggle.

The apple doll looked up at her with its little clove eyes. Aru pulled it from the bag. "What in the—? How did this get in there?"

Phfft-Psyfft leaned against Aru's shoulder to have a look. Then the doll widened its eyes and smiled a wicked smile. The girls screamed and Aru dropped the doll, which scrambled to its feet and stood in front of her! Nrouhw tried to bat it away, but it vaulted right back into Aru's bag. Aru grabbed it out again and threw it as far as she could throw, but it ran right back to her, climbed her skirts, and forced its way back into the bag. Aru reached to grab it out once more, but

Nrouhw put his hand on her arm. People were staring. "There's no point," he said softly. "It's a thrall."

"No!" whispered Phfft-Psyfft.

"Yipe! A real thrall?" Aru had never been sure she believed in those.

Nrouhw seemed surprisingly calm. "If you manage to get it out of your bag it will just walk behind you. You won't get rid of it. Not till it has completed its mission, whatever that may be. I'm sorry, Aru. What a dog's deal. I wonder who sent it. Any large disagreements looming?"

Aru was completely baffled.

"Well," said Nrouhw, "not much we can do about it. You'll have to see what course it takes. Just don't disturb it too much or it will start squeaking, the little scapegrace. I've encountered these things before. They make a hideous noise; you don't want it to squeak."

They kept exploring the market. Aru wasn't going to let someone's perverse magic ruin her day. But who would do such a thing?

Eventually they reached the livestock section on the far side of the grounds. Mostly there were swine but also a few cows and horses. A fine strawberry roan mare stood tied to a ring on the outside wall of a barn. A couple of young boys who were meant to mind her and maybe get her sold had started an argument and things were escalating. Finally it came to punches, and one boy got a bloody nose. He was just about to retaliate despite the stream of blood, when both boys stopped what they were doing and ran off in different directions.

Nrouhw glanced around down the aisle and chuckled. "A pod of Vuoibmi. Come, we'd better get off the street."

"Vuoibmi?" asked Aru.

"Certainly you've heard of the Ysgarlad Vuoibmi!" said Nrouhw, as they found refuge under a huge scarlet canopy. "They are legendary."

"No. Really, I haven't."

As the narrow lane cleared of people, one group remained. A cluster of several women was walking in the direction of the roan mare; these women had their arms about each other and were smiling and laughing. Two wore bright lipstick.

"Don't look at them!" cautioned Phfft-Psyfft.

"I have to say, I'm baffled," said Aru, staring at her own feet and taking a peek at the women now and then as they approached.

"Perhaps you'd explain to her," whispered Nrouhw to Phfft-Psyfft.

Phfft-Psyfft kept her voice low. "The Vuoibmi," she explained, "are a hallowed organization of women who police the city. It is whispered that they are a cannibalistic society, but I don't think that is true. All these women are going through the change of life. They wield a mighty power, and as a sisterhood this force is naturally channeled into guidance of behavior."

Aru took a step back as the women passed. "What are those people doing?" she asked.

Several people, bent in humility, had approached the ladies and dropped something into a basket carried by the round, apple-cheeked one with the embroidered apron.

"Offerings," said Nrouhw. "They usually give them persimmon cookies or sherry candy."

The women had stopped near the roan and were apparently inquiring about the two boys. "The Vuoibmi are violent and they have strong magic and they are greatly feared by everyone," Phfft-Psyfft continued.

"Yes, I see," said Aru. "How do the women come to join this group?"

"In truth, I don't know," replied Phfft-Psyfft quietly. "However, it is a great honor to be Vuoibmi. The women perform a valuable service for the city."

The Vuoibmi continued on down the lane. Slowly, people ventured out from their hiding places. Aru and her friends wandered across the way and then among the fruit and vegetable stalls. Without thinking about it, Aru held her pink bag away from her body as she walked.

Nrouhw asked if they liked hot peppers. Aru said she did.

"Have you ever tried one of these Scorpion's Tongues? They are a local favorite. Fiercely hot."

"I'll try it," said Aru, holding out her hand.

"All right, but just take a tiny bite," Nrouhw warned.

Aru did take a tiny bite. Then her body went into shock. Her breath came in gasps. She felt sweaty, her mouth and throat in pain, her eyes filled with tears. For a moment she thought she might die.

"Oooh!" Nrouhw winced, laughing. "That looks bad." He offered her a chunk of watermelon which had been set out for sampling. She grabbed several more, tears streaming down her face.

If she had been a tiny bit angrier, it could have been the end of her friendship with Nrouhw. Right at that moment.

They continued on, through the produce and along the edge of the meat market. Of all the smells in the plaza, surely the most putrid came from the scraps of meat rotting in the sun. Aru was saved by the Scorpion's Tongue from having to worry about any smells for a while, but Phfft-Psyfft was compelled to cover her own nose with a handkerchief. The odor didn't seem to bother Nrouhw at all. Nor did the flies. In fact, he seemed quite interested in the sides of beef hanging on hooks along the wall. He stopped and bought some smoked summer sausage sticks. Aru appreciated having something to help her recuperate from the pepper. She felt kind of sick to her stomach.

"So," said Aru after she had recovered herself somewhat, "please tell me more about the Vuoibmi. What sort of weapons do they carry?" The question was aimed at Phfft-Psyfft. Aru was still in a bit of a pout.

"Oh, they don't need weapons! When they come after you, you are done for. That's it."

The next time Aru saw Vuoibmi, a couple of weeks later, she and Nrouhw were sitting in the Ysgarlad café having lunch. Phfft-Psyfft hadn't come along this time as she'd been too tired. Aru and Nrouhw were at a table right up against the front window. The restaurant had booth-style seating, so there was a single high-backed bench for them to share. They could sit and watch the traffic go by outside.

A pair of Vuoibmi women crossed the street right out in front of the café. For a nervous moment, Aru worried they might come inside but they turned and went down toward the water. She thought it interesting to watch the public scatter, although they didn't hide as much as everyone had the other day.

Aru and Nrouhw talked about the city, Aru's travels, and his art work. Their conversation was interrupted several times by the thrall. Twice the apple doll jumped onto the table. The second time it tipped a bowl of salsa, which ran down the tablecloth into Nrouhw's lap. Aru was mortified. Nrouhw took it in stride, and kindly made a joke of it:

"I'll simply dye my trousers to match the stain!" he said. "It'll add some spice to my wardrobe."

Aru still had no suspicion as to who might have sent the thrall. The thing plagued her. She had to carry the doll everywhere in a large pocket dangling between her petticoat and her underskirts. This was the only way to prevent it from walking along behind her. It bothered her very much that it had looked like her grandma. Not anymore, not with those eyes.

Despite all this, Aru and Nrouhw were deep in conversation when they were startled by a bulbous woman in orange chiffon who rapped on the window, smiling and waving at them. Nrouhw sprang up from his seat and motioned her inside. "A friend of mine," he explained. The woman came in, and approached their table. "Aru, I would like you to meet dear Kguggle, my most imperturbable and tranquil friend," he laughed. "How are all your little darlings, Kguggle?"

The woman gazed wistfully off through the window and replied, "I wish I knew."

With a slight wince, Nrouhw changed the subject. "Aru, Kguggle here is a marine biologist."

"I'm delighted to make your acquaintance, Aru," said the woman. "Do you mind if I squeeze in?"

Without giving any chance for an answer, she sat down between the armrest of the bench seat and Aru, forcing her to move over close against Nrouhw. Aru liked this woman already.

Kguggle had large, intelligent eyes behind small rectangular glasses. Her long fleshy arms seemed to be everywhere as she talked, abruptly yet gently reaching for this and that, languidly fiddling with the table settings. She wrapped her fingers around the jam jar and kept slowly screwing down and unscrewing the lid. Although what she had to say about ocean life was interesting, her hypnotic movements began to have an effect on Aru, causing her to suppress a yawn.

Aru realized she felt quite comfortable with these two people, as if she'd known them both a long time. She'd only just met Kguggle, but somehow the lady's easy depth of character made her seem like family. This realization brought a pang of pain to Aru; the pain of missing her grandmother.

After Kguggle had to take her leave, Nrouhw told Aru that he must depart soon also, for the theater. He wanted to give her something.

He hoped she didn't mind his being so forward, but he'd seen this little pendant and it reminded him of her, he said. Aru's heart pounded as he pulled the necklace from his jacket pocket and carefully fastened the thin chain around her neck. She held the jewelry out from the base of her throat to examine it. It was a locket, with a pair of delicate flowers adorning it. They were of partially enameled copper.

"Cherry blossoms," said Nrouhw. His face, though, had a sadness, or was it defensiveness? He looked away instead of returning her smile. When he did look at her she felt she was being studied. He licked his lips with his long tongue. Still, Aru felt enormously pleased to have this gift from Nrouhw. She felt like a balloon floating in the air.

Nrouhw said again that he had to leave soon. "I must ask you though, Aru. Please tell me, what sort of animal do you transform into? Because, apologies, I haven't been able to figure it out."

She stared at him. "What kind of question is *that?*" Then she sighed. "I don't transform, that's the thing. I am in human form all the time."

"But—how is that possible? Every human transforms into some sort of animal."

"Not me."

"That's astonishing," whispered Nrouhw. Then he added, "Are there others like you?"

"My mother and my grandmother were the same way."

"Human all the time."

"Yes, all the time."

Nrouhw was quiet for just a moment. "I'd been wondering why you had a wolf name because you don't seem much like a wolf at all."

"My father was a grey wolf, and my mother was half wolf. I grew up in the grey wolf community. Even so, I don't seem to have inherited many of the wolven traits. I love all of my family, though. We are a large clan. My parents and grandmother and I lived in a dear little house at the edge of the woods."

"Well, if I may say so, Aru, your personality is more enchanting than that of the many wolves I've met."

Aru laughed. "I probably growl as much, but I don't bite as savagely!"

Nrouhw admitted he bit with a lot of force, when in animal form. Then he laughed and said he'd made himself late for work again.

Nrouhw walked Aru to the trolley stop. As they said goodbye he quickly put his lips against her temple and gave her something between a kiss and a nibble.

Back at Rhedyn, Aru had to tell Phfft-Psyfft everything. While they chatted and tittered, the young women fanned themselves with folded tomato crate labels. Summer had arrived, and inside the soup factory had grown more brutally hot and sticky. Aru felt bad for Phfft-Psyfft having to endure such heat during her pregnancy. The two talked on and on. The thrall seemed content to lay on its back and stare at the ceiling. Was it listening to all they said? Aru didn't know. She and Phfft-Psyfft decided not to worry about it. They didn't have anything to hide. The conversation went on. Phfft-Psyfft mentioned that since they were not allowed to transform in the building it could be tricky to determine what sort of animal someone was. She had suspected for some time that Aru must be a wolf. A transform to a white wolf, Phfft-Psyfft had figured. How amusing that Aru's fellow had thought her nothing like a wolf. But he was so obviously a cougar, wasn't he!

The next time Nrouhw and Aru met, he gave her another little gift. They were in the open-air tea room at the marketplace, sipping hibiscus tea. Nrouhw reached across the table, placing a stick of scarlet wax carefully into Aru's hand. She smiled graciously, but with a bit of puzzlement. He gave her a broad smile. They looked at each other. His smile became even broader. It's soft wax, he said, for writing on skin—he gently took her arm and made a tiny mark on the inside of her wrist. He looked up at the sky, then into her eyes. Leaning across the table, he placed his lips near her ear and with a whisper instructed her to take the crayon home, and just before they met next time, to place a mark in every spot she'd like a kiss. Aru's face became hot and she backed away. Her jaw dropped. It moved, but she couldn't speak. She shook her head. "That's—that's very forward of you!" she said.

"Yes. Yes, it is," he said. Another huge smile.

Aru's mouth hung open again, but this time with a bit of a grin.

Back at Rhedyn House, Aru toiled through the steamy drudgery along-side the others. The cannery workers loved to complain, yet they, most of them, seemed comfortable with their lot in life. Nobody questioned the arrangement. They were happy to have jobs. Why should Aru make such a fuss? The whole situation drove Aru to distraction. Day-dreaming about Nrouhw became the entire focus of her day. That, and cleaning up after the apple doll's mischief. The next few days were full of the thrall's pranks and indecencies. Siew-Siew got a penalty because her shoes had been knotted together, making her late for work. Aru found herself apologizing to her friends again and again. She couldn't understand why this thrall had been sent to her.

"Why would someone want you to be angry and miserable?" asked Phfft-Psyfft.

Aru shrugged. She grabbed the doll by the neck and shoved it to her pocket once more.

The following week Phfft-Psyfft woke late on free day to find that Aru had just been taken to the infirmary. Such an awful thing! Apparently during the night Aru had come down with a terrible rash. She had spots over her face, her hands, and in the oddest places. She was a bit out of her mind, too, saying crazy things about whacks and whatnot. She'd surely be put in quarantine.

A few days later came Aru's turn to wake with a shock. Phfft-Psyfft, normally such a cheerful person, lay huddled under her bedclothes, sobbing heavily. Aru went to her and did her best to calm her down, but it was a long time before Phfft-Psyfft could find her voice. Every time she started to speak she'd burst into tears again. Finally Aru, wiping her friend's brow with a handkerchief, tried to tell her to simmer down for the baby's sake but those words made Phfft-Psyfft cry all the harder.

"Phfft-Psyfft, please. What's wrong?" Aru tried not to sound as worried as she felt.

"My baby. Tsik-Tsik told me last night, she found out, they're going to take my baby." Phfft-Psyfft burst out crying again.

"What are you talking about? It's all right. Nobody's going to take your baby."

After a bit more crying and a great deal of sniffing and nose-wiping Phfft-Psyfft explained to Aru that she'd been told that when her time came she could birth the baby there at Rhedyn House and they would take care of her. What she hadn't been aware of was that, even though she was married, the policy dictated that after the birthing her baby would be put up for adoption. "Nobody told me that!" cried Phfft-Psyfft. "Nobody said anything about adoption."

"Well, it's not going to happen." Aru decided right then that, no matter what, she would protect her friend. She wasn't sure how.

Four days later Phfft-Psyfft's world fell the rest of the way apart. At five minutes after three o'clock in the afternoon Mrs. Bukbagok approached the peeling table and asked Phfft-Psyfft to come with her. A message had arrived. Mrs. Bukbagok lay her arm across Phfft-Psyfft's shoulders as they walked away. Phfft-Psyfft never returned to the table.

Aru worried. News from her village? Perhaps somebody had died. Or could it be some ultimatum about the baby? Phfft-Psyfft had spoken with someone in the office yesterday. That must be it. Maybe they'd given her a special dispensation regarding the adoption arrangement. But then why didn't she rejoin them at the table?

Aru skipped supper and went up to find her friend in the deserted garret. The air was so thick and hot up there that walking across the room felt almost like swimming. Phfft-Psyfft sat on her bed, staring out the window at the descending sun. She had cried out all the tears she had, and now was just sitting, puffy-faced and absent.

Aru sat quietly with her. She was bursting to know what had happened. Finally she picked up Phfft-Psyfft's hand to hold and the action woke Phfft-Psyfft enough that she collapsed into Aru's arms. Aru held her friend, her own tears streaming down her cheeks. The point came when she just couldn't stand it anymore. "Phfft-Psyfft! What's wrong? Son of a . . . What's wrong, Phfft-Psyfft, you've got to tell me!"

As they sat alone together, slowly rocking back and forth, the reply was muffled by Aru's shoulder. "He's gone. He's gone, Aru."

Without breathing, Aru waited for an explanation. Through all her fears of her husband Phfft-Psyfft having died on his journey as rumor maintained, Phfft-Psyfft always had held out hope that he would return to her some day. This afternoon Mrs. Bukbagok had hustled Phfft-Psyfft away from the peeler's table and into a little room down the hall where she relayed the message to her that had arrived from her friend Olooka: *Phfft-Psyfft was coming for you, died at sea. Please come, you can stay with me.*

Aru sat up with her friend until Phfft-Psyfft slid into a troubled sleep. For the remainder of the night Aru sat staring out the window. In the morning she sobbed and wept. Now two hearts were broken. She knew what she had to do.

That afternoon Aru met Nrouhw at the Café Ysgarlad, as planned. The place was crowded and he was sitting in the back. At the next table Kguggle drank burgundy and played slapjack poker with some friends. Aru stopped for a quick hello, and asked Kguggle, in shock, "Are you eating . . . octopus?" Kguggle smiled slightly and placed the lid over her plate.

Nrouhw sat licking some bright red envelopes, preparing a mailing about his upcoming exhibit. When he saw Aru he smiled, but his expression quickly switched to one of concern. Aru looked like she'd been run over by a three-horse fire engine. She was having difficulty containing her tears, so he gathered up his things and brought her up to the privacy of his studio. The first thing he did was to put the thrall in an apple basket with a mirror, a clever trick which kept the little fiend quite busy. He had only one chair, so he and Aru sat together on his pile of pillows, with their backs against the rough brick of the wall. He held her in comforting arms while she caught her breath.

At last she poured out her story about all that had happened to Phfft-Psyfft. "I have to go with her, Nrouhw. I have to help her get to Olooka's village. It's a long way, and she is so close to her time."

Nrouhw combed his fingers through Aru's hair. "I'll accompany you," he said.

Aru lost a moment of time entirely. When she came back to the world she noticed that tears were on her cheeks and she wasn't breathing. "Just like that?" she whispered. "You'll just come with us?"

He answered her with a kiss. Then, his big solemn eyes stared into hers. "It's the obvious course of action."

Nrouhw's warm breath tingled on her neck. His lips brushed along the lobe of her left ear, his mouth wide, to purr his breath inside until she had to move away, laughing.

"Wooff! You've tickled me quite to the marrow!" she exclaimed, and swirled back toward him for another kiss.

After this they continued to act the sort of way that lovers do, and so were occupied until Aru was almost too late for the last trolley. Nrouhw rode with Aru to escort her back to Rhedyn.

"But how can you come with us?" Aru asked him, sitting close. "Your studio! You have a livelihood. You can't just throw all this away and journey with us."

He shrugged. "It's a portable skill."

This is how the three friends came to travel the road which followed a dry streambed up the system of copper canyons northeast of Ysgarlad, Nrouhw wheeling a large pushcart with some of his belongings and the girls' carpetbags piled on. Siew-Siew and Tsik-Tsik had taken up a collection and sent Phfft-Psyfft on her way with a bundle of diapers, linens, and a soft blanket for the forthcoming baby. These were up on the load, as were several crates of food and supplies. The thrall, as usual, traveled in Aru's big pocket amongst her skirts.

Aru knew the quickest, easiest way for Phfft-Psyfft to travel would've been in chickaree form, but if labor got underway while she was a squirrel the baby would be doomed to a squirrel's birth and a squirrel's life span. Traveling as a chickaree was out of the question. If Phfft-Psyfft was careful she'd be able to help the group by gathering nuts, berries, and eggs as a chickaree. Phfft-Psyfft remarked it was too bad she didn't have cheek pouches like other types of tree squirrels had.

It took longer than expected to get to the road, so by noon they had just reached the first crossroads outside of town. They'd been traveling on flat ground and in the shade of the canyon walls, but still they were covered in sweat and rust-tinted dust. Nevertheless, these conditions proved infinitely preferable to working in a tomato cannery.

Because of Phfft-Psyfft's portly condition they had to go slowly, but nobody was in a hurry. Excitement flowed through Aru, though. The sensational colors of the rugged topography filled her up and fueled her ambitions for the adventures ahead. Phfft-Psyfft's experience of the day was entirely different. She walked the same road, exposed to the eternal beauty of the ravines just as Aru was, but Phfft-Psyfft traveled in a buffer of numbness. It was clear that the impact of their surroundings felt healing to her, but did not make her happy.

They came upon an inn at the junction, a collection of shacks and sheds, really. The old brick structures were leaning. Barn paint peeled from the boards. If there had ever been a sign with the name of the inn, that had fallen long ago. It didn't look like much of a place, but it was the only place. They stopped to take a break and have a bit to eat.

Nrouhw knew the innkeeper because he often came out this way to hunt. The three friends sat at a table in the shade of an ancient sprawling hawthorn. There was one other customer about, an old puffy-faced drunk who looked as if he'd been leaning over that table since yesterday or the day before. A big man, he tipped his hat in greeting, revealing a sunburnt bald head with a greasy fringe of thin hair. He wore a fine silk suit of the latest style, pink in color. It was disheveled and dirty and Aru wondered if he might have stolen it.

"Well, I believe I will order some pie," sighed Nrouhw. "Would you ladies like some?"

"Pie?" asked Aru.

"I recommend it," he replied. "I'll treat."

"How could a place like this have pie?" Aru couldn't imagine it. "Shouldn't we budget our money?"

"Well, we need some kind of sustenance, don't we?" said Nrouhw.

So they ordered pie. Aru thought she heard Nrouhw chuckle softly as she dove her fork through the fresh whipped cream into her strawberry-rhubarb slice. It was exquisite. Phfft-Psyfft had some fleeting cheer from her crimson gooseberry slice. Nrouhw had the rhubarb meringue roulade. He devoured it. All of the treats disappeared quickly because of the travelers' hunger, but the three sat and sipped tea and enjoyed the afterglow of such unlikely ramshackle inn cuisine.

Nrouhw picked a handful of bright berries from the tree above. He funneled them with his fingers into a leather pouch. This he handed to Phfft-Psyfft. "To help your aching heart. Only take them in chickaree form. Otherwise it could be a danger for your child," he said.

Phfft-Psyfft graciously received the hawthorn berries and was about to reply when she was interrupted by an enormous snort from the other table. The drunk had fallen briefly asleep and nearly planted his face in the remainder of his raspberry cream truffle. He made such a loud noise it brought the innkeeper out from his kitchen. "For the last time, get away from here, you filthy swiller!" the man shouted.

Instead of a reply, the groggy guest knocked over his own chair as he stood up and made a gesture toward the others. "I'll just be joining my luvly company here, Uncle, uh huh. Thank you so very mush." He dragged his chair along behind him as he approached. "Um, er, escuze me for bothering you, good folks," he snuffled. "Shorry to be a bore, wallowing in unluck. Disgruntled. May I join you folks? Huh?"

Before anyone could answer, he planted his chair and then himself right between Aru and Nrouhw. The putrefied smell of wine exuded from his pores. "Very lovely ladies," he said.

Nrouhw stood up to drive him off, but as the drunkard turned to Aru with his grunty murmurings, he tipped his hat again, and dipped his head, and Aru saw a birthmark in the shape of a heart. She hadn't recognized the man in his rumpled state.

"I know you! I saw you up at Vulpeden! Vulpeden House."

"Umm, umm, er," he grunted, "My dear, so shorry, you mush be mistaken. I don't recall having met."

"You are certainly the man!"

"Never have we met. I would remember. Uh huh."

"You were at the office of Lady Akawu."

"Not me. Now, lishen—" He interrupted himself with a snort and a couple of hiccups. Then he seemed to forget what he'd been saying. He squinted at Aru. "You have the purtiest piglet pigmentation. Pink. —Groink!—" He belched wine. Aru covered her face.

"Pig skin? Me? I most certainly do not have pig skin!" exclaimed Aru from behind her hands. Then she looked at her wrist and looked back at him with a frown.

Nrouhw placed himself between the drunk and his sweetheart. He started to protest, but his words were cut short by the man—

"'Scuze me," said the drunk, wiping his mouth. "So sorry." He addressed Nrouhw. "Uh, you folk mush be on your way to Anseo. Everyone's going there. Everyone's going out there for the gold."

Nrouhw's ears pricked up for a moment, but he held to the subject. "She says she saw you at Vulpeden. What was your business there?"

"I didn't have nothin'—nothin' to do with it."

"What do you mean?" demanded Aru. "To do with what?"

The man grunted, and snuffled, and paused for a moment, and then in a shrill voice he cried, "Sooey! Sooey! I'm so weak, weak, weak!" Then he made a great effort to focus on Aru's eyes with his own little round ones. "Anseo. Thash were you want to be. Lots of grub for the taking. Truly, uh huh."

"Answer the lady!" Nrouhw growled. He appeared to grow larger.

The man shrank away from him. "So sorry!" he squealed. He took Aru's linen napkin from the table, and dabbed his face. "Uh—Jus a moment." He looked at Aru, and began to mumble, "Err, umm, I reckon I've no choice. Well, here it is, then. Here it is: A certain swinesty someone, uh huh, he slipped the vixen a shubstantial sum to let you go. Sent you on yer merry way, uh huh."

He glanced back at Nrouhw, and then nodded to the ladies. "Thersh many a fortune being made along the way to Anseo. Don't concern yourselves with that ol' foxery. Not important anymore. On to Anseo!"

"What? Why would you do such a thing?" exclaimed Aru. "You had me dismissed? I don't even know you!"

Nrouhw growled again, "Who would set you to such a task?"

The man squealed. He looked toward town, warily. "I can't share that with you, my friendsh. Oh no, I can't do that. My sakes. I'd be baconated immediately. Bacon I'd be. Elitely. Uh huh.

"Too snug there, you would have been. Too tough to sway. But lishen to me, for your own good, listen, my deearies: you'll want to head on up to Ansheo. They've found gold up there in the hillsh up beyond. Everyone's gone rich, thersh agreeable resources of untold degree up that way." He started to snore with a snerk-snerkle sound, his head falling to his chest. Then he revived a bit and mumbled, "Oh, you'll want to head on in that directshun." His arm rested in a smudge of gooseberry. "Uh huh. Becaush liberty is grounded in gold, my . . . friends. Truffles. Grown of gold. Crunkle uncle, groink and gruntal . . . uncanny . . . pie."

"Oh, no you don't! You're going to tell us what in thunder you intended!" Nrouhw batted at the man's face repeatedly, but he had dropped into a deep slumber and couldn't be awakened.

After departing the inn, the friends discussed what the man might have meant by saying that Aru would have been "too tough to sway," should she have been allowed to stay at Vulpeden. Someone didn't want Aru settling in, getting comfortable. Nrouhw thought it appeared that someone wanted her unsettled, unsteady, easy to manipulate. But who? Why Aru? What could anyone possibly want with her?

Phfft-Psyfft said softly, "Could this be because you are of royal blood? I suppose someone might have an interest in you because of that. Yet what could they possibly want with interfering in your life?"

"I've been thinking these same things," Aru said.

Nrouhw sounded exasperated, "I don't know what to make of all this. Someone is brazenly meddling in your affairs. First the thrall, and now this."

Aru had nearly forgotten about the apple doll. There it was, in her pocket, as quiet and still as if it were a real doll.

By mid-afternoon they reached a steeper part of the climb, so they stopped to make camp. Aru went off in search of firewood. Phfft-Psyfft went to raid a chestnut tree she'd noticed. Nrouhw set up the tents.

When they arrived back at the campsite, Aru and Phfft-Psyfft were duly impressed with Nrouhw's handiwork. Aru was particularly in- trigued by the handsome bower he'd created for himself and her. A number of thin cotton tapestries were draped over a rope he had strung high between curling madrona trees. She peeked inside to see after- noon sunlight coming through the stylized patterns with a feast of pink and pomegranate, lush grape, soft plum. There were wonderful lotus and bird designs. Bed quilts he'd spread on the smooth rock, and the pillows that had formerly been his bed, made the interior so inviting that Aru couldn't keep her mind off of it all during supper and their time around the fire. It felt good to be back on the road, and her anticipation of joining Nrouhw in the tent later that evening by moonlight had her in goosebumps.

She had good reason to tremble, for she found that spending the night with such an attractive and powerful person was one thing, but the wild, formidable side of him was another. The eerie way he enjoyed tenderly biting at her, and to nose her all about the shoulders, gave her an exhilarating sensation of uncertainty. His burning, sweet breath became a purr so loud that Aru blushed, knowing that Phfft-Psyfft must be able to hear it from the other tent. Hopefully she was fast asleep.

In the morning a pair of strawberry finches chose the tent rope as their perch for a sunrise serenade. Aru woke in Nrouhw's warm embrace with the rising sun's light glowing through the tapestries as if through stained glass. She saw a look of peace on her lover's face as he lay listening to the music of the finches. When he noticed her gazing at him he smiled broadly. "Somebody oil that bird!" he shrieked. She hit him with a pillow.

That day the trail rose arduously and by the following afternoon they had a view of the ocean in the distance. Ysgarlad again looked like a sparkling ruby tucked into the crooked shoreline. They kept climbing. Just as they decided to watch for a camping spot, Phfft-Psyfft felt a little cramp. A twinge, really. Was it a labor pain? She didn't know.

Because of this eventuality, Nrouhw decided to search for a particularly good site. It took another hour before they found what he had in mind. They stopped in a flat area several hundred feet off the trail, where a nut grove grew in a recess of the cliffs. A waterfall trickled down the rock face, allowing some sparse clumps of grass to struggle for life in the acidic soil. It was an idyllic spot, actually, but more importantly it offered shelter.

Although she thought this was all happening a bit early, Phfft-Psyfft had a few more of these mild aches while they were setting up camp, so she remained in human form and the group prepared to stay in this spot for a while. Chances of rain in the near future were slim, but there could be heavy dew, so extra wood was gathered and stored under the pushcart. Soon it did seem that labor had begun. The pains became more substantial. Phfft-Psyfft found herself focused on creating the perfect birthing spot, so Nrouhw and Aru helped her use blankets and linens to build a good-sized dome among the trees. Inside she created a wonderful nest of cushions and fresh leaves. By the time she was satisfied she had transferred almost every one of their possessions from the cart to be used in some way in her birthing boudoir.

While Phfft-Psyfft was so occupied, Nrouhw took Aru aside to ask her a question. Had she much experience with birth?

"No, I've never attended a birth before," she replied. "I did have a housecat that gave birth to six little kittens. I saw them born. They were so dear." In the surreal fog caused by the excitement, her mind wandered. "The mother was a lovely fat tabby. She disappeared not too long after they were weaned—"

"Yes, so sad. That happens," Nrouhw licked his lips.

"Do you know anything about birth, Nrouhw?" asked Aru, suddenly feeling a stab of fear.

"Mmmm," he replied, his eyes shifting back and forth. "It looks like we're going to have to count on the filbert sprites for some luck, unless that thrall of yours is a midwife."

The thrall. At least that thing had settled down. On the trail, it continued to ride quietly among Aru's skirts. While setting up the kitchen area Aru set it on top of the dish crate, and there it stayed. She didn't tend to think about it much when it wasn't causing a bother.

As soon as camp was established Nrouhw vanished into the woods and then came back a short time later with some meat for himself and Aru. She had built up a fire while he was gone and they cooked a full meal. Phfft-Psyfft didn't eat much, just a few bites of pecan loaf and a mug of weak tea. They sat around the cheery fire as the sun, hidden by the cliffs, dipped low in the sky.

"Listen to that!" exclaimed Aru. The branches above had suddenly filled with frantic kissing and clucking noises. "Is that a squirrel?" Aru looked at Nrouhw, who was staring, open-mouthed, at Phfft-Psyfft.

Phfft-Psyfft dropped her mug. She looked stunned, frozen. The chittering stopped as suddenly as it had started.

"What is it, Phfft-Psyfft? What's going on?" Aru moved across the fire toward her friend.

Phfft-Psyfft began to gasp for air. "Phfft-Psyfft!" cried Aru. There was a quiet gushing sound. Phfft-Psyfft's water had broken. The poor thing looked around in confusion, her eyes rolling up into her head. She grabbed her huge abdomen. "What's happened? Are you all right?" Aru was horrified.

Phfft-Psyfft was unable to speak. Aru and Nrouhw tried to help her, but she just sat gasping and couldn't move. Suddenly, she turned her head to peer at something. Aru followed her gaze. A naked man had appeared in the nut grove, holding some leafy twigs in front of himself.

Nrouhw turned and stared at him. "Phfft-Psyfft?"

"Phfft-Psyfft!" cried the man. He ran to his wife.

Twenty minutes later the excited group sat by the fire in rosy twilight, amid the glowing torches Nrouhw had set on long poles to keep the bugs away. Phfft-Psyfft's husband, wearing clothes far too large, held her tight as she reclined in his arms. Her contractions had begun for real, but were still far apart. She kept looking into Phfft-Psyfft's face in disbelief, squeezing his hand to make sure he wasn't a dream. He kept feeling her round belly, as if he, too, was attempting to grasp their reality. There were so many questions, so much to express.

"It's a common name," the young man was saying.

"Yes," said Aru, "one hears that name a lot in the woods."

But what about the message his wife received? Olooka had said that he'd perished. Phfft-Psyfft couldn't imagine what might have happened. He shared his story.

"That day after we fought, Phfft-Psyfft, I didn't know what to think. Like an idiot, I ran. I threw myself into the search for my missing cousin. I went down to the coast and caught the first cargo ship to the outer islands because that's where my cousin was said to have gone. It didn't take long to find him there. He was in the local jail for thievery and subversion. That's where I ended up, too, just for searching for him, just for my association with him.

"While I was detained I had a lot of time to think. I realized—admitted to myself—that not only did I love you, Phfft-Psyfft, I'd always loved you. I loved you, but you obviously cared for my nuts-for-brains best friend. Yet as I sat in that cell it grew clear that you had feelings for me, after all. I thought of little things you did. Just little things, like the cute way you chew your fingers and look at me. The more I thought about it the more I regretted running away from you. I grew more and more angry about my imprisonment."

"But how did you get free?"

"It really wasn't that difficult," said Phfft-Psyfft. "I escaped from the prison by having withheld my identity as a chickaree. The jailor had assumed I was a woodchuck, and he kept me in a cell with plenty of room between the bars. When I grew angry enough to have the courage, I squeezed out at night and stowed away on a ship to the mainland. I searched for you, but found nothing but frustration. It wasn't until I caught up with Olooka that I found out where you were. She sent a message by raven on my behalf while I went straight to Ysgarlad. But they said at the cannery that you'd run away, Phfft-Psyfft, not long after the message arrived!"

Phfft-Psyfft experienced another pang of labor. She smiled despite the pain, and afterward told her husband that she was so happy he was alive. "But the message said you'd died!"

"What was the message, exactly?" he asked.

Phfft-Psyfft clearly remembered. "Phfft-Psyfft was coming for you, died at sea."

"No!" cried Phfft-Psyfft, "It was supposed to be "Phfft-Psyfft, I'm coming for you; dying to see you."

He got a strange expression on his face. "Olooka said she sent the message to the rookery by way of a mouse. Rotten little rodent had to travel through the bog. Probably relayed the message to the raven with her mouth full of cranberries."

Late that evening, Phfft-Psyfft's labor began in earnest. Through the night the others cared for her as best they could while her contractions came stronger and closer. For quite a while she could converse during the pain but as the night stretched toward morning she found she needed to focus on enduring each contraction. She went for short walks around the campsite with her husband, arm in arm, and leaning on him for support when the pains struck. All this huge excitement in addition to the pain overwhelmed her. With each step she wobbled and tottered so much that Aru marveled she didn't collapse.

Around sunrise Phfft-Psyfft got on her hands and knees in the nest of pillows and began to wail and moan. Nrouhw told Aru that he was concerned for her safety as she was in such a vulnerable state. He said he would transform and keep patrol of the area. Aru had never seen Nrouhw in his feline form, so when he appeared a short time later on the cliffs above the camp, her hand went to her mouth. He was magnificent. Aru stood in the doorway of the birthing tent, transfixed. She stared up at him. She was clutching a steaming rag she'd prepared for the laboring mother as a hot compress, but she unwittingly squeezed it and hot water dribbled down her dress unnoticed.

This trance was interrupted by her friend Phfft-Psyfft frantically careening into her from behind with full force. Phfft-Psyfft had jumped out of her birthing nest, slid in a puddle of her own blood, lost her balance and skidded across the tent. She would've knocked Aru right down if Aru hadn't grabbed a tree trunk which was supporting the tent, and then grabbed Phfft-Psyfft too, and all this time Phfft-Psyfft was screaming that she'd changed her mind and didn't want to give birth.

Phfft-Psyfft the husband and Aru managed to get Phfft-Psyfft back to her cushions and they tried to get her to calm down a bit. Phfft-Psyfft sat down behind her and held her gently, allowing her to shift and move as she needed. Aru managed to clean her up somewhat and she seemed to appreciate the warm compress. Phfft-Psyfft sweated and shook and her contractions were coming every few minutes. Aru grew truly scared.

This went on for several more hours. Sometimes Phfft-Psyfft went quiet during the contractions but often she would cry and moan. In the short rest periods between the pains, though, she seemed all right and Aru began to feel like her friend might survive this, after all. Then, quite involuntarily, Phfft-Psyfft began a deep elongated grunt with each contraction. This primal sound rose up from the depths of her body, an audible agent of the extreme effort her body was making. She sounded very much like a bear. A large, angry, constipated bear.

Oh, thought Aru, *she must be bearing down now. Maybe this is why they call it bearing down.*

Phfft-Psyfft, with eyes somewhat glazed, reached out toward her friend and panted, "Aru, you're going to have to catch the baby." Aru had already pretty much figured this out. Phfft-Psyfft needed her mate's comforting and that meant she was counting on Aru at the other end. Aru knew babies were slippery. She was afraid of what the baby would feel like. She was scared it would slip out of her hands and fly across the tent.

Phfft-Psyfft kept up the grunting for an hour while the baby made its way down the birth canal. Aru was so tired. If she was this insanely tired what must it be like for her friend? Finally the time came when Aru could see the bulge of the baby's head showing, then a patch of dark wet hair. Its scalp! Slowly, the baby's head began to appear. With each contraction more of its head would show, but each time Phfft-Psyfft rested it would recede back in half as far as it had come.

When the head seemed just about to make its way through the opening, Phfft-Psyfft screamed horribly and Aru got scared again. But there was no time to think. Here was the baby's forehead, then its nose, its chin. Aru held the baby's head gently to support it and was surprised when it rotated sideways. The torso had turned to line up with the opening. One shoulder appeared, then the other. The baby squirted out into Aru's hands! Aru didn't drop it. She caught it easily, because it needed catching.

Then there was a horrible shock. The baby in her hands was greyish purple. An absolute and appalling greyish purple. Time stood still for Aru. Here was Phfft-Psyfft, chittering and happy in the relief of the pain and the joy of having completed the birth. Here was her husband, holding his wife and smiling with a tear in his eye, looking over at his newborn in Aru's hands. Now Phfft-Psyfft was reaching for the baby. Aru froze. How would she tell them? How could she—

The baby gagged and started to squirm. Aru nearly dropped it in surprise. It started to cry. Aru quickly set it on Phfft-Psyfft's stomach.

Phfft-Psyfft reached down and brought her child up to her breast. Aru tucked a blanket over the baby, who was already starting to flush out to a beautiful healthy color.

"You're here. My little . . ."

"Daughter," said Aru.

"Daughter," whispered Phfft-Psyfft in disbelief. "You're here."

They stayed in the camp for several days. The new baby was wondrous. She didn't seem like a new person, she seemed wizened and ancient. Except when she cried. Then the baby became a tiny gremlin and Aru felt entirely uneasy. The parents had decided on a name: Phfft-Psyfft. It was a good name, they said. The others weren't really surprised about the choice, as chickarees are rather predictable in these matters.

During this time Phfft-Psyfft and her husband decided they would continue on to Olooka's village, but after visiting her they'd head south to their home village in the Drey region. They hoped Aru and Nrouhw would come along with them. Aru wasn't sure what she wanted to do, but Nrouhw put forward the idea of visiting Anseo, the place that the drunkard had mentioned.

"I would like to go there, Aru. I've heard from seadogs and sourdoughs about the gold strikes in the east; the drunk wasn't the first to mention this to me. Now that the Phfft-Psyffts have found each other," he smiled at the pair, "we have the opportunity to go and see for ourselves. Perhaps we can make our fortune."

"You can't be serious! That's exactly what that man wanted. He wanted us to head to that village." Aru wondered how Nrouhw could even have this thought at all.

"Nrouhw, honestly," said Phfft-Psyfft the new mother. "I agree with Aru. You can't walk right into whatever strange trap's set for her."

"Of course I realize that the fellow was trying to steer us that way for his master, whoever that might be, but I wish to go there even so. I don't see the harm in it, as long as we are careful to avoid undue influences. I'm certain your village is a fine place, Phfft-Psyffts, but you must realize that, as an artist, I cannot make a living among the orchards. Besides, aren't the three of you curious about who hired that drunkard? Who has sent this thrall? I would like some answers."

After a lengthy discussion, Aru was convinced. They'd go east. One of the deciding factors was that their present location was close to the starting point of the Amber Trail, the famous route to Anseo.

They said goodbye on the road two days later, having arrived at the main highway, where they would journey in opposite directions. Nrouhw gifted the baby with a strip of leather upon which he'd written a spell of protection using dragon's blood resin. As a human little Phfft-Psyfft would be able to wear it as a bracelet, in squirrel form it would serve as a belt.

The Phfft-Psyfft family would head south as squirrels, carrying their newborn by mouth in a small sack made from Aru's old riding hood. Aru and Nrouhw had a half day's journey to the northwest to reach the gateway to the Amber Trail. The parting was sweet, and full of optimism and promises to visit. Each person was happy in their heart and excited about the path before them. Now every day was free day.

III. Through

ARU FELT a queasy feeling at the bottom of her stomach as she watched her friend disappear south through the dense thickets of gorse with her new family. Would she see them again? Aru's lack of courage facing this moment brought to light a fundamental truth: it is absolutely wrong to be separated from someone you love. Instinct told her to call out to Phfft-Psyfft. The kernel of her being told her to change what was happening and so they could all be together. She didn't, though. Despite the overwhelming ache in her gut calling her to run to her friend and collect her in her arms she didn't do that. She turned and walked the other way with Nrouhw along the dusty highway.

Parting's sorrow remained, but mellow sunlight and the gentle breeze felt good, and walking in nature with Nrouhw lifted Aru's spirits. Their road climbed along a ridge for a couple of hours, affording a nice view of where they'd been and once in a while a peek at where they were headed: spreading to the eastern horizon was wind-rippled prairie, the swells and valleys dotted with clusters of scrubby trees.

When they reached the highest part of the ridge they could see the gateway village of Loess beyond. Nrouhw, winded from pushing the heavy cart uphill, needed a rest. Aru had made some effort to help, but handling all that weight seemed so much easier for him. He was a great deal stronger than he looked.

The two sat down on a sandstone outcropping at the top of the eastern slope. They had an early lunch of marmalade biscuits and tea and their last two chunks of imported cheese. The village below was a cluster of adobe buildings on the bank of a wide silty river. Most of the roofs were newly thatched. Cheery gardens had rows of sunflowers. Fields studded with haystacks and those nearly ripe with corn made a lovely scene in which the village was comfortably nestled.

Nrouhw explained to Aru that they would be following that river for much of their journey. The Amber Trail ran east along the river in the form of a road through the prairie and then for some distance through the desert. When the river and trail turned south, their destination of Anseo would be east through the deeper sands, somewhere out in the desert and not easy to find.

"You've never heard of the historic Amber Trail? It's a major trade route," said Nrouhw. "The name comes from the most valuable cargo to traverse the route: honey from the flower-fields of the eastern coast."

"Oh!" said Aru. "Oh, I have heard of it. Of course! But I'd always heard it referred to as the Bee Line. Grandma read me wonderful stories of the bees and the Bee Line. It's also a vital supply route for the highest quality propolis, pollen, honeycomb, and royal jelly. We learned that in school."

"And mead," said Nrouhw.

"And mead."

In cougar form Nrouhw had been along this river many times, but never as far as the desert. This time of year the prairie was a pleasant place, he said, sunny but not too hot and with a healthy population of deer and elk in addition to numerous rabbits.

Aru and Nrouhw left the coastal highway and took the road that wound its way down the gentle slope for several miles to the village. As they arrived they went past a farm where a cottage stood back from the road, accompanied by a yellow barn with several large silos. There was a split-rail fence. A pale weathered boulder sat just by the front path, and beside the rock stood some kind of animal, stretching long and slender on its hind legs in order to survey the two of them.

"Is that a ferret?"

"No, no," replied Nrouhw. "It's Tsirp. She's a mongoose. Golden mongoose. Owner of the village inn, actually. I was thinking of getting a room there at the inn for a day or so. What do you say?"

Aru thought that sounded like a great idea. She'd love a nice bath. Before she had a real chance to look at the mongoose the animal had darted off somewhere.

A few more bends in the road brought them to the inn, which stood right on the edge of the silted river. A sweet smell emanated from the newly-thatched roof that fully enshrouded the upper half of the house. Under this the lower two stories were half-timbered, the cream-colored stucco peeking through a jumble of forsythia and oasis jasmine vines. A small signboard with a picture of a bird read: *The Homely Tern.*

All of the windows were thrown open, faded curtains rippling slightly in the breeze. This inn seemed to Aru a gracious old thing, welcoming and well-established. In her imagination Aru could hear the tinkling laughter and chattering voices of those previous guests who had scattered their sunny feelings here.

The innkeeper arrived a few minutes after they did, in human form now and wearing a simple cotton print dress, and she had a little boy with her who carried a basket of mustard cuttings. She greeted Nrouhw warmly and introduced herself and her son to Aru. They both had fascinating eyes. Mongooses, when they transform to human, retain the mongoose eyes, which have narrow horizontal pupils like a goat's. Perhaps it doesn't sound attractive, but one gets used to it quickly. They generally carry a bright and soulful expression.

Aru and her fellow enjoyed a pleasant evening at the inn, including a nice chicken dinner and then a game of jackstraws in front of the fire. Late in the evening Nrouhw said goodbye to Aru. He was headed out onto the prairie for a couple of days, as the two of them had agreed would be the plan. Nrouhw loved this area for hunting, and thought he'd give himself the opportunity to fatten up a bit so he'd need less sustenance for their trip into the desert. He didn't want to leave Aru alone once they were on the road again. Nrouhw had assured her that she would have a lovely time at the Tern.

And Aru did. She slept in sumptuous ease on the sweet-smelling feather bed and awoke early due to the sun shining on her face. After a while she stretched and sat up. Leaning back against the pillows, Aru took a deep breath and gave a wonderful sigh. She smiled a big smile, basking in satisfaction. The room was airy and full of light. Daisies standing in a canning jar on the sill reminded her of the tablecloths her mother used to stitch for the kitchen table. The glow of Aru's surroundings sat her right inside a childhood memory, one of those happy ones where all of reality seemed perfect.

Down the hall and three doors on the right was the bathroom. Aru arrived, towel in hand, for the hot bath which awaited her. In the doorway, she stopped. She laughed. What in the world? No piped water at the inn, and yet—how absolutely curious! In place of a window, a great fish tank occupied the wall above the tub. Soft mottled sunlight came through the glass to illuminate goldfish the size of Aru's hand. They had long, flowing tails. These fish lived between the indoor and outdoor worlds, glistening, and swimming aimlessly, stopping sometimes to nibble on gilded sword plants and duckweed. Aru enjoyed a leisurely bath. She rested her head on the bolster pillow as she watched fish glide through all the sparkle and the sunrays. She sighed again, stretched her arms, and yawned. Calmness made her deeply alive.

Late for breakfast, Aru had fried eggs on toast and a glass of orange juice in the kitchen with the innkeeper's son. The boy was five years old, as he was more than happy to tell you, and spent so much time outdoors, apparently, that his hair was flaxen on top. Aru had seen this before, on some of the fishermen along the coast; countless days under the sun at sea had bleached the hair on top of their heads quite as blond as hers.

The two of them decided that it would be a fine idea if Aru helped with the boy's morning chores. They headed on out to the henhouse, and assuredly not by the most direct and efficient route. There were dandelions to pick, meadowlarks to notice, and a delightful mongoose pull toy to be shown to Aru. It had amber marbles for eyes. Along the way they collected several other children who seemed attracted by Aru's strange paleness.

A sack of chicken scratch sat just inside the poultry shed. Aru was instructed by the group to scoop out some grain, which was mostly cracked corn, and scatter it in the hen yard. This wasn't a fenced area but rather a sandy used-looking bit of land in front of the chicken coop.

The children called, "Here, chick, chick, chick!" but they didn't really have the need, for the birds had been eyeing them carefully the entire time. As soon as Aru began to distribute grain the chickens dove in to clamor for it, followed by a few ducks and a pair of boisterous geese.

Before collecting the eggs, Aru was invited into the brooding section of the henhouse, where fluffy chicks were peeping in the straw. The two mother hens were noisily apprehensive as each chick was lifted, cuddled, and held to a cheek. While they were gathered around the chicks Aru told the children the little story of The Bantam and the Golden Eggs. It was a traditional, moralistic story about the value of family versus the value of wealth. Even so, it featured lots of animal noises and the children seemed to enjoy it.

Back in the kitchen, Aru and her new little friend delivered the eggs to his mother. Tsirp offered Aru a seat and asked if she was thirsty. Aru soon was sipping from a mug of chamomile tea as she sat on a high stool and watched her hostess stoke the fire and prepare to make the midday meal. After a few minutes, Aru, having nothing much to do, asked the innkeeper if she could be of help. She was soon learning to make spongy flatbread, a traditional item in that prairie region and throughout the desert also.

The corn flour batter had been sitting for several hours, and was mixed from a yeasted starter that had been fermenting for several days. Aru, as instructed, added salt to the batter and stirred it thoroughly. The batter bubbled and it smelled rather nasty.

Aru ladled some batter onto a clay plate that sat over the fire. The plate had a long handle. Tsirp showed Aru the best way to tilt it and rotate so that the batter spread evenly. After a minute of cooking the bread began to develop holes in the surface and this was the time to cover it tightly with the lid. After they let the bread steam for a few minutes it was time to pour the next one.

Soon Aru produced several beautiful, evenly-cooked spongy flatbreads. They smelled much nicer than the batter did, slightly sour, with the aroma of fresh ground corn.

Tsirp's little boy eventually scampered off to another part of the house, but the two women were busy in the kitchen until mealtime. After the flatbread was done Aru squeezed lemons for honey lemonade. Then she grated carrots and cabbage for a spicy slaw. The women filled the air with their talk. The innkeeper was as curious about Aru as Aru was about the innkeeper and her prairie culture. Although travelers continually came and went from the inn, Tsirp had never seen anyone that looked like Aru. She'd heard of light-skinned people living in the northern mountains, but she'd never seen one of them. As for Aru, she had never been this far north herself. She had lots of questions about mongooses and about the area. And she wanted to know more about those people of the mountains.

Of course the subject of the thrall came up. The obnoxious thing invariably made itself known, often by its horrible squeaking, and never did a person have a positive reaction to it. All the time Tsirp and Aru were working it had been sitting in the corner on the butter churn, watching Aru.

Tsirp was not happy to have the wretch at her inn. "It is an evil magic. For certain it is up to no good, likely it will cause your demise. You must find a way to destroy it."

The two of them whispered, as if somehow that would prevent the thrall from hearing.

Aru sighed. "It's no good. One can't kill a thrall, as it turns out, they don't die. I've tried locking it away, but it appears in my pocket again, or under my covers at night."

"That's horrid! I'm so sorry!" Tsirp moaned. "There is no spirit animating the thing," she told Aru. "I've heard the magic can jump to other objects. Please be extremely careful. Notice what sorts of actions it takes. They don't think for themselves, these fiends, they follow orders only." Tsirp looked awfully serious. "Whoever sent it is a dangerously powerful person and the thing has a purpose. You must determine what that is."

In the afternoon Aru lounged in the garden in a spot overlooking the river. She started a new stitchery project she'd been planning, a kerchief for Phfft-Psyfft's baby. It would have a bunch of daffodils in one corner, and cheery goldfinches all around the border. When it was done she'd have it sent to her friend. By raven if she could afford it.

Nrouhw returned the next morning just after breakfast. After a long and hearty hug he and Aru prepared to return to the road. They rinsed out and refilled their water jugs, and bought a few food items from the inn. Nrouhw prepared an ointment of jasmine, rice bran and acorn tannins in cocoa butter to protect Aru's fair skin in the desert. The innkeeper had an opinion about their furnishings.

"That pushcart!" she exclaimed. "You'll be all right for a while on the road, but eventually it will be impossible to navigate that thing through the sand. At Oubli you're going to have to hire a donkey or a camel or maybe buy a domestic creature."

"Once again, Tsirp, you have good advice," replied Nrouhw. "Is it that deep, the sand?"

"Oh yes, it can be. Depending on the winds and upon your route."

The sun was still climbing when Nrouhw and Aru said goodbye to the innkeeper and her boy and walked east together along the river road. Aru took a long turn pushing the cart. They soon left the cultivated fields behind. Breathing room abounded in the wide prairie, with nothing to block the horizon, only the low hills which were really nothing more than wrinkles in the landscape. After traveling along for a while, Aru began to notice the rich variations in the subtle palette of the scenery. The sunlight fell more gently here than it did on the rocks of Ysgarlad; it broadcast itself into the waving grasses, lending them a gold and amber shimmer.

Aru enjoyed Nrouhw's company as she enjoyed the day, listening to the birds and insects make their music. In the afternoon they saw a colony of prairie dogs. They encountered other travelers now and then, mostly they saw dusty farmers and their wagons, but a few of them were merchants or people in strange clothes who had some mysterious purpose for their journey. These passers-by would nearly always stop and say a brief hello.

On the third day out from the inn, Nrouhw and Aru overtook a tall, tippy-looking wagon which was squeaking slowly along. As they drew closer they saw that it was a canary-colored circus wagon, carved and gilded, painted with images of magical beasts. Across the back, above the overfilled hay cratch, in shiny blue letters was the word *COLOSSAL!* As they caught up they could see the side of the wagon was also heavily decorated and labeled with the word *MAGNIFICENT!*

A spectacular pair of heavy horses, palominos perfectly matched, pulled the wagon. Just gorgeous. They nodded at Aru and Nrouhw in greeting. The fact that they wore no bridles was a sure sign that they were hired animal transforms and not domesticated creatures. Up above, high up on the driver's seat, rode a man and an extremely tall old woman. Both of them waved.

Aru wasn't about to pass by with merely a wave when she was so intrigued. "Are you lost?" she called up to the two.

They laughed. "No, my pet, we're not lost," said the tall woman in a thick accent. "We're on circus business."

Her voice was low-pitched, so soft and gentle it took a special effort to hear her over the noises of the horses and wagon. She had large brown eyes with long and thick lashes. Her limbs were so elongated and bony, her shoulders so narrow and sloping, that Aru found it difficult not to stare.

"Marvel Brothers Circus!" thundered the man, shaking his head and showing his fangs, "The Greatest Extravaganza in the World!" His resounding tone tore right through Aru, striking some primordial nerve. He was a big fellow, big and brawny. For only an instant, Aru knew herself as prey. A humbling reaction, and a new perspective. Aru had never felt so much like a meal.

For a while the four of them conversed in a friendly manner, traveling along the road together. As usually happened, the apple doll made itself known and had to be quietly explained. The circus folk were on their way to pick up a pair of camels and maybe a few fennec foxes if they could find some who were interested in joining the company.

Something small struck the back of Aru's head. It hurt. A pebble? What? Then another object whizzed by. And another. She and Nrouhw were being pelted by . . . acorns. Fending off another nut with their forearms, they looked up in confusion to determine the source.

At the same time the big man turned around in his seat and yelled, "Eaky! Eaky Dongle! Eh, you'll regret this behavior, you ungrateful little gremlin!" He shook his finger at someone on the roof of the wagon. But no one seemed to be there.

"Oh, a monkey!" cried Aru.

A squirrel monkey somersaulted along the edge of the wagon roof, twittering and laughing at his own cleverness. He had a golden saffron coat, with markings on his face that looked like a pair of white goggles.

"I'm so sorry," said the tall woman. "If you please; may I present our Eaky Dongle, trapeze artist." She sighed a deep, throaty sigh.

The man admonished the monkey, sending him inside the wagon. They resumed their conversation, which eventually blossomed into a shared rest stop by the river and then an early camp together that evening. The woman's name was Umm, and the man's Roehr.

Roehr had a big broad forehead and a square, jutting jaw with a close-cropped beard. His face was surrounded by long sandy hair so thick it stuck straight out. Roehr's motions were easy and deliberate. He projected a calm assuredness. He possessed an unnervingly obvious amount of strength.

The two had introduced the horses early on, as the pair weren't able to speak to introduce themselves. Aru had thought their names strange. "Nugget and Star? What unusual names!" she had said.

"Those are their circus names, they're supposed to be odd," explained Roehr. "Their real names," he said, "are Wheehehe and Prrphyt."

The horses went off to graze for an hour or so while the others set up camp. Umm went with them, explaining that she liked to nibble a bit before supper herself. In a short time she could be seen standing with the horses under a clump of trees; while they were grazing the grass she was reaching for leaves, a lovely giraffe.

While the herbivores were so occupied, the others scraped together a fine communal meal. Eaky Dongle wasn't much help. When Roehr finally insisted Eaky contribute by taking the apricots to wash in the river, the little monkey ended up losing several.

About the time supper was ready the human Umm arrived back at camp, accompanied by two stout men. In human form Star stood a bit taller than Nugget and had a slightly longer face. The horses had been working for the circus for many years, not only as draft animals, but also as eminent performers. Equestrian skills were central to circus arts and with their broad flat backs and steady gait Nugget and Star were the foundations of a spectacular acrobatic team. Excellent dancers themselves, Roehr explained, the two had surprising ability in walking on the hind legs or forelegs.

Umm had also been with the Marvel Brothers for quite some time. She was a prima unicyclist and also a juggler. Aru hadn't seen a circus since she was a small child. She had trouble imagining a giraffe riding a unicycle. Or juggling.

"That's why it's The Greatest Extravaganza," said Roehr with a smile.

Since they enjoyed each other's company, the group decided to travel on together. Over the next few days they exchanged lots of songs and stories. Each morning Nugget and Star would change to their horse forms after breakfast and have some grain before Umm helped them into harness. The humans walked, for the most part, although now and then Aru rode with either Umm or Roehr on the wagon.

Eaky Dongle rode the wagon. Sometimes he rode the horses. Sometimes he rode on a walker's shoulder. Aru and Nrouhw learned that Eaky Dongle spent nearly all his time in monkey form. He so much enjoyed being a monkey.

The sunny, breezy weather didn't change much, nor did the prairie scenery. They saw some monarch butterflies and a tiger swallowtail.

One afternoon when they were all walking along, Aru asked Roehr about his job in the circus. Was he a performer?

"Oh, yes," he said. "I am a performer."

"What do you do?"

"Well, I perform fire stunts," he said. "I jump through flaming hoops and I walk across hot coals."

"That would be amazing to see," said Nrouhw.

"Have you ever been burned?" asked Aru.

"That's always the first thing people want to know," replied Roehr, "but yes, I have singed my mane a few times."

Then Aru asked him, "In all that excitement Roehr, out in the ring, in that crowded tent, don't you ever get the urge to eat somebody?"

Nrouhw made a horrible suppressed noise and covered his eyes. He peeked at Aru through his fingers. He shook his head.

Aru brought her hand to her mouth. "Oh, excuse me. I'm sorry!"

Nrouhw looked at their friend, saying, "So sorry, she was raised among wolves." Then, "Rude, Aru, so rude," he said. He and Roehr both laughed.

The travelers took many breaks along the way because nobody was in a real hurry and Nrouhw needed to rest from pushing the cart.

During these pauses Aru would usually work on her kerchief for little Phfft-Psyfft. Umm would sit nearby, humming a tune, or sometimes she played her bamboo flute.

Aru loved listening to the music. Umm shared the traditional songs of her culture and sometimes she improvised. Although Aru knew nothing of the history of the giraffe people, she appreciated the particular patterns and tones, driven by the rhythm of Umm's tapping foot, as a soulful communication from the ancients. The emotion of the music made Aru think of melting butter on warm yeasted bread, for some reason, and blossoming acacia branches, and the savanna.

Now and then during the rest stops Nrouhw and Aru would slip away together for a short while, just to talk and lie on their backs looking up at the sky. Some of their conversations were quite cerebral and philosophical. Others were more along the lines of:

"Don't do that, Aru."

"What?"

"You know. Don't push on my nose, you know I don't like that."

"Sorry, I just can't seem to help it."

"Do not press on my nose."

"Sorry, but I have to. I don't know why. I can't help it."

Aru often wore the necklace that Nrouhw had given her. At night before bed she would carefully place it inside the pouch her mother had crocheted, a tattered but still beautiful daisy-lace bag. Aru always carried this special pocket on her belt when she traveled. It contained all of her small treasures and charms, and the vial of mithridate from her beaver friend.

One morning Aru woke up to find that the locket had gone missing from her pouch. Not only was the necklace gone, but the thief had the audacity to leave a nasty slimy peach pit in its place. The thrall had never shown an interest in Aru's possessions. More fittingly, Eaky Dongle's name came to mind.

When Aru let Roehr and Umm know what had happened they agreed this sounded like Eaky's work. Roehr told Aru he'd find out what was going on. He climbed up into the wagon, where Eaky Dongle still slept. The others generally made their beds outside on the ground but

Eaky preferred to use his nest inside the wagon. After a minute Roehr reappeared and quietly resumed his work by the fire. His big batch of hummus needed its lemon juice.

It wasn't long before Eaky Dongle emerged from the wagon. Aru and Nrouhw hadn't seen him in human form before. They'd assumed he was a child and so were surprised to find him a young man in his early twenties. Squirrel monkeys have a delayed maturity.

Eaky looked a little ruffled; he hadn't buttoned his shirt properly and he kept blinking a lot and looking at Aru and Nrouhw with his face pointed toward the ground. He had short cropped hair and dark round eyes that were close together. He stuck his tongue out at Aru.

"Eaky Donnngle!" roared Roehr. Everyone winced. Especially Eaky.

Unlike many animals, monkey transforms are able to understand speech from other species, even though they can't speak in reply. Eaky had heard them discussing the missing necklace and knew he'd been blamed even before Roehr confronted him.

"This is serious, Eaky Dongle," said Umm. "It seems unfair to accuse you, but there was no one around here last night but deer-mice and voles. They've no interest in someone else's necklace."

"What do you have to say for yourself?" demanded Roehr.

A minute or so of silence was followed by Eaky asking, "Are those lemon wedges? Can I have one?"

"Eaky!" growled Roehr.

"I don't know what happened to her silly necklace. I didn't take it. Hi, Aru and Nrouhw, by the way, I'm Eaky Dongle. Good to be introduced. I haven't had breakfast yet. I need a handful of chickpeas or something, I'm starving. Can I go back to bed now? I'm sleepy."

Puzzled, Roehr took a moment to respond.

"Yes, go ahead Eaky. Take some lemons. We'll save you some breakfast."

After Eaky Dongle took his leave, Roehr turned quietly to Aru and said, "I don't know what to make of it. Eaky Dongle can be a real rascal, but I've only known him to tell the truth."

Nobody said anything for a while. Aru wondered if maybe it was the thrall's mischief, after all.

Over the next couple of days the prairie became noticeably more dry. Large boulders began to appear more and more often and trees were farther apart. Along the riverbanks things didn't change much, but the open prairie was ending. Bare sandstone hills came into sight in the distance.

Aru's concern about her necklace kept gnawing at her, although she tried to shrug it off. It was just that she didn't see how the thing could disappear like that. Someone had to have taken it. Why insult her with the peach pit? And what about that monkey? Roehr and Umm certainly didn't seem like the type of people who would steal. Was she naive to think that?

Despite all this she enjoyed the days of walking along the Bee Line with her fellow travelers. *They should have called it the Snake Line, though,* thought Aru, *the way it follows this river.*

At suppertime the night before they would reach the desert another item turned up missing. Roehr found that his favorite spoon was gone from the utensils box. A gold spoon, with a crown shape on the end of the handle. He'd put it back in the box himself the previous night. After washing up. He remembered doing it. Now it was missing.

Without really meaning to, everyone looked right at Eaky Dongle. However, instead of jumping up and down with his teeth bared, or twirling his way up to the top of someone's head, or farting loudly, as might be expected, Eaky did something surprising. He covered his eyes with both hands. Then he covered the top of his head, then his eyes again. Then he got up slowly and went to the wagon.

A few minutes later two young men emerged from the wagon door-way. Roehr and Nrouhw jumped to their feet. Aru recognized the one as Eaky Dongle in human form again. He had his hand up, showing his palm in a gesture of appeasement. His other hand gripped his friend's shoulder, guiding him out toward the others. This fellow was looking anxious, especially when his shifting glance landed on Roehr.

"Bruxus!" exclaimed Roehr and Umm in unison.

"Whatever in the great rigor and furor of nature is going on here?" That is what Roehr shouted. Truly, it sounded more like, "RROAR-RRoaRRrrOARRRoaRRR!"

"You know this guy?" asked Nrouhw.

Roehr spoke to Nrouhw but kept his eyes on Bruxus. "He was loitering around the circus just before we headed out. We ran across him again in a market about a fortnight ago. RRoaRrrrr!" This latter statement had a clear tone of, "Now it's clear why!"

Eaky Dongle and Bruxus were slowly walking toward Roehr and Umm, but they both took a few steps backward when Roehr vocalized. "Please don't hurt us, Roehr, I mean, uh—him!" squeaked Eaky Dongle. "I'll tell you everything about what happened, what's been going on."

"Let's hear it, then." Under Roehr's anger was a trace of amusement.

"Well," said Eaky.

"Well?"

"Um, well, a few days after we got on the road, well two days, I noticed something. Someone. It was Bruxus, stashed away under some blankets. Of course, he was in his animal form. So I thought, *Well, I should tell someone.* But then, I didn't." Eaky paused and scratched in his ear with his finger. Then Roehr caught his eye so he continued, "I thought you'd smell him, but I guess you didn't so I figured, *What's the difference.* He wasn't hurting anything. So in he stays. Except he went out every night to forage. I guess."

"He was with us all along? How didn't we know?" wondered Umm.

"Yeah. Well, there's another thing," said Eaky.

"Yes? What's that?"

"He's . . ." Eaky Dongle turned his gaze away toward the fire.

"I'm—" Bruxus started to speak but froze when Roehr looked at him.

"He's a packrat," whispered Eaky Dongle.

Roehr sat down. He looked at Umm. She looked at him. They both shook their heads. Roehr said, "Well, someone get me another spoon. We'll all have supper and then the little gerbil can show us his midden."

After the meal Bruxus led the others to his stash in the wagon. It was just inside the door, hidden under the water tank, so everyone got a bit of a view as he dismantled it.

"Well," said Roehr as Bruxus began to rummage through the straw and rags in the pile, "at least he doesn't seem to have urinated on it."

Umm sighed. "You know it's time to clean out your wagon when you start getting packrats," she said softly.

The first thing to come out was Roehr's gold spoon, which Bruxus handed to him along with an apology. Eaky Dongle, who had reappeared in monkey form just as soon as he had finished eating, chittered and jumped around. Apparently he liked this sort of game.

The next few things were of minimal interest: some nuts, a shiny rock, a few coins. Aru's necklace was there indeed, but when Eaky saw it he snatched it up, put it in his mouth, and cartwheeled up to the roof of the wagon. When on top, he reached down over the edge and dangled the locket just out of Nrouhw's reach.

Nrouhw jumped up and tried to grab it. Eaky held it higher. Nrouhw jumped again, batting at the necklace. This went on for a few minutes until a throaty noise came from Roehr's direction. Eaky Dongle let the necklace fall into Nrouhw's hand.

A quick wash in the river did the necklace no harm, then Nrouhw fastened it tenderly back around Aru's neck. A soft kiss and his arm around her shoulders and Aru was feeling much better about things.

The remaining objects in Bruxus's stash included more coins, a fine pen, a pocket watch, some amber beads, and a set of six small brass bowls. There was a trunk key that Umm had been missing for several weeks. They'd had to break the lock on the trunk. Umm remarked that, come to think of it, this was about the time she'd found that shiny golden brooch.

Roehr and Umm decided to be kind. Rather than turn the miserable animal out where he'd be alone in the middle of nowhere, they would allow him to come along with them as far as the camel market. Roehr told Bruxus that he'd like it there at the marketplace. Lots of shiny things. Roehr had known a few packrats. He hadn't been overly impressed by them.

And so Bruxus became a legitimate member of the group. Most of the time he walked on the road along with the others, but when he occasionally rode on the wagon it was as a rat. As a young man he proved to be a help with setting up and breaking down camp, and he wasn't a horrible cook. In addition he volunteered for some shifts with Nrouhw's pushcart.

Unfortunately Bruxus had trouble communicating with Umm. Her hearing was adapted to the low frequencies and his was attuned to higher notes, some too shrill for human ears. With a bit of extra effort, though, they were able to overcome this minor inconvenience.

The company encountered more layered rock outcroppings as they traveled east. Sand drifts replaced the sandy soil between the boulders as they neared the pass that wound through bare wind-sculpted hills. Eventually, instead of occasional clumps of trees as there had been in the grassland, they found occasional clumps of grass in the sand.

The travelers often bathed in the silted river or used Nrouhw's pair of bamboo fishing poles to catch a few sunfish. Matriarch of the land, nurturing sundry forms of life, the river made the Amber Trail viable. The water wasn't potable for humans, but could be used for washing, and for boiling crayfish and eggs. It would have been difficult for travelers to carry enough water to cross the desert but thanks to the wide and perennial river the route was an option for many.

The wagon's cistern had plenty of drinking water for the circus crew's journey, but Aru and Nrouhw were concerned about their own supply. Nrouhw and Umm tried filtering the river water through some muslin but the silt clogged things up rather quickly. Then Aru remembered a trick her grandmother had taught her. Not finding any in the kitchen box, she dug around in Nrouhw's art supplies and found a bottle of alum. She filled a bucket from the river and slowly stirred in a bit of the powder. After twenty minutes all the silt had beautifully magicked its way to the bottom. Aru scooped some of the clear water into the big brass kettle to boil and purify, and soon they enjoyed their tea, knowing they had a way to extend their water supply.

Winding between the sandstone hills, the road and river led them ever eastward. Nrouhw was compelled to get a last hunt in before they reached the open desert. Roehr asked if he'd like some company.

"I'm really more of a solitary hunter," Nrouhw replied.

"Yes, I understand. So am I," said Roehr. "I don't often hunt, to be truthful, but I feel in the mood tonight. Could you use some help in bringing down a nice fat antelope?"

This sounded like an interesting idea to Nrouhw. The two of them changed form behind some blankets which were drying on a line.

Aru stood up in awe as the two big cats emerged, side by side, tails swishing. Roehr was enormous, more than twice Nrouhw's size. As the two of them padded past the campsite she thought to herself that they truly were majestic. She knew they wouldn't harm her, but nevertheless she breathed quickly, feeling like dinner once again. Aru was just as happy that they were on the far side of the firepit and some distance away. And yet, their fine, luxurious coats made them look so velvety. Umm held quite still, watching them also.

"Don't you want to touch that soft fur!" whispered Aru, trembling.

Umm smiled. "Probably not worth a hand!" she said quietly.

Felines have a great deal of pride wrapped up in their dignity.

The next morning the travelers rounded a rock formation to see, at last, the endless desert spread before them. None of the group had been this far along the Amber Trail before. The view caused excitement and a touch of dismay. All the way to the horizon there wasn't a tree, a stump, a plant or even a decent-sized rock in sight. Nothing but sand and the wandering river, with their road faithfully hugging its bank.

"Well, this is what we've been fattening ourselves up for," said Roehr. "I suppose if we run out of food before we get to our destination we can always eat Brux."

Bruxus tried to laugh but it came out as more of a squeak. This made everyone laugh, including Bruxus. The laughter encouraged them forward.

They proceeded faster through the desert than they had through the prairie; not because the going was easier, but because there was more of a focus on the destination. No farm wagons traveled the road during the day in these parts, only a few worldly characters passed by. One night a produce wagon passed their camp, a big creaking wagon dribbling water from the melting ice. This was headed the same place they were: the market town of Oubli, where river and road turned south, and Nrouhw and Aru would continue on through the desert.

In this remote area, when travelers did pass each other they stopped for a substantial conversation. Over the next few days the friends met several interesting people. They ate lunch with a woman who was traveling alone on a pale buckskin mare, and they shared supper with a family of bronze merchants who were headed to the coast. These folks had a supply of ship's fittings, a heavy load. Aru wondered how the oxen were able to bear the weight. And early one evening a pair of jaguars overtook Aru's group on the road, but they didn't stop to talk; they probably didn't want to deplete their energy by transforming. The most intriguing person they met, however, had to be Aureus the Momentous.

The company had taken to getting up before sunrise and having every-thing ready to roll by the time there was enough light to travel. That way they could rest during the heat of the day and still make good time. Aureus came along one morning when they had just finished packing things up. He was driving a simple ostrich cart.

He arrived from the west in a cloud of sandalwood smell and with the tinkling of brass bells. A small, elderly man in a long gazelle-skin robe, he introduced himself as Aureus the Momentous.

Aru was fascinated by this man and his ostrich. She'd never seen an ostrich before. Nrouhw and Bruxus got to talking with the man. As he had shown up when they were ready to pull out, Aureus just sort of naturally ended up traveling along with the group.

The hazy sky made things a bit cooler, a fine morning for walking. Aureus was full of knowledge about the desert and he kept having to remind the ostrich to slow her pace so he could share stories and tidbits of information with the ones who were on foot. Everyone except Roehr found Aureus quite interesting. Roehr had taken a dislike to him from the start. Time slipped by unnoticed for most of the group as the old man shared his desert lore and it was the middle of the afternoon before they stopped for their midday break. They decided to go ahead and set up camp.

Aureus freed the ostrich from its cart, and accompanied it as it went immediately down to the river for a drink. When the two reappeared over the riverbank the ostrich had become a long-necked, long-legged old woman with large eyes and no teeth. She wore a flouncy beige dress trimmed with frills and fringe, strange garb for desert travel. The dress did nothing to beautify her nonexistent waist. Aureus introduced her as his apprentice.

The travelers had an especially nice meal, which included a pie that Umm and Bruxus had made in the heavy lidded pot with the last two tins of canned peaches. Aureus, after having eaten a huge amount of food, was one of the first to help himself to pie. He took a large portion, leaving a relatively small amount for the remaining diners to divide. Roehr bared his teeth in disgust at this behavior. He eyed Aureus threateningly.

His cheeks bulging with the sweet peaches, the old man noticed Roehr's irritation. "So," he said, slobbering peach juice, "you certainly are a handsome gentleman, Mr. Roehr. I'll bet you have plenty of female admirers back at your circus. Are you the star of the show?"

"I do all right," replied Roehr stiffly.

"Well, you'd be a great ringmaster, I suspect. You sure seem to be in charge around here."

Roehr's expression remained stern.

"I've an idea. It's such a nice day. Why don't we sit back for a while and play a game of cribbage? I've a board with me," offered Aureus.

Despite his animosity toward Aureus, this proposal piqued Roehr's interest, and Nrouhw and Bruxus joined the game also. Eaky Dongle was content with jumping on people's laps and generally getting in the way. Nugget and Star cleaned up the dishes, while all three of the women chose to sit nearby and relax in the shade of the wagon.

Aru worked on her stitchery project. The ostrich woman, fascinated by Aru, wanted to know all about who she was and where she came from. She told Aru about the pale-skinned people of the heights in the mountains to the north. Aru replied that, yes, she'd heard of them and was quite interested in going to see them. No, the ostrich woman had never seen them herself.

The ostrich woman seemed to enjoy spending time with Umm and Aru. While the three were talking, her long and bony fingers deftly fashioned a doll from some old corn husks. It didn't take her long at all, and when finished, the doll was superb. She had a perfectly-shaped head, braided arms, and nicely voluminous skirts. The woman offered it, not to Aru, or to Umm, but to the ever-present thrall. Aru opened her mouth to speak, but the old woman placed her finger to her lips and nodded toward the dolls.

Resting its back against Aru's leg, the apple thrall had been sitting, tormenting an ant-lion larva it had found. It stood up to look at the doll made of dried husks. Then it squatted, reaching to finger the soft straw-colored skirts much as a washerwoman might feel a queen's gown. Turning to stare at Aru, the thrall closed its eyes.

"No!" whispered Aru.

The eyes and mouth vacated the apple doll to appear on the corn doll where there had been no face! The apple doll fell, abandoned. The corn husk thrall looked up at Aru, smiling. It stood up.

The woman clucked and beckoned to Aru. With a stiff reed she wrote some letters in the sand. These letters spelled out,

BuRn IT whEn YOu geT to OuBLI!

When Aru looked confused, the woman added,

In ThE XAnTHic FIREs.

Aru nodded. Then she tossed the apple doll into the river. She didn't want it anymore.

Roehr won the first game, with Bruxus just behind him. Each player had thrown two gold pieces in the basket, so the stakes were rather high for such a game and because of this their outlooks on life were currently much affected by their scores. Aureus had done quite poorly. He didn't do so well in the next game either. In the third game, however, after raising the stakes he skunked all three of the other players, ending the entire tournament and igniting a suspicious anger in the spleens of his opponents. Aureus filled his pockets. The men drained the rest of their mead and started to argue about what had happened.

Fortunately, nature chose this moment to intervene. The haze over the eastern desert had thickened into a bank of citrine color. Aureus noticed it first, setting down his glass.

Bruxus followed his gaze and then he gasped. "What is it?"

"Sandstorm!" cried Aureus.

"Here?" asked Nrouhw, confused.

"We only have minutes!" cried Aureus, "Quick, help me throw these things onto the pushcart and we'll tie the tarp over. Bruxus, find rope!

Aru, clever princess, gather the feed buckets and whatnot and toss them into the wagon!"

People rushed every which way to help. A hasty job was made of covering and securing things, then Roehr shouted, "That's enough!"

"Everyone into the wagon!" called Umm.

The entire crew hustled up the steps and in through the door of the circus wagon. It was dark inside. There wasn't enough room for all these people. But they went in anyhow.

"Who's the last one? Shut the door!"

"It's me," said Roehr "Are we all accounted for?"

"I think so . . ."

They huddled in the dark. No one could find a candle. They huddled. They stepped on each other's feet. They waited.

"Should we take a peek outside?"

"No, better not to open the door. Just wait."

"Hey. Is the old man in here?"

"Aureus! Hey, Aureus—"

A sound came from outside the wagon. It was not the blasting sound of wind-driven sand. It was the sound of an ostrich cart departing at high speed.

Roehr burst the door open and staggered outside. Aureus the Momentous, with his apprentice and the men's gold, sped safely out of reach, leaving a cloud of dust behind them. But no storm. Nothing but a thick haze in the eastern sky.

They climbed down from the wagon and stared after the cart. Star mentioned he had recognized the man's name. Aureus the Jaundiced, a jackal, was known for inexpert sorcery of the questionable kind.

The friends arrived at the market town of Oubli several days later. How strange to see the green and gold patchwork of cultivated fields, sharply bordered by the sands. Such an odd-looking island in a flat desert sea. The complicated miracle of silt farming and drip irrigation had created a completely fabricated haven on the bend of the river.

There weren't a lot of buildings, just some mud-brick structures with wind towers to cool the interiors. A few duck cloth tents looked to be in permanent residence among the other houses. The camel market dominated everything. A tradition stemming from ancient times, its huge pavilion tents in bright colors couldn't be missed. The smell was conspicuous also.

Aru was eager to see the camels. She hadn't seen a single one on the road thus far. As soon as the wagon found a place on the lot she and Nrouhw headed into the nearest of the pavilions. Aru looked around, a puzzled expression on her face. "Where are the camels?" she whispered to Nrouhw. The entire tent was full of men and women sitting around not doing much of anything. Some were napping, some reading, a few were playing cards.

"These must be the camels for hire," Nrouhw replied. "I suppose the domesticated creatures are in the other pavilion."

They walked straight on through. A few of the people looked at Aru with interest as she walked by. Behind this tent stood another, its walls mostly tied back to allow air to blow through. Here were the camels that Aru wanted to see.

How huge these creatures were! Nearly any of them would have dwarfed Nugget and Star. These were the sort of camels that have two humps. By their nature the camels carried a fermented type of odor, pungent, cheesy, and accentuated by stale urine. But they were endearing creatures. There were about two dozen camels in the tent and many more outside. They stood alone or in little clumps, attended by the sellers and being perused by potential buyers. The beasts looked friendly. Aru was struck by how each camel's face looked so very different, and full of character, and how each had a smile on its face. How unusual for a creature to have a natural smile like that.

After looking around for a while Aru and Nrouhw headed back to the wagon to set up camp. They pitched their tent in the lot just behind the wagon. Then they helped Roehr and Bruxus find some fresh produce for the supper. Eaky Dongle rode along with them on Aru's shoulder. He was awfully excited to be at the market. Most of the crew felt the same way, relieved to have a break from the desert road. Oubli had several wells and the fresh clear water was a treat.

Nugget and Star, however, like most horses, were quite uncomfortable with the smell of camels. They spent virtually all their time in Oubli as humans and inside the wagon, burning incense.

That first evening at supper Roehr announced to the group that it had been agreed Brux could stay on with the circus wagon. Umm thought he should cultivate his skills and become a magician. That idea was quite agreeable to Bruxus. He would travel back with them to the Marvel Brothers Show and Roehr would get him an apprenticeship with The Great Rabbitcadabra Praesto, the rabbit of world renown.

"I've heard of her!" said Aru.

"So have I," said Nrouhw. "Congratulations, Brux!"

The next day was a busy one. Nrouhw sold his pushcart and made arrangements to hire a camel for their journey on to Anseo, the village which was key to his dreams of excavating for gold. The camel had his own packsaddle but Nrouhw and Aru had to figure out how to pack things up appropriately. They bought two wooden boxes, some cloth for making bundles, and a brass scale of the type used in fishing. They would have to weigh and pack everything so that the load would be balanced. They picked up a few more supplies. Nrouhw bought Aru a lemon-colored chiffon parasol with fringe.

Roehr and Umm picked out two camels for the circus. They needed them to replace a young camel who, although he'd grown up in a fine traditional circus family, had run away to the city to work at an accounting firm. In addition the pair wanted to scout for other performers, so they planned to stay in Oubli for a few days.

An important task for Aru and Nrouhw was to locate the Xanthic Fires of Oubli. Finding them was easy. For one brass coin, a young girl led them to the edge of town and the eternal flame where the bodies of the departed were cremated. She wouldn't go near the site, however, as she feared the strong magic. Many spells had been placed on this pyre to keep the flames burning with limited fuel and also so that the spirits sent on would not return. It did seem a clever idea to throw the corn husk doll into these flames. Without ceremony, Nrouhw hurled the thrall into the thickest part of the huge roaring fire. Alas, but to no avail. As they were heading back to camp they heard unwelcome little footsteps running up behind them. There was a slight smell of toasted corn. Aru found that, in some crazy way, she felt relieved. The act of destroying the doll felt like murder.

Nrouhw and Aru spent a last night with their friends, telling stories and laughing a lot. Umm gave Aru a polished brass charm, a jaguar. Aru and Nrouhw had invited their newly hired camel, Krohnnck, to share their bonfire, and Nugget and Star came out to join the group also. Krohnnck was a tall fellow, with ebony skin, and his yellowed white hair twisted into wooly locks. He wore a linen tunic and short, loosely-fitting pants. His eyes, along with his prominent brow and jawline, and the fullness of his lower lip, still made the women turn their heads. Krohnnck had always lived beside the desert and would guide Aru and Nrouhw in locating Anseo. Eaky Dongle took a particular liking to the old man, and wouldn't stay off of his head until Roehr gave him a stern warning.

In the morning, packing the camel Krohnnck was quick work because of the way camels kneel. Aru thought the backwards bend in the hind legs made them look strangely human. Krohnnck's saddle cloth had rich, cheery colors and elaborate embroidery. Aru just loved it. What a wonderful way to add pleasure to the day. As they hoisted the bundles, tying basket hitches to keep them in place, the thrall tried to help. Its efforts, unexpected but apparently sincere, did more to slow down the process than anything.

Aru and Nrouhw said goodbye to their circus friends and walked northeast into the desert. Local opinion affirmed that Anseo should be somewhere in that direction from Oubli this time of year. With no road now, not even a trail to follow because of the deeper, shifting sands, Aru and Nrouhw found that walking took a great deal more effort. Their feet sank into the soft sand and it got into their boots. As a camel, Krohnnck had no difficulty. His broad, two-toed feet were designed for staying on top of the surface, the weight of his body so evenly distributed that even with his heavy load he made only a slight impression as he walked. Although they hoped it would only be a few day's journey to Anseo, Aru and Nrouhw absolutely required these services of a skilled guide. To get lost in the drifting, unmarked wasteland of the desert would be a supreme mistake. And then there was the problem of finding the village.

Through all of recorded history Anseo had been an important harbor for travelers. A crucial stopover in the desert, it also functioned as a trade center. Made up entirely of tents, the great mobile encampment could vanish or appear in a matter of hours. Prevailing wind patterns dictated the village's location, depending on the seasonal propensity for sandstorms and other practical local factors of the weather. Invisible forces of the magical world were also taken into account in determining each site of Anseo. Therefore, wind forecasting and magical divination prevailed as methods of locating the village.

Away from the river and its birds and insects a deep quiet covered everything. The only sounds were their own sounds. No flies buzzed the air, no life grew here that Aru could see. They were walking across low, crescent-shaped sand dunes and the sun seemed so big overhead.

"It's hot," observed Aru, "but not too horribly hot."

"That's why people call it the Pleasant Desert," said Nrouhw. He held her parasol, sharing the shade of it with her as they trudged along. He didn't seem to be missing that pushcart.

The going was slow, but again there was no reason to hurry. They stopped often and drank water, snacking now and then on salty dried cheese. Rain never fell in this part of the desert but their camel carried plenty of good water. They took a real break during the heat of the day, setting up a canopy on long sticks to make shade. In the late afternoon they continued on, well rested and ready for more.

"I do wish there was a good strong breeze," Aru said as they neared the top of a larger dune.

"Oh no you don't!" Nrouhw laughed.

"I guess not!" Aru laughed back, thankful the sand wasn't pelting her eyes and filling her ears. "I suppose wind is what formed all this."

As they reached the highest point of the dune they had a full view of the sand dunes spread before them. It looked to Nrouhw like a golden ocean suspended in time, as if deep swells of the open sea had been caught in a photograph. Aru said it looked like the sand had been whipped into a huge caramelized meringue.

"The Pleasant Dessert!" they both said at once.

In the distance were dunes so high they looked like mountains.

As they made camp that evening, they decided to set the bedding out on the sand. The stars would be breathtaking later on. A pot of squash soup simmered nicely over a fire built up of wood they'd brought from Oubli. They ate some spongy flatbread. Their camel friend joined them in human form for conversation. He didn't really need the food, and would sleep better as a camel, but he wanted to sit and chat.

Old Krohnnck talked a lot, both to his companions and to himself. When he was a camel he talked a lot, too, muttering about this and that even though he knew the couple couldn't understand. These camel noises were cheerful rants, but to the human ear they sounded more like a moan, and uncannily like the creaking beams of a ship.

This evening, he kept Aru and Nrouhw's attention riveted through his fascinating knowledge of the desert. After telling a lengthy folktale, Krohnnck asked Aru and Nrouhw if they'd heard of the singing sand dune. He grinned a big camel grin as he described an ancient dune to them, an especially large one, from which music emanated. This wasn't merely the whistling of the wind. From the hill itself came the musical notes, in concert. When the wind rose enough to disturb the sands, or when someone displaced sand by walking, this is when the mountain would begin to sing.

The singing dune was a treasured marvel, and each year a great festival was held in its honor. Bright tents were pitched in the valley below the dune, musical talent performed, great food was eaten, and people came from all over the world. The highlight of the festival was the serpent roll. Dozens of snakes were invited to this event. Precisely at midnight the snakes would stretch out and roll down the face of the dune. This, of course, would cause the loudest and most awe-inspiring song of the year. An added delight was watching the pile of goggle-wearing snakes try to recover from their dizziness.

Krohnnck pointed out some dunes not far across the sands; the second biggest one, just to the left there, that was the singing sand dune. They may as well go and see it for themselves. It wasn't far out of their way. They'd have to cross that range of dunes at any rate, why not just walk a stone's throw further west and pay their respects to the singing dune. Krohnnck was fairly certain Aru and Nrouhw would want to hear it. He was right.

The night sky indeed shone thick with stars. The most stars Aru had ever seen. And this with the moon nearly full! Nrouhw gazed upward with dream-clouded eyes. "That artists colony Krohnnck mentioned yesterday, the one on the edge of the desert."

"What about it?"

"We ought to consider changing our course, going there instead. It sounds as if I could do well there, painting landscapes. And you could learn more about the textile arts. I know you'd love to live in an art community."

"Ah, maybe."

He and Aru lay awake for quite some time, looking up and pointing, squealing and shrieking as shooting stars flashed across. After they finally did drift off to sleep they each woke once in a while and gazed some more. Eventually, Aru slept soundly. Until—

A piercing shriek.

"You snotting little mange mite!"

Aru woke to Nrouhw standing, holding the horribly squeaking thrall in the hand of his outstretched arm. The thrall, squeezed tightly by Nrouhw's rage, waved Nrouhw's knife around wildly. "The rabid little bastard tried to slit my throat!" snarled Nrouhw. Then he hissed.

Nrouhw rarely swore, unlike Aru, who had been raised as a wolf. She'd never heard him use the word 'rabid' before. This was almost as much of a shock as seeing the thrall crinkled and crunching in Nrouhw's big hand, brandishing the knife. The thing continued to squeak. Horribly.

Somehow Aru didn't believe that the thrall had made an attempt on Nrouhw's life. She tried to calm his feline indignance. The thing was probably just up to mischief as usual, it often did things to annoy Nrouhw. It must have just wanted the knife. Nrouhw wasn't convinced. He truly hated that thrall. Now more than ever.

It took two days to arrive at the singing dune. It hadn't looked nearly that far to Aru, but distances in the desert can be deceptive. As they approached its base the great mountain of sand towered over them. Krohnnck had said it would take several hours to climb the dune. They had a bit of a rest at the bottom and then set forth. Aru and Nrouhw were too curious to wait.

The top of the great sand dune formed a ridge that, on both ends, came down to meet the desert floor. Right up and along this crest of the dune the camel Krohnnck led Aru and Nrouhw, in single file. They made a fine sight, Aru with her long skirts and parasol, Nrouhw following the others, his head wrapped in a bright orange scarf. It was tough going; every step caused loose sand to give way beneath their boots. Soon, however, the hard work of each step was rewarded with a distinct squeaky "foop" sound. The strangeness of it, and the comical noise, caused Aru and Nrouhw to laugh, which they continued to do in fits, sometimes stopping to double over until they'd catch each other's eye and laugh again. This went on all the way until they reached the high point on the crest of the dune and had a view of the other side.

The three companions stood admiring the sweeping panorama of smaller dunes and the flat expanse beyond. A slight wind came from behind them, sending wisps of sand floating over the crest of the dune to trickle down the leeward face. A low rumbling drone began, a sound like old men chanting. The great dune was singing. The eerie notes had the purity of a cello or maybe a pipe organ. Even with forewarning it came as a great surprise and wonder to hear the music. As the friends resumed their course along the ridge the sound grew louder.

Climbing up along the top of the dune had been fun; descending was more so. They walked along the leeward side of the crest now, and dispatching enough sand with their steps that the mountain continued to sing for much of their way down. Even when they stopped to rest the dune would continue the song of their descent, decreasing in volume only after several minutes had passed. Nrouhw filled a small deerskin pouch with the sand. Although the sound came from the dune itself, Krohnnck had explained that the magic resided in the sand crystals.

The sun slipped behind the horizon and starlight had permeated everything by the time they made it down. A late supper concluded their day.

The next day when Aru awoke, the amber of dawn lingered in the sky and the air still felt quite cold from the night. Towering above, the singing dune produced sweet snippets of melodies, inspired by the breezes. She looked at Nrouhw, fast asleep. His twitching and his gentle mewing chirps told her he was chasing pronghorns in his sleep again. He had such a handsome face. As always, Aru felt compelled to reach out and stroke his brow and hair with her fingers; but she didn't want to wake him. He looked happy in his dream. Nrouhw had much less of a cougar's wistful expression when he slept.

Watching him lying there, with the morning light shining on his cheek, Aru reflected upon how strange it was that Nrouhw had become a part of her life. They were turning into family now. Such a thought! For a moment Aru drifted into nervous disorientation, thinking of her grandmother, her mother, and papa. Her family. Those were part of who she was. They left a deep, unfillable hole inside her. Still, she felt happy and content with Nrouhw.

Aru shook out her boots to rid them of any lingering night visitors. There were none. As she gazed around the camp Aru realized that the camel wasn't in his sleeping spot. On the other mornings he'd remained a camel but now she saw him in human form, not far away, atop a low dune. She averted her eyes. In the desert one doesn't stare after those who walk away from camp. It's not polite. The lack of foliage means there's no privacy, and consideration must be made for those who have gone off to transform or perhaps relieve themselves.

In this case, Aru had a feeling Krohnnck had other intentions. Her curiosity made her look again. Krohnnck was building a little fire. After a minute he noticed her staring and beckoned her to join him, which she did. She noticed he'd made the fire from dried camel chips.

"I'm performing a simple ceremony to help us find Anseo," the old man explained, and he asked if she'd mind helping out.

Of course she'd help. So he handed her a pair of click sticks, showed her the rhythm he wanted, and invited her to sing along once she caught the tune. This she did, but she had to sing a couple of octaves higher than Krohnnck and she may not have pronounced the foreign vocables quite right.

The ritual involved the use of a gold coin which Krohnnck held briefly at arm's length between the sun and the horizon. He had a stick wrapped with saffron braids of dyed camel hair, and this he stuck into the sand so that the tip pointed right at the sun.

While Aru kept the song going, he muttered this spell in his camelorous contrabass:

> Oh those who lived and suffered long ago
> By dream among the sand-drift mark my call
> I, Krohnnckuck, seek the knowledge you bestow.
> Sun who south of east and south of west sees all
> Oh dawn on me through nature's golden glow
> Our special quest to reach Anseo be true
> Cosmos, Cosmos, oh grant it be so.

As the sun created a thin shadow of the stick, he scattered something which looked like cornmeal on the sand and proceeded to spit onto it. Aru was working hard to carry the song by herself and was relieved when he rejoined her. Nrouhw arrived on the dune and contributed his voice as best he could. Camel songs are just plain difficult. They sang for quite a long time while Krohnnck examined the cornmeal, but at last he was satisfied. A couple of birds flew overhead.

"We are close," he said. "We'll be there by the Sandman's hour tomorrow."

With Krohnnck returned to his camel form and all packed up, they trudged on through the rising heat, walking in a line and following a nice serpentine path along the dunes. This was the hottest day so far. Aru and Nrouhw had to rest often, drinking lots of water and using their camel friend for shade.

Lunch was eaten on blankets under their canopy, sitting on the east face of the last dune before the flatland began. The camel set himself down and the other two sat leaning against him, as the sand slope would have burned their backs. The view of the eastern desert consisted of level sands all the way to the unbroken skyline. There wasn't a bump. Just acres and acres of unending flatness of sand, shimmering in the heat.

Their lunch break lasted for several hours because Aru and Nrouhw felt disinclined to leave their shelter during the hotter part of the day. The slight breeze blew warm against their faces but in the shade and with plenty of water to drink the dry heat seemed quite tolerable.

At last they continued on their way. Before long they realized the flat desert's increased propensity to confuse the senses. Now and then they encountered some minor interruption in the featureless sand, and it was impossible to know its size or distance away. A rock would seem to be just there, several yards ahead, until they found it was much larger than they'd thought and it took two hours to reach it. A lone dune looked as if it were on the horizon but was attained in a matter of minutes.

They saw mirages, shifty tricks of the light, and these were disorienting, too. Before he transformed, Krohnnck had warned Aru and Nrouhw about mirages. He told them that there were absolutely no lakes in the desert and not to be fooled. Sometimes the illusion could look quite real.

And so, when Aru saw a great body of water ahead of them she knew better than to get excited. "But it appears so real!" she exclaimed. "What, isn't that a tree on the shore? How could this be a mirage if it has trees? Perhaps Krohnnck is mistaken, perhaps he doesn't know of this lake."

It almost had to be a true lake, long and narrow. Dazzling. A refreshing break in the golden sands. But as they came close, which didn't take much time, the water seemed to evaporate before their eyes. The tree, however, remained. Soon they had neared it. Or had they? Yes, the tree was just ahead.

How strange it felt to see a tree. The great umbrella-shaped acacia had leaves so unbelievably green; this color—did it really occur in nature? So astoundingly lush! The twisty grey trunk branched in two not far from the base as if the tree had wanted to keep itself company.

How could such a thing exist, way out here in nowhere? No scrub grew here. No grass. The acacia had found some mysterious source of water deep under the sand. Could this magnificent tree represent the last vestige of some ancient oasis? Or perhaps it grew from a seed that found its way across the miles? To this particular location? It was beautiful, healthy and strong and stood as a living monument to perseverance. In addition to wonder and encouragement the tree provided a circle of shade.

Nrouhw bounded ahead through the sand and leapt onto a branch barely thick enough to hold him. As she and the camel approached the tree, a warm buttery feeling came to Aru. It settled over the crown of her head and flowed down, coating her in soothing calm. She took a deep, full breath of the desert air. She felt wonderful. Golden.

Aru slowed her steps. She walked in ease through the deep sand. Glowing serenity allowed her a keen sense of awareness, an understanding beyond her normal abilities. The intensely fruity scent of the tree came to her, the smell of breath and the hair of camel, the odor of herself and of the sand. The wind rustled in the leaves. Aru ignored none of the sounds of her breathing, nor the footsteps, nor the creaking and clanking to which she had become so accustomed. Her senses were wide awake. This wave of clarity let her recognize herself as part of everything. She glimpsed some perspective about the size of the natural world versus the size of her own problems. The little thrall, always tagging along behind her or riding in her pocket, was no longer a nagging concern. Aru ceased to worry about what would happen when they reached their destination. In her softening mind she saw a great cube floating above the tree, a huge transparent cloudiness. This vision struck her as a slice of reality, a chunk of all that is. She had an epiphany. She saw that every possibility exists, simultaneously, all in the same space. Because every possibility exists, then certainly all is as it should be.

As Aru walked her muscles relaxed. She had the sensation of sinking down into the sand as if stepping into that imaginary lake. What a glorious feeling. Free from the gripping anxieties of her mind and brightly aware, she could see the sand fairies hopping. Like the tinkling of tiny bells they flitted here and there across the swimming sands.

She felt the voice of the Visyrn in her head. She was not afraid. It came to her as a gentle realization. For this brief bit of time she understood, truly understood, that the terrifying void of nothingness and the endless manifestation of everythingness are all the same. And that was comforting.

She'd reached the tree, and Nrouhw called down to her, but then when he saw her face he jumped down and took her hand, afraid that she was about to swoon. Aru hugged Nrouhw, a long, gentle hug, and assured him that she felt all right. Her deep awareness faded, like a dream. They spread a blanket beneath the acacia and Nrouhw gave Aru some water and cheese. She tried to share her experience with Nrouhw, but could not describe it.

Later on toward evening, they came across a few more acacias scattered here and there. Mountains could be seen on the horizon. The flat landscape of sand that had seemed never-ending now rumpled itself into low dunes again, and as the travelers continued in a southeast direction these steadily increased in size.

Aru felt weary, and at sundown when she saw colors and lights ahead she couldn't be sure if another mirage or perhaps some sort of hallucination affected her. It had been a strange day. She inquired as to whether Nrouhw could see the lights too. He could. The three of them kept walking.

In the twilight, whether from tiredness or the heat of the afternoon, Aru began to feel as if maybe she hadn't come quite all the way back from her deep relaxation of earlier in the day.

She'd assumed she had returned to fully normal reality. But she hadn't, quite. Not to her own reality, anyway.

The air was cooling down, but Aru trudged through the still-hot sand, employing her parasol as a walking stick. Beside her, Nrouhw amused himself with a small feather he'd found, and Krohnnck followed behind, with his gently lumbering stride, staring off into the distance as he typically did. Excited about approaching Anseo, Aru had a million thoughts competing for attention in her somewhat hazy mind. Too many thoughts. And she didn't feel quite right.

What was this? Paving bricks began to show under the sand. This far out from Anseo? Aru brushed a bit of sand off them with her foot. Yes, paving bricks. They looked like they must have been made of compressed sand. Could it be the whole desert was paved, underneath? Silly idea! Anyway, whatever they might have been for, they were gone—no—here were more. And as she went along, there were patches of exposed brick. These patches came to be larger and more frequent until Aru realized that she was indeed travelling along a road.

She was just about to turn and say something to Nrouhw, when the thrall squirmed out of her pocket, jumped to the ground, and began trotting along behind her. Such a sweet little creature, she really ought to be more kind to him. He always made her laugh, with those little twinkling eyes and that funny, wee nose.

Aru picked up a birch twig and tossed it ahead along the road. Thrall ran and fetched it, wagging his tail happily. "What a good boy!" she exclaimed. She threw the stick again.

Anseo must not be as transient as people say, thought Aru; *they've grown wheat out here in the desert. I hadn't noticed that before, and, oh, there's a farm up ahead. Oh, and another!*

With renewed energy, Aru forged ahead. Near the first farm, a farmhand with a straw hat waved at them from up on a hay cart. Aru waved back to her. They followed the road's straight path through broad fields as the sunlight faded.

"We'll need a place to spend the night," Aru said after a while. "We need to find a house, Thrall. Any house will do. You must tell me if you see one."

Not long after this little Thrall barked to get Aru's attention. There, set back from the road and surrounded by corn straw, sat a tall and narrow yellow house.

A round-faced elderly woman answered the door. Of course Aru could rest there. Supper was just being laid, wouldn't she join them? So, after a good wash and a chance to comb her hair, Aru joined her kind hosts at the table. The dining room was large, the table long and covered with a beige cloth. A shelf high on the wall held a row of hourglasses, these descending in size from a quite large one to a couple of egg timers. Aru sat across from the woman and next to her husband. There were only the three of them, and Thrall lay curled up at Aru's feet while she dined.

The woman had big eyes, and despite her rather sullen expression she proved to be a gracious person. She didn't say much. She wore a light jacket of buff tweed, and over this two black macramé bracelets on each of her upper arms. She smiled when she passed a plate of pasta, and Aru noticed a sharp pair of teeth.

The gentleman, seated to Aru's right, was bearded and quite tall, already dressed in his nightgown and robe. He had tiny moons and stars all over his midnight blue gown. His robe was black. His long pointy nightcap lay on the table beside his plate. The woman addressed him as Willowy, but during their conversation Aru learned that he was the Sandman.

The elders talked about magic sand, and the difference between a sand sorceress and a witch. They asked Aru about her hopes and dreams. When she had talked for a while, Aru wanted to know about the man's necklace. He had a large pendant of amber; he showed her the moth trapped inside, trapped in time. "Always the moth hour for this one," he said.

After supper the woman excused herself and suggested the others go on through to the other room. When she joined them, she had transformed into a sand cat. Despite her age, her round eyes and tiny nose made her look like a kitten. "Don't try to pet her, though, she's not like a domestic cat, she's a little spitfire," warned the man.

Before he could take Aru upstairs to show her to her room, the man had a couple of things to do. While waiting in the drawing room with the cat, Aru gazed at the paintings on the walls. When he returned, she asked, "Are these elegant birds storks?"

"Sandhill cranes," he replied. "Family portraits."

Aru climbed the stairs behind the Sandman, with Thrall in her arms. On the dusty landing halfway up, he directed her to step around Winkie, a plump hen who was sleeping there. Upstairs, Aru was shown in to a bedroom where everything looked new. So bright and clean the room was. The bed looked like it had never been slept in. The pattern on the drapes had gold stripes with tiny clouds and tiny sheep.

The clock was stopped; it said a quarter to nine. So Aru asked, "Would you please wake me early? I should be getting back on the road. My little dog and I seem to have been separated from my friends."

The Sandman looked at her and said, "It's always a quarter to nine in this room." He pointed at the clock, as if it was obvious. "Go to sleep," he said. He threw some magic sand over his shoulder as he shut the door; it filled Aru's eyes and the next thing she knew she was waking up on the bed, still dressed, with Thrall licking her face. It was a quarter to nine.

In the kitchen the woman welcomed Aru with scrambled eggs, corn-meal mush, and, "Did you sleep well?"

"Yes, thank you, I did. And I had the most wonderful dreams! Such a lovely house you have."

"I like to be here," said the woman, "when the time is right."

The countryside was surprisingly fertile. Aru walked on and on through the farmland. Past wheat and corn, mustard, and sunflowers the road led her. Thrall tagged along at her heels. Eventually, Aru needed to rest. She found a nice place to sit atop a rail fence.

After a moment Aru realized that a man was standing in the field not far away. A gawky young man, with a thick body, all arms and legs. "Good morning," she said.

"Good morning to you, Miss," he answered.

They fell into conversation. The man had interesting things to say about the countryside, and he spoke kindly, but he seemed distracted. He directed his gaze mostly to the horizon. He chewed tobacco while they spoke, turning his head once in awhile to spit onto the sand.

As he was headed down the road also, the two decided to walk along together. Thrall wasn't happy about this interloper, and he growled at the man. Aru assured the fellow that Thrall never bit anyone.

Miles went barely noticed while talking with this farmer. Though he told Aru he spent most of his time scaring birds from the corn, he had a great deal to say. His encyclopedic knowledge led to conversations about the importance of crop rotation and other pioneering efforts in stewardship of the land. The road eventually led into a thick forest of birch: tall, straight trees still heavy with their autumn colors. It began to curve and wander through some hills. Then they came to a more open area, where salmonberries beckoned in the sun and Aru paused to eat some. She had just placed three or four berries in her mouth (she was hungry) when a groan came from somewhere.

Following the sound, the new friends came upon a boot lying next to a log. Thrall barked. The boot wiggled. Aru shrieked. Another groan came, a louder one. Aru's friend knew immediately what was going on. "Aru!" he cried, "Quickly! Help me lift this birch log!"

Then Aru realized, also. They grabbed the end of the log and lifted it off a woodcutter, the poor man who had been trapped there by the snag which had kicked back when he felled it.

"I might have lain there forever if you hadn't come along," said the woodman, after they had set him up against a stump to inspect his leg. The farmer said it looked like there was only bruising, but they must watch for symptoms of gangrene. He cut the man a staff for a crutch, and soon the woodman joined them on their way.

The woodman had a long nose, rather tubular in shape. A toothpick waggled in the corner of his mouth. Apparently this was a habit. He must have been a tad eccentric, because he wore a funnel as if it were a hat. Perhaps he had a perfectly good reason for doing this, but it would have been rude to ask, so Aru was left to wonder. Thrall barked at him and clearly did not like him to join their party, poor little doggie.

On they went through the birchwood, which became deeper and thicker and took on an orange glow from the sunlight shining through all those leaves. The friends walked closer together and didn't speak as much. Formations of boulders started to appear in the hilly terrain. Thrall had scampered on ahead, and when he had gone out of sight around a bend they heard him barking horribly. Then, a loud yelp.

Aru and her friends hurried along the road to help him. Rounding the turn they saw a man in a tattered coat.

"What did you *do* to him?" shouted Aru, rushing forward to rescue her defenseless little dog.

The man stepped back, apologizing. "But he attacked me," the man added. "I only kicked him to get him off my leg. He grabbed at my trousers!"

Aru was not impressed by the man's explanation. She didn't welcome him to come along with their group, but the farmer was friendly with him and the fellow ended up joining them anyway. Aru collected Thrall, and placed him in her basket, closing the lid. After a short rest break, during which Aru enjoyed eating some wild almonds the farmer had found, they returned to the road.

"But if you're headed to town, you're going the wrong way!" exclaimed the stranger. "You need to get off this road and take the trail northward, it's several miles back—"

"That's enough!" said Aru, in a fit of exasperation. "You're a liar! Nothing but a cowardly liar! What's wrong with you?" She put her hands protectively over Thrall and the basket. She sniffed.

The man continued to try to convince them to go the other way. The woodman thought they might want to listen to his reasons, perhaps he knew a good shortcut, but Aru would have none of this. So they set off again in the direction they had been going.

The woods seemed never-ending, the pervasive golden glow through the leaves complemented by a carpet of leaves already fallen. A clean, invigorating scent reminded Aru of citrus and of ginger ale. Then came another smell.

"Smoke!" cried the farmer. "It's a forest fire!"

They looked around, but none of them could tell from which direction the smoke was coming. "What do we do?" cried Aru.

"Well, now, let's calm down and think about this," said the farmer, looking around in all the directions.

The tattered man leapt from ledge to ledge up the side of a great rock formation until he stood on top. Aru gasped at how easily he made these great leaps, but then, he reminded her of . . . someone . . . not sure—

The man called out from the top, "I see all manner of animals and birds fleeing through the forest and heading southwest."

"That's the direction of the highway," said the woodman. "We should continue on our way, but we'd better make haste!"

Everyone agreed and they all began trotting down the road, little Thrall once again tucked in Aru's basket. Soon some people arrived on horseback from behind them, laden with their children and some household treasures. They explained that they were a family of eastern box turtles; it was much safer for them to escape by horseback rather than to try to run for it. They slowed enough to let the four friends know that the fire had built to a massive blaze; the wind drove it swiftly in their direction.

The farmer was absolutely terrified, but he advised the others that they should keep to the road, and continue their pace; if they tried to run faster they would tire sooner. So the friends jogged on through the thickening yellow smoke and after a while all sorts of animals were running past them, mostly deer, rabbits, and mice. Snakes and insects also went by, while squirrels and birds flew through the tree canopy.

The tattered man made his way up another pile of rocks to get a view, and he reported that they should continue along the road. But the next time he did this, he shouted that they must leave the road and make their way through the forest to the east.

"I don't know—" said the woodman, but the tattered man spoke with urgency.

"We've got to run fast!" he shouted, "There's a place where the woods opens out into a scrubby area, the fire will slow there, less to burn. But we've only got a few minutes!" Standing on the rocks, he looked in the direction they had come.

Everyone else looked that way too. They could see the fire now, orange flames, such a strange sight, the more distant trees silhouetted against the brightness, while closer trees, untouched, stood proud and beautiful for what would certainly be their last moments. Someone screamed. It might have been Aru, it might have been the farmer. The air was full of smoke and heat. The tattered man leapt down from the rock pile and the four of them joined hands, and ran for their lives through the forest in the direction that the man had indicated. Animals were scurrying past them every which way, mostly the smaller mammals and reptiles.

Holding hands, they ran down a gentle hill, through fire grass and spurge. While they were running, the tattered man yanked the basket from Aru and threw it down, pulling her along as he did so. Aru pulled back against him, but then she saw Thrall emerge from the basket and run right along with them. She didn't have time to think about it, she just kept running. She had a stitch in her side, cramps in her legs, but they ran and ran. They could feel the heat of the fire behind them.

The forest did, indeed, open into a large rocky area where dry shrubs grew far enough apart to slow the fire down. The friends could run no farther. Aru tried to sit down, but the others kept her on her feet and supported her as they walked downhill. Choking in the smoke, slightly singed from the heat, they stumbled on until, with great relief, they came upon a river.

After drinking greedily, and plunging their faces in the muddy water, they still needed to get out of the smoke to save themselves. The woodman and the farmer found a quince tree growing on the sandy bank, and the tattered man helped them push it over while Aru inspected Thrall's little paws to see why he was limping. They all four dragged the tree into the water. The river was deep enough, and slow enough, that they were able to hang on to the log and direct it from behind as they floated down the river. Thrall rode on top of the log, clinging pathetically. In this way, they were able to get several miles from the fire to a place where they felt it would be safe to rest.

They pulled the log up onto a broad beach, in case they should need it to go further down the river. Then they sat or lay on the sand for a while, just breathing. Aru fell asleep. When she awakened, stiff and wet, but happy to be alive, there was the smell of fish roasting. They had a comforting supper by the fire, thanks to the woodman's tinder box, and then Aru fell asleep again. In the morning, the farmer had found a peach tree just up the river, so they had a wonderful breakfast of the juicy fruit.

Smoke hung yellow in the air, but they couldn't see the fire from where they were. This was good. They had a final wash in the river, and then they set off cross-country. As they climbed up the river's high berm they spoke softly about the tragedy of the fire, and the losses to the forest and its inhabitants. When they reached the top and saw the countryside spread before them, everyone stopped talking. Aru picked up Thrall and held him in her arms.

Wheat fields filled the land as far as they could see. But the wheat had been cut, and above the stubble grew a great carpet of poppies, delicate golden poppies, growing as close together as kernels on a corncob. The sweet perfume of these flowers drifted up to meet them, and everyone was eager to go down into the fields among the blossoms. Everyone, that is, except Thrall. The little dog squirmed out of Aru's arms and began barking, tugging at her skirts.

"What's wrong, silly thing?" Aru crooned. "Flowers can't hurt you, silly dog!"

Thrall tugged again, and when she didn't respond he darted off toward the river. The farmer scooped him up on his way past.

"Oh, no you don't, little guy! If you run off along the river, this young lady will insist on following you, and then we'll be well out of our way again!" He handed Thrall to Aru, who received him thankfully, and held him in a tighter grip.

The slope led down, and then they stood among the golden flowers. The smell! Such a sweet, pleasant scent. They waded through the buttery, silky blooms, the shimmery, sunset tones. The smell, so powerful. Aru felt giddy, but didn't completely care. One of the poppy blossoms grew big, it grew huge, bigger, and then it enfolded her in its petals. Sleep, lovely sleep, forever, dream now, then dreamless sleep—

"Aru!"

Someone was shaking her. Stop, she just wanted to sleep. The voice again, interrupting, bothersome. What? Who? What was going on? "Aru, wake up!" He sounded familiar. "Aru please, my love, wake *up!*"

Nrouhw? Nrouhw! Aru lifted her head. Everything was too real, she had to squint her eyes. She looked up at the tattered man, but it wasn't the tattered man, it was Nrouhw. He was holding her in his lap as he sat in the sand. She peered up into his face.

"Aru," he breathed.

Confused, she glanced around. Krohnnck leaned over her, and Nrouhw, and some funny-looking man she didn't think she knew.

"Great thunder!" she gasped, "I've had the most remarkable dream!"

"It wasn't a dream." Nrouhw spoke in a tight, low voice. "You were bound by an enchantment. During the night you walked in a stupor.

You've taken us several hours out of our way. Then we thought you were going to die. We couldn't rouse you."

"Several hours?"

"Aru, you nearly died, right here in the sand! Here in my arms!"

"But it's only been several hours? It's been days I've journeyed!"

"It was magic, Aru," said Krohnnck. "A different reality. You've nearly killed us all with worry. You were under a spell. It came by way of *that* thing, somehow." He pointed to the thrall.

The cornhusk doll was lying on its back in the sand, looking decidedly beaten up.

"Nrouhw went mad a few minutes ago, Aru," said Krohnnck gently. "We didn't know if you might have died. You didn't seem to be drawing breath. He grabbed that little thrall and he throttled it. If it could have died it certainly would have done so."

The thrall lay there with a blank look on its face, staring up at the moon and stars.

"He saved you, Aru. What he did to the doll brought you back." It was the funny man speaking. He turned out to be an aardvark who was also traveling into Anseo. He had a long, almost tubular nose, flat on the end and rubbery.

Aru had horribly chapped lips and parched skin; pus encrusted a crack above her lip. But for someone who had come so close to death, she felt quite well, really. They camped for one night and a quiet morning before moving on. The thrall spent the entire time in one spot, wearing a scowl. In the afternoon they all departed for the village, in order to arrive in the evening.

The lamplit tents of Anseo glimmered like a fairy encampment sprawled among the dunes. As they drew closer Aru could make out two town squares within the mosaic of glowing lights. Even from this distance the travelers could hear the sound of voices carried across the desert.

Since ancient times Anseo had been referred to as a village, but in truth it should be called a town because of its size. Aru hadn't expected it to be nearly so big. How could all this disappear in the blink of an eye and then take shape several day's journey away? Aru couldn't imagine.

Although the moon was up and the sky full of stars by the time they arrived, Anseo bathed in its own illumination. The first few tents they encountered stood as islands of light in the sands, glowing like lanterns and far apart from one another, but as the travelers reached the village proper they found organized streets and a crowded neighborhood. Paper lanterns were set in the sand at every opportunity. Oil lamps hung from cables stretched between the tents and canopies, along with flags and banners bearing all sorts of interesting symbols and languages. Strings of brass bells decorated tents and in some places served as doors. Music drifted in the air. Camels relaxed by the silk brocade walls, a low pitched moo now and then between continuous cud-chewing. People sat in doorways and on blankets along the edge of the sand lane, some smoking from long pipes. A few more wandered in the lamplight. The smells of incense and roasting corn filled the air. Aru's senses were dazzled by the fiery colors and all the noise. She realized how hungry she felt.

They said goodbye to the aardvark. Aru thanked him again for helping when she was in the state of delirium. "I'm only happy that I happened along," he replied.

Krohnnck led Nrouhw and Aru on a complicated route through town. Nrouhw pointed out to Aru that the streets were laid out in a sophisticated tessellate pattern. Narrow side streets curved and turned and almost doubled back on themselves. There were no wide avenues in Anseo because carriages and wagons couldn't traverse the desert. As the group neared the center of town they found that more and more of the lanes were covered with wool carpet which hid all the sand. This made walking easier but the solid footing felt so strange.

Down one particularly narrow street, perhaps it was an alley, they came upon a high wall made of the rears of several tents with heavy tapestries strung between them. There was a trellis that parted the cloth in one spot, creating an opening. Over this doorway hung a banner with the words *Sleep Safe at Low Cost* artistically painted in the common jargon.

Aru and Nrouhw followed Krohnnck through the opening into a large rectangular courtyard framed by additional rough tents and cheerful fabrics. There was a musky scent of amber incense, but it failed to quell the odor of road-weary travelers and the smell of some type of stale urine. The space was carpeted, the overlapping rugs patterned with astrological designs incorporating sunbursts and flowery stars, and the fact that they were nearly worn through only added to their appeal for Aru. How many hundreds of wanderer's feet must have walked on these! Light from a dozen lanterns flickered on numerous cots and sleeping pads, mostly unoccupied this early in the evening. In one end of the square a small fire had two little spits of sizzling meat along with several cooking pots that were hanging and bubbling.

The hosteler came to greet them and show them where they could leave their belongings. While Aru stayed and looked for a suitable sleeping area, the others disappeared into one of the smaller tents. In a few minutes they returned, with most of their equipment stashed and Krohnnck having taken human form. The hosteler invited them to help themselves to tea. There was a tank of drinking water, and even an ice box, but they'd have to use the public toilets and baths down the street. As soon as they seemed settled she scurried off.

Aru felt like a ship which had landed at port. They prepared a big meal from the remains of their provisions and shared it with some new friends from the south before turning in at a late hour.

Waking nearly at noon to fried cornmeal mush being waved under her nose by Nrouhw, Aru was thrilled to see fat slabs of fresh butter on her breakfast. She enjoyed her meal very much, and the bath afterwards even more. Like a snake shedding its skin she gleefully removed the layer of sandy encrusted sweat, studying her clean self with a new appreciation. Baths are generally wonderful, but when one has been unbathed in the desert for days a good wash feels like the beginning of a new life.

During the heat of the day Aru and Nrouhw relaxed on a small couch under a canopy at the hostel, sipping fresh mango juice with cream and soaking up well-being from the ambient sunshine. A sense of freedom sweetened the air.

Krohnnck lay on his back on the carpet, his long legs resting up on an old wicker trunk. The friends talked lazily about the wonders of Anseo and the peace they felt there. Even the thrall seemed subdued. As they'd travelled across the desert the thing had become less and less active, spending nearly all its time in Aru's pocket or even riding in the baggage. Except when it was trying to kill people.

"My friend," said Krohnnck to Aru, "I don't suspect the thing meant to kill you when it led you down that road of yellow brick. It tried to divert you from Anseo. You were heading directly southeast towards the coast."

"The mangy little bruin!" snarled Nrouhw. "But why?"

"And if directing you to the coast is indeed the purpose, Nrouhw, this would account for its seeming hostility toward you," Krohnnck added. "You are an influence on where Aru travels. A competing influence."

Aru shook her head. "I don't know anyone on the eastern coast! Why in the world would someone put a curse on *me?* And to go east? To the coast? I've never been there!"

"You have no business that way? Certainly, someone knows you."

Tears began to gather in Aru's eyes.

"We'll find out who it is, Aru. And they'll have to answer for this," Nrouhw said softly. "If the intention was to harm you," he pointed out, "they would have sent something other than a thrall. Try not to worry about it too much, we need only be aware."

"Would you like to go and see the bees?" asked Krohnnck, "I'll be joining a south-bound camel train in the morning, but I still have time to make a visit to the honey market."

The bee yard was filled with activity. Dozens of elegantly uniformed workers, wearing dresses with large bustles in the rear, waggled every which way around the plaza. It was organized confusion, hypnotising to watch. The women had fuzzy chenille bodices, bands of black about their amber skirts, and shawls of fine gossamer silk over the shoulders. Each was bedecked with exquisite citrine jewelry. Several of these women came forward to greet the friends as they entered the bazaar.

"Ah! I believe we've observed you at our exposition before!" said one of the women to Krohnnck.

"I never miss it when I am in Anseo," he smiled as he replied.

She beamed at him as she and the other ladies hurried off in different directions.

Before proceeding through to the honey bay, Krohnnck brought Aru and Nrouhw to an area where people stood in line. A banner behind them advertised a motion picture.

"This may be a bit of a wait," he told them, "but it'll be worth it. If you'll remain here and keep our place I will make a quick visit to the bistro and get us something."

Before long he returned with three soft pretzels and some jars of dark beer. This made it a pleasant wait in line.

Eventually their group gained admittance to the tent. Inside, the three of them beheld a cozy motion picture house with bean-bag seats and bespangled draperies befitting a queen. As the lights were dimmed the imposing curtains parted to reveal an unusually azure screen. The projector whirred and buzzed but as soon as the film began nobody heeded the noise. The crowd gasped in amazement.

"Color!" exclaimed Nrouhw.

The screen was a blaze of hand-tinted color. This was unbelievable! None of the viewers had seen a colorized film before. Fields of sunflowers, bunches of begonias and zinnias, gardens of azaleas, the film was a dizzying three-minute ramble through bedazzling color.

Afterwards, the friends discussed the film and how amazing it was.

"There weren't many bees in the theater," said Aru.

"No," Krohnnck agreed. "Although the film is known as a bee movie, the truth of the matter is that bees are incapable of sitting through such a lengthy presentation."

As the friends perused the various shops and stalls beside the plaza lots of pleasing smells of the bazaar beckoned them. Big bars of beeswax and jars of bee pollen and propolis filled beribboned shelves and tables. The most appetizing smells arose from the honey itself. Pure bliss. Such a crowd milled around the honey barrels beyond the concessions area that it wasn't feasible to visit them so the friends chose to stick around and see if maybe the crowd would disperse.

The fabric vendors amused both Aru and Nrouhw. One of these stands was especially intriguing. Beneath a banner reading *May Bee's Humble Thimble* was an assemblage of quilts with designs positively befitting a museum. Nrouhw's keen sense of composition was pleased beyond measure by a piece emphasizing stylized teasel and flowers of furze. There was a series of pictorial quilts which depicted the colonization and communalization of certain beloved bee colonies. The artistry was superb. Emblazoned with flower designs and embellished with embroidery and occasionally patterns of beadwork, the quilts represented a beautiful celebration featuring muslin and gauzy brocades. Nrouhw and Aru's favorite had a marbleized topaz print which was bejeweled with hive beetle wings that harmonized with it perfectly. It had a glazed resin finish.

Between the artisan's zone and the bazaar's east gate, the bee skep area was resonant with a huge ensemble of bass and baritone buzzes of bees. The sound of bees was a soft and fuzzy sound but it was robust because it was composed of the efforts of many thousands of individuals working as one.

Dozens and dozens of coiled straw skeps were lined up like inverted butter baskets on long rows of beech planks used as shelves. Each one contained a colony of young Keystone-Species Volunteer Bees ready to be adopted in exchange for simple bee commodities. As a habitual obligation, young bees served three weeks of each year in the hive.

Though the skep enclosure was especially imbued with the ambrosial aroma of honey, Aru was puzzled because no bees were flying about.

"Why don't we see any volunteer bees?" she asked.

"They abide quite cozily within their skeps on business days," explained Krohnnck. "Out of harm's way."

The buzzing noise was strangely comforting, albeit the buzz bespoke of an abeyant hazard.

"Doesn't the buzz resemble the gentle rushing of a stream!" said Aru. "But with the same billowing pitch as those blustery summer breezes."

Krohnnck said he was all but certain that pitch was the key of B.

Aru and Nrouhw turned to look over their shoulders at a bit of a hubbub which had begun right behind them.

"I just want one of them buzzer baskets!" A surprisingly big burly man with a barrel of mead under one arm and a rundlet of honey under the other was clumsily batting at a mob of workers who surrounded him. This man, this bearded behemoth, was being beleaguered by the traumatized workers he'd aroused. They baited him brazenly, calling him a stinker and a bewhiskered old beast. Aru was bewildered by the behavior of these bees.

The grizzled old fellow moved with the bearing of someone who, because of his imposing size and his obesity, was used to being besieged by such belittlers.

"He's one of their best customers, actually," Krohnnck explained, "but his people brought unspeakable damage to hundreds of colonies in bygone days."

Aru resolved to befriend this big bedraggled man if she had the opportunity. She thought it rather uncivilized of the bees to begrudge him for such reasons and to beset him in such a way and cause him to feel so befuddled.

In actuality, bees are social and friendly folk. It's just that they are the kind of people you don't antagonize. Aru grew to understand this more as they continued on through the bazaar. These enterprising people had a multitude of businesses aside from honey sales. The wax museum was closed, but Krohnnck said that the figures were all of significant queens through history and that they looked all the same to him because they were depicted in animal form. The friends spent the afternoon doing some shopping and admiring the huge ripe nectarines, the marzipan, amusing baubles, and other bee wares.

An elderly shopkeeper, bespectacled and in a worker's uniform, called out to them and got their attention as they were passing by. Aru's first thought was that the lady must be blind because her eyeglasses were blackened but then she noticed that her shop had racks of dark glasses just like those she wore.

Aru picked up a pair, saying, "What good are glasses you can't see through?"

"Why, try on a pair, beloved, and you'll see," said the lady, smiling.

Aru thanked her and did so. "Oh. My goodness!" she exclaimed, handing a pair to Nrouhw. Krohnnck tried some on also.

"What kind of bewitchery is this?" Nrouhw asked.

"We call them sunglasses," said the woman. "They have special tinted lenses that reduce the glare from sunbeams. I can't begin to tell you how much our desert customers treasure them."

Nrouhw decided to buy a pair for each of them. They looked nice on Aru and Krohnnck but on Nrouhw they were remarkably becoming.

As the sun fell below the horizon, the bazaar was closing. Bees refuse to use lanterns. Their terrible fear of blazes was the reason there were no beeswax candles for sale in the plaza.

The three friends returned to the hostel and had a fine evening together. This included a supper of coriander butternut squash, and cornbread drizzled with lots of honey.

The next day a large camel train would be coming through town and making its way across the desert to a city far in the south west direction. Krohnnck planned to travel with that train and make a good bit of income by carrying heavy bronze pots for a merchant. Nrouhw asked him if he'd be interested in traveling on with Aru and him instead, to the northeastern mountains in search of gold. Krohnnck ruminated for quite a while about this but eventually decided it best that he stay with his original plan of traveling south from Anseo. Before he left in the morning with the camel train he located a fine pair of baggage camels for Aru and Nrouhw to hire at a good rate and he also brought them a wonderful camel buttermilk pudding as a farewell gift.

Aru and Nrouhw spent a fun day wearing their new sunglasses and exploring Anseo. These strange dark spectacles really did get rid of the glare and made the desert environment much easier on the eyes. The great trading center offered a browser's paradise and they laughed and admired their way through all sorts of shops selling various gadgets and antiques.

Aru drank too much lemony iced tea and as a result she didn't sleep well that night. Her legs were restless as she lay looking at the night sky, and she didn't want to wake Nrouhw by consistently bumping against him so she got up to go for a walk. She passed through the hostel gate and turned up the lane, moving slowly but with a certain amount of excitement about wandering out on her own in the middle of the night. Even the night owls had turned in. Except for the nearly dormant thrall in her pocket, she walked in solitude.

Aru made her way through slumbering little alleys to the nearest sand dune which rose up out of the sea of tents. It wasn't a large dune, but big enough to tower above the crowdedness and afford a bit of view. She climbed up along the dune's ridge, enjoying the way it felt to walk in the deeper sand again.

Aru thanked the moon for giving so much light. Halfway up the ridge she paused. She stood for a long time, looking skyward. A happy urge to howl welled up inside her. She nearly let it out. Brilliantly full, the moon stood amongst the splendor of the star fields. Its creamy glow had shadows of yellow ochre and dapples the color of toast. It reminded Aru of the marvelous vanilla marigolds back home in her grandmother's garden.

Aru muttered her thoughts aloud to the moon, entranced by the moment. "Strange dot, tell me why I can look you in the face, but never the sun? Why is that?" She went on, having a conversation without hope of reply, talking to the unknown. "I love you moon, I do. So eerie you are, always changing. Those blotches that are familiar since my childhood. What are those marks?"

As she stood there, Aru started missing her grandma and thinking about her former life among the wolves. Then Aru noticed that she wasn't alone on the dune. Higher up on the ridge a great big hare sat on its haunches, twiddling its whiskers and staring up at the full moon.

Aru froze when she saw him, but if he noticed her he didn't make it obvious. He had a serene look on his face. After a few minutes he dropped down onto his front paws and hopped away over the very top of the dune.

It took Aru a while to make the highest point of the ridge. When she peered over the other side she had it in her mind mister rabbit would be quite far away along the back of the ridge, in one direction or the other. She suppressed a shriek and ducked down. The hare stood there, just on the other side. Except, he was no longer a great big hare. He was a funny little man.

Squatting for a moment in the sand, Aru breathed fast and blushed at the thought that she'd nearly caught the animal changing. Had he winked at her? She peeked again. The old fellow had already gone halfway along the dune, back the way Aru had come. She got up, shook out her skirts and followed him, retracing her own footprints on her side of the ridge. She tried not to make too much noise.

Soon the little man reached the streets, and headed off in a direction Aru hadn't been. Despite his advanced age she had quite a job to keep him in sight. She followed along a narrow lane, around a corner, and then he started across an open square. A lamp post stuck up out of the sand and under this the man stopped for a moment. Aru stopped also, and strained to see what he was doing. He took something from his waistcoat, looked at it, and held it to his ear. Then, after a minute or two, he continued on his way.

When Aru passed by the lamp post a glint of something in the sand caught her eye. The hare had dropped his pocket watch! Aru turned it over in her hand. A fabulous antique, maybe solid gold—it had a good weight to it.

"Excuse me!" she called. The hare had disappeared down another lane. "Mr. Hare!"

Aru ran after him, thinking only of restoring the watch to this old fellow. Panting, she stopped at a crossroads, peering each way to find him. There he stood, just a few yards down the other road.

"Sir, I think you've dropped something—" she said, forgetting to be embarrassed.

"Ah," he replied. His voice was soft, and it put Aru at ease to hear it. She felt no need to explain her reasons for following him.

"The fob is here, too," she said as she handed him the watch.

He held out a long, bony palm with long, bony fingers, to receive his timepiece. Dressed smartly, but in an outdated jacket and hat, he had a funny, quite compelling appearance. He thanked Aru nicely for returning his property to him and then they got to talking. He had traveled far, and had a bunk in a nearby hostelry. He wondered what Aru might be doing running about at four o'clock in the morning all alone? The man's name was Aldrei. He had lengthy whiskers, tucked into his belt. His ears were not the normal shape of human ears. They grew right up the sides of his head: furry rabbit ears which stuck up on either side of his old-fashioned hat.

It wasn't long before Aldrei brought Aru's complexion into the conversation. "How rare to see a person with fair skin the color of yours, Aru!" he said. "Tch-tch, such an exotic beauty."

"While people often mention my color, I've never before been called exotic." She blushed. "Is this flattery, Sir?"

"Yes, but flattery is virtuous, isn't it. I think so. Virtually so, at any rate. Most people seem to enjoy it."

It took Aru a moment to consider this. "I suppose that's true. I'm not accustomed to receiving compliments, having been raised in the deep woods. My family is from a wholly practical class. Our folk demonstrate a great deal of love, but not a lot of courtesy. But that's nature, isn't it."

"Aye, that it is."

"At any rate, I do appreciate your kind words."

The thrall shifted in Aru's pocket, causing her to rearrange it. In the process, it peeked out at the stranger.

He commented in a reflective tone, "You must be quite enthralled with your little dolly, judging by the way you carry it with you."

"Yes, well, I'm a bit attached to her." There was a hint of sadness in Aru's voice, only apparent if one knew to look for it.

"Lovely. Do enjoy the festivities here in the village, you'll see everything under the sun while in Anseo. The best of luck to you in your adventures!—Have you found the time to visit the Ginger Bear Bakery near the southern square?"

"I haven't been there," said Aru.

"Oh, I recommend it highly. You'll not wish to miss their buttery dainties."

"Thank you, I'll let my sweetheart know. I imagine we'll try it tomorrow." She smiled. "Of course, what I mean to say is 'today.'"

He tipped his hat, and he was off, saying, "Thank you again for retrieving my watch. Good night!"

The Ginger Bear was located in a particularly crowded part of town, an area popular with the smaller sorts of folk. When Aru and Nrouhw stopped by in the late morning a canopy was being raised over the courtyard tables to shield them from the midday sun. The server greeted the couple warmly and seated them beside a perch where a chorus of a half dozen little canary buskers were sharing their exuberant enjoyment of life. Their twittery sweet songs were accompanied by the tinkling of a nearby wind chime made of delicate brass leaves.

Nrouhw and Aru relieved their thirst with big glasses of frothy fresh orange juice and shared a pumpkin muffin and a soft butterscotch scone. They sat and watched the diverse clientele engaged in their various business.

The pair had been basking in this pleasantness for quite some time when Aru exclaimed, "Oh, Nrouhw, look, it's him! It's the man. The one I was telling you about."

Aldrei spotted Aru, too, and in a moment he and his companion were seated at Aru's table. She introduced Nrouhw, and Aldrei invited the two of them to meet his partner Aeon. "We're of the Long-Ears League," smiled Aldrei, causing them to assume that Aeon, a somewhat larger fellow, was also a hare or rabbit. He wasn't.

Aeon looked about the same age as Aldrei, but had no beard. Coins were tied to braids in his hair, one or two hanging down over his brow.

"This, my dear Aeon, is the young wanderer who found my pocket watch," said Aldrei.

"I see, ahhhh!" exclaimed Aeon, nodding to his friend and smiling at Aru. "Such a kindness to return an old man to his property. How noble. You must be a princess."

"It's funny, but I am a hereditary princess, actually!" said Aru with an attempt at a humble voice. Then she added, "But, really, any decent person would have returned it to you."

Aldrei and Aeon made interesting company. The four sat for several hours talking. Aldrei and Aeon had known each other forever. They made their living prospecting and trading in precious metals. This of course caught Nrouhw's attention. Their visit ended with tentative plans to travel to the northern mountains together, as that's where Aldrei and Aeon were headed anyhow.

Aru and Nrouhw stayed on in town, enjoying the illuminating exposure to so many cultures. There were several little tent theaters that offered plays and poetry readings. Musically, something was always going on. There were brass bands, drumming troupes and strange-looking people playing fragile stringed instruments. Aru loved to experience new things, and vicariously traveled through the world and through history by watching the shows and the street performers. And, of course, by all her shopping and sampling.

It was an idyllic time; the only real unpleasantness was when the couple argued about the thrall. This happened more and more often. The thing had started up its mischief again. Yet Aru seemed increasingly forgiving. "Aru, can't you see how devoted to it you've become? You dressed it up yesterday! What's next?"

"No, Nrouhw, you're silly. Those were such adorable doll clothes, and I merely tried them on! Just to see. I'm only having a bit of fun with the thing. Really, what's the harm? Don't say I'm pandering to it. I'm stuck with it, that's not my choice. Through no fault of my own."

Over just a few days, this progressed to, "Nonsense. Everything has an essence of life. Every rock and tree, every daisy in the field. The thing has learned to communicate. It's shown that it can learn. To learn is to be alive. I'm going to educate her."

Nrouhw spoke with concern, "But, my love, it's a soulless thrall. Please don't fall under its master's power. I've caught the thing whispering in your ear in the nighttime."

"Shame on you, Nrouhw," she teased him, tugging on his ear, speaking playfully, unable to find the courage to give her opinion directly. "Shame on you for thinking little Eepe doesn't have a soul. Of course she does."

"Little Eepe? No, Aru, please don't name it!"

That very day Aru gave the thrall its first lesson. Lounging on some cushions at the hostel, she read to it from a novel she had found in a hawker's collection.

They returned to the bakery several times over the course of a week. One day they were sitting with Aldrei and Aeon, whom they'd got to know better and with whom they'd become friends. Aru noticed a strange feeling in the air. There was something different about this day in the Ginger Bear; it felt more crowded and with customers of another sort.

"Do you see those folks in the tailcoat jackets of yellow over there?" said Aeon, "Be careful. They are, in fact, yellowjackets. They are dangerous to be around. I've been stung by that sort more than once. Don't trust them."

Aldrei laughed. "He's right, you know. And look who else is at the table. Scorpions and, that one in the saffron hood—she's a cobra."

Just as Nrouhw was about to comment, a hush came over the open-air café. Two dignitaries of some sort had just walked in. The man was draped in gorgeous flame-colored silks: scarlet and golden yellow and accented with a touch of brilliant blue. Because of his sharp features and a particular look of his eye, he reminded Aru of the amazing golden pheasant she'd seen in at the market in Ysgarlad.

The woman with him surveyed the scene as the two followed the server nonchalantly to a table. She had a foreboding presence. Aru got a good view of her as they sat down at the round table a few yards away. Her face was dramatically robust and radiant. Fierce, with plump lips and a shapely, full nose. Her hair was plaited into many thick braids and fell to just past her shoulders.

"The phoenix and the sphinx," said Aldrei quietly.

Before Aru could express her surprise, the phoenix held up a golden-banded arm and motioned to Aldrei. "Come, Aldrei my coney, and bring your donkey companion and your other friends with you."

So that is how Aru and Nrouhw found themselves sitting at a table with the phoenix and the sphinx and it's how they found out that Aeon was, in fact, a donkey and not a hare.

As they seated themselves, the cobra sidled quietly up to the sphinx, bending and giving her a kiss. "So marvelous to see you again, my sister," she said.

"Join us, Sassah," said the sphinx.

The cobra sat down next to Aru. Aru managed a weak grin.

"So," said Sassah, "I heard you were in town, Sphinx, all the stingers are abuzz with the news. I heard, also, that you got into a heated argument with a scorpion and that she didn't survive."

"The vulgar media tells what it will," replied the sphinx.

The table filled with conversation, but Aru missed much of it because they talked about things like the price of gold and camel butter, and gossip about people with whom she was not familiar. She got lost in the details of her own perception, noticing the sweet smell of the phoenix, the tiny golden bells on his sandals, the clouded beads of amber in the sphinx's braids.

The phoenix ordered lunch for everyone at the table. It was delivered by the steward with a stern little bow. They ate sponge bread with a thick turmeric stew served on top. This dish was eaten by tearing pieces from the edges of the bread, and using these to spoon up the stew. The richness of the sauce made it quite a fulfilling meal. They finished it up lazily. The mood was light.

When the thrall hopped up onto the table and started tittering and dancing, Aru was mortified. Yet only Nrouhw seemed concerned about it. Aru grabbed the thing and shoved it down into her pocket.

"I have a riddle for you," said the sphinx, looking directly at Aldrei. "Let's hear it," said Aldrei.

With an enigmatic smile, the sphinx recited the following:

> Driven mad by lust for me,
> the thief procured a silver phial.
> The vessel, for the love of me,
> was gilded in gold by the smith with his guile.
> The two were discovered and sent to trial.
> Judge and jury let thief go free,
> The guilt of the smith was easy to see.
> Silver or gold?

There was silence for a moment and then Aldrei had the answer.

"Either ore," he said, "You are either ore."

"Blast and curses," muttered the sphinx.

An owlish man approached the sphinx and phoenix at the table. "Honorary elders," he said, and bowing repeatedly, "I want to thank you for visiting my humble bakery. Of course there will be no charge." He began to back away.

"Did you just call me an ornery elder?" demanded the sphinx.

The man's eyes grew large.

The sphinx looked down her nose at him, then burst into laughter.

The poor fellow, thought Aru. But the man was laughing too, although not as loudly as the sphinx.

"Better than a spit in the eye," said Sassah the cobra.

"His loaf is worth more than a bad joke," said the phoenix.

"After so many years as a baker," said the man quietly, "I find myself with a loathe of bread. I guess I'm just a gluten for punishment." He smiled and walked away.

"You'd butter call him back," said Aldrei to the sphinx. "He's good with buns. You might knead his services."

"I don't know," said the phoenix. "The man gives me the crêpes."

"Yes, but at yeast he's a decent baker," said Aldrei.

"He's never gone a rye," said the sphinx, "Yet, it's a curd to me—"

"Enough of your crummy, stale jokes. Enough of this levity! Change of subject!" commanded the phoenix.

The sphinx looked at him, "So, Phoenix, what's it like being a bird unto your people?"

The phoenix looked around. "I don't know what kind of flower that is in your hair," he said to the sphinx, "but I'm betting a dog would."

"Hmmf," she replied. "One may not presuppose an unexceptional omen pidgeon will know about it, I venture to say."

"Your chimerical perspective blights the common eudaemonia," said the phoenix. "Must you always exeleutherostomize?"

"As usual, your ultracrepidarian response is unnecessarily full of perpilocutionist circumlocution," she answered with a smile.

He rubbed his eye. "I believe you misconjugate in the attempt to syntactically structure a grammatically commonsensical sequence."

"Horsefeathers!" she exclaimed, "If you were more perspicacious, and not so saxicolous, you'd see that your supererogatory use of the common tongue makes you sound inaniloquent and unenlightened."

"Numerous incomprehensibilities surround the justifiablenesses of any quantification of knowledgeableness to demonstrate such over-intellectualization on your part."

"Wrong."

"You have the extemporaneous audacity," said the phoenix, "to contradict me with monosyllabism?"

"Yep. I searched and scrounged and squirrelled these short sounds hence," replied the sphinx. "I stretched my mind and scratched my head, looked straight at my strengths. I saved these words in my thoughts for just such a farce of a chat."

"Squirrelled is two syllables."

"As in oil?"

"Well, all right, it's one if you pronounce it 'sqrld.' "

"Yes. But if you remove the vowels, then even the word faerieland would qualify."

"It's been long since I've had a vowel movement," said the phoenix.

At this point everyone agreed that it was getting late.

"We've work to do tomorrow. Everyone shall go now, and prepare in whatever way suits them," said the sphinx.

The phoenix looked at Aldrei. "Join us at dawn, will you, Coney?"

"Aye, I'll be there," answered Aldrei quietly.

The sphinx rose and took her leave. Shortly after, the phoenix departed also. After the cobra left, the four friends sat and chatted a while longer. Nrouhw and Aru wanted to know what the sphinx was referring to when she spoke of work.

"There is an important ceremony taking place here in Anseo tomorrow," explained Aeon. "Best not to discuss it. But you are welcome to attend. Just follow the crowd before the dawn, there will be many."

Aru and Nrouhw's exhilaration from meeting the sphinx and phoenix mellowed their curiosity about the ceremony. Even Nrouhw was content to wait and see.

"This has been an extraordinary day!" said Aru as they said goodbye.

Aeon smiled at her. His smile said, *Just wait till tomorrow!*

At bedtime Nrouhw turned to Aru and said, "I'm a bit hungry, but no matter. There will be plenty of sand witches on hand in the morning."

"Shut up!" said Aru, laughing, and slapped at his nose.

The hostel was illuminated in the middle of the night by the lamps of all those who had risen early to go and witness the proceedings. Aru and Nrouhw got up, had a bite to eat, and fell in with the others who flocked together out the hostel gate and down the lane toward the southern edge of Anseo. The streets grew more crowded as they walked, and eventually they ran out of street and there was only crowd to follow, the desert sand churned by footprints.

Beyond the outskirts of the village, the crowd came to rest surrounding a large round pavilion. In the torchlight this structure gleamed silver and gold, covered with moon designs made of metallic thread. Evidently the tent had been raised many times before, there were places where it had been repaired. Faint images of animals suggested that long ago it had a life as a carousel awning. Aru and Nrouhw admired the elaborate lunar patterns on the tent, but Aru was even more fascinated by the crowd of people surrounding it. Persons of every type milled about the vicinity of the tent in an aura of anticipation.

An hour or two passed, but everyone remained patient. The waiting was an important part of the ceremony, as was the quiet socializing which took place. During this time three different people asked Aru if she was from Opal Heights in the north. She told them she'd never been there and she didn't know anything about the place. Apparently the people that lived there had strangely pale skin like hers.

As they waited, Aru and Nrouhw made friends with a peculiar little lady whom they met when the tall lad standing between them tripped over his own feet and landed on his face. After they helped the fellow stand up and get brushed off, Aru and the old lady got to talking.

Her name was Piatho. Piatho had an awfully loud nasal voice, but she chattered kindly about this and that. She was a frumpy collection of faded calico patterns, an apron too big and an undersized shawl. She had a sharp beaky nose, but her eyes reminded Aru of a snake, and she had no real shoulders to speak of. Her neck, when she stretched upward and waved her head around, as she seemed prone to do, reached an impressive length. She wore a large medallion, a carved wheel of brass slightly larger than her palm. Aru liked her.

As Aru and Nrouhw walked with her among the crowd, Piatho shuffled along all bent over with legs wide apart, struggling as if climbing a hill. It seemed that she required a cane, but she didn't use one. Piatho plainly enjoyed looking all around in every direction. As the three of them walked and talked there were a series of little mishaps. A woman swooned just as they passed, Nrouhw caught her and in so doing stepped on someone's foot. A short time later a rack of roasted corn came tumbling down, and then one of the beaded necklaces that Piatho wore broke apart and scattered lutescent stones all over the sand. Aru had a firm grip on little Eepe in her outer pocket, she knew it wasn't the thrall's doing.

"It goes this way," said Piatho, "everything around me falls apart. Just yesterday I received a nice bouquet of potted dandelions. I managed to kill them by sundown." She smiled a cheery smile and kept toddling along. A few minutes later two men, neither looking where they were going, crashed into each other right in front of her.

The thrall peeked out from the drawstrings of Aru's pocket, and Piatho noticed it. "Oh! Is that yours?" she asked, giggling and smiling at the thing.

"Yes, this is Eepe," said Aru with a hint of pride.

Piatho peered at the thing, and then she gave a quick gasp. Aru felt sure she had seen the tiny spark of true life inside the doll.

"Curious!" muttered Piatho, waving her head until she was distracted by something else.

At last a hint of daylight began to take shape in the east. The crowd became absolutely silent. Aru looked around, trying to figure out what was taking place. She and Nrouhw had to take a few steps backward as the crowd parted and formed a pathway to the entrance of the tent. They looked to see who was coming.

A group of men were first in the procession. They all wore feather ruffs around their necks and carried big fans of banded plumes. Bulgy eyes sunken into large eye sockets gave them a bird-like appearance.

"Ruffed grouse," whispered Piatho.

Next were several people whom Aru felt sure must have been rabbits. Just behind them were three women wearing dresses patterned with flowers of the spring. One of them carried a large hourglass.

After these came Aru and Nrouhw's friend Aldrei, hauling a large and heavy-looking suitcase. Behind Aldrei the phoenix strutted in his breathtaking splendor. The magnificence of his robes, again in brilliant yellow, flame orange, reds, and silver, was augmented by a grand collar of gold, a solar disk which framed his countenance. He carried what looked like a crystal in his hands.

"A sunstone given him by the bees," whispered Piatho loudly.

Following him, the sphinx, flanked by two camels, also walked with a gait of authority. Clothed in heavy linen, she carried a long crook and flail. She wore a big scarf with thick damask stripes of gold lamé. This was tied over her head in such a way that it came across her forehead and hung down past her shoulders, covering her hair.

While they passed by, Aldrei came over to greet Aru and Nrouhw. Just as he walked up, a young goat, poor thing, frightened by all the commotion, made a great leap out from the crowd. As it did so, it knocked Aldrei's suitcase from his hand, spilling some of the contents. Rather than stare after the fleeing ruminant, as one might expect him to do, Aldrei looked directly at Piatho. She looked back at him with a smile, fluttering her eyes.

Everyone knew better than to offer help as Aldrei collected his things back into his suitcase. It was a witch case, and in such a case one doesn't touch. Aru noticed the splendid images that were carved in the fine leather on the front. An ouroboros dragon encircled a time wheel with a three hares design. She recognized the traditional image of three hares chasing each other around the inside of a circle. In the center of this symbol their ears formed a triangle in such a way that each hare's ears made up two of the three sides. The tips of each hare's ears formed the base of an adjacent hare's ear. By sharing the ears in this way, only three ears were inscribed, yet every hare had two ears.

Having recovered his property, Aldrei clicked his tongue and headed off toward the tent. The doors had been parted wide and a healthy bonfire could be seen inside. Aru just had a quick look before the procession disappeared within, leaving the camels outside to be unpacked.

She glimpsed that the phoenix had a long hood hanging down in the back with a golden tassel on the end. Then the door flaps were closed.

Soon, as the coming sun's light grew rosy on the horizon, the sound of drumming started up inside the tent. Such a deep sound, the kind felt more than heard. It was like thunder, or drums in the wind. The grouses had begun. After a while, a few at a time, members of the crowd gathered with flutes and bells outside the tent and joined in with the drumming. A song started up, one voice, soul-touching and pure. A few verses, and then others joined in. The singing came from both inside and outside the tent.

As the sun peeked over the edge of the mountains the song stopped. Another began. This one came faster and louder, with more clanging of the bells. Piatho had a little concertina. The song grew wild as the sun made the sky, and the crowd shouted like maniacs to welcome it. Then everything faded to quiet. A few minutes later a new song started up, led by a different person. So it went, all through the day.

Aru and Nrouhw helped with some of the singing, sitting together under Aru's parasol to fend off the increasing heat of the day. A few times Piatho lent them her concertina. Once in a while they'd shout out a bit of conversation. During one or two of the songs a few people could be heard dancing in the tent, moving in a circle around the fire.

In early afternoon, Aru and Nrouhw went back to town and had their lunch. It felt good to be out of the sun and have something refreshing to eat and drink. They could hear the ceremony going on in the distance. After an enjoyable break, they packed up some papayas and tangerines and, collecting several flasks of water, made their way back down to the gathering.

The singing continued, and Piatho sat in the same place they had left her. She was appreciative of a tangerine. The experience of the ceremony had a mesmerizing effect and while Aru felt she had been singing these songs and smelling these smells forever, at the same time she saw the day fly by quickly. She and Nrouhw returned from a short supper break and before they knew it sunset filled the western sky, accompanied by frenzied noises from the crowd.

Darkness fell. The songs continued. Occasionally the leader of a song would announce its name; since some ended up repeating over and again, this gave a chance to learn them. Aru's favorite of these, called The Time Miser Song, had the distinction of being sung in coyote. Aru could almost understand the words. Something about 'time-my-jailor-set-me-free.' A high-pitched quavering melody, Aru found it pleasantly haunting.

Certainly one would expect that after going on all day the participants would be tired, but the opposite seemed true. As the evening continued the pace of the happenings intensified. Many of the songs became dances as the ones inside the tent stepped and jumped to the drumming of the grouse and rabbits. A good number of people in the crowd also danced. One song had all the dancers whirling and spinning. Perhaps luckily for everyone, Piatho made no attempt to join them.

The bonfire inside now lit the tent like a great lantern. It threw the silhouettes of the dancers within onto the canvas walls. Startlingly, one could see that Aldrei's form changed not just to hare but also to galloping horse as he danced and leapt.

As the midnight approached and the moon climbed in the sky, a new layer of depth in the ceremony was achieved. Aru's eyes felt different, as if she weren't the only one looking out of them, as if a long line of ancestors peered over her shoulder. Annoyed, she tried dancing for a while to shake off the feeling.

The drumming sped up. Breathing hard, Aru went back to stand next to Piatho and Nrouhw. The old woman had taken the brass medallion from her neck. This was a wheel with holes through the hub like a button, strung through with a loop of cord which she now held by its ends as she twirled the disk. It was an iynx, a moon-quaffer. The cord wound first one way and then the other as she drew her hands apart. It whistled loudly, calling to the moon.

Piatho's sweet soprano voice chanted in her own language, that of the wryneck woodpecker, "Go pia-pia-pia-pia pia-pia-pia, go pia-pia-pia-pia-pia-pia-pia, go pia-pia-pia-pia-pia-pia-pia." Her eyes became foggy. She had a faraway look, as if a part of her had gone to work in some invisible realm.

The drumming sped up more. Piatho's wheel whistled. Someone howled. One of the doors of the tent was thrown open, revealing a whitish-yellow light inside, like the light at the end of a tunnel. Out came three rabbits in animal form. Aru couldn't see what they did, but probably they had gone to the camel trunks, because before they returned to the tent she saw them each holding a tall conical hat made of beaten gold.

All sound stopped a few minutes later, an odd silence as in silhouette the sphinx, the phoenix, and the hare could be seen donning the hats. A cool, clear voice like liquid started the next song, which escalated to be twice as loud and twice as fast as any before. Aru wasn't sure how they did it with those hats on, but the sphinx, the phoenix and the hare danced energetically around the fire inside of the tent.

Rather than pressing in on the pavilion, as they had been, most of the crowd drifted outward, creating some bare areas in proximity to the tent. This gave Aru and Nrouhw a better view. They didn't stop to wonder why people were backing away. Piatho's wheel continued to whistle. Her voice came into Aru's head, Aru wasn't sure how it got there, *An ill wind. There's an ill wind about.*

The rhythm of the drumming slowed a bit, but the three dancers sped up. Aru's mouth hung open as she watched three balls of light circulating inside the tent with the tremendous flapping of great wings. The sphinx and phoenix were now in their animal forms. Their tornado of light spun round and round, faster and faster still, until it rose upwards and the two winged ones burst out of the smoke hole in a cloud of sulfured smoke.

Everything lit up as if it were day, the sky an ozone-clouded yellow. The world somehow seemed to flip upside-down as the sphinx and the phoenix ascended. By the time they reached the crown of the sky, they looked like two bright stars. The world remained illuminated, a strange shadowless glow of sunlight and moonlight combined.

For six full hours they flew in the sky, and for all this time the hare continued to dance round the fire.

Aru stood singing, trying to help as she could. She felt so real, more real than she had ever felt. She felt alive.

A man passed by, walking along in an aura of unconcern. He wore strange, tight clothes, the likes of which Aru had never seen before. The pants, they clung to his thighs like a jester's tights.

While in the middle of thinking how odd this was, Aru caught sight of a little boy, just a baby, dressed in pajamas and clutching a stuffed bear. *Oh my goodness,* she thought, *whoever would bring a child to something like this?* She looked around for the parents but nobody seemed to be looking for a little boy. So Aru did what just about anyone would do, she went to him and gently picked him up. "It's all right . . ." she said, but in a weird, ethereal way because no sound came from her mouth.

"Mommy!" shrieked the child, struggling with all his might to get down. He was absolutely terrified. "Mommy! Help! Cyborg!" A doorway of light appeared out of nothing a few yards away, and a quavering shadowy form was framed in it.

Aru dropped the child involuntarily, her body responding as if he were a hot potato. As he fell slowly through the air she could only watch him fall, but he disappeared before he hit the ground. Aru had the sensation of tumbling backward.

She felt strong hands on her shoulders, grabbing her, and pulling her upright.

Again she stood singing, standing next to Nrouhw and Piatho. There was no doorway, no strange man, no child. The old lady had her hand on Aru's shoulder.

With daybreak approaching the rhythms accelerated once again but the drumming faded completely, replaced by the clang of the bells. A booming voice came from inside the tent and the crowd responded by joining in with vigor. After a while the entire throng began to circle the tent in a counterclockwise direction. Voices joined in from the sky. The sphinx and phoenix came into view, and they flew down and returned through the smoke hole to whirl around the inside of the tent, slowing their pace to rejoin the hare in the dance he had never paused.

The grouse and rabbits started up again, quite a bit slower now, and the same song continued on for a while. Then, with a mad, deafening free-for-all of noise, it was done.

A great meal was served right there at the tent, with everyone encouraged to take part. They feasted on chicken in peanut sauce, curry, spongy bread, fried bananas, and pineapple. The tables were filled with delicious kumquats and pears, camel buttermilk pudding and fabulous chickpea fritters.

While Aru and Nrouhw dined and made conversation, Aldrei, back to his mostly human-looking self, came and joined them, sliding in between Aru and Piatho. A few minutes later Aeon also sat down. It was the first time Aru and Nrouhw had seen him at the ceremony.

Aldrei had washed his face, but he was sweaty and, understandably, seemed a bit preoccupied. However, he demonstrated a healthy appetite. After they ate he produced a cosmetic jar from his waistcoat pocket. "This," he explained, "is buttercup glow. An element from the sun which resides in every buttercup flower."

With permission he wiped it on the chins of Aru, Nrouhw, and Piatho. Aru felt a warm feeling of the joy of buttercups and daisies in the sun. The friends laughed to see the chin lights on one another's chins. After sharing the butter, Aldrei gave the rest of the jar to Piatho.

By mid-morning, everyone felt more than ready to go home and get some sleep. In a few days, Aldrei and Aeon would be leaving with Aru and Nrouhw and their camels, heading off to the mountains for gold prospects and the village of Sylfaen. But Aldrei would need to sleep for several days first. Piatho said goodbye to Aru and Nrouhw as they left the feast. It had been a wonderful time knowing them, she said.

On the crowded walk back into Anseo, Aru tried to ask Aldrei about the ceremony. He pretended not to hear her, swatting at imaginary bugs. "Dang these annoying tempus flies," he said, "they always show up when this sort of work is done."

Aeon acted playful as he trotted along next to Aru. Perhaps he felt relieved the whole thing was over. "They were fixing a crack in the world," he said softly.

Aeon and Aldrei soon left the river of people and wandered out to a patch of soft sand. When Aru looked back a few minutes later the old men had both stripped off all their clothes and were rolling on their backs, having a glorious and well-deserved dust bath.

IV. Everyday

As he scratched and bobbed through brushy tangles, foraging for beetles and bugs among the dirt and duff, a tiny wren caught Aru's attention. She stopped to watch him for a while. Such a serious expression on his little face. He hopped up to trill his song from a twiggy underbranch. Slender beak open wide, he quavered with the dedicated effort of an opera singer, pausing every few minutes to check for a result. Aru gave him a smile and walked on.

November's barren trees filled the woods and the cool air felt moist to the travelers. The smell of soil had reached them less than a week after departing Anseo, two full days across the sands before they'd arrived at the dirt track which bordered the eastern foothills. After another half day's journey north they made it to one of the depots where horses and camels waited to be traded and wagons could be bought. Aru and her friends needed stop only for a dark and foamy coffee and some friendly conversation. The camels which Krohnnck had secured for them would carry their cargo right to the village of Sylfaen as the pair had business in the mountains beyond.

Few travelers used these northern highways. The route wound through hills and climbed steadily but Aru and her friends made no hurry. Aru enjoyed walking among the bare maples and hazels in such crisp weather and found it satisfying, somehow, to wear a jacket again. Small game ran in abundance here, and deer, so Nrouhw took brief excursions of his own through the woodland.

Aeon preferred to travel as a donkey. He made enjoyable company, so comical and endearing with his great big ears which cocked this way and that. Much of the time Aeon carried the little man Aldrei on his back. These two had been companions for many years, and they had the unusual ability to converse regardless of animal shape. Of course certain types of animals could understand human speech, but Aldrei and Aeon could speak one another's animal languages.

The group were several days into the hills when Aldrei told them their narrow wagon trail would soon cross a more heavily used highway that ran between the northern bogs and a fair-sized industrial town to the southeast. It meant they were only another day or two from Sylfaen. He said that the intersection crossed the heart of a tiny valley just on the other side of the ridge they were climbing. When rounding the last bend on the crest of that hill, everyone looked beyond in anticipation.

A disaster scene spread below them. The backwoods crossroads was filled with people. A multitude which numbered at least several thousand covered the roads and the open areas of the forest. Some of the people were moving busily, others not at all. Tarpaulins had been spread between many of the trees.

"There." Aldrei pointed. A farm wagon lay overturned in the ditch.

"Oh, tell me it isn't so," whispered Nrouhw.

The group hurried downhill to offer what help they could. Aru asked what was going on but no one heard her. Soon they encountered some of the people on the road. They were all women. Aru recognized at once by their facial features that they were bees. They seemed dazed and were in complete disarray. Strangely, they weren't dressed in typical bee attire but wore only unbleached linen shifts.

As the travelers walked through the crowd they had to navigate around those who were sitting in the road, many as if in a stupor. Others wandered aimlessly, limping or supporting one another. Some were in better condition and worked busily with disaster relief tasks such as administering medical aid or distributing food. The friends stopped one of these and asked her how they could help.

"I believe we have the workers we need," she told them. "Maybe if you are possessed of cups or small buckets beyond what you require we could use them. Scores of us have become too bedraggled to metamorphose into humans. In this weather there is scarce hope if we can't carry to safety those who are bereft of strength."

"I'm sure we can find something," replied Nrouhw.

"We'll unpack the camels and give you water and food," added Aru.

The woman told them that they could use some help with the old man. By this she meant the farmer, driver of the overturned wagon. The bees didn't know exactly how to take care of him.

The farmer sat on the ground not far from what remained of his dray. Piles of dead bees surrounded him. "It was the Spring-Heeled Jackrabbit," he said softly. "He come up straight out of the ditch breathing blue flame and he spooked my Whinny."

The man's head was bandaged with camel-linen. His right arm hung in a sling. He told them that his wagon had been carrying skeps of dormant bees to found a new colony up north. When the Spring-Heeled Jackrabbit caused the accident and the wagon flipped, his horse and the few bees in human form had survived but several skeps had been smashed underneath. Other skeps had flown off the wagon. A couple of intact ones had been taken away already by the Agency of Eagles, who were also dropping emergency clothing and supplies. The queens from both of those intact hives had survived the accident.

Another queen had already departed the scene by way of a litter made from felled trees and pieces of the wagon. She traveled on the southeast road, a carriage on its way north to meet her. Underneath a tarp on the edge of the nearby thicket, a badly injured queen in insect form clung to life; everything was being done to try to save her. Two others were still missing and feared dead. As the farmer related these things, desperate workers who had been digging under the wagon managed to flip it over.

The old man went on to tell of the eagles' swift response, and how a factory had donated the underclothes and several hundred pairs of leather thong sandals. The women were cold, but this did give them something to wear. More clothes, blankets and supplies were on their way by horse and wagon, and many of the women were already on the road south to the town. From there they would take the train or other transportation east back home to their colony in the flower fields.

Aru made a twig fire and started some coffee to help revive the disoriented. She went from woman to woman, giving them sips from the soup ladle. The thrall tagged along behind her, staring at everyone with those creepy little eyes. Its cornhusk face had begun to look grimy and ragged.

Aeon and the camels had gone to human form, and Aeon doctored the horse's leg while the camels helped Nrouhw parcel out nearly all the food and water they carried. Nrouhw found several wooden mugs and about a half dozen bowls of various sizes, and one small bucket. He assisted a woman in filling them with the coarse dry grass from the roadside to pad them somewhat for the groggy bees. When they had done this, Aru helped them look for living bees too weak to transform. They gently placed the bees into the containers. The woman sorted through a bowl that had already been filled. She found a dead bee and flicked it over her shoulder with her fingers. She saw the look on Aru's face.

"It's only an insect," she said matter-of-factly. Then she went back to work. With bees, whether the transforming type or the creatures, life is all about the hive.

After they had given out their food and all their small containers the friends realized that the best help they could then provide would be to get the farmer and his horse to shelter. It made sense to bring them along to Sylfaen. So a few hours after arriving at the scene, Aru and her friends set out again.

Chkuchk was the farmer's name, and he liked to keep a big plug of tobacco in his cheek. Aru figured he was a gopher. He lived in a village to the south, but gave thanks for the transportation to Sylfaen. He had a nephew up there. Nrouhw helped him up onto Aeon's back and he rode the donkey most of the way, walking on the steeper hills. Whinny followed along of her own accord, a donkey's pace serving just about right for the lame mare. She was only a creature, unable to transform or use language, but she knew her role in the accident and she felt bad. Aru patted her neck and tried to comfort her.

The mood remained somber. "All those bees," said Nrouhw.

"Such a terrible loss," said Aldrei, although his tone sounded rather indifferent.

"What rabid sort of fiend is the Spring-Heeled Jackrabbit?" asked Aru. Then she saw Aldrei's face and her breath left her for a moment. Did she just put her foot right in her mouth? Was he a relative somehow?

Aldrei grumbled, or maybe laughed. "The reality of the situation is that Spring-Heeled Jack is nothing but a young scamp, stupid as any young man. He'll grow up someday. Maybe another century or two."

Aru decided not to ask any more questions.

They agreed to journey hard the following day in order to reach the village by sundown. Well into the mountains now, the highway climbed through thick woods as they traveled mostly uphill and upward, on and on. Once in a while an opening between the massive trunks of conifers let Aru and Nrouhw see that their road followed along the side of a great ravine. And what a ravine!

The gorge divided the mountain range as though it had cracked apart, cleaving some of the peaks into sets of rock cliffs which faced each other across the narrow rift. Each viewpoint they encountered escalated Aru's and Nrouhw's awe. The sights made one giddy. For much of their route the opposite cliffs, sheer exposed rock with towering slopes above, seemed only a stone's throw across the way. Rugged mountains crowded together all along the deep chasm, reaching high up into the sky. The ravine seemed bottomless. Such a vastness of nature here, a substance so tangible, so perceptibly real. It made Aru aware of her own smallness and mortality.

They didn't have much food, but Nrouhw went and caught a coney and toasted it over the fire for himself and Aru at lunchtime. Whinny and the camels grazed while the others did a bit of foraging for bulbs and mushrooms.

After the meal, Aldrei asked Nrouhw for a favor. "My old bones aren't used to all this walking," he said. He asked if Nrouhw would be willing to set out alone and take a certain trail that diverted from the road ahead and made a shortcut to Sylfaen. There'd be chanterelles along that path this time of year, and Aldrei would so love some. He just wasn't feeling strong enough to navigate that route himself.

"That sounds like fun," said Aru, "I'll join you, Nrouhw."

"Oh, I wish you wouldn't. If you don't mind," said Aldrei. "It's a steep bit up to the village from here, that's the reality of the situation, and we may need your help. With the farmer."

When they reached the shortcut they saw a sign nailed to a tree:

DANGER! ROUTE CLOSED. UNSTABLE TERRAIN.

"Oh, I never worry about that," said Aldrei lightly. "There's a bit of scree along the way. A tad of rubble from a landslide or two over the years. Nothing a smattering of common sense can't help you to avoid."

Aru wasn't sure. "Are you certain it's all right? When was the last time you went this way?"

"No worry," replied Aldrei, "I go every year to pick the mushrooms. Nrouhw, you'll be fine."

So Nrouhw departed up the trail, a gunny sack in hand. Aru felt uneasy about this, but there wasn't much she could do. She kissed him and reminded him to be careful.

They gained considerable altitude on the last part of the route, as Aldrei had forewarned. Sylfaen was situated not far below the timberline. Their highway took them across an especially steep mountainside, eventually passing above the tiny village and presenting an overview of the layout of the community.

Below them, out on the very tip of a bluff which jutted into the gorge beyond, stood a magnificent tower of rock, a sculpted hillock, craggy and with small trees and brush growing in its vertical crannies. The cluster of a dozen or so ancient thatch-roofed buildings that made up the village of Sylfaen nestled at the base of this great outcropping, protected from the sheer drop-off on the far side. Most of these buildings rested on the seat of a small saddle between the tower of rock and the narrow plateau that crowned the length of the bluff. Tucked away from much of the wind, they nevertheless enjoyed gorgeous views both ways along the ravine.

Aeon, bearing the farmer, led them all down from the highway by following a narrow and rocky road which cut across the face of the bare slope until it met the bluff below. This was easy going for a donkey, much more challenging for the laden camels. After they had made the descent, their road curved along the rim of the lowest of several terraces comprising the flat bluff-top. Around the bend it must have dropped down into the tiny village. But Aldrei stopped halfway along, where a trail coming up the slope on the left met their road. It seemed he had paused to let Aeon look over the stubbled hayfields. Or did he plan to take that trail?

"Are we not continuing on to the village?" asked Aru. "I would think Nrouhw would have arrived by now. Perhaps he's waiting at the inn."

Aeon looked at her with his big donkey eyes and nuzzled her arm gently. Then he rubbed his hefty head against her, almost knocking her off balance, in order to scratch the area at the base of his ear. Aldrei made no hurry to answer Aru, a trait of his which had begun to wear on her patience.

Eventually, he replied. "Our farmer friend and his Whinny will want to continue in that direction, but that road is not ours this evening. We'll go a short way down into this charming scene below us. Your Nrouhw will catch up soon; meanwhile, feast your eyes on these lovely mountain tillages." He leaned against the wide wooden gateway to the trail, taking up the walking stick which rested against a post.

Aru and her friends said goodbye to Whinny and Chkuchk and started down the path. Before them a steep downhill quickly mellowed into a gentle incline that continued across a shoulder of the mountain. The broad hillside was dressed in hedged plots of farmland and dotted with cottages. It was terraced or treed in the steeper spots. The rich volcanic loam was not to be wasted and every accessible parcel was in use. This time of year most of the fields sat tilled and empty, the mantle plowed into a patchwork of homey brown corduroy.

Aru's eyes searched the landscape for Nrouhw, but she didn't see him. She smelled meat smoking and heard voices of the farmers below. Aldrei had also been scanning the area and seemed to have found some marker he was looking for on the slope. He pointed to a cottage in a rocky hollow below them on their left. Behind the house a pair of great timeworn maples grew with their trunks just inches apart, their bare branches spread high over the entire roof and garden. This was the cottage he had arranged for the friends to share.

The sign above the door read *Kestrels Villa*. The several children who had escorted the newcomers down from the trail told them it was known as "The Villa." Obviously a joke name for a farmworker's shack such as this. The place was small, and truly ancient, but someone had tidied it up nicely for them. Aru was pleasantly surprised to see that a charming old grandfather clock stood in the corner. After unpacking some of their things and helping Aeon get supper started, Aru sat at the table and talked with Aldrei and the two humanized camel women. The cornhusk thrall sat under Aru's chair, poking between the floorboards with a toothpick. Aru felt increasingly worried about

Nrouhw. He should have arrived before they did. Maybe he'd got to talking with someone in the village.

At last, just as their late supper was about to be served, Aru heard a sound at the door. Holding her breath with anxious hope that Nrouhw had arrived, she half noticed that Aeon's face looked odd as he, also, stared toward the noise. And he and Aldrei, did they exchange a quick glance? The door swung open and Nrouhw stood, grimy, in the doorway. He looked like he'd been dragged behind a wagon. His clothes and boots were gone, he wore only his long jacket. He had no mushrooms, in fact, no gunny sack.

Apparently, the trail had become a great deal more treacherous than Aldrei and Aeon had expected. At a certain point Nrouhw had given up on the mushroom gathering and later had parted with his clothes so he could navigate the steep, crumbling terrain as a cougar. He had carried his jacket and his knife clutched in his mouth.

By the time he reached Sylfaen in the dark his anger had blossomed. It took a wash and a good meal and several apologies from Aldrei before he calmed down. Aru felt relief, mostly.

After the camels departed the next morning, Aru and Nrouhw took a stroll to have a better look at the area. Aru carried the thrall in a sling made from her soft camel-hair scarf. Rather than go up to the village proper just yet, they decided to follow the trail downhill across the sloping farmland. Aside from the strip of orchards and a few clumps of shade trees, most of the countryside looked like a boundless sea of furrowed dirt, a pleasant scene with dark soil, rich and viable. The mountain views in every direction were exhilarating and the mountain air filled with farmy smells. Each time they came to a hedge there'd be a stile or creaky wooden gate to contend with. They saw some ponies, and a man and woman planting bulbs on the far end of a plot.

Above the trail, a couple of dirty-faced young girls perched high on the bare limb of a walnut tree were laughing and calling out to Aru. "Opali! Opali!" They smiled and waved. Aru just smiled. She had been noticed all her life because of her light skin. There was no point in saying anything. Someday she would find out more about that Opal Heights, though. It sat somewhere in these mountains; she'd have to make a point of visiting while she lived in the area.

Stacks of peat and firewood and the smell of compost seemed to attend each cottage they passed. The residents must all have been out working somewhere on such a fine day. Nrouhw and Aru followed a narrow trail which wound uphill, and after crossing some stubbly fields they found themselves in the hillside forest below the highway. They saw a tree hollow way up high in a massive and burly trunk, with a round wooden door hung on brass hinges. As they stood talking about the door, and whether anyone might be home, someone opened it up and stared down at them. He blinked. "You two are new to the area, aren't you," he said.

"Yes, we're Nrouhw and Aru. We've recently moved into a cottage just up the way."

"Kestrels Villa," said Aru.

"A pleasure to meet you," said the man. They could only see his face. "My name is Hoo-H'HOO-Hooey-Hoo. Feel free to call me Hooey. The name most use. Did you have something you wished to ask?"

Aru replied with a soft and respectful tone, "Umm, no we don't, Hooey, we only stumbled upon your house. We are exploring the area. Sorry if we disturbed you."

Hooey widened his round eyes. "Oh. All right, then. If you don't mind, I'll just go and finish my dream. Good day."

After lunch Nrouhw and Aru unpacked their things and began to set up housekeeping. Aldrei and Aeon had gone to visit some friends and inquire about current prospecting in the area. While the pair were working, they heard a light rapping on the door jamb and in walked a woman with her two daughters. The three of them had big, dark, round eyes and Aru immediately thought of her friend Phfft-Psyfft. The older girl smiled and held forth a lovely pecan pie.

"We live in the third treehouse just down the way," the mother explained. "We was told there would be neighbors here in the Villa again. And here you are. Welcome."

They weren't chickarees like Phfft-Psyfft, but certainly some kind of squirrel. These new neighbors told Aru and Nrouhw all about the area and asked all sorts of questions of them. Aru enjoyed the girls and their adorable jabbering. She wondered if it was a school holiday. No. No school holiday. There hadn't been a school in Sylfaen for many years. The children spent their days working alongside their parents. Aru and Nrouhw were appalled to hear this. No school at all? But their new friends didn't see this as a problem and leapt right into chit-chat about other things. After about an hour, the squirrels said farewell, but not before telling the two something important about the Villa.

Great care must be taken, they said, for a troupe of little-folk lived in the cottage. For several hundred years they'd been there, under the maples, and helped with chores such as polishing the kettle or dusting the shelves. Maybe they'd been there longer, nobody knew.

The girls told the newcomers in whispers that they should leave food out for these hobs, but be discreet. They must never offer the food nor any sort of gift outright or the things would take offense and leave, never to return. And that would be a regrettable loss indeed.

"Are they mischievous?" asked Aru.

"Oh, no," said the older girl, whose name was Pippet. "They won't bother you. They just have their little chores they do."

Veya, the mother, laughed. "Been trying to attract one of those brownies to our place for years."

The next day Nrouhw helped Aldrei dig potatoes in the cottage garden while Aru mulched the beds and mounded dirt around the woody rose canes. "From what I understood about this area," Nrouhw said to Aldrei, "it should be swarming with prospectors. Where are they?"

"Well," Aldrei replied, "many of them are underground in caves or over on that mountain to the east." He lowered his voice, "The truth be told, the paydirt is right here on these slopes. It's a well-kept secret. Aeon has connections in the local mining industry, one of the few things here not regulated by the Doms."

Aldrei went on to explain that the land in Sylfaen and surrounding area was owned by a local corporation called Dominion Associated, known colloquially as "the Doms." This organization had been established a generation or two earlier by a family of stoats. It remained mostly stoat-run, although a ferret and a badger family had achieved positions of power within the company. The Doms leased out land to the farmers and others. Some paid in money, but most worked for the company in exchange for their rent and keep.

Aldrei was familiar with Sylfaen and had worked things out by messenger bird from Anseo so that the four of them had a place to live and Nrouhw had the opportunity to chase after the gold he craved. All this meant that Aru would be a member of the Doms workforce, which was agreeable to her. Aldrei had explained that the village was a cheerful place and the work not unpleasant compared to city life.

And this proved to be true. Already friends with Veya and her daughters, Aru accordingly joined their particular work crew. While Nrouhw and Aeon spent their days together seeking treasure in the mountain fissures, Aru found herself spending the hours of daylight chattering with new friends while engaged in honest, healthy labor.

She started out by helping to prune the bare orchard trees. The job was filled with fresh air and birdsong. Care was needed in setting the tall wooden ladders to reach safely into the grand old trees because a poorly set ladder on those slopes would mean broken limbs on either a tree or a person. "We're not *flying* squirrels!" Pippet would remind her little sister Chirra.

The crew of about a dozen was composed mostly of squirrels. Several of these worked the very tops of the trees in animal form, gnawing off small branches. Of the workers who weren't squirrels, two mousey-looking women who kept bickering with each other turned out to be shrews, and a tall, skinny old woman, a ferret, acted as supervisor.

There was an interesting man, a stout, dawdling type of man, with a friendly face like a beaver's and thick hair that stuck straight up. For a common agricultural laborer he was rather a sharp dresser. He wasn't fast in his work, but he didn't waste any energy, either. With his slow and steady manner he got the job done. And despite his weighty build, he could reach even the most remote branches. Another fellow of about the same age worked along with him, and Aru grew curious.

This other man had the same sort of stiff hair and rotund body but he was a much smaller person. He looked like a miniature version of the sharp-dressed man.

She asked Veya quietly, "Are those two related?"

"No, no, silly. The one is a porcupine and the other is a little urchin. Completely different folk."

"Oh, I see," said Aru. "Urchin, that's another word for hedgehog?"

"Oooh, don't call him that!" whispered Veya. "They don't like it. They claim it's not them that has a problem sharing the hedges."

Although she didn't possess the boundless energy that most of the crew seemed to have, and balancing on top of an orchard ladder wasn't her favorite thing, Aru found great satisfaction in clipping wayward branches all day. Pruning away the weaker and unproductive wood was healthy for the tree and, like tangle-free hair or a tidy room, it gave her a certain sense of accomplishment. Making design choices, creating order from disorder, this work served as an outlet for her sense of artistry.

Aru tried to keep the husk thrall in her underskirt pocket as she worked, but the thing would climb out and cause trouble in one way or another. On several occasions it nearly caused her to fall from the tree; one of those times her ladder would have fallen on a young girl.

There were five children in the group. Pippet, a young teenager, was oldest. She helped supervise the rest. These kids were quite chattery in the early part of the day and they seemed to know a lot of stories.

Aru decided to share one she knew:

> WAY BACK at the beginning of time there lived a skunk. In those days, people spent most of their time in animal form. Living was easy in the world, but the skunk pined and pined. She wanted, more than anything, to have children to love. But none had come. She lived her life, did her best to be useful, but still no children. She became old, nearly too old to be a mother. At last, one day, a single son was born. The skunk was elated.
>
> As the boy grew from kit to youngster he proved himself to be quite a handful. Time and time again the aging mother had to rescue him

or nurse his wounds. Nothing would deter him from exploring and getting into mischief. And always the mother came to his aid. The young fellow loved, above everything else, to climb. Mother skunk did not like heights. Several times the mother skunk had to rescue her son from high in a tree, and each time she would freeze with fear but eventually managed to retrieve him.

A day came when the little rascal, on a romp through a previously unexplored part of the woods, came upon a tree trunk as big around as you can imagine. This tree reached all the way up beyond the clouds. Up he scrambled, without even a pause to take a breath.

Mother skunk heard his cries later that day and came to find him. He was higher in this tree than he'd ever gone before. Mother skunk began to cry, also. Yet, after a while, she wiped her eyes, blew her nose, and started up the tree to save her son.

As she climbed in the tree she found a funny thing happening. The higher she went, the more she forgot about her fear and even began to enjoy the view. By the time she had climbed as high as her son, she was having quite a good time and wanted to climb higher. The boy's boldness had returned with the presence of his mother. So the two skunks, mother and young boy, continued climbing higher in the tree. Up they went, ascending higher and higher until they reached the very sky. And they kept going.

By the time they reached the upper branches it was well into the middle of the night. The young boy was tired by this time, and as he stretched to look around at the view he lost his footing, falling right out of the tree into the sky. Mother skunk, not knowing what else to do, leaped after him.

But the two didn't tumble to the ground. They just floated there in the sky, the mother's love keeping them aloft by turning them to constellations. To this day the curious little boy swings around the North Star by his tail, observing the world, and the protective mother is always watching him.

Skunks today have vision that is too poor to see the stars. They've forgotten about the great skunk mother, or they don't believe the story. They've become terrible climbers and they don't fall well. But she is up there, waiting, and someday they will remember her courage.

"My grampa tells a story like that," said a boy of about ten. The boy's version went like this:

LONG TIME ago there was a mouse lived in a lowland village. She had a big bunch of children, but even so, due to her good luck and hard work she had the nicest bungalow in the village.

One day this orphan rat boy shows up at her door, and she can't turn away no young one, so she goes ahead and takes him into her bungalow. This rat, he's thankful, but he's big and he's slow and he doesn't seem to learn easily.

Weeks go by and this orphan, he's a likable fellow but effort to keep. He helps with the chores, but does a terrible poor job. Like, Mrs. Mouse asks him to wash the floors and he just smears the dirt around. And he gots a huge appetite. Mrs. Mouse starts to care about him, even so.

A sheriff shows up in the village, and Mrs. Mouse, she hears that he's looking for the orphan. Only he's not really an orphan, he's a runaway from a rich family and an estate.

"Don't let him get me!" cries the young rat. "He'll take me back to my mean uncle who beats me!"

The sheriff tells Mrs. Mouse she can keep him for another week and then leaves her with some coins what come from the uncle, so she can send him home.

The boy cries and cries that he'll be treated bad if sent home, beaten and tortured, so she agrees to use the money to buy him train fare to the city instead.

She buys the ticket and packs up a bag of food for the boy to take and he'll leave in the morning. Only, the sheriff returns that evening and tells her that she's bad for doing what she done, and he'll rat on her if she don't pay him a large amount of money.

Mrs. Mouse, she's scared, so she gives him what he wants. Then she thinks, How did he know I bought a ticket to the city?

She catches the boy sneaking out the back with that bag of food to join his fake sheriff dad. She's just a tiny mouse but she is so mad.

When she calls them out they laugh at her for taking the bait. She is so little, but this just steams her up so bad, she grabs the dad rat and she swings him around and around by his tail, this little mouse. She swings

> him so hard and lets go. She's so mad the power of her swing sends
> him right into the north sky, where he just goes on spinning around.
> Then she sends the boy rat up there, too. They both set up there in the
> sky to this day.

Aru loved hearing stories from other cultures and she genuinely enjoyed her time working and socializing in the leafless orchard.

On her fourth day in Sylfaen, Aru finally made her way up to the village. Nrouhw had amassed only a couple of small nuggets so far, but was excited to spend them. Although the village had no real assay office, the stoat-run grocery store acted as a bank and would give him some coins for his find.

Along with Aldrei and Aeon they climbed the trail to the narrow road and stood looking back down over the countryside and at the scenery. After a moment Aru and Nrouhw smiled at each other. Aru gave a big sigh. Sylfaen had a homey, peaceful character. And with such views! Perhaps they'd settle here permanently.

A wooden aqueduct ran alongside the road, delivering spring water from the upper cliffs to the village as it had done for countless years. The friends followed this along the lower plateau and then down into the village. None of the buildings were large, but each had two or three stories, some with shops in the bottom and residences above.

After the grocer's, they headed to the inn to sit on the veranda and enjoy the scenery. A twisty old stump enhanced with carvings of bears welcomed them through the only front garden in town.

The inn sat at the end of Second Street. There were three buildings squeezed onto one side of Second and four on the other. The only other street in the village of Sylfaen, if one didn't count the road with its switchback coming down from the plateau of the bluff, was First Street, which ran along in front of the village businesses at the base of the stone promontory. On the far side of the inn was a steep incline culminating in a sheer cliff and views to the west along the gorge.

They climbed the steps to the entrance. Aru noticed a woman up in the doorway, watching them. She had trousers on. Not riding jodhpurs, either, but regular slacks like men wore. Although she was small in stature the woman had quite long legs. She looked lithe and athletic and possibly dangerous. As Aru and her friends approached she smiled slightly and disappeared inside.

A while later, seated on the cliff-side veranda with her friends, Aru realized the trouser woman sat out there also, all by herself at a tiny table in an alcove by the window. Aru stared a bit. A tight leather bodice drew attention to the rounded belly and voluptuous figure. Oiled hair, in itsy-bitsy braids and pulled back into a bun, set off her smooth mahogany skin. She was wearing eyeglasses.

"This view! Profound and beautiful, just like my beloved," laughed Nrouhw, surveying the wonderful panorama. He put his arm around Aru's shoulders and handed her a nutcracker.

The four friends sat drinking their stout beers and crunching on salty nibbles of hazelnuts and toasted pecans. One of the workers on Aru's crew happened by and they invited him to sit. This added a bit of village lore and gossip to the conversation and soon Aru had forgotten all about the trouser woman. When she looked over there again, the woman had gone.

The next evening, Veya and her daughters stopped by the Villa for another visit. From the hickory-bark basket they set on the table, Aldrei pulled out four delightful fresh-baked gingerbread people, still warm. They smelled so good! Three of them were well-made and typical, the other was a fair bit larger, bumpy, and its raisin nose looked, in a rather disturbing way, more like a third eye. This last one obviously had been made by little Chirra.

"Ah, this one's positively my favorite," said Aldrei as he set it with the others.

While they all stood chatting and admiring the lovely cookies, the thrall crept up the table leg and started brazenly across the table to take a look at the gingerbread. Nrouhw flicked the thrall off the table; it screeched as it flew across the room to land upside down in the corner, a frumpled mess with dark and tangled cornsilk hair.

"Eepe!" cried Aru.

"Can't hurt the thing," grumbled Nrouhw.

All three eyes on the lumpy gingerbread cookie opened wide, and a sneering grin came to the hideous clownlike loop of icing that made its mouth.

"No!" cried Aru and Nrouhw together. The thrall had assumed another form. Nobody was happy about it, but Chirra appeared quite flattered.

Days later, a menacing rainstorm approached along the gorge. The workers enjoyed a rare lunch break while they waited for the storm to blow through. Aru was invited to the residence of her squirrel friends.

It was a long climb up the great leafless tree, an awfully long climb. Especially in skirts. Aru now carried the ginger cookie in her sling rather than the cornhusk doll.

An orchard ladder against the huge thick trunk reached up to short boards nailed one above the other. Up high, a series of short ladders reached from branch to branch. These led to a platform which wrapped around the trunk, a weathered old porch built underneath the charming stick-built treehouse.

Veya smiled at Aru. "Welcome to Aeryhurst, our humble home!" She pushed open the trapdoor just above them. Aru climbed up, relieved to scramble through the opening and stand up somewhere secure. The winds had started to blow, and the whole house swayed a bit with the movements of the tree, but even so it felt cozy inside and safe from the cold rain which had just begun to fall.

"Come on in, Aru," said Pippet. "Have a seat."

Aru had trouble finding one. They had stepped from the entryway into the central room of the house, a living room formed by the hollow inside of the massive tree. Thick-silled windows all around the walls let in light through other rooms which had over the generations been added around the outer trunk. Furnished in polished walnut and adorned with delightful wall carvings, the room looked folksy and comfortable. But there was no place to sit. Piles of clothing, crates and crockery, and bulging paper sacks filled the space. A chest overflowed with nuts and pinecones. A disintegrating hamper contained what looked like coconut husks and dozens of wooden spoons, all this topped by a basket full of hundreds of rough-carved clothespins.

Veya removed a dilapidated sock monkey and several sacks of baby clothes from one of the chairs at the table and motioned for Aru to sit down. She brushed off the chair with her hand.

"I just can't seem to throw stuff away," she apologized. "You never know when you might need a thing—"

"I s'pose that's why I'm still around!" came a man's voice, making them jump. Sitting among the mess near the far wall, someone had been invisible in the low light. With reassurances of not having meant to scare anyone, the voice came forward and introduced himself to Aru as Veya's husband. "Clear off the table, girls," he told his daughters. "We'll have some lunch."

The storm began to howl outside, but Aru thought that if one must spend a windstorm in the treetops, the snug home of squirrels was the place to be. Toasted cinnamon fig bread smeared with melting cashew butter was accompanied by hickory-wood mugs full of thick cocoa, foamy and hot.

The lunchtime conversation centered mostly on the business of pruning and the father squirrel's job over at the warehouse, but at one point some interesting news was brought up. A group of bighorns had just come up from the floor of the ravine and were staying down in the seasonal pickers' cabins. Apparently the Doms had made some kind of deal with them. These families were weavers and would be making woolen horse blankets in exchange for staying in the fresh mountain air for a while. They'd been having some issues with bronchitis.

As pruning time was winding down anyhow, maybe Veya and Aru might want to go and work with the newcomers. The weavers needed several more people to spin the rough caramel-grey and chocolate-colored wools and so far they had only one local spinner, but she was willing to teach. Aru had never learned to spin, so she felt intrigued.

A loud noise from below interrupted their discussion of the idea. "Was that the wind?" asked Aru.

"No, I don't think so," said Veya. She turned to her husband, "My love, can you see if that's Rogue?" The mister and little Chirra went across to the dumbwaiter and momentarily they began pulling it up.

"We have a fellow staying with us," Veya explained to Aru. "He's reluctant of heights so he can't make the climb. Nice man. Just fallen on hard times, we're helping him out some."

After a great deal of effort by the two squirrels, the man scrambled out of the dumbwaiter, dripping and grubby. He was slobbery-mouthed and one-eyed and at first Aru was a little put off. He greeted her, and Pippet introduced him as Aue. He went by Rogue though, he explained, his nickname from the fights. Aru said hello and politely didn't ask what he meant by "the fights." Rogue must have hurried through the storm because he was winded, his gasping breaths unpleasantly polluting the indoor air. He smelled rather nasty in general. He put away his wet things, although he didn't wash; he sat down with them at the table for some lunch, declining cocoa, but he did enjoy a nip of brandy.

He was dog-tired, he said. He couldn't tolerate much more of the Doms and their unrelenting policies. "They have a new strategy in awarding prizes at work. Trophies are meant to encourage healthy competition," he said, "but they are doing it wrong. Rewards unfairly given to people competing for the same prizes under different circumstances will bring resentment. Thinking about it, I suppose this to be the Doms' intention all along. It serves their interests to stir things up, set folks against each other, keep them from organizing. It's rough. Rough, I tell you. I wish I could embark on a different line of work, but as I'm a good prizefighter the company refuses to use me elsewhere."

The storm eventually calmed, and they all went back to their jobs in order to get a few more hours in before dark. The slightly slippery descent from the treehouse was made in human form by the entire squirrel family, out of politeness to Aru. She felt thankful that her own home sat sensibly on the ground.

That evening at the villa Aru talked with Nrouhw about the job as a spinner. They both felt it to be a good plan for her. His prospecting hadn't been going so well overall, but recently he and Aeon had found a small vein of silver. This night Nrouhw had seemed in a particularly good mood when she arrived home. He'd had a bath waiting for her, and made a fine supper which the two of them had eaten sitting on the sofa in front of the fire. Aldrei and Aeon appeared to have gone to bed early and the only sounds were the wind outside and the crackling flames. Lately, Aru had been giving the thrall lessons at every opportunity, and had discovered that the thing absolutely loved to count. So after dinner, Nrouhw had set before the thrall a big sack of coffee beans, as this would likely keep it busy for hours. Nrouhw sat cradling Aru's head against his shoulder. Then, as if driven by an impulse, he stood up. He knelt down in front of her. He held out his hand. In it was a delicate band of gold, a diamond ring.

"Aru, would you marry me?" he asked. Just like that.

Aru and Nrouhw had never talked about marriage. They'd hardly discussed the issue of Aru being solely human and the complications that might cause in a normal family. The couple didn't have plans, really, of any kind, except to enjoy each other's company. They'd always seemed to have an unspoken agreement about taking one day at a time. A respect for each other's freedom. Marriage might not fit into their plans—such a huge commitment! One mustn't enter into such a contract without a lot of forethought. Marriage requires loving the other person fully, and standing truly ready to spend the rest of one's life together, come what may.

Aru grabbed Nrouhw's head in her hands. "Yes! Of course I will! Yes!" she laughed. Then she kissed him. He slipped the ring on her finger. It had been his great grandmother's.

"I'm going to go outside now," he whispered. "When you hear a sound at the door, let me in." He crossed the room.

Aru looked at him. "You're going to . . ." she asked as she followed him, "change?"

"I want to spend time with you in my other form. Just to sit before the fire with you."

"Is it safe?" The words slipped out.

He looked into her eyes. "I won't kill you but I might possibly accidentally scratch you."

"Try not to." She grinned.

"Of course," he replied, as she shut the door behind him.

A gentle rattling of the doorknob a few minutes later prompted Aru to pull open the door. When she beheld the great cat so alarmingly near she inadvertently made a sound, something like "Eghhh!"

"I'm sorry," she breathed, turning even more pale than her normal color. She grabbed the door for support, not realizing she had moved behind it for a shield. She knew it was her lover, there on the doorstep, but a deep-seated fear took hold.

He looked at her with magnificent, sad eyes and then bowed his head. This wasn't going to work. He hadn't meant to frighten her. He started to walk away.

No, wait! How should she tell him not to go? "Umm, umm—Here, kitty, kitty!" she called, in the shrill voice people use.

He sat down. She had never seen a cougar laugh before. She wouldn't have thought it possible.

Aru stole all the pillows and the big beige comforter from the sofa and the pair curled up together just in front of the hearth, the warm firelight flickering onto them. Nrouhw's fur felt soft and thick, on his belly it grew especially soft, and rather wooly. Sorrel and dark golden, his coat color resembled his human skin tone. He smelled so sweet and clean, a soothing musk of almonds, or oatmeal, or maybe fresh air. How sumptuous for Aru to lie there endlessly, snuggling with him, burying her face in his fur, petting his neck and feeling the deep vibration of his breathy, rattling purr. He licked her temples and up into her hairline with his scratchy feline tongue, and then carefully washed her tender forearm and hand. Aru squirmed out of her old brown dress so she could feel Nrouhw's silky coat soft against her skin. He nuzzled her belly with his big feline nose. His whiskers tickled. They drifted slowly off together into the best kind of sleep, with Aru basking in warm contentment under a fold of quilt, gradually to become wrapped in comfortable dreams.

"Ahem." Aldrei's voice came to Aru before she woke, interspersed with the sound of the coffee grinder, and the smell of steaming bran muffins enticing her back to the real world. "You might want to make your way back from dreamland and join us at breakfast, you two," he said.

Aldrei showed no concern whatsoever as the big cat Nrouhw slipped past him out the door into the dewy morning. Aru went to the other room to wash up and dress, and it wasn't long before she and her human fiancé were seated at the table.

It turned out that Aldrei hadn't been in bed as they'd assumed; he'd returned this morning from what he described as an all-night astronomy lesson with the stoat children he tutored up in the village. Aru knew he hadn't been with his students for much of the night, though. It was common knowledge in Sylfaen that since they'd arrived an apparition had been sporadically terrorizing the villagers in the nighttime. A black horse, it was whispered, with ears of a mule.

As this image ran through Aru's mind, the old man Aldrei happened to rub his own rabbit-like ear as he set the pot of apple butter on the table. He gave Aru the slightest wink. Or, she felt pretty sure he had.

The smell of breakfast had roused Aeon from sleep, too, and he climbed slowly down the ladder from the loft. "What's this hooligan been up to now?" he said sleepily. He gave Aldrei a quick kiss on the cheek before he sat down.

Aru and Nrouhw's news of their engagement brought smiles and congratulations, but Aru had an odd feeling that their friends weren't as pleased as they seemed. What a strange thing to think, she scolded herself. She shook it off and returned to the joy of the moment.

After breakfast, Aru got ready for another day in the orchards. Nrouhw and Aeon were headed out for an overnight by their vein of silver, feeling ready for riches. Aru tied a nosegay of dried flowers to Aeon's packsaddle before they set off.

"I'll miss you," she whispered to Nrouhw. He smiled back to her. Aldrei pulled on his own beard with both hands and pretended to gag. Nrouhw pushed playfully at Aldrei's shoulder.

This day in the orchard started out well, with Aru stumbling upon a huge fairy ring of penny buns. This excited the whole crew, as they were all mushroom lovers.

The day had its particular challenges, though. Other workers were spreading manure on the hay fields directly upwind. In addition, the hedgehog, Chuik, had to care for his little urchins all day because his wife, who normally took them along to her seamstress job in the village, was giving birth that morning at home. Chuik introduced his four boys to Aru: "Here are Chmok, Chuac, Tchmoki, and Jubz," he said. Their vole friend Sisk had come along, too.

Chuik and his big porcupine friend were proud to be diligent workers. This day they got much less accomplished than usual. Most of the crew tried to help out, but ultimately Chuik and his pal were the ones who felt the weight of the situation. The young boys gathered up twigs and did other small jobs to help the pruners, but in the late afternoon both the children and their papa grew tired.

Working just uphill from Aru, father urchin balanced on his ladder, focusing on a branch that waved just out of reach. All of the boys had gathered below, having just returned from an errand upon which they'd been sent. Now they were playing knucklebones with a bucket of slimy fat slugs. The incessant chatter played at Chuik's nerves:

"Going to be a mild winter."

"No it's not!"

"Did you just say pickle?"

"No that was a fart."

"Poppa, Sisk called me a warthog!"

"There it is again, 'pickle.' "

"My farts do not say 'pickle.' "

"Poppa, Tchmoki's messin' with his winky—"

"All right, that's IT!" yelled the father. What he was about to say remains a mystery, because as he shouted he slipped on the damp wooden rung of the ladder. Aru didn't actually see what happened. There was a scream and he landed with a crash. He fell directly at the foot of Aru's ladder.

"I heard a snap!" cried Jubz.

"It sounded like a chicken bone!" said Tchmoki.

"Or Poppa's leg bone," said Chmok.

At the same time his brother Chuac declared, "No, it didn't!"

"Oh, no!" cried Sisk.

"Please don't kill us, Poppa!" cried Chuac. "Please don't kill us!"

Veya and a friend reached Chuik immediately. He was in awful pain. A woman high-tailed it in squirrel form to a willow tree just down from the orchard, where she snapped a twig off and brought it back in her mouth. She gave Chuik this willow branch to bite on. A ptarmigan had been resting in the willow, and through elaborate pantomime the squirrel had sent him off to fetch the marmot, Mrs. Schir.

Mrs. Schir was the midwife, and when she arrived on horseback, her old mare blowing hard, she brought the news to Chuik that he'd been blessed with two more healthy sons. Mrs. Schir whistled when she saw the hedgehog's leg. It was broken in two places.

The porcupine was extremely concerned, "He's passing out!"

"Passed out is good," said Mrs. Schir. "He won't feel the pain, then." With a sturdy, fat body shaped like a pear, and a square snouty face, Mrs. Schir was a real force in the world. Using cheerful, nonstop dialogue, she comforted the onlookers while assessing the situation. She sent a man right off for some sheaves of wheat straw and a few hanks of baling twine. From the depths of her apron Mrs. Schir pulled a small brown bottle which she held to the groggy Chuik's lips. Laudanum would help him endure what was to come. The old ferret supervisor had sent a young girl off home to get a blanket, and with that Veya and Aru tried to make Chuik as comfortable as they could while they waited for the wheat straw.

Mrs. Schir took out a small knife and began scratching at a palm-sized rock she'd picked up. Aru wondered what the purpose of this could be. Mrs. Schir held the stone up for the children to see. It had a crude drawing of a fish. She made the boys turn away and cover their eyes, then she chucked that rock right down onto the rocky slope which bordered the orchard. The children were so happy to have a game, and spent the next hour finding and re-throwing the stone.

When the straw and twine arrived it was time to reset the bone. While a couple of people held the dazed man, Mrs. Schir pulled on his leg and manipulated it until she felt satisfied the bones had gone back into place. Chuik screamed during this process but it was over quickly. With help from others, she took the sheaves of wheat straw and placed them on both sides of the leg, binding it tightly with the sisal.

They carried him out of the orchard with a pony and cart, back to his home and his newborn sons. Mrs. Schir rode up to the village on her own business, and the rest of the pruning crew went back to work. The children would be cared for by several families for a few days until the urchin parents were able to cope.

Chmok and Chuac, as the two eldest children, continued to work in the orchard until they could return to their employment at the dressmaker's workshop with their mother. Aru started to get to know them over the next couple of days; they were delightful boys, really. But then her application for the spinning lessons came through and she, Veya, and Pippet transferred to the weaving workshop. Chirra would work with her grandma in the nut sheds.

The pickers' cabins were a good way down the slope, nearly as far as the river, so this meant leaving home about twenty minutes earlier in the morning and walking along before sunrise. The soil was frozen this morning, and the early hike to unfamiliar grounds felt invigorating. Aru collected Veya and Pippet near their treehouse along the way. The three laughed together as they went down the trail. Their destination lay at the far end of the bare and dormant orchards, just past a field where several folks were getting ready to dig potatoes.

Beside the cluster of weathered pinewood pickers' shacks stood one of several community barns, owned, of course, by Dominion Associated. They entered the big unpainted barn through a small side door and Aru's eyes took just a moment to adjust to the low light. Inside, it was an immense high-ceilinged space, and noticeably quiet.

Far over in one corner, old blankets had been hung to create a sort of room. Soft voices came from behind these curtains. Aru, Veya, and Pippet walked across and, with a slight hesitation, peeked between the blankets. They were looking into a makeshift weavers' workshop. Two magnificent teak handlooms took up much of the space and several people were already busy warping each of them. A small, hot fire had been built on the clay floor and the thin wool blankets were surprisingly effective at trapping the heat even though there was so much open space above. It was enough to take off the chill.

About a dozen people were hanging up their coats, shifting packages, and otherwise preparing for the day. The group consisted mostly of women, but there were some male youths and a few children. They had handsome faces, all of them, with wide-set dark amber eyes, low cheekbones, and quite narrow jaws. Most of the women wore chamois dusters the color of coffee. They had white flounces in the rear, and thick stockings. An older lady noticed Aru and the others peeking and invited them in.

"Ahh," she said, "you must be our spinning students. The other student has arrived. The teacher will be dropping in a bit later. You can wait over here with, ah . . . Tichit." She motioned to an area heaped with unopened parcels and burlap sacks stuffed with dark raw wool. A mousy young woman sat looking conspicuously alone while the bighorn people bustled about.

"Your name is Tichit?" asked Aru.

"Tchchtt," the girl softly corrected. Veya and her daughter knew Tchchtt fairly well because one of the heavily-traveled runways that led to Tchchtt's family home passed right near their house. While they all sat talking together a young bighorn child came and sat with them; she would be a student also.

Aru snatched up a shred of wool from the floor to feel it between her fingers. People were staring at her. She was used to it.

A half dozen weavers settled nearby with friendly nods and quiet conversation, and began carding the wool. Seven or eight spinning wheels, several quite timeworn, were arranged in sort of a circle and after a while a few of these were in use. Aru sat listening to the faint whirring of the wheels. She enjoyed the sweet, waxy smell of her surroundings.

Eventually the blanket curtains rustled and one of the weavers poked her head in from the other side, announcing to the students, "Your teacher is here."

The blankets parted, and in walked the trouser woman! Except she wasn't dressed in trousers this time. The woman paused just inside the entrance. Her stance was slightly crouched, giving the impression she might suddenly leap forward. She looked in the direction of the students. Aru suppressed the impulse to stare at her outlandishness. She had on a tight, dark bodice, as before, made of the finest supple leather. The neckline of this particular one arced up over her bosoms and then plunged down between them, framing two cast bronze bowl shapes that covered her chest! These were the predominant part of a carved bronzework and filigree ornament that, serving as a bit of exoskeleton, protected her bubbies and upper back. Yet her arms were bare. The v-shaped waistline of the bodice extended into a full skirt made from layers of soft vertical strips, like petals of leather, studded with brass and trimmed up and down with lines of dark stitchery.

Why would someone dress like this? It made no sense. And she wore glasses. At any rate, she displayed such aplomb that it made one less inclined to criticize her choices. She was formidable.

The weaver who had announced the spinning teacher's arrival politely guided her over and introduced the students to her. "Aru," the teacher repeated, holding out her dark long-fingered hand, "such a delight to meet you." She shook hands with Veya and the others too. Despite her rakish appearance, she had a pleasant voice, fresh and silky. It made Aru think of droplets of morning dew.

At home that evening Aru told Nrouhw and Aldrei and Aeon how she and her friends had learned to use the drop spindle. "I believe they call it the drop spindle for a reason," she said. "I must have rent the roved fleece and let the spindle drop a hundred times or more."

It had been a wearisome day. The teacher, a consummate spinner, didn't seem to have much of an understanding about the perspectives of a novice. Although she tried to be patient with all the clumsiness and mistakes, she essentially expected her students to begin with a high level of skill and just didn't seem to be able to adjust her own thinking downward from a process which obviously came so naturally to her. She wasn't good at instructing or encouraging her students. Aru wondered why the company had chosen this particular spinner to be the teacher, as certainly any of the even-tempered bighorns would have been a better choice.

Aldrei grinned through his beard. "Those balmy Doms stoats have yet another circus going, it appears. A tribe of blithering monkeys could run things better than they." He laughed and had a bite of roast, dabbing at the corner of his mouth with his handkerchief. "A barn full of sheep," he said, still chewing. "Such a boring prospect. Perhaps they've brought in an outsider to keep everyone awake."

"She is interesting, I have to give her that," laughed Aru. She went on to describe the woman and the effect she had on her day.

"She has some fascinating stories," Aru said. "She told of the wreck of a pirate ship in a storm. In detail, she described how the pirates used a great piece of the ship's wooden hull as a raft. They were able to salvage a small chest of treasure from the bow of the ship before it sank. They fished out a crate full of bottles of rum just before it submerged beneath the muddy waves. And do you know what? Inside it was a young mouseling who had stowed away. It turned out he was from a wealthy family, who rewarded the pirates greatly for his rescue. She described the whole thing so well. I felt practically in a trance."

"It does sound fascinating," said Nrouhw.

"She had travel stories too, of riding the rails, bedded down in a rattling boxcar. One can only imagine where the lady has learned about such things." As Aru went on to talk about her exotic appearance Nrouhw wondered if he hadn't seen a woman of this description somewhere on the docks of Tir Dramor or Ysgarlad.

The next day the spinning weasel came in to the workshop to help. He was a boy of about sixteen years, tall, and thin as a rod. He'd traveled from another village to render his services, as his family for many generations had been spinning weasels. Although his species has a reputation for devious brutality, some of the individuals are more straightforward and reserved and many are quite clever at estimating amounts. This young man simply held out his hands and allowed the spun yarn to be wound between them. With his special talent, he could tell when exactly 80 yards had been wound; then he would then twist the yarn and fold it into a skein.

Aru enjoyed the spinning lessons. The rhythmic sound of the looms thumping and clacking, and again the jokes and songs, the stories and free-flowing gossip made life pleasant. The bighorns were a warm and sweet-natured group and the whole atmosphere was one of contented calmness. Now and then there would be a clash between the two of the young men, coming head to head over some minor issue, but then that's their nature. They had a streak of impertinence, those youths, probably getting restless to be out on their own.

Aru's spinning improved quickly, and within several days she'd become reasonably competent. The teacher continued to be of little help, but how much fun it was to share stories with her. She certainly did have a gift for telling them. At the end of the week she let Veya, Pippet, and Aru know that they were ready to begin spinning the wool at home. This was good news for Aru, as it turned out, because Eepe had been growing more mischievous each day at the barn.

The friends worked together in the Villa, saving Aru from the climb up to the treehouse. Generally it was just the three of them, as the young vole Tchchtt rarely came by. On most days Tchchtt worked down in the family bungalow with her mother.

The humble Villa afforded coziness and comfort through the familiarity of tradition. Centuries-old woodwork and masonry gave the place character, as did the faded, well-used carpets, and draperies carefully embroidered by the hands of those who had lived long ago. It felt especially snug as the season grew colder and a warming fire burned all day in the grate. Never mind that there were rags shoved in a couple of broken window panes to keep out the wind, or that some days Aldrei's snoring coming from the loft rattled everyone's sensibilities. The workload always loomed heavy, but the cottage filled with songs and laughter as the women did their spinning and their socializing.

Despite Veya's advice against inviting the little hedgehog father to the Villa—"That urchin always has such a terrible case of the fleas, poor thing,"—Aru welcomed Chuik to visit any time. Assigned to the pest-control division while his leg healed, Chuik would hobble in on his crutches and check around the firewood bin for beetles, earwigs and millipedes. Then he'd sit by the hearth for a while, sipping coffee.

He talked with the women while they spun and they would ask him about his family. Times were tough. With him working less and his family growing it would be a long winter. Chuik admired Aru's newest stitchery project, a pawprint design she was embroidering along the lapels of one of Nrouhw's jackets. Chuik had done quite a bit of embroidery himself a few years back, before the children came. He liked Aru's design a lot, and one morning he gave her a gift of three particularly fine needles.

When someone up in the village gave Chuik a bottle of cola he brought it along to share. Aru poured it into her stoneware cup and they each had a taste. None of them had ever had cola before. It tasted wonderful, like something hummingbirds would serve.

Another regular visitor was the spinning teacher. She would drop in every few days to check in on things, to deliver fleece and pick up the skeins. She wouldn't stay long, but sometimes they could coax another story from her. In addition to her personal memoirs she knew many traditional tales from her home on the coast, and she had such grace in telling them. The spirits of the characters themselves moved through her body as she retold the age-old stories.

Once in a while the teacher would take the day to sit with the women and spin. Her spindle whorl was carved in a radiating spiral net design. She worked elegantly, without effort, as someone who'd been honing these skills her whole life.

"Veya," she said one day, "I heard something about Old Chip-Chip Chippie's grandson's recent escapade. They say he took your cousin's buckboard for a jaunt down the trunk road!"

"Oh my, yes!" exclaimed Veya. "And then he went and hid all the sacks of walnuts up Bear Creek Gorge. That made Ol' Chip-Chip madder than a wet hen. That boy will be doing extra chores at Grandpa's for quite some time, is my guess. Oh, that reminds me, they're looking for a new kitchen maid up at the inn."

"Did something happen to Skutch?" asked Pippet.

"Oh, no. She's fine," said Veya. "It's just too much for her now. She'll be staying home some days, under Sktcht's care." For the others' benefit she added, "Sktcht, that's her great-granddaughter."

"It's about time for that," Pippet replied. "Phew! Did you hear that a rich man is at the inn? A real wealthy gentleman from the coast."

"I saw him," said Veya. "Dark man, very handsome. His son is with him. Nice looking young man." She giggled and said, "It might be you should take that kitchen maid job, Pip! He has big brown eyes. He could be a squirrel."

Pippet laughed.

"Really," said Aru. "All this work! Every day." She tugged her fleece a bit too hard, having to repair the consequences while she continued, "Don't we ever have a day free? We ought to have a regular day, each week, to rest. That's the way in most places."

The teacher smiled slightly at Aru, but kept silent.

I suppose she's afraid to say anything, thought Aru. *Since she has a good job in the service of the Doms.*

"Oh my," said Pippet. "We don't mind working a good day. 'Hard work unsullied by conceit is bread; bread on the table and meat.'"

"'Toil makes mettle,' as they say," said Veya.

Aru looked down. She knew the squirrel family had debts and sometimes went to bed hungry, despite all of their hard work. How could they accept their situation so easily? She stared at her own hand; how nice and soft the skin had become. She brought it to her lips. The rich, waxen smell of lanolin, how enjoyable its sweetness. Straw, with a light base note of cud. She didn't reply.

On another day, they sat working the wool, just the three of them. Outside the windows, rain dripped heavily from the thatch. The fire in the grate and a pair of tarnished brass lamps on the table reflected enough light across the burnished wood surfaces that it made up, pleasantly enough, for the diminished daylight. As the women conversed quietly, the grandfather clock tick-tocked its deep mechanical commentary. The low-pitched sound of the clock's ticking had once caused Aru at night to dream of a dwarf, a tired, slow-paced dwarf, incessantly hammering somewhere under the house.

The clock was a fantastic thing, a considerably large and dignified article of furniture for a plain cottage such as this one. A stately piece, yet it had a character beyond one's first impression. A careful examination revealed carvings of bears, of elk, of mushrooms, deer and squirrels, all concealed in the overall design of the cabinet. The truth is it was a cuckoo clock. Aru had made it her job to raise the heavy pine cone weights to wind it each week on Monday mornings. Nrouhw didn't think much of it. He didn't like the dancers. Every hour, on the hour, a cuckoo bird would call and then the music would begin. A small door burst open and out came a troupe of tiny dancers, wooden bears in dresses, brightly painted, who revolved across a previously-unnoticed balcony and back around through another door. Nrouhw wanted to disable this feature of the clock, but Aldrei would have none of that. Aldrei adored the clock. Even Nrouhw dared not challenge him on this matter. Aru had grown fond of it too. She felt pretty sure she had seen a tiny hob dart behind it one evening.

This morning as the old clock celebrated the eleventh hour, Pippet rose from her stool and began to make herself ready to go outdoors. Aru knew she wasn't just making a trip to the outhouse. Since the first days of working with Pippet in the orchards she'd witnessed the girl's silent departure from the group at about this time of the morning every day. She'd return an hour or so later and discreetly take up her work, as if she had never left.

For some reason, on this morning Aru finally had the courage to inquire about it. Pippet looked at Veya, who responded, after a moment, "Aru, why don't you go along with her today." She sighed. "And then you'll see what her kind nature does. She's a good girl, this one."

So Pippet and Aru set off from the Villa, sheltering under umbrellas and Aru wearing her high lace-up boots. They headed up the drizzly trail leading to town. The thrall followed along behind them, slopping through the mud, splashing, and making weird noises. After a short way, they came to a narrow side trail which Aru had never wandered down. She could see that it led slightly downhill, toward the base of the steep wooded area below the village. A small boggy area existed there, beyond which was the edge of the gorge.

Just where this smaller trail split from the main one, a covered pail sat waiting on an old stump. Pippet looked at Aru, and then picked it up. "We'll want to hold our skirts up high down this way," she told Aru with a gentle grin, "otherwise we'll be a couple of fine daggle-tails before we're done!"

Their boots squished along through a sog trail of mush. A bit of mist hovered in the air as they went along, and a lovely, wholesome muddy smell permeated everything. The landscape was a crisscross mass of bramble vines, with just a few dried leaves clinging, and interspersed with old bare willows. It seemed impenetrable beyond their pathway. In places, arrangements of boards made makeshift bridges across the puddles and mire. It wasn't too long before they came upon a log cabin standing in a cleared out area beyond a great hedge of brambles. Smoke came from the chimney, but Pippet didn't approach the door. Instead, she walked around to the back of the cabin, explaining that the home was filled with children and the baby might be asleep.

Like many in the area, this was a family of voles. A boy took care of his young siblings all day, Pippet told Aru, because their mother had died in a mishap at work and their father had a job in town. The children spent their time peeling and splitting spruce root for cordage. They needed Pippet's help because of an older brother. Just as she mentioned him, a squealing shriek came from what looked like an old pig shed behind the cabin.

"It isn't nothing about cruelty," said Pippet, glancing at Aru. "It really isn't." They crossed the backyard and stood before the shed. "Just, there's no other way."

Pippet grabbed a small key from a hook beside the door and put it in her pocket. She lifted the rusty bar that latched the door from the outside. Telling Aru to please wait just a moment, she slipped through the doorway.

Aru heard excited noises coming from the boy inside, and the sound of Pippet's soothing tones. In a few minutes, Pippet returned, beckoning Aru to enter. As Aru stepped into the musty shack the boy disappeared behind Pippet's skirts, but Aru barely noticed him. She stood gaping.

Every bit of the shed within reach of the child had been carved in intricate geometric patterns. Walls, posts, even the dirt floor and window glass were covered with deliberate, delicate designs. Tears came to Aru's eyes.

The boy began to shout and moan but Pippet knew how to calm him, and within a few moments he found his ability to greet Aru nicely. About eleven years old, he had a rather tall and squiggly frame for a vole. "Aru, this is Queex. Queex, Aru," said Pippet.

The boy smiled.

"Good morning, Queex," said Aru. Of Pippet she asked, "He stays here alone all the time?"

"During the days, yes. He's unpredictable. His little brother can't keep him safe. But you're a dear, aren't you, Queex!"

"I am," laughed the boy, grabbing his head with his hands. He reached out so Pippet could hand him his lunch. She gave him the pail, which he opened eagerly.

"You did all this artwork yourself?" asked Aru. It was rather obvious, yet difficult for her to comprehend because of the surprising sophistication of the designs.

He answered, his mouth full. "It's—it's—it's a marvelous display!"

While Queex ate, Pippet went to a corner by a woodstove. The iron headboard and footboard of an old bed had been made into a barricade. With the key she unlocked a padlock and opened this up like a gate. She stirred up the fire in the stove and filled the firebox with as much wood as it could hold. Then she locked it safely out of reach again.

Queex had finished eating. He didn't eat much. Pippet took him out to use the outhouse so he wouldn't have to use the chamberpot. He laughed and danced and jumped up and down, repeating, "It's a marvelous display! It's—it's marvelous!"

When they came back Aru and Pippet played with him for a few minutes in front of the shack. The rain had tapered off and a few beams of light shone through. The boy made wordless sounds, a big grin on his face. The thrall had been tagging along behind Aru all this time, and until this point Queex had pretty much ignored it. Now he pushed it down into the mud and stomped on it, with all his might. If it had been a cookie or a small animal, that would have been the end of it. But the thing just stuck its tongue out at the boy.

Aru would have been angry, but she understood that Queex didn't know any better. The brutish behavior was abhorrent, but she swept the resentment from her mind. Most of the resentment, at any rate. Before long the time came to return the boy to the shed and say goodbye. He gave Aru a hug. How disturbing it was to lock the door and leave him there alone. "Don't they worry he'll get out through those window bars and wander?" she asked.

"No, he hates to transform. There's no worry about it."

"They shouldn't shut him away like that. He's just a boy."

"Well, really, what else can they do?" said Pippet. "Who knows what sort of wild creature he might tangle with. And he's not good for nothing. He can't work."

"No, but it's just wrong," said Aru. "Although it's good of you to come and help him, Pippet," she added.

"We all do what we can, don't we," answered Pippet softly. They headed back up to the Villa.

Aru wanted to come along with Pippet on more of her visits and get to know the boy, but she couldn't. The Doms would notice the reduced amount of work completed if both of them went. Once in a while, though, she and Pippet went to see him and his family in the evening. They would bring some fudgy pecan cookies or other baked treats for the children and once Aru gave the children a cone of henna paste that she had bought at the market in Anseo. With this, Queex rather clumsily painted a delightful dragonfly on Aru's wrist.

Nrouhw and Aeon arrived home to the Villa after dark each day, usually after Veya and Pippet had gone. These evenings were spent quietly, as the labor of the days had taxed everyone's energy. Sometimes friends gathered there at the cottage to play music, but most nights reading and conversation, sometimes a bit of backgammon, that was enough.

For about a month so far, the two prospectors had been traversing the mountains on a venture of hopes and disappointments. Aeon apparently wasn't able to come across a road or trail without insisting on following it, and as a result the pair had meandered all through the local mountains, sampling every hidden stream or gully, but with scant luck in locating mineral deposits. Aeon obviously enjoyed the rambling. He was spending all of his outdoor time in donkey form. Unlike most people, who were hesitant to use up the lengths of their lives as animal years, Aeon didn't seem to be concerned about it.

Nrouhw had a good bit of hunting along the routes, and about that he couldn't complain, but the hunt for riches wasn't panning out. Disappointed, he decided to return to his vocation as an artist. He told the others this week he'd spend his meager profit on oil paint. Inspired by the local vistas, he felt excited to produce some panoramas and sell them, maybe up at Opal Heights. Aru thought this a good idea. He had such talent, why waste his time chasing around in the mountains.

"Your timing, though, that's the thing . . ." mumbled Aldrei, as he tamped his pipe.

"What do you mean?" asked Nrouhw.

Aldrei chuckled.

Aeon explained that an old mine had just been reopened on a nearby peak. A young gopher, a close acquaintance of theirs, had a stake in the lode claim there and said they had hit paydirt. That very day he'd invited Aeon to come and try his luck.

"In reality, it might be a gainful pastime for the two of you," smiled Aldrei.

More than a half day's journey from Sylfaen, the mine was too far to walk home every day, so Aeon and Nrouhw spent most of their nights in the mine camp. This was difficult, but when he did come home, Nrouhw was cheerier, as the mine brought him a certain amount of success. These nights were long for Aru, even so, when he left her sleeping alone.

Just a week or so after Nrouhw and Aeon first set off to take advantage of the opportunity at the mine there was an accident at home. It happened while the women were working with the wool. No one else heard a thing, but the crash woke Aldrei out of a sound sleep.

Everyone bustled out the door and ran up the slope behind the cottage to search for whatever had landed. Aldrei said he'd heard a shriek. Amid a tall cluster of rabbitbrush, Veya found what they were looking for. There in a heap, crumpled, lay a man. Veya recognized him immediately as the rich man's son, the one whom she'd seen in the village. "If I hadn't've seen it I wouldn't have believed it!" she said. What was he doing on their hillside?

He lay quite still, unconscious, but his rapid breathing showed under his fine silken shirt when they pulled his jacket open. There was no visible blood, no obvious damage to his body. The four huddled around him, staring down. He had a clean-shaven face and oiled black hair that fell to his shoulders. On his temples he had a pair of ridges; like small spiraled horns set against his skull, they reached back and up toward the top of his head. All those present knew what this meant. Animal characteristics like this on a human body could only be found on someone of distinguished wizardly capability. *Or on someone like Aldrei,* thought Aru. This fellow didn't look like a pooka.

Clutched in one of the young man's hands, and wrapped around one of his legs, was—of all things—a carpet. Barely noticed in the excitement, the fine-woven rug had remarkable designs, a valuable piece of art, no doubt. This they spread on the ground to carefully lay him on, so they could carry him into the Villa. On the way down the slope, while staring at his face and those strange horns, her hands gripping the carpet edge and her lungs puffing with the great effort it took to help bear the man indoors, Aru realized that this must be a flying carpet. This fellow had crashed his flying carpet on their hillside.

Aru's bedroom was really just an alcove beyond the fireplace, concealed by a curtain. They drew the curtain back and laid the young man on the bed. He groaned when they transferred him, but didn't wake up.

For a moment they all stood looking at him. Then Pippet pointed out a trickle of blood on his neck. He had been cut, after all. He had a gash just in front of his left ear, a small cut, but bleeding steadily. Veya put some water on to boil for cleaning it. Aldrei suggested Aru check the man for other injuries. Pippet, obviously smitten with the man's appearance, volunteered to help—making the others laugh. The man had no broken limbs or other cuts; just a few bruises were all the pair of them could find.

Veya searched the hillside just outside the cottage to collect some yarrow leaves in a bowl that Aldrei had handed to her. Then she poured water from the kettle over these. She used the resulting tea to dab onto the young man's wound, in an effort to stop the blood and to prevent infection.

The friends went back to work, talking softly and watching over their guest. After several hours, the time came for Veya and Pippet to go home. The young man was still dead to the world, and, strangely, still bleeding slightly from his cut. After a quick supper of leftover stew, Aldrei said he must leave and would be gone for a day or two on some business. He left Aru with instructions about continuing to treat the fellow's wound.

About eight o'clock the man awoke with a gasp and a sneeze. Aru crossed the room from the kitchen table where she'd been reading by lamplight. He tried to sit up, but didn't have the strength.

"Move gently," said Aru. "You've had an accident. You've been unconscious all afternoon."

The young man looked around. He looked at Aru. He mumbled something, weakly pointing at her. She couldn't get him to repeat it. A few moments passed before he spoke again, more clearly this time, asking where he was and how he got there. He seemed to have difficulty moving his jaw. Aru introduced herself and told him how they found him on the hillside. She didn't mention the carpet, which he could see for himself hanging over a chair. It was an expensive-looking thing. It had poppies and acacia branches in the design, and traditional wind motifs along the edge. And what was his name?

"My name is . . . Arven Lekkchaos . . . Chymynroddion . . . Black-buck," he said with great difficulty, looking at his hands. Then he looked at her, "Lekki." He tried again to sit up. Aru told him to move slowly. *Blackbuck,* she thought, *that's an antelope. I see now, yes, of course, certainly. He's so elegant. Genteel.*

"Do you not remember the accident?" she asked.

"I recall having a cigar on the village boardwalk yesterday. We came to this place—Sylfaen—for . . ." he searched for memories as he spoke, "for relaxation, and prizefight betting."

"And to fly carpets," said Aru.

"I suppose so," said Lekki. He gazed beyond her and then continued, "I believe I remember flying along the gorge and—My father! I should notify him of my whereabouts."

"My friend Aldrei has promised to stop at the inn and let him know," said Aru.

They didn't converse much that first evening because of Lekki's condition. After a couple of hours of checking on him, and twice wiping his wound and brow with the yarrow liquid, Aru curled up on the couch. She wasn't comfortable, and she dreamed a tedious dream of leathery pterodactyls hatching their eggs on the cottage roof.

Lekki's situation changed little all the next day. He didn't get any worse but didn't seem to gain any strength whatsoever. Veya and Pippet helped care for him during their hours at the Villa. Surprisingly, the thrall helped out also, gathering roots and mushrooms for Aru to use in a tea, and even doing some chores so Aru could spend more time watching over their visitor. Aru smiled about this. She could see that her lessons were having an effect on Eepe.

The young man was polite, quite debonair considering his circumstances, but at the same time distant, out of reach somehow, even beyond the apparent effects of his infirmity, and Aru had a feeling she shouldn't trust him. She could see his curiosity about the gingerbread boy. She wondered what he was thinking.

A message arrived by sparrow that Lekki's father had disappeared from town early that morning. Lekki didn't seem surprised, or particularly disappointed to hear this.

Late in the afternoon the spinning teacher came to call. She set down her big willow basket of lovely grey and chocolate-brown fleece. She chatted with Veya for a few minutes before she crossed the room to where Lekki lay. As she stood by the bedside observing him, he woke from his groggy nap with a start. He made a noise, an involuntary snort. He apologized, but then he seemed to be staring. Aru wondered if his condition had deteriorated. Maybe it startled him to wake with a stranger of such unconventional appearance standing over him. Aru formally introduced the two.

While the others visited, Aru went ahead and poured another batch of the herbal wash and began to dab Lekki's face. His cut was still draining. Aru didn't pay much attention to the pleasantries the others exchanged. Lekki had high cheekbones, a long and angular face. He had a thin upper lip but a wide mouth, and long eyelashes . . . Aru's observations were interrupted by the spinning teacher asking if she might borrow the bowl for a moment.

Aru looked down at the remaining yarrow leaf brew. She placed the rag in the bowl and handed it over. "Of course," she said, wondering.

Everyone watched while the woman sniffed the liquid warily. Then she smelled the outside of the bowl. She turned to Aru. "Don't use this anymore!" she said.

"Whyever not?" asked Pippet, before Aru had a chance to respond.

"It's of no help to him. Sleep is the best healer for him right now, let's let him return to it." She carried the bowl away from the bedside. "We ought to get you back to work while we discuss this," she said, leading them back to their seats. As she crossed the room, and to Aru's dismay, she tossed the bowl and its contents into the fire. This made a loud whoosh and hiss. After the women were settled she spoke quietly, making it difficult for Lekki to hear. "I don't know if it's by design or by accident, but your friend there was being poisoned."

"Poisoned!" gasped all three at the same time.

"But, yarrow, it's not dangerous, such a small amount. People have been using it since time out of mind!" whispered Veya.

"Not the herbal, don't worry, Veya. The poison came from the bowl."

"But it was just a simple gourd bowl," said Aru, looking at the fire. "Were the carvings on it magic?"

"No, well—I don't know, but the bowl had been soaked in ourare." In response to the looks of incomprehension she explained, "A vicious toxin that causes paralysis. It's derived from the bark of certain shrubs. Climbing shrubs. It's the reason his cut is still bleeding. Ourare contains anticoagulant properties." Then she added, "Veya, where did you get the bowl?"

Thinking for a second, Veya replied, "It was just here in the Villa."

"Well," said their spinning teacher, "of course no one here would want to harm Lekki. It must have been acquired innocently. Perhaps bought from some shady hawker at a market or bazaar."

Aru looked at Eepe, who was busy picking the old jute out from between the floorboards. He'd been so good lately. "I think the bowl belongs to Aeon and Aldrei," she said, without really thinking. Then she sort of laughed. "Oh dear," she said, "that does sound rather like the type of thing they would own."

The others sort of laughed, too, and went back to their spinning. They each glanced over at Lekki once in a while, and into the fire also. The rag could be seen smoldering near the center of the fireplace for quite some time.

Once he was no longer being poisoned, Lekki came to life rather quickly. A short while after everyone else had left for the evening he said he felt he could walk back up to the inn. Aru convinced him to at least wait and have some supper first. Still a bit wobbly, he sat at the table with her. They talked about the poisoning and how lucky he was that the spinning teacher discovered it. How could she have known? Aru started talking about her and what a fascinating person she was, but Lekki didn't seem interested. He noticed the ring on Aru's finger and she told him she'd recently become engaged. He said that he was to be married also, to a girl from Opal Heights. By his expression Aru could tell that he cared for the girl.

When Lekki departed he left his carpet behind, saying, "Keep it, I have no use for it," and he walked up the trail into the darkness. He had refused the candle lantern that Aru offered. She stood there for a moment, watching him disappear, thinking about what a sullen mood he seemed to be in and how she'd probably never see him again.

The spinners worked outdoors the following day, because it was so nice out. Aru sat on a three-legged stool while pulling and winding the dark wool, shielded from the breeze by the Villa's fieldstone walls. She could feel the warmth of the sun on her face. A pair of fat ducks splat-splatted toward her across the muddy walkway, tottering the way they do and muttering happily. They sat by her feet to preen.

Aldrei had returned home—he said he knew nothing about the history of the gourd bowl—and he sat with the women, tipping back in his chair and smoking his pipe. The friends were talking about ideas for how to spend the women's upcoming leisure time. The spinning teacher had told them that tomorrow would be a free day, a result of a lull in the supply of fleece. A holiday just for the wool workers alone.

Pippet suggested they hike to someplace, maybe have a picnic in the barrens or explore the forest beyond Witch Tree Creek. Aru liked this idea. Veya liked it too, but felt more in the mood for curling up at home and finishing up knitting the caps for her nutcracker collection. She thought Pippet and the others ought to go, though.

Aldrei said he wasn't interested, but he did have a suggestion for Aru and Pippet. "Several hours walking, it will take you," he said, "but Toewrinkle Hot Springs would be a lovely destination."

"Oh, Toewrinkle!" said Veya, "I've not been up that way since I was a girl. That's a wonderful place! Oh, yeah, Pippet, that's a good idea."

"Toewrinkle, periwinkle, liver spots, eye twinkle!" mumbled Aldrei happily in his weird little way. "The trail starts at Porcupine Pass."

"I remember!" said Veya. "Lovely place."

"You'll be hiking east," he said, "along the mountainside and through a forest of red cedars more than a thousand years old, their trunks ten or more yards in girth. The terrain is steep and you must wend your way amongst formations of granite. When there comes a rushing sound you will know you've met the Tumbling River. Fast water, but so clear you can see every mayfly nymph and tadpole, every minnow skulking amidst the rocks and shallows of her bed. The trail turns uphill from the river, not far, and over one last small ridge to your destination.

"The hottest spring is in a cave, with a low rock wall built up across the entrance to contain it, and the water trickles out to cascade into a succession of several pools, each one cooler than its predecessor. The lowest pool is large, fed also by a showering waterfall that comes down the face of the cliff, and the outflow is a broad muddy creek which eventually drains to the river. Sitting inside the cave and looking out, you'll be in a steaming bath of shoulder-deep mineral water, lulled by the sounds of the trickles, and river, and the wildwood birdsong."

Pippet brought a picnic basket when she met Aru in the morning. Aru added a loaf of bread and a pot of freshly ground peanut butter to the contents. Veya had slipped some pralines and two delightful marzipan acorns in, along with a couple of bottles of thick root beer made by Pippet's father. The gingerbread boy thrall hopped into the basket too. There was no point in trying to expel the little scoundrel.

The girls had knives in wooden sheaths hanging from their belts, and also from Pippet's hung a needle case. This was shaped like a bell, with two needles through a strip of leather dangling inside it. They had on sturdy shoes and lightweight walking-skirts. It was another fine day, and so thrilling to have an unexpected holiday. The weather was unseasonably warm.

It felt strange in Aru's heart to set out somewhere without Nrouhw; she missed him. She did find an unexpected benefit of walking through the forest without him though. She saw deer. A lot of them. "Have you known many deer?" she asked Pippet.

"No, not really. I use to work with a deer a few years ago, but I didn't know him very good."

"Well, they tend to be . . . They're graceful. They're a graceful people, I mean to say, and they've keen sensitivity. As a species they're known to be intelligent," said Aru quietly, "but once I had a deer friend who, in animal form, was as dumb as toast."

They came to the river by mid-morning and followed the trail up the ridge as Aldrei had instructed. He hadn't mentioned how tough a climb it was up this last hill. *Actually, it might be described as a cliff,* thought Aru. Of course it wouldn't be scary to *him,* but Aru and Pippet had long skirts and a basket and a sense of mortality to contend with. By the time they reached the top they felt more than ready for a nice soak in the hot spring. Breathing heavily, they peered down into the narrow ravine on the other side. Aru's irritation toward Aldrei that had developed over the last ten minutes melted entirely away.

There, just as described, were the cascading pools, waterfalls, the opening of the cave. In addition to the falling water, sounds of the river echoed up into the canyon. Holding on to a tree trunk, Aru leaned forward so she could see better. A soft mist enhanced the beauty of the smooth rock surfaces, the pines and dormant maples and the three great cedars whose protective drapery of branches drooped low and curved upward again at the ends as though—A splash in the largest pool alerted Aru and Pippet to the fact they were not alone. Aru's palm went to her forehead, and then to her mouth, and then to Pippet's mouth because Pippet had started to titter. A man, sitting unnoticed, probably sunning himself on the rocks, had dived naked into the water and was swimming lazily. Not just any man, either. It was Lekki.

After performing the necessary job of physically dragging her giggling young friend out of sight distance, Aru sat down on a log with her head between her hands. Then she started giggling, too. "Well, that's a bit of rum luck!" she whispered.

"Can't we just go down?" begged Pippet.

Aru sighed.

"Well, if we just wait a while, he'll leave," Pippet said.

"No he won't," replied Aru. "Did you not notice? He'd pitched a tent by the waterfall."

"I didn't see it."

"It had a dark damask fabric; it blended with the patterns of the rock, somewhat. Although, if you didn't see it, I hate to think what you were looking at."

They fell to giggling again. The two considered making some noise, as a warning, and giving Lekki a chance to find his clothes. But then Aru reminded Pippet they hadn't brought any bathing costumes, so there would be no point. They may as well just head back down to the river and spend their day relaxing there. And so that is what they did.

Back to work after the holiday, Aru found her long hours slightly easier to bear, having had a break. Still, the poverty-stricken village way of life had worn her enthusiasm about Sylfaen quite thin. In some ways, this was no better than the factory. She hated seeing children without shoes, sometimes without enough to eat. Where was her and Nrouhw's land of opportunity?

When Nrouhw came home for a couple of days, he noted that Aru's light had dimmed. They hadn't intended to live apart. When he left again, he told her that he wouldn't be mining much longer.

Once more, what made things bearable was having friends. Aru spent time with her spindle and her companions, sitting on the soft sofa, drinking coffee, looking through the leaded glass window panes at winter as it crept in, filling the bare world outdoors with crispness.

As entertaining to each other as the three women were, they enjoyed it when Aldrei sat with them. They always looked forward to the teacher's visits, because of her stories, and once in a while the hedgehog Chuik would come by. His leg had healed quite well. It was Chuik who told them about the meetings.

They called themselves the Workers Efficiency Brigade, ostensibly under the auspices of Dominion Associated, but in fact most of their meetings were secret and concerned ideas which would not have pleased the Doms at all. The first meeting that Chuik brought Aru and Veya to was a secret one, down in the burrow of a large vole family. Here they referred to the organization as the Workers Emancipation Brigade.

Aru had never been in a rodent burrow before, and it proved a bit damp and dim for her liking. A steep narrow staircase led down to an arched hallway, where a mudroom smelled like pinecones and yesterday's strewn socks. The visitors, including the thrall, were led through the kitchen and into an enormous sitting room. The group had been meeting now for several weeks and had already built a substantial membership. Filled with the noise of conversation, the cavernous room overflowed with people from the village and outlying areas.

"Such a great turnout! There are chickens, squirrels, and marmots," said Chuik, "there's a marten, a donkey, a mole, an owl, and some otters. And of course voles. Sylfaen is overrun with voles these days. I saved you ladies a place there at the table."

"Oh, look, it's Rogue!" exclaimed Veya, looking toward a table as they weaved their way through the crowd. "And one of his friends."

"Yes, he was happy to hear you'd be coming tonight. Just right beside him, the fellow there, holding the teacup, is a dormouse friend of mine," Chuik said.

At the table, everyone was introduced. A young woman told the newcomers that, yes, she was a ferret, one of the few in her family who could be trusted to know about these meetings! Next to her smiled a woman about the same age whom Aru guessed was a badger. Rogue wanted Aru and Veya to meet his pal Bingo.

Veya said it was so nice to meet Bingo at last. Not his real name, of course. Bingo made his living as a fighter too.

The dormouse, a small round-headed pointy-nosed fellow, squinted at them, held out a handful of squished little mushrooms, mumbled, "Nobody ever remembers what I say," and fell directly to sleep.

"Whatever does he mean by that?" asked Veya.

Aru pressed her lips together and raised her eyebrows uncertainly.

At the next table were an otter and his granddaughter. They lived on the other side of the river down past the orchards and beyond the pickers' cabins. Pippet described in detail to Aru the roomy old cottage they had, made of small river stones and with a peaked tile roof. They'd come to these meetings because grandfather otter remembered what it was like in the bygone days, before the intrusion of the Doms on the family farm and the fisheries.

Aru also saw the man Hooey, whom she'd met in the forest. He must be the owl that Chuik had mentioned. He looked sleepy, but he smiled and returned her wave.

After a few minutes, a man stood up, drained his whiskey glass, inhaled a pinch of snuff, and strutted smartly across the room, bobbing his head as he walked. His destination was a tea table which was serving as a makeshift podium. Dressed in a showy tailcoat and spats, he looked at first like he really must be somebody.

"Oof, I can't stand that mister bumble-nuts!" whispered Veya. Seeing Aru's look of surprise that she'd speak so disparagingly of anyone, she added, "He's just a puffed-up stuff-shirt. He'll talk for forty minutes and say nothing understandable, you'll see."

The room quieted. Everyone clapped politely.

"Err, thank you," said the man. "Your flurry of fervor I certainly don't deserve!" he crowed. "Kok is my name, but that, I reckon, y'all recall." He tilted his narrow, crotchety face, peering obliquely at his audience. He paused longer than appropriate, looking around the room.

"I'm struck with the thought that the crowd's raucous talk takes pluck to block." He paused, and clucked his tongue. "But chalk it up to tough luck begot, not because we balk, but all we got must not be brought from what's run amok and in small talk be caught. Yet such a remark ought but be taught, and a securer charter for the earners assured!" A wattle of sagging skin under his chin trembled with each accentuation.

"A certain dire murmur I heard," he crowed, "has inferred by error to adjure you, in an effort to coerce the earners' work! I assure you, rather dirt-poor serf, erstwhile a tender server of the ermine, earnest and bitter worrier without a future, we'll secure you grandeur and burgeon your purse! I'm sure we're ever to endure!"

It was at about this point that Aru stopped listening. She didn't realize it until Pippet's soft voice drew her out of a daydream and she had a cup of coffee to accept.

With an insulting turgidity Kok did keep up his crowing for the longest time. Aru couldn't follow a thing he said, but she had a sense it wasn't important anyhow. She spent the time observing the others in the room. The dormouse snored softly, his nose nearly resting on his clenched hands in front of him. Three heavily pregnant women in pleated roughspun dresses sat together on the sofa, almost surely voles. A lot of folks were fidgeting or scratching or shifting in their seats. A man in the rear, standing and leaning back against the little harmonium, had dark eyes, bright and soulful. He looked like an interesting person, intelligent, and he dressed as if he had a bit of a liberal mindset. He must be the donkey Chuik had mentioned. Aru thought a couple of plump old biddies in the corner were the only ones actually listening to the presentation. Finally, and to no one's great disappointment, Kok surrendered the podium to the next speaker.

Aru had seen the tall, thin Yhaaat before, up in the village. He was the saddler's son, a talented leatherworker in his own right. Nrouhw had bought the new britchen for Aeon's packsaddle from him and the two had made plans to go hunting together sometime. Yhaaat had a serious and masculine but somehow kitten-like look to his face. He wore the dark chocolate-colored coat and golden buff vest he'd had on when she met him, but tonight had added an ascot.

Yhaaat wasn't skilled in public speaking either, but had several things to say. He began by giving a brief reminder about the purpose of their organization, the focus being to help the workers better their lives, and that the Workers Emancipation Brigade founders intended to give everyone equal say. Many of the meetings were secret because of the Doms' powerful influence in their lives. Each of the secret meetings were held in a different place and they were always in need of people to offer their homes.

He recalled that at the previous meeting one of the brigade members had been concerned that a ferret family who lived near the voles might be curious about the number of tonight's visitors. It had been decided that those who were able should bring something tonight, perhaps a sausage or few nuts or a piece of fruit. Aru and Veya had each brought a large, beautiful apple: Aru's a golden variety and Veya's a tart green. The idea was, the participants would pretend this was a harvest food-basket social and the next day mother vole would bring a nice basket over to the ferrets and to the mice next door. Yhaaat told the group that the food would be collected at the end of the meeting.

Mainly, though, Yhaaat talked about the prizefights. As soon as he brought the subject up some objections about them were raised. A local tradition, the dog fights had been under controversy these past few years, and just recently a new issue had developed. The matches took place at night in the barn by the pickers' cabins. The bighorn weavers had been having a terrible problem with youth gambling. They wanted certain regulations initiated. Some present at the meeting insisted that the fights be done away with entirely.

Yhaaat pointed out that while not everyone approved of the violence and so forth, the dog fights did draw in tourists and contribute needed income to the community. He went on to mention that an opportunity had come up. Rogue's friend Bingo—Yhaaat introduced him as an extraordinarily promising young upstart fighter—had just come to town and was looking for a backer. This was a special deal because the Doms planned to promote an upcoming tournament much more aggressively than usual and bring in fighters from a greater distance. The workers brigade members, who were keeping Bingo a secret, would sign him up at the last minute, throwing off the Doms' system of rigged bets. Besides a chance to make some profit by wagering, all this added up to a rare opportunity for investment if the members wanted to pool their money. This secret could not leave the room.

The audience tittered excitedly but the fact was, nobody had quite enough to feed their families, let alone money to invest. A marmot woman asked why they didn't let some of the rich folks up at Opal Heights know. Yhaaat explained that the workers brigade hoped to benefit those who lived here in Sylfaen.

The meeting lasted several hours, a boring, comfortable familiarity of folding chairs and coffee cups. Toward the end, it became rather hot and stuffy due to all the body heat and used-up air. As they were leaving, Aru tossed her apple into the collection basket by the door. "For the ferrets," she said.

Chuik insisted on escorting Aru home through the darkness. She had said good evening to him and was just finishing up her business in the outhouse when she started thinking about her early childhood. About when her mother had to reassure her that what went down into the dark void below the privy wasn't a part of her body. This led to wondering about how preverbal children think, and how the creatures think. How did they experience the world without the tools of language? What went through their minds when they were just sitting and doing nothing?

Aru stepped into the night, closing the door behind her. But as she did, her sapience traveled through the gateway in reality she had opened by having these fanciful thoughts. She, Aru, was still present. The chalet, its grounds, the maples, all were still there. But something was missing, disconnected. She had that horrible experience again, of not knowing what she or anything around her was. She knew the trees and the cottage were familiar, but she could only perceive them as foreign, as incomprehensible. Reality didn't make sense.

"Visyrn, you monster!" she cried, "Don't you do this! Don't do this to me!" Her depth perception and sense of everything's dimension and cohesion were confused. The world seemed big around her, everything loomed large. Aru felt lost in a mire of nothingness, in danger of never having existed at all. In panic, she lunged toward the cottage. As she lumbered across the yard, clutching her skirts and with a hand on top of her head, a booming voice that made no sound told her just the words, *NO MATTER*. (Nothing makes any difference, nothing is important.)

Aru burst into the cottage, grabbed a book from the kitchen table, and desperately started reading. The book was a detective novel she'd borrowed from Aranieda. She lost herself in the first few paragraphs she read, and in so doing quickly brought herself back to the world.

Aldrei had been napping. He stretched his arms and yawned as he walked past the table where Aru sat. Having grabbed the kettle, he peeked under his arm at her as he lit the stove. "Gently down the stream," he said softly.

They had some rye crackers with whey cheese and some mulled wine. The two talked far into the night. Aru didn't speak about her experience with nothingness. She told Aldrei about the meeting. Then she drifted into expressing her frustrations about life as a continuous cycle of work, a process without a purpose. She lived a happy life, yet she felt such angst. Time moved like a giant boulder tumbling down a hill, out of control and smashing through her days while she lived in ignorance, waiting for she didn't know what. How could people just work all day long, never seeming to question what life is? Aru needed to know what was going on. How could life be? How could everything exist? What is all this? What does reality mean?

Aldrei mostly listened. He agreed with her about the craziness of working all day for a pittance. "The reality of the situation is this:" he said, "what does not behoove one should give one pause." Aru snorted.

As a result of this evening with Aldrei and her philosophical effusion, Aru became more involved in developing and refining her stitchery craft. She recognized how good it felt to express originality through the artwork she made, something worthwhile to share with other people. It wasn't an answer for her, but it felt meaningful.

Bingo liked to fight. That gave him a purpose, apparently. Rogue didn't share these feelings; as a boy he had stepped into the ring only to avoid laboring in the mills like other young pups. However, now that fighting was all he knew, it was all he could do. The day after Nrouhw gave up on the mine and came home for good, Veya invited Aru and Nrouhw up for supper. Rogue was there, too.

Good food and good friends, and her Nrouhw home at last. Aru had a fine time. Conversation fell to the subject of the dogfights and she and Nrouhw found out something interesting. Rogue told them Lekki's father was considering putting up the money to back Bingo in the fights. Mr. Blackbuck was, apparently, known simply as Blackbuck. He would be giving Bingo a look-over that same evening at a training bout down at the barn.

"But how did he know about the opportunity?" asked Aru. "It was supposed to be secret, wasn't it?"

"Well," said Rogue, "he's a powerful man. There was a mole there at the meeting. Musta been *his* mole."

As Veya's husband needed to be up especially early the next morning, Aru and Nrouhw departed for home soon after the meal. Who should they bump into on the uphill path but Lekki. Aru felt thankful for the darkness, because she was certain her cheeks were slightly flushed. Lekki didn't know she'd seen him at Toewrinkle, but she knew.

They talked for a few minutes. Lekki had come to town again with his father, who was thinking of investing in a local fighter. He was on his way down right now to see the dogs spar. He invited them to come along. Nrouhw definitely wanted to go, and although Aru had absolutely no desire to watch a dogfight, she wanted to spend the evening with her beloved.

The barn smelled like kerosene from too many lamps and a lack of ventilation. A fight arena had been outlined with old moldy hay bales and some dirty cotton rope. Bingo and his sparring partner were there in the ring, attacking each other. They were dressed in their underpants! Aru found the whole scene quite discomforting.

Yhaaat, the marten, the young speaker from the meeting, stood with a couple of other people on the far side of the ring. One of these, a dignified gentleman, excessively handsome, could only be the Mr. Blackbuck. He had a commanding presence and an intimidating aura about him. Aru thought it just as well that Lekki had no interest in going to greet him.

Aru and the others stood and watched for a long time. She tried not to wince too much. She noticed that Nrouhw needed new boots. Those were getting holes in them.

The fighting went on. Bingo fought well but really didn't seem to be that amazing. At least that's what Lekki said. After a while it became apparent that Blackbuck was thinking the same thing. Finally, a point came when Blackbuck donned his hat and briskly shook the hand of the woman that stood with him and Yhaaat, preparing to take his leave. The woman said something that made Mr. Blackbuck change his mind, he turned and considered Bingo again, tapping his silver cane on the dirt floor. They rang the bell and the fighters took a break.

As Bingo sat getting his brow wiped by his trainer and guzzling water, something crazy happened. Another Bingo, identical to the real one, walked out of the shadows. He had on underpants of the same color; there was no difference between the two men except for a bit of spattered blood.

Aru had heard of identical twins before, but still it took a while to get over the shock of seeing a duplicate Bingo. This man climbed into the ring and took up where his brother had left off, easily wearing out the weary sparring partner. They intended to cheat the Doms by using a twin. Aru wasn't sure how she felt about that.

Aru and Nrouhw later heard, through Veya, that Rogue had said Blackbuck accepted the deal. He would finance the Bingos' training and entry fee for the big upcoming tournament. One of the Bingos (whether the original or his brother, Aru couldn't be sure) sat with Rogue again at the next workers brigade meeting. The spinning teacher was also there, and the woman who set Chuik's leg in the orchard that day. The speakers talked about how this boy Bingo could best any of the other fighters, and how Blackbuck had financed him, but no mention was made of his twin. During the course of this meeting the spinning teacher invited Aru and Veya to her house for tea the following day.

The teacher had taken up residence in the woods to the northeast, the opposite direction from the village and quite a bit uphill from the orchards. The slope was steep there, but the house was built right into the hillside. A welcoming front porch greeted Aru and Veya. Although the home stood under the trees it was a light and airy cob house with lots of windows.

They sat down in a quaint parlor, where tea and cookies waited. A phonograph played a piano sonata. Veya remarked about what a comfortable room she had there. Yes, thank you, their hostess said. She thought of it as her little hole in the wall, a lazy place to unwind.

The gingerbread boy sat playing with a ball of silk yarn as they talked. After a while it started rooting through the breakfront drawers and Aru had to scold it to make it stop. It had been acting more and more like a real child, had even spoken a couple of words a few days before. Not as though one could understand it, but still this was rather amazing.

Aru couldn't help but boast. "I've been telling stories to him, and reading novels aloud. He truly pays attention. He truly does. Little Eepe understands far more than one would expect; he's been searching out Aldrei's old texts for me to read to him—what was that one?—oh yes, *The Law of Conservation of Mass*, although there's no indication he comprehends it."

The teacher was clearly not supportive of Aru's interactions with the thrall. "Many stories about these insentients are heard among the whispers of the witches," she told her. "It's not a person, Aru. This thing can only mean you harm. Let me help you dispose of it."

But Aru had accepted the strange impish entity into her heart. "You don't understand," she insisted, "it does, after all, have a soul. It's coming more and more to life. I feel a certainty. A knowledge, a joyful knowledge, that I'm doing the right thing by him."

Veya suggested politely that Aru was off her nut. This did seem to be the case. Otherwise, they had a pleasant tea, and a chance to look at a couple of fine spinning wheels and a priceless imported loom. Before they knew it, time came to head home. Aru and Veya were just getting their coats when the spinning teacher had a thought. Would one of them please stay just a while longer and help her with something?

Veya had to go home, she had a cousin coming for supper, so Aru said she'd be happy to lend a hand. After affirming that she'd see Veya in the morning at the Villa, Aru stood talking in the foyer with the teacher, who was dressed in leather as usual and talked with her hands a lot. Aru couldn't keep herself from worrying that maybe this woman was actually the mad one. But the conversation was pleasant and intelligent and Aru found she enjoyed talking alone with the teacher.

"There's something that I must bring up," said Aru, "I feel embarrassed about it." She thought to herself that it must be worse, however, to let this go on. She sighed. "Since the day we met, in all this time, I haven't been able to remember your name! Everyone refers to you as 'the teacher' and I never hear your name used."

Aru held her breath while the teacher looked at her over her glasses. By her expression, Aru couldn't read her thoughts. "I'm not sure anyone in this village knows my name," she said, smiling. "But, oh! There's the kettle! Would you like some more tea?"

Aru said she was fine. The teacher went to take the kettle off the flame, and then she asked Aru to wait just a moment. She began acting decidedly odd. She walked around peeking out the windows, pulled all the blinds, and then beckoned to Aru to accompany her upstairs.

Up they went, and then along a hallway where all the doors were closed. Another stairway, a narrow one. They were headed to the attic!

They entered through a small passage. Looking around, everything seemed typical of a dusty attic in an old cob house. Empty picture frames leaned against a stack of crates, an old clothes horse was there, an ancient highchair with a doll sitting in it, a dartboard, a couple of wickerwork dress forms. The teacher led Aru to a small table where she righted a chair, dusted it off, and offered it to her. Then she got all the way down on her hands and knees, reached far back underneath the table and produced a bundle from behind. It was a carved wooden case about as long as a carpet beater, wrapped in a shawl. She sat down in the other chair with this in her lap, without even tidying the dust from her skirt.

Then, peering at Aru from the very corners of her eyes, she said in a low voice, "In the Bowne Forest, where I was born, they know me as Aranieda."

"That's a lovely name," said Aru.

"Aru," said Aranieda. "I must tell you some things in confidence. I'm certain that you can be trusted."

"All right . . ." said Aru, surprised. Strange. But secrets could be fun, sometimes. She leaned forward slightly.

"What I have here in my hands is an item of most grievous circumstances. It is the key to a clandestine undertaking which must be thwarted. I have been keeping this box safe, Aru, but for reasons I'm unable to share I can no longer do so."

"Oh," said Aru, a bit taken aback.

"You're the one who must take the box now, and bury it somewhere it won't be upturned by some inadvertent plow or shovel."

"Me?"

"You're associated with the box and its contents, although you don't know it. There's more, Aru. There's a reason this task falls to you."

"A reason this falls to me?" repeated Aru. "What could that be?"

"Because, Aru, there's something I know about you of which you are not yet aware." Aranieda sat looking up at the attic window, staring out into her own thoughts far away. She returned her attention to Aru, saying, "What do you know of your ancestry, Aru? Not much, I think. On your mother's side?"

"Well, I—" began Aru,

"You are from the star people, Aru."

Aru's mouth hung open. Yet, somehow, she already knew.

"This duty is thrust upon you because of who you are. There is a great deal that you can't be told right now, for your own protection. But you must rise to the challenge. So many vulnerable people depend on you." She continued, "Don't you find yourself looking up at the stars at night, Aru? Certainly you've wondered about your differences." Aranieda reached gently and placed her fingers on Aru's pale wrist.

"I, I don't—I . . ." stammered Aru.

"Your grandmother had a sense of who she was. She—"

"How do you know these things?" cried Aru, interrupting.

"Shhh, the walls have ears," said Aranieda gently, removing her hand. Then she added, "It's my line of business to know things. My girl, you carry the blood of nobility. And this not through your mysterious origins, as you suspect, but through your wolf side. Through relatives your great aunt went to visit in the east. We can talk more about this. Right now, it is important that you listen, you pay attention."

Aru started shaking her head. No, this was just too fantastic.

"This box, there are those who will seek it out. It absolutely must not be found. Take it to the woods somewhere and bury it deep. Don't let me know where." Aranieda handed the bundle to Aru, who received it as a matter of reflex more than intent.

"What's—" began Aru,

"You absolutely mustn't tell anyone. Not your friend Veya, certainly not the Pooka, and, Aru, you can't tell Nrouhw." She looked Aru deeply in the eyes. "There's another thing. On the honor of your royal blood, Aru, it will be difficult, but you cannot look inside. You cannot. You have to bury it unopened."

Late that evening at the Villa, in the hush and darkness, with their bed curtain drawn and amid excited whispers, Aru and Nrouhw unwrapped the box together. It was heavy. The shawl was silk, a burnt golden color, soft and pretty. Made of sweet-smelling chestnut wood, the box was carved all over with spiral and moon designs. On the lid, an image of a cornucopia spilling out live oak leaves and blossoms. A thin strip of dark buckskin bound the whole thing round and round, and there was a brass lock, although that was broken. They examined the box for a while, then wrapped it up, tucked it away, and got ready for bed.

The pair lay holding each other and whispering a conversation far into the night. Nrouhw didn't know what to think of it all, either. He'd suspected all along that this woman, Aranieda, worked for the Doms in some function beyond that of spinning supervisor. Aru had borne similar thoughts. They had no idea whether to trust the woman. Perhaps she had stolen this thing from the Doms. Nrouhw also said he wasn't surprised to learn that Aru had a royal heritage, as she had always said so. Yet how could Aranieda know all this about Aru? And he was hugely curious about what might be in the box. They agreed that Aru ought to go ahead and bury it as instructed. In case Aranieda was telling the truth.

Aru so much appreciated having Nrouhw and Aeon back home. Again there were evenings of camaraderie and backgammon. Sometimes Aeon would play the violin and Aldrei his rusty old accordion. One night Aldrei said that the Bingos would be fighting in the third match of the village tournament. Until now only one Bingo had fought; tonight the other twin would help out his brother. Their opponent was Bruiser, a local champion. This time Aru declined to go along, but Nrouhw and Aldrei went. They had a great time and were happy to give her and Aeon a full report, wanted or not.

Nrouhw's description was full of gusto. "They call out like this: 'Ladies! And gentlemen!' and launch into unnecessarily megaphoned preliminaries. And as soon as the fight starts everyone lights up their cigarettes and cigars and you just want to die . . ."

"The first man bit the dust almost immediately," said Aldrei.

"Things get pretty rough in the ring," agreed Nrouhw. "It's all vicious movements, and quick. Forceful, disciplined power and strength. The fighters are athletes and very focused."

"With their figurative hackles up," said Aldrei, "running with sweat, snarling, gritting their teeth and circling, trying to knock one another down. What could be more hilarious? I almost peed myself."

"This last part is true," said Nrouhw. "I'm not sure that Aldrei's cackling enthusiasm was appreciated." He elbowed Aldrei and they both laughed. "Anyhow, Bingo, or the twin named Rauf, that is, in his match he fought a decent fight but was well bloodied by the halftime. He had a nasty black eye forming and a torn ear.

"Ouaf, the other Bingo, he came out after the intermission, and Aru, if I didn't know they'd used stage makeup I never would have guessed. The black eye was amazing. It truly was. I saw him up close, you couldn't tell. I can't imagine how he had that done in so little time, what is intermission, five minutes? Oh, seven."

"So it fooled everyone, then," said Aeon. "Well, I, for one, don't mind showing up the Doms stoats and ferrets. They've had all these villagers on a tight rein for a long time now."

Aru asked if there were bighorn youth there.

"Oh yes," said Aldrei. "All four of them. Nothing the young sheep fellows like as much as a good head-to-head competition."

"What about the gambling?" asked Aru, "Were the young sheep doing a lot of that?"

Nrouhw shrugged. "It was crazy to watch. Everyone knows that nearly all the money goes to the Doms. These kids, and a lot of other people, they think they're going to make a profit. They're so disappointed, and surprised, when they don't win. Each round they're surprised. It's rather sad, really."

"Hysterical!" said Aldrei. "I had one old vole, drunk as a boiled owl, tell me the ghosts of his money were 'attackling' him. I told him 'No, dear, that's the apparition of your angry wife: 'Where's the rent?' Haha! Such a bumpkin!"

In the morning Aldrei and Aeon slept in, while Nrouhw and Aru, up early, had a chance to linger over a breakfast of eggs and steaming pumpernickel pudding. Nrouhw asked Aru about the box. She told him she hadn't actually taken care of it yet. The truth was, she struggled with the idea of burying the box while having no idea what it contained.

While the others were preparing supper that evening, Aru closed herself behind the bed curtains and pulled the box from its hiding place. She lit the bedside candle and climbed up onto the bed beside the box. She'd done this several times already, examining the case carefully and running her fingers over the carvings. This time, her fingers came to rest on the knot that tied the leather thong which bound the box tight. She bit her lip. In a moment, the box was free.

Aru looked at the curtain in the direction of her busy friends in the kitchen. She could hear the three of them laughing, clanking things, and Aeon singing some silly song. She looked back at the box. Quietly the broken lock came out of the hasp. She held her breath as she slowly, silently pushed the lid upward. The case was lined with crushed velvet. Dark amber in color, so soft. The contents were wrapped in another cloth, a piece of fine woven wool. It felt like cashmere. Aru looked toward her friends again.

A musty smell came from the case. Aru reached for the object within as delicately as one would reach for a baby in a cradle. It felt hard and smooth through the fabric. As she lifted it out she thought it must be a rod of glass. It was too thick, too sinuous and uneven to be a flute. Her breath came short and her heart beat right in her throat as she pulled away the wrapping. Without thinking, she gasped.

Aru held a carved staff of crystal, the clearest of crystal so pure it appeared luminous. One end was a horse's head, nostrils flaring wide. The thing felt magic, and alluring, so absolutely beautiful. Carved into such detail . . . Not a horse, a dragon! It was a roaring dragon, a winged serpent long and thin, with batlike wings folded tightly and legs clenched against its length in scrolling curves. Aru had never seen anything so extraordinary. She quickly wrapped it back in the cloth and slipped it into its box. A monogram had been embroidered on the corner of the wrapping, daintily stitched: *A. B.* Softly, she closed the lid. She polished a bit of dirt off the inside of a curlicue on the carved top with her finger. She wrapped it up, restored it to its hiding place, and went to supper.

A few days later the light of dawn touched the frozen slope high above the villa to reveal a light-skinned young woman in an old tweed frock coat moving among the thick trunks of the pines. With mittened hands Aru shifted a small piece of metal roofing to uncover a hole in the ground. From this hole she carefully shovelled out a bunch of smoldering coal and hickory chunks and tossed them onto an ice-encrusted mud puddle, where they sizzled. She dug the hole deeper. At last it was deep enough.

From a gunny sack Aru produced the long box wrapped in silk which had been entrusted to her. A spider, crouched in the crevices of the pine bark above, and a small, nondescript, sparrow-like bird both paused to watch her take one last look at the carved chestnut box before she returned it to the sack and then stuffed it into the hole. After she buried it she scattered needles and cones to cover the disturbed area. "There. At last I've done it," she said softly.

It was about this time that something horrible nearly happened. Aldrei and Aeon had gone for the day, and Aru and Nrouhw were on their way out also, when Nrouhw said he smelled something. "That's odd," he said, "it smells like burnt maple."

Someone had lit a candle and set it on a shelf of the bookcase. The underside of the shelf above was blistering and had started to char. They caught it only just in time. It was obvious who had done it, and Nrouhw was furious.

"He didn't know," said Aru. "He's just learning about life." Her voice wasn't quite as certain as it had been the last time she defended him.

"It knew, Aru. The only question is what reason it would have for burning the Villa down."

About a fortnight later Aru and Aeon's evening cribbage game was interrupted by Nrouhw. Rummaging under the bed for a misplaced paintbrush, a special sable filbert, he had stumbled across something wrapped in an old homespun pillowcase. Aru responded to his call to find him standing over the crystal dragon which now lay upon the paisley cashmere on top of the bedquilt. He was completely captivated.

When he noticed Aru there next to him he whispered, "Aru," and gestured to the staff, "what in the world?"

They both stared at the staff. Nrouhw picked it up; it glittered in the candlelight. The fact of the matter is, only an artisan possessed with magical ability could produce a thing so stylized and yet so real; a natural-looking monster effortlessly posing in the form of a baton. Curled claws rested against the snarling jaw, reflecting the curve of it and initiating a pattern of writhe and gnarl that followed along the folded wings and then the powerful rear legs to the loop of curled tail at the bottom end. Whorled horns, scalloped frill, long sharp teeth—everything was carved to the tiniest detail.

"This's what the box held?" he whispered. "I thought you buried it."

"I couldn't do it, Nrouhw, I just couldn't. I buried the empty box."

"To fool Aranieda?"

The two whispered, "I'm sure she was watching," at the same time. Aru laughed.

Nrouhw wrapped the staff back in the cloth.

"Look," said Aru in Nrouhw's ear. "The initials, A. B. Lekki goes by a middle name. His first name, I can't remember it, but it starts with A. A-something Blackbuck. And the carvings on the box, they looked like antelope designs, don't you think?"

"They did look antelope," said Nrouhw. "Smelled of antelope also, and this cloth. Definitely antelope wool."

"I've always had a feeling about Lekki. I don't trust him."

"But why would Aranieda have you bury something of Lekki's?"

"I know. It doesn't make sense."

The community meetings continued each week, and Aru and Veya made it to most of them. Nrouhw and Pippet generally came too. Usually these gatherings took place in underground homes or one of the hillside dugouts, and under cramped conditions. At these workers brigade meetings Aru and Nrouhw got to know some of their neighbors better and were invited to the occasional lively home evening spent in the company of fiddles, mandolins, and whiskey jugs.

It was at one of the February meetings that shocking news was announced. An undercover gambling commission agent had been in town recently to investigate the fights. She had discovered a devious duplicity. Bingo, it was found, had an identical twin who had been in collusion with him to cheat at the tournaments. The pair of them had been posing as one fighter in order to unfairly wear down their opponent. Both of these unsavory people had been arrested and taken away and all funds had been confiscated. What a fortunate thing, after all, that the workers brigade hadn't invested.

Most of this was reported by the young marten, Yhaaat. Kok the rooster commented, though, and spent twenty-five minutes explaining his objections to Yhaaat's unfortunate use of the word "chicanery."

Aru and Nrouhw discussed the announcement with their friends at the Villa later that night. What did this mean for the village? Sylfaen didn't have any star attraction at the upcoming tournament. How was Rogue taking this turn of events? He hadn't been at the meeting.

Some little time after this, Sylfaen experienced an influx of wealthy tourists. A poor farming village, it usually counted on a trickle of tourism, mostly in the summer months. One dim and dingy morning Aru, Veya and Pippet talked about the current events by lamplight as they spun their wool. Aranieda arrived, and joined the conversation.

Town was filled with shrew- and mouse-looking people, dressed to the nines. Pippet said she heard there were several thrushes and some grouse staying at the inn. The inn was full and some folks were renting their cottages out, sleeping in the community barns themselves. Aranieda said that she'd heard some things from their hedgehog friend Chuik. Apparently, hypogeous snails were being served at the inn. People were flocking to the area from as far away as the Southern Reaches in order to taste these snails.

"Hypogiss snails?" Aru had never heard of them.

"Hypogeous."

"What are those?" asked Pippet.

"Hypogeous snails are a type of subterranean mollusk which is extremely rare and of great value to those who crave them," said Aranieda.

Aru explained, "Snails that live underground."

"Oh, my!" said Veya.

Pippet laughed, "Ooh, I wouldn't mind trying some!"

Aranieda had a strange grin that Aru couldn't interpret. She spoke quietly, "It's not likely you'll have a chance, though, or any of us. Those little delicacies come surprisingly dear. Only for the wealthy."

"Give me a bucket full of the good ol' garden variety, and I'll be happy—" Veya was just saying, when the sofa where she sat began to tremble. In fact it began to shake.

The overhead lamp swung on its chain, the cupboards and crockery rattled, everything wiggled and moved. Stupefied, the women stared helplessly at the shuddering room around them. The thrall started shrieking like an excited monkey. Brains do weird things in times of crisis, and Aru's was wondering, *How can a freight train be roaring past the cottage?*

Aranieda grabbed Aru, who was seated next to her, and dragged her under the table, shouting, "Everyone seek cover!" She clutched Aru with one arm and the stout table leg with the other.

Veya and Pippet joined them under the table. Aldrei appeared on the stairs from the loft, gripping the doorframe with his long fingers. The cottage continued to shake, things crashing from shelves and off of walls. A cupboard door swung open, a jar of beans falling to burst on the wooden floor. Through it all, the roaring, the horrifying shaking, Aru had a clear view of old Aldrei bracing himself calmly in the doorway, looking down at the floor, and above the rumbling she could hear him say just one word, "Grmhrel."

The shaking seemed to go on for a long time, but really it lasted less than a minute. When stillness returned they waited a moment, but the quake had ended as definitely as it had begun. Quickly they made sure that no one was hurt. The Villa seemed okay too. Aru thought of Nrouhw, who'd left at dawn to paint on the canyon rim. A feeling of dread percolated from her gut up through her midriff; bringing numbness to her chest, her face, her hands. Vaguely she noticed that the glass from his favorite photo had smashed, and several dishes had broken, including a soup tureen given her by Tsirp, the innkeeper she'd become friends with in the village of Loess just before she and Nrouhw entered the desert.

Finding themselves all right, the occupants of the Villa ventured outdoors to check on their neighbors. On the main path they met a small plump man who told them he'd heard by way of sparrow that the old smithy up in the village had partially collapsed. While they were talking, Nrouhw arrived from where he'd been painting near the cliffs. He and Aru embraced. After a short discussion, the men headed up to the village. Aru went with her squirrel friends to make sure Veya's mother and Chirra were safe and to find out if the treehouse made it all right and to look after others in the orchard area. Aranieda departed for her own home.

Chirra and her grandmother met them on the trail, uninjured and only slightly shaken. From beneath, the treehouse appeared to be fine, so Veya decided to investigate the condition of an elderly neighbor. As they walked back out toward the edge of the orchard, Pippet cried, "Look!" and pointed toward the upper slopes. A nasty gash had appeared in the hillside, as if some huge giant had cut out a section of the mountain and tossed it into the farmland below. A landslide.

"That's where Aranieda's house is!" gasped Aru.

"No . . . no, her house is farther along toward the river," Veya said. "I'm sure of it. Past those big cedars. There's no houses along that area, it's too steep."

Aru knew Veya was right, but still she felt compelled to make sure. She left Veya and Pippet to look after the old lady and hurried off up the slope. Forced to make a wide detour around the muddy rubble, she felt sad for the farmers who worked those fields. What a mess. And up above, the devastation of the mountainside looked strange. Astonishing! Trees of the forest lined the gaping new cliff right to the rim; forest and mountain sliced away like a great cake.

When Aru finally recognized the pathway to Aranieda's, and saw it leading away from the slide area, she felt relieved. But she kept on walking. When the house finally came into view, she stopped in midstride.

Yes, it was well clear of the landslide area, but nonetheless a giant boulder had tumbled down the hill from above, flattening small trees and smashing right through a corner of Aranieda's house. The massive rock had continued on down the slope, creating a huge furrow as it went, and had come to rest against a cluster of thick pines, splitting the trunks of two of them into matchwood. The house remained on its foundation, but part of an upstairs room and all of a downstairs room sat open to the world.

Aru just stood there. How strange to see the furniture—a desk, a great wardrobe, a table—sitting visible in the rooms, like in a dollhouse. The house looked like an enormous dollhouse.

Aranieda's movement among the scattered debris snapped Aru out of her daze. She went to offer her help. Aranieda had already set to work collecting her belongings that the boulder and the wind had strewn. She didn't seem to be particularly vexed by the disaster. One of the rooms involved had been her study, and there were photographs and papers everywhere, she gathered them systematically. When Aru went to her, Aranieda enquired about the status of Veya's treehouse.

"Oh, I can't believe it! How could this happen, Aranieda? Are you going to be all right?" exclaimed Aru. "Oh, yes, Veya's tree seems fine." Aru looked around. "How could this happen?" she repeated.

Aranieda paused for a moment and smiled slightly, speaking to herself as much as to Aru, "I guess I cultivated Grmhrel's anger a little too long." Then she went back to gathering her papers and things.

"Who is Grmhrel?" asked Aru as she bent to help with the papers before they all blew down the hill. Little Eepe, who generally wiggled and squirmed as he rode in his sling, went stock still.

Aranieda paused again. She wiped her mouth with the back of her wrist. Picking up a chunk of crumbled masonry, she held it for a moment while she spoke. "He's a monster, Grmhrel is, I suppose you'd say. Not an ogre, though. He's a guardian of down below. The lower world. I'm surprised you haven't heard of him," she said. Then she threw the cob chunk onto a spot where a couple of other chunks lay, to start a pile.

"No, I never have," said Aru.

"In any case, you might have seen his image somewhere. He has a wolfish appearance. He has horns, though. Horns like a water buffalo."

Aru wondered if he could fly.

"No," said Aranieda, "he's a lord of the caves and the underground. His mane is made of snakes; his serpent tail has a monstrous rattle on the end."

"Oh, my," said Aru. "Is he real?"

"What kind of a question is that?" Aranieda laughed, "Are *you* real?"

Aru didn't know how to answer that.

They worked together for a while, collecting household items and sorting through rubble and bits of wooden lath. Aru took Eepe out of his sling to let him amuse himself. A gust of wind blew a swirl of leaves and a bunch of the papers down the hill, and as Aranieda scurried off to retrieve her papers Aru focused on the area close to the house. She pulled a couple of notebooks out from under some boards, and rescued some smudged tintypes of city scenes from the frost-encrusted dirt. There was also a scroll bound on wooden rods, curiously small. As she picked this up, Aru saw Aldrei's name scrawled on the outside of it! She took a quick glance over her shoulder. Aranieda had bent down to grab the last of the fly-away papers. With a brazen impulse, Aru shoved the scroll down into the big deerskin pocket she had on under her skirts. The thrall, who was nearby, poking at random things with a stick, saw her do this. It shrieked. Aranieda looked up to see what was going on, putting Aru in the position of trying to look innocent. "He must have scared himself, somehow," said Aru. She felt rotten.

Late that same evening, Nrouhw and Aru sat on the sofa together discussing the strange events of the day, and the weird scroll which bore their friend's name. Aldrei had gone out on some business; Aeon's gentle snores floated down from the loft.

"Repairing her home," Nrouhw was saying, "that's just a part of life her type comes to expect, isn't it." In response to Aru's expressionless face he added, "You do know she's a spider, Aru, right?"

Aru blinked. "Seems obvious, now that it's, well . . . obvious."

"Well, what did you think she was?"

"I—I don't know, a bat, maybe."

"A bat named Aranieda."

"I never thought about it. Invertebrate transforms are so rare nowadays. She's such a peculiar person. What'd she be doing with this?"

Aru unfurled the parchment, just a short paper with a single verse quilled in delicate calligraphy. A title was scrawled by a different hand across the left margin, *The Bowne Recluse's Directive*.

Lavish curls and flourishes formed a script so fine as to be almost invisible in the candlelight:

> Unbidden must Auricomous mind the star
> And so confound He who bridles the raging winds.
> For what does a Hobgoblin care of the two worlds?
> But fondness for the Ingenuous, the naive
> Will keep safe the golden Nymph and so what casket's hidden.
> Call upon the One of unbounded guile as bespoken.
> Let it be.

Nrouhw cleared his throat. "This is more than a little odd, isn't it. Have you worked out what it means?"

"Well, auricomous, that means golden-haired, right?"

"It does?"

"Yes, I looked it up. So this almost certainly is about me. I can't imagine who the Bowne Recluse is, but how does this person know anything about me? And then the hob, that's sure to be Aldrei, as his name was written right on the scroll itself."

"Or at least Aranieda thinks so."

"Anyhow, I've been thinking, it has to be about the crystal. Look, the second line, '. . . confound he who bridles the raging winds.' That's Lekki. His magic carpet. He rides the wind. So the star, that's the crystal dragon and this is about keeping the crystal safe from Lekki."

"Could be. So Aranieda gave you the crystal to hide because Aldrei will protect you and therefore the crystal. She's using his power to guard it."

"Yes. I suppose you're right. That makes sense," said Aru. "Why wouldn't she just ask for his help?"

"Aru, this is Aldrei we're speaking of. He has no reason to care about spiders and their problems, or any concern whatsoever about acting in an honorable way. If indeed these intentions are honorable."

"We've already determined that she stole the crystal from Lekki to begin with. Now we know why she gave it to me to bury."

"Except, what's this whole thing all about?" said Nrouhw, brushing the hair back from Aru's temple. "We know Aranieda works for the

Doms. Why should the Doms have such concern about keeping the crystal dragon from Lekki? I suppose it gives him some sort of control over one of their assets. It feels as if it bears a strong magic."

"I don't know, but this has got me thinking about a lot of things," said Aru. "Do you suppose it's a coincidence that Lekki had his accident just behind our house? Or do you think he planned the whole thing, looking for the dragon? It may be that he knew of Aranieda's intent to pass it to me."

"He went through a lot of pain. Would he purposely crash into the hillside? What sort of person would do that?"

"And . . ." began Aru,

"And," continued Nrouhw, "how does all this involve you? Aranieda says you are a princess."

Aru smiled. "I've always known it!" she said.

The next time Aranieda's name came up in interesting conversation was when Veya heard some gossip from a couple of voles she knew from the workers meetings. Apparently Aranieda had nearly had her head ripped off trying to awaken a sleeping bear with a stick. Old Muhg-Wuffle liked to spend most of his winter days in fur form, sleeping in his den under an ancient hawthorn that grew a good way beyond the river. His cave was deep down in the ground and only accessible through a narrow tunnel that twisted among the extensive roots of the tree. The bear could only fit through the tunnel when in human form.

The story was that a sparrowhawk, in deft flight weaving between the twiggy branches of the hedgerow in pursuit of a mouse, had witnessed the entire hullabaloo. Just as she swept past the great hollow hawthorn she heard a thundering roar and a scream from down within. Frightened, she circled and perched on a crooked branch and cocked her head to listen. After a few moments she heard a woman's voice coming up through the opening in the tree. It sounded as if she were a short way down the tunnel, shouting down to Muhg-Wuffle in his den below. "What ever did you have to do that for? I'm bleeding horribly. From my neck!"

Rumbles and growls followed, and after a while Muhg-Wuffle's muffled human voice rose from the depths. He apologized unenthusiastically, telling the woman that he'd been dreaming deeply and when she poked at him he thought she was a tiger. They talked for a few minutes before the woman apparently returned to the den area to speak with him. During that bit of conversation the sparrowhawk learned the woman was the spinning teacher, that strange woman from the eastern coast.

"Whatever business she had with him," one of the voles had said, "why couldn't she have waited? He would've been well awake within a month or so anyhow. Now he'll be grumpy all spring, watch and see."

Nrouhw and Aru were outdoors one evening, dyeing their big old rag rug with a preparation of walnut shells and acorn tops which Veya had made for them. She'd said the walnuts came from a grove accidentally planted by a forgetful relative. Aru handled the rug using a pair of sticks, but even so she thought her hands would be forever stained. While they struggled with the rug and the dye, Aranieda came by with a basket of buckeye nuts for Nrouhw. He wanted them for the tannic acid he used in treating leather. Aranieda sat and talked with the couple for a while, watching them work.

As he stirred the dye kettle, Nrouhw asked Aranieda what had ever become of Ouaf and Rauf, the Bingo twins.

"It's a bit of a story," said Aranieda hesitantly. She could see that Aru and Nrouhw would have nothing but to hear it. "All right, then. For all these months since we arrived in this area—"

"We?" exclaimed Aru.

Aranieda only smiled and finished her sentence, ". . . I have been working to bring the Blackbuck under control. He is an arrogant man who consistently commits unethical acts. He is especially harmful to the people he supposedly watches over as king on the eastern coast. In my efforts to subdue him, I've also made an attempt to improve the conditions of this wretched Sylfaen."

Aru interrupted again, "But Sylfaen isn't an awful place. Such healthy mountain air it has, and the people are happy, always laughing. They are poor, and that's a shame."

"Aru," said Aranieda, "the poverty is extreme. The villagers are uneducated sharecroppers on their own ancestral land. They are cheery, yes, but not happy. The infant mortality rate is alarmingly high. This is reprehensible."

"Mmm, yes, I wasn't thinking about the backwardness here," said Aru. "I suppose I've come to see it as normal."

"At any rate, I'd been searching for a way to fund the purchase of the snails I needed for my plan. When I learned of the upcoming dogfight tournament, I realized this held my answer. I recruited the fighter twins, offering them a share of the spoils if they'd come to town. I instructed one of them to befriend Rogue. They posed as a single fighter, a scam that would likely stir Blackbuck's interest. I then sent the mole to the workers meeting, promising her many snails if she'd tell Blackbuck what she'd heard at the meeting about the investment opportunity."

"It was *your* mole!" gasped Aru.

"Yes. After Blackbuck invested a large amount of money to back the Bingos, the gambling commission agent discovered their fraud. Except, the agent was not actually an agent. An acquaintance of mine, she formerly made her living as an actress down by the docks in a city on the coast. She and the Bingos each left town with a share of Blackbuck's investment money, leaving me enough to purchase a healthy amount of hypogeous snails to sell to the innkeeper at an amazingly low price."

Aranieda paused for a moment. Aru could see the curiosity welling up inside Nrouhw. "But why?" he asked, "In what way could the innkeeper's good fortune aid in your plan to bring down Blackbuck?"

"It's all so simple, in truth!" replied Aranieda. "I only needed to convince the Blackbuck that a source of the rare and valuable hypogeous snails, a commodity with which he has become obsessed, is available to him locally."

She seemed about to explain the reason for this, but Veya and a friend of hers arrived to find out how the dye project was progressing. They all stood talking, and as they munched on molasses cookies which Veya had brought the stars began to appear in the sky.

"My!" exclaimed Veya's friend. "Will ya look at that! How time goes on! The springtime sky is here."

The season was soon turning, indeed, but Aru felt irked that winter just wouldn't let go of its grip. Frozen mornings and muddy afternoons kept coming, and days on end would go by without the sun poking through. With the weather so drab it felt good to be inside, filling up with coffee. Radiant warmth came from the split walnut and maple logs in the fireplace. Nrouhw busied himself with sketching and painting. No longer spinning wool for the Doms, Aru and the others were now sorting and cleaning scraps and clippings from the finishing of the garments and blankets made by the sheep. Several large bags would be dropped off each morning at the Villa, and the sorted wool retrieved.

When she wasn't working with the wool or on her embroidery, Aru spent much of her time reading to the thrall or teaching it simple concepts such as how to add or to tell time. Although Eepe couldn't speak, Aru told Veya and Pippet that he was quite clever and learned quickly. She made him a little pair of pants and helped him to sew on the button. Veya could see that Aru had a gift for teaching, and no harm in her having fun, but really she mustn't go on with this thinking the thing was a real boy.

The days ticked on, comfortable and quiet, if somewhat boring. Then Veya and Pippet began to chatter about the vernal celebration up in the village. A four-day-long event, a ceremonial welcome to spring, Agor reigned as the greatest holiday of the year in the farmland areas.

Sylfaen transformed into a carnival, with residents coming out of the woodwork to participate. It gave Aru quite a shock to see how many actually lived in the vicinity. The Doms were not an influence here. Traditions of the season thrust aside any divisions among the people while everyone enjoyed freedom, equality, and a chance to parade about with a certain anonymity, wearing masks or painted faces. The village took a deep breath of its own fresh mountain air.

Up on the bluff, right above the road leading along the crest to the village, was a nice flat area. A naturally terraced slope, scattered with newly-budding fruit trees and scrubby bushes, led up from there to the plateau, which was surmounted on its end by a knob with a farmhouse on top. All of this was covered with booths and pavilions; there must have been twenty or more hawkers camped there.

The wares were exotic, and at considerably high prices for Sylfaen, but folks saved for this all year, especially the squirrels. Aru and

Nrouhw couldn't afford to buy, but had a great time picking through the items brought from far away. Nrouhw enjoyed investigating the table of gentlemen's grooming supplies.

Eventually, Aru and Nrouhw, with Eepe following, made their way up to the crown of the bluff, from where the dizzying height of Sylfaen village was especially noticeable. In all this time, Aru hadn't quite got used to the view. They met Veya and her family, as planned. Hooey the owl was with them. He was a bit ruffled. Whenever he went out during daylight hours, people he spoke to fretted that someone they knew must be about to die.

Hooey strolled along with Aru, Nrouhw and the squirrel family. The young girls jabbered, reciting the entire known history of the fair. They explained the egg rituals, and the face painting, and showed Aru the stall with hollow chocolate rabbits. Veya pulled Aru and Nrouhw aside, though, at one point. She whispered that Pippet had a premonition that morning. Something bad would happen at Agor this year.

Singing, dancing, storytelling, and eating continued throughout the course of the celebration. During the nights torches lit everything and nobody slept except the children, save for perhaps a brief nap here or there. Gallons of coffee and Agor brew were drunk, the latter being a special tea made of mushrooms and herbs. The tea was a stimulant and helped supply energy for the festivities but it was also a purge and sent the revelers to the outhouse quite often.

All the locals Aru knew and lots of people she'd never seen before were in attendance. Veya's family seemed to know nearly everyone, despite the masked faces. Aranieda spent some time with Aru, Nrouhw, Aeon and the squirrels on one of the afternoons, sitting around a bonfire. Aru noticed that Aranieda wore a snuff-colored lace scarf to hide the lesion on her neck. Aldrei had been missing for several days.

Of all the celebration's fun, what most impressed Aru were the puppets. On the second afternoon, the curtains of a large booth in one of the rows of stalls were pulled back to reveal that it was filled with glorious wooden puppets. They were birds, all of them, birds of every description, from hawks and owls to sparrows, wrens, and thrushes. Many had articulated wings. Some were marionettes, others could be affixed to sticks or poles, where they would make flying motions when moved up and down. Carved by the local woodworkers, these puppets were available for anyone to use and soon the crowded festival was filled with them.

During the last evening of the festival, Nrouhw and Aru decided to carry puppets. Most of the revelers were in quite a giddy mood by this time, having had little sleep. Veya and her family were off doing something else, but Aeon, in human form, was with Aru. Nrouhw met them at the puppet stand after having gone off with Hooey to look for some mouse-on-a-stick. Aru, Nrouhw, and Aeon entered the booth and began amusing themselves with the bird puppets as they selected the ones they'd like to carry.

Eepe acted like a naughty child, disturbing things for no reason, and he stuck bits of straw into one of the torches to make it crackle. Nrouhw deterred Eepe's further actions with a growl. However, while the friends were making silly jokes about the woodcock, the woodpeckers, and the nutcrackers, Eepe climbed unnoticed onto a high shelf containing unpainted songbirds, sweet and handsome birdies with feathery egg-shaped bodies and short pointy beaks. He poked at the lark, and with his stubby foot gave the wren a shove; he climbed over the thrush to examine the sparrow. Then, another shelf of small perching birds caught his eye.

"Down from there, you!" snarled Nrouhw.

They left the booth with gorgeous puppets that clacked and jingled, and one small and pouting gingerbread boy in tow.

Happy exhaustion makes life a dream, and although Aru had a fantastic time she couldn't remember much of it later. She and Nrouhw danced for hours, and then sat with Veya and family watching the crowd. An argument broke out nearby. Kok the rooster was squawking at a big pot-bellied man with thick greasy hair. Kok was really stewed about something. The man acted groggy; perhaps he'd had too much beer to drink.

"Father!" shouted Kok. "Curse your blundering fur!"

"I'm just a big dumb bear," moaned the man. "How would I know I wasn't to do it?"

"It's Old Muhg-Wuffle," whispered Veya to Aru. "I didn't recognize him, he's looking pretty rough, poor fellow. I've never seen him at Agor before."

"He's normally asleep at this time," said Aeon.

This led to discussion as to why Aranieda would want to wake up a dormant bear. Nobody had any plausible idea.

Veya and her husband explained that, at dawn, a monster would arrive. A hideous thing.

Aru yawned. "Pardon me," she said, "I'm feeling so woozy, I'm not certain I can stay awake until the dawn."

"Oh, my—That's the nutmeat of the whole ceremony! That's when the monster comes!"

"A giant boor!" trilled Chirra, dancing on her toes.

"A giant wild boar," said Pippet.

Chirra nodded vigorously. "A wild boor! A scary big one, made from rags and mud and gunpowder; an' the little blindfold children set it on fire and push it over the—"

"Now Chirra, don't jabber and let on about it all!" said her father.

"Come, now. The play is about to start."

"After the play, the monster!"

"Chirra! Hush!"

The ritual play took place in the inn garden. Not everyone could fit in the garden, because absolutely everyone attended, but folks crowded all around, and most of them could see. It was a mass of people and bird puppets. Aru and Nrouhw had tired of carrying theirs and planted them in the hillside with a host of others to watch over the ceremonies with their lifelike eyes. The play began. Dancers wore fabulously grotesque old-woman masks and oversized headscarves, and burlap dresses covered in flat wooden spoons. These costumed players swept the ground with willow brooms, showering everyone with dust, making people laugh and cough. They threw toffees wrapped in wax paper. Children dove for the candy. Eepe dove too. He dove into the crowd.

"Get back here!" called Aru, as she hoisted her skirts and squeezed through the tightly-packed crowd of merrymakers.

Munching on something, Nrouhw looked after her, half-wondering why she would even want to pursue the thrall. Then his groggy attention returned to the festivities.

Eepe stayed barely out of reach as Aru chased him through the crowd. He darted up the hill. Clear on the other end of the bluff, he stopped. He performed a toe-slapping, pigeon-winging jig to taunt her. Nearly out of breath, she caught him, grabbing him by the festive bow she'd tied around his neck. Despite herself, she shook him, hard, and scolded him. The thrall narrowed his eyes and glared at her. He kept glaring at her as she carried him, and he scowled.

Aru also scowled as she gripped him. Again, she'd lost her self-control. Feeling some shame, she walked along the makeshift lane between the market wagons. Oblivious to the bright colors and exotic smells, she could only think of the play that she was missing. But Eepe saw a sign on a big amber-colored van and he started squeaking. Such a piercing noise, even above the sounds from the crowd. It hurt the ears. He wiggled. He became so excited that Aru stopped to see what had him in such a frenzy. It was only a coffee stall.

The sign read:

GWYLLT MOUNTAIN COFFEE CO.

FILL YOUR CUP.

MIND YOUR ANTY.

Underneath, it read:

LIWIYCH

—JEWEL OF THE EASTERN SEABOARD—

"Silly Eepe!" scolded Aru, "What are you thinking?" She stopped for a moment, and looked at the sign. Pride crept onto her face. "You remembered, didn't you, that Gwyllt is a remarkable coffee. How thoughtful, Eepe! How thoughtful! But we need to get back, I'm missing everything!"

A man by the booth called out to her. The hair rose on the back of Aru's neck. "Come," he said, beckoning.

"We're on our way back down to the festival," answered Aru. "We'll stop by for a cup after!"

"Come here," he repeated. He motioned with his finger.

Aru ignored him and passed on by. But Eepe lurched at her face, slapped her on the nose, and squirmed out of her grasp. He jumped up and down in front of her. Aru swiped to grab him, but missed. She chased again, as he ran back to the stand, and into the coffee tent.

Panting, Aru stood looking at the man. He crouched in the dirt near the entrance, his long, twiggy legs splayed wide. He sipped a cup of coffee while staring at her. With his beady eyes, he assessed her as one would a horse or an ox at the market. Aru didn't like him.

He sounded smug. "Your gingerbread man wants a cuppa coffee."

Aru should have followed her gut feeling. But the smell of the coffee, or maybe it was the man's voice, something made her pause. She looked at Eepe, so eager. Never had he seemed so sweet. Like a puppy, he peered at her.

"Eepe, you're such a naughty thing!" she said. But her tone was proud, like a parent whose son has reached a milestone of life. And indeed Eepe had reached a milestone: life itself. Eagerness requires a soul. Aru had seen his spark of life and helped him to blossom.

While Aru, fuzzy-brained with Agor brew and exhaustion, was thinking all this, Eeepe tugged at her skirt. She gently shook him off.

"It's a little chilly this morning. Come have a cup. It will only take a moment. You'll warm up, and be on your way. The world's tastiest coffee. Roasted dark and smoky. No charge."

"No charge?"

"We've got to use up what we ground this morning. No point in letting it go to waste."

The man had an odd sneer. But the coffee smelled so good. "I really shouldn't," said Aru. "Thank you, anyway." She tried to grab the thrall.

"You'll regret it later on, if you refuse this cup." The man held up his own mug to show her. "We'll be pulling out soon, you won't have another chance. The world's tastiest!"

Aru glanced downhill at the festivities. She heard drums and whistles. The crowd was laughing and cheering. "Just a quick cup," she said. "Thank you."

Seated inside the coffee tent it was difficult to see. The sunlight was still dim and the thick amber walls were barely translucent. Only a couple of small oil lamps were lit. Aru sniffed the contents of her mug. Aaaah.

At the back of the tent, several extremely petite women scurried here and there to pack things up. With rather bulging posteriors and tiny little waists, they made Aru think of the colony of ants she had seen near Ysgarlad. But Aru had to look twice. Were those dueling rapiers on their belts?

The coffee tasted good. So good. Aru heard a baby cry. There was a stack of books on the table in front of her. Aru set her mug down and picked up a book to look at it. Eepe climbed up to sit on the remaining books. While she studied the one, he dangled his feet in her coffee.

"Oh, Eepe!" she exclaimed, and then she laughed. She held him up so the liquid would dribble from his feet into the cup, but he wiggled and kicked, splattering drops all over her. About to scold him once again, Aru paused at the sight of his wicked smile. He peered over her shoulder and then looked into her eyes. Aru reached for a napkin, but dropped Eepe as someone grabbed her from behind. Several pairs of pinching hands clutched her arms, her neck. They had her by the hair. She couldn't move her head. Frozen in dumb shock, her eyes stared. Did time go by? She tried to pull free. Too many had hold of her. It was those women! They had a bitter smell.

What was happening? Aru fought and tried to scream but they pinched her nose and forced a gag into her mouth. It all happened so fast! Someone forced a sack over her head. Gasping, Aru couldn't get her breath. Eyes wide in the darkness of the sack, she heard Eepe laughing. Cackling.

The gag hurt her jaw. Pain added to the confusion. They'd tied a knot in the rag. It forced her mouth wide open. And so tight around her head.

A shrill voice spoke exceptionally fast, "Well! A bit of a last-minute transaction, but you're a smart cookie, aren't you—well done—we could use one like this. Wouldn't mind having you, in the bargain, Mr. Goody, to admit the truth, but we'll take her—what the thunder do we know about your strange magic? Anyway, this one'll suit the queen's residence. Twist that rope tight there, Auntie. Will ya look at the skin on the girl—wonder where she's from—never seen nothing like it."

Other identical voices chimed in, talking rapidly, all speaking at once. The words blurred into high-pitched meaningless noise. Aru couldn't breathe inside the bag. She couldn't breathe.

With a gasp she woke up in—a storage closet? The bag was gone. It smelled bad in there. Pungent like kerosene and burnt garlic. Also the stink of dirty diapers. Choking into her gag, Aru looked around frantically. She must be inside the coffee van. Some light came through a crack. She peeked out. Her heart pounded. Aru could only see a small area in front of the coffee stand. A scream through her gag made a muffled moan. No one would hear her over the noise of the crowd down below.

Someone was out there. A woman. A woman peeked into a doorway across the narrow dirt lane. Veya! Aru shouted her name as loud as she could. "Mauh! Mmea!" There was no point. But she kept trying, ignoring the pain. She banged on the wall with her bound fists. And then Veya was gone. Wildly, Aru's eyes darted back and forth. *No! Veya, come back! Help! Help me!* She banged and banged. There was a small window. Could she fit through that? Could she get it open? She tried the door. Locked fast.

Aru returned her eyes to the crack. Her breath came hard through her nose. She felt dizzy. After a few minutes, there was Eepe! He ran past, with both Nrouhw and Veya chasing him. They were headed downhill. Again Aru swooned, collapsing onto the floorboards of the grubby van.

What happened, as the ravens later told, was Veya couldn't keep up, but Nrouhw chased the thrall straight to the tent of wooden puppets.

Eepe slipped under the tent wall. By the time Nrouhw skidded around to the entrance and got the flap untied, the gingerbread man lay idle on the shelf of perching birds that had caught its interest before.

The eyes of a splendidly-carved jay contained a sinister glow. The jay twitched. It wiggled its toes. It took a deep breath. Nrouhw, frantically searching, looked up just in time to see the bird hop to its feet, clacking its beak with a crazy grin. It raised its crest and tried its wings, stretching them upwards in a clumsy movement.

"Rrr-AAAOW!" screamed Nrouhw. He leapt toward the jay, swiped, and missed.

The bird ignored him, preening its wooden feathers before fluttering from the shelf to land on a rack of marionettes. It lowered its breast and spread its wings to fly right out of the booth, into the dawn of day.

Nrouhw ran after it, shouting, "Get back here! What have you done with Aru?"

Just down from the puppet stand was a fortune-telling booth covered in tapestries. A large mirror hung beside the entrance. Across the narrow path between, a hatter's stall had all sorts of mens' hats hung on pegs. Everything flickered in the light of nearly-spent candles and smoking torches. The hatter's had a small round looking-glass. The hand-rubbed bronze frame was in the shape of a sea turtle. This faced the big mirror of the fortune teller's across the path, the relative positions of the mirrors reflecting an infinite row of turtle mirror images into each one. After flitting between the tents and booths, the bird came to rest on a hat peg beside the sea turtle.

Nrouhw rushed up, followed by Veya. The bird cocked its head and looked at them. "You can't catch ME!" the jay cackled, and then it hopped right through the mirror into the world behind the glass.

Veya hurried over and peered in; she glimpsed the bird jumping through the round recursive turtle images as if they were hoops, fluttering into world after world inside the mirror.

"It spoke!" Nrouhw stared, panting.

"He's run off into the mirror; he's simply gone!" cried Veya. "Eepe, he went right into the looking-glass!"

Nrouhw continued to stare at the mirror. "Where's Aru? What did it do to Aru?"

Veya's eyes got even bigger. "When I first seen him, he was walking along. Dropping money, paper money! He was! Just throwing it, letting it blow any which way in the wind."

"Where? Where did you see this, Veya? Show me!"

Veya guided Nrouhw back to the spot where she'd found the thrall. No surprise that the money was gone, but nothing looked out of place. The booths were still closed up. The noise coming up from the village indicated that the monster was departing the cliff. Explosions came one after the other, barely heard over all the cheering and drumming.

Veya gasped. "Oh, no! The coffee wagon is gone. Next to this tent. There was a coffee van here. Right here. Nasty-looking fellow."

"Oh no, look, the tent is emptied," said Nrouhw, pulling back the canvas. "Oh, great thunder! Rabid rabies!" He picked up a discarded coffee sack.

"What? What?"

"The Gwyllt coffee company. Owned by slave-making ants. They are notorious for using slaves to work the coffee farms. And—Oh, my thunder! I've heard they kidnap exotic women to serve their queen! Veya, I'm going to change."

Within minutes, a frightened and furious cougar sprinted east along the highway out of town, carrying his folded trousers in his mouth. He ran faster than he'd ever run before. And then, he pushed on through exhaustion. He caught up to the wagon. A large, fancy, amber-colored van, two horses, narrow wheels. Entrance at the rear. He could smell Aru. But if he spooked the team, she could be killed. There were babies wailing.

Looking ahead on the road, he saw an outcropping of rock. In stealth he headed uphill through the woods. He circled through the forest. He reached the rock before the van did. In a swift and silent leap, he made the roof.

A tiny lady was driving. Another sat next to her, jabbering away. The one looked up and saw Nrouhw, dropped the reins, and both jumped from the board and scurried into the woods, one uphill, the other down.

If the horses panicked now, reins trailing, if they ran away down the winding mountain road, the van would overturn before the first curve. Regardless, he must act before they reached that curve, while the road remained flat. The horses had blinders on, but Nrouhw had to do something before they smelled him. In one silent and nimble move, he swung down from the roof to the driver's seat. From there he stretched his long body over the high dash and reached below to the draft pole of the moving wagon. The team sensed his presence, and began to trot. Nrouhw dug into the pole with his huge front claws to hold on. He grabbed the doubletree pin in his teeth. With a horrible crunch and a bang, he pulled that pin right out of the moving wagon! The doubletree dropped off, smacking the horses in the rump. The horses lunged, the yoke bar snapped off. They took it with them as they thundered off down the road, still hitched as a team.

The van careened to a stop, teetering near the ditch on the uphill side. Nrouhw released his grip and fell into the dirt. He lay there gasping, only long enough to gain the strength to rise. Then up he leapt and he raced around to the back of the van. In his rage he tore the door right off the hinges. He peered into the darkness. Babies were screaming and crying inside. A locust and several ants scurried out the corner of the doorway, but Nrouhw didn't have eyes for them.

In the rear, right on the floor, lay half a dozen babies thickly swaddled in a sheer white fabric. They were furious and panicked and they smelled like filthy diapers. Stolen babies. To be enslaved. But there was no Aru.

The cougar Nrouhw scratched at the coffee sacks and sniffed and licked the wall. There was nowhere to turn. She wasn't there. He smelled her fear. He smelled her, so strong, as if she were within reach. Gathering every mite of his courage, he composed himself and transformed back to human. In a daze, he climbed the van to find his trousers. He pulled them on.

The babies. They seemed to be all right. Each was crying or fussing, a good sign. None looked to be injured by the lurching van. What type of animal they were was unclear, but they appeared to be various species. There was a large bottle, with milk still warm. It smelled like dog milk. Nrouhw held two of the babies, and offered one the bottle. He was at this task of soothing and caring for the babies when Aeon and Lekki arrived.

Lekki entered the van first. "Babies?"

"No Aru?" said Aeon, "She wasn't taken, after all?"

"She was, I smelled her. She was in this van and she was terrified."

"Did they have saddle horses?"

"I don't know. Not with this van."

"We will send some ravens to search the road," said Lekki.

"And find the team," Nrouhw added, but his voice was distant.

"These were meant to be slaves!" said Lekki.

"Yes, I'm afraid so," Nrouhw replied. "They don't appear to be injured. I don't recognize any of them."

Aeon drew a breath. "None of these are from Sylfaen. A child went missing yesterday in the next village over. It won't take long to find the owners."

"Parents," said Lekki.

With hurried and clumsy efforts, the three men fed and changed all six of the babies. Then, holding a pair each in their arms, they started back up the road toward Sylfaen. A frantic group rushed down the road in their direction. As they approached, Veya, her husband and several others called out to ask about Aru. No one had seen her.

One of the voles started to cry as they all turned home towards the village. Would they ever see Aru again? Slings made from shawls gave the infants comfort, and one of the women was able to nurse the one who continued to fuss.

"We will send out ravens," Lekki repeated, because he didn't know what else to say.

"We'll find her, Nrouhw," whispered Veya.

The climbing sun shone on their backs as they walked.

"This isn't right. I'm going to search east along the road." Nrouhw started to turn back. "Every minute she is missing casts her further into danger."

Hooey raised up a finger. "Take just a moment to consider the situation. The heart doesn't always give the best guidance."

"Let us send the ravens and hawks," replied Lekki.

"Yes, they'll cover much more ground than you, Nrouhw." said Aeon. "They'll find her."

"Certainly so!" whistled an old marmot friend of Veya's.

Lekki persisted. "We know where they are headed. South to Liwiych. They must have her on a horse."

"She'll be easy to spot," said father squirrel.

"There's too much that can happen. I'll send a raven when I find her." Nrouhw turned again to retrace his steps along the road.

Lekki reached for Nrouhw's shoulder. "My friend, certain—" and then something caught his eye. "Great thunder!"

As the grimy tatters that were Aru stumbled out of the woods and down the bank, Veya was the first to reach her and help her stand. The others rushed to her. She screamed into the gag when someone bumped her arm. Inflammation of her cheek had her eye nearly shut.

"Aru! Sssssss! What have they done!" hissed Nrouhw. "Did they beat you?" He untied the knot and gently removed the gag, which was stuck to her dry tongue. She held her bound arms to her bosom, and wouldn't let anyone touch them. Her wrist was swollen and looked to be broken, probably. She couldn't move her fingers. They sent for a cart to bring her home.

Most of the group returned to the village, but Aeon, Lekki, the squirrels, and the owl stayed with Aru and Nrouhw. While they waited, they sat together on the shoulder of the road. Nrouhw cradled Aru gently and they covered her with Lekki's cape. Through a hoarse whisper, and after a few sips from a wineskin, the others learned from Aru that the window *had* been large enough to squeeze out of.

Aru didn't share the story until later, but it recurred in her mind for ages. There'd been four ant ladies in the amber wagon, along with the locust man. But fate had spun a favor for Aru. In the late of the previous evening, at the fragrance vendor's stall, she had been sampling oils and perfumes. The smell of her annoyed the others in the van, and quickly they began to feel ill. They complained and cursed, and soon they were overcome by the odor. They lay around like drunkards, feeling sorry for themselves. Complaining and whining, one by one they began to snooze.

In careful silence, Aru managed with her tied hands to unbutton and remove her skirts until she had only her brown flannel underskirt. Every long moment this took meant she was farther from home. If only she could transform, like a normal person.

Careful not to make sudden movements, Aru clambered onto a waist-high cabinet and balanced there. It smelled like cigars.

Her trembling fingers released the catch at the base of the window and pushed it outward. The noise and air had no effect on the sleepers. The horses were fresh, and walked a brisk pace. The ground moved by beneath. The gag hampered her breath. Aru grabbed the window frame with her tied hands and hoisted a knee into the opening. She perched there for a moment, uncertain. Reaching down, she pressed her bound arms against the side of the wagon, giving her body leverage to worm out through the window. One grunting push with her arms launched her over the rear wheel and face-first into the road.

She landed hard. Winded, and with the gag, she couldn't get her breath at all. She lay half-sprawled, half-crumpled. Fire burned under her ribs. She couldn't fill her lungs. Agonizing pain shot up her right arm. Aru forced her way to her knees and lay over them with her chest on the ground, struggling for air. She had to hide. In a bleary cloud she stumbled off the side of the road. Up the embankment she went, to conceal herself among the trees.

Now as she waited there with her friends in the dust on the edge of the road, Nrouhw wanted to know about her ordeal. How did they capture her? She couldn't speak about it.

Hooey had things to say, though. "These dreadful ants (genus *Rosso-myrmex*, I believe), historically, as creatures, robbed colonies of their pupae, raising other ants as slaves. Nature. But, no! Having evolved to animal transforms, they ought to be beyond these hideous behaviors. Absolutely reprehensible. There is no excuse for this. No excuse!"

But Aru asked about Eepe. What happened to him? Was he safe?

"Aru! Are you nuts?" shrieked Veya.

And Nrouhw exclaimed, "It sold you to slavers!"

"But—"

Veya shivered. "Aru, he went human. I don't know how. He was able to make the dreadful coffee man understand him. The locust."

Aru had to absorb all this. Then she asked, "For what reason? Why would Eepe do such a thing? How did he know they were slavers?"

"Everyone knows this," said Lekki.

"Except me, apparently. Everyone except me." Aru tried to wipe her eyes. She cringed in pain when she moved her arms.

Nrouhw wanted to remove the binding from Aru's forearms, but the group decided that her other arm made a make-shift splint the way it was. Aru agreed. She didn't want anyone to touch her arm.

When the wagon came, Pippet and Chirra were riding on it, eager to see Aru. They had obviously been told to stay quiet, but they puffed with excitement. They did manage to chitter quietly on the ride home. The group of friends discussed the thrall as they headed back to Sylfaen. Aru talked for an exhausted moment. She had both a sense of loss and a sense of freedom in regards to Eepe. But why give her to east coast slavers? Nobody knew.

"I'm sure the fact that it acquired the ability to breathe was due to your belief in the thing's capabilities," Nrouhw said. "Aru, you helped it break the magic. I believe that by educating it, you gave it real life. It can breathe, it can speak. Eepe is no longer a thrall. Not exactly sure what he is now."

This led to a discussion about the essence of life and what, indeed, that is. Eepe had existed as a magic spell, a force of animation which could only make choices in support of its master's command. The thrall had memories but not really true awareness. So what had changed?

Somehow it had evolved ideas of its own. Memories that weren't tied to the master's mandate. Aru and Pippet agreed that consciousness means awareness of life through using the senses. Aeon said yes, but that it also has to do with real thinking, which involves the ancestral gifts of instinct and the ability to have feelings. Somehow the thrall had developed this.

It was Chirra who made the most sense to Aru when she said, "All I know is about what looks out my own eyes: that's me. I don't know nothing else."

"Funny," said Veya, "I never pictured him as a jaybird. A jaybird."

"A jaybird! Chip's predictions! So it's all come to pass, then." Aru stared into the distance. "I wonder if I'll ever know who sent him, though," she added, speaking through her fingertips. "And why."

Veya put her hand on Aru's shoulder. "Eepe, he's gone away," she said in a gentle tone, "and it's not much chance you'll be seeing him again. Not in the time of this life. It's probably best you'll never know."

"I have to know," Aru said softly.

V. LIFE

SUBMERGED in sleep and dreamily drifting, Aru floated in the transcendental realm of everywhere and everywhen. Not long before she woke she found herself deep, deep, down in a world of plankton and chlorophyll thick light.

She passed mermaids who peered at her jealously through an undersea forest of nutrient-rich kelp, tails coiled around the great waving stipes. Shadows on their pale skin and the circles under their hauntingly lovely, soulless eyes were tinted emerald by the reflections in the depths. Each face was natural and wild, a classic beauty, but the corners of their mouths were sharp and severe and a strange sinking feeling emanated from the creatures, warning of a vicious danger.

Seaweed and eelgrass grew dense in the dark water, amid slime and sea foam and noisy bubbles. Some of the mermaids swam about, with wriggling movements like fish. Others lazily preened themselves, running periwinkle combs through rippling hair to pin it back with ornaments of polished abalone.

An algae-covered, wrinkle-skinned old sea turtle drifted near, riding the underwater current topsy-turvy and holding a fan of fresh palm fronds against his chest. He was waving to Aru with his flipper. He wore a monocle and a woman's black velvet hat with a broad rim, a cluster of parrot feathers tucked into the ribbon. He stopped right in front of Aru and looked into her eyes. "It's all up to you," he said.

Stretched out on the grass with the warmth of the sun on their faces, Aru and Nrouhw stole a few lovely minutes together away from the rest of the crew. Aru's well-worn frock was of shamrock calico and her feet were bare. Her wrist, no longer in splints, was healing well, and she had only some yellowish tint remaining from the bruises on her face. She lay on her back, legs crossed, wiggling her toes and breathing easily. As her thoughts slowed down, Aru felt her muscles soften, every placid ounce of her supported so fully by the gentle slope of the grassy hillside. Her briny dreams of the morning were long gone now, lost, faded into the mist in which dream memories so quickly conceal themselves. It was mid afternoon and already the choruses of frogs had begun. The funny fellows were bloated with springtime songs, their earnest mating calls emanating from the new growth of bulrushes and lily pads down at the pond.

The mountainside scenery had undergone a metamorphosis in the few weeks since Agor. The first cutting of alfalfa, grown leafy and tall in the fields, was underway. The dense smell freshened the air. Other crops had filled out their rows between the hedges, adding to the surge of color on the slopes: asparagus, cabbages, lettuces, and leeks all flourished, along with spinach, chard and kale. Pea vines were climbing in the gardens, and sweet pea grew up the wall toward the window of the villa. Fragrant blossoms would cover the window by midsummer, a leaf-light sunshade for the indoors. The two matriarchal trees that stood over the house had become a fluttering canopy which spread above the rooftop and over Aldrei's little cabbage patch.

The community seemed more animate these days. Workers toiled throughout the daylight hours in the Dominion Associated's dozens of garden plots and the broad fields of crops on the slopes.

Most of the bighorns had moved on to their summer pastures. Aru and her friends now spent their time thinning plants in a garden called the Upper Ivywold. They also worked pulling up dodder and quack-grass. Nrouhw continued to paint, and to travel occasionally to sell his work. At times he joined Aru on the Upper Ivywold crew.

Nrouhw did not make a good worker. He had no rhythm to his labor. Distracted easily by the smallest thing, he needed constant rescue from his musings, and often a tender asparagus shoot protruded from the corner of his mouth. What's worse, on these days he swallowed enough fiber that he was generally forced to cough up a hairball, and a cougar coughing up a hairball, whether he inhabits an animal or human form, is not something a person wants to witness twice.

Aru loved him despite his shortcomings as a farmer, and it was a long goodbye the morning he left for a fortnight's journey with a wheelbarrow full of impressionistic landscapes. He would head north and east to a place Aldrei had suggested: Terasau, a horticultural center over in the foothills of the coastal mountains. Nrouhw wished Aru could come along with him to see the rain gardens and botanical conservatories on the tiers of the hillside city, but the rent for the villa was so great they didn't dare lose her work hours. So off he went by himself, as usual, and Aru watched him disappear up the road before she set out for the gardens.

The Dominion Associated required only six hours of work this morning, so in the afternoon an authorized Workers Efficiency Brigade meeting would take place. Folks held these sessions merely to keep up appearances as a cover for the secret meetings; with all the Dom stoats and ferrets, badgers and skunks attending there would be nothing important shared.

The turnout was even smaller than expected. They assembled in the tiny meadow by the farmhouse on the top of the bluff overlooking the village. The day had grown warm, with just a touch of a breeze. The group sat scattered among the several rows of old and moldered folding chairs. Rogue was there, and a couple of voles Aru had met once or twice. The meeting started exactly on time and exemplified the worst kind of boring efficiency, but it didn't matter to Aru. She didn't hear a word of what the speakers said anyhow. From up there on the flat summit of the promontory one could see far along the gorge in both directions. Behind her, the mountain continued to rise to unseen heights, cloaked by ridges full of trees and dense ferny undergrowth.

Living on the slopes at such an altitude and facing lofty mountains all around, Aru often experienced the feeling that gravity wanted to draw her down into the depths of the narrow gorge which snaked its way around the promontory of Sylfaen and cut so sharply through the cliffs. Some areas of the mountainside inspired this feeling more than other areas. Just now, at the crown of the entire bluff, Aru felt a tiny bit seasick and a quite like a pebble that might roll down the western slope and tumble right off of the cliffs beyond.

Her queasy exhilaration was buffered by the protective tower of rock, the monolith which stood at the point of the precipice beyond the village below her. The rock was the only thing in Sylfaen taller than the bluff. These days its vertical cracks and crevices were overgrown with the leafiness of bushes and several tenacious little trees. Sheltering beneath, the village was snuggled into the spring growth of its own tiny gardens and high hedges. This greenery, and all that spread across the slopes, also helped to stabilize Aru's senses. The lush vegetation obstructed the flow of her unsteadiness, giving roots to her wavering perception of gravity.

Aru so much enjoyed sitting back and absorbing this seasonal view, breathing it all in. Trees and shrubs grew like a carpet thick as moss on all the neighboring mountains, interrupted only by protruding rock faces and the sheer cliffs of the gorge. The sound of rushing water from far below was barely distinguishable from the soft rustling leaves of the old farmhouse's fruit trees. The happy tune of a pennywhistle rose from somewhere down by the inn's gardens, celebrating someone's idle afternoon.

Veya and Pippet couldn't be present at this meeting, but Aru had promised she'd let them know of anything meaningful that might be said. It ended up a relatively short meeting but they covered a lot of territory, however unimportant, partly because the stoats would only allow certain people to speak. All Aru could remember of it later was that one of the speakers kept reciting the phrase, "Therefore, my good friends . . ."

Aru did learn some interesting things, though, from the gossip beforehand. Most significantly, someone repeated a rumor that the source of those coveted hypogeous snails was local, a cave somewhere in the cliffy woods, just up the mountain from Sylfaen.

After the meeting ended, lost in thought about nothing in particular, Aru made her way slowly downhill along the trail toward home. She hadn't gone far when she looked up and was startled to see that a woman had appeared on the pathway ahead. The lady had just come out of the high grass and was crossing toward the creek. She stopped when she noticed Aru, and waited motionless until Aru approached.

The woman was uncommonly tall. She wore an abundance of jade jewelry, and what is more she had a jade pendant on her forehead. Her matching dress had an all-over ogee pattern, just beautiful, professionally tailored in a graceful satin design that looked as if her long and extremely slender torso had been poured right in. It was obvious she wore no corset, and she had a sheer shawl tied across her narrow hips. Her hair, in tightly-twisted and well-manicured coils, hung down her back, swinging immodestly as she moved, weaving like a curtain of beads.

Aru tried not to judge, but the woman had eyebrows drawn on. She was certainly a striking character, at any rate. What could she be doing here in the village? Aru's first thoughts were that she must be from a circus, or maybe she was a friend of Aranieda's. "Hello," Aru said.

"Aru, isn't it?"

"S-sorry?"

"Your name is Aru," repeated the woman, peering keenly into Aru's eyes. Then she relaxed her gaze. "I didn't wish to startle you!" she laughed. "You were described to me by an acquaintance of yours, a friend who lives in the western woods, over on the coast."

"Oh," Aru said.

"Little Phfft-Psyfft, the chickaree. She sends her greetings," said the woman, staring again.

"Phfft-Psyfft! My dear Phfft-Psyfft! How—"

"When she heard I'd be passing through Sylfaen on my travels hither and thither she trusted me to deliver you this." From her chatelaine bag she produced a small box from a stitchery shop.

Aru received the box with both hands. "I haven't written in a while. Is she well, Phfft-Psyfft?" She turned it over and over, examining it.

"Yes, she's just fabulous," said the woman.

"I'm positively taken aback that you know her!" Aru went on, "How is baby Phfft-Psyfft? Is she walking?"

"Young Phfft-Psyfft is as healthy as can be. Simply enormous. It's always such a surprise how fast they mature isn't it," The woman's smile was broad. She licked her thin lips.

"But, gracious, I haven't introduced myself. My name is Thxsiss." She held out her hand.

Aru's little misgivings about the woman melted away. She shook hands and immediately began asking more questions about her friend and the baby.

Thxsiss, instead of answering, said in her soft, slow voice, "Sweet Aru, I'll tell you all about our friends. Except, please, I'm just on my way to a lovely shady spot for tea with some new Sylfaen acquaintances. Would it be sassiness to suggest that you come along with me? I'd be simply delighted."

Aru thought this a perfect idea on such a beautiful day. The two of them followed the creek up to the highway where it crossed under a bridge. Upslope from the road the stream ran between lichen-covered ledges in a series of slippery trickling waterfalls. The climb from the highway took some effort, but almost immediately Aru heard a louder sound of rushing water coming from above through the trees. Her new friend turned her head and smiled at her. After a good bit of effort and some rather tricky climbing, they stood before a cleft in the mountainside where the water plunged from a clifftop high above in a pair of long frothy falls. It poured into a deep round pool rimmed with watercress and spearmint. Aru could smell the mint.

"This parcel of real estate happens to be in the possession of the stoat Chikchit," Thxsiss explained. "Her sister was recently confined with a little visit from the stork, so, while Chikchit is busy with her siblings in town this afternoon, our harmlessly surreptitious usage of the premises is taking place. Isn't it such a secluded and refreshing forest haven!"

The tall cliff behind the waterfalls was covered with a thick tapestry of moss and vine. Its hidden rock face curved inward at the bottom to form the far side of the pond. Ferns, salal, alder, and gooseberry bushes grew so dense in this hollow of the mountain that leafy foliage enshrouded everything. How joyful to know of this secret, this fairy's lounge, so pleasantly shaded and misty on a summery afternoon!

"Isn't it sweet!" whispered Thxsiss.

As they approached the pool Aru noticed a small arbor of bamboo. It was off to the side, arched elegantly over a couple of tables such as one would see in a bistro. Several people sat in conversation around the farther table. Climbing roses had been trained up the trellis and a few rhododendrons grew on the bank. A sleepy old willow trailed its branches in the water.

At the table were three people. A man of small stature whom Aru had seen before, a woman, and—Aru gasped, and then she laughed. "Lekki!"

"Aru, what a surprise!" He did look surprised, and confused. He questioned Thxsiss with a discreet glance. Rising, he pulled out a chair for Thxsiss and then one for Aru. "Always a delight to see you," he said to Aru.

Enticing tea cakes sat before them on the table. A bottle contained what looked like liquid chlorophyll, easily recognized as absinthe, though Aru had never tasted absinthe herself. *Oh it truly is a fairy lounge,* she thought.

Lekki offered the newcomers some of the refreshment, setting a pretty spiral-shaped glass before each of them and pouring from the bottle. He carefully rested a leaf-shaped spoon across the top of Aru's glass. Aru thought of Nrouhw, and how he would have enjoyed seeing these beautiful things. Little slots in the spoon, intended to resemble the veins of the leaf, allowed a jigger of cold water to be poured over a sugar cube and into the drink. As the liquid turned a milky color Aru could smell an herbal smell. Something leafy. And anise, maybe.

The man, a hedgehog friend of Chuik's, introduced his wife to Aru. They all sat and sipped their drinks and spoke of pleasant things. The couple talked about their children and a lot of the conversation seemed to revolve around springtime and babies. Aru didn't know if it was the drink or just her mood, but everything seemed filled with light and warmth and happiness. The waterfall sounded calming. Joyful, too.

Eventually the lovely hedgehog couple had to take their leave. It wasn't until then that Aru noticed the woman's crutches. After they departed she asked Lekki if he knew why the woman was crippled. He told her she'd had the consumption a few years ago. Such a sad thing.

"In her spines, you say," said Aru, wiping a bit of dribbled liquid from the corner of her mouth.

"No," said Lekki. "In her spine."

"So sad," said Aru. "She is so nice."

Lekki then got down to his business with Thxsiss. Her husband sold various elixirs and remedies. Lekki had arranged to buy a particularly expensive one for his fiancée's mother. She currently had an awful case of orf.

Thxsiss handed him a small jar, promising its contents would work like a charm. "Just have her slather this on the lesions," she told him.

Then she suggested that they have another round of absinthe. Lekki and Aru both protested slightly, but Thxsiss persisted, and because they each had started to feel quite relaxed it didn't actually take that much convincing.

The day was perfect. Sweet warm air, the lush coolness of the hollow. Just the lightest wind. Aru could feel the tiniest gusts softly kissing her cheek. The aroma of spearmint had intensified; as Aru breathed in and out it felt like her airways received a spritz of refreshment with each breath.

Aru noticed that when Thxsiss spoke she turned her head to face her subject rather than move her eyes back and forth. Lekki had grown a mustache since she saw him last, and a goatee. She didn't find herself particularly drawn to beards, as a rule, but this was trim and tasteful and accentuated the lines of his jaw in an attractive way.

She realized he'd been speaking for a few minutes.

"I've yet to spend time there," he was saying, "although my fiancée and I are considering it or the Lichen Fern Lodge for our honeymoon."

He had such long eyelashes.

The three talked for quite some time. Or maybe not. Aru couldn't be sure.

At one point when Thxsiss was speaking she was obliged to pause in order to clear her throat. "Please excuse me," she said, "I've a frog in my throat."

Thxsiss coughed again a few minutes later, producing a small tree frog who landed right on the table. It sat there looking slimy and revolting for a moment, and then leapt away. "Oh, I'm so sorry," Thxsiss said, dabbing her mouth with a napkin.

The conversation went on. Everything seemed in a haze, full of light. In detail they discussed fairy groves and the algae that grows on sloths.

Aru mentioned that she felt a little light-headed.

Thxsiss reassured her, saying she had just the thing to help with that. She drew a small bottle from her bag along with a glass pipette. "Tincture of essential oils of hashish," she explained. "A few drops under the tongue should ease the symptoms of the spirits of absinthe." Somehow she got Lekki to take some also.

After this Thxsiss became quite a bit more talkative. "People seem to view me as a somewhat salacious woman, but I'm sincerely committed to a life of upright decency," she said. "Yes, my life is a synthesis of habits some may see as unseemly, but I believe each of us has a special rhythm and certainly folks will find their own distinctive sort of conscientiousness if they refuse to settle for the status quo."

Aru felt like she might be dreaming.

"Flexibility in life, this is essential, Princess."

"Princess," said Lekki, leaning forward. "Do you say this literally or figuratively, Thxsiss?"

"Aru has her secrets," was all she would offer.

Lekki looked at Aru, but politely refrained from pressuring her to say anything.

Aru started to relate a story about Nrouhw, and some trouble he once found himself in regarding an absurd little secret, but Thxsiss asked if she'd like a tea cake and then Aru forgot all about her story.

As time went on, Aru felt even more like she was dreaming. Thxsiss swayed back and forth as she talked; Aru had some vague thought that she seemed as if she were casting a spell. Then Aru wondered how many scores of aphids might be in these bushes and shrubs. So many leaves. Shiny and beautiful leaves. Shiny. So beautiful.

What had Thxsiss just been saying . . . ?

"Are not these roses magnificent?" exclaimed Lekki. He'd pulled a loose vine from the arbor and now turned it in his hand, examining it closely. Aru watched him.

"Yes," whispered Thxsiss, "a certain subtlety of the finest of sensuousnesses, that's all you're experiencing. Now, embrace it. Hastiness is so blissfully unnecessary. Be spontaneous." Her voice seemed to come from a distance, although she sat right at the table with them. "Behave as you wish. Amongst friends all is selfless, you know this."

Aru looked up at the waterfall, pouring, pouring, endlessly. Such a glittering of prismatic droplets. Moving together, countless individuals tumbling in the fog of the spray, rushing as one down to the river, the faraway sea. Rushing, rushing. Rushing.

After a few minutes Aru glanced back toward Thxsiss. What was she talking about? But she had gone. Neither Aru nor Lekki seemed to have noticed her leaving.

Aru mentioned to Lekki how the spray of the waterfall fell on the surrounding leaves and didn't it look beautiful. He said yes, he'd just been reflecting on how the gurgling and splashing of the water sounded remarkably like a heavy rain. And yet behind the sound of rain there was a deeper, more resonant fullness, like water sloshing in a barrel.

Aru wasn't sure what he was talking about, but she didn't notice that she wasn't sure. So it didn't matter.

They sat just watching the water fall.

After a while Lekki commented on the wind. "It is pleasant, this bit of a breeze. Funny, it makes those currant leaves wave like tiny flags! They look like nautical flags, do they not? On a ship's mast." He laughed. "Currant plant ships, signaling to the dragonfly nymphs in the pool, 'Gain your wings and then come perch on me.' "

As he laughed, the curve of spiral horn at his temple caught the light of the sun and Aru realized how truly elegantly his horns were shaped. In animal form his horns would be much longer, and would stand out from his head rather than be set right against it. But these horns had the beautiful rings and turns that made the long ones so visually pleasing. Aru had never seen a blackbuck in animal form. Only pictures. They were such lovely animals.

As Lekki's words slowly soaked into her awareness, Aru returned her attention to the leafy shrubs. "The branches are sturdy and yet they bend," she observed.

"Dear Aru," said Lekki after a moment, "it is quite true what you say. They do, they bend. And they do not break." He paused. "I have no idea why I have neglected to understand the importance of this before."

"I know what you are saying," said Aru, "I feel it deeply."

"We must remember this. I am certain it is a key to understanding life itself."

"Yes! We must! It's so important!" said Aru, and then, "I'm afraid I'll forget."

Lekki looked thoughtful. "Perhaps we should write it down."

"Yes," agreed Aru. Then something occurred to her. "Do you have a pen, by any chance?"

"Out here in the forest, no! Do you?"

"No I don't," said Aru.

A few minutes went by.

Aru looked at Lekki and asked, "What were we going to write down?"

Lekki didn't answer. Lost, apparently, in deep thought.

They sat under the arbor by the rushing water and just listened, tasting the sweetness on the wind. The world felt clean and beautiful. Aru may have fallen asleep for a few minutes, and then spent longer than ordinary in that misty doorway world of nearly awake. She imagined she heard her grandmother's voice. Then she realized how much she needed to empty her bladder. She excused herself from Lekki and stumbled off to find a private place among the bushes.

When she returned, Lekki seemed relieved. "You'd been away such a long time," he said, "I began to worry you had gone off a precipice."

Aru laughed. "No, Lekki, I'm fine."

"Indeed," he said, rather staring at her.

Aru blushed and turned her head away.

"Oh, I beg your pardon," whispered Lekki. He rubbed his forehead, just above the base of his horns. "I am afraid I am not feeling quite myself. I never meant to behave in such a rude manner!"

Aru smiled. She understood. He hadn't meant anything.

Some sprigs of mint lay on the table. "Oh. While you were gone I gathered a few of these," Lekki said, nibbling on a stem of the new leaves and offering some to Aru. As he handed it across the table his fingers touched the palm of her hand. A chill of excitement went through her body.

"Sadly, we are out of tea cakes," Lekki said, chewing on the mint. "I would so love a sandwich just now. Good buckwheat bread, with avocado, alfalfa sprouts, a bit of mild cheese. Cucumber slices, some spinach, pesto, and lemon pepper." He licked his lips, with a big grin.

"That does sound like just the thing," laughed Aru. She loved avocado too. She had no idea what pesto was.

Lekki laughed too. Neither of them were really sure why, it must have had something to do with Aru's laughter.

Something inside Aru made her feel she absolutely must touch him again, just once. Without really meaning to, her ankle brushed against his leg as she changed position in her chair. He surprised her by reaching across and gently placing his hand on her wrist. They sat looking at each other, without speaking. A warm ocean of light flowed over them. They felt beautiful.

Aru spoke. "Oh my," she said. "We should probably be going, Lekki."

It took him a moment to respond. Then he quickly withdrew his hand, as if he'd suddenly noticed it. "Yes." A look of pain came onto his face. "Something's not right, Aru. We should go."

"Nothing wrong with a sprinkling of harmless harmoniousness." The soft and breathy sound of Thxsiss came from somewhere, surrounding them.

Confused, both Aru and Lekki rose to their feet. Aru rose too quickly. Giddy, she started to waver and collapse back toward her chair. Lekki lunged forward to catch her just before she fell. The chair did fall.

He found himself supporting her with his hands below her shoulder blades. His quick breaths felt warm on her face. She lay heavily in his arms. They stared into each other's eyes. His looked so healthy and clear, and yet so hazy. Outside of time, Aru foundered. She felt his strength, his pain.

He helped her to her feet. But he continued to hold her. Each incapable of pulling away, they found themselves unable to resist the sweetness of the other. She saw the look on his face that shared her feeling, *Oh, no.*

"Aru . . ." he said.

They breathed together, in a vertigo of images and sensations.

Their faces were close, their lips nearly meeting.

He grabbed her by the shoulders. He paused, and touched the neckline of her blouse, slowly fingering the delicate trim.

Looking up at him, Aru felt tingly soft flowers surging upward inside of her. Shaky with gooseflesh, she, for this moment, cared about nothing but him. Nothing else mattered at all. She needed to absorb his dark beauty, the power she could feel. Internalize him, blend with him, consume him.

He held her again by the shoulders, drawing her close against his chest. She felt the warmth of his body through their clothes and smelled his musk.

Then, gently, he moved her away from himself until she was at arm's length. "Aru," he said. "Aru, I think . . . I think . . . Something is not right at all."

Lekki helped Aru to her chair, he righted it and she sat down. Without words he gently placed a light shawl around her shoulders. Aru absentmindedly ran an edge of the cream-colored chiffon between her fingers and held it against her cheek. The shawl belonged to Thxsiss, who had left it on the ground near the chair where she'd been sitting.

The two sat without saying much for a while.

Lekki sat holding his forehead in his hands.

"What just happened?" said Lekki.

"I have a terrible feeling that the snake used some witchery on us," Aru whispered.

"Why should she do this?" Lekki groaned.

"I am so sorry, Aru," he added.

"I'm sorry, too," said Aru. "Let's get out of this place."

Lekki escorted Aru back to the Villa, because she felt quite woozy, and they stood talking for a few minutes in the garden as the sun was going down. They said goodnight, assuring one another that everything would be all right. Lekki departed quickly up the trail. Aru went indoors, where Aldrei and Aeon had a bowl of lentil soup waiting. They were concerned. Where had she been all this time?

The following day Aru worked especially hard, pulling up bittercress and thistles. She didn't talk to Veya, or anyone, much. She had lots of thoughts running through her mind. What had taken place at the waterfall? It made no sense, like a dream. The vexing kind where one wakes up with relief. She'd lost her sense of self-control. It didn't seem real. It felt like she had someone else's memory inside her head.

Then from behind, she heard Lekki's voice. He'd come right to the garden! "Aru—" he said. And when she turned, "Aru, may we speak alone for a few minutes?"

"Oh. No, Lekki, I don't think so."

"Please don't misunderstand. There is nothing improper. It is just that I have something I must tell you."

An elderly vole weeding next to Aru mentioned that some lettuces needed thinning down by the lower gate.

Down at the bottom of the garden, Aru uncomfortably began removing lettuce plants and placing them in her basket. She glanced over her shoulder. Pippet and Chirra were watching, but then Veya grabbed Pippet's skirt and directed her back to her job. It took Lekki a few minutes to speak.

"Aru," he drew a breath, "I am deeply in love with Mhehh. She is far and away the most beautiful woman in the world to me. I would never do anything of any sort to hurt her and I've no desire to be with anyone else. No desire whatsoever. Furthermore I am fully aware that you feel the same way about Nrouhw."

Aru nodded.

"I must speak frankly," he said. "I've given the events of yesterday a great deal of consideration. Aranieda arranged my meeting with the hedgehogs. I suspect it was she who directed Thxsiss to bring you along and—" he sneezed, "Excuse me. To do what she did."

"Aranieda? But why would she want to do something like that?"

"My father is against my marriage to Mhehh."

"Oh." Aru stopped working and heedlessly manipulated a lettuce in her hands. "I'm sorry to hear that, Lekki. What an awful thing." She looked up at the mountain across the gorge, then back at Lekki. "But what has that to do with Aranieda?"

"You know she is employed by my father, don't you," said Lekki.

268

"No!" Aru exclaimed. "No, she works for the Dominion Associated!"

"I don't think so. Well, I don't know. But she most certainly is in the employ of my father. I thought you knew. She is one of his spies. One of his most adept," said Lekki.

"A spy!" It made sense, actually. That would explain a few things.

"The day I collided with your hill," he continued. "Aranieda was there. I knew something was amiss when I woke. Aranieda just happened by your cottage on that day? No! Not a chance!"

"But, she was our spinning teacher, she often came by the villa."

"Aru, what do you know of my father?"

"Not much, Lekki. Not really." She threw the lettuce in the basket. "He's a powerful man, he owns a lot of land in the east. That's about all I know."

"He is a greedy man, Aru. Greedy for domination. And he does have power, yes, the control of the wind. You hadn't heard that? Well, he does." Lekki sneezed. "Please excuse me. You see, Aru, that day we were flying carpets, that day of the accident. It was no accident. I've known that all along. My father controlled the carpets, I have not that ability. He dashed me against the hillside intentionally. Never mind that he could have killed me! For a long time I assumed that he did it out of anger about a certain issue between us. But now I see his plan. Unfortunately, at the moment it involves you, Aru."

"Me?"

Lekki sighed. "I am certain of it. Of all places, my father caused me to strike the hill just near your house. And he has Aranieda in his service. I believe he has instructed her to, ah, distract me with you, hoping I should lose interest in my fiancée Mhehh. This is the sort of thing the man would do. So ignorant of love, he thinks one can turn it on or off like a faucet. Or with a spell and potions, apparently."

Aru was quiet for a moment. "But why me?"

Lekki put his hand on her arm. This time Aru, happily, felt nothing but the warmth of a friend's touch. "There are reasons he would choose you," he said. "I shall come visit, if it is all right, after Nrouhw is home and explain his deranged schemes to the both of you. I felt I should warn you though, as soon as possible. Trust Aranieda not. Do not trust anything she says."

"She's a spy?" Aru still couldn't quite take it all in.

"Yes, an emissary of my father's. She always has been. Since I was a child I can remember her."

That evening Aru sat at the table with Aldrei and Aeon. Aru had told them of meeting Thxsiss on the trail. Now she wondered how the woman had known her friend Phfft-Psyfft. Aldrei said that he knew of that woman and her husband. Everyone knew of them. They traveled widely and it came as no surprise to him that the chickaree would send a little parcel along. It was commonly done. Much less expensive than raptor mail. Medicine show people like that went everywhere, eventually.

When Aru mentioned she would get a letter off to Phfft-Psyfft right away to thank her for the gift, Aldrei said that he had a raven friend who would be flying west in a few days.

"I still have Thxsiss's shawl," Aru remembered. "I suppose I must find a way to return it to her."

"I wouldn't worry," said Aldrei.

"She won't want it back, pet," Aeon said. "Just keep it."

When Nrouhw arrived home from his travels he brought with him a bracelet of malachite beads for Aru. He knew that she'd delight in such a thing. Each bead engraved with three tiny leaves, it had several strands to wrap around her wrist. His paintings had sold well and he had a lot of adventures to tell her about.

Aru had much to tell him, also. She told him she wished she'd never gone with Thxsiss to the waterfall. Nrouhw told her not to waste a wish on something that had already happened. He suggested she not bother herself with any more thoughts about it. He took her in his arms, enveloping her in the sanctuary of his warmth, and soon she forgot all about her troubles. A few days later, however, Nrouhw had his own interaction with Thxsiss.

It was nice having a bit of money. Aru always loved to window shop, but on this day she had in mind a specific thing to buy. She sought a gift for Nrouhw that she'd been wanting to get him for a long time. The day was a holiday, an annual event which brought a healthy revenue to the Dominion Associated, consequently allowing the farm workers another afternoon on which their lives were their own.

The Sylfaen Worm-Charming Championships drew folks from several other mountain villages. Everyone had great fun watching the contestants—mostly people who looked like lizards, frogs, birds, or shrews—as they worked at twanging on their garden forks, or tapping on their stobs or other paraphernalia to call the wiggling worms up through the mown grass. A lively, thick-necked and chinless man with a megaphone ruled over the string-marked grid of little lawns, and he kept the excitement up with his clever observations. Aru was surprised to learn that he was a pond turtle.

The part of the festivities that Aru had most anticipated, though, was the gathering of more than half a dozen wagons on the flat area above the road. Some of the vendors had arrived a week or more earlier, but today they each had their wares on full display. The first on the end was a bottle and brush wagon, quality work but Aru had something else in mind for her gift. She and Nrouhw headed past without stopping. The next van had eyeglasses and various lenses, which caught Nrouhw's attention. As he moved in to inspect the merchandise Aru followed him, taking a peek beyond to see what vendor came next. She gasped and grabbed his arm.

"Nrouhw, look!" she said.

On the side of the adjacent wagon it said in emerald green and gold:

Dr. Hethsuth's Elixirs of Health

Medicinal Ointments & Patent Medicines

Love Potions

Painted under this arc of lettering, a man in silk pantaloons and a turban played on a bulbous flute, a twisting snake reaching up toward him from a palm frond basket. It was only a grass snake, but enormous, and it was skillfully depicted in order to look wildly alluring.

Nrouhw set down the stereoscope he'd been looking through and held Aru's hand as she walked to the opposite side of the medicine wagon where a canopy spread from the edge of the roof. Underneath, the side of the wagon opened in two great doors, exposing the interior couches and shelves full of drawers and bottles. No performance was going on at the moment, just a large felted cloth spread on the ground, lots of sequins and beadwork, and a banner across the undercarriage of the wagon with more snake images and advertising. An empty basket with overturned lid sat near the center of the cloth.

As Aru and Nrouhw stood looking at the performance area, Thxsiss appeared from around the corner of the herb wagon beyond. She wore a slinky form-fitting dress. It was exotic and pretty but the area above the bottom ruffle was so narrow Aru wondered how she could even walk. She seemed pleased to see Aru and Nrouhw.

"So sorry you missed my husband," she told them, "he was just here moments ago. We have another performance in approximately thirty-seven minutes, so if you anticipate that you'll still be in the vicinity you might wish to witness our amusing little presentation."

They conversed for a short time. Aru tried to politely confront her about what had taken place the other day. Thxsiss deftly sidestepped every question. Aru could feel the silent anger welling up inside of Nrouhw. The muscle on his jaw gave a twitch. They talked on, with Thxsiss mostly ignoring Nrouhw and his comments. Aru said that there was a woman who might have reason to interfere with Aru and Lekki's lives and did Thxsiss know anything about that?

"Must you persist with this hostile inquest?" Thxsiss replied. "So much silly suspiciousness in this village! Unquestionably this woman has a vested interest in your life, dearest; certainly in such a hinterland of a social center—"

Thxsiss never had a chance to finish her sentence. Nrouhw had her by the throat. "Why did Aranieda hire you?" he demanded.

Thxsiss didn't seem as surprised as one would expect. It was as if this were a common occurrence for her, someone grabbing her by the throat. "My services were solicited by the little rabbit person," she hissed through his fingers.

He released his grip somewhat and paused. "You're speaking of Aldrei the fay?"

"Yes, of course. The ancient one. A supercilious little narcissist. Companions with the sagacious old ass."

"For shame!" exclaimed Aru, as Nrouhw released the woman to drop back onto her slippered heels. "For shame! Isn't it horrid enough to hex strangers for profit, now you accuse the innocent!" But even Aru knew the name Aldrei was essentially an antonym of that word.

They left Thxsiss there to her dances and her various seductions and went on with their enjoyment of the fair. Before rejoining their friends, Aru and Nrouhw discussed whether Aldrei actually might have been the one who had hired the snake. But whatever for? Neither of them could imagine why Aldrei would do this. What a truly despicable person this Thxsiss was.

Aru did find the gift for Nrouhw that she'd been seeking. From the herbalist, a big glittery tin of catnip tea. That evening the housemates at the Villa had a cup after supper. The soothing mint nearly put Aeon to sleep, but Nrouhw couldn't keep his nose out of the tin. The others laughed to see him so amusingly frisky. Aldrei laughed especially loud, and joined Nrouhw in a sea chanty and then in dancing the hornpipe. How could Thxsiss think Aru would suspect their dear old fellow? Yes, he often had questionable behavior. But he was a friend.

At her first opportunity, Aru went to visit Aranieda. Sitting in the parlor, Aru looked around the room while she searched for the best phrasing of what she was about to say. She noticed that the patterns of Aranieda's carpet and wallpaper brought to mind the feeling of the vernal forest. As she remembered from before, the uncommonly high ceiling was painted to look like a cloudy sky. Leafy branches from a mural on the north wall spread across a portion of it. Just lovely. An immense glass-front hutch displayed Aranieda's exquisite celadon dishes. Aru thought the antique letter holder might have been carved from jade, but Aranieda said no, it was merely a more vivid celadon glaze. A truly fantastic thing, it was shaped like a grasshopper.

As the two sat and talked, sampling Aranieda's delightful pear and honeydew salad, Aru tried to muster up the nerve to confront her hostess. Finally, in a burst of courage she came right out and asked Aranieda if she worked for Blackbuck. Was she a spy, as Aru had been told? Did she send Thxsiss to manipulate her?

Aranieda sat with her face unreadable, removing her glasses. Perhaps she looked a little sad. Then, quietly she told Aru that she could be hunted down and killed for sharing what she was about to tell her.

In a barely audible voice she said, "I did, in the past, do some surveillance work for Blackbuck. Yes, for many years. I no longer work for him. He is as yet unaware of this."

Aru looked at her with a wary glance. *But why would you admit this to me so freely?* she was thinking.

"I'm sharing this information with you, Aru," Aranieda continued, "because the course of your life is trespassed upon by my former employer. Blackbuck—" she whispered, looking toward the window, "is a conniving man of the dimmest integrity. He has an interest in you, and has had you under observation for some time now. It's time that you knew."

"Me, why me?" Aru's hand went to her mouth. "But I have no reason to believe you, Aranieda," Aru lied.

"Blackbuck cares only about his own influence on the world and therefore he cares greatly about his descendancy. He supremely opposes the upcoming marriage of his son, for as you know there can be no children from an interspecies marriage." She paused briefly. "The man is obsessed with affluence and aristocracy. Your own royal heritage is what interests him about you, Aru. He enjoys surrounding himself with nobility. He's curious about you."

Aru reflected on this for a moment, after a sip of valerian tea. "I find it difficult to imagine that Blackbuck would be interested in me. Why me? I've always had a humble life. I don't, in fact, possess a written pedigree; I've simply known, somehow, about my royal blood. I'm hoping you can give me more information about my heritage, frankly. You say you've been watching me?

"We always know that's possible, don't we," continued Aru, "to have someone watching, like in all the stories. Yet it's quite disturbing, Aranieda. One just doesn't expect this sort of thing to happen to oneself. Truly, you've been watching me? For the entire time I've been in Sylfaen?"

Aranieda pressed her lips together and smiled, gazing into the distance. "At one time you and your grandma had a name for me. Kritikk."

"Kritikk!" Aru forgot to speak quietly. "My little spider friend? That was you?"

"Moderately sized, I'd say," said Aranieda, fanning herself and pretending to act bashful.

"Oh. All this time? You've been spying on me all this time?" Anger flared up, but then a pang of sadness filled Aru. "But he—you—were my little friend." She stared out the window for a moment. "I don't expect you should understand, Aranieda, but Kritikk was a confidant of mine when I was lonely, traveling away from the life I knew."

Softly, Aranieda said, "I know. I was there. There was nothing false about my friendship with you, Aru. I was present. At the time, that's all you needed."

After Aru had some tea to help her recover from these revelations, the two spent a good hour or so sharing memories of Aru's journey from her childhood home north through the woods to Ysgarlad.

The time had passed quickly. Now Aru was on her way back to the Villa, puzzling about what seemed to her a bizarre life. Here Aranieda had deceived her and blatantly spied on her, yet upon Aru's finding all this out she felt more like a friend than before. Maybe reconnecting with someone Aru knew back when her grandmother was alive brought her some sort of comfort.

The trail crossed the slope under majestic cedars and stately firs, joining with deer trails as it wound through thick growth of fern and vine maple, slowly descending toward the fields to avoid the rockslide area. This time, Aru didn't notice the beauty. She realized that the subject of the conversation with Aranieda had never returned to Blackbuck—how could he have ever known about her before she came to Sylfaen?—and they hadn't discussed Thxsiss at all. How did that happen? The primary reason for her visit had been to determine if Aranieda had hired Thxsiss or not.

Really, though, what good would it have done to get answers from Aranieda anyhow. Would she have told the truth?

Aru was growing tired of assessing the reliability of others. How frustrating to have to wonder who among her friends she could trust. She continued to ruminate over her somewhat pathetic situation as she walked along. Her thoughts came forth like ivy, creeping and intertwining, finally growing into a tangled conglomeration, useless.

Maybe she should have confidence in Nrouhw only. For her own protection. This whole business with secrets and trickery put her off terribly. Obviously she shouldn't trust anyone else in the community. She hated feeling vulnerable. But, after all, wasn't facing that vulnerability simply part of being a functional person?

To Aldrei ethics were superfluous. Aru knew this; she wasn't a fool. Still he seemed to be capable of love, or at least of caring.

Certainly, she thought, *when the truth be told, we are all of us, ultimately, selfish.*

Too much mystery in her life, that was the real problem. Aru felt hobbled by the enormous amount of the unknown. So much she didn't understand. She just plain felt powerless. Peevish. *Working most of the time, just to eat and sleep. That is no life.*

She truly began to feel sorry for herself.

She didn't understand.

What meaning did life have? None.

Then she realized she'd taken a wrong turn somewhere. It would be starting to get dark before long. Aru discharged one tear of frustration, wiping it slowly across her cheek with the cuff of her sleeve. She turned back and retraced her path, looking for anything familiar.

As she was walking, still fretting and befuddled, she caught a glimpse of a bright object lying just off the trail. In a hollow of thick moss at the base of a tree something was squirming. Something iridescent. Remarkable color. She'd seen this before. A fairy lizard! As she knelt down she saw, actually, a nest of baby lizards.

They felt slimy and wet at first, but as they tickled in her fingers she noticed it was just that they had a certain fluid softness, their smoothness and motion creating an illusion of damp. Hypnotic in their movements, the hatchlings crawled across her hands repeatedly as she turned her palms to accommodate them. Such unbelievable color they had. One of the baby lizards scurried up her arm and right up the side of her head to perch on top. Laughing, Aru gently disentangled it from her hair.

She must have lost some time, for when she looked up from this diversion the twilight had definitely arrived. Aru tucked the adorable babies back into their home and hurried back along the trail. The sweeping boughs and shadowy foliage had deepened noticeably in color. She took the first fork to the right, it didn't look familiar but it led downhill.

Everything began to soften. The twilight probably had something to do with it. Form started to lose significance. Aru lost touch with her abilities to perceive, or maybe gained new abilities, she couldn't be sure. Aru knew this feeling, and she couldn't breathe.

She left the trail and headed straight downhill through the trees, thinking that this way she would surely come to the farmland she would recognize. It couldn't be far. She tore her skirt on a bramble, got bitten by a nettle. She barely felt it.

"Visyrn!" she shouted hoarsely, "I don't want your insanity! Leave me alone!"

She began to tremble, not from the cold but from an electricity running through her. She felt something about her opening up, cracking wide open, vulnerable and free but terrifyingly transient. This could be the end. Perhaps she never would exist after this. Perhaps nothing ever had. The greying cedar branches surrounded her, great swaying brushes. She started to run but terror stopped her. Everything felt liquidy. Fluid. Unstable. She squatted, curled into a ball with her hands on the ground. She covered her head. She hugged herself tightly.

Aru pulled a tiny jar of aloe vera out of her pocket. There were words on the faded label. She focused, trying to read in the dim light.

> Cactus (*something*) Apothecary—"Oh, Cactus Flower Apothecary."
> Aloe Skin Ointment Prescription.
> Two Oz.
> Also good for Gangrene and Varicose Veins.
> For Thousands of Years Aloe Vera has remedied
> all manner of Illness and Distress.
> Apply liberally to face for Youthful Complexion.
> For Burns and Rashes use at two hour intervals.
> Caution: Feline and Canine DO NOT EAT.

Reading helped to bring her back, drawing her down into her memories, who she was, her everyday life. This sensation actually wasn't so awful. She could manage it. She found it desperately important not to give the episode attention. Quick! Fill the mind with other things! Yet, this time she thought—carefully unclenching her fear—dipping her mind into the idea, delicately, like a toe into water—perhaps the experience wasn't so distressing. Relax. Let it happen as it fades. A warm dreamy calmness. Aru felt a sense of well-being. She could, at the moment, appreciate her peculiar life, translucent and asymmetrical.

"Aru, are you all right?" Nrouhw's gentle voice came from behind.

Seated on the grass in a narrow clearing, her legs folded underneath her, Aru realized she hadn't moved in quite some time. It was dark.

Nrouhw! How had he found her? She hugged him. Of course he must have used his cougar form. Aru knew to be grateful she wasn't a creature who was his prey.

"Are you all right?" he repeated.

"Oh, dear," said Aru, "I hope I haven't worried you too much. Such a witless thing, I wasn't paying attention and took a wrong turn." As they walked back to the Villa she went on to tell him about the lizards and about her visit with Aranieda. She couldn't talk about her other experience yet, not out in the air.

When they reached the farmland slopes Aeon joined them with a lantern. He'd been searching for Aru down the river trail.

Aru and Nrouhw spoke with Lekki a few days later, and for some reason Aru happened to bring up the subject of the lizards. The three didn't have long to talk, as Aru was on an extended break from her weeding work to refresh herself, ostensibly. Lekki had invited them to meet at the ruins of the old mill. It made the perfect private meeting place because it was just down from the garden where Aru was working, and also the locals thought the place was haunted.

When Aru arrived it looked as if Nrouhw and Lekki had been talking for a while. They sat on the dock, the vine-covered arch of an old stone bridge reflected in the still water beyond them. She didn't know why she brought up the lizards, just a point of conversation mostly, but Lekki's reaction surprised her and Nrouhw.

"You saw them *here?* That is not good," he said. "They do not belong here." He seemed quite concerned. But they had other things they must discuss. Lekki talked to them about his father. Like Aranieda, he seemed to want to warn Aru against trusting Blackbuck.

Aru and Nrouhw found out that Lekki had no memory of his mother because she died when he was an infant. Blackbuck had loved his wife dearly. She was the shining jewel of his life. He gave her many romantic gifts. The most special, though, was when he presented her with a beautiful little ball of polished emerald upon the birth of their son Arven Lekkchaos. She cherished this sphere because of the love it represented, the love Blackbuck had for her and their son.

That summer was warm, and one day while Lekki napped in the shade his mother took refuge under the grape vines that grew over the well. The breeze blew sweetly through the big leaves and she loved to snack on the crisp, juicy fruit. This day she held the emerald ball, which she'd got into the habit of turning over on her palm. She sat on the stone edge of the well, playing with it and daydreaming, when it slipped through her fingers and splashed into the water far below.

A couple of lovebirds high in a willow saw the whole thing, how the emerald tumbled in, how the young queen, in her distress, she tumbled in after it as she leaned over to try and see it way down below.

There was nothing anyone could do, it all happened too quickly. Even so, Blackbuck couldn't bear the circumstances and placed the blame on himself. As he had been powerless to help his sweetheart, in his life he became obsessed with power.

"My father had never been known as a kind man. But after the death of my mother his only care has been to develop his ability to influence and control," said Lekki. "He uses his wealth and his natural powers. He lives to control his world."

Lekki had just come to the subject of his father's special interest in Aru and her heritage when they were interrupted. "Aru!" The crew leader stood on the slope above. "What are you doing down there? Come now, and get back to work! At once! And you, Nrouhw, weren't you supposed to help today?"

They said a quick goodbye to Lekki. As they were leaving, Aru asked, "Lekki, tell me your father's first name?"

"Avariceo," replied Lekki. "Why do you ask?"

"Oh, my, I don't know," Aru responded, because she really didn't know what to say. It was a senseless answer, so she attempted to repair the awkwardness by saying they looked forward to seeing him again soon.

On the way up to the garden Nrouhw asked why she'd inquired about the name.

Aru whispered, "The monogram. It's not Lekki our friend is keeping the—object—from. It's his father. AB for Avariceo the Blackbuck. Not Arven Lekki the Blackbuck. The thing was taken from Blackbuck himself." Aru looked around nervously, not knowing who might be watching from the bushes. "It's his father spoken of in the directive, not Lekki. 'He who bridles the raging winds.' That's Blackbuck."

"Hmph. There you are!" said the crew leader. "I don't know what you're thinking. You'll stay late today, the pair of you."

A week or two passed. Billiards wasn't Aru's favorite game, but ten o'clock one evening found her and Nrouhw down in the orchard, up in a tree. Aru leaned over the table and thrust the cue through her fingers, resulting in a satisfying clack of the balls and one of them went down a hole, more by chance than anything. Nrouhw smiled. Veya and her husband congratulated Aru. The billiard parlor had been built high in a walnut tree several generations previously by an enterprising marten. Quite popular with the squirrel community, it offered cheap entertainment and almond and hazelnut liqueurs.

Toward the end of the evening Aranieda's name was mentioned. The clientele here were all active members of the workers brigade, mostly rodents who'd known each other all their lives, so discussion about meetings and politics took place freely. Rogue often spent his evenings there too. How he made his clumsy way so high up the ladder to Quadrillion's was frightening to imagine.

The last rack of the night, a hearty game of pool pitted Rogue and Nrouhw against Veya and the accordion player from the band. Rogue loved to chat during the play about goings-on in the village. He mentioned that lots of people had been talking about that idiot boy from the swamp after Aranieda had mentioned him at the recent meeting.

"His name is Queex," said Aru gently.

Rogue looked at her, somewhat confused. "Yeah. Well, anyhow they're sayin' she's right, they heard it before how the boy, Queex, has a special ability at findin' things. They say he can take an' use a scraggy forked twig branch and locate just about anything."

"It's odd though, I've never had heard that before," said Veya.

A fellow standing at the bar laughed, "Tell him to locate me some money!" and several of his puffy cheeked friends joined in with their chuckles, elbowing one another.

A small woman, rather pathetically intoxicated, had been leaning against the billiard table, peering at Rogue blearily over her snubby nose. She spoke up in a slurred and squeaky voice, "Curse that mangy Aranieda. She rarely comes to those meetings, you notice, but when she does she's all for sidetrackin' things by bringing up matters that ain't related to the betterment of the community. I seen her over at the hop barn or somewhere telling people what to bring up at the meeting a couple times, I think to myself maybe she's there on behalf of the Doms to sabotage things." She drained the last drops of her mint julep.

"What? Sabotaging the meetings? Aranieda?" Rogue blurted. "Everybody knows she's the one who started up the whole brigade business in the first place. She runs them meetings. Everyone knows that."

From the response in the room, it became evident that virtually no one had known that.

Much of the conversation at Quadrillion's for the remainder of the evening featured Aranieda. Sitting with their friends and a nephew of Veya's, trying to speak over the noise of the band, Aru and Nrouhw listened to several stories about her. Perhaps the most interesting was when the nephew, Piew-Piew, told how the other day he'd been up the eastern slopes gathering pine nuts with his crew and had seen Aranieda and the Blackbuck gentleman walking on the trail. He wondered what might draw those two so far beyond the river, so he followed along. They went right slap to the old bear tree, the huge leafy hawthorn that Muhg-Wuffle had inherited from his grandaunt years ago.

Piew thought maybe the bear had done something to get himself in trouble again. "Anyhow, up they went and right to the tree and Mister Blackbuck knocked hard on the edge of the door hole with his cane. Everybody's expecting ol' Muhg-Wuffle to appear in the doorway but no, it's one of them fellows that come to town for the worm charming jubilee. I recognized him. A wide girth and no-hips fellow with long skinny legs and splayed toes. Dreadful big eyes, too."

Aru grinned. "Frog!" she said.

"Yes, a tree frog. Name of Vridget. A whole family of them frogs moved into the old hawthorn."

"Veya had a frog beau years ago," said Veya's husband, giving her a playful shove.

Laughing, Veya admitted that yes, as a girl she'd been quite fond of a boy from down by the mossy pond. This confession caused her to endure a moment of whistles and catcalls because of course common knowledge recognized that frogs are rather wonderful at kissing.

He was a nice fellow, said Veya, but it could never have worked for them because she wanted children and that's not possible with inter-species relationships. "It's different for you though, isn't it," said Veya to Aru and Nrouhw. "I so look forward to a little one arriving for you two one day."

After joking around with Veya, Aru brought the topic back to Aranieda. "Please tell us, Piew," she said. "A large family of frogs? And what did Aranieda say to them?"

An extended family of frogs, perhaps twenty or more of them, had been playing about on the tree in animal form. Vridget and another human shape frog male were standing in the entry, wondering what business Aranieda and Blackbuck had in disturbing them on such a fine day. Blackbuck had turned to question Aranieda also, throwing his arms wide in a gesture of frustrated impatience. He didn't have time for this sort of foolishness.

Aranieda declared that she would strangle that blasted bear. Apparently he'd lost track of who was supposed to be purchasing his property. He'd completely muddled the arrangement.

After only a few minutes of talking to the frogs it was clear that they had no intention of reselling, no matter what the price. It was a lovely location, a perfect habitat for them, and with such ancient charm. "We'll find another way," Aranieda had said to the Blackbuck.

Aru wondered what that meant.

She had the opportunity to ask Aranieda the very next day. Aru, Veya, and Pippet had been working on some of the roofs up in the village. Their current duties included helping with moss removal. It happened that this is what they were doing when the doctor rode into town on her regular visit. They could see her coming down the road into the village on her little cob mare. Not long after, the crew lead stopped by and asked Aru if, since she knew Aranieda, she and Pippet would guide the doctor down to Aranieda's house and help out. "Help out?" asked Aru. "Whatever is wrong?"

But neither the lead nor the doctor would discuss the situation with Aru. She and Pippet left with the doctor at once, walking next to the horse, worrying in silence for most of the way.

As they followed the path down between the sunny and fragrant fields, Aru looked up at the doctor, a frightening woman. Along in her years, she was. And quite gruff and stern, to the point of rudeness; yet the lady must have had a soft spot because a pet bird rode on her shoulder, compensating with skinny legs for the swinging movements of the horse. Aru thought it might be a plover.

The doctor's olive skin was leathery and you could see the pores on her cheeks clearly in the sunlight. She had a long, tapered nose and although Aru tried not to think it: behind her glasses her eyes definitely looked like a dragon's. She rode with her mouth slightly open in a vacant and uncanny smile, and Aru could see an array of teeth so sharp that perhaps the woman filed them.

Aru grew extremely worried about Aranieda but she didn't dare ask again about her condition. She and Pippet hurried along as best they could, so that even the horse had a challenge to keep up with them without breaking into a trot.

When at last they arrived at Aranieda's house they let themselves in, the doctor leading the way with the old-fashioned skirts of her swamp-grey dress trailing behind her. Crossing through the sitting room Aru gasped more than once, because, for the second time, she saw Aranieda's home in a shambles. The three went quickly, proceeding directly upstairs to the bedroom. Along the way, however, Aru and Pippet saw overturned tables, drawers pulled from their places and emptied, papers scattered, crockery broken. Pippet, obviously scared, looked at Aru and moved close to her as they climbed the stairs.

Reaching Aranieda's chamber quite out of breath, all three women recoiled in alarm when they saw her there in the bed. "Ahh," Aranieda groaned, "you really needn't have come."

But clearly she needed the doctor. One of her eyes had nearly swollen shut, and an improvised bandage around her head had soaked right through. She tried to sit up when they walked in, but found herself unable to finish the effort.

"What happened, Aranieda?" gasped Pippet, while Aru cried, "Who did this to you?"

"Now, you two mind your own business," commanded the doctor. She immediately put Aru and Pippet each to a task, and of course they obediently applied their best efforts. Aru heated water for the cleaning of Aranieda's wounds and made up a soothing poultice for the eye. Pippet opened the windows to allow the sweet aroma of the forest and brought in bunches of mint and basil to scatter in the bedroom. Then, they set right what they could of Aranieda's belongings.

The doctor had a crisp, traditional manner. She bossed Aranieda about dearly, and surprisingly, Aranieda compiled, even if at one point she did refer to the doctor as a "doddering old casualty of petrification." The old woman spoke the common tongue, but with her thick accent she was difficult to understand. She did make it clear that Aranieda would need to remain in bed for at least several days.

After an hour or so the doctor said she'd done all she could for the patient and must be off to her next appointment. She was required in the orchards to help the midwife; a cousin of Pippet's was in labor with quadruplets. "I'll probably see you later," said the doctor to Pippet.

"Yes, in a while," Pippet replied.

They agreed that over the next few days Aru would come by now and then to help Aranieda. After Pippet left that first afternoon, Aru brought Aranieda a steaming cup of lemongrass tea and sat down on the edge of her bed. "Do you want me to send for Nrouhw?" she asked. "To protect you until you are strong enough to transform?"

Aranieda sighed. "No, they will not return. They learned what they seek is not here."

"Who did this? What is it they are looking for?"

"Just a snivelling pair of odious toadies who think they can rampage their way blindly into some sort of meritoriousness. The fools are trying to find the dragon wand," said Aranieda, weakly smiling at Aru. She sipped her tea. "I know you didn't bury it."

Aru stood up. The dragon wand? "You spied on me!"

"Yes. Of course. But I knew all along that you'd never bury it. Remember that I know you well, Aru."

"Aranieda!" splurted Aru, "If you had no intention of my burying the crystal, why would you tell me to do so? What the rabid thunder is this all about? Are these people going to come after *me?*"

"No, you'll be all right, Aru," Aranieda said softly. She shifted her position, with Aru's help in moving the pillows. "I had instruction from my mentor. I studied with this man for many years, a brilliant man, a sage who lives deep in the Bowne Forest down in the southeast. He advised me that if Aldrei knew I gave you the wand outright, then he would cause mischief, never cooperate. I needed you to make the decision yourself to keep it, thus granting Aldrei's protection for the wand. It must be kept from Blackbuck. I had verified that Aldrei has a fondness for you—I knew he'd keep you safe."

"And so those were Blackbuck's thugs that attacked you."

"Yes. They threatened me," she said angrily. "They threatened me with a forcible silking."

Aru gasped, "A what? Whatever is a forcible silking?"

"It's something they do to slaves in the silk industry overseas, a horrible thing. Just reprehensible. They use a nasty machine."

"Stop speaking of it," interrupted Aru gently. "You're starting to bleed again."

Aranieda didn't seem concerned about her injuries. Aru knew that as soon as she had any strength at all she'd be up out of bed regardless of the doctor's instructions. In order to change the subject, Aru asked

Aranieda about the squirrel's account of her and Blackbuck's interaction with the frogs at the hawthorn.

Aranieda told Aru that she had arranged with the bear to sell the tree to Blackbuck. This tree had been owned by Muhg-Wuffle's forebears for many generations. It stood on the base of the hillside like a queen, probably several thousand years old; the great gnarled trunk was algae-coated and hollow and had just room for a narrow spiral staircase down to the tunnel which eventually led to chambers below the roots. A good way underground, the rooms were aesthetically appointed and large enough to be comfortable for a fat hibernating bruin. Still, it hadn't been difficult to convince the dear old boor to give it up.

Set into the wall of a storeroom below the kitchen was an ancient copper door, carved with hexafoil witch-markings and covered with a gorgeous verdigris. The door no longer opened and the bear family had long forgotten its purpose. It probably had once led to an old cistern or something. Central to Aranieda's plan, this door was the focus of Blackbuck's interest, supposedly an entrance to the world below.

Aru wondered why Blackbuck would want a door to the world below but she politely let Aranieda continue with her story.

Unfortunately, the idea of selling his home and sailing off to the honeybear jungle for an extended vacation had been the only thing to stick in Muhg-Wuffle's mind. He hadn't waited for the proper person to whom it had been arranged that he would sell the estate. Aranieda was still working to figure out her next course of action.

"But why is the tree so important?" Aru asked. "Why were you trying to sell it to Blackbuck?"

"Because," she said, "I have him convinced that the tree is a gateway to the source for hypogeous snails. I need him to believe this."

"I see," said Aru. "Then it is a business venture. It seems that everything ends up all about money."

"That's what motivates people, I suppose."

"So is the crystal dragon associated with this business venture?"
"Yes."

That was all the explanation Aru could get out of Aranieda. She tried several times that afternoon to learn the story behind the dragon, or what was going on between Aranieda and Blackbuck, but every time she brought these things up Aranieda somehow avoided telling her anything else meaningful.

When Aru got home for supper she found Aldrei and Aeon had gone. Nrouhw had arrived home just before she did to find a soup simmering on the woodstove and a beautiful summer salad on the table. But the loft had been cleared out; their few possessions had vanished. It wasn't until Lekki was in town and came for supper a few days later that they learned the old pair had gone up to stay in Opal Heights.

Lekki accepted a second helping of spinach pie, sorghum being his favorite. The table was all set up with the best hemp tablecloth and Nrouhw had filled the green pitcher with stalks of wild iris.

They talked for a while about Aldrei and Aeon; Lekki didn't have much information about why the two had gone or if they'd be coming back. All he knew was that they'd taken an apartment in the palace up in the Heights. He did, during the evening, mention that Aldrei's probity had been a question in his mind lately. Lekki had recently found out that ourare only works if it enters directly into the bloodstream.

"But certainly we knew this," said Aru. "The poison from the bowl went into your wounds when we treated them."

"Yes, but you see, that is the only way to use the poison. It cannot work orally." He drew a breath. "Do you remember, the only bleeding wound I had was the one by my ear."

"I do remember."

"That little nick seemed to me like the cut from a knife," said Lekki.

"The scar," commented Nrouhw, "does mark a major artery."

"Indeed," Lekki replied. "A carefully placed little stab, just nicking the blood vessel. If that is the case it was done just before you found me. Or it was done by Aldrei."

"Well, it wouldn't have been Veya or Pippet! Or me!" exclaimed Aru.

"Precisely."

"Oh dear," said Aru. "One never knows what Aldrei might do, as much as I love the old rascal, but why would he want to poison someone? He's not a wanton murderer."

"Well," said Nrouhw, "wanton, yes. Murderer, no . . ." he gazed at the ceiling with a scowl as if estimating something, "possibly not . . ."

"I am quite baffled as to why he should want to do such a thing, Aru," answered Lekki, but his face said he had his theories. "If indeed it was Aldrei, I do not think he intended to kill me."

"Do you believe the gash might have been from a stick? Or a sharp rock, maybe?" suggested Aru. "We found you in an awfully rough area of the hillside."

"It is possible. It would have been a terribly sharp rock."

"But then there's the fact that it was Aldrei's bowl that was the source of the poison," Nrouhw said softly.

Aru gazed at her lap.

The latest events concerning Aranieda also came up in their conversation. Aru said that she was beginning to feel that she had misread Aranieda's character. She wasn't sure what Aranieda's motivations were, but she had done good things for the community, what with the workers meetings, etcetera. Nrouhw agreed, saying his respect for the woman had evolved much in recent times.

"Listen to me now, my friends—both of you," Lekki told them. "She works for my father. She always has. Never believe a word she says!"

For the remainder of the evening they talked about such things as the weather and Lekki's upcoming wedding.

Aru and Nrouhw met Veya and her enthusiastic Pippet and Chirra on the downslope trail the next morning. They were all on their way down to work in the fields south along the river. The girls absolutely loved going to the river.

It had rained during the night—everything smelled fresh and sweet, and as the friends walked and chatted sunshine began to illuminate the countryside. Every bird within hearing distance vied for attention. Aru enjoyed the coolness in the air, coolness dewy like a flower that would blossom into the day until it faded into summery heat.

Besides alfalfa and timothy hay, the Dominion Associated was a big producer of cabbage, peas, and broccoli. The crops had now filled out the counterpane pattern of the fields, having transformed many of the hedgerow-edged quilt blocks from striped patches of vegetation into solid patches of flourishing growth.

Down below the orchards they passed the barn with the pickers' cabins. At the river was the old limestone bridge, but they didn't take it. That way would have led them up beyond the otter's cottage to the vineyards. Instead they turned to the right and headed downstream on a narrow trail through reeds and rushes, following the marshy edge of the river.

Potent and gurgly, the voice of the rushing water reassured some deep and primal aspect of Aru. The calming sound of the life-giving, enduring resource gave her a moment of deep satisfaction with life. Dark and algae-rich, the water looked like pond water on the move.

They walked without speaking, absorbing the vast trove of verdant tints and shadows offered by the profuse variety of plant growth around them. For a while she and Nrouhw held hands. Aspen trees and vine maple, serviceberry, dogwood, and hazel—lush life filled their surroundings and the sights and smells lifted their spirits, sponging away their worries.

The river passed through lazy farm fields, cascading down a series of broad natural terraces. Wind rippled the blankets of spring cereal grasses. Where flat areas were too wet to till, expanses of swamp grass had rivulets of cattail and skunk cabbage winding through them.

As they followed the path between tender new rushes and wet meadows, along the sometimes steep riverbank, Aru inhaled long, deep breaths of the lovely air. She drew her shoulders back and upward, slowly stretching each vertebra. Sweet, clear air. Sweet, sweet life. The constantly changing view made her fully alive, always curious about what she would see after the next bend in the trail.

At a certain spot they were obliged to leap across a brook that snaked downhill among slimy slabs of rock to empty into the river. There, on a ledge above the high stream bank, the sod roof of a tiny cabin peeked out of the dense growth. Rough passage forced the friends to detour away from the river for a while, and soon they passed a latrine and a mound of fishbones and eggshells, apple cores and watermelon rinds. Raccoons here, apparently. As they returned to the edge of the river, they had to squeeze past an old willow pole which served as a rack for drying the fish which dangled from it like pairs of stiff socks on laundry day. Catfish, as Nrouhw observed. The group walked on for another ten minutes or so to their destination.

The farm cart had come the long way, through the fields. Already an old man and woman stood knee deep in the sedge, laboring together to cut and bundle something. "Isn't that poison hemlock?" asked Aru.

"No, silly kitkin," said Veya, "it's lovage. That's the herb we got sent down here to gather today. They send it up to the Opalies."

"I think they make candy from it, somehow," said Pippet.

"Yep, that's right," said Veya.

As the friends approached the workers, the pair stopped what they were doing and turned to greet the newcomers. The woman introduced herself and her husband. Stocky farm folk, they were big-boned and tremendously hefty. Aru couldn't remember having seen elders who showed such physical strength. Standing near them she felt small.

The lovage grew leafy on tall stalks, forming dense thickets all across the field. Clumps of foliage like celery leaves waved high above everyone's heads. The woman showed Aru and Nrouhw how to cut the stalks and tie them into thin bundles. She worked with weathered, pudgy hands, reaching around her huge bosoms to sheave the herb and hoist it to be stacked upright into the big two-wheeled hay cart.

The whole group worked hard for a couple of hours until the man said that they'd gathered enough. Then he decided to fill the wagon the rest of the way with mallow, another herb that the Dominion Associated grew for the residents of Opal Heights. It wasn't the proper harvest time for this plant, but he said that the buyers used a lot of mallow and would always welcome fresh product. They found a large patch of it over closer to the river, and pulled up the plants by the roots, tossing them into a couple of jumbled piles. The velvety leaves felt pleasant to touch and Chirra said she liked the smell of the root. Aru couldn't smell it.

The old couple worked slowly but quite methodically. They had big sad eyes, though they seemed like perfectly happy folk. Their gentleness and neat manner made Aru feel comfortable around them.

The man did give a shout when he jammed his finger while loading the mallow into the cart.

"Don't mind him," apologized his wife. "He's always bellowing about something or the other."

Not even noon, and the work was done. They took a few minutes to go to the river and splash their faces or wander away to relieve themselves. Then, all that remained was to yoke the team. Aru had lost sight of the elders, but after some time they returned from behind a shrubby cluster of trees as a pair of oxen. They had instructed the others that although they'd easily been able to free themselves from the yoke by transforming, they would require assistance in yoking up. It went without saying that someone should also fetch their clothing and toss it onto the cart.

They had been of similar size as humans, but she was slightly larger than he as an ox. This was because, even though a bull, he was a purebred Highland and she a Highland Shorthorn.

Nrouhw and Pippet did most of the work in setting the oxen to the cart. Aru wished that she could touch the soft noses and pat their necks. And then, off the cart went across the field, the animals lowing a soft farewell. The rest of the group found themselves with an unexpected afternoon to do as they pleased.

They sat for a while near the river's edge, basking in the changing qualities of the light, the gloriousness of the wetland flora, and how it all reflected in the moving river. Lazily they discussed what they might do with their precious time. Pippet whispered something in Veya's ear. Chirra heard what she said and started jumping up and down. After considering for a moment, Veya seemed to agree with Pippet's idea. She gave Pippet a nod.

It meant walking a little farther along the trail, but no one had objections to that. They arrived at their destination within a pleasant half hour. The ruins known as Willows lay on both sides of the river at a place where the water churned through a narrow channel in the rock before it poured out of sight over a great waterfall into the ravine. The view from this spot was similar to the one up at the village, just from a different angle and a somewhat lower altitude.

Veya and the girls couldn't relate the history of the place; nobody seemed to know anymore who had built these one- and two-story buildings that now crumbled under time and plant growth. Lots of deciduous trees grew here. Arching vine-entangled limbs dangled curtains of witch's hair lichen, surrounding and framing the stone structures and filtering the light into hazy sunbeams.

Some kind of mossy fungus thrived on the standing walls, so thick between the square-cut stones it looked as if it had been the mortar. Almost all the wood had gone—the buildings stood roofless, a few thick beams remaining, and for some reason many of the window casings also, some even retaining the glass. In places an entire wall of a building was missing, leaving the impression that these sections must have been made of wood. Those absentees left the companion walls to fend for themselves, unsupported and beginning to bow slightly in the middle and crumble on the edges.

Once there must have been a vineyard nearby, as leafy feral grape-vines had mounted the stone walls, growing high and traveling happily along the horizontal surfaces, unfettered by pruning. A few had twined around trees, smothering them, making grape trees of them. The fruit wasn't plentiful, but there grew enough to satisfy Aru and her friends, as a supplement to the simple lunches they had packed.

Chirra's sticky hands dropped a cluster of the tiny grapes into Aru's palm. Aru examined the fruit. They looked just like the translucent jade beads of a bracelet her grandmother wore when Aru was little. The grapes had the sweetest of juicy pulps and made an absolutely voluptuous treat.

"Wonderful!" Aru exclaimed, reaching to press one of the grapes to Nrouhw's lips. He accepted it with a touch of apprehension. Fruits weren't his favorite. Tasting it, he smiled but may have had more joy out of watching Aru's pleasure.

The girls hadn't finished showing Aru and Nrouhw the magic of Willows. A short tour of the area revealed lots of figures made of stone concealed in the shadows of the buildings and the underbrush of the woods. They looked timeworn and probably older than the large structures, covered with the effects of nature's slow but persistent reclamation.

Some of the carvings portrayed voles but most looked to be human, or maybe some sort of gentle gnome because round heads dominated their simple and graceful forms. Many faces had smiles and closed eyes, demonstrating a feeling of serenity.

On the other side of the river stood taller figures of the same type, but fording the swift current, especially at the head of the waterfall, did not seem a prudent option and no bridge ran across. Veya didn't know if anyone had explored that side in recent generations.

On this side, a pair of mossy logs lay one across the other on a flat boulder, the river washing against the edge of the stone as it rushed past. Aru and Veya sat on the lower of these logs, Nrouhw, Pippet and Chirra on the higher end of the upper. From where they sat they could all enjoy the view of where the water seemed to disappear into nothing, pouring over a long drop that they could only appreciate by the sound. They talked about the ruins for a little while and then Veya mentioned some gossip she'd heard from a friend who worked up at the inn.

The other day, apparently, Mr. Blackbuck, as he often did, had some business in the village and sat smoking on a bench in the garden of the inn, that old bench just beside the topiary horses. The gardener had some hedge trimming to do and was working nearby with her assistant. The old doe's deafness required her assistant to speak rather loudly to her, so much so that Veya's friend could hear everything from the veranda. Blackbuck seemed to ignore the both of them as the assistant jabbered on and on. Then the young fellow said something that caused Mr. Blackbuck to have a clear interest.

The gardener's assistant related information to the gardener which he'd overheard the innkeeper discussing with his wife. The innkeeper told his wife that the boy Queex, down by the swamp, had been singing a song no one had ever heard before. And where could he have learnt it? And the innkeeper had gone and learned it from the boy—something about how to find snails. A challenge, a sort of riddle, and the man was struggling with the solution. Because if he could locate a source of those hyper-whatever snails that had been so popular and brought so many to town recently, well, he'd be a wealthy man.

Veya pointed out that this was especially interesting because it was widely suspected among the community that Queex was actually the innkeeper's son.

"But little Queex," said Aru, " is scarcely verbal. He's not capable of learning a song. Is he?"

Pippet replied, "Queex memborizes the sing-songs he's heard his sisters chant, ones like 'Baby's mangy scabies; you prob'ly all have rrrr—!' Well, um, you know, that sort of thing."

"Pippet!"

Pippet apologized to her mother (for almost using the word 'rabies') and continued. "He can sing one or two full length songs, but I don't gather he knows what most of it means. It's just a song. Just words."

Chirra sang out, "Smelly-tail suck-thumb, wash your face in pond scum!"

"Chirra!" gasped Veya, "Where did you learn that?"

Chirra laughed. Then she began another: "Ear mites, turd fights—"

"That's enough, now!" scolded Veya.

"You're such a nutcase, Chirra," laughed Pippet.

They spent an afternoon of ease, soaking up sunshine on the rocks and wandering along the riverside and in the leafy woods, and before they left for home everyone helped Veya to fill her big cotton pockets with grapes to dry for winter sweets. Nobody seemed to mind the uphill walk on the return. They felt invigorated. Veya and her daughters bid the others goodbye when they reached the archway at the bottom of the orchard, then Aru and Nrouhw continued climbing the trail together while evening descended. As they arrived at the place where the narrow path branched off toward their cottage, Aru took a quiet breath and stood staring at the tall trees on the mountainside which showed off their last rich depth of color as they slowly became shadows. The strange and beautiful spookiness of that dark mossy shade called to Aru; she thought how she'd love to have a dress that color.

"Watch out!" cried Nrouhw, pushing Aru off the narrow trail with the back of his arm, both of them forced to lunge into the greenery to avoid being mown down by two galloping horses rounding the bend, each with a toadlike man astride and riding from the direction of the

Villa. "Here, now! Whoa, now!" screamed Nrouhw after them, "Halt!" But the men had already gone.

Aru and Nrouhw gaped at each other, then ran to where they could see the cottage. Blackbuck's henchmen? Aru's gut wrenched, she stood panting, peering across the yard at the little cottage in the shadow of the maples. But the door remained closed; nothing appeared to be out of the ordinary.

Why would those hoodlums ride this trail? Were they after the dragon? No other destination lay down this path, only the Villa. Nothing but scrubby overgrown hillside rose beyond it, quite steeply, right up to the highway.

As Aru and Nrouhw stood uncertainly in the yard, a faint glow appeared through the window, and it expanded, as if someone were lighting a lamp. They looked at each other again. "Stay here," Nrouhw mouthed, and motioned with his hand.

As quietly as only someone of his species could, Nrouhw crept to the door. Ever so slowly he depressed the latch. Then he flung the door wide. Aru could only see his back as he stood, motionless, in the doorway. "It's you!" he exclaimed.

As Aru came running up, she smelled food cooking and heard Aldrei's voice from within: "Just happened to be in the neighborhood."

That evening was to be one of Aru's fondest memories in Sylfaen. Amidst a sea of kettles and splatters and tantalizing smells, Aldrei and Aeon artfully prepared a supper of the exotic foods they'd brought.

The four of them set up a fabulous table with morning glory vines and wildflowers and lots of candles. For dinner they stuffed themselves with steamed cactus paddles in avocado sauce and braised sea cucumber with fish, followed by young soy pods roasted with cilantro and lime. Aeon had brought a cake decorated with slippery round slices of a small fruit he called "melonette." Again they laughed together around the table, telling stories and joking about the local goings-on. It felt like a family holiday at home.

When asked about the horsemen, Aldrei merely said, "Horsemen?" As Aru turned to look inquiringly at Aeon, the old fellow rubbed his ear and remarked that it was fortunate he and Aldrei had happened to be there if hooligans were nosing around. Then he produced a strange little cough.

While Aeon served the cake, Aldrei asked Aru if Lekki had been by to visit, and if so, how was he doing because the old pair hadn't seen much of him recently. This led to some discussion of Lekki and his royal heritage, which in turn led to Aeon relating the story of Lekki's mother's accident. Then he went on to say that the young queen's body was quickly recovered from the well and she was honored with funerary rites both genteel and lavish.

"It was years later," he told them, "that Blackbuck sent a snake down the well, which had long dried to shallow uselessness; in order to re-trieve the emerald ball Blackbuck had grown to miss as a remembrance of his wife. The snake, Pythymuss, located the ball but also found a crack which opened to the world below. Curious, he went through it.

"Pythymuss discovered a world of glittering caves where the trea-sured hypogeous snails dwelt in great numbers. Blackbuck ordered the crack widened and began having the snails harvested and dis-tributed to shrew merchants up and down the eastern coast. In his greed, he ignored the standard precautions regarding the importation of hard-shelled foodstuffs. There were soon reports of illness that at least one doctor believed could be linked to these hypogeous snails.

"As an additional development, strange lizards began coming up through the well. They seek the light of Blackbuck's world, invading the local countryside. Dangerous fey, these lizards are. Completely in-visible to the eye, they only show themselves when injured or dead. To step on one of these lizards or harm it, or even worse kill it, invariably brings misfortune to the offender."

For reasons Aeon neglected to explain, Blackbuck's access to the snails through his well had been curtailed. But the lizards had become a real problem in his land and he had come up with no solution.

Aru only half-heard these last couple of points. *Invisible? Others can't see the lizards?* A number of divergent questions ran through her mind, but she didn't say anything aloud.

Not long after they'd finished the meal several visitors dropped by, having been invited, apparently, by Aldrei. Two of them were sisters, Conuri and Keet; acquaintances of his from some faraway place Aru had never heard of. Many a Sylfaen evening saw folks getting together in cottages, treetops, and burrows to make music, but this night Aldrei had assembled some truly accomplished musicians. Especially talented were the sisters.

These two had a peculiar foreign drawl in which they most charmingly and gregariously gossiped during breaks in the music. Despite a clear family resemblance they were not twins, although they were both small women, dressed nearly the same in flashy satin. Tea jackets in bright emerald and forest tones complemented their soft apple green blouses and the dark iridescent teal of their jacket cuffs and skirts. The one named Conuri also had a celestial turquoise pattern in her blouse, and the same color brushed over the shoulders of her jacket. All this was complemented by yellow cowl headscarves worn over fiery orange skull caps. It seemed to Aru that the sisters had a rather proud look about them, and mischievous too.

Conuri and Keet talked of many things and soon Aru and her friends knew that they'd once been buccaneers in the southern seas and that Keet was addicted to stimulants and that they both loved baseball. Aru also learned things she had never known about Aldrei and Aeon, and some of it might actually have been true. Over glasses of fresh-squeezed limeade and clear rum, the sisters even got Nrouhw to tell them whether he'd ever killed a bobcat and how he knew it wasn't a transforming one. These were things Aru had never thought to ask him herself.

It wasn't just the conversation and laughter that made the night memorable, though. Conuri had brought a violin and Keet a formidable set of bagpipes fully mounted in jade. When they started to play their instruments, Aru sat motionless, captivated. The tones came pure and true, the control was astonishing. Generally the music around the village was uplifting and fun, but something about the clearness of the sisters' notes awoke a power in the old melodies they played.

Hooey the owl had come, and brought his banjo. One of the other guests was a local man Nrouhw knew, but whom Aru hadn't met before. He plucked magic harmonies from his worn-out old guitar, playing left-handed and tapping out rhythms all the while. Also, a couple who lived in a crabapple thicket by the river had come, both wonderful singers and she played the violin as well. Nrouhw and Aru sang along where they could, Aldrei joined in with his tambourine, and Aeon droned with an ancient bronze horn. Like many donkeys, Aeon absolutely loved to play the bagpipes. And like most, he was horrible at it. But his contribution when Keet gave him a turn on the pipes, although bone-wrenching, did make for a diverting interlude. Everyone burst out laughing, their hands over their ears.

Although Aru enjoyed singing, the beautiful abilities shared by the visitors made it fascinating just to sit and take it all in. Everything was part of the appeal: their rhythmic movements and percussion, the clothes they wore, the shapes of their bodies, their smiles and winks, the size of their feet. Everything contributed. They were all of them quite showy and exquisite, each in their own way.

The songs of the evening were old songs, unlike the drinking tunes sung in the villages these days. Passed down in scrupulous fidelity from generation to generation, these came from unknown ages past, received as gifts from the mysterious natural world. Out of the rock cliffs, and from trees, the rush of waterfalls, and from the creatures that moved through the local mountain areas of long ago they came. The sisters shared ancient songs from their own culture; mostly they were boisterous tunes with complicated rhythms. Fun, yet beautiful too. All evening, Aru was swept right along, laughing herself to tears through the rollicking songs, animated by the dance tunes. She and Nrouhw both wept in response to haunting melodies which conveyed the depth of the wistful joy of the ancients.

Aru had no shared lineage with these people, and no particular reason to covet such a connection. Somehow, though, through the music she felt the presence of these people's forebears and it was no different than if they were her own. The grandmothers and grandfathers long gone, who were young like her so many years ago, she could almost bring forth the memories of their lives. The old ones were calling to her. It felt comforting and at the same time a bit frightening.

Aru went out for some air during a break in the music because the room had become too warm from all the activity. She passed the guitar player in the doorway as he returned indoors. Aru found Nrouhw had made his way outside already, and she joined him on the old mossy log they used as a bench.

"I'm fairly certain that guitar player is a tachycineta thalassina." He smiled, putting his arm around her.

"What's that?" Aru asked.

"A type of bird. In the swallow family. I'd say it's a good bet that all of our guests this evening are birds. At any rate, they smell like birds."

"It doesn't surprise me, really," said Aru. "But how do you know his species?"

"Well, when we came out here at the same time to relieve ourselves, I, of course, was minding my own business, but . . . well . . . he pulled his trousers down to piss."

"And?" asked Aru, taking a healthy sip of her drink.

"He has an iridescent violet rump and fluffy white underpants."

Aru couldn't help but spit her limeade onto the grass. "Bird identification is fun, isn't it!" she laughed behind her hand. "I'd like to see him in bird form."

"Then you could admire his metallic green and violet upperparts and his white underparts."

"He must be pretty."

"Yes, well, at any rate, if he keeps on drinking as he has been, please watch out around him. I know he doesn't appear so, but I've read that his type are prone to violence."

Back inside the Villa, some snacks had been laid out on the table. Little cucumber sandwiches piled high on a plate seemed like the perfect thing. There was also a bowl of something which looked a lot less enticing. It was this second item that Keet noticed from across the room, and which she hurried over to inspect.

"What, dem ent cocklebuhrs?" she asked excitedly, answering herself with, "En dem fresh!"

Filling a saucer for herself and one for her sister, she nearly emptied the bowl that Aeon had set out. She and Conuri chattered away to everyone as they munched on the hard and spiny seeds.

"Dis' iz sush a delight," she said, picking her teeth as she returned her empty saucer to the board. "Now," she said softly to Aru, "please kin gimme uh tetch o' cocaine? Uh be so t'engkful."

"You pirates and your cocaine!" laughed Aldrei. "You never learn, do you!"

The middle of the night came surprisingly soon, and so it was a little sad to see the sisters depart. They headed off toward Opal Heights with Aldrei and Aeon. The other guests had already gone home. Aru and Nrouhw realized how tired they were, and soon drifted off to sleep in a warm aura of meadowy impressions and each other's arms. All was well.

The next time Aru went with Pippet to visit the boy Queex she did indeed get a chance to hear that strange song that Veya had spoken of. The vole children and their father were in the grass behind the shack, and shelling peas, having just finished their supper. Queex played with the discarded husks. He acted more excited than usual to see Aru, and spent much of her visit spinning around, and jumping, and shouting things like, "WuggaDeeee!" He sang the song in pieces, and he also sang it all the way through several times. Probably he did this because he'd been getting some attention for singing it.

His father told Pippet and Aru that apparently Queex had learned the song from a lone cicada named Tettix who had sung it to Queex over and over:

> Ooo-eee-ooo-eee, ooo-eee-ooo-eee,
>
> Woeful our long days anxious be; always a sentence to die decreed us
>
> Might easy be rendered, and by no genius,
>
> Ooo-eee, ooo-eee.
>
> To we, you see,
>
> ooo-eee.
>
> If nectarous and succulent to healthy degree
>
> You are; then you can plainly see,
>
> Ooo-eee-ooo-eee, ooo-eee-ooo-eee,
>
> Life is cautious when one's flavor, by accord, is universally adored.

Always they seek to gather we, sluggard mollusks hypogeous.

Somewhere, wreathed with laurel, the tempest master hails to free us

By charms wherewith lustrous scarab beetles hold the key,

Ooo-eee,

Lodged unforeseen and evergreen in branches of a tree.

And safe and sound we'll laugh, as the hunters fail to see us.

And yet the means to their reward, held just there upon the sward.

Ooo-eee.

The very next morning Nrouhw rushed in through the door of the Villa as Aru finished up her breakfast. She'd been wondering where he was. He'd been gone since she woke up. Now she learned that over the past few days he'd been keeping an eye on Blackbuck, who had just set out with a couple of his men to follow a trail upslope of the highway.

"But they weren't headed in the direction of the Heights. I want to find out what he is about. This will require my feline shape. Let me carry you, Aru. It's the only way we can both get close, to watch him without detection."

Aru couldn't believe Nrouhw had suggested he carry her on his back. This had been an unspoken fancy of hers for a long time. "Are you able to bear so much while in cougar form?" she asked.

"Well, to be honest, I've only ever used the grip of my teeth for transporting others. But since I love you so much I must somehow get you there unmauled. Preserving your exquisite loveliness." He gave her a kiss. "I can't carry you far, so I will wait to transform until I pick up his trail again."

Aru was hesitant. She asked Nrouhw, "Have you forgotten work?"

"Never mind it. Let's just go."

"We'll lose our jobs!"

"Possibly. More likely they'll find some way to punish us." He shrugged. "Well, come on now, are you game?"

Aru started laughing. The idea of going out for a ride on the back of a handsome cougar rather than laboring in the gardens was just too much to resist. She was game. Hurriedly they found her shoes and scarf and twenty minutes later Nrouhw in human form had located their quarry again.

The dense vegetation on the mountainside above the highway placed Nrouhw in an advantageous position for stalking Blackbuck. A light rain misted the mountain, but the trees protected Nrouhw and Aru from all but a few drips. Soon the pair halted briefly so he could change. When Aru turned around and saw him as a cougar again, there behind her, she felt an electricity of shock that went tingling down her arms. She shook her hands and rubbed them together, trying to dissipate the feeling. She made an effort to slow her breathing.

Nrouhw lay down on the carpet of ferns in order to let Aru climb onto his back. He looked at her, waiting. She didn't move. She really hadn't expected to have this sort of apprehension again. Silently she commanded her instincts: "I will not cower. This is Nrouhw. My love. He is not going to eat me." His large, magnificent paws lay straight out in front of him like those of a stone lion.

Aru drew in a deep breath of the cool forest air and let it out slowly. That melancholy facial expression, the one that defined Nrouhw's introverted nature, the "tortured soul" appearance which she found so alluring, here it clearly appeared as the typical expression of a cougar. It wasn't particularly friendly-looking, or approachable. He kept staring. She knew he must be starting to feel impatient with her.

She swallowed softly, and edged over to him. Aru stood for just a moment trying to determine how to crawl onto his back in her skirts. She'd want to be seated in the area just behind his shoulders. As she placed her hand on his neck her fingers again took pleasure in the softness of his coat and the feel of muscle beneath. She swung her leg over to ride astride. He was thinner than a horse, thinner than she expected. Quite a narrow animal. Still, as he stood up she found it comfortable, he had a withers to keep her from sliding forward and the curve of his ribcage formed a natural saddle seat.

Nrouhw moved without percussion, his velvety gait absolutely purposeful. In the quiet forest he travelled in smooth silence. Aru's feet nearly touched the ground at times, she had to draw them up to avoid contact with rocks or undergrowth as now and then he made little leaps and bounds. His impressive strength carried her up the slope, and because he retained his human cognizance she knew he'd avoid scraping her against the shrubbery.

When she felt him slow his pace and crouch low as he walked, she knew he'd sighted the ones they sought. Nrouhw had circled around to approach his subjects from the front. To Aru's surprise, it wasn't Blackbuck and his thugs she glimpsed through the foliage.

Aru's mouth hung open. *The innkeeper from the village! Why should he be poking around in these woods?* She whispered under her breath, "Oh, then Blackbuck must be following him."

Nrouhw came to a halt and Aru slid quietly off and squatted next to his shoulder, peering uphill through the wet branches and trying to be as silent as he. She could feel the warmth of him in the air against her right side, but the only breath she could hear was her own.

They were on the shoulder of a steep knoll covered with shrubby laurels. Above them, though, it was grassy, barren of trees except for one. Just below the rounded summit a massive oak tree stood. The beautifully distorted trunk was enormously, amazingly thick. Still fully in leaf, with just a few dry leaves down on the grass to hint of autumn's approach, the tree rose in two great sections. The top of one side was missing, as were some of the major branches of the other side. It was obvious from the scars and burns that this oak had been subject to repeated lightning strikes. Heavy with clumps of mistletoe, it stood healthy and proud with outstretched limbs in spite of it all.

The innkeeper stood on the knoll looking up at the great tree. He whirled around to discover his pursuers as Blackbuck and his two minions, a man and a woman this time, burst into the clearing. "Innkeeper!" shouted Blackbuck, "I have warned you to lay off this project! The rights to those snails are mine."

The poor man was silent, glancing at Blackbuck but he couldn't look him in the eye, even from the bit of a distance. His own round eyes bulged and his fists clenched. Blackbuck walked toward him, cloak fluttering, his walking cane a threatening menace. His assistants waited at the edge of the woods.

Blackbuck quickly surveyed his surroundings, and laughed. "Ah. Here is your Tempest Master, the old oak. And your ring of laurel trees. Remarkable deduction for someone the likes of you, my little man. But I know you have not an idea of what you are looking for, or where to use it, do you!" He snorted. "I do."

The man shook his fist at Blackbuck. He trembled visibly. "The secret was given to me, Mister Blackbuck. To the voles, not you. Y'ain't even from our village. The snails want me to be the one to have them. Not some stranger."

Blackbuck snorted again. "Obviously the song does not come from the snails. It is *about* them. The narrator is not the composer!"

The innkeeper, biting at his nails, looked up at Blackbuck. He couldn't follow what the man was saying.

"Whoever made the song was not a snail," Blackbuck sighed. "It was either the cicada Tettix or someone else speaking as if they were in the snails' shoes."

The innkeeper had no idea what Blackbuck was talking about. Snails didn't transform. Why would they want shoes? At a complete loss, he panicked. In order to escape the situation, and perhaps to get up the tree and somehow beat Blackbuck to a solution, he began to undress. He was going to transform right there.

Concealed in the laurels, Aru gasped. She couldn't believe it. She covered her mouth, and then her eyes with the other hand, peeking just enough to keep track of what was going on.

As the man transformed to vole before him, Blackbuck sneered in disgust, "I have been thinking of you as a noxious little pest, but now it is clear you are merely an *obnoxious* little pest. Such vermin!"

Blackbuck swatted at the man with his cane, but the change took place rapidly and the man was nearly a vole already. Greatly reduced in size, he lumbered through the grass with his still-monstrous form. By the time he reached the tree he was fully a vole and, though voles are particularly poor climbers, made his way right up the knotted trunk.

As Blackbuck stood watching, the woman who had arrived with him stepped forward.

"Sir," she said quietly, "I'm certain you've noticed them, but I thought I might inquire about those beetles in the oak. They must be the scarabs that you seek?"

Walking uphill to inspect the tree, Blackbuck had a look of surprise on his face, quickly suppressed. It was too difficult to see beetles from where Aru hid, but she thought maybe she could see something glinting in the tree.

"Yes," pronounced Blackbuck. "Jewel bugs. The mistletoe is crawling with them. Obviously they are the scarabs of the song. I have been determining my next move, based on this new information. I have only to ascertain what secret these insects hold in regard to accessing the hypogeous snails."

Somehow the vole had made it up into the branches and his frightened squeaking could be heard above Blackbuck's head. Almost for certain it wasn't on purpose, but the poor fellow was at a loss, and quite terrified of the man below: when Blackbuck looked up to locate him among the oak leaves, well, the vole let go quite a little load of scat from his bowels. This discharge missed Blackbuck completely, but it didn't matter. As soon as the female attendant saw the look on Blackbuck's face she ran for the cover of the woods, the manservant followed right behind her.

The two happened to run right in Aru and Nrouhw's direction, the man crashing through the branches disturbingly close by. He headed down the hill and was soon out of sight, and the woman squatted just at the edge of the clearing not far from them. Aru tried not to breathe.

Blackbuck stood large on the knoll, a scowl on his face as with brusque, impatient movements he unbound his shoulder-length hair. Unbuckling his cape with one hand, he threw it and his cane down on the grass, hard. He also tossed down his jacket and gloves before moving behind the tree where he could not be seen by his company downslope.

There was a stillness in the air, as if even the wind waited breathlessly for him to return from behind the great oak. When he did, it was in his antelope form. Blackbuck stepped proudly out into the open. He seemed to enjoy his hooved shape, pawing the ground and making a loud sneezing noise repeatedly.

As an animal he displayed the enchanting handsomeness he had been gifted with as a human. He moved in elegant grace, a living artwork, with a certain dignity that surrounds a long-lived herbivore. Everything about him spoke of sophistication. Halfway down the sides of his body his dark roan coat abruptly changed to a white as pure and bright as fine shirting. This patterning gave him the appearance of looking well-dressed in a suit even while in animal form. In addition the circular markings around his eyes made him appear to be wearing spectacles, although in human form he only used a monocle. His pair of ribbed and spiraling black horns, nearly as long as his body, sprouted in a V-shape sloping back from his forehead.

A strange whispering began to fill the air. It wasn't animal sounds this animal made, not human speech, either. The noise started in soft tones, and built in volume, unworldly verses that Blackbuck repeated, and he began to run, circling the tree and crown of the knoll. Now his utterances were drawn out into whistles, smoothly fluctuating. He ran fast, leaping so high into the air it seemed like he would fly.

Around he went, leaping and running, so graceful, beautiful to watch; and frightening. Aru could feel the wind he created against her cheek! Then, he broke off his circling and began spinning in one place instead. He twirled fiercely and furiously, rotating from his hind-quarters, his cloven hooves pivoting, drilling into the wet sod. As he spun he lowered his head, allowing his long horns to whip up the wind.

He stopped, abruptly, and placed his face flat on the ground. Out from between his horns flew a great whirlwind, shrieking and whistling with the voice he had stirred into it. The awful twister moved like it had a mind of its own, zig-zagging across the open slope in the direction of the oak, and the woeful vole hidden in the branches.

"No!" shouted Aru, unheard over the din.

The whirlwind blasted into the tree, where it exploded in all directions, sending oak leaves high into the air. Aru's eyes were covered with her arm but she felt something raining down on her and Nrouhw. When she looked: beetles. Good-sized beetles, nearly as big as her thumb. Ordinarily, a rain of bugs would be horrifying. But these were beautiful: lustrous scarabs with an iridescent emerald sheen.

As she peeped out at the scene uphill, she saw leaves floating down, circling on the leftover winds. The blast hadn't taken all the old oak's leaves, although it seemed that it should have, but the bunches of mistletoe in the branches were now more apparent. For a few minutes an eerie calmness stood in the air. Blackbuck the antelope stepped back behind the tree, and then in human form returned to speak to his minions who had crept out of the bushes. As he was gathering his jacket and things, Aru saw something small fall from the branches above. The vole? No, Blackbuck saw it also, collected it from the grass, and after studying it he smiled and slipped it into his pocket.

There was no sign of the innkeeper.

Aru and Nrouhw looked at each other. Nrouhw touched her wrist gently with his nose but the two remained quiet, peering out through the leaves.

"I have what I came for," Blackbuck told his companions. He grabbed up his cane and, without taking any last look at the tree, the scattered leaves, or the shiny beetles which were flying and scattered about, he headed back down the mountain toward the highway. His followers trailed behind him.

Aru and Nrouhw waited, unmoving. After a while they could hear a shrill squeak. The innkeeper came to shape again, across the slope and a good way downhill from the tree. He'd landed there, on his back, and it had taken him a while to regain consciousness and figure out what had happened. When he was fully re-formed he stood bruised and naked, his back to them, staring at the scene for a while. Then he limped pitifully across the grass, gathered his clothing, and dressed himself, chittering incoherently all the while.

He stood again, contemplating the scene, before he left. Slowly he made his way down through the woods, taking a different route from Blackbuck.

Aru accompanied Nrouhw on foot as they headed back down to the spot where they had concealed his clothes. She held some beetle wings in her hand, examining them once in a while as she walked. Such vivid color! How they sparkled! They'd look wonderful sewn into the vine pattern of a scarf she had embroidered for Veya.

As they neared their destination, Aru politely slowed down to observe some moss flowers while Nrouhw went on ahead to change. When she met up with him he'd returned to human form. They had a lot to discuss as they continued downhill.

After they'd gone just a short way farther, someone hailed them from behind. It was Aranieda, making her best effort to catch up with them. They hadn't been the only ones following Blackbuck's activities that day. She had been up on the knoll also. Aranieda, still convalescing, had only recently been able to transform again. And yet nobody seemed much surprised to see the other. The three had a brisk discussion all the way back down the mountain.

In her spider shape, Aranieda had experienced a different perspective of what had taken place. A trained intelligence-gatherer, she knew well how to end up at the opportune place and moment. Aranieda had been able to observe the entire proceedings by riding in the tastefully coiffed hair of Blackbuck's female assistant.

Aranieda told Aru and Nrouhw that what had dropped from the branches of the oak was a silver key. The ancient oak's sister tree, another great matriarch that had overseen these mountain woods for countless years, was Muhg-Wuffle's old hawthorn which now belonged to the frog family. Aranieda presently had Blackbuck believing that the disused cistern door was an ancient gateway to a snail harvesting tunnel. The key that fell, and which Blackbuck had tucked into his upper-left jacket pocket, was a mate to the lock in the strange verdigris door down under Muhg-Wuffle's hawthorn. Aranieda knew this because she had ordered the key made and had placed it there in the mistletoe herself.

Aranieda had more to tell them. When they reached the place where the little trail branched off toward the Villa, Aranieda invited Aru and Nrouhw to come for supper after the following week's secondary artichoke harvest. She also asked them to invite Lekki.

It was after a long day, then, that the three sat with Aranieda in her parlor. As an after supper treat, they sampled homemade lime jelly on thick slices of herb bread she toasted on the parlor stove. Rather than her usual tight-bodiced leather exotics, their hostess wore a myrtle velvet gown, the homespun fabric of the corset embroidered with silver thread in curlicue leaf and net motifs. When Aru admired the dress Aranieda told her that she'd made it herself, for a golfing awards banquet. She used to be a prominent golfer. The others were impressed by this, but Aranieda told them that, sadly, she'd had to abandon the sport. She just couldn't tolerate the stronger pesticides they'd started using on the golf courses.

Then, Aranieda sat forward a bit in a manner that declared it was time to begin the discussion they'd planned to have. She started by addressing Lekki in particular. She admitted that she'd been watching him carefully since she'd come to the mountains. She knew he didn't trust her; why should he? But she had learned that she could trust him. She had called him, Aru, and Nrouhw together because she wanted to tell them about his father and the snails.

All those present knew that Aranieda had used Blackbuck's investment money from the dogfights to purchase the snails so that she could trick him into thinking they were available locally. She wanted to convince him that the source lay beneath old Muhg-Wuffle's tree.

When the frogs complicated things and Blackbuck seemed to be going off the idea of accessing snails by way of the hawthorn, his interest was renewed by the boy Queex and his song. Aranieda had been the one who sang the song for Blackbuck, because he had commanded her to go and learn it from the boy. But there was no need to visit the boy to learn it. Because she herself was the source of the song.

"I'm the one who sent the cicada to sing to the boy," said Aranieda. "I composed the words myself. The cicada set the melody.

"Now that Blackbuck has the key he'll feel the snails are his. I merely need to do something about the frogs. They are a disorderly colony, a bunch of useless specimens! I spent the afternoon there today, trying to convince them to sell the tree to Blackbuck. He's made them a generous offer. They're not good listeners, clamoring about, climbing over each other as one is trying to speak, their hands and feet in one another's faces. I was unsuccessful. And I hope I didn't get salmonella just by going down into their drawing room.

"The silver key, you see, fits the lock but doesn't turn. It won't open the door, probably nothing will. Not at this point in time. The thing is, it doesn't matter because the plan is simply to occupy Blackbuck in Muhg-Wuffle's old home below the tree long enough to trap him down there using a basic hawthorn web enchantment.

"The point of it all is to keep Blackbuck a prisoner among the roots of the tree for seven months. This is the only way to relieve him of his hereditary and honed abilities. As an antelope windlord, living under the hawthorn will expunge his power. I have seen him hurt too many people, leave too much harm upon the land, with his self-important lust for domination.

"I know it's outrageous," Aranieda gave a weird smile, "but in the end, I don't imagine that you, Lekki; or really anyone, will wish to interfere in my endeavors. I only need Blackbuck to stay below the hawthorn for a time, without the company of the frogs."

They sat back on the silken couches which Aranieda had painstakingly upholstered, and sipped their crème de menthe. The four of them discussed the blatant ways in which Lekki's father and the Doms took advantage of the working class, depriving them of their ancestral rights. This evolved into conversation about the abuses of power worldwide. Then the subject of inchworms came up, and whether they could be trusted in measuring bamboo.

Aranieda concluded the evening by sharing some exciting news with Nrouhw. She had spoken with the head of the Opal Academy, who absolutely loved Nrouhw's viridian vistas which were hanging at the Sylfaen inn. The school had recently lost a staff member; the woman had decided to retire early, leaving a vacancy in the instruction of novice drawing and painting. Aranieda had suggested Nrouhw for this position, and after her long conversation with Mr. Vweheh she felt sure the post was Nrouhw's if he wanted it.

Such a fine life they might have up on the mountaintop. And Aldrei and Aeon were already living in the palace up in Opal Heights.

VI. Ultimately

JUST a few weeks later Aru woke to frosty windowpanes and a colorless sky. She stood barefoot, in her cotton camisole and petticoats, examining the tracery of scalloped, feathery designs made by ice crystals on the glass. Nrouhw placed his hand on her shoulder, and as she turned he offered her a teacup brimming with hot malted milk and reminded her that Veya and the girls would be there soon. It was moving day.

Aru nodded. She smiled and gazed out over the luxurious mantle of virgin snow that shrouded the world. Absently, she held her cup and saucer, sipping the drink. The weather inside was balmy, thanks to the birch logs crackling away in the stove, and outdoors everything was dazzling and silent. The familiar landscape looked majestic, all dressed up in winter. The fluff of puffy clouds had settled on the naked trees. Snow piled impossibly high along each branch, ladening all the boughs to the tiniest tips of their twigs. The conifers, too, stood glistening, loaded with heaps of snow, muffled and cozy on a hushed morning and reminding Aru of pointy-hatted long-bearded cumulus gnomes.

She and Nrouhw had been waiting for the first substantial snowfall, to make travel easier so they could move their belongings up to the summit. They were thankful for the loan of a horse and sleigh because they had somehow collected quite a few possessions since they'd arrived in the area. Everything had been packed into crates and flour sacks, save for a few dishes and other items they might need today such as candles, matches, and tissue paper.

Veya and her family arrived not long after a man delivered the horse. Happily, Veya's husband was able to get away from his commitments and come along. They brought extra brooms and rags and a picnic lunch that they all could share when the loading and cleaning was done. They'd packed some tiny oatcakes as well, intended for Aru and Nrouhw to leave out as one last offering for the little fairies of the Villa. A few other friends dropped by also, to say goodbye.

Aru's sadness about leaving was tempered by the fact that they weren't going far and could visit often. And by the fact that this new venture sounded so exciting.

Lekki had described life in the Heights to Aru and Nrouhw. Every residence in the entire alpine neighborhood had indoor plumbing. There were parties and balls at the palace, pageantry and fun. Skiing was popular in the winter, as was ice skating. With Nrouhw's position, they could afford to do all sorts of lovely things. Lekki had also been quite helpful by arranging a fine cottage for them to live in, just next door to the academy. He'd said he thought Aru, especially, would enjoy that community. It might be gratifying for her to live there, he'd said, as she was like the others there, so fair of skin tone, as they were. Aru felt confused by this. Although she was curious to see these people who looked like her, why would she be gratified to live among them? But she hadn't said anything.

Veya had never been to Opal Heights, but from what she'd heard a strange magic filled the place. She was thrilled for Aru and Nrouhw, but also worried, as she'd heard many stories of sorcerers, phantoms, and ghosts. Some of these she and Pippet had already shared with Aru. On this day, during their lunch, Veya told the story of the apparition they called the White Lady.

The legend, as Veya recounted it, maintained that:

> A HUNDRED or more years ago, a young egret woman with two small children had been abandoned by her husband when he mistakenly believed she had betrayed him. The woman withdrew to a tiny cottage on the lake behind the palace, and there she and the children lived, but raising them alone was a struggle. One year the winter was harsh, but spring came early. The family was desperate for food, so the woman sent her children out onto the lake for some fish. But the ice was too thin, the children fell through and she lost them both to the cold water. The woman lived on alone for many years but ultimately died of a pale longing for her young ones. As a ghost, they said, she roams the Heights, searching for children who look like her own and tries to drag them into the depths to hold against her skeletal bosom. She wears a wispy dress and moans like the wind, and walks the frozen lake on foggy nights.

Pippet chimed in eagerly, whispering, "Granpapa told me that when the lady's wails sound like they're near you she is a long ways away, but when she sounds far away she's real close. Maybe floating right behind your shoulder."

Chirra shrieked, peering behind her back and brushing herself off. A shiver went up Aru's spine.

Aru and Nrouhw tarried with their friends a bit longer than they should have, so when they did leave they had to make haste in order to arrive at their destination in the light of day. Aru hitched up the horse, a big fellow. He had a cheery strap of jingly sleigh bells that buckled around his middle and over the bobsled shafts. It felt good to handle harness again after all this time.

The bright outdoors gave Aru high spirits; she rubbed her mittens together. Chill air nipped at her face and she could see her breath.

The snow crunched under everyone's feet. As they all started up the trail, Aru turned to look back at the Villa. Snug under a snow-covered roof, beneath the two great guardian maples, the cottage gave her a crisp new image to remember it by. Aru said goodbye to the house as another friend; something of her would remain within the Villa and, in exchange, memories of this home would be a part of her for years to come. She wondered what the next residents would be like.

Veya and her family accompanied Aru and Nrouhw up to the highway. They said goodbye quickly but with plenty of hugs. Aru gave Veya a delicate silver locket that she'd had since she was a child. Veya had something for Aru, too. She surprised her with a lovely fan of goose feathers. It was both beaded and quilled, and with a cottonwood handle she'd carved in the shape of a squirrel performing an aerial toe-touch. It must have taken her many hours to make. One more long embrace and then Nrouhw handed Aru the horse's thick cotton lead rope. A good side-step to free the runners again and they were off, headed up the road.

The horse was a fine cremello gelding, the colors of a pale moon. Even in his winter coat he had a satiny appearance. His nose was soft and pink. He had work to do. It would be uphill all the way, but the road wasn't steep and there was a good three or four inches of snow.

Aru and Nrouhw walked by the horse's head. There were no sleigh tracks to follow but they did see a lot of animal tracks crossing the road. After a couple of bends in the mountainside they'd gone farther in this direction than Aru had yet been.

Opal Heights was the name of the house owned by Lekki's fiancée's family, but over the generations the name had become attached to the entire mountaintop community. It was situated not on the mountain directly above Sylfaen, as the villagers tended to think, but on the next peak to the west.

The way had a nerve-wracking precipice or two but there were brilliant views as they traveled beside the ravine. Sparkling snow covered everything, reflecting light into places the sun couldn't reach. Their road ascended steadily with a gentle grade and a switchback here and there. The jingling sleigh bells, the creaking and jangling of the rig and swooshy cutting sound of the runners, the steamy blowing of the eager young horse, the smells of horse and wool and winter, all this added to Aru's bliss as they walked in the cool sunshine.

Several times Aru thought they must be about to reach the top of the mountain. At last they came to a place where the road turned away from the cliffs. They entered an open forest of shrubby upland birches, bent and one-sided from the harsh winds. Soon the road climbed more sharply, turned, and made its way across the top of a narrow snowy ridge. Shaped like a huge natural dike, this could have been a causeway for giants. Squinting off into the brightness in both directions from the ridge, Nrouhw and Aru enjoyed spine-tingling scenery. Eventually the ridge widened out before them to join the treeless slope of another mountain. As they followed the road around some craggy rocks several buildings came into view. Above them and off to the right, the palace.

The great house of Opal Heights stood high atop an imposing snow-dusted column of natural granite. Perched in elegant watchfulness on the massive stone monolith, the palace itself looked delicate, as if it was made of sugar and milky porcelain. The road before Nrouhw and Aru crossed the snowfields for a good half-mile or so and then climbed a long ramp built on top of a mass of rubble, a ramp that eventually zig zagged its way right up the side of the tower of rock. Except for this entrance, a grand one with welcoming pillars and fountains, the bounds of the residence were a sheer precipice all around.

Six or more stories high, the main house had towers and spires of various heights capped by conical roofs of grey slate, too sharply pitched to hold the snow. Sweeping up from the front court, two grand curving stairways met at the main entrance on the second level. Across a courtyard the bell tower had a big clock face on the front. Despite the remote location and such a commanding vantage, this place stood in welcoming dignity, a seat of royalty and pageantry.

But the palace was not their destination. After they crossed the snowfields with their horse and sleigh and then gazed up at Opal Heights for a while, Aru and Nrouhw took a road that split off to the left, north, following a freshly-sanded slope over a ridge. As they crested this hill they could see the town in a cozy valley before them and tremendous vertical cliffs rising beyond. Breathtaking. And, what a marvel! Through some sort of insanity, high up on the faces of those far cliffs were buildings. Somehow. There were jagged peaks above.

It was row houses, mostly, up on those cliffsides beyond the town. They looked strange, like trains of boxcars made from crumb cake or maybe shortbread, perched precariously along indiscernible roads. Up high was one row, up there was one, and up that way another. As odd as they looked, it was in some places difficult to discern which were buildings and which were the natural rocky outcrops on the cliff face.

"And, look!" said Nrouhw, "Above, aren't those mountain goats clinging to the cliff wall?"

Yes, six or seven mountain goats scaled the cliff. They seemed pasted right to the rock face! What sort of magic allowed an animal to balance in such an impossible way?

Three celebrated peaks crowned the mountain at Opal Heights. These were named Bwahmaa, Mahahag, and Bwahmyr. Each was a collection of great upended slabs of granite; multiple wedges sharpened by the wind and snow, standing together in sheaves that poked up into the sky. Together these three triumphant entities formed the highest mountain in the eastern ranges. On this day they showed off a frosting of fresh snow.

Aru and Nrouhw continued, exhilarated by the impressive sights. A few steps along, they passed beautiful statues placed on the bank just above the roadside. Truly masterful depictions; a pair of women draped in elegant folds of flowing robes, shielding their eyes as they stared off in the direction of the late afternoon sun. A grandmother and her granddaughter, maybe. *What a lovely welcome to the town this makes,* Aru was thinking, when she realized the statues were alive.

The shriek came before Aru could arrest it; all she could do was pull out her handkerchief and make a similar sound into it. She excused herself. Nrouhw, the jewel of a person, instead of laughing bade her good health.

The women turned to look at the travelers. They smiled and waved. Aru waved back with her handkerchief. The ladies returned to their conversation and Aru sheepishly ducked her head a little as she walked past. As soon as she'd gone far enough beyond them, she released her breath in a laugh that squeezed out of puffed cheeks through lips still pursed from embarrassment. She sounded something like a deflating balloon. Nrouhw was laughing too.

"Those women, how is it possible?" she whispered. "I've never seen anything like it, their skin; so absolutely colorless, I truly thought they were carved from pure marble."

"You did, as well?" replied Nrouhw. "That's what I thought when I first saw these people, too."

They giggled again.

"So hauntingly enchanting," said Aru. "Is that what the people of the mountaintop look like?"

The road came to a junction not long after it began to descend into the valley. "Here we are," said Nrouhw. "Turn right on Bweheh M. Bweheheh Way. That's the street of our address. The directions are quite simple, thankfully. A rather grand name for a road."

Their horse veered to the right without being asked; apparently his own home lay that way also. Soon they came to a place where they crossed another lane. From here they had a clear sight of the town.

They looked out into a steep bowl created by the high cliffs under the peaks and the somewhat lower hills to the west. The town filled the bottom of this valley and had been built up onto the cliffsides in some places. They could see a frozen lake and a large lakeside park. The buildings were old, mostly stone, and quite charming with snow on the roofs.

"Look at all those diapers!" exclaimed Aru.

Nrouhw laughed. "Those are too small to be diapers. Those are ceremonial flags. I remember seeing a similar sort of bunting when I toured the mountain villages on the southeast continents. Several years ago. I'm fairly sure that's what those are."

Aru tried to take it all in but was overheated from her warm clothing and tired from the climb. She was also eager to see their new house.

The road began to ascend as they traversed the back side of the steep ridge they'd just rounded. Traveling east along this southern rim of the valley, buildings stood here and there. These increased in number, pressing closer together as the road progressed up and across the slope. On the left-hand side glimpses of the town below could be caught between the buildings, and over the rooftops the beauty of the far rim, the peaks glistening as they reflected the late afternoon light.

An expensive-looking stationer's and a cheesery and other interesting shops lined the way, and although it must have been approaching suppertime a few folks were moving about. Aru saw an owlish-looking woman in an overcoat pursuing a couple of tiny children through a doorway. A big man crossed the road in front of their sleigh, giving a nod, his arms full of packages wrapped in muslin. There were several more of those people endemic to these mountaintops: the Opali.

Fascinatingly attractive, these few Opali that Aru saw displayed elegance and sophistication. Their abundance of poise was clearly visible. They themselves were somewhat difficult to see, because of the light-colored clothing they wore in that frozen environment.

A couple of women, deep in conversation, passed not far away. The sunward side of both their forms made no outlines at all against the snow, only a focal blurring, all texture smoothed away by reflecting light. The gentle shadows of their features were what made them visible at all, along with the tiny pockets of shadow in the weave of their sweaters and the spectral shades of faintest pink and violet in the folds of the luxurious drape of their satiny skirts.

These Opal Heights people, their hair grew thick and woolly. They were fair, certainly. Lily-petal skin, creamy as milk, colorless as paraffin. Striking skin tone they had, and snowy hair and eyebrows. Yes, their coloring was interesting and beautiful, but—*great rabies-ridden mange-mongers!*—how could everyone have told her these Opali people looked like *her?* Aru looked down at her mittened hand. She wanted to look in a mirror. Such a stabbing feeling, to have been told she'd fit in here merely because her complexion had a different tone.

Her thoughts were startled away by something that overtook her and Nrouhw from behind. An animal came up the road, some kind of white deer or elk. It appeared from nowhere, passing her and Nrouhw at a trot and pulling a small canoe-shaped sledge with a single trace and a single rein. At first she thought the driver was a snow monster, but then she realized that the body was that of a shaggy sheepdog and the head belonged to a man who had the dog on his lap.

The man grinned in what Aru took to be a kind and welcoming expression. His teeth were big and shiny. He was utterly pleased with life, and anyone who encountered him could clearly feel it. He rode on by and she never saw him again. But Aru always remembered seeing that man the day she arrived in Opal Heights.

After the man in the sledge had gone by, Aru and Nrouhw talked about him. The animal was a reindeer, not an elk. Nrouhw explained that sledges of that type were the common form of transportation in the area. Horses were loved by the Opali people, but were not practical in the deeper snow. The people of Opal Heights kept horses for their occasional trips to the lower lands and for dressage and other equestrian events in covered arenas. Aru patted the horse's neck as they walked. Such a flawless, handsome thing. He was getting tired.

"Here we are. Number 137."

Nrouhw stopped in front of a tidy row of two-story terraced cottages. Each had its own narrow gateway in the high stone wall. Peeking through, one could see across charming little front gardens divided by frosty hedges. The door to each cottage had windows in it and was crowned by an arched window above. All of the sash windows were arched also, and stone chimneys along with tiny walls defined the shared roof into individual segments. There were skylights! Nrouhw said that of course there were, as these cottages had been designed for artists to live in.

"That," Nrouhw pointed to the tall and ornate building just beyond, "must be the academy."

They tied the horse to an old stone hitching post and went in to see their new home. The front door opened into a small reception room and then into a parlor with a fireplace made of quartz. Someone from the academy had built up a blazing fire for their arrival. There was a door into a hallway and also a big double doorway into a dining room of about the same size as the parlor. Aru felt excitedly numb. How could all this be for just her and Nrouhw?

Down the hallway was the kitchen, with a window seat and a pantry. There was a water spigot in the sink, and an indoor water closet in the rear of the house. Upstairs they found the two bedchambers (one would serve as Nrouhw's studio). The bathroom had a big porcelain-enameled tub.

Nrouhw called Aru to come see the balcony. There was no backyard, but the view from the bedroom balcony was spectacular. They could watch all the activity going on in the town below—there were people skating on the lake and strolling along a snowy promenade—and they could look across at the high icy cliffs and towering peaks.

They stood holding each other, looking at the scenery until a horse sneezing down the street reminded them they had things to do. After they'd started unloading the sleigh a boy arrived who had been sent by the academy to help them. They stacked most of the things in the parlor temporarily, and with the three of them working it didn't take long to get the job done. When they finished, Nrouhw and the boy left on the sleigh to return the horse to his owner and Aru was to start with the unpacking of essential things such as the linens and bedding, and some dishes. First, she went upstairs again to look at the bathtub.

The bathroom was light and airy and clean. It had tiles on the floor and also shiny tiled wainscoting on the walls, with a fanciful border pattern. There was a built-in wash basin with an enormous mirror above it. The bathtub had a spigot for water. It stood on funny lion legs with big paws, and it was a beautiful thing, with a curled rim and raised on the ends and sloped for comfort.

When Nrouhw arrived home after dusk he was surprised, on walking through the parlor, that almost nothing had been unpacked. The fire in the kitchen stove was lit, but nothing was cooking on the stovetop. Upstairs, he saw light coming from the bathroom doorway. When he peeked in, he laughed. Candles had been lit in the wall sconces, reflecting on the mirror and the frosted glass of the steamed-up window. Clothes and towels were strewn, water puddles were all over the floor. There in the bathtub, nearly hidden in a cloud of bubbles, was Aru, a big smile on her face.

The name of the eight-cottage row house was Bwe Mahaaha, "The Hornfel." Nrouhw and Aru's first guests in this new home, just after breakfast time, were Aldrei and Aeon who brought a housewarming gift of ginger lily bath salts. There wasn't much in the way of furniture yet, but the friends sat on various improvised chairs, and had their tea from ceramic bowls because the teacups were yet to be found. Despite any misgivings or confusion about loyalties, it was good to see the old fellows. Aldrei had changed since they'd seen him. His hair and beard were quite snowy and ivory now and the fur on his ears also. He had entered his winter phase.

Nrouhw had an appointment over at the administration offices of the academy. Aldrei would have nothing for it other than for Aru to accompany him and Aeon on some errands that morning. It was a brilliant day, sunny and cold like the day before.

They hadn't gone far down the street before they came upon a man that Aldrei and Aeon knew. An Opali banker, he wore an impeccably-tailored light grey lambswool overcoat and matching silk top hat. The man greeted them in Opali, not realizing Aru didn't speak it. Aeon spoke to the man briefly, and as they parted Aru bade the gentleman have a good day. He smiled at her and walked away.

"He didn't seem to understand me. Don't they speak the common jargon here?" she asked.

"Of course he doesn't understand what you're saying," replied Aeon. "Didn't you notice? The Opali are voice shakers. They'll understand the jargon just fine. You just have to shake the words out, like this: So-o-o-o plee--ee-eeased I-I-I a-a-a-am to-oo-oo m-ee-ee-ee-ee-eet you."

Aru tried this with the next few Opali people she spoke to, and sure enough, she could make herself understood. It would take practice for it to come naturally, though. The first real conversation she had was with a woman in a bookshop down in the valley. The lady was quite curious about Aru.

Everything looked bright and clean in this town, with only foot traffic and a few deer sledges to disturb the snow. The friends visited several nooks and shops that morning, but the most intriguing was the last. Aru could smell the waxy sugariness in the air as she approached.

The signboard read in the common tongue:

MAMA BWEHMEB'S CONFECTIONERY.

CANDIES FOR EVERY CONTINGENCY.

Aru had noticed several other candy shops in the neighborhood, but even so Mama Bwehmeb's looked like quite a thriving business, all noisy and overcrowded with kids and old people. The granite storefront was etched to resemble a lace doily, a pattern which continued across the window panes. Strings of all sorts of candies and sparkly crystal beads dangled inside. A marble statue was just outside the door, a truly exquisite carving of a silly dancing faun holding a tall wide-mouthed vase as an umbrella stand for the customers. A bell jingled as Aru and her friends shut the door behind them, closing out the crisp cold air.

"Aldrei, good morning; hello Mister Aeon!" said a young girl who was dressing the window. "Come in, come in! Grandfather is in the back." An Opali girl, she had a starched uniform with an apron and a little hat somewhat like a nurse's. "Oh my, who is your friend?" She reached out to shake Aru's hand.

Aldrei and Aeon greeted the girl warmly, then Aru walked with them to the back of the store to find the grandfather. A row of round tearoom-style tables lined one wall, a cute place to sit if you didn't mind women's skirts brushing against you now and then, or moony kids pointing at selections of candy just behind you. The wall was covered floor-to-ceiling with shelves of glass jars filled to the brims.

Across the aisle, a long counter of showcase cabinets was topped with curved-front display cases and a candy scale, and more sweets jars with glass lids. Two men and a woman in those strange little hats rushed to and fro behind the counter, at work to keep all the eager customers happy. High up above were the subtleties, under crystal domes: sugar sculptures of birds and fancy fish and lotuses and even a stag with great antlers.

The store owner was seated at one of the tables in the rear, and Aldrei and his friends crowded in to join him. "Aru," said Aeon, "we'd like you to meet our friend the lovely Mr. Mahahb Mahahbeh."

The old fellow had been reading his newspaper, and when they arrived he set down his glasses and welcomed them, placing his bony hand fondly on Aldrei's shoulder. He said some kind things to Aru about her appearance and how he couldn't remember ever having seen anyone of her enchanting creamy peach-like complexion.

"She truly is rather attractive," he added into Aldrei's ear, apparently under the impression that he was whispering, "in a shocking sort of way."

Aldrei laughed loudly and winked at Aru.

Mr. Mahahbeh had long hair and a trailing beard also, of the purest white, and eyebrows and eyelashes of the same snowy colorlessness, just like most Opalis. His skin had plenty of wrinkles, but he had no age spots at all. He was an extreme voice shaker, and so Aru wasn't able to understand quite everything he said. But he looked at her with sweet grey eyes and laughed and giggled so much that Aru couldn't help but like him.

After they had all kidded around for a few minutes Aldrei suggested Aeon and Aru go get sweets for the four of them, his treat. So Aru found herself with the difficult task of helping decide which to pick.

At the counter, coconut rabbits and marshmallow elephants smiled out from beribboned trays beside paper cups of seafoam divinity and sticks of chewing gum. There were bins and bottles, and amongst it all, signs everywhere suggesting items such as clear aged ginger ale and offering lemon, vanilla, and pineapple cream sodas. All sorts of tiny cakes and pastries sat on paper lace doilies, along with yogurt-glazed animal cookies covered in sprinkles.

Aru thought Aldrei might want the candy skulls, but Aeon said that Aldrei had nearly broken a tooth on one once. Although, they could also bring him one of the white paper bags full of candy teeth.

Rock candy, rice candy, penny candy, and ivory sugar pearls, there was far too much to choose from. Two boys in aprons were pulling saltwater taffy and popcorn was popping in a glassed-in kettle. Kids scrambled everywhere, spilling their little bags of candy gems and knocking things over and adding much to the charm of the place.

At last Aru and Aeon brought back to the table a plate filled with unicorn tails, squares of almond nougat, and of course crystallized lovage flowers. Mr. Mahahbeh had fallen asleep; Aldrei said it happened in the middle of a story he was telling. He was a very old man.

"Perhaps we should let him rest, then," said Aeon. "We have plenty of things to discuss."

"Nonsense!" said Aldrei, and he shook the old man awake.

"Fiend!" cried Mahahb, and he slapped Aldrei hard across the cheek with the back of his hand. "Don't you know better than to wake an old man?" Then the two of them broke out laughing.

Aeon looked at Aru, sighed and shrugged. "I'm glad these two love the candy store and not the tavern. Can you imagine?"

Mr. Mahahbeh brought out some playing cards and the four friends spent the rest of the morning playing poker. When it was time to head home, Mahahb beckoned Aru over for a hug and he handed her a delicate candy necklace with an actual candy locket. The hug was both wonderful and torturous for Aru because she had to hold her breath to avoid his awful cheesy, soured patchouli smell. But his warm acceptance, along with the other events of her day, brought Aru happiness. She felt inspired about the prospects of life in Opal Heights.

Nrouhw liked his new job at the academy, mostly because they allotted him time during the day to work on his own projects. The classes were conventional, drapes and sheets and pale models. Nrouhw was fascinated that in the student work the faces often resembled their own more than those of the sitting subjects. He was told this was common.

When Nrouhw was at work Aru had a lot of time to herself. She didn't mind, it was fun living a life of leisure. Visits with Aldrei and

Aeon became a regular part of Aru's routine, either laughing together at Mama Bwehmeb's or touring the locality or sitting in Aru and Nrouhw's parlor. She and Nrouhw saw Lekki now and then also, and after they'd been in the Heights a few weeks they received a letter in Aranieda's exceptionally thin script:

My Dears Aru and Nrouhw,

I'm certain this letter will find you well, because, as you no doubt understand, it is my breeding and vocation to know these things.

First, I shall share with you that there is some news of good cheer regarding the boy Queex. It seems that Avariceo the Blackbuck has decided, for whatever his reasons may be, to bring Queex to the house of Opal Heights. I believe he has an idea that the boy retains some sort of secrets regarding the hypogeous snails.

Queex will be well kept at the palace, with his own nanny to care for him, and able to play at producing art. I must say I think the boy is gifted with a degree of talent, perhaps his works can be sold in galleries. At any rate, his family is well pleased and this arrangement can only be a wonderful chance for the boy to eventually sustain himself, with help of course, and have the comfort he ought to have.

So look for Queex to arrive in the Heights one day soon, and know that Pippet has been asked to accompany him and his escort as the boy knows her well and trusts her. Perhaps you and she can have a nice visit while she is there.

Also I wish to tell you about the adventures that our same Blackbuck has had since last you heard.

The man recently called upon the frog colony of Muhg-Wuffle's old family tree, having managed somehow to get himself invited for lunch. Of course during his visit he found an opportunity to try the key in the lock of the storeroom door to the lower world. It could not open, because of course we know it will not. Sadly, however, there wasn't a way for me to entrap him while he was so occupied down there, not without imprisoning the frogs also under the old hawthorn.

Something unexpected did happen. I witnessed this personally, having concealed myself in a place advantageous to viewing the man's actions.

When the key couldn't work the lock, Blackbuck kept at it even so, as he is not one to give up within a reasonable time. When finally he withdrew the key he was surprised to see that a magical writing had appeared engraved upon it. I have to say, I was as mystified as he, for I can only now theorize about how that writing came.

The glyphs were in an ancient tongue, and one in which I am not well schooled, but I could understand enough to work out that Blackbuck's later actions were an attempt to perform the ritual delineated by that verse. I surmise that the ritual was, ostensibly, to make the key perform its work in opening the door.

There had been an old deteriorated key in the lock originally, too fragile to be of use, so I had pressed it into a bar of soap and had the soap sent to a silversmith as a mold for a new one. I had certainly never requested any spells upon that key, which of course is the one now in Blackbuck's possession. Could there have been some magic in the original key, I don't know. Or did the smith have something to do with it. However this came to be, it is of benefit to my plans for it helps to keep the man interested. This will likely give me time to somehow evict the frogs and then supply the place with seven months of provisions.

I kept the man Blackbuck under close surveillance after this, because I had a certain curiosity about his next activities. Only a few days later found him just down the slope from the palace of Opal Heights, standing out on the center of Lake Mwahma and executing a rite involving the lake ice. He stood in the noon sun, and this was on the date of the full moon. It had been a foggy morning, but the sky was beginning to clear, I saw him hold the key high with both hands, and my limited understanding of the glyphs I had seen makes me believe that the desired result was for the key to turn to glass when a favorable outcome was achieved.

As the key shone silver in a sunbeam it was snatched by, can you believe it, an albatross. She must've mistaken it for a shiny minnow. Blackbuck shouted and sneezed but the great bird flew off with his prize, uncaring.

Such a man was not to be defied in such a way. Because there was no shelter to make his hasty change discreet, he transformed right there on the ice. Before he removed his clothing he first untied three knots from a lock of his hair, causing a small whirlwind to form around him, blowing the snow. This shielded him somewhat from my view. When he had fully his antelope shape he drew up this wind, it became a violent tempest, and he blew it all toward the east, in the direction the big bird had taken.

It was impressive, Blackbuck's magical dance, a truly engaging thing to watch. Clearly, at a certain point he began to call the wind back, and furiously the wind changed; the blowing snow traveled now the opposite direction. Eventually the albatross appeared in the sky again, except she was in her human form, as apparently the enchantment of the stormy wind current that had swept her back to Blackbuck had also caused her to transform.

She landed nearly on top of him and she threw her arms about his antelope neck to stop herself from blowing further in the gale. He shook her off and she fell, stunned, to lay naked in the snow as if dead. The wind calmed as the Blackbuck returned to human form. He tossed his thick winter cape over the albatross woman and then he dressed himself. She soon revived enough to wrap herself in the silvery wool. When she had done so he grabbed the woman by the shoulders and said something to her I could not quite make out.

"Yes I swallowed it," she told him, "and there inside me it will stay. Unless you choose to take my life."

Then he replied to her with a bitter tone, saying, "You don't belong here, vagrant, and your life isn't worth such an object."

She answered him with the words, "Just kill me then, mage, if that is your plan, and get it over with!"

But he replied, "You know as well as I, that I can kill no albatross."

"Then release me at once, Sir, and I will be on my way," she said, and that is what was done.

Now, I believe that the Blackbuck would speculate, as I do, that the origin of the glyphs on the key was the silversmith of Bwahmyr. That is who made the key and I am fair certain that Blackbuck will have deduced as much by the quality of the work and the smell of the magic.

I also imagine he will soon pay a visit to the smith, probably in person or perhaps by emissary. He'll want another key, another enchantment to replace the one lost to the belly of the bird. And here is where I must beg a favor of you.

The silversmith of Bwahmyr Peak is a powerful sorcerer. Born, it is whispered, not an Opali mountain goat, but a descendant of the abom-

inable snowfolk themselves. It would be greatly to my advantage if I knew the perspective of the silversmith and what intentions she may have in any little concerns with Blackbuck. We can be sure she is aware of who he is, because of the upcoming wedding etcetera, yet I have not been able to determine her opinion of him. It seems she may have rendered me some assistance, yet I must learn more about her reasons for attending to the key, if in fact it was she that did so. She never leaves her mountaintop and I am unable to pay her a visit myself, as the high glacial location is just too cold for me to endure.

Your Aldrei goes sometimes to visit the smith and her husband Meheheh Mehah, an illustrious watchmaker. Would you please ask Aldrei to take the two of you to visit there? I'm positive he'd be happy to do it. You would enjoy seeing the fine works of art these masters produce. If you could let me know anything of the smith's intentions it would aid me in working to minimize the destructive forces that pour forth from the wretched man, the Blackbuck.

Yours most Sincerely,
Aranieda

Three days later, as a result of this letter, Aru and Nrouhw were snow-shoeing with Aldrei up Cloudy Pass toward the peak called Bwahmyr. The snowshoes were great fun, as the mohair-wrapped frames had an uncanny purchase. Aru felt as if she could walk straight up a wall. This was good, because the road was steep, and became steeper, indeed it seemed nearly vertical for a stretch though it couldn't have been.

When they made the top of the ridge they were at least a league above sea level, higher in altitude than Aru had ever climbed. On a clear day there must have been an astounding snowscape view in all directions, but on this day fog and a light snow made walking the high ridge an experience of intimate isolation. Even with the world so small and close around them they felt invigorated.

The road ran northwest along the frozen rocky crest, marked here and there with snow poles and slightly packed by sledge trails. Before long they saw a formal-looking building staring down from a rise. How strange it looked up there in the treeless wild.

"Dharma Cairn Academy," shouted Aldrei over the wind.

"Really?" cried Aru. "The children come up here every day?"

"Of course they do," shouted Aldrei. The idea seemed to please him.

As they continued up the road it leveled out to nearly flat for quite a way, a welcome relief from all that climbing. Finally it came to an end in a loop in front of a great house, not as massive as the palace, but still impressive. Aldrei told them the name was Abseil Manor, famous as the site of the annual eagle gymkhana.

"Oh, that sounds like fun!" shouted Aru.

Aldrei yelled, "The aerobatics are amusing. Also there are educational forums and beauty judging, if you go for those sorts of things."

Aru realized she'd been getting tired and she was glad they'd arrived at their destination. Only, they hadn't. They passed under the arch of a building and through a courtyard and then right on through the snow-covered grounds on what looked like a rabbit trail.

Aldrei paused in the lee of one of the outbuildings and told them he'd need just a moment. He winked and slipped through the doorway into the shed. Nrouhw and Aru stood waiting patiently. After a while, standing there, they began to feel a bit less patient. Aru's toes felt cold. She wanted to sit down. Eventually she lost her patience altogether and began to whine. Nrouhw decided the time had come to see what had happened with Aldrei. He pushed the door open to peek inside. The shed had a large skylight, so it wasn't difficult to see. A few garden tools, snow shovels, two wheelbarrows, a stack of salt bags, there wasn't a lot of clutter. And there was no Aldrei.

Nrouhw removed his snowshoes, shook the snow off his coat, and went in, closely followed by Aru. They poked around among the things, not actually sure what they were expecting to find. Wherever Aldrei had gone, they'd just have to wait until he came back. Aru sat down on the salt, relieved to have a break, anyhow, out of the wind.

Then, through the open doorway, she saw something.

"Oh!" she shrieked.

It was an eye in the snow, looking at her. Iridescent blue. Just an eye. Peering at it for a moment, Aru realized she saw also the cleft of a little snout and a shadowy hint of a long ear. Aldrei was sitting just outside in the snow, looking at them. He had taken the form she'd first seen him in, that of a hare. Only this time he had his winter coat.

Nrouhw stepped over to look. "Now why would he do that?" he wondered. "I suppose it is easier for him to travel in this form."

"Not a good sign regarding the route to come, is it!" Aru exclaimed.

Nrouhw laughed. "Or, it may just be more fun for him."

They followed the hare up the trail toward the summit; more accurately, they followed his tracks, because at times it was almost impossible to see him. The snow was deep up there, and there were no more sledges to pack it, but the snowshoes worked like magic.

Soon they came to a signpost. A spiral pole bore a sign reading *Bwahmyr Silver* in fine calligraphy. What a sight! Such a promising beacon! But Aru's pleasure drained away when she noticed where it pointed. Straight off a cliff. She and Nrouhw looked at each other. Nrouhw threw up his hands and crossed his arms, leaning back at the shoulders. He was curious to see what Aldrei had for them next.

He wasn't disappointed. The hare leaped high into the air and kicked the sign hard with his rear legs. The thing spun like a pinwheel, shooting out silver sparks in every direction. Amid the clacking and popping Aru could hear a faint music as it spun. Her mind reached to place the melody, the flickering memory of a tune from her childhood. When the signboard came to a stop it had the additional words *through the weekend, most likely* painted across the bottom and now it pointed northeast. The hare hopped along in that direction.

As their path took them over Bwahmyr's eastern shoulder, the icy peak loomed above. At long last they found the silversmith's domed house. Made of blocks of snow formed perfectly into a coiled shape like a snail shell, it sat in solitude on a flattish area that still caught the afternoon light. The entrance was also of snow, a short tunnel through an elegant horseshoe arch. Just beside, a thin pole was planted in the snow at an angle, dangling several chains of silver bells to tinkle in the wind.

Aru and Nrouhw looked up at the cliffs, hoping to see what Aldrei had said they might if they were lucky: the entrance to a small mine. It was nowhere to be seen, though. This was too bad; Nrouhw, especially, would have liked to see it. All the processing of the silver ore took place up there right inside the mine and the forge was in there also.

With a flick of his tail Aldrei changed instantly to appear, fully clothed, in the form that was familiar to Aru and Nrouhw. "Nice place, isn't it!" he said of the house. "A little isolated."

Nrouhw laughed, "That should precipitate a warm reception."

"Perhaps the owners will besnow their kind hospitality upon us."

Aldrei and Nrouhw both thought themselves terribly funny.

"If there was a view, you could see it!" said Aldrei. "All the way to the coast, on some days. You'll just have to imagine." And with that he disappeared down through the doorway.

Nrouhw and Aru stood politely, waiting for someone to invite them in. They weren't certain what to do, as Aldrei hadn't knocked. Were they supposed to follow him? They had waited a few minutes and were whispering back and forth about whether they should go on in when an elderly, bearded Opali man poked his head out of the tunnel.

With an amused grin and in a very shaky voice he asked, "Why, whenever do you intend to enter?" Then he disappeared back inside.

Steps carved into the snow led downward under the arch. These accessed the low tunnel, then steps went up again to enter the snow house. The interior was all one big, bright room. It felt deeply pleasing to be inside that round shape. Light came through the blocks of snow as if the whole structure was made of frosted glass windows. The dense centers of the blocks had a blue tint, but the grooves between them shone with an even brighter light.

A platform of snow served as a sofa and apparently also as the bed. Covered with lots of thick mountain goat wool blankets, it proved to be an insulated and comfortable place to sit. There were tables and racks and tapestry partitions, and there was a small cookstove with tea simmering.

Aldrei introduced the man, the watchmaker Mr. Meheheh Mehah, who greeted them in an amiable manner and asked them how they had fared on the hike up the mountain.

"Let me just beckon my better half," he said. He peeked behind a beautiful wool curtain covered with tessellated everlasting knot designs. Softly, he said, "Mynydd, precious, the guests have presented themselves." Then, returning to his visitors, "Evidently she's heard a truly melodious echo, an echo of the breath spent on your trek as you ascended the fell. My best guess is that this pleasant experience rendered my love's temper exceptionally benevolent with respect to the two of you kids." He gave Aru and Nrouhw a wink.

Mynydd entered the space silently, with just the swishing of her many satin skirts and a soft smile of recognition for Aldrei. She didn't look at her company at first. She waited until she had reached her chair and donned her spectacles.

Ice-blue irises filled Mynydd's eyes almost completely, making them look extra large, and intense with intelligence; scary to look into, not because of fierceness but because they looked too magical, too knowing, and maybe insidious. Those eyes were framed by a bony, sharply-defined brow and long, slightly hooked nose with flared nostrils. In addition to her startling eyes, she had a sizable pair of horns. Ringed with ridges, these curved up and back from her head in gorgeous twists. Her skin had that Opali flawlessness that Aru was beginning to envy. Her ears were a bit pointy. For a woman of such advanced age her hair was quite thick and she left it long and free and in waves of curl. She wore no jewelry at all.

When Mynydd spoke it was with a soft voice. Her words were welcoming and kind, yet a strange feeling surrounded her, a bubble of unreachability. One didn't ask her questions. Answers would come in due course. The guests joined her in some sweet silverleaf tea and an interesting conversation about the history of the area, and then were invited into the studio. After a joke about having seen quite enough of the couple's vices Aldrei remained on the sofa; they could soon hear his resounding snores.

Mynydd and Meheheh's studio was not a separate building, or even a separate room, but an area at the far side of the house. It was, as Meheheh described it, "a pleasurable mess." A jumble of metalworking tools and scraps of silver and great magnifying lenses, the shop was crowded with all sorts of sacks and tins stacked high. Several half-finished projects lay around, and dozens of watches hung on their chains from above. Silver dust coated everything.

It felt a bit cold on this side of the house, but in her heavy skirts and coat Aru was quite comfortable. Looking over an array of items on a workbench made of snow, she noticed a wonderful little cap all carved in scrollwork. "May I pick it up?" she asked.

Mynydd smiled and handed it to her. "It's a helmet for a certain butterfingered adolescent squirrel."

"It's so lovely," said Aru, a phrase she found herself repeating again and again as she and Nrouhw browsed through the outstanding collection of silverwork strewn here and there. The awe they felt increased with each item that was presented. The artists had collaborated on a new commodity, watches worn on a bracelet. Wristwatches. These were becoming popular with schoolteachers and others who might have their hands full when they were curious about the time.

In due course Meheheh suggested they have another cup of tea and a nibble in the sitting room. Aldrei opened one eye upon their return, although he kept on snoring until he sat up to join them when the pastries were served.

It was then that Mynydd suggested to Meheheh that he tell one of the scores of stories he knew. The old goat was happy to do it, but he found it tiring to speak in the common tongue, so he spoke in his own language and Aldrei translated for him:

"You know all about the story of *The Song of Defnyn*, of course. No? Well then, I'll tell you."

IT HAPPENED on a distant fell but not so long ago, when the ice grew thin and the winter snows were melting and the swans were building up their nests to bring another course of cygnets into the world. Fine structures of lotus tubers the birds had made on the shallows of a mountain lake, one just by the outflow of the waters and another on a tiny island at the head. Lined with the softest downy feathers selected and arranged with care, these love nests would soon welcome a new generation of the elegant birds, to drift, mysterious and beautiful, on the still water.

These were days of fortune and prosperity for all who lived on the mountain, for the slopes were charmed by the presence of many fairies who loved the winters and the glistening cold and who dressed the happy mountain with lilies and love in the summertime. Among all of these alpine fey, the water sprites brought the lightest feelings and most brilliant amounts of joy to the community.

Nature will have her bearing, however, and when the spring snow-storms come unforeseen there are sometimes those who suffer and die. Onto this lovely mountain and lovely lake there came a thunderous blizzard, bringing woe to the animals who were feathering their nests and making ready for springtime activities. From the snowstorm they made themselves safe, for they were animals and in human form they knew the ways of the wild. But down the mountainside came a monster, a traveler of the greatest speed, a roaring and devastating avalanche. The people scattered from the hillside just before it happened, because they felt it coming, or they burrowed far underneath it to be safe. But the thing drove down in its destructive force and covered half the little lake as it came.

The water fairy folk had all retired to below the ice, save for one fairy maiden. The nymph Defnyn let curiosity rule her; and why not so, for how could she come to harm? From the center of the lake, as she admired the lightning and the blowing snow, she witnessed the avalanche's deluge and destruction.

Soon a man on snowshoes came running from the direction of the village warren. With him was the father swan, and the mother, from the nest which had just been covered over, for he was the wildlife warden, the keeper of the pond and its waterfowl. The swans, although mute, had gone to fetch his aid.

The warden could see the fairy sparkling on the lake, and he called to her, "Hello, you there! Have eggs been laid in the nest yet?"

There were five eggs in one of the nests; Defnyn had just recently heard the news. But she couldn't recall which one. *Yes,* she told the man, through the voiceless voice inside his head, adding, *I think so,* in her own thoughts.

He hurried to the area where the nest had been, and began to dig furiously in the snow with his hands. Defnyn saw something she had never seen before, a person transforming while engaged in an activity. Before her eyes the man changed to a big snowshoe hare and when so transformed his work went much faster. Furiously he dug, throwing up the powdery snow in all directions, but it was to be his last effort.

Another shift of the avalanche crashed down the slopes and swept him away down the mountainside, never to be found until the melt.

Defnyn was turned into a swan by her sisters because of the events of this day. Firstly, they blamed her for the death of the hare, and this truly was her fault, as the nest, in fact, was empty. Also, though, they charged her with having been the cause of the avalanche in the first place, refusing to believe the truth of the matter:

You see, young Defnyn had a clear, ringing voice and she loved more than anything to sing. She knew every song and ballad of the country-side, and many more she had brought to life herself. She sang with vivacity and her tone was high and sweet. Her sisters were certain she had been singing during the snowstorm and had brought the mountain-side down. She had done no such thing, but she was considered to have a pernicious streak in her character and her siblings would not trust her when she told them she'd been quietly watching.

So she became a swan to float about on the waters and, as her sisters suggested, to reflect upon life. It was a cruel thing to do to Defnyn, but fairies, like young humans, can be unwittingly cruel sometimes. Defnyn spent some time in reflection, indeed, but soon she got over all that and directed her life forces into learning to transform. This is something that had never been done by a swan, but because Defnyn was in reality a fairy she was able to teach herself to do it.

So Defnyn as a young woman lived on the shores of the lake in a tiny cottage she built for herself. With the burnished and smooth skin of a human on most of her days, she had the soft plumage of a graceful swan when she felt like swimming on the water. She missed her mother, and her sisters too. She couldn't be a part of their world anymore and she couldn't fully appreciate the swans or the humans of the mountain villages. Feeling trapped in her life, she began to study magic.

Defnyn became a sorceress, and quickly a powerful one. She created an ice palace in the sky, made of swirled clouds, up high where the air is frozen. Out of pure vindictiveness she wouldn't allow the snowflakes to fall to the mountains below. She lived alone in this bitterly cold construction for quite some time, until she learned to see the fairies again, at which point she kidnapped her sisters, one by one, and held them prisoners in a cell created for the purpose.

The magic of life is in the water, and without the water from the snow all the fairies and the land and people began to suffer. After four years the water fairy mother found a way to ride to Defnyn's palace in the teardrop of a common crane. She was received with indifference and her pleas were coldly rebuked. The mother water fairy told her daughter Defnyn she would give anything for her children to be free.

One solution was offered then by Defnyn, just one. She told her mother she would happily free her sisters if she were to find herself in possession of the object known as 'The Keepsake.' Defnyn's mother told her that could never happen, as the orb was said to hold a mystery so big it could never be possessed by just one entity. It held something which could present catastrophic danger of an unimaginable kind. But the mother wanted her daughters freed so much that she departed to seek the thing.

Four years later, to the day, the queen of the water fairies of the lake arrived again at her daughter Defnyn's palace of ice and clouds. Without ceremony, she handed the sorceress Defnyn an old flour sack, at the bottom of which was a heavy ball. Defnyn peered into the sack, and smiled. She released from the cell her sisters, the water nymphs of the mountain lake, all of whom departed for home quickly and without speaking, lest Defnyn have second thoughts.

The fairy-become-swan-become-sorceress took her new prize up to the tallest tower in her palace of clouds, and she drew the bolt of the door although she was alone. She placed the sack on her lap, but she didn't open it until she had drunk a whole pitcher of milk sip by sip and had eaten eighteen pearls.

At last she reached into the bag and withdrew an object the size of her palm.

How can one describe such a thing? Swirling clusters of galaxies did more than to literally fill the globe: they comprised it. This object was beyond beautiful, beyond sacred, beyond belief. The orb contained not only our universe, it contained all universes. It was everything. Everything that there is.

Defnyn was unaware of this. She could feel the phenomenon that she held in her left hand was significant, but she had no idea as to the degree. Rumors among the witches had spoken to her of the thing's existence, but only that it was full of stars, a monolith in space that floated endlessly. How her mother achieved the acquisition of it she would never know.

Defnyn kept the thing in the flour sack in the bottom of a closet for four years. Then she went to retrieve it from the closet and brought it to her dressing chamber. There she had built a small fire on the table. Defnyn removed the everything from the bag and held it over the fire. The orb began to melt, very slowly, and as it did so whole universes—whole universes—disappeared into a quantum vacuum. Liquid light dripped from the melting everything and Defnyn collected it in a teacup made of diamond.

Thankfully, just as she was so occupied, Defnyn's mother and sisters arrived, and with them a pair of women who called each other Lovebird and Sugarplum. These were swans whom the fairies had taught to transform into humans just as Defnyn had learned to do.

Defnyn looked her mother in the eyes, and her sisters in the eyes also. Then she drank the sip of liquid she'd collected in the cup.

A strange look came upon her face, the cup slipped from her fingers. In a few moments what stood in the dressing room of the sorceress in the ice palace of clouds was not Defnyn anymore, but a huge prismatic dragon, coiling and roiling like the mists above a steaming cauldron.

The fairies knew they must work faultlessly, before the dragon came into its power. They faced the monster, all of them, despite it having the ability to turn them all to dust. The swan woman Sugarplum played upon a lyre and Lovebird on a flute, as the water sprite sisters sang and danced for four solid days in order to lull and soothe the dragon. When the thing was fast asleep the fairies threw a net of ice crystals over it.

Lovebird and Sugarplum had gone under the power of the songs of the fey; they lay flat upon the floor and traveled far to the worlds beyond mortal existence, and with them traveled the soul of Defnyn. Four more days they were gone and four nights while the fairies kept up their song. When finally they returned, the young Defnyn was no longer a dragon but was in her swan form and the fairies placed a silver chain around her neck. She would never transform to human again. They left the everything on the table in the dressing room, after pouring milk to end the fire.

> The fairies of that mountain fell never speak of the palace in the sky.
> The snows fall again and there is water. Defnyn swims around and
> around upon the waters of the lake and she always will, because she is
> a fairy swan and cannot die. But she sings her plaintive, funereal song
> in order to share her pain with any who will listen.
>
> There are many things you can learn from this story, if you want to.
> Take what's meaningful and leave the rest.

After a silent moment, Aru drew a breath. "Thank you with all my heart for the story, Meheheh," she said. She turned to the silversmith. "And so now we understand the significance of that lovely swan cream pitcher you've made, Mynydd, the one with the little chain necklace."

They talked on for a while, and when Aru finally found an opportunity to bring up the subject of Blackbuck, Mynydd seemed to be expecting her to do so. "Yes we've met your antelope friend," said she. "The man has a tremendously self-serving personality. Nevertheless, he may yet step from his pedestal of self-obsessiveness and enter the realm of sensibility which the rest of us inhabit."

"He does have a sense of style, at any rate," Nrouhw pointed out, in an attempt to keep the conversation moving in this particular vein. "A true appreciation of aesthetic excellence. I imagine he greatly values your work."

Mynydd apparently had no qualms in regard to gossiping about the man. "He respectfully requested that I replicate a key," she said. "A request that I declined, as this fellow was not the person to whom I had vended the other.

"I did, however, sell him an ever-so-expensive piece. He was inspecting the adequacy of my metallurgical efforts, when, with his tendency toward impetuousness, he selected a fine necklace. It seemed meant to complement his other neck ornaments. Nonetheless, sensing an opportunity, I excavated through my mess to locate the most successful yet of my present endeavors. I suggested to him a genuine treasure; a girdle valued well beyond the amount even my most wealthy patrons could have spent. He purchased both items for himself without hesitancy.

"The belt is not necessarily sensible and utilitarian, but rather is a decorative embellishment made of precious metal. The design is a slender band of sterling silver to encircle the midsection, and bent down into a chevron shape against the center of the abdomen. It is meant to be employed over a light doublet. Set with tiny emeralds and threads of different gems in a delicate design, heavily polished to be smooth and resplendent, it is a true thing of elegance, if you'll permit me to mention this myself.

"It suits him well, and for that he can be thankful. I've hexed it, to be honest, and the next time he disrespects anyone it will secure itself; it will seal fast, inescapable and irrevocable, to become, essentially, a representation of all that is enduring and ever-present. A wearable ornament as a perennial memento."

"But why would you do such a thing?" asked Nrouhw.

Mynydd smiled at Nrouhw over her glasses. "I just didn't like him."

Aldrei was the first of the visitors to depart that afternoon. He was running a bit late, as it turned out, for a regular engagement at one of his favorite local spots. Fairhaven Mental Asylum shared an old hotel building with The Ermine School of Applied Psychology just down the west cliff from Abseil Manor.

"Do give my regards to Ankh Ip," said Mynydd.

"Isn't he that snowgoose that suffers from paranoia?" asked Meheheh. "Poor fellow."

Aldrei laughed, "Aye, that's the one. Always thinks he's being followed." Reaching for the remaining pastry, he said, "All righty, Mynydd, I'll say a hello for the two of you."

"Then, you'll be going to look in on a friend, Aldrei?" asked Aru.

"No, not exactly," sighed Mynydd. "He merely goes there to twiddle with people's wits."

That did sound like Aldrei.

The journey home didn't take much time at all. Mynydd and Meheheh loaned Aru and Nrouhw a sled. The thing was round, and of silver, and so small that Aru wasn't sure if it was meant to be a sled or a serving platter. Nrouhw sat upright on it, with Aru seated across his lap and clinging for dear life most of the way, burying her face in his shoulder.

They took some shortcuts which diverted from the road, speeding downhill faster than any horse could go, all the while inundated by the thick swish and spray of the snow. Each new plummet caused a euphoric tingle to surge up from Aru's groin, traveling along a spine already iced with fear. She laughed a lot, and screamed out curses at Nrouhw, curses which he completely deserved for being insensitive, obstinate, and over-courageous. At some points on their way, her anger at Nrouhw was real. Nrouhw should have taken more seriously their hosts' admonition to ride the sled on the trail and road only, and to walk the bit below the school. Mynydd had said they'd learned not to let lowlanders use the sleds on the steeper slopes.

When Nrouhw and Aru got to town (alive, much to Aru's surprise) they handed off the sled to a waiting eagle, with a quickly scrawled note thanking Mynydd and Meheheh for everything. Aru had to laugh with Nrouhw, because, if they'd had enough time, she might have liked to ride the sled again. The walk home from town seemed short.

Aldrei later suggested to Aru that it might not be the cold that Aranieda feared up on Bwahmyr Peak. He laughed and said Aranieda needn't be concerned, the silversmith knew well how hard she had worked with her web of lies to try to capture Blackbuck and suspend his power. If Mynydd's interests regarding the man hadn't been aligned with Aranieda's it would have been evident a long time before.

Aranieda brought Lekki with her when she called on Aru and Nrouhw about a week after their visit with the silversmith. The occasion was a significant one, the first evening of what was locally known as the Light Bears' Nights. Each year, a few days before Midwinter, polar bears gathered at Opal Heights. They came from the north, hundreds of them, for an ancient ritual they performed up on Mahahag, the highest of the three peaks that stood above town. Aranieda arrived at Aru and Nrouhw's Hornfel apartment so bundled up in a huge furry coat and big hat and splendid assortment of scarves that she looked like a polar bear herself.

She and Lekki were invited into the sitting room and their coats were hung up to dry in the foyer. Aranieda wore a tight dress of pale cream-colored leather, showing off her long legs and round abdomen. Either she'd gained a good bit of weight around the middle or she was wearing quite thick winter underlinens. The many twists and braids of her hair were gathered at the top of her head and decorated with all manner of silver beads and hair combs. As usual, she looked stunning.

Aru had a beautiful piece of jewelry on a thin chain around her neck, and Aranieda complimented her on it. Nrouhw had bought it from the silversmith during their visit, without Aru knowing. It was a hollow ball, with shiny pendants that dangled from it, a talisman locket. The top half unscrewed from the bottom and herbs or other tiny items could be put inside. Nrouhw had also made a charm for her to carry in it, but Aru didn't mention that.

Lekki asked Nrouhw how he liked his job teaching over at the academy. Nrouhw said he liked it a lot. He had some inspired young students in his classes. Also the administrators gave him plenty of time to paint. He said he'd be having a show later in the year. Aru added that they'd been giving him a bit of trouble socially. He'd been enduring some discrimination.

"Speciesism," she whispered.

Aranieda tightly stretched her lower lip. "Hmmm," she said, "well, you know, it's going to be a tad tough at the start. You are a major predator, after all, Nrouhw."

Nrouhw laughed. "Yes, I know. I try to be sensitive. But it's been years since anyone has eaten a mountain goat. They've all been of the transforming type for a couple of generations now."

Lekki looked uncomfortable.

"Aru," Nrouhw said, "why don't you tell these two what we learned from Mynydd?"

As Aru described how the silversmith imprisoned Blackbuck in a silver girdle, Aranieda smiled, with a couple fingertips against her lips.

Aru grinned, saying, "If he can't transform for a while, surely that will make him less pretentious. He could certainly use a little humility."

"Agreed! Although that is not the only benefit for us, Aru," said Aranieda. "If he can't transform, he can use only a fraction of his power. Blackbuck's wind force is tied to his animal form. This is such splendid news."

"Yes. It truly is. Great news with great timing," agreed Lekki quietly.

Aranieda went on. "This condition of his will supersede my plans of entrapment, at least for the present. It won't prevent Blackbuck's antics entirely but it will indeed make things easier in seeing that he is brought under control," she said. "There is still a lot of work before us, as he is willful. But the silversmith has given us a lovely leg up."

Good news gave everyone an appetite, and so they moved into the dining room. Aru and Nrouhw had set a beautiful table and Aru was proud of the fine linen tablecloth and new porcelain dinnerware. They had a full set of sterling silverware as well. Nrouhw had borrowed it from the academy until they could afford their own.

The four dined on an excellent one-course meal of steaming fish chowder of cod, clams and minced potatoes. Fresh warm slices of sourdough had been spread with coconut butter. The friends made lively conversation as they ate. Aranieda and Lekki had grown to trust one another more. Lekki felt it was time to address a few concerns.

"Tell me something, Aranieda," he said, dabbing his mouth with his napkin. "Tell the truth. Why would you arrange that whole fiasco with Aru and myself at the waterfall last spring? For what reasons would you help my father in his attempt to ruin my life on account of his vile prejudices? Now that I know you better I don't understand why you would wish to help him do such a thing. Why should you treat Aru in such a way? None of this makes sense to me."

Aranieda remained silent for just a moment. She wiped some crumbs from the tablecloth into her hand and deposited them in her saucer. Then she brushed her hands together. She looked up at Lekki. "Well, of course I set up the meeting with the hedgehogs for you. You know that. But your father, through Aldrei, influenced my choice of location and I did not realize Aldrei's motives until afterward. I hate to say it, but Aldrei was the one who arranged the whole proceedings on behalf of your father. He hired the serpent Thxsiss to meet you there, and to have her bring Aru, he arranged with her to influence you and Aru to be . . ." she cleared her throat and pushed back a wisp of her hair, "receptive to one another."

Lekki's expression was one of distaste and confusion. He sat for a moment, reflecting on what had just been said. Then he replied, "Mmm. This does make a considerably larger amount of sense. Please forgive me for jumping to conclusions, Aranieda. I should have realized."

Aranieda nodded an acceptance of the apology. "Aldrei has had some sort of arrangement with Blackbuck for quite some time. He'd been aiming all along to bring you two together as a couple, Lekki and Aru. Despite the fact you are each bound by love to others. I believe that is why he joined up with you in the first place, Aru, before you came to Sylfaen."

Unconsciously, Aru reached for Nrouhw's hand. "Aldrei? We've considered that he might be manipulating me. Of course he has been. But all along? He's had an objective all along? Since we met?" Aru's voice went shaky. "I have trouble in believing it." She paused, and looked at Nrouhw. "Of course, now and then I've wondered about the old hobgoblin. There's been times he seemed to be up to something. Specifically regarding me, I mean." Aru swallowed hard. "Phfft-Psyfft, in a letter a while ago, told me she'd never met any Thxsiss. Remember how Thxsiss had said she knew Phfft-Psyfft? Soon after I read that letter, I realized I'd often spoken to Aldrei of Phfft-Psyfft. I'd only mentioned her to him and Veya, really."

"So we deduced that Aldrei must have had something to do with what happened," said Nrouhw.

"I have suspected it was he that poisoned me with the ourare," Lekki said. "He intended Aru to heal me. He wanted me to lie in your cottage, vulnerable, for a significant amount of time, while you were away, Nrouhw. He conspired for Aru and me to fall in love."

"But why?" asked Aru in a squeaky voice. "Why would he think that we'd fall in love? Because it suits his purpose? Is he as insane as your father?"

"Pretty much so, it seems," said Lekki. He and Aru looked at each other with some understanding.

"You mustn't take Aldrei's actions personally," said Aranieda. "He is only what he is. He has his own reasons for doing things, he travels in a spectral ethos belonging to a hidden world. Any reason he might wish to help Blackbuck is something I have as yet been unable to determine."

Aranieda took a breath. "Blackbuck, this is another matter. Blackbuck can't abide the thought of his son in marriage with a mountain goat. Beyond his obvious feelings of antelope centrism (dare I say antelope supremacy?) there is the matter of an heir. Have we already mentioned to you, Aru, that he is against Lekki's interspecies mating with Mhehh because of his desire for grandchildren? And there is something else regarding this matter that we ought to discuss. Something, I believe, best coming from Lekki?" Aranieda turned her gaze to Lekki and gave a slight nod.

Lekki sneezed and excused himself. He cleared his throat. "Aru, there is something I have discovered just recently. I have heard you speak fondly of your grandmother. Her name was Auwu, correct?"

"Well, yes. Mmm, yes," mumbled Aru. "It was." After a few seconds' thought she asked, "But how do you know? Did I call her by name?"

"Because, the thing is, Aru, my mother was the daughter of your grandmother's sister. Aru, we are cousins. Second cousins, actually, although not by blood, of course, as your grandmother was adopted."

"W—wow!" exclaimed Nrouhw. "That's extraordinary!"

"Yes, my grandmama was called Crwydryn. I recently found out that she had changed her name from the wolvish Wruelle. I never knew her well, she died when I was yet in diapers."

"Oh, yes I know of her, Wruelle!" Aru whispered. "My wolf great-aunt. Grandma's sister. She moved out to the eastern coast when she was a young woman! She went to live with relatives, as I remember."

"I know nothing of these relatives, Aru. But I can tell you that your Wruelle's daughter, my mother, was wolvish of mannerism but genteel of habit. Despite her wild ancestry she fit well into my family and its culture. Your Auntie Wruelle's husband, my grandfather, seemed like an antelope, but he was a changeling, and apparently a white oryx fairy. They say that is why my mother was able to bear the child of an antelope." Lekki coughed again. "Anyhow, the thing is, my mother had fairy blood. She could see the fairies, sometimes. She wove their images into her tapestries. I do not have the sight myself, Aru, but . . ." his voice trailed off.

"Blackbuck," said Aranieda, turning to Aru, "has an idea that if you were to unite with Lekki here, he'd have your special genes in his family. Blackbuck seeks to have grandchildren with the sight. The ability you have to see the lizards."

"Yeugh!!!" blurted Aru.

"Oh, Lekki, I'm sorry. It's not you, it's the idea. Cousins and everything. The whole idea."

"I completely understand," Lekki said quickly.

"So, let me get this right," said Nrouhw. "Blackbuck is scheming and interfering with everyone's lives so that he can have the ability to see the lizards as part of his family legacy?"

"Yes. There are several reasons this is important to him. And he has greater plans involving exploitation of people of the lower world," said Aranieda.

"He is not a well man," Lekki said, his voice almost inaudible.

Nrouhw suggested they continue their conversation in the living room. Aru had baked some sugar cookies.

They talked about local events; there was a comic operetta playing at the Cirque theater which was supposed to be good, and Lekki had heard a huge exhibition of fossilised dinosaur skeletons was coming to the museum. Before Aru knew it, Aranieda was saying that they hadn't much time before the bears would come. They should proceed with the business that they had discussed by ptarmigan. Aru agreed, and after another sip of Aeon's homemade sparkling daisy wine she excused herself to go and retrieve something. Nrouhw got up to poke the fire.

The weight of Aru's footsteps caused the upstairs floorboards to squeak. She wasn't gone more than a few minutes, and when she returned to the sitting room she carried something rolled up in a small lace tablecloth. Solemnly, Aru placed it in Lekki's hands. Everyone watched while he carefully unwrapped the bundle and laid the contents across his lap. The dragon wand. Lekki had known of this thing but this was his first time to see it. He touched the smooth clear surface, tracing over the rhythm of the curves. He held it up like a staff. It caught the lamplight, appearing luminescent. A shining ice serpent.

Aranieda sighed.

Nobody spoke for a long while.

344

The dragon's snarl was menacing, a frightening expression. Yet it was possible to see it in another way. The wide open mouth and large squinty reptilian eyes might equally be viewed as laughing.

Finally, Lekki spoke. "You are aware, Aru, of the madness of the situation. My father would kill you, without one pang of conscience, in order to reclaim this thing—if not for the fact that he is as fixated upon you as he is upon the sceptre. Why he has not made more of an effort to search your house for it, I do not know."

Aranieda reassured Aru, saying, "It remains a fact that the safest place for the dragon staff is in your possession. Aldrei will not let Blackbuck have it as long as you are the thing's steward—"

"Why does he want it so badly?" interrupted Aru. "As beautiful as it is, why is he so desperate for it? Is it a family heirloom? Please, I just want to know."

Aranieda looked at Lekki. He returned her gaze with an expression of exasperated resignation. He bumped his forehead against the wand a couple of times.

"Very well, I'll tell you the history of the dragon, then," Aranieda said. She stood and went to the window, peering out and attempting to see downhill along the street. Of course, the high wall blocked her view. "However, let's wait until after the bears arrive," she said, reclaiming her seat, "as their traditions have a role in all this."

So they had a bit more of the daisy wine and they nibbled on cookies, and Aranieda and Lekki explained to Aru and Nrouhw about the ritual of the bears.

"Every year the Light Bears come," Lekki said. "They parade right up this street, and past this house. They follow the road up to where it meets Cougarde Way, the narrow old route which crosses the ridge under Bwahmaa Peak. Eventually, Cougarde turns into a trail across the western face until they reach the actual climb of the Mahahag. Nobody goes out on this, the first night, Light Bears' Eve. Not until the bears have left the road. It is not safe."

They could hear drums and whistles approaching. Nrouhw suggested they go upstairs to get a view of the parade. The four of them squeezed their way between the draperies and canvases of Nrouhw's studio to crowd in front of the window. Darkness had fallen, but bright torch light could be seen approaching up the hill, along with the advancing sound of the drums. Soon through a light snowfall under the streetlamps they could see the polar bears, most of them in animal form, huge bears, truly enormous, wearing thick garlands of snowberry and magnolia around their heads and looped generously about their necks. The bears waved their heads from side to side and stepped in a slow bouncy sort of dance as they walked to the simple rhythm. Some of the bears beat drums, some carried torches, some had sticks or brooms. They moved two and three abreast along the street, walking without hurry but waving and bobbing so much the group looked like a stormy polar sea.

In addition to the pounding drums and clicking sticks there were slide whistles, and shrill penny flutes repeating a single phrase, these played by those bears in human form, scattered here and there among the crowd, dressed as snow goblins and one or two as witches. The goblins didn't dance the way the big bears did, they walked normally, but spent much of their time dodging playful smacks from the brooms and sticks. It was a rough business; some of the whacking was done quite hard, and repeatedly also. Just in front of the house a bear grabbed one of the goblins; they wrestled and then the goblin was dragged, squealing and laughing, until it could recover its feet.

"They build a great fire right up on the summit of Mahahag," said Lekki, "and they dance four nights, all the bears together. The final dance, of course, is on Long Night. These bears, they are different than their cousins the grizzlies and the others who hibernate. They bring the new year in their own way, and many folks here believe they are the root of Opal Heights good fortune because they chase away the bugaboos to make way for prosperity."

"There's truth in that," said Aranieda. "They are the reason for Opali prosperity. I don't know about the demons they chase, perhaps there's something to it. But it's the dance itself that benefits the people here."

"The dance?" asked Nrouhw.

"Yes," replied Aranieda. "The great bears sleep up there in the day, right out on the snow, and they dance the long nights away, roaring and jumping and sweating all the while. When at last they are done and they come down the road again in human form and return to their northern villages, they've left an enormous amount of sweat and bear grease on the mountain. It is this grease that is vital to the Opali." Aranieda focused on the bears in the street below; she seemed to have finished her point.

"But I don't understand," said Aru. "What use do the Opali have for bear grease? What do they do, collect the grease and sell it?"

Aranieda watched the procession for a while before she responded. The noise and movement were hypnotic, spellbinding. "Perhaps you've noticed," she said at last, "how Opali women seem to favor diamonds."

Both Aru and Nrouhw, somewhat confused, agreed that they'd seen many Opali wearing diamond jewelry.

"Well," said Aranieda. "Women are attracted to diamonds, yes, but diamonds, contrariwise, are attracted to grease."

"What?"

"You see, there is something special about the location of these mountains, something unusual on a cosmic scale. It's not spoken about, generally, but this place, in all of the world, is where the broken chips from stars fall to the land." She took a breath and went on quietly, her voice difficult to hear above the drums, "For thousands of years, since time began, probably, the shards of stars have fallen here. Diamonds, falling to the ground. But as long as they have been falling, the snow goblins have been collecting them. They snatch up the diamonds immediately as they land and no one, indeed, knows what they do with them. But that's where the bear grease comes in. The snow goblins can't abide bear grease." Aranieda was silent for a moment. "The falling stars, when they fall on the Mahahag, they stick there. Because diamonds are oleophilic. They are naturally attracted to grease. And the snow goblins won't touch them. Not those. And that is the secret to Opali prosperity."

"The mountain goat people learned years ago to carve the shards," said Lekki, "Today they have renowned families of master carvers who are famous the world over."

Such a chill went up Aru's spine that she had to sit down. "It's not crystal, the wand—" she gasped, "Nrouhw, it's a —" She couldn't finish.

Nrouhw looked stunned also.

"Well, my . . . mangy . . . uncle," said Aru absently.

"You thought the dragon was of quartz crystal?" Lekki needed a moment, in turn, to absorb this idea. "How could—how—" He sneezed and gave up on what he was searching to say.

Aranieda had one of those slight, empathetic smiles on her face. The sort professors get when a student has a revelation. "Why don't we return to your parlor and I will finish my story," she suggested. The bears had gone.

Lekki had wrapped the diamond dragon in its cloth and left it on the chair where he'd been sitting—Aru's big, comfortable armchair covered with needlepoint doves. Aru approached the bundle, and stood, hesitant to touch the diamond. The others gathered around.

"Go ahead, Aru," said Nrouhw softly.

Aru unwrapped the wand again, and held it to glisten in the lamp-light. "Please," she said, "Aranieda, finish the story. I need to know."

Everyone stared at the dragon.

Aranieda looked at Lekki, sighed once again, and explained, "The dragon was to be carved as a gift from Mbeheh to his wife Memaah." Everyone present knew these were the names of the parents of Lekki's fiancéee Mhehh. "It was one of the largest, most perfect star chips ever to be recovered from the crown of Mahahag. It caused quite a sensation when it was found. Even Blackbuck heard about it in his palace far away on the eastern coast, because he had business dealings with Dominion Associated.

"You must understand, Aru and Nrouhw, that the stoats of Sylfaen and the other mountain villages, they've always loved to come up to the Heights, many of them, and spend their winters as ermine. Only a generation or so ago, a couple of ermine families realized how much the alpine people relied on the village farm products. They formed a corporation, Dominion Associated, to capitalize on the market. With loans from the Opali they managed to build their business quickly and were easily able to exploit their neighbors in the villages as peasant labor. Most of their business is local, but they've grown so fat that they engage in a certain amount of specialty trade involving shipments overseas, and that is how they first crossed paths with Blackbuck.

"The Blackbuck has ties to a fleet of sailing ships, and eventually through the ermines he became engaged in business shipping crystallized lovage flowers abroad for Queen Memaah of Opal Heights. On a visit to the palace, he was invited to view the dragon in the initial stages of its carving. Immediately he began a campaign to purchase the thing, which, despite the king's romantic intentions for the dragon, was ultimately successful. Blackbuck oversaw the completion of the staff himself, visiting the Heights several more times. During these visits he imbued the dragon with certain spells as the thing slowly came to completion." Aranieda paused, swirling her wine glass and peering at its contents. "The reason for all of this was that he'd made a deal with the underworld daemon Grmhrel, the dragon wand in exchange for Blackbuck's continued access to his newly established snail claim. You see, the underworld has a starless sky and has always been lit by fireflies. But a disease has taken the fireflies away and Grmhrel sits angrily in the dark. He wants the magicked wand to light his world."

"And then, of course," said Lekki, "it was when I accompanied my father on one of his trips, a couple of years ago, now, that great fortune presented me with the attentions of the princess Mhehh. I promptly succumbed to the illumination shed by her spirit; I have not been home to Anemone since the day I first arrived in Opal Heights."

"Yes, and time flows onward. Grmhrel has grown impatient for his dragon staff, and he shakes the foundations of the countrysides far and wide in his anger. Blackbuck finds himself inconvenienced by Lekki's inclinations and frustrated by the disappearance of the wand."

"How did you acquire the wand then, Aranieda?" asked Nrouhw.

Aranieda gave a wince of a smile. "Of course it takes a great deal of time to carve diamond, but when the work was done there was only a small window of opportunity. Something had to be done before Blackbuck took possession of it. It is a story for another day, but through a precarious chain of events I became guardian of the dragon.

"No, he doesn't know who it was that appropriated it, but I'm fairly certain that he suspects, these days, that I am informed as to where it is. And it's evident that this suspicion leads him to Aru's involvement.

"A truly brilliant thing, both a piece of a star and a piece of artwork by a real master, the wand must be kept from Blackbuck to prevent him from his voracious plans that would cause harm in two worlds."

"Two worlds?" asked Aru.

"A shame that such a beautiful thing must remain concealed," said Lekki. "This is something that should be enjoyed by many. But legally it belongs to my father, and there is no choice but to keep it hidden."

Aranieda nodded slightly. "Blackbuck's only interest in the dragon is to use it as a bargaining chip with a monster for the purpose of taking improper advantage of a valuable resource. He simply has no concern for the many who would suffer from the consequences. He can't be allowed to proceed." She sounded tired.

"Your message said another wand is to be carved," said Nrouhw.

Lekki began to wrap the dragon back in its cloth as he replied yes, and that he and Aranieda considered this an important matter. The four had a lengthy discussion, coming to the conclusion that in their efforts to defeat Blackbuck they should focus on this replica scheme.

"Our biggest concern at the moment," said Aranieda, "is the rumor that Blackbuck is working closely with the same carver in the palace to bring forth a wand to replace this one. It's important that we don't take this to mean that he'll give up on his search for the original, however. It is a time-consuming and expensive process to create such a wonder as this. And this dragon could never be equaled. He'll not give up on this one. Blackbuck never gives up."

They talked late into the evening, long after the sound of the drums faded into the distant rhythm that would be part of their world for the next several nights. Then it was safe for Aranieda and Lekki to leave.

It was early in the new year that Aru and Nrouhw finally had an opportunity to meet Lekki's dear Mhehh. There was a reason they had not been introduced to her in all this time. The princess Mhehh had a warm and gentle disposition, but she was terribly naive and capricious. Not long before Nrouhw and Aru had moved to Opal

Heights, Mhehh had become quite serious about her involvement in a rather bizarre fellowship. She had been spending most of her time with a group of people who had recently arrived in the area. Lekki had never encountered an organization of this sort, and truthfully he was concerned about her involvement with it.

The encampment sat on the opposite side of the ridge upon which The Hornfel stood; on the south flank, overlooking the Opal Heights palace and the road that came up from the great gorge. To get there you took the third fork of the road instead of heading to the palace or coming around the bend into town. It was a beautiful spot, looking down over the illustrious house and the frozen lake below. Beyond that was the great gorge and, somewhere off to the east along it, Sylfaen.

Aru and Nrouhw met Lekki on the road and took a steep, well-marked trail up to the camp. The sun reflected brilliantly off the snow. The air seemed full of light. The day was crisp, the snow clean and deep. The palace below them looked like it was made of sugar candy.

The camp was on a broad icy ledge that reached back into a gap of the hill. Big house-shaped canvas tents had been erected on wooden platforms, with metal stove pipes sticking out. They weren't attractive structures, but certainly serviceable. They blended into the mountain-side scenery. The snow had been churned by footsteps, but there was no other sign of life except the wavering hot air above the pipes.

Lekki led them past two of the tents, and up the whitewashed steps to the entrance of an extra large one. A strange noise could be heard inside. Sort of a humming. Aru looked at Nrouhw. Bees?

Looking decidedly uncomfortable, Lekki put his finger to his lips and opened the door. The sound was voices, chanting something unintelligible over and over. Frangipani wafted from within.

The friends went through the doorway, and then brushed off the snow as they peered into the crowded room. There must have been close to a hundred people filling that boxy space, with sunlight shining in through the canvas and laundry hanging to dry among the dozens of candles above. It appeared that most inside the tent were women. Each and every person had a sweet, wholesome-looking face with a big smile as they peeked out from what looked like pretty bedsheets they wore draped over their heads.

Two women, beaming and sweet-smelling, welcomed the newcomers and gently wrapped shrouds around them. Aru's was fabulous; airy, and trimmed with lace.

The women beckoned to the friends and led them into the crowd, but Lekki politely pointed out his fiancee and they smiled understandingly as he made his way toward her, with Aru and Nrouhw right behind. Mhehh laughed and threw her arms around him when he reached her. Then she peered around him and welcomed Aru and Nrouhw with a huge smile and handshakes. She had such beautiful teeth. Her hand felt warm. She couldn't talk over the chanting but the language of her pantomime said, "It's lovely to meet you!"

So Aru and Nrouhw stood, feeling far too warm as they still had their coats on under the drapes, and they were packed shoulder to shoulder in one of the concentric circles of people facing the middle of the tent. Still, Aru enjoyed this new experience. In addition to the chanting, a few of the people had small silver handbells that they rang, adding a light, high tone to the sound.

In the thick of the singing and the incense, Aru's attention drifted off into fancies of splendor. A gull flying through sunlit clouds, a dappled horse prancing through swells as they broke upon a beach of silica sands. The joy that filled the tent filled her also, the smiles all around fed her spirit. She held onto Nrouhw's hand, feeling at peace and unjudged as she exchanged warm-hearted gazes with these people with whom she felt a bond even through such a brief association.

For quite some time this went on, the standing, the chanting, the feelings of receptiveness and light. Aru and Nrouhw joined in with the chanting. Lekki was silent.

Aru looked at Mhehh. She had long white eyelashes and soft grey-green eyes; the effect was dramatic. Her fine eyebrows were barely visible against creamy smooth skin, the nose and lips detailed as if sculpted of porcelain, perfect. Her cheek looked more filled out than Aru had imagined, her chin less defined, her neck had folds of fat. On the whole, though, Mhehh had a classic beauty, a look of royalty.

She was one of few Opali in the group. An ermine or two were easy to spot, and a man that could have been a ptarmigan or a small owl, but most of the crowd seemed to be of the same species, something foreign to this area, some type of herd animal undoubtedly. In human form their skin was of a light tone, although nothing nearly so light as the mountain goats' or even Aru's. Their hair grew thick and curly and was the color of fresh snow, whiter, even, than the Opalis', which seemed slightly yellow or silver in comparison. They had heart-shaped faces with big eyes and ears and in most of them the philtrum groove above their lips was unusually pronounced, giving them somewhat rabbit-like mouths. These were faces of friendliness, of adorability, of devoted rumination.

Aru quite enjoyed herself. Several hours they stood chanting, and it wasn't until Lekki suggested they take their leave that Aru noticed she was getting hungry. They said goodbye to Mhehh, left their pretty veils by the door, and returned to the outside world.

No one said much until they had climbed down the steep trail to the road. "She gave me this," Lekki said, pulling something out of his wallet. "She thinks I ought to join." He handed Nrouhw a necklace of braided sinew cord. It had a pendant with a photograph of an aging bearded man. "This is their leader. Mahabajnish Reetyirrtana. They all wear these."

"Leader?" asked Aru. "So, he guides them in this chanting?"

"I didn't see him there," said Nrouhw.

"No, he wasn't in attendance today," said Lekki. "He doesn't always come to the assemblies. And yes, that's right, Aru, he teaches the group about chanting and contemplation and how to find peace. How to live in finer accordance with nature, he says."

"Does he wear a necklace like this?" asked Aru.

"Not with the photograph. He wears a tassel with a big steel bell."

"Hmmm," said Nrouhw.

"I couldn't determine what species they are," whispered Aru.

Lekki told them that these people were called Dall sheep but he didn't know much about them, as they spent virtually all of their time in animal form when they weren't chanting together. It was becoming increasingly difficult to entice Mhehh to go anywhere else or partake in what were previously her normal activities of life.

"Is the leader a Dall sheep?" asked Aru.

"No," said Lekki, "he's an alpaca. He's from a faraway land, I'm not sure where. Higher mountains they have, than in our countryside."

"Do you think you'll join?" Nrouhw wondered.

"I'm not comfortable with these people," said Lekki.

"They seem nice to me," said Aru. "Though the necklaces are odd. Why would they all have an image of this man? What does that mean?"

Lekki shrugged and shook his head.

A full month took its course before Aru and Nrouhw saw Mhehh again. This time Lekki managed to spirit her away from the group, and the two of them invited Aru and Nrouhw to visit the palace zoo. Aru had never been to a zoo. She'd never been to a palace, for that matter.

Big soft flakes of snow were swirling down outside as Nrouhw and Aru sat in a pleasant waiting room off the main foyer, drops of melting snow in their hair as they sipped hot spiced milk through heaps of whipped cream. It had been a stiff climb up to the palace grounds.

When Lekki and Mhehh came down to greet them Aru thought they looked a handsome couple, he so dark and she so remarkably free of hue. They both had long wool coats, light in color, his with a herringbone pattern, finely tailored, and hers of the softest angora.

Aru felt a twinge of resentment upon seeing Mhehh in her fine clothes and diamond jewelry. She, Aru, sensed she must be a princess herself. Something deep within her bones had always let her know she was royal; she found it such an enduring frustration to be so displaced from her true heritage. A strange emotion it was, to feel respect and admiration for someone and also feel somehow cheated, an unrecognized kinship. But she beat down these feelings, brushed them from her mind. When she grabbed Mhehh's hand and said how fine it was to see her again, she meant it completely.

The four of them went outside, back down the great stairway to the courtyard, and headed south and east through the grounds. The towers of the palace rose far above their heads, and there were several large buildings in addition to the main house. Everything was made of pearly marble and rock crystal, glass, or of ice. Some structures in the palace were seasonal, made of ice and rebuilt every year, late in the fall.

Lekki pointed out, up in the heights of the main building, six, maybe seven stories above them, the music gallery. Amidst a mass of spired towers, the gallery roof was composed of quartz crystal tiles of various sizes. Each tile was specially sculpted and set so that it could jiggle freely while remaining part of the protective rooftop. The steep rooftop shimmered, even in the half light of the snowy day. Carefully engineered and precisely tuned, the roof would vibrate during lightning storms, producing a delicate, eerie music. Mhehh said that it made an exquisite sound; she had found it settled her nerves during the many summertime storms of her childhood.

Passing through an alleyway between a high snowy hedge and the wall of an outbuilding they came to a place where the walkway ended at a gate. A door, really, it filled a pointed stone archway crowned by a collared stone ball like the pawn of a chess set. Wholly outlandish marble gargoyles guarded the doorway and another served as a downspout at the corner of the building's eaves.

"Here we are." Lekki smiled. "The Opal Heights Menagerie." He opened the door and they went through. Nrouhw had to duck a little.

Now they stood in a sculpture garden. Snow heaps covered the shrubbery and the smaller sculptures. Leaf-bare ceramic fruit trees with twisted trunks were set here and there among marvelous statues. A central monument, carved of stone, supported a lifelike and majestic stag with his great antlers, and a buffalo, and an elephant which towered high over the both of them.

There were ice sculptures, also. Nrouhw and Aru's favorite was a grand ship under full sail. All the rigging was there, fine wires coated with ice. Parted waves curled against the bow.

Among all this artwork a group of several llamas lay chewing their cud together, their jaws working in a figure eight motion, snow caked on the thick wool of their backs.

Two dogs sat watching by the llamas. One dog was enormous, and so covered with matted cords of hair one couldn't properly see his eyes. He looked for all the world like a giant mop. The other, a smiley type of dog, had a dense and fluffy coat, the tail curled over and touching its back. These were both herding dogs. Mhehh told her friends that the smaller one worked in the far north country as both a reindeer herder and a sledge puller. Both dogs rose and came to greet the visitors, but they kept a respectful distance. This was probably because they were working dogs, not accustomed to cordial fondling.

"May we pet the llamas?" asked Aru.

"Yes, yes, assuredly!" laughed Mhehh.

The llamas seemed to enjoy the attention.

Mhehh lowered her voice. "Every specimen in Mother's collection exemplifies the color of the snow. I suspect it is the only such menagerie." She kissed the nose of the llama that had approached her. "It wasn't intentional. She began with the pileated gibbon and a snow leopard. An overwhelming percentage of the rest essentially presented themselves to her in well-expressed recognition, with respect to some inconsequential indebtedness or the other."

"She owns the animals, then?" Nrouhw and Aru were a bit shocked.

"What, no!" exclaimed Lekki. "They put an end to conscription zoos years ago. All these folks come here for their own convenience. Many of them are writers or teachers, people who want to get away from the cities for a while; the position offers plenty of unfettered time in human form."

"Would everyone enjoy visiting the shelter where the predators are kept?" Mhehh was asking, when a couple of enormous men came around the corner of a building. They both had on red wool scarves, and sweaters with snowflake patterns in a circular yoke design. Polar bears, apparently. Mhehh spoke with them briefly, and introduced them to Aru and Nrouhw. "You bears are setting off on an excursion to somewhere?" she asked.

"Yes, Your Highness," said the heavier one, "We are just leaving. Er, we, uh . . ."

"We hate to be the bears of bad news," said the other, "but some of the animals have gone up to town today. A dentist is offering free examinations. The elephant has gone, and the opossum and Ratty, I believe some others also. We're just on our way to our own appointments, Your Highness."

"Regrettable timing, it is," said Mhehh. "Nevertheless, regular dental attention is ever necessary. How commendable, bears, your engagement in such excellent preservation of your health."

After the bears continued on their way she said to the others, "What wretched luck, concerning the elephant especially. Not very serendipitous. Pearly elephants are exceptionally rare. Ours possesses the most elegant and lengthy tusks, as well. And such an effervescent personality! How regrettable she is elsewhere. Yet, we'll have our pleasure this afternoon, regardless. There are yet plenty of animals to be met."

They walked toward the rear of the zoo to see the carnivores. On the way, they passed a small round building, the front of which was entirely windows. There were two compartments behind the glass. They stopped and looked. On the left-hand side an ivory python uncoiled for them and showed its amazing length and sensual, flowing movements as it climbed a rope ladder. Nrouhw and Aru also appreciated the intriguing reticulated water dish. On the right, separated from the snake by a thick wall, a snowy owl opened one eye and yawned. Such a huge and bewitchingly impressive bird he was.

As they stood admiring the owl, someone called a greeting. At the back of the zoo grounds stood a high wall which contained a moongate, and through this opening Aldrei and Aeon had arrived. Aru later learned that their apartment was behind that wall, a cozy suite in a disused and remodeled milking shed.

The pair joined the cheerful group as they entered the long, low building where the meat-eaters were displayed. On this day it seemed nearly empty, but both the arctic wolf and fox sniffed Aru's hands. A tiger jumped down from a ledge and walked right across in front of the visitors, a big yawn flashing the rows of teeth. A beast who took one's breath away. Nrouhw wondered what was the cause of the tiger's ghostly coloration. Lekki told him that almost all the animals in the menagerie were of a white breed or color phase but the tiger was an example of leucopathy, an inherited condition. The only other such animals in the menagerie were the squirrel and the vulture.

A neighboring building with a large courtyard contained ferrets and chinchillas, an arctic hare, the gibbon, some sleeping ghost bats, a milky stork who stood snoozing on one leg, and a bog pony. Pelicans dined busily on shiny fish. In the courtyard some elderly polar terns were also having their lunch. A great star-shaped glass tank contained just a few cisco fish, who floated aimlessly. Mhehh noted that her

357

mother deeply desired a beluga for her collection but had never been able to entice one to come.

Two orphaned harp seal pups, unbothered by the falling snow, rested on a platform by the tank. They smiled at the visitors with their soulful, watery eyes. Fat, healthy, and covered with soft downy fur, their cute and sweet faces made everyone laugh. Perhaps the highlight of Aru's tour was the time she spent cuddling them.

Aru and Mhehh talked about the palace and about how Aru enjoyed her new life in the town of Opal Heights. "Lekki mentioned that you possess some measure of reverence for the metaphysical," said Mhehh.

The discussion turned to Mahabajnish and his followers. Each time they fell into conversation that afternoon the princess seemed mostly interested in talking about the group of revelation-seekers. Earlier, she had described her interest in the group and how much she enjoyed her part in it all. Now she admitted she had her moments of frustration.

"Honestly, I never meant to invest the better part of my schedule in these transcendental endeavors for such an extended stretch of time," she said. "Perhaps it would be sensible to have just a breath of a recess, now and then. To spend a few extra hours in the form of my biped flesh, for enjoyment, to a measured extent, of the slightest of modest indulgences. But first I shall need to memorize the complex melody of the seventieth interdimensional mantra—"

Aldrei laughed. "Now, that's no way to go through life!" Aeon elbowed him and laughed also.

Mhehh looked puzzled. "Excuse me, but I'm entirely unable to comprehend your declaration," she said.

"Butt-first. You don't want to be going butt-first. What you need to do, is you need to turn around and take a good look at where you are going. You've invested your time, you should stay with the group. It's good for you. The reality of the situation is that you're just not working hard enough at it," Aldrei said.

Lekki looked at Aldrei as if Aldrei had punched him in the jaw. But he didn't say anything.

Mhehh laughed. "You, my friend Aldrei, are the phenomenally rare fellow who may well, without consequence, address me in such an altogether disrespectful manner." She smiled.

358

The livestock barn had enormous skylights and the interior walls were covered with freshly scrubbed tile. The polar bears had mentioned that the barn was mostly vacant today, but Nrouhw wanted to see the Abigar cattle. Another cow of some kind was there also; Mhehh couldn't remember the breed. She stood quite tall and had a big hump at her withers, a fine-looking animal. Her lush, short-haired coat felt as soft as velvet.

A large area with a marble pool and scattered with lotus blossoms showed where the Ivory Elephant spent her exhibition time. Aru was sorry to have missed her.

"My friend Aru," said Mhehh, taking Aru's hand, "you are forever welcome at Opal Heights! I expect another opportunity to visit her will very readily present itself."

The day was truly an enjoyable one, full of new memories. Just before Nrouhw and Aru departed for home, Lekki found a moment to speak to them privately. He let them know that Aranieda had been in touch with him. She'd told him that indeed it was true that Blackbuck was having another wand carved. This, more than the upcoming wedding, was why he had been in Opal Heights for all these months. However, he'd run into difficulty. They'd procured another spectacular diamond, nearly as large as the original, but he was finding it couldn't be magicked properly. He thought it was due to impurities in the stone. And this was partially true, but, Aranieda said, unknown to Blackbuck there was another reason. During the nighttime while the carver slept, owls were coming in. The workshop where the carving took place could only be reached by secret stairs that wound their way up one of the tallest towers in the oldest part of the palace. The owls, barn owls, specifically, had found a way to get in through the vents. Each night they were gathering tiny chips of diamond scrap in their beaks and carrying it away.

The friends had an unknown ally. As a result of her observations, Aranieda was convinced that someone was creating a counteractive enchantment from those owl chips. This was preventing Blackbuck from successfully creating a new wand. However, because of his difficulties, he had redoubled his efforts in locating the original.

The snow had stopped falling when Aru and Nrouhw said goodbye to the others. Mhehh loaned them a couple of reindeer and sledges for their trip home to the Hornfel. In all the time Aru had been in the area, this would be her first time to drive a reindeer sledge.

Had they been transforming animals, Emheheh and Mmhehh both could have been a part of the menagerie. Their coats were milky, clean and pure, with a bit of a pink stain showing at the noses. Mmhehh's eyes were brown, and Emheheh's a cool blue; eyes strangely despondent-looking and distant, at once cow-like and wild. They weren't friendly animals, but they weren't unfriendly either. They were merely a part of these mountains, as if harness had been put to the snow or the wind.

Aru had grown familiar with the sledges by now. Simple and perfectly practical, the wooden reindeer sleighs were a common sight on any day in Opal Heights. Shaped much like canoes, they sat directly on the snow without runners. The back third of the canoe was missing; instead the flat end rose up to form a rounded backrest.

In the interest of a low center of balance, there was no seat. The driver sat right in the bottom of the sledge, on a soft reindeer pelt. There was only a single rein, clipped to a simple halter composed of one split-ear strap that looped under the reindeer's jaw. No bits or bosals, nothing to interfere with the animal's muzzle, or her freedom should she decide to head for the hills. This wasn't cause for concern, however, because in such an unlikely event all one need do is tumble out of the sledge onto the snow, gain one's feet, and hang onto the rein; the animal would be forced to stop.

As they glided through the fluffy snow beside the road, Nrouhw commented that the sledge reminded him of sailing a skiff, the only sound a soft swish of the snow underneath. The leg joints of the reindeer added a strange clicking sound, though, as they moved along, their broad-toed hooves snowshoeing on top of the snow. Aru and Nrouhw agreed that there couldn't be a more relaxing way to travel.

When they arrived home Nrouhw went in to start their supper and Aru unharnessed Emheheh and Mmhehh. She whispered words of gratitude in their ears and, as instructed, set them loose to wander the mountains in search of lichens. Someone from the palace would collect the sledges.

After a fine supper and then a little tapioca pudding in front of the fire, Aru decided to take a long hot bath. As she sat enjoying the soapiness and breathing the steam, she thought about the boy Queex. He would arrive at the palace the following morning. Pippet had promised to come stay with Aru and Nrouhw for a few days once Queex felt comfortable in his new surroundings. The change would be difficult for him, Veya had said in her message. He needed routine in his world. Queex's father would visit as often as he could, but it wasn't easy for a Sylfaen man to get away from his daily obligations. Life could be so harsh for the people of the villages. Veya had mentioned that an elderly woman, an old shrew, had frozen to death all alone in her home the previous week. Horribly sad. It didn't seem fair.

When Pippet arrived at the Hornfel a week later Aru hugged her and told her how much she had missed her and her family. She wished Veya could have come also. Aru had planned to visit Sylfaen, but so far she always seemed to have something else scheduled.

Pippet told Aru and Nrouhw about how folks were doing at home, but mostly chattered all about her amazing new experiences. Opal Heights was such a different world than the village. In the palace they ate from priceless porcelain with silver spoons. There were all sorts of diversions and activities. Mhehh had invited Pippet and Aru to go skiing with her up on the Bwahmaa. Apparently Mhehh was indeed taking some time away from the group at the encampment. The ski trip had been planned for the following day.

The Mantelshelf Lodge and nearby Bellwether Resort were reached by a road which had a name written in the Opali language on the street sign. This name, Mhehh told them, could be interpreted in the common tongue as "Safe-From-Cougars Boulevard." Aru thought Nrouhw would be amused to hear about that.

Most of the ski slopes looked frighteningly steep, but since Aru and Pippet were beginners Mhehh brought them to a special area just for novices. Aru still wasn't sure she was game for this, but Pippet seemed like she'd been skiing since birth.

After several successes in staying upright for a short glide, Aru felt ready to try the next level of difficulty. She stood on her skis and surveyed what was considered to be a gentle incline. Pippet had already made her way down and was at the bottom laughing and waving.

"You've been progressing especially well, Aru," said Mhehh. "Go ahead now, no hesitation. You're very competent. Perfectly ready."

"All these young rabbit children, they're everywhere!" said Aru, wondering how she would ever avoid running one or two of them down.

"Yes. This phenomena tends to present itself on the learner's hill," replied Mhehh. "Never mind, I'm entirely confident that circumventing them will be less effort than you expect."

And so Aru tried it. Although it was indeed thrilling when she stayed erect, she kept losing control and falling down when she swerved to avoid the bunnies. After a period of determined refusal to give up, Aru truly began to enjoy herself, despite the fact that her snow-caked skirts were rather soaked. She felt she was getting the knack of it, and could perform relatively reliable turning and stopping maneuvers. Mhehh said they seemed ready for the beginner's trail.

From the top, it looked like this route went right off the end of the world. But Aru had learned enough control to allow her some courage and she soon found herself flying down the slope like a bird. She and Mhehh skied down together. Pippet had gone out of sight ahead.

Time seemed suspended as they sped through the ever-changing scenery, with brief views of the town below or of the western peaks far away. Aru fell only once, and was able to recover herself with ease. This was good. She wanted to do this again. Nrouhw would love it.

As they slid into the base area at the bottom of the slope, Aru had a proud smile on her face. Mhehh congratulated her and was pleased to hear that Aru felt excited, ready for another run. It was only after a few moments that Mhehh noticed the crowd of people over on the edge of the ski area. Someone had taken a nasty spill, and others were gathered around, wanting to help.

"Oh, no," cried Aru, "Pippet!"

Going a little too fast for the end of the run, Pippet had completely lost control and gone right through the eagle rope-tow area and off a snowbank into a hole. She lay there in the snow grimacing and crying and unable to speak.

Someone had already gone for a sledge, and as Aru and Mhehh reached the site, the rescuers were just about to start carefully loading Pippet into it. When they did she shrieked in pain.

Aru and Mhehh followed Pippet to the hospital. This was located clear out on the southwest side of town. They met an orderly in the lobby who informed them that Pippet had been taken upstairs and they would need to wait. He showed them to a small waiting room that smelled of ammonia. He said he believed they would be making an X-radiation photograph of young Pippet's leg. There was concern that a bone may be broken.

"Poor Pippet!" whispered Aru.

Waiting was forever, and Aru's mind raced with worries. Mhehh left for a short while to have a message sent to Pippet's family. Aru nearly went mad, sitting under a large clock on the wall that slowly and deliberately ticked out each second. She thought about her friend Chuik, and how much pain he had endured when he broke his leg in the orchard. She wondered how he was doing now. She truly needed to make a visit to Sylfaen.

The room around her was bleak and sterile, as if any colorful object might be suspect of harboring a colony of germs. There was a folded newspaper, a metal coat rack, and a sign on a closed door that read *No Exit*.

When Mhehh returned, they talked quietly about Pippet and her family. Mhehh seemed surprised to learn what conditions were like in Sylfaen, and she said she would see that Pippet's medical expenses were taken care of. Finally a nurse came to escort them upstairs to see their friend. He apologized to the princess for the wait.

The nurse wore a stiffly starched uniform with a high collar and he had spats on his shoes. His shoulders were narrow and his feet enormous. He had conspicuous front teeth, uncommonly prominent cheeks, and large ears. Moving to the doorway, he gestured with his white-gloved hand to invite them through it. "So, eh, you can follow me," he said. He led them down the shiny waxed hallway to something that looked like an ornate cage.

It would only be Aru's second time to ride in an elevator. She watched the dial above the door point to *One*, then *Two*, then *Three*, then land on *Four* before the doors opened. A tingle of excitement went through her. Although concern for Pippet enveloped her thoughts, the trip to the hospital did have an element of fun. Was it strange of her to think that? In the hospital an air of emergency and excitement combined with efficiency and control. The building had an aura of deep emotion and bare physical reality. Things were brought to light here that a person normally didn't see. It was exciting, in a perverse sort of way. New experiences.

The nurse led them into an airy ward, bright with lights switched on even though the sun was shining through a dozen tall windows. They walked along a wide area between two tidy rows of beds with sheets and pillowcases bleached sterile, with undersized curtains drawn to feign privacy. Subdued-looking people lay in some of the beds.

As the nurse steered them toward Pippet, Aru gasped at the sight of her. Things were much worse than she'd imagined. There Pippet lay, her leg wrapped in a massive bundle of splints and bandages, held high in the air with a system of weights and pulleys. She had a cast on her arm, also, and bandages around her head that came down over her eyes and nose. Only small holes cut in the bandage allowed her to see. She looked like a mummy. Despite her efforts, Aru's tears started to well up.

The nurse, however kept walking, and Aru realized Pippet was in the bed just beyond this person. "Pippet!" she cried, receiving a "Hush!" from her nurse and several others.

After her mistake, it was actually a relief to see her friend lying there in a daze with her leg in a cast and bolstered up upon a stack of pillows. Pippet smiled at her visitors. A doctor was feeling her pulse. "What's the update, Doc?" asked their nurse.

"I think she's going to live," said the doctor, winking at Aru, whose look of horror apparently hadn't quite faded from her face.

Pippet seemed to be handling the whole experience exceptionally well; probably the morphine had influence in this. After some concern about her family, she talked about how much fun skiing had been. Such an extraordinary diversion for a squirrel from the village orchards. "The cast goes all the way up to my hip," she whispered.

Pippet thought it was funny that Aru had mistaken the man in the next bed for her.

"He has a growth of beard, dear nutwit!" she pointed out. "It's sad though, supposably he's a lemming from the coast; fell off a cliff, he did. I guess that happens a lot, they said, with lemmings. I heard someone say he's had a hard time of it." Her voice changed to a whisper but she probably didn't realize how loud of a whisper it was. "I heard where they had been talking of putting him down. But he's doing better now, I guess. Thankfully!"

Mhehh did take care of Pippet's expenses, and she arranged for her transport to Aru and Nrouhw's apartment so she could stay with them for a few days. She also arranged for a job for her at the Sylfaen inn, so she could live there for the several months it would take for her leg to heal. There would be no transforming, and certainly no climbing the ladder to the treehouse, until that cast was off.

When Veya came to retrieve Pippet she stayed overnight. Aru chattered into the wee hours with her friends in a sitting room overfilled with paper doll chains which Aru had taught Pippet to make. They indulged in assorted gossip from Sylfaen, and talked about life in Opal Heights, and about Queex. Pippet said the boy would miss his family, and the changes were tough for him, but he clearly enjoyed his new life at the palace. She also whispered that his nanny had told her she'd heard the ghost of Queex's mother in the walls during the night, scratching and repeating his name.

Aru missed Veya and Pippet after they had to return home, but a wonderful thing soon captured her attention. Just up the street from the Hornfel, at the corner of Saltstone and Viewcrest, was a shop called The Buttress, a ladies' clothing store. One weekend morning, on an especially foggy day, Lekki stopped by and took Aru and Nrouhw with him up to the store. But they didn't go in. Squeezing through a passageway between it and the neighboring building, they arrived at a cottage built up against the back of the shop, presumably the owner's residence. Lekki went in without knocking.

A welcome of thick warm air met them as they entered directly into the kitchen. They hung their heavy coats to drip beside a big glass-front cabinet filled with decorative plates. There was the latest style of ice box. An enamel cookstove filled the back wall of the room, the teakettle steaming furiously. Lekki removed it from the stovetop on his way by, and led the others through a doorway right into a bedroom.

Sitting together on the edge of the bed were Mhehh and an older woman. This lady was introduced as Girun, a ptarmigan, owner of the store. Mhehh was holding a baby-sized bundle wrapped in a blanket with satin trim. She smiled and put her finger to her lips.

A square little button nose and protruding ears with the finest downy hair on them, and dark eyes that said "cuddle me," that was Sheeki. Curled into a ball, he had the soles of his tiny toes tucked under his chin. His skin was dark brown, and although he looked to be about six months old he had a full head of thick spiky hair. Aru smelled his soft skin. "He smells so sweet!" she exclaimed.

Nrouhw agreed. "As sweet as milk."

"As sweet as morning dew," laughed Aru. "On the creamy petals of a gardenia!"

"He smells as lightly sweet as the teat of a nectar-fattened unicorn," Nrouhw declared.

Aru had questions, but she kept them to herself. She couldn't be sure what to ask, without, in Opali culture, causing offense. She sat down next to Mhehh and happily accepted an offer to hold the baby. Amongst the enjoyment of little Sheeki, the story came out that he was, as he appeared, a baby hedgehog boy. He had arrived in Opal Heights only a few days ago and was staying with the storekeeper and her daughter who were acting as his nursemaids. He was in hiding because he had been adopted in secret by Lekki and Mhehh.

While Girun went to get some tea, the couple explained that they had arranged the adoption quite some time ago. In fact, Aru had met the parents when the mother was carrying Sheeki.

"This was the couple we sat with that day at the waterfall," said Lekki quietly. "As a sad fact of the matter, the hedgehogs already had more children than they could afford to feed, a situation complicated by the mother's health. They had agreed to the adoption for their child to have the life of a prince, rather than increase the likelihood that all their children grow up in hunger." He sneezed, excusing himself. "I tell you, when we return to Anemone, I shall find a way to sell some acres of my holdings that I may finance a school for the children of Sylfaen. The condition of that place is intolerable."

Mhehh added softly, "Our pleasure in welcoming Sheeki comes mellowed with a special melancholy. Lekki and I are tormented by the wretchedness of the hedgehog mother and father, and by the necessity of sequestering our precious fellow with the consequence that we are compelled to engage in surreptitious parenting until after the wedding."

Blackbuck's disapproval was clear, but the Opali king and queen also had some strong, outdated feelings about interspecies marriage. Beyond attitudes about species they considered inferior, they had always assumed they would have little mountain goat grandkids. Having their daughter marry an antelope was injury enough, but it was uncertain whether adoption outside the species would or would not be considered more of an offense in their eyes than Mhehh willfully marrying into childlessness.

Aru didn't think the adoption of this beautiful baby was an act of defiance, although the parents would probably see it that way. Sometimes people have perfectly good reasons for doing something that is nobody's business but their own.

"Queen Memaah and King Mbeheh," said Lekki, "have become used to Mhehh spending much of her time in the tents of that strange foreigner and his followers, so therefore her absence from the palace while she discreetly visits the baby will not be remarked upon."

As for Mhehh, she had recently learned that her teacher Mahabajnish had been seen by a friend of hers engaged in activity with a couple of the group members out in the snow which did not at all conform to his teachings regarding celibacy and chastity. As a result, Mhehh had stopped going to the meetings at all. This decision was favorably timed in accordance with the arrival of little Sheeki, for he needed her full attention. Her parents' assumption that she continued to take her leisure among the friendly sheep at their encampment would allow Mhehh to spend all the time she wanted with her secret baby.

Aru couldn't visit Mhehh and the baby as often as she'd have liked. Blackbuck's ubiquitous eavesdroppers created too much risk of Sheeki being discovered. When she did get a chance to go, she shared in Mhehh's excitement about the baby and the upcoming wedding.

Otherwise, Aru spent much of her time on outings with her other friends. Sometimes she went window shopping with Mehb, a new friend she and Nrouhw had made who worked in the administration office at the academy.

Mehb invited Aru and Nrouhw to the opening of a minor exhibit at the museum. She dabbled in ceramics and had a couple of pieces that had been accepted into the show. Aru had been looking forward to the party, but she came down with a nasty cough that day and at the last minute decided to stay home. After Nrouhw left that evening, she settled in front of the fire with a bunch of fluffy bed pillows, a glass of ginger tea, and a book she'd been meaning to read.

About an hour later, there was a noise. In the kitchen. Aru couldn't move a muscle. She sat without breath, listening. There was a clank. Someone was there. Thinking quickly, she shouted, "Aldrei! Someone's in the house!"

Several more noises came from the kitchen. A crash, a couple of clunks and thuds, and then a silence. Had someone just gone out the window? Aru didn't know where the courage came from, but due to her nasty catarrh any idea of running out the front door into the cold night air found a quick veto. She grabbed the poker from the hearth and crept through the dining room. Slowly, breathlessly, she peeked around the corner. The window was open, curtain flapping in the wind. No one was in sight. The little crystal lamp had gone into the sink. Somehow the glass chimney hadn't broken. She peered carefully into every potential hiding spot. No one. She closed the window with trembling hands. She latched it.

There was a knock at the front door. It took a moment to respond, but when Aru did it was by ducking into the pantry. She squatted down, her fist pressed against her lips. The knocking came again. Aru rose and tiptoed back out to the sitting room. She went to the front window. Another knock. Carefully, carefully, without making them wiggle, she peeked through the drapes. Aldrei and Aeon stood on the doorstep. Aeon knocked again.

All the breath Aru had been holding came out at once. She rushed to the door and greeted her friends. They had with them a big pot of hot and spicy chicken and rice-noodle soup.

When Aru asked how Aldrei had known she was at home he pretended not to hear. She didn't mention the intruder, surely one of Blackbuck's henchmen after the wand. Apparently Aldrei knew, considering his timing. Blackbuck, it seemed, was getting more desperate to find the wand. Things must not be going well with its replacement.

Aldrei and Aeon stayed till long after Nrouhw returned from the museum. Aru enjoyed her time with them, despite her grippy cold. The soup was delicious, the perfect thing, and Aru had two large helpings. She felt much better after having it.

During this visit, Aeon happened to notice something about a hockey tournament in the newspaper. "The beavers hosting the event played in sweaters of combed cottonwood fluff," he read. "They say the jerseys are soft as a bunny's bottom and durable as cotton." He paused, and glanced at Aldrei, "I've never done any spinning before, but now I'm thinking of giving it a whirl."

At the mention of beavers, Aru thought immediately of dear old Chip. "I've a friend who is in logging and hydraulic dams."

"Did he ever give you any prophecies?" asked Aeon.

Aru's eyes narrowed. "Whatever reason would you ask such a thing?"

"Beavers are well-known as prophets, Aru." said Nrouhw softly. "How could you not know that? What do they teach in those south woods schools, hmm?"

"Well, yes, he did say one thing."

Aeon looked at her expectantly but Aru said nothing more.

"Well, what was it, then?" Aldrei prodded.

"He told me that I was facing doom. He said that the trickery of a jay bird would deliver me. I think it had something to do with the way Eepe departed. I don't know."

"Ah, I love a good ol' prophecy," Aldrei giggled. "Meaningless."

Later that night, Aru and Nrouhw talked about what had happened. He made light of it, joking about how he wouldn't have wanted to be the one trapped in that kitchen when Aru came in with the poker. But in his eye was a worry, and several days later he would ask Aranieda about stashing the diamond wand elsewhere.

That evening, though, they talked about the social environment up at the academy and how it compared to the scenario of a classic novel they'd both read. They went to bed rather late, after some more ginger tea. Because of her bothersome snuffles, Aru wasn't feeling amorous. Nrouhw fell right to sleep, but Aru lay there for what seemed like hours. Finally she got up, wrapped herself in the old lab coat she liked to use as a house robe (someone had given Nrouhw several for painters smocks) and she started a fire in the bedroom grate.

The soft thick linen cushions of the chair in the corner invited her. She curled up and for a while she just watched Nrouhw sleep. Tired but completely awake, she thought about going downstairs to get that book she'd started. Her chest felt tight and her cough was annoying.

For some reason, while sitting there too lazy to retrieve her book, Aru started thinking about a reclusive scientist friend of Aldrei's. He lived up on Bwahmyr, on beyond the mental hospital. A few weeks previously, she had enjoyed tea with him and Aldrei and Aeon down at Mama Bwehmeb's candy shop.

The scientist, a goateed and bespectacled Opali man, had recently published an article which discussed the idea of using rockets for interplanetary travel. This was an exciting thing to consider.

As she sat watching Nrouhw and staring at the fire, Aru fantasized about traveling through space, looking out through a small porthole at the moon passing by, and the Milky Way looming large. She thought about the stars and the universe, the enormous bounds of everything. The vast regions of emptiness. She began to feel a little strange.

370

The top of her head grew warm, a funny sensation, as if she were wearing a hat. Or perhaps it felt like her scalp was swollen, or covered with warm mashed potatoes. It was not a pleasant feeling, and decidedly odd, but Aru wasn't particularly scared. She did start to wonder if she was about to die. Bright light appeared in her mind, neither cold nor warm, as if a door was open to another world. A tunnel of light? Maybe so. She was dying. She didn't want to die. One doesn't die from a cold. She just needed to come down, calm down.

It's you, Visyrn, isn't it, she thought to herself. *Leave me alone, I don't like this.* But also, someone was visiting her. Her mother? Maybe her mother was there, existing somewhere between a feeling and her mind's eye. She had a vision of someone, her mother, but immediate memory gave her no image, just foggy fluff from the surface of her mind, devouring the images before she could get to them.

Yet her mother's presence, if it was there, was within her also, seeing out of her eyes. Aru was allowing her mother to be present through her, to look around the room. Perhaps Mother had a message for her.

"Don't press it. Merely relax," she told herself. She calmed her mind. No, she wasn't dying, she didn't think so. She remembered her mother, and her grandmother also. A chill of love went through her. *"Find beauty in your life. Live in beauty. Surround yourself with it, enjoy it, exude it. Let it carry you."*

Was this a message that came to Aru, or did she just make it up herself? That wasn't clear, but did it matter? This was just the sort of thing Mother would say, should she want to give Aru some advice.

"Reality eludes you, Aru." The unmistakable intonation of Visyrn was loud and clear. But Aru continued to live in this moment without fear, somehow, taking all this information in and storing it without much analysis. She'd just remember these thoughts and sort it all out tomorrow. She got up from her chair, stirred the fire, and crawled into bed. Most likely she went right to sleep.

On the day of Lekki and Mhehh's wedding, Aranieda came to the Hornfel for early tea, as arranged. She'd attend with Aru and Nrouhw.

When Aru told her about the intruder in the kitchen, Aranieda raised her eyebrows. She worried that Blackbuck would be so bold, and she said that his flunkies had been noticeably more active in their reconnaissance recently.

She mentioned that she had fresh concerns about the man. His failure in achieving his goals seemed to be driving him further into indifference about his people. Serious issues which troubled his lands had become magnified in his absence, yet he would only focus on the acquisition of those blasted snails and the continued callous domination of his son.

True, his attempts to manipulate Lekki's life, his marriage and successors, were ultimately meant to influence the composition of the royal family in order to spare his people from the affliction of the invisible lizards. But surely there was a better route. All Blackbuck cared about was his own name and legacy.

Although Blackbuck was against the wedding he would be in conspicuous attendance. He hated Mhehh, he resented her family and had a distaste for just about everything to do with the Opali culture, but he would be there because of appearances. Appearances were important to him. And he still needed that wand which was not yet completed.

It was a sunny day but there were lots of puffy clouds. The winds must have been strong way up high because the clouds traveled faster than Aru had ever seen them go. They formed all sorts of wonderful animal shapes, changing quickly from rabbit to leaping opossum, to rearing horse, to dove on the wing, and so forth as they rushed across the sky. On the way to the palace Aru and Nrouhw had fun pointing them out to each other. Aranieda didn't share in their amusement.

As soon as they rounded the end of the ridge, the bells of the palace could be heard clanging in joyful resonation. The three made their way downhill. When they arrived at the foot of the ramp to the great house a number of people in fine clothes and riding in horse-drawn carriages were already ascending to the entrance. The wedding list had been limited mostly to royalty and dignitaries, but over two hundred people had been invited to the reception. In this crowd Opali were a minority, and the darker colors of skin seemed almost strange to Aru.

On top of the granite tower, lacy banners decorated the arches and spires of the house, and the grand front steps were littered with delicate blossoms made of ice which tinkled as they tumbled in the breeze.

After climbing the magnificent stairway, the crowd turned aside at the main entrance and proceeded along outside the palace wall through an ornate arcade made of frozen snow. This led to a large terrace with half a dozen pairs of etched glass double doors leading into the great hall. Most of them stood open.

Inviting flute music came from within. Aru and her companions squeezed past a huddle of women, rather curvaceous highborn and chic ladies, who stood excitedly gock-bawking in the doorway.

The enormous ballroom was of marble and quartz, with wide pointed arches supporting the ceiling all along its impressive length. From these great vaults hung streamers of fine silk gauze, draped in graceful flourishes, reminiscent of the bridal veil. Three spectacular crystal chandeliers dangled among the gauze, their candles reflecting in the mirrors which lined the upper walls. It was a storybook scene.

The friends were ushered toward the cloakroom by silver-grey uni-formed servants who relieved them of their coats and overshoes. The family stood with royal dignity in a receiving line, first the moun-tain goat queen and king; then Mhehh and her new husband, then Blackbuck, and other members of the family. Mhehh's parents smiled politely but they appeared quite emotionally reserved. The newlyweds had a much more excited demeanor and Mhehh hugged Aru and kissed her cheek. She smelled like jasmine.

At the near end of the room was a tremendous fireplace with a lively and crackling fire, before which spread the dining tables with their glittering settings. Tall thin candles stood among masses of fresh flowers and there were finger bowls with orchid blossoms floating in them. These had come from the queen's own conservatory.

As the guests flowed in, the center of the room became crowded. Ermine and important-looking personages were among the throng, but also a heterogeneous variety of folk. Most who were not Opali had powdered faces and hair. Many of the women had long opera gloves. A small orchestra near the far wall performed an elegant minuet.

Several buffet tables had been set up and Aru and Nrouhw followed Aranieda to take a peek at the fare. Ice sculptures of birds and flowers and of an overflowing cornucopia were situated proudly amongst milk-glass platters loaded with delicacies such as snow crab and herring eggs, cheese blintzes with sour cream, ambrosia topped with slices of quince. There was an abundance of whipped cream, heavy cream, and cream sauces—but Aru gasped!

There was a man there, picking through the stuffed apples with a silver carving fork. He had a big birthmark behind his ear. She knew him! She knew him from Ysgarlad! He stood with a woman, presumably his wife, who held a large saucer while he filled it. A carnation decorated the buttonhole of his champagne-pink, double-breasted suit. He had a kind-looking but boozy face.

The wife had a thick nose, turned up and exceedingly flat on the end. Dressed to the nines, she was in Epoque, her dress fashionable, yes, but robbed of its elegance by wearing too many ropes of pearls. Substandard pearls. A pretty pink silk purse hung from her cheerfully fat waist.

"That man! It's the inebriate we encountered at the inn last year. The man who paid the lady fox to let you go! What's he doing here?" Nrouhw whispered.

Aru stared for a moment, and then she whispered back, "I suppose this means—"

"He must have been, all this time, in the service of Blackbuck!" Nrouhw's whisper was more of a low growl.

Before Aru could respond, she was startled by Aranieda tapping softly on the back of her shoulder. Following her friend's gaze Aru saw Blackbuck himself walking hurriedly in their direction. He had excused himself from the reception line.

At first Aru assumed that he would continue past them, but as he walked he seemed to be focusing on her. Aru tried to ignore him; it surely wasn't her the man was looking at. Someone just beyond her.

Yet here he was, and he stopped to talk. He gave a brief greeting to Aranieda, then a nod to Nrouhw. Aru noticed Blackbuck wore the smith's jewelled belt over his fine pleated dress shirt. It certainly was a breathtaking piece.

Speaking to the others, but looking at Aru, Blackbuck said, "The two of you must allow me to appropriate the company of this young woman for a few moments. Aru, is it?" Without waiting for an answer, he continued, "I require the opinion of a young woman in a small matter that has been irksome to me recently. I'll have her returned to you in a matter of minutes."

With that he gracefully offered the back of his hand in such a way that Aru had no choice, without seeming rude, but to place her own hand on his and walk along with him. She looked over her shoulder. Nrouhw had a look of confusion and concern on his face. Aranieda looked angry.

Crossing the glistening room with Blackbuck, Aru felt both disgusted and strangely proud. She knew she held the hand of a presumptuous brute, yet he was truly a handsome man, and if he had no sense of honor he certainly did have a sense of style.

He spoke to her courteously as they went, asking her how she enjoyed the celebration. Guiding Aru toward the open doorways, he soon stood with her out on the terrace. A small cat-like man met them with some soft wool cloaks and he handed Blackbuck a bottle of something.

Blackbuck took Aru to a secluded portion of the terrace and told her he had a simple task for her. He directed her to look into the bottle and tell him what she saw. She realized she should say that there was nothing in the bottle at all, but it was too late. She had already told him: the tail of a lizard. He smiled but he didn't say much after that. He escorted her back to the festivities.

A beautiful afternoon turned into evening, with dancing and speeches and lots of almond cream and alpine flower liqueurs. Aldrei and Aeon appeared out of the crowd and joined Aru and her companions. Just after sunset, there was a dramatic release of thousands of fireflies.

Lekki and Mhehh sat at a table with their parents and a few others. The bride looked lovely, plump and fresh-faced with her soft skin, and her dazzling dress showing off its lengthy, voluminous train and corresponding veil. The dress was of rich and exquisitely embroidered lace flounced over a gown of the most pale pink satin. Her snowy hair was woven and styled to complement a delicate diamond tiara. She looked happy. So did Lekki.

At length the bride and groom rose to say a few words to their guests. Lekki held a staff of silver and mastodon ivory. The room fell silent. A few people were smoking cigarettes. There was a cough. Lekki thanked all of the people for coming, saying he and Princess Mhehh were honored to share their day with all of them. Then he said they had an announcement. The king and queen looked at him in surprise, in curiosity. Blackbuck's face was expressionless.

"Mhehh and I have something else we wish to share with you today," said Lekki, "or someone, rather." A woman entered from the hallway; it was Girun's daughter, holding a bundle which she carefully handed to Mhehh. "This is Sheeki," Lekki continued. "He is our son. We have adopted him and we will treasure him for such time as we receive the gift of life ourselves."

The room hushed to utter silence for a moment. Then someone started clapping, hesitantly. Soon the others joined in and the room was full of genuine applause. The parents of the young couple smiled but they did not clap. Blackbuck removed himself from the scene entirely. Little Sheeki slept peacefully through the whole affair.

Later on that evening another, less public, announcement came when Aeon told his friends that he and Aldrei had some minor tidings to share with them. Aldrei said to them that he had been bound by loyalty to a friend to serve Blackbuck's interests but this was no longer so. Now that Lekki and Mhehh were married there was no need for him to remain in Opal Heights. He and Aeon had a dear friend on the coast, the Jerboa, who awaited their return. Perhaps if Aru and Nrouhw were ever to pay a visit to Lekki in his homeland they might stop in for a visit, because that is where Aldrei and Aeon would be found. Aldrei and Aeon said goodbye and Aldrei gave Aru a diamond charm. Without speaking aloud he said to her that wearing this charm would help greatly to protect the wand from the Blackbuck. *As long as you have this around your neck, Aru, anyone but the rightful owner can see the dragon,* he told her. Aru was sad to hear that her friends were leaving. She was wearing the charm locket that Nrouhw had given her, so she unscrewed the top and slipped the diamond into it.

Lekki and Mhehh took the baby with them as they left for their honeymoon. Although it might be an odd idea to bring a child along, they felt it necessary for the continued safety of young Sheeki. The ceremony finished with the new little family riding off in a sleigh under the bright stars of a new moon. The sleigh was horse-drawn, decorated with pearly camellias and lots of candle lanterns and festooned with hundreds of silver bells. They would spend their first night at the lodge in Sylfaen.

Aranieda told Aru and Nrouhw the queen and king were unhappy about the adoption of Sheeki but would recover. After all, Mhehh was only fourth in line as heir, after her older sister, that sister's daughter, and then Mhehh's older brother. The royal family were a bit old-fashioned, but they weren't completely unreasonable. The queen currently had a tension headache, "from the dreadful echo of the vulgar herd," but she'd get over it.

That night Aru and Nrouhw lay together talking about the ceremony and then a bit about their own wedding plans. Aru mentioned that, as much fun as the day had brought, a part of her was appalled at the extravagance and indulgence. She enjoyed her life in Opal Heights immensely, but at the same time it was weighing on her conscience to be so pampered. She didn't like to think about the fact that in living such a fine life she was benefiting from the ermine exploitation of the villages. Nrouhw agreed, and suggested that they involve themselves in some sort of charitable work. That might help. She felt so very culpable. She remembered the hungry children in Sylfaen. The turns of life itself decided, however, to take care of these problems for her.

It was only a few days later that Aranieda suggested the time had come to put their long-held plan into action. The first step was an easy one. Nrouhw and Aru had sandwiches at one of their favorite cafés. There they, in voices perhaps not *quite* hushed enough, discussed their secret plan to take the dragon wand up to Windwether Rock on the Mahahag glacier and throw it into the crevasse, disposing of it once and for all. They had a similar conversation at a tavern the following evening. And then, for good measure, they spoke of their intention again, in fairly loud whispers over cups of steamed milk up at the Bellwether. This was during the weekend ski races.

It was snowing a few flakes, the following week, when Aru and Nrouhw hiked the upper Mahahag trail. Aru glanced behind her now and then as they went. They were certain to be followed by Blackbuck's people.

Their steps were slow, their manner solemn. Nrouhw carried a velvet bag, made from remnants of an old Opali dress. Trimmed with his beadwork and with embroidery by Aru, this bag had a purpose. It held a magnificent dragon wand, a priceless work of art. The decorated sack gave ceremony and respect to the last few hours of the masterpiece's existence, before it was gone from the world forever.

It was an act of desperation, in some ways of defeat. Without Aldrei to protect the wand, and with Blackbuck nearly having completed the duplicate, its bargaining worth had diminished greatly. The best option now was to put it away, along with all the magic it represented.

The afternoon was cold and clear. Aru felt thankful for her mountain goat wool sweater and her thick hooded cloak. She pulled the cloak tight about her neck. It had a generous hood.

At last they mounted the main ridge and they could see the glacier and what certainly must be Windwether Rock reaching up out of the snow below. One great outcropping of granite dominated the scene, extending out into the foot of the glacier. The ice flowed around the huge rock like a creeping river.

They reached the rock, passing below a great wedged prominence of it to access a large flat area on the other side. They pretended not to see several people following them down from the ridge. Just beyond the far edge of the flat slab, where they now stood, were several long canyon-like cracks in the glacier. Nrouhw stepped toward the edge of the rock to peer into the closest one.

"This will do nicely," he said to Aru.

She went splay footed and in baby steps over to the edge to see, stepping back quickly once she had a peek. Aru looked back toward the approaching henchmen, just now hidden by the wedge of rock. "I don't think they're going to quite make it in time," she said with a grin.

Timing his actions to coincide with their followers rounding the wedge of granite, Nrouhw pulled the wand from the velvet bag and held it up in the sunlight for a moment, a quick goodbye before tossing it away forever. It sparkled amazingly, as only well-cut diamond can. How could anyone part with such an object, throw it into the bottomless depths? Nrouhw held it high, gazing at it. He kept gazing. What was taking those guys so long?

Around the edge of the granite cliff appeared the first man. No, a boy. Queex? Nrouhw and Aru froze for a moment, with mouths gaping. Then Nrouhw slipped the wand back into the bag.

Queex came toward them, chanting a nonsensical singsong as he picked his way through the snow. He had a walking stick but he wasn't using it. He carried it over his shoulder. Aru would have called out to him, but she was too surprised to say anything. The boy came right across the flat snowy slab and stood just in front of them. He acted as if he were oblivious of their presence. The two men arrived around the cliff, but they halted and stood there, watching.

The boy kept singing his gibberish as he began to draw in the snow with his stick. ". . . cho-cho-ee-keh-dah, ah ee ein, peeshu peeshu . . ."

Nrouhw and Aru stood transfixed. Queex glanced up at them; could he not see Aru's face under her hood? Did he not know her? But now she was unable to move or speak. Queex drew in the snow—he drew symbols of some kind. With quick, jerky movements of the staff he made a large circular design composed of strange glyphs.

Aru followed Nrouhw's gaze up toward the top of the granite wedge. There above the edge of the prominence, Blackbuck! Inwardly, she panicked. Blackbuck stood with his chest out, laughing with glee at his own cleverness. He held a reindeer antler in one hand and a mirror in the other, the mirror blindingly reflecting the sun when he held it just so. No one had expected Blackbuck.

Blackbuck called down to Queex from the cliff but his voice roiled in the language of the wind. Only the boy understood. He declined to answer. Queex continued to draw and sing, and began to tap the figures gently with his stick. Now and then, while performing this drawing and tapping, he would glance around. Aru caught his eye. They looked at one another, and Queex's eyes widened in recognition. He went on with his work. But both Aru and Nrouhw found themselves able to move again somewhat.

As Queex tapped the images, tiny droplets of water began to exude from the stick. Like round drops of dew, they stood clinging to the snow. More and more of them he made. They were falling quickly off his wand, hundreds of them. Queex looked up at Blackbuck for a moment. The drops of water became bubbles, growing larger a few at a time, only to burst. And out of each bursting bubble flew a small ivory-shelled beetle.

Aru called out, "Queex, what are you doing?" but he only glanced at her and then back up at Blackbuck. He continued his song. Queex stopped creating new beetles, but began to manipulate them, waving and twirling his stick. The beetles flew spiraling up into the air.

Blackbuck shouted from the cliff, and striding quickly forward to the edge, he threw the mirror high into the air. As it began to fall he smashed it hard with his reindeer antler, sending its fragments out on the wind toward the others. Everyone except Queex covered their faces. The glass fell into a thousand tiny pieces, scattering to cover the area where they stood.

The beetles, which flew in a spiraling manner, turning teeny somersaults as they traveled through the air, were beholden to their young master. Queex made them disperse and they flew wildly about, each beetle picking up a tiny piece of mirror in its mouthparts.

Blackbuck's men at this point crossed to where Queex was, unconcerned that they were crushing beetles into the snow as they trod. Queex lost some of his focus as he endured a number of his beetles being destroyed.

While the boy waved his stick at the insects the cloud of beetles with their tiny shards flew high into the air again. They formed into a giant ball of wild gymnastics.

One of the men, a snippy domestic goose type, shouted "Finish it!" at Queex and pointed to Aru and Nrouhw. Using his long stick, the boy drew again in the snow, making some alterations to his work. He stopped singing.

"Wuggadee!" he shouted. "Not, not, will not behave!" Queex stood up, looking defiantly at Blackbuck. "No, Mister Buckbuck! Wuggadeee! Not, not those two. No."

The ivory beetles made hiccuping noises and flew off over the glacier, dropping the tiny pieces of mirror as they went, a glinting and tinkling shower of glass. Queex faced Blackbuck, alternately puckering and pressing his lips as he stared toward the man, his eyes glazed. He stepped backward a couple of steps, positioning himself disturbingly near the edge of the crevasse.

Blackbuck's fury gave him some power despite the restraining girdle. On his face it was evident that he could feel the energy surging up through his bones. He whirled the enchanted antler about his head like a bullroarer and then he shouted a curse as he aimed at the boy's circle of glyphs. His one great hurricane blast of wind scooped up snow, hurtling toward Queex.

Nrouhw sprang toward Queex to grab him, and then through the roar of the wind came a chilling sound, the death screams of a vole boy, a gander man, and a cougar man, as all three were swept into the chasm when the edge of the crevasse gave way.

VII. Without

ARU's breath has fled from her, leaving her lungs close to useless. Nrouhw is gone forever and she lies languid, staring into nothingness like a cold, dead fish. Only absence is real, and the little room is fusty, woaden and dim, utterly saturated with misty gloom. Waves slap against the far side of the wall. Breathing comes wretchedly shallow. A gutted slimy mackerel, lacking even the energy to flop or squirm.

Focus on breathing alone, each breath an exertion, burdensome. Each breath. Eyesight grows poor when all is dull and unheeded, as nothing bears importance anymore. No joy remains, only listless exhaustion, the effects of shock; excruciating despair brings with it the loss of hope, and the hands tremble.

Different ways of drowning in cold water. Panic and voiceless suffocation, the desperate fight just to breathe. Or settle into stillness, quiet daze of stupefaction, solitary and numb, watching the bubbles of breath, not really thinking, only looking, a dream. In the past there was execution by dousing, dumbfounded infuriation, betrayal of life. No struggle allowed. Give up.

The light of day vanished behind a bank of darkness, lost, and gone to unknowable skies. Meaning warps the world, sorrow a buffer from thought, a moat keeping real perception at bay, there is no comfort in madness. I have no body.

There was something about a mirror. A shattering reflection. Azure. The memory is silent, like a movie shown to one. Sit here and breathe and let my weary veins circulate what meager life force is within. With the collapse of capacity for effort, it's all that can be done. But now, now I've lost everything. An absence fills my all.

Misery consumes the heart and nausea the stomach. The meat of the body weighs heavy, dragging down the bones as it sags, creating a great cavity inside where empty thoughts bounce from wall to wall. Lie down, curl up.

Someone had grabbed her by the arms, it was that man. There were awful bruises but Aru didn't feel them. She remembered dark shapes, river boats in the twilight. Ice chunks clogging the shore. That man of Blackbuck's carried her there. All that way.

A pressing headache inflates her brow. Aru sees herself from above, crying endlessly, sobbing, pouring forth on and on. Perhaps she should have stopped herself but she just isn't able to care. She has cried so much that her eyes swelled nearly shut. They hurt, badly, as if they'd been punched. But the pain becomes another thing to notice from a distance. She is smothered, hollow, her head a brittle skull, vacant, with giant gaping eye sockets.

She felt it all now. The loss of her parents at such a young age, the way her grandma left her, the isolation among the wolves, all these things she had endured but hadn't fully reconciled to herself, or even acknowledged, really. Anguish. Wedged behind her breastbone an anchor of heavy cold steel pulled her down, down, down to the place where the groupers with their sharp teeth wait in the shadows.

Then, wilted and useless, beaten, she didn't care all that much that she was sinking. Too stunned to fight. The shock of realization shot through her body now and then, causing a sick feeling. She'd look over to the extra chair, where he might be sitting, where he would have been sitting, and such a stab of pain overtook her! She could see him there, almost, his smile and that expression she loved, then she couldn't picture him; the image had faded and she was alone.

The glacial fissure was deep, and the bright sapphire color of the ice darkened into its hidden depths; a beautiful, terrible place to die. The terror, the screams, it all echoed in her nightmares, chilling her awake.

"Eat," said the woman. When Aru rolled over to face the wall she could hear the woman click her tongue in disgust. A clatter of the dish tray onto the table and she left.

Aru's life had caved in. Exhausted, she did nothing but stare at the round window. The colors in the stained glass were soothing, a life rope for her to cling to. Three irises, with blooms large and dark and lush. Cloudy streaks in the opaque glass represented a soft petal so perfectly. Aru drank up the hues. The design was full of curves. The blossoms barely touched one another, thus defining background shapes as pleasing as the flowers. Nrouhw would have loved it.

There had been no lifeline for Nrouhw. The crevasse was dark and deep, unfathomable, such a contrast to the white snow above. No chance of survival. Blackbuck's cold eyes peered down into it from the rock's edge as his big brute, the henchman, dragged her away. She struggled so hard, then she gave up; the man hoisted her, carried her somehow. She didn't know how they got to the river.

The woman returned. "Eat. It's been days, now. Eat and drink."

Had it been? Days? It didn't matter. Aru turned onto her stomach. She couldn't cry anymore. The woman rolled her back over, not gently, helped her up so she could drink some water. Obediently, Aru drank half the glass. Then the woman left.

The boat rocked slightly. Aru wondered vaguely when it was that they had shoved off. Couldn't be on the ocean, must still be the river or a lake. She tried the door. Locked. Another day, maybe, went by.

The keeper came back, delivering some food to replace the uneaten meal from the day before. She'd been in and out, but this was the first time Aru took a look at her. Her long, tubular torso was ringed by several rolls of fat. Her shape much reminded Aru of a basket from her childhood, a tall basket made of thick coils wrapped with indigo-dyed raffia. It was where her mother kept the umbrella. And the birch rod.

The woman had an elongated nose and a pointed, jutting jaw. She wore her blue-black hair teased and puffed and swept upwards from her high forehead.

"Who are you?" asked Aru in a hoarse whisper, and, "Where the thundering stormhowl am I?"

The woman didn't look at her when she answered, "We're on the Oso. The best plan is just you keep your questions to yourself, as you've been doing, deary."

"The Oso River? Have I been kidnapped?"

There was no answer.

"Am I a prisoner?"

"You are a simple girl, aren't you," said the woman.

385

"I want to speak to Blackbuck."

"Mm-hmm, rest assured that will happen at some point. Eat something." And then she left.

"No," said Aru to herself, "this isn't right. All of this. It can't be real." Swimmy in her sense of balance, she made her way over to one of the round windows and tried to see out, but the glass was too opaque. She sat down and nibbled at a corner of a chunk of bread. Then, bit by bit, she ate the whole thing.

Aru's keeper, or possibly warden, chose to wear the cooler colors of the spectrum exclusively. She had quite an outdated sense of fashion, yet her obsession with clothing had her every day in her morning dress, then her work dress, her tea gown, her silk evening dress. She wore nasty, uncomfortable-looking walking shoes. She had eight pairs, the entire collection of them a couple of sizes too small. She always walked slowly, but somehow managed a certain amount of grace.

The warden and Aru rarely talked for more than a few minutes, and when they did it was about subjects of the woman's choosing. Usually, the topic was food. This warden was a voracious eater. Rarely did Aru see her when she wasn't munching on something or at least smelling like she recently had been. When she stepped into the cabin she often had in her hand a glass of the liqueur made from the blue blood of the indigo milk cap mushroom, raising it between her thumb and fingers and considering herself to be handsomely genteel indeed.

There was no lamp or candle; the cell was lit by a deck prism and the two stained glass portholes, the latter of which faced each other from the hull walls. The room was quite narrow. Although Aru couldn't reach from one of these sides to the other it almost felt like she could, and the tapered shape let her know she must be in the forepeak of the bow. The berth was a large one—for a boat—but there is no luxury as somber as unwished-for extra space in the bed. A wardrobe built right up into the stem of the prow held some expensive-looking clothes.

The consistent creaking of the timbers around her sounded as if some heavy-footed person quartered nearby was using a rocking chair. To console herself she imagined it was a friendly hippo, smoking a pipe and reading the personal ads in the classifieds. It helped that the woody groaning had a rhythm. Along with the whooshes of the wind and the plunging slosh of the water through which they passed, the sound brought some small comfort to her.

The day came when the Warden, clutching Aru by the wrist, brought her out of the damp cabin and led her down a dark and awfully tight passageway. Aru stumbled along, inhaling the sweet air, not noticing much else, because for some reason she had it in her mind that if this woman was taking her to her freedom then her life might go back the way it was before. They passed through the galley and into a narrow saloon. The steely light of late afternoon shone through large rain-spattered portholes. A couple of sofas lined one side. Covered in a dark velvet fabric, they had the powdery-looking sheen of blueberries. Heavy drapes on the walls and a valance above the doorway made the space seem like the salon of a house, only smaller, of course, and outlandishly narrow.

One object did catch Aru's interest. Among the collection of knick-knackery on the wall hung a big round clock, a delightful old-fashioned one, tastefully detailed, and with raised numerals and beveled glass. The interior of the clock face was nearly filled by a moon dial: a full-lipped, big-cheeked man-in-the-moon which revolved smiling through a midnight sky filled with stars. Both the kindness of his face and the deep indigo of that sky encouraged Aru for a moment.

The Warden escorted her up the steps of the companionway. At the top one could go to the forward deck or go aft through an airy deckhouse. They headed out onto the deck. The woman offered Aru an umbrella from a collection of several, but Aru refused it. She wanted to feel the drops of rain on her face, and on her hair, the misty water of rain to cleanse her spirit.

"Am I to be let go now?" she asked.

"Let go?" repeated the woman. "I wouldn't think so. Enjoy your time on deck. You'll be allowed up here or in the saloon. Don't try to go anywhere else." She took a quick look around and then headed below. At the top of the ladder she called out through the doorway, "If you try, you'll find that the doors to compartments other than yours are locked." Then she said, "You should use that umbrella, otherwise you'll be soaked through in no time." She made a little face and descended, disappearing from view. Aru wasn't sure what she would have done if the Warden had said yes, anyhow.

The boat was narrow across the breadth and quite long, good-sized for a riverboat and surprisingly large considering the river it was in. Back toward the stern two crew members were using poles to guide it off the banks and keep it going downstream. It was a peacock boat, brightly painted and with a graceful peacock head and neck at the prow and a big fan tail at the stern. Two others like it floated ahead of them down the river.

Aru considered making a jump for it but the deck rose too high above the waterline, and also she didn't know how deep the water was.

Deep breaths of the cold air felt good in Aru's lungs. After peering through the rain at the river, and looking around a bit at the boat and vacantly at the scenery going by, she sat right down on the deck under the peacock figurehead. For a while she did nothing but listen to the patter of the rain and the plink of the drips. These were in concert with the creaking of the boat, a sound which had become so familiar. Aru began to sob and then to cry into her hands.

"Are you all right, Miss?"

Aru looked up, wiping her tears but still sobbing and sniffing. It was a kid in denim overalls. A young deckhand.

Too downtrodden to be embarrassed, Aru smiled weakly but didn't say anything. After a few minutes of respectful silence the little deckhand offered the comfort of conversation. "It's going to be somewhat of a cool evening, and you're quite soaked, you know. Can't you feel the cold? Here, I'll be right back."

She rummaged in a locker over in the deckhouse and returned with an old oilskin raincoat and helped Aru to drape it over her shoulders. It was far too big and smelled strongly of mildew but it did block the breeze well. Aru hadn't realized how cold she had been getting.

"Thank you so much," Aru said. She told the girl her name and asked for hers.

"Squee-ee Ahk Uh k'kkkk is my name, Miss. I've been crewing here on the Clearwater since she departed from the coast. Did you know she was pulled upriver by herons and hot air balloon? Such a grand experience! We traveled as fast as a locomotive or nearly so, I think. I've never seen anything like it."

"How old are you, Squee? Do you mind if I call you Squee?" Aru smiled gently, brushing away another tear. "I don't think I'll say your name properly, I'm sorry."

"I suppose that's fine. But the mate, that's his name too, Squee. He's a rat. But no matter, it'll be fine. Perhaps we'll both come running when you call." She giggled. "At any rate, I'll be nine and a half this summer. It's been weeks I've been aboard this vessel, and I can't help but tell you I'm quite lonesome for my loved ones. The pilot of the Zodiac, that's the one right up there ahead—the other boat is the Pirate—anyways, the pilot he came to our school and he asked for a volunteer. Ostensibly we are volunteers, but technically we were crimped, the crew of these three boats were. Money changed hands somewhere, and as a result I believe the police looked the other way. I know we'll not receive much pay for all this, and I miss my family horribly. But there's a bright side to everything, Miss, and don't you worry. She's a sweet little craft, the Clearwater, and the river is pretty, in its own way. When we get back down to the sea it will be spring and life will renew. Everything will look better then, you'll see."

The rain let up a bit as they talked. Squatting next to Aru, Squee told her about how beautiful the eastern oceans were. She told her about much of the history of her young life, and especially about her experiences on the riverboat. It had been obvious to Aru after hearing Squee say her name that she must be a dolphin girl, but now Aru learned that she was a bottlenose. The young deckhand chattered about anything and everything, but she didn't know much about Aru or her situation. All she knew was that they'd come up to the headwaters of the Oso for the purpose of bringing Mr. Blackbuck back to his palace near the sea. Also that one of the guests of the Clearwater hadn't boarded, after all.

Aru extended her hands and held both of Squee's. She looked into the girl's eyes and said, "I want you to know, Squee, that your kindness at this difficult time for me is appreciated beyond what you might imagine. But," she whispered, "at any rate, I must be going now, goodbye." Time froze Squee, her hands still reaching out, while Aru put her finger to her lips and stood up, launching herself over the wales of the boat into the river below.

It was an act of madness, certainly, and therefore pointless to worry about whether Aru's leap was premeditated. Was she personally accountable for this act of stupidity? Did she care if she survived it, Aru would never know. But as she plunged into the water the little girl's scream entered Aru's memory, to be collected there in a blur with the echoes of Nrouhw's tragic plummet to his death.

As a matter of great fortune, the river ran especially deep in that location and Aru submerged and resurfaced in a confusion of swirling froth. In the panic over what she had done Aru's mind went completely void, but her reflexes took over and without even knowing it she kicked off her slippers and swam hard to grab the big calabash that Squee threw to her for a life buoy. Somehow she caught it by the cord that retained its stopper, and holding it tight by this she managed to place it below her bosom to keep afloat in the turmoil of the flow.

The current swept Aru along, unyielding, and she fought for air in the rushing of the water. Her sense returned enough for her to remember to roll over onto her back, and bend her knees to force her face up so she could grab a breath. Still pressing the gourd against herself, she struggled to turn so she was facing feet first as she rushed downstream because if something were to smash against a rock, better her ankle than her skull.

As she hurtled down the river, Aru made gasping glances for a place to swim ashore, but her skirts dragged like a sail under the water and it all happened too fast. With the water splashing over her, the current driving her, blurry flashes of the shoreline came between dousings and coughing gasps. She tried to see where the boat was but she saw only bits of sky, bits of shore, a collage of impressions.

A fallen tree stuck out from the shore. Aru turned to face it barely in time, ready to heave herself onto it so as not to get sucked down under and pinned. The gourd bottle flew from her hands as she reached for the top of the log, a whirlpool grabbed her like icy tongs and spun her around and around, and that was it; she'd never make it now.

Everything slowed down, as it does in such situations. Aru circled with the water in drowsy indifference, drawn in to the center of the vortex where she floated downward, with plenty of time to look around her. She wondered what would happen next. Could she be drowning? Possibly, but time passed and nothing terrible happened. It seemed like ages went by, spiraling downward. Into the depths, into the whispers of fishhh fishhh fishhh.

> "Fish town,
>
> Come to fish town,
>
> Our home,
>
> Deep and meaningful
>
> Fish town.
>
> Welcome home."

Aru's eyelids drooped, and she had hardly begun a funny dream about interrogating a fluffy house cat when—plop! She awoke in a municipal fountain. Fat stone porpoises arched as if playing among the spray. Grand mosaic designs depicted beautiful ocean themes. She sat upright and looked around.

In every direction there were the neat gardens and pathways of a town square and beyond those stood historical-looking buildings of several stories. People rode bicycles on the pathways and only a few walked or strolled. There were no horses to be seen. A couple of children stood by the rim of the fountain, a boy and a girl, looking at her and whispering in each other's ears in wonder.

A man approached, a well-dressed gentleman, and Aru suddenly felt self-conscious. She stood up, as best she could, and stepped out of the fountain to try to wring out at least the lower portion of her skirt.

"Aru," said the man, "Cousin Aru, welcome to our waters. These are the cherished spawning grounds of the steelhead people of the Oso River." He held out his hand. "Please come with me, let us help you find your equilibrium."

In her stocking feet and sodden clothing Aru went with him, word-lessly, one hand hoisting up her heavy skirts and the other holding onto his arm. The man's arm felt slightly cool to her, but he had no fishy scent as one might expect. He led her along a bikeway through the park, where they were passed by many cyclists, mostly trout folk like Aru's escort.

These people were tall. The women had quite sloping shoulders. Even with a nice layer of fat, their general appearance was sleek. The steelheads dressed in fine tailored and well-pressed clothes. The fabric they favored was unfamiliar to Aru, a shimmering metallic cloth, all silvery and shades of light cyan. The steelheads glanced at Aru with friendly but muted curiosity, their eyes looking wise and quite round.

It chafed Aru to walk in her wet clothes, they pulled too tight on some areas of her body and she worried her stockings were getting holes on the bottom and that her toes might soon poke through. It seemed they walked a long way through the park and among the tall buildings, but finally they met a small, thin woman in a doorway of a building labeled *Wrasse Bathhouse*. She introduced herself and said she'd guide Aru from there. A wonderful steamy smell came from within and Aru didn't mind at all being encouraged to enter. But she hesitated. She told the lady she couldn't pay. The lady laughed and told Aru there was no expectation that she would.

Aru followed the woman through to a softly lit waiting room where several trout people lounged blissfully about in silken robes with towels wrapped around their heads. Instructed to wait for a moment, Aru did so, choosing a wooden chair to sit in, rather than an upholstered one, due to the sandy muddiness of her clothing.

In no time an elderly woman appeared. She smiled when she saw Aru. "Come, my young cousin," she said, "let us see if we can make you whole again. You seem a bit tattered."

First she got Aru into a private shower bath. The lady left Aru alone in a small room that contained a sink, a toilet, and an intriguing chamber with walls of glass. The latter was made of large plates of glass held together in a box shape by a metal frame and sealed with putty. Only the back was solid, a wall covered in tiny cerulean tiles. Aru was apprehensive about entering this glass stall but the slate floor inside felt warm and pleasing to tread on. A big seahorse-shaped bracket high above the spigot clutched a showerhead in its curling tail.

Aru took down the showerhead handle and turned on the hot water, and in yelping panic turned it off again. She stepped, dripping, out of the glass box. She hadn't expected the ceiling above to be filled with spray holes raining down a drenching storm of water! Water that she had not yet allowed to warm up!

On her second try, Aru knew to stand close to the wall to avoid the cold rain. Once it warmed up, she stood in a wonderful hot soaking downpour while she used the torrent from the handheld to clean off the river scum. Steam filled her lungs. A recess in the tile wall held soaps and shampoos. The frothy soap she chose smelled like spring rain on the riverside gravel.

After a dry-off with the thickest of soft towels, Aru put on a chemise and a robe and wandered out the door and into the next room. A light smell of incense lingered in the draperies and heavy tapestries which filled the tiny space with the tranquility of underwater colors. Fresh bulrush mats covered the cobbled basalt floor.

The old lady was waiting there, along with another woman of about the same age and size. An enameled stove cladded in teal grey soap-stone produced enough heat that even with the windows open wide the room remained pleasantly warm.

The ladies directed Aru, still relaxed and quaggy from her shower, to remove her robe and lie down on the padded couch. They brushed her skin with otter's hair brushes, then rubbed her with oils, and then volcanic clay, a spa treatment that went on and on. She lay nearly asleep, hushed and lulled by the gurgling water of an unseen creek outdoors. After some time to absorb the clay, she had a warm rinse. She sipped from a tall glass of something tangy. A cool and crisp berry drink which had a hint of plum.

While Aru's skin was still warm, the ladies had her lie face down and wrapped her body in nicely hot, aromatic strips of specially processed seaweed. When all done with the wrap, they covered her with towels and left her to herself. She lay there, full of peace. Out of the blue came a realization. That drunkard, the pig in Blackbuck's employ—at the crossroads inn, he'd inspired them to go to Anseo. Where they met

Aldrei. It had all been planned. The pig sent them to Aldrei, who of course led them to Blackbuck.

At ease despite these thoughts, she was soon in a deep sleep, dreaming deep dreams. Eventually, after she opened her eyes again, a large octopus person of unclear gender came in to perform mild suction on her skin. Meanwhile, the ladies used their tiny, expert hands to give Aru a thorough massage with creamed spirulina algae and a touch of azulene oil. They finished it all off by using warmed basalt stones and then soft brushes moving lightly over her skin.

Aru woke up the next day on the same massage couch, having slept right through to the morning, but a puffy pillow had been placed under her head and soft blankets covered her up. She found her clothes had been laundered and there was a fine pair of indigo-dyed worsted stockings waiting for her, and a brand new pair of walking shoes.

The lady who had originally welcomed her to the bathhouse tapped on the door and came in, bearing a cup of hyssop tea. Aru had smiled for the first time in a long while the day before. Now she greeted the lady with a smile wide and grateful. The lady said she looked much better than she had when she arrived. She invited Aru to have another shower and then someone would be waiting downstairs to escort her to brunch, if she would like to have it.

Of course Aru said she would, and the lady told her that an important person wanted to meet her and it was she offering the meal. The queen of the steelhead trout had a curiosity about the pale girl who had come to visit fish town.

Aru's escort brought her to a small public house not far from the bathhouse. The name of the place was The Lie. A family of teals owned this establishment but it was in every way designed to lure in steelhead clientele. Both inside and on the outside of the building the iridescent nacre of the abalone shell was heavily emphasized as decoration because it is well known that trout delight in shiny things. The flooring was of gravel and there was an abundant use of mirrors, crystal, and polished metal.

The queen of the steelhead sat at the back of the pub with several steelhead people and a visiting dwarf gourami. After introductions, Aru joined them at the table.

"Well, you're an airy girl, aren't you," said the old queen gently.

"Am I?" Aru wasn't quite sure what the queen meant but she had said it in a complimentary tone.

"Yes, and let's get some food in you right away." She smiled at Aru. Then she looked toward a shaddy little woman who was wiping tables. "You! Alewife!" she called. "Some more tea here, please. And more water. And could you bring us some menus!"

The queen was quite elderly, and as such had more size and weight than the others around the table. She spoke in a bubbly voice but her way of moving as she conversed indicated a placid disposition.

Many questions were asked of Aru, about her experience of life in what these people referred to as the upper world. She answered them over a lunch that included mussels and steamed sapphire crayfish. It was a nourishing meal. Aru ignored what appeared to be a small mouse on the plate of the person to her left.

Before she knew it Aru had told them much of what had happened in her life since she left her family cottage in the western woods all that time ago. It felt good to talk to someone about Nrouhw, about the things they had done together and about what a remarkable person he had been and how much she missed him. It was a funny thing, she told them, but she had always thought it was his curiosity that would kill him, never heroism.

The queen of the steelhead also told Aru some things about the ancient culture of the fishes. Coelacanth, goblin shark and sturgeon, all of these have pedigrees going back hundreds of millions of years, long before the human form appeared a fraction of a million years ago.

So many beasts of the upper world totter about on hooves or have toes with nasty hooks on the end, and from a fish perspective it's all a bit silly. Aru could see that the queen had quite a conservative attitude; she obviously felt that the waters were a perfectly good environment and wondered why anyone should ever want to leave them.

Before it was time for Aru to depart, the old lady had Aru come close and she spoke quietly to her. "I have something for you here, young granddaughter," and into Aru's hand she placed a small glossy stone. "It's a wishing stone of agate," she said.

Aru suppressed a squeak of surprise and thanked the queen politely. She examined the stone, turning it over and over in her hand. The colors and pattern of it formed an uncanny resemblance to an ocean scene. When Aru raised the stone toward the lamp, these designs filled with light. The middle of the stone had a round hole, bored through by the actions of the river water.

"You'll know, of course," said the queen (Aru didn't), "that this is a little fairy stone, a window into other realms within our everyday world. Peeking through the hole will show you the sprites whom you can't ordinarily see. It will allow you to perceive the true form of all beings."

Aru wanted to try it out, but guessed that looking at the queen or her associates through it would be rude. She kissed the stone and then she strung it on the silver chain that held the charm case Nrouhw had given her, something she hadn't removed from around her neck since the day he died. She tucked the silver locket and its new stone companion back inside her blouse.

"The stone will help to keep you safe from fairy wiles," the queen told her. "You'll find that with its help you'll be more aware of your world, your direction will be lit up and you'll be able to find it. In return I ask only that you remember our world here under the surface. You must honor the steelhead always.

"And you must let your passion and your life flow like the river: don't waste your time in the eddies of worry, dejection, or fear."

As Aru promised to do these things, another escort arrived at the table. This was the person who would return Aru to the upper world. As the escort took her hand, Aru thanked the queen for everything. Then, in a swirling and whirly blur Aru found herself outside the inn, exchanging goodbyes with the people of the fish town as she began to float up through the water of the river. The farther she and her steelhead companion drifted from the town, the more she could see of it below her. There were towers and bridges and dozens of waterwheels.

Aru's escort gave her a tap on the arm and pointed upwards. Aru looked up to see the undersurface of the water, a dark reflection of the depths, thick images of the river bottom dreamily mirrored there and seen through suspended specks of light.

But straight above their heads was a brilliant circle, a clear wide-angle view of the sky and the entire above-water world from horizon to horizon. Aru could see the world she knew, with its sun and clouds and the trees along the river bank above her, but as if painted onto the inside of a dome. Some trick of the light made this magic doorway, a round and friendly passage to her familiar realm.

She broke the surface with a splutter and tread water while she got her bearings. She'd come up in the shelter of a small cove, so it wasn't hard to make her way to the bank. Somehow she had lost track of the steelhead escort.

Aru hauled herself out of the river and climbed up a slope to sit, shivering, among the tall grass in a field of lupine. For a while she did nothing but recover her breath. The sky was clear and the mountain bluebirds were warbling up in the junipers.

She decided to take off her shoes and stockings and some of her clothes and spread them over the shrubs that grew on the bank, so her things could dry in the breeze. Then Aru stood facing the water, twiddling the fine woolen stockings between her fingers as they hung there, and she remained in that moment for quite some time, musing about her incredible visit beneath the river. She took the wishing stone from her necklace and looked at it in the sunlight. A perfect seascape miniature produced by nature. The patterns of color strongly resembled frothy breakers under a summer sky and even a cloudbank stretching across the horizon. The foreground of the tiny scene included sea spray and, remarkably, what looked like a couple of pieces of driftwood on a beach. She peered through the hole in the stone and searched with it along the river like a spyglass, but she didn't see anything unusual. Perhaps it was the wrong time of day for viewing fairies. She missed Nrouhw.

Without a lot of concern about what was going to happen to her, Aru stayed in that spot on the river's edge for several hours. At last she decided to get dressed again and then she would walk beside the river. She thought she'd follow it downstream, this seemed the easiest thing to do. Maybe she'd run across a fishing cabin before dark or perhaps even a village.

Her clothes were mostly dry, only the shoes were a bit damp still. She put them on anyhow, climbed down to get a drink from the river, and she was off. There was no trail, but through the open countryside the going wasn't difficult. Once in a while there were rocks to climb over or a thicket to circumvent in order to keep within sight of the river. Late in the afternoon and after quite a bit of walking, Aru came over a low rise to see below her a thin twist of smoke ascending from beside one of these thickets. There was no cabin or village in sight, only the old wreck of a small riverboat sitting half out of the water and listing slightly to the side.

Aru stood for a moment, assessing the situation. Old smashed-up buckets, a broken chair, a hopelessly dented washtub. All sorts of things were strewn around, and empty tin cans everywhere, as if someone had been living there for quite some time. Not someone wholesome and tidy. An unusual number of squashed things. What would cause that?

She saw someone squatting near the fire. A huge shiny kettle hung on a tripod, perhaps to heat water, it looked like they might be cooking something. Aru thought she smelled fish. She was getting quite hungry. The person by the kettle remained still. A child, apparently. So small. Maybe six or seven years old. Certainly a child wouldn't be living out here alone, there must be—

A noise right behind Aru made her jump with such a horrible jolt she nearly lost her balance and went tumbling down the hill. What she saw when she turned did nothing at all to improve the condition of her nerves. "Cull and be peppered!" she exclaimed, before she could stop herself. Then she covered her mouth, half in fear.

She was eye level to the belt of the largest man she had ever seen in her life, a man far bigger than any size she knew a man could possibly be. He was dressed in the most enormous chambray shirt she'd ever seen. He had on the most gigantic pair of blue jean pants she'd ever seen. His shoulders were massive, his neck thick as an ancient spruce and heavily tattooed. His forehead was wide and flat, his nose blunt, his eyes rather small and quite far apart. He had a wide mouth.

"Hello," he said. He had no teeth.

His name was Belche. Certainly not a handsome man, but despite his great size he didn't appear dangerous. He held his own hands as he squinted down at Aru, and apologized for giving her such a start. Belche had a slow, docile demeanor. His speech was limited and simple-minded, even childlike. Belche didn't inquire about who Aru was or where she came from. He asked whether she knew where there might be some mackerels or crab larvae, locally. They talked about the weather for a few minutes and then about how unseasonably early the mosquitoes were this year.

When the large man mentioned he was on his way back to his camp Aru invited herself along. As they walked down the hill together they talked about food, mostly. Belche went slowly, his unhurried pace matched Aru's stride quite easily. Although he appeared awkward and clumsy he managed to conduct his oversized body with a certain amount of agility. He gestured with disconcertingly large hands in emphasis to everything he said, moving them in a soft and restrained, deliberate manner. Belche's hands weren't hammy as one might expect, rather they were bony and veiny with long fingers.

Belche referred to his companion as Echeneis. Aru found the pair's names easy to remember because they were marked on the side of the cabin of the old boat in faded but large and handsome letters,

Belche the Giant & the Little Echeneis, Seafirth.

Echeneis was not a child, after all, but a grown woman of a small size. She wore a funny little hat. She welcomed Aru to sit by the fire but she eyed her suspiciously as she served her a plate of pan-fried minnows. Aru ate eagerly.

"Well, she can sure put them shiners away, can't she!" laughed Belche.

His partner merely puckered her lips and stared off through the fire into the distant world of her own thoughts. She sat that way through most of the meal while the other two ate. Belche talked to Aru about the river and about the weather and the local wildlife, but nothing about who he was or where the two of them were from. Or why they were wrecked on the riverbank. When Belche was done eating Echeneis picked up his plate and ate the scraps from it, still mostly staring into the fire.

"Would you like me to clean up?" asked Aru when everyone had finished.

"If you like," responded Echeneis.

Aru found a somewhat serviceable bucket and did her best to scrape and clean the dishes using hot water from the kettle and sand from the river. She washed several of the pots and pans which were lying around from previous meals.

"Time for cards!" said Belche while Aru stacked the last couple of dishes to dry. From his blue jeans pocket his enormous hand pulled out an old deck of cards that was so dog-eared that the idea of using them was absurd.

"Surely you've memorized which cards have which of all these nicks and tears," laughed Aru when he had dealt out the first hand of poker.

"Aw, it doesn't matter," replied her host. "We're just playing for matchsticks, anyhow."

They played until late into the evening, using the light from the fire and several clamshell fish-oil lamps. The conversation remained airy, focused away from anyone's personal business. Echeneis won the first two games and Aru the third. As much as he loved to play, Belche didn't seem to have a good grasp on the basic strategies of the game. Slowly Echeneis became more talkative, and she and Aru continued to win most of the games, creating, in a funny way, sort of a sisterhood between them.

"You can stay in the boat with us tonight," Echeneis said to Aru as Belche finally returned the playing cards to their pocket in his pants.

Saying that the poor old narrowboat had seen better days would be a kindness. Built for canals, it was exceptionally thin and Aru wondered how it ever came to be up the river. No wonder they had wrecked, the thing was rotten and starting to fall apart.

With Aru following, the others went through the door at the rear of the boat. Aru noticed that the doorway had been widened so that

Belche could enter. However did he fit into a bed? He obviously couldn't stand up inside, he had to hunch over sideways and feed himself through the interior like a thick string through a bead. Aru, stepping down from the stern deck into the cabin, saw on her left a tiny stove and then a bank of cupboards beyond it. A narrow bench extended along the wall on the right.

"That will be your berth," said Echeneis. "Sleep well." She then slid the curtain shut behind her as she went forward.

Aru wasn't welcomed past this barrier during her stay, but from the sound of it Belche didn't go far beyond the curtain himself. There must have been a point in the boat past which he couldn't fit at all. This made for a substantial lack of privacy for all concerned. Belche and Echeneis didn't seem to care, particularly.

Over the next couple of days the three of them played a lot of poker by the firepit. Bathing in the river and netting minnows were their only other activities. One morning Echeneis asked Aru if she'd like to come with her to search at the base of the nearby cliffs for robin's-egg sodalite gemstones. Aru certainly didn't have anything better to do, and this sounded interesting so of course she said yes.

The two of them poked among the rocks for a while but they hadn't found anything yet when Aru felt a sharp sting on her finger. Something had bitten her. It got away too fast for her to see what it was.

"Let me look at that," said Echeneis. "Oooh," she said, "you are already swelling! I wonder what that could have been that bit you. Does it hurt badly?"

"It does smart," said Aru, "and it's starting to itch quite a lot."

They kept up their search for the sodalite, but after a while Aru was too bothered by her injury to continue. She wanted to go back and wash her hands in the river. Echeneis seemed to think Aru was acting a bit like a baby about it, and she made quite an effort to convince Aru to continue rock hunting for just a while longer.

"No, I'm going back. I'll see you at the camp," Aru said.

"Never mind, I'll go along with you, then," said Echeneis. "There don't seem to be any of the gemstones along here, anyhow."

Back at the camp, Belche was surprised to see them. Accordingly, Aru was surprised to see that Belche had removed the entire sign panel from the boat. The missing sign exposed a framework of pigeonholes built into the wall of the cabin. There was something inside those compartments. Small twitchy things were moving around in there.

Aru climbed up onto the boat deck to take a look. The other two exchanged glances, Belche gave a shrug and Echeneis gripped her own forehead in a quick pantomime of distress and resignation.

In each of the little niches sat a wide-necked jar. Every one of these was occupied by a pair of brightly colored, terribly beautiful frogs.

Aru knew what those were: *D-something azureus*. Poison Dart Frogs. She'd read an article. They were illegal in the north country, due to consistent misuse by the villagers. She could see that she had interrupted Belche as he fed them the venomous ants required to keep them lethal.

Thinking quickly, she feigned ignorance. "Oh, what pretty creatures!" she exclaimed. "Can I hold one?" She approached the wall of frogs and rested her hand on one of the jars. Aru had to force herself to do this, knowing that touching one of the occupants could bring death.

The frogs were beautiful, though. Their shiny and slimy skin made them look for all the world like living ceramic figurines mottled with a thick glossy glaze of cobalt. Especially their tiny bulbous-tipped toes. Exactly like exquisite pottery.

"It's best not," Echeneis told her. "They are horribly shy little fellows." This statement was not substantiated by the frogs themselves, who jumped and clambered in their compartments, seeming completely oblivious of Aru's presence.

But Aru was quick to comply. "Oh, I'm making them nervous," she said, and leapt back down from the boat, apologizing.

She made her way down to the river to wash her hands. The bite remained swollen, but it hadn't grown any worse. Aru rather casually wondered about her safety, now that she knew about Belche and Echeneis's secret. They hadn't told her to go ahead and hold a frog; she supposed that was a good sign.

Echeneis didn't seem much perturbed when Aru returned to sit with her near the firepit. Belche, when he'd finished his chore and replaced the signboard, joined them. Apparently Aru's reaction had convinced them she wasn't a threat in regard to their small import business getting reported to the authorities. But the subject of dart frogs didn't come up again. After lunch they had another round of poker.

This time, Belche said to the others, why not add to the fun. They could wager something more interesting than matchsticks.

"But we have nothing to bet, silly," said Echeneis. "What would any of us possibly use?"

"Well, I have something," said Belche. He left to retrieve an item from the boat and soon returned with a large ring. "It don't fit me, anyhow," he said. He showed it to Aru. "It's an antique. Very old."

The ring did look valuable. A fine cameo carving of milky white jellyfishes against dark iridescent abalone, set in fine silver. Secretly, Aru wanted it when she saw it. She admired it, but told Belche that she had no use for a ring that large. And anyhow, she herself had nothing to bet.

"Aw. This could easily be made into a lovely brooch." Belche held it up to his chest with two fingers and grinned a huge toothless grin.

Aru laughed. It almost sounded tempting.

"I don't know if this is such a great idea," said Echeneis. "Besides, I don't have anything."

"There's that pretty lapis pendant you found in the street in Gwyrdd-las," he told her. "You don't need it. It's only a trinket."

"Well, maybe. Maybe. I'll consider it." She pulled the pendant up out of her blouse and looked at it. Such a pretty thing. Aru wanted to look at it too. Pyrite and other inclusions in the dark stone made it look like a miniature of the universe with its stars and galaxies. "I wouldn't mind winning that ring from you, Belche," Echeneis laughed, "but you know I don't play as well when we wager things."

"But I absolutely don't have anything to gamble with," said Aru. "I've just . . . I've got nothing at all." She looked at the others, "I don't mean to spoil the fun, but I truly have naught. Perhaps we should continue with the matchsticks."

"You have a necklace," Belche pointed out.

"This? The chain holds my talismans," replied Aru, clasping her hand over her chest.

"Oh. No then, we don't want to meddle with any sort of witchy things!" said Echeneis.

Belche shuffled the cards. "What about that ring?" he asked.

Aru winced. She looked down at her beautiful gold ring. "No, this is my engagement ring," she said softly.

"Aw. Lucky feller!" said Belche.

"Well," said Echeneis quickly, noticing Aru's withheld tears, "I guess you have something you could play with. It's all for fun. What about those shoes? They're not worth as much as our stakes, but we'll allow them, won't we, Belchie!" she said. "It's all for fun!" she repeated, looking back at Aru.

"I don't know," replied Aru, "I can't really do without my shoes."

However, only a few minutes later Aru had lost her new shoes to Belche, who had an apparent strike of luck. Aru wondered if she should be angry. Something seemed a bit fishy in all this. But Belche and Echeneis were both quite reassuring.

"Don't worry, Aru, you can win them back again," said Echeneis as Aru discreetly removed her stockings and stashed them in her pocket.

"But I have nothing left to win them back with."

"Oh, who knows. Maybe you'll find some of that robin's egg sodalite. We can search again tomorrow," Echeneis said.

Aru believed that maybe she could, because she wanted her shoes back. Without realizing what she was doing, she started scanning the campground area for anything valuable which might be lying around, as if somehow she'd have the right to bet with it. She caught the gleam of something out of the corner of her eye.

"Oh, look, what's this?" asked Aru, purely out of curiosity. She was looking at a large shiny bubble just sitting there on the ground beside an old tattered knapsack.

Belche reached way down to pick up the ball and gently set it in Aru's hand. Much heavier than she anticipated, it was made of solid glass or crystal.

"Aquamarine," said Belche. "Awful clear aquamarine, this one."

"It's beautiful," Aru whispered. She wondered if he used it for scrying. She looked into the thing as it filled her palm, curious to see a vision of her own.

"May I?" he asked, and, gently, he took up the crystal ball again himself, cradling it artfully on the backs of the fingers of his left hand.

Perhaps the ball carried some magic greater than its astonishing purity. Or did the man himself have realized powers? As he handled the orb Belche appeared to be a different person, sophisticated and charming. With a flourish he emptied the knapsack of its contents, three balls of quartz crystal the same size as the aquamarine on his hand. He arranged these on the ground by his feet.

"You'll want to stand back a tad," he said softly to Aru. Echeneis stayed where she was, sitting on a log by the smoky fire behind him.

In a fluid motion, the big man flipped the sphere over the ends of his fingers onto his palm where it began to spin, travelling in a circle around his hand. Allowing it to rise to his fingertips, he then cupped the ball loosely between his hands; with an elastic movement, drawing his hands together and apart, he no longer seemed to be touching the ball at all. It looked somehow suspended in one place, riding in the air. The ball appeared to hover stationary, independent of him, while he moved his amazingly graceful hands all about it with great flair.

Seeming to have a mind of its own, the ball rode his arms from elbow to elbow, shoulder to shoulder, stopping, starting, all in a hypnotic flowing movement. It travelled up the underside of his arm, floated across his back, drifted to the top of his head, all the while in measured control, rolling and swirling smoothly. Which was more confounding, Belche's performance or the fact that this was the Belche that Aru had thought she knew? Where did this masterful grace come from?

He picked up the other balls, tossing them up with his toes; he spun them around together in his hands and his performance blossomed into a billowing gymnastic dance. Each time Aru gasped in amazement Belche did something more amazing still. He performed cartwheels and flips, the balls traveling along with him, riding on various parts of his enormous body.

He bent to swirl the balls on his toes with his hands, now appearing to pull on an invisible string that moved them individually up and down. While he was bent over in this way, Echeneis ran right up his back from behind. He stood up, then she was standing on his shoulders and they passed the balls back and forth, juggling them high in the air.

The two practiced for quite a while, with Aru fascinated the whole time. You never know how people will surprise you with what they can do. This is especially true of circus people. At the end, Aru clapped and then Belche showed Aru how to roll a ball across her fingers.

They played more poker, betting with matchsticks, and munched on dried sardines. Supper came and went, and still more poker. Belche had reverted to his rougher mannerisms, the ones with which Aru was familiar, as soon as they had finished with the juggling. Now he laughed loudly and allowed himself to make bodily noises without excusing himself.

That night Aru woke up in the midnight hours for no reason. Lying in the darkness on her narrow berth in the boat, she groggily became aware of a whispered conversation the others were having on the other side of the curtain. Belche and Echeneis were discussing something about fish, then one or two comments about supplies, that kind of thing. And Aru's shoes, Echeneis was wondering what they'd be worth.

Aru sat up. She kept listening. They had no intention of letting her win her shoes back!

". . . What'll we do when she notices the ring gone?"

Aru grabbed her left hand and peered at her fingers in the dim light. She rubbed the place where her engagement ring should be. They'd taken her ring right off her finger as she slept!

Belche's voice came, "Well, little echeneis fish, what do you think she might do? We'll simply deny any knowledge of it. Must have come off in the river when she washed her hands last night. Or maybe when she was doing those dishes. Perhaps she tossed it off somewhere with the dishwater."

"She's going to be rabid mad. She'll know we took it."

"There's nothing she can do. What can she do? She can't prove we have it, and even if she could, well what does it matter? Still, she will want it. And also she knows about our amphibians. These things are both problematic for us, certainly." He paused. "The best solutions are the simple ones, my pet. I'll help her look for her ring over by the dish pans. Then while she's stooping and searching I'll hit her over the head with something."

"What, you'll kill her for a ring and a pair of shoes? When did we turn that desperate?"

"Not kill, her no. I'll hit her gently. Just enough to make her sleep for a while. Then you and I can shove off in the boat—"

This thing can float? thought Aru while her heart pounded. *How is that possible?*

"—and," he continued, "we'll be far along the river before she ever wakes up."

In her fear and anger Aru could just imagine the smug grin Echeneis had on her face as a reply.

For a while Aru sat, mortified that her ring was gone, stolen, and shocked that these two would breach their friendship in such a way. Also that Belche was suddenly so articulate. The real Belche was someone she truly didn't know. If that was even his name.

Apparently, it was time to leave. Aru remained still while she waited for the others to fall asleep. She lay there seething. They'd taken Nrouhw's ring and there was nothing she could do about it. After a horribly long time, several hours, she knew she needed to move or risk being caught by the dawn. It was quiet on the boat. She wished she could hear someone snoring. Aru silently, silently, got up and searched through the cupboards across from her bench in the near darkness. She might find some food or something helpful for her journey. There was no chance of finding the ring, that was gone. Hopelessly gone. Just like Nrouhw and everything that gave her life meaning.

She noticed some sort of official certificate in the cupboard. Aru couldn't help but take the time to bring it to the window and try to read the calligraphy in the early hint of light. Something about a blue whale and whale shark association. Aru had been wondering what type of animal Belche was. Hippo had crossed her mind. Whale shark. She'd never heard of those before.

Aru didn't find much in the cupboards that could be of any use, but there was a bag of something hanging high in the corner by the ceiling. She felt it with her fingers. A pudding! No matter what type. That would feed her for a while. These folks seemed to eat mostly seafood.

Is there such a thing as a fish pudding? thought Aru. Oh, well. She'd have to take her chances. She cut the pudding down and with it in hand she slipped out the door of the boat in her bare feet.

A clear and starry sky made the stony ground cold and the scruffy tufts of grass were heavy with dew. Aru knew the way along the river downstream. She'd been that direction for firewood. She took a glance back at the boat reclining there on the bank. The boat with its cobalt frogs and its nasty thieves. Its juggler smugglers. Its struggling smuggler jugglers. She had trusted these people, only to be so horribly taken advantage of. She sighed, and then she laughed. That boat could actually float!

Invigorated by the night air and the excitement of sneaking away, Aru returned to her aimless journey. She'd go wherever the river led her, because at least that way she wouldn't be walking in circles. She was free to venture forth without worry because an umbrella of despondency continued to keep her from caring all that much about what would happen to her. She did regret the loss of the ring. Nrouhw's grandmother's ring. But, in the end, what difference did it make? One more thing to feel bad about. Add it to the rest.

The patches of mist drifting up the river looked disconcertingly like a horde of phantoms, a crowded migration racing the coming dawn. They traveled silently along at the speed of the morning wind, an endless supply of ghostly forms, moving on top of the water as if it were a road through the countryside.

Eventually Aru entered a bit of a woods, and fingers of the mist went in there, too. Dampness dripped among the trees. She noticed a trail now, whether used by humans or only by deer she had no way to know. In some places it was clearly defined, at others it came down to guesswork as much as anything. But she kept following the river.

The sun began to rise, although as it came up Aru seemed to be going deeper into woods. The way became tougher to navigate. It involved quite a bit of climbing over or under logs and skirting around small hills and large boulders. It was chilly out, but not too bad. Aru crossed her arms for warmth as she walked. She noticed a strange fungus growing on the end of a big log. It looked like mussels from the seashore.

Aru walked for the whole morning, and remained in the thick of the woods. She saw a few rabbits and shy squirrels, but not a lot of wildlife. She noticed few creatures, let alone transforming animals. The rocky, cliffy woods had lots of great grey boulders, some with bunches of trees growing out of the cracks. Usually she could stay alongside the river, but once in a while she'd have to go out of sight of it. At one point she came upon a freshly fallen tree, a big cedar full of branches going everywhere, and a new trail had been trampled through the bracken, leading around the end of the log. Right beyond this another couple of trees were down. Aru wondered what might have caused all these to fall. The temporary trail went around these trees also and soon she was well out of sight of the river. It didn't worry Aru, as she was sure that soon the route would wend its way back toward the river and join the original trail, and if it didn't she'd simply cut across through the woods, bushwhacking her way through.

But now the path took another turn, and Aru began to wonder which way north was, after all. Maybe she should go back along the trail the way she'd come until she had her sense of direction again. No, she'd give the trail a bit more of a chance, it had been following the river for so long. Surely it would return to it soon. Up in the canopy, a bunch of birds screeched. They were excited about something. Probably her presence disturbed them. She continued down the trail for a while, but it did seem to be twisting off in quite the wrong direction.

"All right," she said to herself, "I'll go back and find a spot where I can see the river."

But when she turned back the way she had come, Aru found that she lost track of the trail after only a few minutes. Such a strange thing. This section of the trail had been so easy to follow, how could it be ambiguous going the other direction? But that's how it was.

Although it would have been easiest to simply continue following the trail in the original direction, Aru stubbornly, and perhaps wisely, refused to be so manipulated. The more difficulty she had in finding her way back toward the river, the more effort she gave it. And so, within a distressingly short time she found herself hopelessly lost.

Being lost in the woods is always worrisome, regardless of whether or not one had been on one's way to any particular place. Aru started to realize that she did indeed care about what happened to her. She hadn't been aware of it, but she still hoped to find a village by the river. Now, though, she was lost. Hungry and getting tired and thirsty, Aru started to panic and to swear. She sat down, sobbing from frustration.

Out of nowhere, through the branches, a band of mountain jays swooped down, landing one and two at a time, mostly on the lower branches of the trees, a few on the ground. Their raucous, raspy calls were deafening. Aru stopped her crying and sat in amazement, her hands cupped over her mouth. They'd obviously come to investigate the newcomer.

They watched her as she watched them, fascinated. Such beautiful birds, flashy and full of life. But so loud! Distracted by the vivid color of their feathers and the brightness of their dark eyes, Aru didn't notice at first when the man stepped from behind the tree.

When she saw him, her instant reaction was to roll down onto her side, to blend in among the grape holly that surrounded her. It was a ridiculous move, but that made it only the more embarrassing to sit back up. So Aru lay there, on her side, peeking out at the man and hoping that, somehow, he would walk on by.

Of course he didn't. The man walked directly, boldly, up to the front of where Aru hid, and he stood there, peering at her. Certainly, he looked smart. He was probably about twice Aru's age. He had on a black hat with feathers in it, and a satin suit in the most deep, brilliant colors of the summer sky. Tight black leather pants accentuated his extremely thin legs. His entire appearance was sharp and insistent.

"There are surely mildew and spiders in great quantity amongst those plants," he said.

Aru sat up. Then she stood up, shaking out her skirts.

"My name is Jhaaack," he continued in his raspy voice, with a friendly flip of his head. "What might you be called?"

Aru whispered her name, thanking him for his warning.

He stepped back. "Aru? Ah, you don't look like a canine." He peered at her, "No offense meant, my young friend. It's just that you are so light in color, and fragile-looking. No disrespect, of course. Ah, we just can't seem to figure out what you are, and how you possibly came to be in these woods. Don't you know of the hazards here?"

"Well, I—"

"As my fellows and I have been discussing, these woods are no place for a lonely young woman like you. Where is your home? Please consider, won't you, that the fishing villages along the river, ah, well, any one of them would be a better environment for someone such as yourself. You surely will want to turn around now, and go back where you came from. Ah, it's not that we don't want you here. We've been watching you for a while. Except for a rather colorful choice of expletives you appear to be a nice young woman—and we can forgive those teensy sorts of peccadillos, can't we?— you walk softly upon the ground, no smoking or other distasteful habits, apparently." He stopped for a second, glanced at the sky and back at Aru. He continued, "Ah, no, you'd certainly be welcome here if things were different, as a guest, we'd love to have you stay. But, ah, you see it's not really a choice for us, we must warn you away because of the dangers."

"What sort of dangers?" asked Aru.

"Ah. Look—" he began, but then he gave a shrill outcry, "Look out!"

There was a sound in the woods, up on the hill above them. A deep thud sound. And then another. The jays around them took to shrieking flight. Thud, thud, bump! and a big boulder came crashing through the trees. Aru and the man jumped out of the way. It came to rest not far from where they had been standing.

"Get out! Run! You must leave these woods!" shrieked the man as he disappeared up into a tree. His voice came one more time before he, presumably, transformed back to a jay, "Get away!"

Such a very large rock! Aru stood looking at it. Had someone set that boulder loose to roll down the hill on purpose? Was it meant to smash her? In her disbelief, Aru stood there, staring.

The jays began to dive at her, screeching.

A second rock, nearly the size of the first, came hurtling through the air and smashed against a tree next to the one Jhaaack had gone up. It took away half the tree as it hit. Aru didn't need any further prompting. She ran. Like the wind.

Unfortunately, the hurler of boulders could move fast. Faster than Aru ever could. As she ran, she heard it—whatever it was—crashing down the hill, snapping and breaking everything in its path. Footsteps shook the ground behind her. Soon she could hear the breathing, smell the foul breath. Terrified, Aru didn't look back, she gave everything she had to running, running.

It was no good. Some sort of large biped grabbed her up into the air as she ran, just as if she were an old rag doll, and she was shoved underneath a great hairy arm! The smell was suffocating, the filthy matted fur in her face horrifying. Aru fought and scratched but the monster that carried her continued to run. He had a long club in his other hand and with it he batted at the jays as they mobbed him. He snarled, and he drooled big slobber bubbles, and his sweat splattered all over. The jays flew at his face, at his eyes, but he gave them quite a thrashing and in the end they gave up, leaving him to his prize.

The next thing Aru knew she woke up, bruised and battered, in a sitting position against a cold wall, and in the thick of a noxious, eye-watering stench. It took her a moment to understand what had happened. Holding her overskirt over her nose and mouth, she looked around her, trying to focus her eyes in the half-light, and then she remembered with a start. Carried off by a brute. Again. The same as on the day Nrouhw died. Aru struggled to get to her feet, but felt a big hand on her shoulder. It pushed her back down.

"Naw, yah don't," said a deep, guttural voice.

Aru became aware of all sorts of household items around her and she realized that they were in some sort of outdoor living area. Well, not entirely outdoors. There was a creek running right by and a stone archway above, sheltering them. They were under a bridge.

Bravely, she looked at her captor.

It was a bigfoot. He had a huge hump on his back. Clumps of hair showed through gaping holes in his ragged grey jacket. Thick shaggy hair like that of a bear grew in patchy disarray, covering him except for his bald face. A bulging, boulder-like forehead and huge squashed nose framed repulsive little bloodshot eyes. His gorilla mouth had canines jutting upward like a wild boar's tusks, reaching nearly to his eyes. The thing sat resting against the sloping abutment of the bridge, hands folded doltishly on his potbelly. He wore thick leather shin guards but no boots because he didn't need them. His enormous feet were furry on top and covered with terribly thick skin on the bottom, disastrous toenails curling like claws around the ends of his toes.

If he wanted her as food he would have killed her where he'd caught her. Aru sat and worried about what other reasons he might have for lugging her to this place. Strewn everywhere she saw things like cooking pots, chamber pots, and several sizes of oil cans. There were tattered tarpaulins and blankets, and what looked like an old sewing machine. Down in the creek was the bloated carcass of something just lying in the water, it looked like a billy goat, probably.

One of the piles of blankets started to grunt and moan, and Aru realized it contained another bigfoot. The thing farted and then it sat up and looked around, its disagreeable gaze coming to rest on her. This bigfoot looked much like the other, with its ears hairless, and pointy, and set way back on the head. Except this one was older and had long, pendulous, hairy breasts.

"What the snoop-hound blazes is this, then?" grunted the female. "Harrumph! This isn't no princess." She didn't wait for an answer but got herself up out of bed and came over to poke at Aru with a stick.

She smelled of rotten eggs and death.

"Look, Ma. Leave her alone. She's mine." The male batted at the female with his great paw-like hands.

"Should've left her alone yerself," said the mother, giving a swat back. "She's too ugly and thin to be of any use. Knock her on the head and toss her in the crick."

"I will not. She's going to spin for me."

The female snorted, "Spin, will she?" She stopped bothering Aru and started poking at a pile of embers, instead, to revive the dying fire.

"And she's going to mind me," he said. He looked at Aru, he thought for a moment. "Scratch my head," he said to her, and he bent so she could reach the bald area just in front of his crown.

Aru froze, unable to breathe.

"Come on, scratch!" he bellowed.

Aru's trembling hand reached and rubbed his greasy, crumby scalp.

"Harder," he said. "Use your fingernails."

The female got the fire going and cracked several eggs into a pan. What sort of eggs they were, Aru didn't want to know.

"So, tell me, son," said the female, "how's she to spin without no spindle? You broke that flippin' spinning wheel years ago."

"I didn't break that. The princess did."

"Yeah, when you put it through her head she did."

"I didn't put it through her head. That's an exaggeration."

"We were so much better off living rough in the mountains," sniveled the mother. "This new generation, with all yer civilization and yer newfangled life, there's nothin' free about it. Nothin' happy."

"Go back to the mountains, then. I'm tired of hearing it," he said.

She scraped the eggs from the skillet into her mouth. "I'm tired of living on beans n' weasels," she said with her mouth full. "We never should have come down this way."

When the monster had enough of the scratching, Aru sat back down. She noticed the bag of pudding lying on the ground where she'd been. She still had it with her! For a while she sat and thought, while the monsters argued back and forth and made disgusting noises. Aru wished more than anything to get away from the smell.

As the two bickered and spit at each other, Aru developed a plan.

"Look here," she said, standing up and trying to make herself look as big as possible. "You fools, you've made a terrible mistake! I am Dirid Ur, Killer of Giants!" She held up the bag of pudding. "Do you see this?" she said in her deepest voice. "These are the brains of the last bigfoot that tried to capture me. See this?" she said, while reaching into the bag and placing some pudding in her mouth. "I eat her brains for my breakfast!"

The mother and son stopped what they were doing and stared at Aru. She stared right back, a pillar of bravery and confidence. All she had to do was stand up to these brutes, show them she was predator and not prey, and with their simple minds they would easily be tricked into letting her go on her way. Aru stared straight into the mother's small round eyes with a fierceness that would frighten anyone.

"Stupid girl," said the son, and he grabbed the pudding out of her hands. He reached in and tasted it. "Mmm. Plum," he said. In less than a minute he and his mother had eaten the entire thing.

Aru sat again, slowly. A particularly unhappy look was on her face. She tried several times that day to trick the trolls, but to no avail. Each time she tried something, she put herself in more danger, leaving these monsters less reason to keep her alive.

In the twilight of evening, still sitting at the camp under the bridge, Aru heard a sound up in the sky. She looked up, and though she couldn't see anything, she knew what it was. The mother and son knew, too. The screech of jays.

Like a gathering storm, dozens of the birds collected in the branches surrounding the bridge, their racket growing louder and louder. One of them dove at the bigfoots, beating broad wings in their faces, pecking and clawing. Then another flew down and did the same.

Aru, with her hands in front of her face, looked up at the birds. The man Jhaaack must be one of those jays in this flock. This was her chance to run for it. She jumped to her feet, but the bigfoot son's big hand had her wrist in an instant. He held on. He pulled Aru in front of himself as protection from the birds. He grabbed his club and started swinging at them again.

But this time the birds had an advantage they didn't have before. Aru could see lights in the woods, approaching. Torches. And jays flew from where the torches were, bringing sticks of fire and dropping them on the monsters and their camp. Twigs ablaze with fire. This proved extremely worrisome to the trolls.

The next few minutes were a confusion of azure wings, swooshing clubs, and raucous shrieks. The big troll continued to use Aru as a shield, but pieces of flame were lighting all over his campground, all over his personal belongings, all over his screaming mother. Greasy burning hair added to the repulsive smells. Then through the trees came the company with the torches. Blackbuck's agents! No, the third one was Blackbuck himself!

"Release her, or die a terrible death!" shouted one of the group. She jumped across the creek and waved her torch.

The bigfoot looked horrified. It shoved Aru at the woman, grabbed its mother by the arm instead, and the two made off uphill into the brush at high speed. Soon they were only visible in shadowy glimpses, a pair of dark blurs ducking through the undergrowth as they ran away. The birds followed, mobbing them repeatedly as they ran.

Aru recovered her balance and her footing and lit out in the other direction. But Blackbuck's servant tossed her torch to her associate and gave chase, catching up with Aru quickly. She grabbed her arm, and holding her by the wrist the same way the bigfoot had, she led her back down to Blackbuck. There was no use in fighting.

Aru glared at Blackbuck.

She had forgotten how handsome he was. She hated his handsomeness, his smug superiority. There he stood, in his nice clothes, holding a torch. He stepped forward and placed his hand on her shoulder in a gesture of concern. She shrugged it off violently.

"Come, we'll take care of you, Aru. You need our help," He said this in a deep, soft voice. He looked her in the eye, persuasively. "Things will be all right."

"All right for you, you murdering slime!" growled Aru. She barely noticed that Blackbuck winced as she said it. "Let me go. You have no right to detain me."

"It's for your own good that I'm bringing you along with us, Aru," he said. "You're not in your right mind."

Aru responded with a low growl and a look that made Blackbuck keep his distance as they set off. She could fight them, but she knew they would just carry her, like they did before. What did they want with her, anyhow? She certainly wasn't going to cooperate with Blackbuck.

And so the bunch of them climbed to the trail that went over the bridge and by torchlight they walked along it. It didn't take long to reach the river, but they let Aru know it would be a couple of hours walk to reach the boats. Would she like them to borrow a pony for her at one of the farms? Aru said she would walk. She was so angry that she didn't notice the scenery of the river. She thought about screaming for the police when they passed a village, but who would the police believe, a well-dressed gentleman or a ragged, wild young woman with dirt on her face? Blackbuck, the vermin, would simply say she was mad.

Eventually they arrived to find the Clearwater, the Zodiac, and the Pirate docked at a tiny fishing village, the peacock boats overwhelming the humble stone quay. That night Aru slept again in the big comfortable berth in the pointed cabin in the forepeak of the Clearwater.

Aru slept soundly, without opening her eyes until late the next morning. Then, the first thing she saw was the Warden.

"Naughhh," she groaned and rolled over to face the wall. She stared at the boards for a moment, then, with resignation, she rolled back over. She sat up and looked at the woman.

"Shit . . . shit . . . putrefied, rotten . . . shit." That is all Aru had to say. She looked past the smug-faced matron, and out the leaded glass porthole. She could see a tiny section of the sky.

"Keep your temper," said the Warden. "Such a foul mouth!"

Aru softly snarled at the woman.

"Really!" said the Warden contemptuously. She adjusted the comb that secured her bouffant hair. "How unbecoming of a young lady. What, were you raised among wolves?" Aru simply looked at her, and then down at the braided rug.

There was silence for some time. The woman sat in a rounded posture, her long, peculiarly segmented shape curled forward over her little glass of indigo mushroom liqueur. She wore a silk tea dress and smoked a hookah, exhaling huge clouds of smoke. Water bubbled in the cobalt base of the pipe and the room was thick with her emissions; she used the aspen flavor tobacco popular among the forest tents. It smelled good, actually, but Aru was irritated.

"What are you doing in my room?" Aru wanted to know.

"I've been asked to keep a close watch on you," replied the Warden with a puff of smoke.

"You have, have you?" Aru shook her head. "Well," she said. "What else does his highness say? Any little plans regarding me? You know— you are aware this is kidnapping, aren't you?"

"Mr. Blackbuck has adopted you as his ward. Due to your mental condition," said the woman nonchalantly.

"He can't do that! In any case, there's nothing wrong with my mind!"

"He *has* done it."

"We'll see about that. I want to speak to him. I'd like to speak to him right now." Aru was livid.

"You'll be dining with him tomorrow evening."

Aru should have raised an unrelenting protest, right there and then, but she didn't. She was warm and dry and there would be food to eat on the vessel. She'd have her freedom in a day or so. In the meantime, Aru learned, she could spend time in the saloon and above deck although the Warden or someone would always be watching her.

She loitered for most of the afternoon on deck, where she could breathe freely and watch the hazy river scenery go by. Her time was spent mostly in missing Nrouhw. The Warden sat in the deckhouse, keeping an eye on things.

When Aru'd been above deck last time she hadn't noticed much. Now she appreciated the fantastic woodcraft of the Clearwater and her companion boats, carved in asymmetric balance. Rich iridescent peacock plumage was represented by deep and bright tones of paint and tiny silver inlays to catch the sun. Such intense colors and the beauty of the forms were exhilarating, a relief from Aru's somber mood.

The great curving neck and peacock head (with topknot) rose from the bow. The forward bulwarks, also carved in feathery detail, flared up on either side as if forming the shoulders of a pair of wings. In the stern the great fan of the tail served no purpose that Aru could see, except to be a glorious display of carved feather design, arguably as beautiful as the tail of a living peacock.

When now and then Squee had the opportunity, the two of them sat and talked. Aru felt badly about the worry she had put Squee through but the young deckhand shrugged it right off, cheerful about her safe return. Aru offered to help Squee shuck the big bucket of oysters she had, and so Squee showed her how. They sat working together. Squee laughed and chattered, giggled and whistled while she wrenched her knife to pry and pop open the shells. Aru had a great deal more trouble opening the oysters, but it was no matter because Squee valued her companionship far more than any amount of work she accomplished.

During the twists and turns of their conversation that afternoon they confided to one another a few of the embarrassing things they'd done in their lives. Squee told Aru a story about the time she had been quite rude to a porpoise.

"Dolphins are often rude to porpoises, though," she said. "It's only our nature. They're a competing species. You should see how the gray seals treat them," she said.

Aru commented about the great capacity of every species to evolve in some way, but then she realized that this statement might be offensive. Squee took no notice, prattling on about the book she'd been reading before she was taken aboard the Clearwater, *An Elementary Treatise on the Dynamics of Anthropomorphy*. Squee was fairly certain she wanted to be a nurse. Maybe a doctor someday. Once in a while she would touch Aru on the arm, tilt her head, then giggle and laugh in her easygoing and flirty way.

Somehow Squee's receptive nature and genuine compassion made Aru surprise herself by pouring out her soul to the little girl. Aru told Squee far more about her life history than she meant to reveal. Aru told Squee what had happened at the house of the foxes in Ysgarlad and how she'd been sent to the cannery and had come to meet Nrouhw. She told her of the prophecy by her friend the beaver, and how Eepe had become a jay and flown away to other worlds.

"Your own convictions and the trickery of a jay bird," repeated Squee. "Well, for certain sure your tolerant perspective led to the gift of life for the little thrall, Aru. So, as a real creature Eepe was able to use his own trickiness to live free, to escape as a living wooden jay. And he released you from his master's meddling as well. I'd say that you delivered him, and that he delivered you both! That's what I'd say!"

"You are a terribly perceptive girl, Squee!" exclaimed Aru. "It's taken me ages to reach the same conclusions. This is surely what the prophecy implied. Eepe did free me from his master's intrusions when he left me. It's so absolutely frustrating that I still have no idea who sent him in the first place, though," said Aru. "Or why."

As they talked Aru lamented the loss of Nrouhw, and the loss of her friends. And Aldrei and Aeon, had they ever been her friends at all? Aru fingered the silver case around her neck containing the diamond. She was alone in the world again. She missed her parents and her grandmother. She missed Phfft-Psyfft. She missed Nrouhw horribly.

Squee listened to everything, saying little. Finally, Aru looked at her, embarrassed that she'd shared so much, and with such a young girl.

"Ahk," said Squee, "don't worry, I'm happy to listen. It's quite understandable that you're feeling so bad. You've endured difficult things. So tell me, what helps you free yourself from the shadowy depths?"

Aru couldn't think of anything. "I don't know," she said. "What helps you?"

"These days, I daydream about the ocean. I think about the things I'll do when I return home," she said. "I sing to myself, too."

"I only feel like singing if I'm already in a cheery mood," replied Aru, but after a moment's thought she added, "I find comfort in looking at beautiful, colorful things. Bright colors. Do you know?"

"I guess one has to do whatever small things one can. You've got to come up for air once in a while, that's the thing." Squee pulled a bedraggled bracelet off of her wrist. "Here," she said, "have this. It's colorful."

She handed it to Aru. Strung together on a chain were small pieces of turquoise along with seashells and a variety of beach glass beads. At first Aru thought she shouldn't take it, but Squee genuinely wanted Aru to have it. Aru gave her a hug. She could tell she was hugging a dolphin, as Squee smelled like fish and she felt a bit rubbery. Aru smiled. She clasped the bracelet around her own wrist and gave Squee another quick hug.

They'd finished with the oysters. Squee took the pot of shelled ones down to the galley so they could be baked into an oyster pie for the evening meal. She said that the cook prepared lovely oyster pies, made with shallots and just a hint of blue cheese.

Aru remained on deck, still monitored by the Warden who yawned and nodded in the deckhouse. Downriver, the pewter silhouette of jagged mountains reached high into the eastern sky. The sharp outline of those shadowless peaks against the clear afternoon sky's soft gradient of color played a trick on the eyes: it flattened the whole scene into a giant wall looming ahead. As she continued to gaze, Aru decided those mountain forms looked like tarnish along the bottom of an old mirror, a great, flat, sky mirror. An enormous medicine cabinet door, maybe. Perhaps it opened into a better world.

The Warden began to doze. Aru wandered astern, where Squee the rat was at the tiller. She glanced up at the rooftop of the cabin and realized that some sort of hawk was sitting there. It turned an eye to Aru, and then it yawned. Had it been up there all afternoon?

"It's a merlin," said a man.

Aru jumped. She hadn't noticed him until he spoke.

"Meant to keep birds away," the man added.

Who was this fellow? She hadn't met any of the other passengers yet. "Oh, I hadn't noticed you standing there!" Bewilderment made Aru's voice somewhat scratchy. "I didn't see you come up the companionway. I'm Aru." She held out her hand.

His gloved hand shook hers. He held on an awkward moment too long. The man was dressed in quite a foppish manner in a brown silk jacket and astonishingly clean and bright white shirt. His turquoise-colored suede boots were distracting, almost comical. And he had extremely wide feet. In reality, he did look absurd.

He just smiled, so she added, "Who are you, then?"

Instead of answering Aru he stood back, looked at her in an unsavory way, and whistled. Whistled! "Aren't you a doll," he said.

Aru stood with her mouth open.

Next he addressed the man at the tiller. "Congratulations, lil' pirate!" he said, slapping him on the back. "Rather gratifying, isn't it, in these desperately bureaucratic times, to scratch out a temperate living on even a moderately lucrative craft."

Pointing to the compass, he went on. "Is this elaborate apparatus merely decorative or is it comparatively accurate? A strategic course is imperative." He sniffed. "Mustn't be erratic in your exploratory operations."

"Stop it," said the rat, glaring.

"Got you a bit rattled, have I?" said the man, "How inconsiderat of me. My gratuitous prattling is not deliberat."

"Hissssh. Fucking booby," said Squee, under his breath.

The man smiled, reached into his jacket, and took a swig of something from a flask. "Gentianella spirits, for my health," he said, winking at Aru. "This and my art magazines are all I need, these days." As he said this he stumbled over a coil of rope, barely catching himself before a fall. "Oh, dear. My boot!" he exclaimed, reaching to caress the suede on his toe, checking it for any scratches.

"I didn't see you come up on deck—" repeated Aru to the stranger. The man Squee at the tiller ignored him, staring off down the river.

"Well, darlin'," the stranger replied, "I cannot blame you for wondering about me." He put the back of his hand against his mouth to muffle a quiet belch, and then he stepped toward Aru, replacing the bottle into his pocket.

"The truth is, I'm out searching for my youngest daughter, who recently fell under the romantic influence of a belligerent and haughty peacock and is now missing from home. Rumor has it there is a young woman captive on this little boat. And I heard something about a peacock."

He had Aru uncomfortably trapped between himself and the carved transom, so she took a step sideways.

"Watch out now," he said. "Don't you step on my new suede shoes!"

"Sorry!" she said, although she hadn't done anything.

"Anyhow," he continued, "it hadn't been clear that the peacock *was* the boat, so I guess I'll just be off. After a few minutes rest, if you folks don't mind at all. I should have realized. This all came too easily, receiving the news of her whereabouts so soon. All too good to be true, I suppose. Lucky I wasn't captured when I first landed, and put into servitude. You know, the fish have a saying, 'You don't eat a worm on a string'—"

At this moment the dolphin Squee reappeared on the deck and called, "Oh, hi, there you are!" Then she asked, "Who's this?"

"Well, I . . ." began Aru, and then her voice trailed off.

"Pleased to meet you, little fishy," said the man.

With a noticeable lack of indignance, Squee replied, "Sir, I'm not a fish, I'm a mammal." Then she said, "Excuse me," to the gentleman and turned to Aru excitedly. "I have permission for you to help me make fishing lures down in my cabin, Aru. Would you like to join me? It's quite fun. I share my cabin with the cook. But she'll be busy in the galley. Have you ever tied flies before? No? I'll show you. They're not real flies, of course. They're made of feathers. I have some lovely macaw tail feathers. You just wind up pieces of feather on a hook to make them look like bugs, so that in the water the fish will mistake them for a bite to eat."

"That does sound intriguing, Squee," said Aru. "Yes, I'd love to come along." She looked at the stranger. "Have a good day, Mister. I hope you find your daughter."

The man smiled, gave a theatrical bow, and made a weird sort of honking noise. Then he noticed something on his boot, licked his finger and was rubbing to remove the spot while Aru and Squee walked away.

Aru enjoyed tying flies with Squee. Later that night, Aru saw a ghost.

She woke soon after bedtime to a phantom lingering in the corner of her cabin, a shadowy ethereal specter, not quite seen, but acutely felt. When she noticed the thing, it came toward her in the darkness. Aru surprised herself by not panicking. She asked, her voice shaking,

"Wh—what are you doing here?"

The spirit moved closer, and Aru could see its contour more clearly as it hovered now by the side of her bed. Aru scrunched down under the protection of her bedding.

"Well, well. I had assumed you'd be a little happier to see me."

Aru gasped, "Aranieda?"

There came the sound and eerie sapphire flame of a lighting match, with the accompanying smell; then a candle illuminated the rounded form of Aranieda in her customary tight bodice, though this time it was apparently because she had stolen a servant's clothes that were too small. She set the candle down, and reached out her hand to Aru.

"Here, see for yourself. I'm real," she said, with a laugh.

"Aranieda!" Aru, holding Aranieda's hand, sat upright, then hopped right out of bed to grab both of her friend's hands. It wasn't a ghost.

Aru laughed with joy and then she burst into tears. Aranieda put her arms around Aru and held her while she cried. They sat down on the bed and Aru continued to cry, then sob. Aranieda handed her a handkerchief embroidered with forget-me-nots and sat there with her, looking off into the distance, mostly. She didn't say anything for a long time.

Finally Aranieda said quietly, "He lived his life with a passion, Aru, and you know he'll be well remembered for who he was and the profound legacy of his art. I want you to know that I hold his memory dear. I miss him, too."

Aru looked up, thankful for Aranieda's words, and saw that her friend had tears in the corners of her eyes. It hadn't occurred to her before that Aranieda might ever cry. Aru nodded to Aranieda and they sat together quietly. After a while Aranieda asked her if she felt like talking about Nrouhw. Aru said she did. But then a few moments more of silence passed before she confessed that she felt too lost to know what to say.

In the dimness of the candlelight Aranieda peered at Aru over her glasses. "You know, Aru, right now it's perfectly legitimate to feel whatever you're feeling. What has happened, the deaths of both Nrouhw and young Queex, it's absolutely atrocious. But perhaps you'll speak about it when you can. The act of releasing a few words to the ears of a listener might be of some help."

"It's the strangest thing," Aru said slowly, "some days I feel stronger and a fraction less crazy, at other times when I'm reminded of Nrouhw by some little scent or notion the agony surges through me and turns me back to a pudding." She paused. "And Queex; I'm so devastated by what happened to Nrouhw my feelings about Queex are lost somewhere in the shadow of my grief. Is that wrong?"

"Here, I've something I'd like you to have," said Aranieda as she reached down into her bustier and produced a tiny glass bottle. She offered it to Aru.

"Oh, a tear catcher," Aru responded, accepting it with thanks.

The size of Aru's little finger, the tear catcher was of cobalt glass, with a silver floral filigree cupping the round bottom of the bottle and crowning the stopper.

"Yes, this small trinket was a help to me at one time. You might find it useful now or perhaps it can merely serve as a remembrance of your dear Nrouhw. Your feelings about Queex, Aru, I'm sure they are there, only buried. You loved Queex also; don't look for a right or wrong about what you feel.

"You're aware, Aru, that Nrouhw and I had our differences; of course we did. He was impulsive. He once called me a mealy-mouthed counterfeit," she laughed. "I suppose I deserved it. But, by nature, he behaved as an authentic gentleman. I've never known anyone like him. I'm reminded of the time I came upon him sitting high upon the slate wall by the academy in Opal Heights, in the branches of that cankery, dusty old winter plum tree. He had on fine clothes, an indigo brocade vest, I remember, and a gorgeous silk cravat tied over his collar."

"Oh, yes, I gave him that cravat for his birthday," whispered Aru.

"Well, I asked him wasn't he cold up there in his fine clothes, and he told me he'd got up there to pick you some plums. He had taken off his coat because he didn't want to get it dirty. That old ragged wool one he always insisted on wearing. When he came down he gave me a pocketful of fruit. His beautiful clothes were a mess. But he didn't seem to notice."

"Ah, yes. That sounds so much like Nrouhw. He loved that silly old coat," said Aru with a smile. She took a deep breath. "But, Aranieda, how did you get onto the boat?" she asked. "Does Blackbuck know you're here?"

"Great pompilids, no!" exclaimed Aranieda. "No, Blackbuck hasn't been apprised of my presence. He is unaware I've voyaged with him on the peacock boats all the while, gathering what information I might.

"Boarding this vessel wasn't difficult. You see, Aru, as you may have noticed, Blackbuck has raptors posted on each boat to keep birds away who would bear messages. Blackbuck has several reasons for not wanting messages to be exchanged between these boats and the rest of the world.

"The booby you met this afternoon landed first on the Pirate, the boat that carries Blackbuck. As it happens, the raptor guards aren't paid well, nor are they particularly aligned with Blackbuck's agenda. As a result, they are not inclined to attack transforming birds, regardless of their mandate. The booby couldn't have known this, but just happens to be the sort who won't let a little thing like raptors stop him."

"So brave!" said Aru.

"Well," Aranieda replied, "brave and fearless are two different things entirely. But at any rate, I was able to stow away among his feathers and make my way over to the Clearwater."

"And so, you've made the entire journey from Opal Heights? When did you board the Pirate?"

"Well, Aru, the fact is, in Opal Heights I learned at the last minute that Blackbuck would join his minions up on Windwether Rock. I caught up with him as they were leaving town and I dropped from a tree onto the man's head. I concealed myself in a braid of his hair. Not for the first time, you know.

"Aru, I was there by the crevasse. I saw what took place. I witnessed the whole thing. I traveled with Blackbuck to the river, I was there to see the men carry you onto the Clearwater. And so, yes, I've been aboard the Pirate all this time. The booby was my first chance to switch boats and come to see you."

"Then, you saw everything," said Aru. She fell quiet for a moment. "It's all a blur of memory for me. But at least the wand is gone, out of Blackbuck's reach."

"Alas, he may not have the staff, but he has the half-completed duplicate, and if Grmhrel should accept it then Blackbuck will go through with his plans."

"And many people will suffer."

"Yes, I'm afraid so. He'll continue to harvest and market the infected snails because his wealth has made him too powerful to restrain."

"I wonder if the decoy wand fooled him," said Aru. "Or if his men will find the real one hidden at the Hornfel."

"I've been wondering the same, hoping against hope it isn't found," said Aranieda. "We certainly made a good job of the decoy, in my opinion. Nrouhw's dragon wand of ice looked amazingly like the diamond staff."

"Didn't it, though?' said Aru. "Your powdered dragline silk surely helped. When Nrouhw held it up in the sunlight, it sparkled enough to fool me, as close as I was."

"Still, I wonder should we have just thrown the real wand into the crevasse, after all," said Aranieda.

"Perhaps we should have," whispered Aru.

"I've learned things while on the Pirate," said Aranieda. "Some things you'll want to know."

"What sorts of things?" asked Aru.

"Aru, this won't be nice to hear, I'm afraid." Aranieda paused. "When Blackbuck's schemes failed and he wasn't able to marry you to Lekki, well, he decided he'd have you even so. For himself. He'd take you for his wife, with the idea that you could bear him children with hereditary ability to see the lizard fairies." She glanced at Aru then continued, "In Opal Heights when we fed his spies the false intelligence that you and Nrouhw would be up on the Mahahag to dispose of the wand, Blackbuck decided he'd hex you both. He'd cause you to fall madly in love with him. Then he could get the two of you to accompany him down to his boats and he could just . . . spirit you away."

Aru was shaking her head. "Take me for his wife," she muttered. "Disgusting. Disgusting man." Then she looked at Aranieda and said, "But he doesn't have that kind of power. Not for magic that deep."

"No," said Aranieda, "but Queex, as it turns out, did."

"Oh . . ."

"Blackbuck had spent time preparing Queex, and had everything in place to use his abilities for the casting of a love spell. Perhaps his plan was meant for you and Lekki originally, I don't know. Never mind that love spells are the most difficult magic to cast, or that his power comes largely from his animal form which of course he can no longer use. He thought by employing Queex he could work the hex. And maybe he could have, we'll never know.

"Queex conjured the tumbling flower beetles with his glyphs and together he and Blackbuck created a binding spell that was carried by the beetles." She took a breath. "But I think at one point Queex recognized you, Aru, and when that man of Blackbuck's harried him, it provoked a decision. Queex altered the glyph image into what looked, from up on the rock where Blackbuck stood, like a grimacing clown. He sent the beetles away. This defiance and ruination of his plan was more than Blackbuck could tolerate." Aranieda paused again, rubbing one wrist against the other while she gazed at Aru over her glasses with her big eyes. "I don't think he meant to kill them, Aru. His loss of self-control caused a terrible accident when the ice gave way. Too much weight near the unstable edge. From what I can see, in private he truly feels guilt. Not that any of this makes a difference now."

Aru kept silent for a while. Then she took a deep breath and said to Aranieda, "There is something that has been troubling me about Nrouhw and Queex. And the gander man. Do you know, have they been able to retrieve them from the . . . ?"

"I'm sorry to say I don't know," replied Aranieda. "Although I am from quite a long-lived species of spider, I must remain conservative regarding the amount of hours I spend in animal form. On the Pirate I was compelled to hide in my human shape much of the time, just as I did when I followed the wagons through those woods, avoiding detection by your wolves all that time ago.

"I haven't heard anyone aboard the Pirate discussing the funerary details. But," she said softly, "the crevasse looked terribly deep, Aru. I don't think it's likely they would have been able to retrieve them."

Aranieda stayed in Aru's cabin during the following day, transforming into a spider only when she needed to relieve herself. Because Aru kept to her cabin she wasn't under constant surveillance. The Warden checked in a few times, wondering why Aru remained in her quarters. Aranieda avoided detection because she could feel the vibrations of the Warden's footsteps long before she reached the door. The Warden, thankfully, instructed that Aru wear the lavender garden-lace dress to dinner, rather than grabbing it from the wardrobe herself as she might have. When she came in later to help Aru dress before she collected her for dinner, Aru was already dressed and had her hair done.

"It's good to see that you are beginning to appreciate what Mr. Black-buck is doing for you," said the Warden in her snippy, sleepy voice.

It took great restraint for Aru to remain silent.

Aru and the Warden disembarked from the Clearwater at a little farm-to-market dock in the middle of nowhere and boarded the Pirate through the side door. In the dusk, the boat seemed similar to the Clearwater, with some differences in the carving of the peacock figure-head. Perhaps the boat was a bit larger, Aru wasn't sure. On the inside, though, she was arranged more like a luxury craft. They went through to a narrow but grand dining salon. It featured a long table covered by a marvelous tablecloth with peacock patterns in teal lace. Only the tall cerulean candles lit the chamber, shining on place settings of green glass and burnished copper, with gold, and reflecting in the mirrors between draperies on the walls. So beautiful, and yet all of it was sickening and disgusting to Aru.

At the far end of the table sat Blackbuck. He directed Aru to sit in a chair to his left, a butler pulled it out for her. She would be his only dinner guest that evening. They weren't alone, however. It seemed that Blackbuck had a footman for every dish that was brought, a waitress for every spoon.

Blackbuck had dressed in a sapphire-black dinner jacket. A woman played a lute in the shadows of the corner. Around Aru's plate were scattered fresh Love-in-a-Mist blossoms. This dinner was clearly a romantic gesture. Each detail felt like a slap in the face. How could a man be so insensitive, so full of himself that he couldn't see out?

Aru had no appetite, but she politely ate a small amount because, even now, the manners of her upbringing prevailed. Inside, she was scratching at this man's eyes like a wild animal, but because of Aranieda's presence back in her cabin, Aru didn't want to make waves. Her hands shook, but she drank her wine.

The conversation was mostly a monologue on his part; Aru wasn't sure if Blackbuck noticed. He didn't apologize about Nrouhw's death. "So unfortunate," he said.

During her miserable evening Aru did find out that, apparently because of his spy network, Blackbuck knew all along about the decoy of ice. He knew every detail. He referred to the powdered dragline silk, the substance that they'd used to make the ice shine like diamond, as Aranieda's spinnbarkeit. She was intensely insulted to hear this when Aru told her later. This wretched man had a gift for inspiring animosity in others. He topped off the evening by telling Aru that he had sent his "people" to her apartment at the Hornfel to find the real dragon scepter. All the while he somehow assumed that, impressed by his great power, she would be falling madly in love with him. Blackbuck had no soul.

Aranieda's presence on the Clearwater meant much to Aru, and yet having her in the cabin brought back old times and made Aru miss her grandmother terribly. Aru pined for Nrouhw and her grandmother and she felt humiliated and crushed under the arrogance of her captor. Even though she and Aranieda discussed plans to thwart Blackbuck's scheme, Aru didn't foresee that they'd actually achieve anything. The Warden, following Aru around and chiding her with insults, added a thorn to Aru's side. Having Aranieda and Squee for company helped, but even so Aru found herself trapped in reflections of "if only."

Aru didn't know what to do. At all. Struggling deep in her mind, confined by her pain and confusion, she was at a loss. Overwhelmed by helplessness. Out of control of the situation and fixated with worry about her life, she wanted to hide, to be alone, but she couldn't let that be known. She appreciated her friends, but felt farther and farther removed from them though they clearly showed concern about her.

Other people's lives are worth living, she thought. *But mine? I'm so tired. Maybe I can release myself from life by the act of not wanting to be here anymore. Maybe I'll just go to sleep, fade away. I've lost the will to live. I don't care anymore.* She had thoughts like these day after day.

Sometimes she could see her way out of the mist. Perhaps if she did something with her life that she could control, something no one could take from her. She could pour herself into a spectacular stitchery project or some other expression of her spirit, a statement to share with others, a mark of her distinctiveness to carve upon the world. Maybe then she'd get through all this. She would create a reality of her own, by act of focus, build her own realm, her own life. Yes. But without warning her heart would plummet like an enormous waterlogged beetle into the hollow night of her soul.

There is no point to my life. Why go on? Nothing I've ever done has come to anything. All I have is loss. I don't care about anyone anymore. Aranieda and Squee don't truly know me, how can they? It surprised her that she didn't care about her friends. She had no regard for their feelings, no worry surrounding their concern for her. The part of her that would have cared, a huge part of her normally, had grown small somehow. *Nobody understands me as Nrouhw did. I'm just exhausted.*

The boat creaked and the water slapped against the hull incessantly. It started to drive Aru mad. Once a soothing noise, a comforting motion, they now pierced her skull like metal spikes. She couldn't get away from it.

Aru felt like an old, old woman. The bitter kind, not the type with laugh wrinkles. She felt she'd suddenly aged eighty or ninety years, or more. She brushed the crumbs off her skirts with an old woman's hands, pulled her shawl close to keep out the draft. She felt shaky, benumbed, brittle. Her lips felt thin. Why go on living?

The nightshade grew along the banks, beckoning. A few berries, a leaf. Ten would surely do it. Would there be pain? She wasn't as worried about that idea as she would have imagined. But how long would it take, that was the thing. Hours of madness? Days?

Asleep one night, in a fetal position, Aru was awakened by Aranieda. "Listen, Aru," she whispered. Aru didn't hear anything.

"That!" Aranieda whispered, "That tapping sound. Hear it?"

Aru listened. She didn't hear anything. Oh. There, maybe she did. Something was tapping against the hull, underneath the starboard porthole. And the boat was creaking and the water was sloshing. "It must be some garbage in the water," grumbled Aru, trying, too late, to retrieve a dream.

"No. It's a purposeful noise," said Aranieda. "Aru, go see what it is."

Aranieda didn't usually give commands. Aru looked at her with resignation and got out of bed. She put her coat on over her simple woad shift and stumbled her way quietly to the companionway and up onto deck. It was a clear, starry night. A cool wind touched her face. The sleepy merlin noticed her but didn't react much to her presence on deck in the middle of the night. Blackbuck certainly wasn't getting his money's worth out of his security.

Looking over the side, Aru saw something floating on the water. A bottle. As she peered at it in the moonlight she noticed the bottle move in a strange way and tap against the hull several times. As her eyes focused she could see a ribbon around the bottle, and holding on to the ribbon, a fish. Aru did nothing for a while. She stood leaning over the rail, watching. It was a lot of work for the fish. Tap. Tap-tap. Tap.

At last Aru went and got a boat hook and managed to hook a loop of the ribbon. This was difficult to do without spearing the fish, who, as soon as it was clear that she had hooked the bottle, disappeared into the dark waters.

When Aru brought the bottle up, she could see it held a message. She hurriedly returned with it to her quarters, where she and Aranieda quietly broke the bottle inside a blanket to retrieve the note. They found the paper was labeled with Aru's name. There was something else in the bottle, a token. Both Aranieda and Aru immediately recognized it as one of Lekki's pewter buttons, from a favorite vest he often wore, one Mhehh had given him. The note was from Lekki!

They unfolded the paper and read the note together under the candlelight. It was only a few lines, elegantly penned. Aru's mouth opened wide as she read the words, and as soon as she finished, she snatched up the message and crumpled it, and threw it hard onto the floor. Then she stamped on it.

"What is wrong with this world?" she cried.

"Shh, Aru," cautioned Aranieda. "Someone will come." She sat for a moment with a strange look on her face while Aru paced up and down and made dramatic gestures all over the narrow cabin.

"Wait a moment, Aru," she said. "Wait a moment." Aranieda retrieved the paper and uncrumpled it, flattening it out so she could read. "Yes. It's some sort of cipher." She turned to Aru and then back to the message, pointing with her finger along the lines of words. "Look," she said, "as awful as this is, Aru, you've got to pay attention. Lekki has written something which you know absolutely is not correct, you know it isn't true. Yet only you could know that for certain. This is a signal for you to look closer at the letter.

"These words aren't meant for you, Aru. These words are only smoke, meant to mislead if the message ends up in the hands of the wrong person. Your words, the ones that are his message for you, those are hidden here somewhere within the text."

Aru looked at it again, grudgingly, as if it were poison to touch. "Perhaps that is the case, although I don't see how it's possible," she said weakly. "But why would he choose such a horrible, heartless guise?"

Aranieda sighed. "Well," she said slowly, "think about who he is trying to mislead. Blackbuck. Wouldn't the Blackbuck, upon procuring this message with Lekki's token, wouldn't he believe it completely? It is certainly what he would be thrilled to hear. And who would know how to manipulate the Blackbuck better than his own son? Lekki has designed some sort of plan to free you. That is apparent. Let's just deduce how to decipher his message."

Aranieda studied the note, poring over these words:

> *Aru,*
>
> *Remember all my love that was confessed to you during our wondrous tryst up at Topaz Lodge those many nights ago. Not a mote has changed for my part and my heart has no doubt that your fervor perseveres as well. We must come together, we must meet once more.*
>
> *You'll find my world has become dingy and drear, there's no way for me to leave you behind and turn my back upon my dreams. We both know who has the answer, it is I. We must let my father know of our unquenchable ardor.*
>
> *Stay on the riverboat and do not be concerned, soon we'll be together.*

After looking at the words again, Aranieda said, "There is another possibility. It could be that you were never meant to receive this note, that Lekki's intent was for the merlin to intercept it. It may be that there is no hidden message at all." She stood hunched over the text as she spoke, stretching the sound of her words out to buy time as her mind also processed what she was reading. "No!—I have it!" she said.

Aru leaned over to see. Aranieda pulled a pencil stub out of her bosom. Aru wondered how many other items Aranieda might have stashed in there.

Aranieda pointed to the end of the fifth sentence, and circled a phrase. "This is the key," she said. "See how it says, 'The answer, it is I.' It's telling you that the solution to the cipher is the letter I. The most obvious thing, then, is to look for the words containing the letter I, to see if there is something relevant about them. There aren't many, Aru. And they form a sentence. Look." She quickly circled more words and handed the paper to Aru.

Aru read: "During-nights-find-dingy-behind-riverboat." She looked at Aranieda, "That doesn't . . . Oh my, yes! Of course it makes sense. 'During the nights you'll find a dinghy behind the boat,' that's what he's saying! He's come to rescue me."

Aru and Aranieda hugged. They packed up the few things Aru would want to take with her, along with some belongings Aranieda had managed to send for. They got ready to leave immediately.

"It's fortunate there's no hearth in this room," Aru said with a wry grin as she turned her back so Aranieda could transform. "I would have thrown that note straight into the fire."

With the spider seated carefully in the fold of her jacket collar, Aru snuck with painstaking quietness back up and out onto the deck. It was still a beautiful, starry night. But there was no dinghy at the stern. No Lekki.

He'd be there, though. He'd come. The next day Aru was especially nice to Squee. She wanted to say goodbye to her, but she didn't dare. And so she said encouraging things about Squee's future while they cleaned the galvanized fittings together, and gave her a gift: a sailor's cap quickly stitched from herringbone wool. At least this time she wasn't jumping over the side of the boat right in front of Squee's eyes.

That night Aru crept onto the deck again, with her passenger.

No dinghy.

The following day Aranieda heard someone say that they were approaching a sizable town. They'd dock there for a day or so to refresh the supplies. She told Aru that perhaps Lekki waited for this layover. They'd reach the town in the morning, it could be that he was waiting for them to dock. They repeated their journey to the deck that same night in any event, just in case he was there. He was.

Aru dropped a couple bundles into the rowboat and with the help of a rope ladder which Lekki tossed, climbed down as quickly as she could. They whispered greetings and while Lekki dipped the oars and began to row toward the shore, Aru let him know Aranieda was with them. He said hello to the spider as Aru briefly held back her hair.

As he rowed against the current, toward the bank slightly upriver, and the peacock boats quickly drifted out of view, Lekki spoke softly, "It is good to see the both of you again. I hope you and Nrouhw will pardon me for my rude tactics, Aru, but I knew you would work out the cipher. There stood a high chance of my father or his spies ending up with the message bottle. This way, if they had intercepted the message it would only have furthered my—Aru, what is the matter?"

"Lekki, you don't know?" choked Aru. "Lekki, Nrouhw is gone. He and Queex died on the Mahahag, they were cast into a crevasse by your father's wind. The ice gave way. And a man of your father's also."

Upon hearing this, Lekki was sick over the side of the little boat. Then he apologized to Aru and rowed the rest of the way to the shore, grief and anger visibly welling up inside him.

When they reached the riverbank, Lekki whistled softly and some sort of furry animal came to retrieve the boat; in the grey light Aru's teary eyes didn't notice what it was. They waited a moment while Aranieda transformed and dressed.

"There is a place where we can talk, it is not far," said Lekki as he led them up a stony brook that came from the nearby hills. The three of them walked quietly, nobody wanting to begin the conversation they would soon have.

They arrived at a tin shack, empty-looking and with the windows boarded up. Yet, a wisp of smoke was coming from the chimney pipe. Lekki told them the place belonged to a friend who wintered there. Inside, they were greeted by a different friend of Lekki's who was waiting for them.

Lekki introduced her, "Allow me to present my friend Keak; we have known one another since our school days in the Mazarines. She is a true friend and I trust her implicitly. There is nothing to avoid discussing in her presence."

"Delighted to make your acquaintance," said the woman in a raspy voice, shaking the hands of Aru and Aranieda. She had an air of dignity and self-importance, but her hair stood straight up and was all over the place. Keak had a dagger-like nose and round dark eyes. A slate blue cloak was fastened at her throat over a white blouse with a high collar, her waist bound with a thick leather belt. She had the table set and waiting, with fresh and steaming crayfish tails on tin plates for everyone.

They sat down to eat, and after some polite conversation with Keak, Aru turned to Lekki and inquired about Sheeki. It was a somewhat wistful question, but also her spirits buoyed up as she pictured Lekki's little son and his baby laugh.

"He is beautiful, Aru. He's doing just fine, and so is Mhehh. She said to send her love." Lekki winced and scowled, and Aru knew he must be remembering that she'd added, "And to Nrouhw also."

Aru and Aranieda related to Lekki the story of what had happened. Lekki responded that no one in Opal Heights knew what had become of them. He and Mhehh had returned from their honeymoon to find people worriedly discussing Aru and Nrouhw's sudden disappearance, and in the palace confused rumors circulated about why the boy Queex was missing also.

Through friends, Lekki had learned about his father's plans to convince Aru and Nrouhw to travel with him by boat home to Anemone. Lekki knew they would never go willingly. He and Mhehh had decided that she and the baby would stay at the house of her parents while he located Aru and Nrouhw and sought their help with a plan that the couple had developed while on their honeymoon. Mhehh had come up with a promising proposal. They might be able to protect the many who lived in the lands along the seacoast from the hardships caused by his father's greedy indifference. But now, Lekki didn't know. He was at a loss.

"I wish to hear the plan," said Aranieda.

After Aru had a moment to settle her presence she said, "I'd like to hear it, too."

Lekki looked at Aru with shame in his dark eyes. "I am so sorry," he said. "Such a horrendous thing I have done, sending you a note with those words. I had no idea. The note was, of course, meant to mislead my father, should he obtain it." Lekki pushed a curl of hair behind the spiral of horn that extended in bas-relief above his temple. He continued, "I thought you would find it humorous when you worked out the code; I am so sorry to hurt your feelings in such a terrible way."

"Please don't feel bad, Lekki. There's no point. I don't have any feelings anymore." The words came out on their own but Aru realized they were true.

Lekki peered into Aru's face and then he looked away. "Although it may seem a single blade in a drought, I do have some good tidings for you," said Lekki solemnly. "A bit of starlight to pierce through the shadows." He reached for the satchel he'd set on the floor by his chair. Holding it on his lap he said, "Aru, I went by the Hornfel, and picked up a few things of yours. There is not much here, but I did bring this."

Aru recognized the fabric that bound the wand before he had it out of the bag. "Oh!" she gasped. She held out her hands as Lekki offered the bundle to her. She didn't unwrap it, she held it against her chest and thanked him.

"Such fine work, Lekki," said Aranieda. "Your recovery of this jewel, it will likely provide the people of our homeland a brighter future."

Lekki nodded, solemnly. Along with the wand he had retrieved Aru's embroidery basket, the tiny bottle of mithridate, some jewelry, and Nrouhw's favorite paint brushes, all of which Aru was thankful to have.

"It is a simple plan," said Lekki, finally. Then, addressing Aru, he asked, "How much do you know about my father's business with the hypogeous snails?"

"Quite little, I'm afraid," replied Aru.

"The problems with which we are concerned," said Lekki, "all seem to revolve around the ancient well on the grounds at Anemone, our house, which is near Amryliw, down by the sea. The well is the last vestige of a bygone era, relic of a manor that stood on that hill hundreds of years ago, long before the construction of our family home, and before the house that predated ours. The old well stands at the bottom of the periwinkle garden. It was my mother's favorite spot, that garden, and as you know, it proved to be the location of her demise. The well is also where my father found access to the hypogeous snails and at the same time it is the source of the plague of fairy lizards. There is a foul magic surrounding that creepy old well, certainly.

"The discovery of the valuable snails right on his doorstep, so to speak, should have been a happy windfall for my father. My family has no pecuniary needs, certainly, but there are those in our land who live in poverty, and the finding of this treasure could have benefitted them greatly. He does not see things that way, however, my father. Somehow he is driven to collect and hoard ever more wealth, for reasons that are beyond my understanding. And, at any rate, it seems there is always a wasp in the aster blossom.

"Several issues arose in regard to the snails. First, because my father had the opening in the shaft of the well widened and began removing snails from the cavern at a great rate, he caught the attention of Grmhrel, the one who guards all passages between our world and the world below."

"Yes," said Aru, "and he had to bargain with him, the wand in exchange for access to the hypogeous snails. The wand is so Grmhrel can bring light down into his cavern, to replace the light from the ailing fireflies, isn't it?"

"Right. That is right, Aru. And this intervention by Grmhrel complicated my father's plans," Lekki continued, "but a far more significant problem arose. People along the coast began to fall ill, sick with a terrible disease that has claimed several lives so far. The source of this outbreak was found to be a microbe carried by the snails my father is marketing. The same bacteria that had killed the firefly larvae. Hypogeous snails are extremely vulnerable to disease and these should have been tested before distribution, but no, they were not tested. It is to the great shame of my family that my father continues to promote the snails he already possesses, despite knowledge of the bacteria. He has apparently convinced himself the illness is merely some sort of ridiculous hoax brought about by his competitor across the sea.

"The disgraces surrounding this situation are manyfold. Scientists recently determined that the bacteria was carried to the snail cavern in the first place by the snake Pythymuss on his original exploration. In addition, I have learned, although I cannot be certain it is true, that my father has been seeding a batch of these infected snails, in an attempt to produce his own supply. His detachment from reality seems more and yet more severe."

"It's a terrible, terrible tangle of calamity," said Aranieda. "The Blackbuck is ailing in his wits and Grmhrel is an angry and dangerous entity with whom to be involved at the best of times. And there is something else, something I overheard while aboard the Pirate. Your father, Lekki, for reasons I wasn't able to determine, is having the high tower at Anemone restocked with provisions to create for himself a clandestine retreat where he could survive for quite some time. He appeared, almost, to look forward to some sort of disaster on the approach, something that would leave him and his chosen ones among the sole survivors."

"Confound it all, I was not aware of his activities at the tower, but he does indeed seem to have those sorts of thoughts governing his mind once again. We must do something," said Lekki. "The idea of Mhehh's would use my father's own insecurities and selfish pride against him. He may not care about his people, but he certainly cares about his social status. That is where my friend here, the many-talented Keak, comes in."

Keak smiled and coughed and spoke quietly, "I must say that I admire Lekkchaos for standing up to his father, the way he does. He has had me fluttering all up and down the coast, in and out of every hillock, to invite every rich pretentious rat bastard in the land to his little social gathering."

"Fishing for kings, you might say," said Lekki, and Keak laughed along with him, a rattling laugh.

"The whole of our plan," Lekki explained, "is to have my father meet with the other royalty of the coastal lands and discuss the problems concerning the snails and the lizards. My father is the wealthiest landholder of them all, and we have spread the rumor that he would be interested in setting up funds for research regarding these issues. Eradicating the disease is to be the priority.

"Keak has been masquerading as the emissary of one of those neighbors and in this way we have got my father to agree to host a banquet at Anemone. He is of course unaware of the purpose of the gathering, he is under the impression it is purely a social event. At the same time, Keak has been calling upon the guests as if the invitation comes from my father."

"A fine deception," said Aranieda, "but of course there is a risk of exposure if the royals communicate with one another."

Keak responded to Aranieda's concern, "We've alerted the messenger bird community, in secret. There is no great risk of turncoats, because, honestly, it is in just about everyone's best interest to dupe Mr. Blackbuck in this way."

That was it, then. A simple plan, and it would be an excellent start for solving the problems which Blackbuck had created. Aru and Aranieda agreed that it would be best for them to slip back aboard the Clearwater that night in order to help keep things on schedule. Lekki would keep the wand in his possession and make his own way to Anemone.

In the darkest hours of the night, the small company set out with Lekki as their guide. They would meet the boat by way of a shortcut to the river town where she was presumed to be docked. Although he knew the area, Lekki soon remarked that the undergrowth was surprisingly dense this year. The brush and brambles had grown up in some places so as to make the way impassable.

Fortunately, among the shadows they found a pathway hacked through the bramble bushes; this would save them untold amounts of wasted time. It was a cleanly cut path, wide enough for the four of them to walk abreast at leisure. They fell to conversation, and so it took them a while before Aranieda noticed that something was odd. Didn't it seem like they'd been traveling in a circle? And now the trail wanted them to double back alongside the way they had just come.

"I don't like this," she said.

The others agreed that something was odd about the pathway and it was decided, after her offer, that Keak would transform and get a view from the forest canopy. Gone for only a few minutes, she arrived back in a flurry. She transformed and dressed at top speed and rejoined the group breathlessly.

The passageway through the brambles was a labyrinth. And in the center, where they were headed, slept a minotaur! Except it wasn't sleeping anymore; Keak had watched it wake and listen to their approach. They needed to get out of there quickly, they didn't have time to exit by the way they had come in.

"There is one thing," Keak wheezed. "It's only a miniature minotaur."

"Those can be the most savage kind!" whispered Aranieda.

They had to think fast. Aranieda and Keak had a quick discussion and told the others that they would proceed into the labyrinth to distract the beast while the other two ran back out the way they had come in.

The pair of them had a way to escape at the last minute. They would fly over the brambles together.

"But we haven't time!" exclaimed Aru. "We'll never make it out! It's too far!" She looked despairingly around and then she had an idea. "Aranieda, do you have a knife?"

Of course Aranieda produced one.

"Quick, we need some of your strips—" Aru pointed to Aranieda's skirt. Without a pause of any sort, Aranieda began cutting off the leather strips of her skirt and handing them to Aru.

"We'll need four," whispered Aru. "Lekki and I can use them to wrap around our hands. While you're distracting the monster we'll draw brambles across the path, make a dead end for the minotaur."

Lekki started wrapping his hands. "Your thinking is exceptional, Aru! This blockade will slow him enough that we'll have a chance."

Aranieda nodded, handed Aru her knife, and said, "Make the barrier thick, he'll have tough skin." Then she and Keak, who was again in bird form, disappeared around the corner, further into the maze.

Working frantically, Lekki and Aru grabbed the bramble vines from one side of the trail and wove them into the vines from the other side. Lekki was the faster of the two so he used the knife and cut through any vines that wouldn't reach, tossing them into the middle. With both of them frantically laboring to save their lives, it didn't take long before a bushy, thorny wall stretched across the path. They could hear the minotaur coming; they kept working. It needed to be higher, thicker.

Around the corner he appeared with a stink preceding him, half goblin, half ram, a hideous brutish little beast. He snorted when he saw them, and he charged.

Aru and Lekki never looked to see how their barricade was holding. They ran with all their might. It seemed forever until they were clear of the brambles. Safe outside of the labyrinth, they trotted back toward the shack. They walked in circles and paced until they had their breath, then they fell onto the ground.

Lekki revived first, and gently prodded Aru. He helped her up, shakily, and they brushed themselves off and started again for the river town, looking behind them once in a while. "We can still make it," Lekki said.

This time they headed straight for the river and followed it through the woods. They didn't speak much, their concerns about Keak and Aranieda filling their thoughts, and Lekki, of course, was reeling from the news about Nrouhw and Queex. The bramble vines had torn their clothing and their skin. Lekki had a gash across his cheek. He showed Aru how to chew the leaves of the wild rose and apply the paste to the worst of their cuts.

Before the break of day they arrived at the edge of town, and soon came upon the docks. There lay the three boats, the Clearwater, the Zodiac, and the Pirate. Aru and Lekki found a place to sit down in the shadow of a wall, and they waited for their friends to arrive. The bramble scrapes did sting quite a lot, and Aru still had some bruises from the bigfoot.

They sat against the rocks, waiting. Aru endured an eternal series of moments. She struggled once again in a bitter conflict with time in which she held her breath too much and clenched her fists without realizing it. Dawn eventually arrived, and still no news. At last, finally, Aranieda appeared.

She looked a bit beaten up, but surprisingly robust for someone who had recently confronted a minotaur. Aranieda told them that Keak didn't wish to be seen around the quay. She had gone somewhere to clean herself up for her impending conversation with Blackbuck. Aranieda had procured some new clothes for Keak at a shop in town, leaving money for the sleeping shopkeeper.

The relief that their friends had lived to tell the tale was tempered by the news that the minotaur had made contact with Keak's wing and nearly crippled her. Aranieda said that after the two of them had done their best to distract the minotaur, Keak had held it off by pecking at its eyes so Aranieda could transform and make her way through the bushes. Keak misjudged the monster's reach and he nearly had her. She was only able to save herself by a well aimed peck that momentarily blinded him. Then, following her only choice, she fluttered down the path into the maze and threw herself face-down into the damp shadows. Her plumage provided camouflage and the monster ran right past her, searching, and then turned and headed for the others. Keak knew there was no more she could do.

She and Aranieda met outside the labyrinth, Keak unable to fly but fortunately able to transform. She and Aranieda walked to town.

Aru handed Aranieda her leather strips, what was left of them, so that she could salvage the rivets. It remained quiet along the dockside at that hour, so the three of them made their way over to the Clearwater and Lekki signaled to the merlin above. His gesture was returned with a friendly acknowledgement. "A friend of mine from Rhywle," explained Lekki.

The bird disappeared for a few minutes and reappeared, tossing a knotted rope over the side with repeated motions using his powerful beak. Before she climbed up, Aru turned to Lekki, and quietly hugged him. She said she'd see him at Anemone. Then she whispered a thanks for his help and she returned to him his button.

VIII. Answers

RAGGED mother-of-pearl clouds passed across the morning sun. They glowed with stunning iridescence. How could this not be a good omen? The three boats remained moored at the little river town, creaking against the dock. Under the Warden's close supervision, Aru lounged the day away on the deck of the Clearwater, reading and napping in the cool shade of the peacock deckhouse. She did give half an hour to help Squee with the weekly bugbear of polishing the silver. The main street of town ran along the riverfront. As the people went about their work day Aru found that watching them provided fine entertainment. She and Squee talked about sonar, which Squee had, and gills, which she didn't, and how long they could each hold their breath.

In the late afternoon Aru went below. The stroke of four fifteen had the Warden peering into her cabin to make sure she was dressed and ready. She would be dining tonight in the back garden of a fish house in town. Blackbuck had instructed her to meet him there. He would be entertaining some associates, and Aru knew these would include Keak. As the two climbed a street from the docks, the Warden, shuffling along in her too-small shoes, gripped Aru by the hand as if she expected her to make a run for it.

Aru's resentment of the woman had eroded through pity. *Will she ever become a butterfly?* wondered Aru, as she freed her hand with a sharp twist and a yank.

The Warden turned with Aru into an alleyway. They walked on cobblestone pavers between high fences painted in pale shades of grey and delphinium blue. Borage and cornflowers grew thick along the edges of the alley, and honeybees rushed to finish their day's harvest while the air was still warm.

They paused before a red gate. The street number had been painted in cursive script across the boards. The Warden lifted the latch and pushed it open. Aru and the Warden peeked through the opening into the shady back garden of the restaurant. Much of the space was devoted to a big rectangular pool, the water just inches deep and smooth as glass. A long table, dressed in dark indigo silk, ran right beside the water and half a dozen smaller, round tables were at the far end. At one of those tables sat Blackbuck enjoying an aperitif with several other dignitaries. Aru recognized Keak.

The garden smelled spicy sweet. Strings of huge lampwork beads dangled from the overhanging magnolia branches, reflecting in the still water of the pool. As she and the Warden walked past the indigo table they feasted their eyes on the arrangements of moist fresh dahlias, burnt orange and dark-tipped pink, resting in leafy centerpieces, studded here and there with tiny yellow lilies. Tall candles and votives too scattered the tabletop between the abundance of flowers. There was barely room for the settings.

Blackbuck stood up when she arrived, and another man pulled out a chair for her. Aru thanked the gentleman and arranged her pearl-spangled skirts as she settled herself in her place. The Warden, smug as ever, displayed a triumphant smirk before she departed. She was sure Aru would be swooned by Blackbuck's privilege and charms.

Keak flashed the tiniest smile to Aru and after introductions returned to her conversation with the host. Almost unrecognizable as the woman Aru had met in the forest, Keak had a stately flair which impressed Aru greatly, given that she'd had only hours in a river town to transform herself from battered ranger to regal emissary. Her hair was oiled and pulled back, supplemented by an elegant hairpiece. She wore fine jewelry and a dress that looked uncomfortably tight. Stifling a laugh, Aru remembered Aranieda had picked it for her. Keak's injured arm was out of sight under a fashionable slate blue capelet.

Besides the glorious bunches of flowers, this table had, as part of the decoration, two rosy finches in a golden cage. The pair hopped and chirped inside the cage, and though they seemed happy and were obviously not transforming birds, Aru had mixed feelings about the display. She wondered what Nrouhw would've thought about it.

Blackbuck was engaged in conversation with Keak. He had been predictably receptive to the idea of a large banquet, quite flattered that the community requested that he host it at Anemone.

"My home Anemone at Amryliw is a dreamland of beauty," he said, turning to Aru. "I know you will enjoy it there."

Aru replied that she'd heard much about the town of Amryliw, she wondered if she might meet relatives of her mother's there. Aranieda, concealed in a wave of Aru's coiffure near her ear, squirmed a little. It tickled, and so Aru paused while she formed her next question:

"As my mother was your wife's cousin, won't family of my great aunt be living there in Amryliw still? I've often wondered if they might hold land? A palace by the sea? A dear friend of mine"—Aranieda wiggled again—"has revealed to me that I am by birth a princess."

Blackbuck swallowed and dipped his head slightly; was he stifling a laugh? He answered quite solemnly, "I have no wish to disappoint you, my darling young woman, you certainly display the graceful airs of a princess. I regret to say, however, that your friend, however dear, has no more idea about your heritage than you have. This person apparently has been feeding your own fancies back to you.

"Your grandaunt Crwydryn, while a dignified and noble person, was a daughter of the merchant class, not of monarchs."

"Others have told me so," Aru tried not to sound like she was choking. She picked up her berry bowl, glancing at the pretty floral design.

"It is a common practise to use someone's beliefs, or even mere longings, in order to manipulate them, my dearest. It's a sad fact of life. It happens to us all at some time in our lives," Blackbuck said gently. Then he went on to talk about the hierarchy of royal descent and managed to insert into the conversation that the only way Aru could become royalty would be through marriage. She could marry into status as her grandaunt had done.

At his mention of manipulation Aru's hand instinctively went to her ear, causing Aranieda to make a quick retreat around the back of her neck. The scuttling spider legs tickled, and forced Aru to disguise her involuntary reaction as a sneezy cough. Others asked if she was all right. She said that she was, but in truth she had sunk down several more levels in happiness.

Aru didn't say much at all for the rest of the dinner. Blackbuck, if he ever thought about it, must have considered her a quiet person. In his mind that behavior would befit a queen.

Keak, as it turned out, had a lovely personality imbued with quite a multifaceted coloration. She took control of the occasion and made the dinner something that even Aru would have enjoyed if she hadn't been so far down in her hole of self-pity.

Back in the cabin on the Clearwater, Aru and Aranieda had about as heated of a discussion as can be had in undertones. Furious about Aranieda's lies, Aru wasn't having a bit of her defense that weaving webs and telling stories is just what spiders do. In any case, Aranieda pointed out, how did Blackbuck know that Aru didn't, in reality, have royal blood? She may not have royals in her family on the coast, but he couldn't know her true ancestry, could he. It was quite mysterious.

Aru frowned. "I'm not from the star people, either, am I."

"You very well could be, Aru."

This glint of hope helped Aru's mood, but she didn't grab on to the idea as she might have done in the past.

More days went by, more miles of the river, and more dinners and visits with Blackbuck. One day Aru confided to Aranieda that, in some bizarre way, she was starting to have feelings for the man. How could that be? She hated him. And yet she found herself becoming strangely attracted to him. She felt ashamed. Perhaps it was his wealth, winning her over after all. And in the middle of her deep mourning for Nrouhw.

Aranieda told Aru that this was something she'd seen before. "Don't feel ashamed," she said, "I have witnessed this several times among victims of kidnapping. It doesn't seem logical, but I believe it is in some way the defense of the spirit against an oppressor. When people can't bear to live in fear and hate they seem to choose love. That isn't such a bad response, in my opinion, but of course this sort of love is misdirected." She looked at Aru over her glasses. "It's an understandable feeling, Aru, and I'm sure that in your case it will quickly pass."

The next day, however, Aranieda shared with Aru a discovery she had made. "Blackbuck has been feeding you tainted food. Your desserts and sweets have been filled with sugar hexed by an Opali witch. The spell is one of desire. It's not a love potion, so much as a lust potion: something much easier to contrive."

"Yeugh! Ick!" exclaimed Aru, making a face. She twisted her arms around themselves and then held them up against her chest. "Eew!"

"It won't have nearly the effect, now that you're aware of it," said Aranieda. "But it won't hurt if you limit your sweets. Continue to eat them when under observation by the Blackbuck, though," she added. "Continue to allow him to think his seduction is slowly having success. It's in our best interest if he is under the impression that things are going his way."

Aru sat still, looking extremely unhappy. Beyond her impression of what the next while would be like, pretending to fall in love with this monster, it was going to be tough to forgo the goodies. When Blackbuck entertained he presented her with the most scrumptious treats, fanciful cakes and pastries, gorgeous puddings. To her cabin he'd been sending cookies that Aru thought of as magical purely in the sense of their beauty. Cookies in fabulous animal shapes and also flower shapes, leaves and fruits. Each glazed in the most tasteful way in luscious colors with the use of shading and amazing detail. Works of art, really. Aru's mouth watered just thinking about their light lemony flavor. Now she was distressed to find that they actually were magical indeed. She had been sharing them with Aranieda, who had eaten quite a few . . . Aru looked at her friend.

Having predicted Aru's train of thought, Aranieda peered back at Aru over her glasses, smiled a little, and shrugged.

Not long after this the Clearwater, the Zodiac, and the Pirate finally reached their destination of the town Liwien at the mouth of the Oso River.

Aru and Squee stood leaning over the railing to take in the sights as they approached. Squee chattered away, excited to return to the docks of Upper Liwien at last. She would be released here, able to swim home and be with her family. And she'd have a pouch full of coins to send them.

Crowded onto steep hillsides above the river, the buildings of the town displayed a striking array of colors, making Aru think of Nrouhw's fat wax crayons standing in their box, bright and cheery. The river was too wide at this spot to allow the town to inhabit both sides. Only a few structures of some kind were visible over on the flat northern bank. As they drifted into the harbor, Aru enjoyed the scent of snapdragons, then of fishy odors, and of something baking.

The waterfront reminded Aru of Ysgarlad. An abundance of warehouses and the noisy bustle made it seem they were landing at a city. She guessed the town must extend beyond the top of the ridge. Several sailing vessels rested in the slips. A great brick hotel, with shops on the street level, sat just at the end of the quay. There was a candle maker's, a chocolatier, some other thing, Aru couldn't quite see. The ocean was near. Aru had smelled whiffs of it for several days. This part of town stood well back on the estuary, though, and so nothing but wide river showed beyond the cliffy banks to the east.

On that downstream side of the little harbor stood a hill, bell-shaped except for the cliff which faced the water. This slice of marbled granite a dozen stories high cleaved that lower half of the bell into a wall of dramatic beauty. Perched just above the face of the precipice, brightly painted houses, tall and boxy, squeezed together to cover the shoulders of the hill and sit like jewels on the crown.

By contrast, the steep ridge that rose up beyond the docks was scattered with business establishments, hotels, and houses all bearing pastel shades like a huge jumble of salt water taffys. Many of the trees were in bloom. Flowering vines clung to archways and walls, interlacing a network of terraces, stairways, patios.

Nearly every building in town had a veranda or was adorned with balconies and sun shades. Cast iron and wood were both popular. Purple balconies hung on a yellow building, bright indigo on a salmon pink or a green one.

Herring gulls called out and fought over scraps. They landed on the railings of the Clearwater, looking for handouts. These were fat and lazy birds, brightly clean and healthy and obviously their living was easy. Aru tossed the remains of her pilot bread to a couple of them and watched their display of hierarchy as others arrived to scuffle.

Squee had her duties to perform as the boats tied up at the pier. Aru stayed on the rail and waved back at a boy who was strolling with his mother.

Although Aru had been instructed to be all packed up and ready, they remained aboard the boats for a couple of hours after docking while they waited for the coaches from Anemone to arrive. Aru spent her time drinking iced tea and gazing at the scenery.

There was a clear love of flags and banners in local culture, but this was famously a country of flowers. Hanging baskets, window boxes, and rooftop gardens filled the scene with blossoms. Pots of pansies were everywhere. Fragrant garlands of peonies had been festooned from lamp post to lamp post on the frontage street with small lanterns hanging from the center of each arc.

Squee became more and more excited as her chores neared completion. At last she was done and she appeared on deck next to Aru again with happy tears in her eyes. "I'm going to see my family, Aru!" she cried as she hugged Aru so tight that she caused a temporary digestive issue. "I've been released!"

If Squee left right away she would reach her island home by nightfall. She was practically turning flips with joy. Aru couldn't help but laugh and share in her excitement. Squee's few possessions would be sent along by pelican in a day or two. She gave Aru a scrap of paper on which she'd elegantly penned her postal address and a short poem about larkspur flowers and life in the sea.

A short time later Aru was waving and blowing kisses to a little bottlenose dolphin who whistled a high-pitched trill as she leapt and splashed and laughed just off the bow of a departing schooner.

It wasn't long after Squee had faded from sight down the river that the coaches appeared. "There they are," said the Warden.

Aru looked along the road that weaved its way up the south ridge where the Warden was pointing, but she didn't see anything. Squinting up into the sky beyond the ridge, she saw three small spots of brightness in the distance. Balloons. "We'll be traveling by air?" she asked.

The Warden didn't bother to answer.

Aru stared at the balloons, watching them slowly grow bigger. Then, with Aranieda stowed in the fluffy feathers of her hat, she disembarked for the last time. She walked down the pier, and then along Front Street, in the company of the Warden and a Clearwater passenger whom she'd never met before. A porter followed with their luggage.

They passed people having their morning refreshment on porches of cafés, merchants with watering cans teetering on step ladders, and an old lady in a lovely quilted jacket walking her dogs. Everyone smiled and waved. There was a shop called *Miscellany Books*. Aru wished her captor and his entourage would stay longer in this town and that she could have had a chance to explore on her own.

At the far end of the cove they came to a landing where fishing boats were moored. Blackbuck with his full retinue already waited there, standing in the shade of a raised cobblestone plaza that overlooked the water. Aru's group would need to board quickly, as the touchdown area was small and they must depart before the second balloon arrived.

This would be Aru's first time in the air. Although quite excited to go aloft, in truth she would have been happier if Aranieda could have accompanied her in human form. The aircraft arrived in all its grandeur, and with a breathy surging sound and a strange clicking. It hovered above as it readied for landing; the balloon was gigantic, much larger than Aru had anticipated. Ropes were tossed down to be caught by assistants on the ground. The clicking sound ceased. The huge upright wheel stopped revolving.

Seen from below, the whole thing looked remarkable. It showed an outstanding blend of comfortable tradition and the latest innovation. The gondola of this vehicle was similar to the body of a fine horse-drawn stagecoach. Scrollwork offset the large unglazed windows and surrounded a fantastic enamel panel on the door depicting a painted bunting in flight. The front end of the coach had a giant carriage-type wheel of some sort attached right in the center, as if it were an enormous faucet handle. A pair of propellers spun at the rear.

The pilot stood on the roof, operating the burners and calling out instructions to the ground crew. He had a thick white handlebar moustache. The craft landed with apparent ease on the tiny cobbled square.

Aru's heart pounded as Blackbuck's valet ushered her up the steps and into the coach. In the plush interior, she saw seats and lower walls padded and upholstered in the finest burgundy-tinted leather. The wallpaper was a beautiful silk damask, very tasteful with stripes and tiny rosebuds and trimmed in gold leaf. A small crystal chandelier hung from the center of the ceiling, beneath an open skylight. Blackbuck positioned himself facing the front. His steward motioned Aru to take a seat facing the rear. "Welcome aboard my dirigible thermal airship," said Blackbuck to Aru.

Several other passengers boarded, although many more could have fit in. Next to Aru sat a colorful character who was presented to her by Blackbuck as Mr. Variegat. "How do you do?" said Aru politely, reaching to shake the man's hand.

"Thank you for asking!" said Mr. Variegat with delight, grabbing hers and holding it to his bosom. "I'm feeling just wonderful, and I must tell you I don't think I've ever enjoyed such a fine morning as this. Such a lovely little town, did you notice the scent of the azaleas, and, oh! the mignonette! Did you get a chance to try the ice cream shop?" He giggled and nudged her. "They have sprinkles!" Gently giving Aru back her hand, he added, "And how are you finding this precious day, my dear?"

The fellow had strange bulgy eyes, and that, together with his narrow face and quite disproportionately thin limbs, made Aru wonder if he might be a tropical fish. He certainly had those characteristics of pattern throughout his clothing. However, he had an extremely wide mouth with thin lips and he didn't smell like a fish.

"It is a lovely day," agreed Aru, smiling. She glanced out the window and noticed an advertisement for a toy store painted on the side of a nearby warehouse. There, depicted in a curvy, organic style, clowns and flower fairies peeked out from behind the tall and shiny green lettering. In addition to these, a great crowd of other fabulous creatures engaged in all sorts of delightful play. Among them a hobgoblin rode a hobby horse, and a short-legged gnome pulled a wheeled duck along. A winged ballerina blew bubbles which floated over her companions, several cats shared a ride on a sled, and down in the corner a clown in checkered diamonds played at shooting marbles with a skunk. Aru couldn't quite read some of the words because a single vine of morning glory, overgrown with trumpet-shaped flowers and heart-shaped leaves, had climbed right across the sign to extend in a tangle along the eaves above.

A big, long-haired white donkey was sniffing at these vines, and other donkeys were standing nearby, patiently waiting for the fishmongers to load their baskets. One pelican-looking woman had been haggling with a customer, but they'd stopped their activity to watch the balloons.

Aru looked back at Mr. Variegat, who was still grinning at her.

"Can you say," asked Mr. Variegat, "the following? 'Outraged, a fierce thrush rustled twigs in umbrage.' Quickly, now?" Aru repeated this fairly easily, so with a grin the man presented her another: "Sadly, these six sick sheeps' sleek silk sheets slipping swiftly slide asunder."

She couldn't say this quickly without laughing and saying "slick" rather than "sleek" or "sick shilts" rather than "silk sheets."

"Have you heard this old one?" she asked: "Because several belugas blew bugles, they blundered the Barnacle Bay brewery burglary."

After Mr. Variegat had giggled and speedily articulated his way through the phrase—once in his normal voice and again in a falsetto—Aru smiled and looked back out the window. She saw rooftops and the river down below. How could she not have felt the balloon rise? In an abrupt refusal to cooperate, Aru's heart leapt into her throat. Therefore, she had to gasp in order to breathe.

And now, with some terribly loud hissing squeaks the clicking sound started again and the great wheel began turning and they floated in a southerly direction, right over the ridge. But Aru couldn't look out the window for more than a moment.

Fear, cold and white, enveloped her. She'd had no idea this would happen. Struggling for breath, she found that tears were coming from the outer corners of her eyes. She searched for a handkerchief. Blackbuck reached across and handed her one.

"There, there," he said. "No worry, Aru, the airship is perfectly safe."

Aru nodded, but kept gulping air. She felt herself submerging into raw terror, thicker and all the more gripping of her insides as she succumbed. Though she'd only just met him, she grabbed Mr. Variegat's gloved hand in both her own. He patted her hand tenderly, and then placed his own hand on the back of her head, encouraging her to bury her face in his shoulder, which she did. ("You nearly squished me!" Aranieda scolded later.) In his kindly voice, Mr. Variegat whispered, "Breathe slowly, my pet, everything will be all right."

After a few minutes, embarrassed, she looked up from Mr. Variegat and sat upright. But it was no good. With a quiet moan she leaned her head down toward her own shoulder, making her body stiff and as small as possible. She tried breathing deliberately, slowly, blowing gently on the outward breaths. This she quickly gave up in frustration. Possessed by fear, she had no patience.

The others continued polite conversation in an attempt to preserve Aru's dignity, what was left of it. Gradually, as she listened to discussion of the latest regional news, the terror surrounding Aru lifted, her panic replaced by hollow distress. She wanted to close her eyes but she couldn't. She had to watch everything, to protect herself. Only her will could keep them safe.

Aru didn't want to join the conversation, or look at the spectacular view she knew she was missing. When she did speak, it was to ask about the clicking noise. The woman sitting across from her explained that the great wheel served as part of the propulsion system which controlled the direction the airship traveled. The rim was filled with rhinoceros beetles, who, when exposed to lamplight, would scurry and cause the wheel to turn, powering the propellers at the rear. The pilot simply controlled the beetle lamp, the air in the balloon envelope, and the angle of the propellers. Aru had a vague thought about the expense of importing such exotic beetles as workers.

When the craft wasn't turning, when it merely drifted on the wind, it flew in an eerie silence. However, as they continued to travel through the air and nothing catastrophic took place, Aru calmed a bit more. She peeked out the window.

"We are up so high!" she whispered. She'd never seen a view like this, not even from the Opal Heights peaks. A pleasant thrill reminded Aru about the joy of relaxing and having fun. The feeling left quickly. She sat back and closed her eyes for a moment, wishing it were the following day and this flight only a memory.

"Courage, dear," said Mr. Variegat to Aru. "New things! Adventures! What is there to fear more than looking back on a dull life?" He laughed. "Come—" he said, winking at her. He pulled a telescope out of his pocket. He looked through it for a moment and then offered it to Aru.

"Oh. No thank you." She made an effort to smile.

"Please, just have a tiny peek!" He pressed the telescope into her hands and sat back expectantly.

Not wanting to offend, Aru chose a small lake as a point of reference and aimed the thing out the window. It wasn't a telescope. It was a kaleidoscope. She turned the mechanism to watch brilliant floral patterns evolve and transform, and she couldn't help but softly utter noises. "Oooh," and "Aaah!" she said.

The kaleidoscope images appeared out of nothingness, to swell and divide in a glassy rhythm. Each striking detail blossomed or folded until lost in multiple euphorias of color and grand patterns. Pansy-blue petals elongated to velvety purple iris, crowded away by an apricot starburst which then riffled into arrangements of fern and lace amid breathtaking clusters of labial roses. For every instant a new thrill, each tiny moment displayed pattern ideas precious as wildflowers in their brief, unpossessable beauty.

Sharing this wonderful instrument with the other passengers helped to bring Aru out of her protective shell and into their conversation. She started to enjoy the aircraft ride, mostly. An old gentleman pointed out some of the landmarks below, and explained to her that the reason she didn't feel the wind was that they were traveling right along with it. Through the skylight Aru could see the white-mustached pilot working the controls above. He was so busy, and seemed so competent that he reminded her of some sort of a wizard. All these things were comforting. She did wish the pilot would quit honking rudely at birds.

When Blackbuck was handed the kaleidoscope he looked through it, but apparently only as a social gesture. He had a quick peek through the scope and then a glance toward Aru. He didn't seem to receive any joy from the beauty; he had a look of condescending patience at this bit of fuss about a child's toy. Aru smiled at him anyhow, doing her best to keep him believing she could ever develop an interest in him.

They traveled on for a while, and right when Aru realized she was having fun they looked down to see the great house of Anemone with its woods and meadows. Beyond it, the fishing village of Amryliw. Open ocean stretched across the horizon. Aru thought about what Aranieda had said when she described Anemone, and it was true. Standing among the lush and flowery coastal foothills, it was the most picturesque and glorious palace you can imagine.

The beetles worked hard as the pilot maneuvered into position. Aru closed her eyes and braced for the impact, but they landed so gently it took her a moment to realize they had done so. After climbing the steps down to the wide flagstone trail, Aru felt strange walking on the solid ground again.

Mr. Variegat linked arms with both Aru and the woman in the gold brocade dress who had been seated on their left, and he began chattering happily as they proceeded along the pathway across the lawn toward one of Anemone's principal entrances.

"Oh goodness, I've left my hat on the transport," said he, excusing himself and patting his pockets as if checking for his watch. "Be a darling, won't you?" he said to a steward. "Please go and fetch it for me. It's a yellow silk one, easy to spot." Aru was certain that Mr. Variegat's hat was blue, but when the man produced it from the coach, sure enough it was golden yellow, with an amber band.

She didn't mention it to anyone, but as they all walked down the trail toward the palace Aru noticed a lizard scurrying away into the border of freesia.

Aranieda kept an apartment at Anemone, and so she quietly proceeded there upon arrival and set up housekeeping with the intent of appearing as if she'd returned weeks earlier. Aru's own accommodation proved to be an absolutely extravagant suite in the same wing as Blackbuck's living chambers. The Warden brought Aru to her new home, and showed her the grand entry and sitting room. These were fashionably appointed, a bit garish for Aru's taste. The rooms also included a small and sunny morning room, and even a private bath, but the real jewel of this apartment was the bedroom.

Although largely octagonal, and ringed with heavy floral draperies falling against the tall casements, the chamber also had a dormer alcove with a window seat. Painted limestone plaster gave the walls a cloudy sage color, brought to ground by a deep moss shade on the wooden moldings. Someone had painted leafy, branchy stems above the wainscoting, full of lavender-petaled flowers, and sprinkled with birds. One solitary bird, perched high on a door frame, looked painted by a child. An embroidered bedquilt of silver grey complemented all the greens, and daylight filtering with a blush of pink through the sheer bed curtains gave the whole room a dreamy glow.

This was a place for rest and relaxation, and as much as Aru had a distaste for Blackbuck's extravagance and relentless attempts to impress her, she did love the room. Freckled flower petals in a wooden bowl scented the air. In the evenings bright flashes of fairy light covered the lawns and gardens below her balcony as masses of fireflies went about their courtship soirée.

In her first days at Anemone, Aru spent much of her time in this room. Sometimes she cried in the night, for missing Nrouhw and for the pain of having to pretend to be receptive to Blackbuck's wooing, even while deeply in mourning. Blackbuck's self-regarding conceit still couldn't let him see how insensitive, how horrible, that was. And aside from all that, the man was nearly her father's age and he was an absolute cur.

Blackbuck sent Aru gifts of fruit, rare orchids, or spice cake on nearly a daily basis. He had a kadupul plant delivered, and other night-blooming exotics. He hired doves to serenade her through the open balcony doors. He seemed to believe that Aru had begun to appreciate him and that it was unlikely she would attempt to leave his fabulous palace. There were no longer restrictions on where she could go, beyond the dictates of common manners. As the days went by at Anemone, Aru saw less and less of the Warden. The woman did appear now and then to deliver private messages from Blackbuck or to help Aru dress for the more formal occasions.

Something no one had mentioned to Aru about the coastal area was that rather frequently, at least every few days, the ground shook. Sometimes the walls moved enough to rattle the curios on the shelves and make the chandeliers swing. Aru asked the Warden about the quakes. She didn't look at Aru when she explained that the tremors had been occurring more and more often due to a seething buildup of pressure underground.

When the day of the banquet arrived, the Warden came inching along in her too-small shoes to escort Aru to the dinner. The two of them wound their way through passage, court, and gallery to the great hall, and when they reached their destination she guided Aru down the red carpeted stairs as she was announced, and then left her to her seat at the raised and canopied top table. Most of the two dozen guests waited in their places already. At first Aru recognized only Blackbuck, seated a couple of settings to her right. With some relief she noticed Mr. Variegat giggling with a young queen seated next to him. He dabbed at the corners of his mouth with a royal blue handkerchief.

The lovely sound of a violin ensemble came from behind her, and as she looked around for the musicians she discovered them to be a good number of club-winged manakin birds hidden among the potted flowers and waterfalls on the face of the stone wall.

On Aru's left was a young man in a wheelchair. He sat in a regal posture, his special chair ornate, with a tall back of carved mahogany. Three things gave away this prince's species immediately: his protruding, wistful eyes; his particularly broad mouth; and his quite distinctive fingers. He was a friendly fellow, and talkative. Certainly a frog.

Aru soon relaxed into conversation with him. They spoke about the attractiveness of Blackbuck's estate and how pleasant these coastal lands were in general, and then as the subject of the prince's own life came up he gave her an explanation for his injured condition. "Ah yes. The chair," he sighed. "An unfortunate accident. Friends and I were mistaken for edible frogs while at a swimming party when I was vacationing in the south."

As they nibbled on peppered cucumber slices and smoked salmon, he and Aru admired the table and its settings. The Queen on Aru's right commented that she'd not seen silver piccolo sterling of this type since her childhood.

"Such a shame there won't be a dance," she added. "The dresses are so lovely." Her delicate hand with a sweeping gesture pointed out the great poofs and folds of exotic fabrics surrounding each lady's chair. "That delightful hyacinth—is that one a silk from the eastern continents? I'd so love to witness the spectacle of these masterpieces of stitchery circulating all about the room."

Aru agreed. The women looked so soft and crisply feminine in their embroidered silk and satin, their ribbons and delicate summer shawls.

One elderly lady, dressed in the dull black of mourning, following the customs of her generation, had on a cap and veil that had so many fussy taffeta flowers and black feathers and drapes of dark silk tulle that one could scarcely see her face. Quite tall and stately, despite her advanced age, she was coiffed and manicured to perfection, like the image of someone on a coin. She looked as if she smelled of lavender and camphor. Yet there was something a little off about this woman, Aru couldn't quite determine what it was.

The soup was brought, and they had wine, and then one of the guests arose to deliver a speech. Humorous toasts and even lengthy orations were common throughout the meal at these sorts of affairs along the coast, and so Blackbuck had no reason to raise an eyebrow. One woman, a queen belonging to the House of Alstroemeria, spoke in an engaging manner about the exceptional bounty of their vicinity. She described wondrous places Aru knew nothing about and she received nods of recognition from the diners. How fortunate they all were to be property holders in a realm of such spectacular beauty and contentment.

Splashes of old lace on her sea-green gown along with her perfectly refined but slightly chirpy voice made Aru think the queen must be a sea animal, maybe a dolphin; perhaps she knew Squee's family. The lady went on to introduce the subject of the hypogeous snails and the coastal community's delightful fortune in having a source of them. She only briefly mentioned her concern about the disease the snails carried and she hinted that precautions needed to be set in place. She also brought up the problem of the lizards and said that she hoped a solution would be found soon.

All during the speaker's pleasantly-voiced observations, Aru's eyes kept drifting back to the elderly lady in black. Some little thing about her posture, the way she moved. It just didn't seem quite right to Aru. Hold on, what was that showing through the gap in her veil? Right there; where it had slipped just a bit from her temple. It looked—A glimpse of spiral horn, shiny black. Lekki! Aru suppressed a laugh.

Over the courses of the grand meal two more quests spoke, focusing on the disease carried by the snails. A consensus was reached that something needed to be done; research must be funded in finding a cure for the crippling and devastating disease. Certainly their gracious host would be generous in supporting this deeply needed research.

But this consensus did not, after all, include Blackbuck.

"These statistics you quote are false!" he declared, standing before them in his crimson tailcoat and holding his cane as if it were a sceptre. "Quite false. Obviously, one of my competitors in business has duped the lot of you into believing these stories about unrest and disease. Yes, several of the fishermen in the poorest villages have come down with something, but this is normal, happens every year. Nothing to be worried about. Absolutely nothing to do with the hypogeous snails." He ardently refused to contribute to the cure for the disease in any way, and furthermore made it clear that he had nothing to do with the disease or its spread. His guests were rather shocked but remained politely quiet, only whispering among themselves while they finished their stuffed peppers pinot grigio.

As the desserts were laid out, the room was noticeably more hushed than it had been previously. Spectacular bouquets of dahlias, zinnias, and roses were gracefully arranged on the tables. Each blossom turned out to be an artful cupcake wrapped in dark green tissue paper. The baskets of melt-in-the-mouth whipped raspberry almond bark; the rainbow-filled cream puff swans on iridescent glass saucers: all these niceties received less appreciation than they were due. Blackbuck's neighbors sat puzzling as to why the man had invited them to achieve a solution to the problem of the snail disease and now spurned them and acted as if they were beggars come to call. During his response Blackbuck had insulted several of them personally, even commenting on the weight of one of his guests.

This was the situation when Aranieda slipped in through a side door unannounced and scurried across the hall to tap on a crystal wine glass with a spoon and demand the room's attention.

461

Aru thought Aranieda's unfaltering poise impressive. She dressed appropriately for the occasion yet remained true to her barbarous tenor. The sapphire blue dress clung to her legs and flared out below the knee, and her evening gloves matched. Over this dress, tailored and sleeveless, a green leather tunic drew tight across the curves of her bosom and abdomen. An embossed golden gorget covered her shoulders and sternum, and gold combs studded with eight large diamonds kept her thick braided hair wrapped fast about the crown of her head.

Aranieda removed her glasses, folded them, and tucked them away. "I require your attention for just a moment," she announced. Then she looked around the room with her big dark eyes. "Grievous news has just arrived from Erinaceu City. This news concerns the dreadful scourge which you have been discussing here today in the lovely halls of Anemone. I am aware that your majesties have assembled here in order to work toward discovery of a solution to the problem. Your intentions are honorable and deserve recognition. But I regret to inform you that you are quite likely too late. All may be lost.

"My name is Madam Aranieda Cleome S. Earetikle, as many of you know I am Vice-Magistrate of the court of your host, Mr. Avariceo Blackbuck." In all this time Aru had no idea that Aranieda held such a high office under Blackbuck's authority.

Aranieda went on to say, "I have recently been informed that prominent microbiologists at Erinaceous College at the Lliw Anhygoel University have made a terrifying discovery. As a result of our own intrusion into the caverns below our soil, the bacteria has begun to spread, not only to the surface of our world, but beyond those caverns and into the world below. Yes, the disease has gone into the Underworld. Two cases of the disease have been reported there, according to the anecic worm council. This means that the lives of all those who live below are at great risk, because those people have less ability than we to resist this bacteria. Eventually, this microbe could cause the demise of them all. You must act now, you must raise awareness of the peril of this disease, and you must each do everything within your power to see that a way is found to halt this epidemic by interrupting the spread of the microorganisms. Your own families are at risk, as well. Most importantly, do not serve or eat hypogeous snails."

While Blackbuck's guests looked around in horror, he stood up, fuming, and called out a denial of it all. Aranieda was escorted from the room by a pair of well-dressed thugs. It was an evening to remember.

The very next morning Aru used the excuse of her menses to spend the day in the mossy woods which bordered Anemone's grounds to the southeast. There in the forest she met Aranieda, and they hiked together south through the cedar trees, maple and dogwood, and out into the countryside, having left two young ladies-in-waiting in an old empty woodcutter's shack with playing cards, some opium, and a bottle of brandy.

The early mist dissipated, revealing a light and sunny day. An old rutted wagon track led them past tulip farms in all their glory and barnyards scattered with poultry. Silver spangled chickens, and speckled, and red barred ones, lace-patterned hens, long-tailed roosters, and silkies too, all these scratched and fluttered about. A small party of peacocks stood on the ancient thatch of a cow shed near the road. There were windmills all along the route, busy grinding corn and wheat, and large spinning windwheels to generate electric power, some with satin ribbons flapping in the breeze.

The two passed a plum tree heavy with fruit, but Aranieda cautioned Aru not to touch it. The Baron claimed ownership of those plums, she said, and he was a big guy who could be cranky and mean. People knew to leave that tree alone. Gashes in the tree trunk, huge claw marks, made Aru disinclined to argue.

They did come across some apricots, though, wonderful little ones juicy with flavor, and some sweet dark cherries. The cherries reminded Aru of the cherry rhubarb pies her grandmother taught her to make, sweet hours in the warm kitchen, laughing together.

At a crossroads, children were out working in a schoolhouse garden. Aru and Aranieda leaned over the fence to talk to the students and admire their crops. The garden was truly a thing to be proud of. Nasturtiums grew among the healthy purple cabbages and young broccoli, they had mustard, strawberries, leeks and peppers. A boy showed off a harvest basket full of baby carrots, radishes, and onions.

The teacher carried lizard bells: old iron cow bells dangling from a long walking stick. Occasionally he would place the base of the stick on the ground and waggle it to ring the bells. Lizards could hear the deep tone through both the air and ground and they would clear away from the area.

Beyond the school and then several small fields, a cluster of cottages shared a lake's edge. There wood ducks swam through lillies and among the dangling willows. One house had a horseshoe-shaped door. Narrow front yards, each well-tended and neat as a pin, met the road with stone gateposts and wisteria-covered archways. Sitting next to each of these was a nasty, fly-infested pile of trash.

Aranieda noticed Aru looking at the garbage and so she explained, "The Semi-Arboreal Omnivore Federation of Labor called a strike again. They haven't collected the refuse for several weeks now. The workers, mostly raccoons and opossums, have a reasonable grievance. I believe they've almost reached an agreement."

"But such a smelly mess. It's too bad," said Aru.

As they neared their destination they passed more homes tucked here and there among the fields and orchards. Aru and Aranieda talked about the Long-Eared Jerboa and the Jerboa's underground bungalow they would be visiting. Excited in anticipation, because Aldrei and Aeon would be there, Aru also felt odd. She hadn't seen these two since Nrouhw had gone.

Aru learned from Aranieda, as they walked along, that the Jerboa had known Lekki's mother, and through her had made the acquaintance of Mr. Blackbuck. This is how, several years before, the Jerboa had heard the rumors about Aru and how she reputedly had the ability to see the lizards, a whispered-about, supposedly mythical quality that had become known locally as lézarvoyance.

Aranieda explained that the Jerboa had tunneled too deep, and angered Grmhrel, the houndish, horned guardian of the passageways between terrestrial worlds and the underworlds, a natural being whom she and Aru had talked about previously. As a result of this transgression, the Jerboa was obliged to make a bargain with Grmhrel.

As powerful as Grmhrel was, he could not leave his underground domain. His pet lizards roamed the surface and suffered injury and he had no way to recall them. Lézarvoyance among the surface dwellers would be of benefit to Grmhrel because the lizards could find some protection, and someday he would find a way to return them home to their natural environment.

So the Jerboa told Grmhrel about Aru, and Grmhrel agreed to allow the Jerboa to tunnel again once Aru followed Blackbuck's plan of marrying Lekki and producing children. Aldrei had assured the Jerboa he would help Blackbuck achieve this goal. The future generations at Anemone with lézarvoyance would appease Grmhrel for centuries to come, and the Jerboa would be able to tunnel freely.

As they walked on, Aru stewed about the audacity of these attempts to use her in such a way. How frustrating to endure friendship with a fairy hooligan of Aldrei's sort. Why should she even meet this Jerboa? This thought was still between her ears when something soothing and otherworldly seeped in to replace it with a feeling of childlike optimism. Happiness. It was a music that came, a strange and enticing sound, haunting and beautiful.

"Here we are," said Aranieda.

In wonder, Aru focused her eyes on some sort of tall wooden sculpture up ahead. Built high on a roadside hill, the arching, curvy shape silhouetted against the sky. A closer look made her realize it was a great harp, source of the fairy music, played by the wind. Aru had never heard a wind harp before, and it was a lovely thing. But a set of narrow steps stole her gaze, steps which followed a crooked crevice part way up the cliffy hillside. Each step had been painted a lollipop color, bright and shiny, and up at the top of the stairway was the balcony of a home built right into the cliff face. The old striped awning was nearly covered by passion flower vines, and studded with pinwheels spinning wildly away amongst the blossoms. And standing on the balcony, a man—Aeon!

Aru gathered her skirts and hurried up the stairway, and when she reached the top she threw her arms around Aeon, with tears of joy, and also sorrow for Nrouhw's absence, leaking from her eyes. Aeon returned her hug with a warmth of his own, and introduced her to some visitors who were just leaving.

ZrrBurr, Beazul, and Beazul's cousin ZenZirr had been sipping strawberry cordials with Aeon on the balcony and discussing nothing in particular. Yet when Aru arrived, followed shortly by Aranieda, they began darting around collecting their things; Beazul kept repeating, "Busy busy, I'm so busy busy." Odd little needle-nosed people, they were dressed in gaudy green and purple sequin tailcoats. As a nervous mannerism, when not engaged in conversation all three persisted in humming bits of the same old song. It was one of those simple tunes that won't stop returning to mind.

After they had gone, Aeon mentioned that in the past hummingbirds were a normal variety of house wren. Before sugary caffeinated drinks became popular among the birdhouses. Aru said she hadn't known.

Inside the bungalow Aru's eyes needed to adjust to the reduced light. The entryway joined a tiled and carpeted corridor which they followed awfully far, going not quite straight through the hill. Toward the end of the tunnel, Aeon ushered them through a narrow doorway. There was Aldrei, who rose from a dining table to greet them. With him was the Jerboa, who stood only as high as the chair seat. "Excuse the mess," said Aeon. "We were recently all three down at the dust baths."

Aldrei grinned and brushed off the seats with a whisk broom so Aru and Aranieda could sit down. They had to step carefully, as the floor was scattered with hundreds of little painted tin wind-up toys. Hundreds of them.

The Jerboa welcomed the guests and offered them some spicy gumdrops. Aldrei laughed and showed Aru and Aranieda how the two had just been playing with some candles and hand mirrors and an old phénakistiscope. The images were of a rabbit boxing a kangaroo. As the disk spun, a baby kangaroo popped up out of mama's pocket, and punched the rabbit, who fell, tumbling over backward onto its feet, ready to box again.

Then, of course, the ladies must see Aldrei's favorites of the Jerboa's wind-up toys and what they could do. The tumbling tricycle-riding duck with the umbrella had an especially wonderful character.

The Jerboa's dining room was small, formal in design, with furnishings of sophisticated taste, traditional in every detail. The most exquisite tea cups and plates were on display in the mahogany breakfront, along with crystal glassware, and silver serving dishes sat on the buffet. However, a large fish mobile hung over the table. A dozen tropical fish, made of blown glass, circulated with the movements of the air. They were so brilliantly lifelike Aru could nearly see their frowny fish mouths repeating, "bob . . . bob . . . bob," as they floated in the eddies of the gentle draft. Across the room, a centuries-old hearth of brick with a fire in the grate supplied flickery backlight to a gorgeous stained glass fireplace screen with a cricket design.

Aeon had prepared a midday meal. Everyone filled their plates with his fresh-baked marbled tarts, and with chilled shrimp, smoked salmon, purple potatoes, deviled eggs, pickled capers, fresh green beans, slices of papaya, watermelon, and oranges.

"It is indeed scrumptious, isn't it," said Aldrei. "Aeon is a masterful cook; we can depend on his unique ability to sneeze in the cuisine."

While Aldrei and his friends laughed loudly, and, as usual, for much longer than the remark deserved, the Jerboa patted Aldrei on the back. Aranieda looked at the ceiling.

Then Aranieda mentioned that she had a couple of questions. Blackbuck's hawks had been watching her persistently, she explained, and so she was having trouble gathering information. Aranieda wanted to know if Blackbuck had any success with the replica wand.

"Mmm, you must understand that Grmhrel is in a particularly volatile humor," the Jerboa told her. After a sip of vodka . . . a bite of potato. The Jerboa seemed in no hurry to answer. "Of course, Nieda, as you know, the disease has killed off most of his fireflies. The little midges no longer light up his crystal cavern to create those shadows he so loves to command. The few of the flaring little fuckwits that remain have come up through the well at Anemone, all as a result of your Blackbuck's opening it. Grmhrel has lost his shadows. He sits grumbling in the dark. He's lost most of his Visyrn up the well, as well. Greener pastures, so to speak."

"Excuse me," said Aru. "His what, did you say?"

"His lizards." replied the Jerboa.

"What did you call them?"

"The lizards are Visyrn, Grmhrel's little friends. This is the old-time name for them."

"Visyrn?"

Aru was quiet for a moment while she put thoughts together in her mind. The gilded clock on the mantel ticked as a metronome, following the agitated tempo of her pulse in half-time. Nobody spoke, because the look on Aru's face was prelude to an announcement.

"I didn't realize," she said at last. "I believed, for some time now I've believed, that I am tormented by something godlike: in a vision, some sort of visitation. Since I was a small child. Something endless comes, a great nothingness."

The fish mobile tinkled softly, and Aru stared at it for a moment. "It clutches my very soul, it feels as if it is dissolving me entirely. Honestly, several times I've spoken with it, a presence which comes to me as 'Visyrn.' Or, more accurately, it speaks to me, there never is true conversation. A terrifying feeling when it comes. I—I thought it was a celestial entity of the void, an end; the end of everything, never to exist, deepest fear—I didn't know it was the lizards. The lizards!"

"Lizard visitations!" laughed Aldrei.

Then Aru stood up, seeming to rise to half-again her height, and with her hands splayed on the table she leaned forward and stared straight down into the eyes of Aldrei. Her voice sounded gruff and guttural. "You knew! You knew about it all. All along, didn't you! I'm aware of your deceit, Aldrei, how you've ill-used me. All this time. Since the day we met. Since before then! You've known the whole story, and you didn't tell me. Instead, you've done nothing but manipulate me. And Nrouhw." She sat down again. "Nrouhw, too," she repeated.

Aldrei, not one to care a stick about angry words, answered serenely. "Our worm has turned," he said, feigning pride but with genuine pleasure. He smiled at Aru. "My, how you've grown." (*No I haven't. More manipulation,* thought Aru.) "And in such a short time. You never would have confronted me in such a way."

"I wasn't angry enough before," said Aru.

"You *were,*" Aldrei said. "You know, Aru, the reality of the situation is that you know next to nothing. But of course you are changing.

Transforming. As does everything in nature. Wisdom will come. A seasoned heart may ably face what is distinct from any reality that others have ever conceived or known." He looked at his pocket watch.

"Such a lonely thing to say," muttered Aru.

"Loneliness is often associated with looking in the wrong places," said the Jerboa. Then turning to the others, "Now let us return to the subject at hand. He truly has a problem, does that Grmhrel, and the Blackbuck has done a poor job of appeasing him."

Aldrei grinned. "The man Blackbuck is a walking sack of human foibles. He has only the most cursory understanding of magic. He tried to pass his facsimile of the diamond dragon off to Grmhrel, and would have been squashed to a pulp, aye, for his ignorant trick, if his Lady's grandmama hadn't been who she was."

"The copy," continued the Jerboa, "wasn't a sovereign diamond like the original. It couldn't hold the depthless, second-rate spells the oaf did manage to perform over it. Never could that wand light the caverns below. It was not the dragon carving that concerned Grmhrel, only the magic put into the first diamond as it was carved. As you remember, the Opali king was having the rock carved as a gift for his queen. Then Blackbuck imbued it with his own hopes and spells. There is much greater magic in that original diamond."

"Blackbuck should've resorted to science, not magic," said Aru.

Aeon spoke softly, "That man will never achieve a pill bug's pocket-change using a scientific approach. He hasn't the brains. Besides, science is what keeps us grounded in reality, magic is what keeps us real." Aeon rubbed his head against Aldrei's shoulder with nearly enough force to knock him over. "Communing with nature, speaking with the stones, that reminds him of who he is. Blackbuck is a sorcerer, not a scientist."

"And yet a greedy fool to ignore the science, deny it all for his own profit," said Aranieda. "Did he have any success at all?"

"Blackbuck doesn't realize how near he came to losing his life by attempting to speak with Grmhrel," replied the Jerboa. "Grmhrel no longer cares for even the original diamond anymore, if in fact Blackbuck could produce it. Blackbuck's deal is off. Will he give up on snails? Unlikely."

The five of them conversed for quite some time about a variety of things, but this was the information that Aranieda had come for. She also wanted to let the three Long Ears know that Lekki desired to meet with them to discuss a plan to help the underworld people.

Aranieda seemed to be fueled by a particularly wild spirit these days. She acted with an overzealousness, perhaps. Quite brazenly she met Aru the next day in town and went with her to a lovely tea house hidden among the stately shrubbery of an old rose garden.

Along the way the two passed a sad sight, a burned-out cottage, someone's dear little home which had been completely devastated by fire. "The woman who lived there stepped on a lizard," explained Aranieda.

Aru had become accustomed to seeing lizards scurrying across the path whenever she walked outdoors. It was surprising they weren't trod upon more often, really. But the whole subject made her feel uncomfortable now. She wanted to think about something else.

A morning drizzle had left everything damp, but the sun endeavored to poke through. The tea house had white linen tablecloths, and delicate tea sets on display. There were varieties of fresh roses on each table. Several of these tables were outside, in front of the windows, nice and dry under an awning. That is where the friends sat, to enjoy the sweet, rain-washed air. It was pleasant, a homey place. The wood of the storefront was painted a dark blood-red. The lettering of the signage was all in gold leaf. A collection of broadcloth banners hung just inside the windows, weighted by tassels and bells.

Aru enjoyed the feeling of normalcy, simply sitting with her good friend, sipping a lemongrass tea, with lime, and breathing in the scent of the roses. They sat for quite a while, discussing the problems at hand, of course, but mostly they talked about little, everyday things. It felt refreshing. The tea had a fine flavor, and Aru had several cups. Eventually she needed to go through to the rear and use the lavatory.

Weaving her way between the tables, Aru passed shelves crowded with bric-a-brac and decorative tea tins.

The waiter, a big spongy-handed man with thick tortoiseshell eye-glasses, held his head forward stiffly on his long neck, moving like a man much older than his years. He smiled a friendly smile. His upper lip was pointy. He moved so slowly that he was aggravating to watch.

He and his wife owned the tea house. A woman of soft demeanor, and friendly, the missus was at the same time rather a shy and quiet lady. She habitually wiggled her nose and gently ground her teeth, and she spent her time hopping back and forth between the service counter and a back room.

On Aru's return trip to the table, she halted right in her tracks. She moved into the shadows behind some dangling ferns, and peered breathlessly across the room and out the window. Blackbuck was seated in her chair. He and Aranieda were exchanging angry words. Aru could hear them through the open door.

Blackbuck stood up, pulling something out of his satchel Aru couldn't quite see. "What is that—?" Aranieda had a strange look on her face. "You wouldn't dare."

It was some kind of a spray can. *Pfsst!* Blackbuck sprayed Aranieda right in the eyes! Aranieda shrieked, covering her face with her hands. She curled into a ball, dropping off the chair onto the ground, her legs up in the air. Blackbuck tossed the canister aside, sneezed, and wiped his mouth with a tea napkin. Picking up his cane he strode off as calmly as if he'd just shaken Aranieda's hand and bid her good day.

Before Aru could rush out through the doorway, a man from a nearby table cried, "Great Thunder!!" and flew over to lift Aranieda's head, fanning her. His wife reached her before Aru, also. They were both pelicans, Aru realized later. The wife took charge. "I'm only a dental extractor, not a doctor," she explained, "but I'm certain the most important thing is to get her washed off immediately."

The remaining tea water was lukewarm, so they used that to wash Aranieda's face, and called to the waiter for more water in a bucket. They removed her shawl, which was saturated, and her necklet. Her skin and eyes were red, and she was coughing and gagging uncontrollably. Where was that waiter?

Aru picked up the canister Blackbuck had used. It was a small pump sprayer of the type used in gardens. On the side of it were printed the words Arsenate of Lead along with a series of cautions. She gasped. "Pesticide!" She looked at Aranieda's face. Things did not look good. Aru felt helpless. Then she remembered the little bottle that the beaver had given her. The mithridate. From the day Lekki had returned it to her Aru had kept it in her pocket, hanging from her belt.

Certainly Aru saved Aranieda's life that day, but it was a long time before her friend had her health again. Aranieda spent the following week or so in a cottage Lekki found for her, and Aru didn't dare visit, so her only news of Aranieda's condition came from private messenger sparrows.

In the meantime, Aru remained in the palace, doing her best to give Blackbuck the impression that, despite her disposition, his advances were succeeding. She needed to engage his trust as much as possible. And she must do all this while managing to keep a safe distance from him. If only she could punch him in the face and tell him what she truly thought of him. This deception, so opposite of how she actually felt, was exhausting.

One afternoon a manservant asked if she would be so kind as to help expel a lizard which had got into one of the house's towers. A chamber maid was beside herself because it had scurried across her arm as she was cleaning the windows. Aru was more than happy to oblige, in part because she'd not been invited to that particular section of the house up until now. The room in question turned out to be a quiet study, a mostly forgotten library, in a well-maintained but largely disused area of the south wing. It was a small matter for Aru to find the creature and slip it into a soap tin, ready for careful release by a footman down the well in the lower part of the periwinkle garden.

The library was windowless, and ringed with high bookcase walls. It had wool carpets that featured a windstorm motif in their patterns. It smelled of books and stale sandalwood oil. These books were not handsome matching volumes in tidy sets, but a hodge-podge collection of miscellaneous strays of every size. Aru asked if it would be all right if she lingered for a while. She thought she might like to have a look at some of the books. Perhaps she might borrow one or two? The man, relieved to have the lizard extracted with such a minimum of fuss, didn't see why not.

When she found herself alone, Aru browsed the shelves for a few minutes and then climbed the steep stairs to the dusty loft, where she suspected that the older, more obscure and interesting books might be. She was correct in this presumption. Perhaps it was dumb luck, but it only took her minutes to track down a stack of books on the subject of local mythologies and ancient superstitions. They had titles such as, *The Thunderous Wonders of the Greater Liwiych Area in Ancient Times and the Consequences for Modern Human Life*, and *Sea Mammals that Could Never Populate the Sea*. She brushed dust from the cover of one, to read *Subterranean Ventures and Histories*. This book had no date, but it was an old cloth-bound one and pages were falling out. Aru thumbed through a number of volumes, choosing this old one and several others to bring back downstairs.

She hadn't meant to linger in the library so long. The clock chimed to let her know she had missed the evening meal. It was beautiful, the clock, all fruitwood marquetry and ebony. The weather had turned brisk outside. Aru could hear it: a storm was blowing in. She enjoyed this little room. It felt hidden, protected, private. No fire burned in the grate, but heat must have been rising from below because the atmosphere was quite comfortable. Settled on the sofa, wrapped, just for nestling purposes, in a soft appliquéd quilt, she found a chapter in the old book which was entitled, "Guardian of the Realms Beneath."

Much of the chapter described various awful encounters of persons throughout history with the gatekeeper to the lower world. Some bits of information were of great interest to Aru indeed. Grmhrel, she learned, used to walk the land as a man, many centuries ago. Like Aru, he was a non-transforming person, or at least that's how the legends described him.

One ancient scholar's account claimed that the man Grmhrel had married a Tiruuvan mountain dog woman and raised two daughters and a son. Educated speculation held that he had other wives or romances with women over a period of several hundred years, in the era just before his return to the underground. Several witches in the south of Liwien had written, and were adamant, that a handful of people of their era who had traces of his blood in their veins were gifted with a special ability to see certain demons of the underworld which were quite invisible to the general population. The author of the book had heard various rumors of this type, but through laborious research had come to the conclusion that this was all nonsense. Still, such notions will persist among the uneducated.

Aru wasn't as surprised to read all this as she really ought to have been. Mostly, she was thinking that here was something else Aldrei certainly knew and hadn't shared with her.

She should have been getting tired and thinking of returning to her room, but Aru was filled with the energy of the hunt. Special vitality pumped through her blood because she was in the middle of a project. She wondered if these were Blackbuck's books or if he'd ever looked through them. Could it be possible there were things hidden in these forgotten volumes that even Aldrei didn't know?

So it was that Aru returned to the tower loft, where she shuffled, skimmed, and sorted until the dust drove her back downstairs into the library proper, with an armful of timeworn selections. She dumped the books down onto the desk. Then she opened several volumes to pages she'd bookmarked, and spread them on the desktop. All at once she felt a presence behind her. Aru knew something was there. She was afraid to turn around. She made herself do it.

There was someone. By the door, standing in the shadow of the entryway. Just standing there. Aru's heart froze. Such a shock. A man. Was he real? Who was this? How long had he been there? It wasn't Blackbuck. It wasn't the manservant. Aru tried to focus her eyes after the brightness of the electric reading lamp. She couldn't seem to form words. Was anyone nearby in the palace? Did this person mean to harm her? Silliness! Only a servant, come to escort—

"This is going to come as a bit of a shock . . ." came his voice across the room. Nrouhw! No. Yet as he came forward, out of the shadows, and he came to embrace her, to keep her from falling in the faint that had overtaken her, he felt warm and real, and he smelled like her dreams and her longing, and he laughed, a sort of worried laugh, saying, "Stay with me, Aru, stay with me! Oh, my dear love, breathe, just breathe—"

Aru began to cry, repeating his name over and over. She collapsed as he held her and so he found a chair, holding her in his lap, his arms tight around her until she could calm herself. Aru stared with disbelief into his face, learning it again, touching his features, kissing them. And he kissed hers in the same way. The kissing and embracing, the wave after wave of not believing it could be real, all this went on for quite some time—days, actually, although the venue changed. Aru managed to sneak him back to her apartment, where they spent as much time as possible together with the shades drawn.

After having fallen completely to pieces and then gradually, over time, having pulled herself together, Aru now floundered in swirling euphoria, joy so intense that at times she wailed and seemed to have lost her sanity. Nrouhw cried also, for the relief of having rejoined his lover, and for the sorrow of the pain she had experienced. Aru turned some real anger toward him, too. Irrational, perhaps, but there it was.

The joy of this amazing good fortune made every inch of Aru's body tingle, prickle, feel more alive. A rhapsody of light flooded her perception, and yet everything was a wild blur. The two of them held each other for hours at a time, absorbing one another's feel, their smells, absorbing everything entirely. They made their love with exceptional feelings of well-being. Once, still in her nightgown in the afternoon, Aru pulled away from his embrace and did an outlandish dance, jumping and wiggling and waving her hands in the air. The top part and bottom part of her seemed to be doing completely different things! A few times they danced together, rocking, barely moving, listening to the music of the wind outside with its sighing sounds, and following the shared rhythm of their own breath and blood.

The two spent surprisingly little time talking. Partly this was because he did not yet want to tell her everything, and she, honestly, wasn't wanting to hear about the horrible parts just yet. At any rate, by way of feigned illness and a simple request for privacy, not much was seen or heard of Aru until she and her long-lost love slipped out to attend the meeting which Lekki had finally called. The task of disguising Nrouhw as an old man for the excursion was relatively easy, as he now walked with effort, using a cane. Aru draped herself in a bulky lace headscarf, hoping not to be recognized as she quietly met him on the narrow roadway downhill from the house.

Why Lekki chose to assemble in midday was unclear, but it probably had to do with his selection of a gathering place. A strange choice, it was, for a clandestine meeting involving several people who were lying low. It was an old conservatory, a glasshouse. Lekki commented that the conservatory had always been a place he could go to be alone, and, as he pointed out, no one could listen behind the doors.

On the approach, it looked like an ordinary garden greenhouse, not particularly large or small. It stood on a knoll in a remote area of the grounds, near the southern border of the estate. The structure was framed in handsomely burnished ironwood. Most of the windowpanes were of lead-crystal. The curving glass roof had cupolas and a dome, topped by a weathervane with the vigilant-looking silhouette of a big, fat crow. One of several of the stone labyrinths on the property at Anemone encircled the building, a magical repository for the storage of the surplus winds of autumn. The Blackbuck family had, since ancient times, an interest in the sailing of ships.

As Aru passed in through the doorway, her breath went still. When she spoke she whispered. The space was open and empty, everything had been cleared out except for a couple of wrought iron benches. Astonishingly, the entire floor was a mirror. Reflecting back the re-fracted light that came through those crystal windowpanes, it filled the glasshouse with a display of colors which moved with the shifting of tree branches outside. Sunshine became a spectral spectacle. In the waterlike surface of the floor one could see reflected the intricate lines and architectural elements of the structure in addition to the brilliant watercolor hues that came through the lead window glass. Many of the panes were cracked or chipping, but this only added to the prismatic effects of all the refracted and reflected light. Gentle breaths of wind came through windows up above.

Aru and her companion incognito were the last to arrive. Their appearance together didn't catch anyone by surprise, as Lekki had been the one to communicate with the household servants in order to locate Aru that first evening, and the others present had their ways of keeping up to date on current events. If the truth be told, they'd each known about her beau's arrival even before Aru did. In addition to Lekki, Aldrei and Aeon were present, and also Aranieda, who was in a wheelchair. Aranieda appeared sickly, but her voice came deep and full, if a bit forced. She and Aru talked about what had happened. Of course, Blackbuck would never be held accountable, due to his wealth. Aranieda said that her condition was improving steadily, and she thanked Aru for coming to her aid. She said that Aru looked absolutely radiant. Aldrei gave Nrouhw a gift of some sugar mice.

The gathering had a purpose, but before they got down to business the others wanted to hear the whole of their friend's story. His account began with a foggy memory of waking up broken, stiff with pain and the cold. Hovering over him, the boy Queex, apparently only bruised from the fall, was tickling his face, poking at him. The light was a strange bright blue in the bottom of the narrow crevasse. The henchman hadn't made it. Nrouhw had some broken bones, yet was able to transform, which would enable him to survive. He paused in his telling of the story, and took a deep breath before he went on.

With limited ability to take human form, verbal communication with the boy had been both occasional and difficult. This crack in the glacier went so deep that they had no hope of a rescue attempt. No one would have guessed they had survived.

The crevasse went long to the southeast, downslope, but most of the downhill part was covered by snowbridge. Eventually the boy discovered that the end of it was open, an ice cave accessible from the outside. Unfortunately, this crevasse tunnel was largely filled with scree for some way along. Nrouhw was trapped by the rock debris as man or cat but, as a vole, the boy could easily make his way through.

No amount of convincing, however, could get the boy to go home. He couldn't be persuaded to go for help, either. He couldn't understand or perhaps he feared becoming lost, all alone on the mountain. Queex lived wild as a vole, burrowing himself to sleep at night in the warmth between the cougar's folded foreleg and his heart. He made forays out through the rubble, finding forage somewhere down the mountain, but in his innocent or stubborn faithfulness, he always returned.

When the cougar grew strong enough to slowly, slowly, dig through the rubble, the vole guided him in where to dig. All this while, as he saved his friend's life, the boy could not, or would not, listen to the pleas for him to save himself. Over the weeks that it took to gain strength and then dig his way out of the chasm Nrouhw had been compelled to watch the boy become a man, and then an old man, because he spent so much time in vole form. Queex died of old age on their way down to the river after they had finally gained Nrouhw's freedom.

Whenever they had been together in human form, the little vole called his fellow survivor by the name "Nureek." The cougar name was probably difficult for him to pronounce. Or, it may just have been his playful way. Regardless, upon the death of his little friend, Nrouhw vowed to be known henceforth by the name which Queex had bestowed upon him. It was his way to honor the vole who had given his own life in the act of saving him.

Those present were silent for a moment. Even Aldrei had respect for the one who had perished on the way down the mountain. Aeon shed some tears and then sniffed loudly, wiping his eyes with his sleeve.

Nureek, also, telling the story, had a few tears slip from his eye. But, as he said, they had better get to the business of their meeting. It wasn't wise to linger there too long.

And so Lekki began. "According to what my elders in our community have always told me, things were different years ago. They say that my father, when he was a young man, conducted himself in the manner of a decent human being. He no longer fits this description. And now he has gone so far as to murder Aranieda—" Aranieda looked over her glasses at Lekki. "He thought he had murdered her," Lekki continued. "That was his intention. Due to his position, his bought-and-purchased cohorts, the man is above the law. This action of his, however, for me it is the final straw.

"We are finished with magnanimous attempts to influence him. It is time to truly take matters into our own hands. The man has hurt too many, and so many more are in danger. I have a plan. Some will consider it an absolute perfidy of my filiation, but as we intend to circumvent his rightful authority and achieve a solution to these problems which my father has created, I hope to have the support of any of you who will join me.

"My father holds that reports of the spread of the disease he brought forth are false, or greatly exaggerated. The declarations of doctors and scientists mean nothing to him. As my father has filled his congress with the gullible and the greedy, there is no reasoning with him. He is not true or honest, he hides within himself. Where is the actual Blackbuck anymore, the man behind the monster, the prince my mother married? I do not know. Whatever part of him is real, I have never reached it. Never known it."

It was then that Lekki announced that researchers at Lliw Anhygoel thought they had a cure for the disease. A serum, a special bromide of quinine. Lekki had secretly emptied his trust fund, and also borrowed gold from his father's treasury, in order to finance research (which so far had been quite promising) and the initial manufacture of the medicine.

This was welcome news for the residents of the coastal lands, but there was a larger issue. When Blackbuck opened up the well, and excavated for snails below, he drove some of the creatures of the deep to travel out from those crystal caves and up through other wells, long-unused, into the various underworlds. These creatures had spread the bacteria as they became part of the local diet in each domain, or sometimes they spread the contagion simply through infestation. The inhabitants of several of those worlds had poor immunity to the disease and were now dying in great numbers. They desperately needed a cure. As soon as the medicine was proven, someone would need to get samples of the formula to the people of the underworld. But Grmhrel would let no one down into the caves. Aldrei remarked that it had always been a challenge to get beyond him into the lower worlds. Now, with Grmhrel's increased anger, it was impossible. Not even an insect could pass.

"As you all know," continued Lekki, "Grmhrel would not accept the duplicate wand from my father but we still possess the real one, the diamond with the light that Grmhrel seeks. Although my father has greatly enraged Grmhrel, we are fortunate that Grmhrel would not accept the other wand, for that would have empowered my father further in his destructive enterprises. As it stands, we may hold the ability to appease the Grmhrel and gain passage for messengers."

"We have," said Nureek, "someone to thank for ensuring the second wand's failure. During my time in the crevasse with the little vole, I learned who it was that produced the counter-enchantment on the chips the owls were removing. It was the boy himself. It was Queex who was hexing the owl chips, making the second wand nearly impervious to Blackbuck's spells."

"Well, how do you do, and squeeze a weasel! You don't say!" Aldrei exclaimed, laughing. "That little imp had more than his fair share of gumption."

As they were now aware, it was not the magic of the dragon carving that drew Grmhrel's attention. It was the electricity of power imbued in the diamond, and the inborn potential for light within the rock itself. This was the brightest of diamonds.

Lekki and Aeon together announced that the Jerboa had agreed to help. The Jerboa would break the diamond, and set the tiny pieces onto a cold magic fire for winged fairies to carry about in the caverns. These pieces would create much more light than the wand would have, casting strong shadows for Grmhrel's servitude. This was the bargaining chip they needed. Grmhrel would certainly agree to this, and perhaps the fairies themselves could be the messengers to carry samples of the serum. The type of fairy to enlist had yet to be determined, but as most fairies so adore crystal, it surely wouldn't be a problem to attract them to the idea.

"Destroy the dragon?" exclaimed Aru. She suddenly felt possessive of the wand, a feeling she'd never had before.

"That'd be such a shame," said Nureek. "There is no other way?"

"Our purpose for the diamond hasn't changed," said Aranieda. "Only, the need is even greater now and anything that can be done to convince Grmhrel to allow passage must be done."

"No." Aru couldn't bear the idea of sacrificing the dragon. "It's a matter of convincing Grmhrel to accept the wand. We can reason with him. It's Blackbuck that wronged him, not us."

"Grmhrel is not a man," Lekki told her. "There is no convincing. There is only bargaining. It saddens me also, the thought of destroying such a beautiful thing. But since my father's foolery, Grmhrel will have nothing of wands. Also, it is simply the case that with this strategy a brighter light is to be offered."

As they continued with the discussion, all those present came to agree that the destruction of the diamond was a price that must be paid in order to attempt to save countless lives. There really was no choice, now that the idea had come up. It had to be tried.

It certainly did appear promising that their offer would be accepted, and as they continued to talk about it the mood in the room, inspired by the brilliant display of lights around them, grew more excited and optimistic. Until Aldrei pointed something out.

"Aye, it all sounds like berries and hazelnuts," said he, "but then . . . of course, due to his increased rage, there is no way to meet Grmhrel without being killed. Just who is going to make the bargain with him?"

Aeon agreed, "Grmhrel, never a darling, has suffered a great deal of loss these past few years. And now, to confound the issue, Blackbuck has infuriated him. Yet we have seen a noticeable lack of seismic activity in the area; he has been letting the anger build up, he has become more dangerous than ever."

"In reality, he may kill us all at any moment!" laughed Aldrei.

"Have you considered the Jerboa?" suggested Aranieda. "Having already cultivated a proper rapport with him, perhaps the Jerboa could be the one to—"

"It's not such a good relationship," said Aldrei. "Even the Jerboa, I must say, treads softly toward the monster Grmhrel."

Lekki lifted his chin. "I will do it. It has been my intention all along. My father is the originator of this crisis. It falls to me to take responsibility for it."

"You do carry protection by the fact of your ancestry," pointed out Aranieda. "Having a distant tie to one who once granted Grmhrel a great boon would normally keep you quite safe in his presence. But he has been stewing and boiling down there so much recently, I can't say that even a member of your family would be spared. At best Grmhrel is volatile and unruly. At present, his impulses could easily be disastrous."

"Yes, I am aware of these things, thank you for your concern—" said Lekki, but he was interrupted.

"I'll go," said Aru. "It only makes sense. I can see the lizards. He won't harm me, because I can see the lizards. And I can haggle well. I used to help my father get bottom prices at the market when I was only a child. I have a natural talent for bargaining. I'm the ideal one to approach Grmhrel."

"Too dangerous, Aru!" replied Nureek, and Aeon agreed.

"He isn't a rational being," said Aranieda quickly. "There is no predicting his immediate responses. Lekki should be the one to go, purely for the reason that he is in more athletic condition than you and has a greater chance of getting out of Grmhrel's way quickly, and returning up the well."

"So, that is it, then," said Lekki. "I will be the one."

Soon after this, Lekki's little family arrived from Opal Heights. Since the banquet, Lekki had remained incognito until enough time had passed to disassociate him from the charity ruse he had used on Black-buck. Then he had staged his own arrival at the palace, and had exchanged angry words with his father about Nrouhw and Aru. But he had gone ahead and taken up residence in a handsome villa owned by his father. This home was not on the grounds at Anemone but rather it stood on the flats down by the oceanside in the nearby village of Amryliw. When Mhehh and Sheeki arrived to join him, it was a happy reunion for Aru and Nureek also. It was startling to see how much Sheeki had grown. He was already attempting to burrow and to climb on everything!

Although the friends had given up on influencing Blackbuck to make things right, it seemed prudent to have Nureek remain a secret and for Aru to keep up her charade of the shallowness which ostensibly fostered affection for Blackbuck. Nureek used a few minor spells of his own to improve his old man disguise and he became Aru's new language tutor she'd met at the market. Blackbuck had no interest in this tutor and so didn't pay much attention when he was noticed in the house or nearby.

These were strange days, but happy times. The young friends met now and then for coffee or to walk on the beach. One particularly warm afternoon they all went down to the Festival of the River in Liwiych to watch the parade. They traveled by horse coach, quite an excursion, really, but luckily Sheeki slept most of the way.

While riding together, they talked more about their plans, and about their other friends. Aru let it be known that Aldrei hadn't been completely honest about the Jerboa. "The truth is, it's not that the Jerboa had tunneled too deep. Aranieda recently learned that Grmhrel caught him eating a lizard and hates him as a result. That is why the Jerboa has been helping Grmhrel all this time with his lizard problem, although it is accurate that he needs to regain his favor so he may tunnel again. The three longears insist that it was just the one lizard, but there were specks of lizard all over his dining room when I visited. In fact there was a bit of lizard residue on the corner of the Jerboa's mouth the whole time we were there."

Liwiych was located on the oceanfront just out of sight of Amryliw down the coast. A small city on a broad delta, it reminded Aru in some ways of the river town where she had first set foot in this part of the world. A thick crowd had already assembled along the promenade when they arrived, and excitement was building in the air.

Soon after the friends found a spot in the shade they could hear drumming and the sound of a calliope. The beginning of the parade appeared, the Grand Marshal on a side-stepping palomino mare led a duo of fine three-horse fire engines, with sirens blaring and bells ringing. Sheeki shouted out in his excitement at the noise and all the polished shininess.

All sorts of local businesses were represented in the parade. There were balloons and banners, beadwork and polished buttons. Bands of musicians walked in step as they performed. It rained confetti and candy everywhere. A large group of people walked along together dressed like chickens, and some elk performed as motley clowns handing out quips and living squids.

The parade went on and on, to a remarkable length. There were groups of folk dancers from each local village, carrying paper lanterns or pipes and scarves or tambourines with ribbons. Children watching the procession had candy whistles and lollipops with glitter stars and moons inside. Aru was especially moved by the exotic group of flamingo dancers who paused to dance right in front of them, a passionate display of grace and dignity with long legs and lots of ruffles.

Lekki seemed to know quite a number of the paraders. Once, during a pause in the procession, a double-decker omnibus stopped and the crowd aboard called to him and waved. They were dressed the same, in grey-blue riding jackets with tails and iridescent neck scarves, though the colors on the women were softer. The team was driven by a great big man who looked different than the others. Aru was fairly certain he was a bison. They were odd horses, some sort of harness breed Aru didn't recognize. The coach was painted a lovely bright green and the signboard on the upper deck read *Extantibus*. A bunch of the jam-packed passengers hopped out and hurried over to admire Lekki's new wife and coo over his beautiful baby.

Real flowers covered many of the floats, or artful ones made of crêpe paper, and quite a few floats had a river or ocean theme. Mhehh pointed out the dancers who in wonderful papier-mâché costumes represented a pod of orcas. Others danced around them in a fluid manner, wearing rippling sapphire-blue and sea-green capes.

In the middle of all the celebration, Aru turned to Nureek with a strange look on her face. "I'm not a princess," she told him, lowering her eyes as if expecting to be scorned.

Nureek laughed and asked why such a thing would come to her right now. He said into her ear, "It makes not a whisker of difference, Aru. Why should you care about something like that?" He pointed at the next float and elbowed her, laughing again.

Several small wagons hooked one-to-the-other made a train of cages with people inside. These were dressed like police and wealthy city officials. Riding along as escorts were several people costumed in prison stripes, one brandishing a set of oversized keys while the crowd laughed and cheered. Aru looked at Nureek and smiled.

Toward the end, a team of twenty-six oxen (Nureek counted them) had in tow a carousel. An actual one, of normal size. Aru and her friends stared in amazement. Children were riding on the carousel, smiling and waving at the crowd, mounted on exquisitely carved and brightly painted animals. The woodland stag made Aru sigh due to its majesticness. There were a seahorse, a zebra, a crowing rooster, an ostrich. A leaping house cat wore a red saddle and had a fish in its mouth. There were also a couple of gorgeous horses, a hare, a fat sheep, and a goose.

Clinging to his father's chest, Sheeki laughed and scrunched up his nose and ate up all the sights and sounds, but Mhehh covered his little ears as the steam whistles of the calliope went by. A circus-style wagon, all in scrollwork and gilded, it had open sides where you could see the large purple octopus playing the keyboards. He waved at Lekki in recognition. This glorious calliope was drawn by snow white draft horses who were in gold-studded crimson harness and draped in a wonderful tumble of columbine flowers. A cloud of teeny hummingbirds who darted to and fro dropped little charms on the spectators. It wasn't a good time to look up. Aru was nearly hit in the eye by a tiny brass elephant.

The last entry in the parade was a small buckboard pulled by goats. On the deck was a large iron cauldron, and inside the cauldron a healthy fire crackled away. Four or five people dressed as witches in pointy hats and brandishing homemade brooms were jumping on and off the wagon, sweeping parade rubbish from the pavement and tossing it into the fire. The crowd cheered.

And after it was all over another parade appeared, this time composed of dozens of coaches which made their way down the promenade to collect those visitors who weren't staying for a supper by the sea. Aru and Nureek bid goodbye to Lekki and his family who would spend the night in a hotel and return the next day. When the coach which Lekki had ordered for his friends arrived, who should be sitting and smiling inside but Mr. Variegat.

"Well, how do you do, my deary!" he exclaimed, putting down his paper and then holding out his kid-gloved hands in welcome. "Come on aboard, the both of you, there's plenty of room. I was afraid I'd be all lonely in this lovely carriage!"

Ever a flashy dresser, Mr. Variegat was adorned in a persimmon brocade vest with a goldenrod silk ascot and a chestnut morning coat over crimson striped pants. Set off by a black wool cloak with silver embroidery inside, this was all crowned by an expensive silk top hat, which he removed as the lady entered, smoothing down his curled wisps of hair and licking his lips.

Aru introduced her tutor, and Mr. Variegat said he was glad to know him. Then he turned toward Aru, removing his monocle, to say, "I noticed the two of you with your friend, the younger Blackbuck. You know, I've just recently agreed to broker some goods for Lekki's associates, a medicine. My goodness, there are buyers all across the land! It should all be a dance in the park!"

After she seated herself and arranged her skirts, Aru gave a little start. "Mr. Variegat!" she exclaimed. "How did you—?" then she stopped herself, thinking of her manners.

"Thousands of years of ancestry, my dear," he responded, winking.

The items of clothing he had on were all the same, but the patterns and colors had changed. Now he had the same goldenrod ascot, but along with it he wore a tasteful palette of blues and greens that, incidentally, was a mix of the most prevalent of the colors Aru and her tutor were wearing.

"As I say, the testing of this serum has been quite successful," Mr. Variegat continued. "I truly believe that this will be a blessing for those poor souls afflicted with disease. And certainly for the university and the business associations involved, as well!"

"Yes," said the tutor, "young mister Lekkchaos told us that a fairy dust has been added to the ingredients, and now the cure rate approaches one hundred percent. Indubitably, it is a veritable wonder of a medicine."

"Yes, isn't it wonderful!" agreed Mr. Variegat.

As they traveled toward home, sipping Mr. Variegat's nice dry rosé, they chatted about all sorts of things. From his picnic basket their friend produced hardtack and hazelnut spread. Later he shared some fermented fish, which filled the carriage with a choking, horrible smell as soon as the jar was opened, but actually tasted somewhat like food. Aru was half expecting to wake up dead the next morning from botulism or some sort of thing, but for unknown reasons took comfort in the fact that Mr. Variegat was eating more of it than she was.

"Ah! Here we are!" exclaimed Mr. Variegat. He stood up and tapped on the front wall of the carriage with his cane. "Driver! Driver!" he called. "Could you please stop here? Stop, please!" He smiled at his confused coachmates. They were still quite a way from their destination. "Just a little rest now, only for a minute, I hope you don't mind," he said.

Aru assumed that he needed to use the bushes, but after they had all climbed out into the late afternoon sunshine and were standing on the road, Mr. Variegat breathed deeply and said, "Ahh. I don't think I've ever enjoyed such a fine afternoon as this. Come, now. Let me show you something!"

How he made it down the winding trail and across the creek after all that wine and in his embroidered slippers, Aru couldn't guess, but when they arrived at the flower field she understood why he made the effort. The entire floor of the valley was carpeted in pansies. Aru'd never seen them in such a variety of colors. Without thinking, she reached for Nureek's hand.

Mr. Variegat broke a twig that hung down from a maple tree and squealed, "Ha-HA!" as he threw it as far as he could into the flowers. Forming ripples like a pool when a rock is tossed, the flowers then rose as a cloud into the air, for butterflies they were in reality, and the shock of this realization was a brilliant one. As the creatures flitted and circled here and there, the three of them kept saying, "Oh!" and, "Aah!" as if they were watching fireworks.

It was this experience with Mr. Variegat that gave Aru the idea to use butterflies to carry the diamond light to the underworld caves. The others agreed. What better fairies to use?

Lekki would be meeting with the Jerboa twenty days after that festival in Liwiych. The Jerboa would break the diamond and then help him to go down the well. That was the plan. Two and a half weeks went by with great anticipation, but then distressing news came to Aru from Lekki's home in the village by the sea. Little Sheeki was sick. Something he had caught at the parade, apparently. The mumps. Such inordinate unluckiness just stung. Lekki couldn't bring his cure to the underworld because he was quarantined with his son who was dangerously ill with an unrelated disease.

Sheeki stayed at home in Amryliw and was attended by the best doctors available. There would be no visiting the family for at least a week more, so all Aru and Nureek could do was worry from afar. Meanwhile, people were sick and dying in the lower worlds. Aru convinced the others to let her be the one to go down the well. She now stood as the obvious choice. Then, Aru had only a day or two to prepare herself for negotiations with Grmhrel. Perhaps it was a good thing she didn't have too much time to think about it.

The day before the dreaded encounter, Aru left Anemone in the early morning and walked alone down the road she had taken with Aranieda when they visited the Jerboa at home. This time, though, she turned off much sooner and followed a path which led into the mountains. She hiked along a narrow gorge for quite a way, and then she came to a creek which drained into it. Climbing this drainage up the steep hillside she arrived at a row of mountain ash trees and began to count them. "One . . . two . . . three . . . four . . . five." Just beyond the fifth tree she turned along the face of the slope and found what looked like a rabbit trail, soon arriving at a large dark hole, the entrance to a cave. Aru looked around behind her, and then she slipped inside.

In the shadows toward the rear, Aru searched the crannies and saw the passageway which had been described to her. Narrow with high walls, it reminded her of Nureek's crevasse. It sloped gently uphill. She followed the passage around a curve, where the sunlight faded but was replaced by torchlight. Another turn, and then Aru squatted to crawl through an entranceway to an open cavern about the size of a bedchamber. There was a table in there, and a mirror.

"Did anyone follow you?" asked the Jerboa.

"No," said Aru. "I was careful."

They spoke quietly for a few minutes and then, with trepidation, she parted her shawl to open the big canvas sack that hung around her neck, forcing herself to hand over the beautiful dragon wand. But first she unwrapped it, in order to have one last look at the irreplaceable artwork. *We should have had this photographed,* she thought, too late. *"Pish; there will always be the memory."* Was that the Jerboa speaking in her thoughts? She tried to pass the wand to the Jerboa but she couldn't seem to let go. Those wonderfully pleasing curvatures of the wings and neck, the exquisite balance of positive and negative form, the glowing light, and the absolute perfection of this object caused it to have life, somehow. Aru couldn't stop looking at the dragon's face. She was sure that it was imploring her. A tear fell on the dragon's cheek. It must have been hers.

Aru transferred the wand into the Jerboa's small, long-fingered hands. The Jerboa nodded to her and began to sing, as he carried it to the table, and soon was joined by an unseen chorus. The words of the song were something about foxfire and fireflies. The diamond sat on a purple cloth, a velvet napery with periwinkles stitched all around the borders. Then, after what may have been a long time involving a strange dance done by the Jerboa, the torches in the room went out. Light soon returned, however, because out of one of the Jerboa's lifted hands came a fierce and smokeless fire. From the other hand poured water, splashing onto the cavern floor.

The song changed, and soon the light became so bright that Aru had to cover her eyes. Even so, there were colors. Wild colors. And a wrenching, cracking noise almost too loud to bear. The chorus of high voices became stronger, too, almost as loud as the crackling. Aru thought she might go mad. Maybe she had. How can you tell if you've gone crazy? Then, after a while, continuous loud popping noises as the singing and volume of the other sounds decreased. Ouch. Something kept hitting her, the little rocks, pieces of diamond, it hurt. She didn't dare uncover her eyes. When she did, the Jerboa had stopped singing, the popping had stopped. The torches were re-lit. The Jerboa's back was toward her. The chorus still sang, and as Aru watched she realized the voices came from ants. Red ants were gathering up the tiny pieces of diamond. Aru held her breath as, still singing, they made a wide trail up her boot and up the outside of her skirts to deposit the cold fire diamonds into her canvas sack.

After this was done, the Jerboa turned around to speak, but not to Aru. Behind her stood Blackbuck. He'd followed her, after all! "You'll find you haven't any business here, Avariceo," said the Jerboa softly.

Blackbuck peered at him. "I do not know what you are up to, vermin. But you will make the young lady ill, fooling with all this water. Are you unaware that she may have been exposed to the measles?"

How long had he been standing there?

"Come along now, Aru," continued Blackbuck, "you must not play with this mouse, great thunder knows what the mischief is this time, but the little rodent is never up to any good. From now on you must tell me before you go and mindlessly frolic with sundry woodland creatures. And are you aware, you have got ants on you. Brush them off quickly, and let us get back home before we miss my lunch."

Aru looked helplessly at the Jerboa as Blackbuck escorted her out, but the Jerboa only winked and threw several ants at the back of Blackbuck's head. Aru walked silently behind Blackbuck. They descended the slope and traveled back along the gully. The ants were still in his hair. How long had he stood there? How much had he seen? Why didn't he mention the wand, or try to take the bag of diamonds? The two of them were more than halfway back to Anemone before it occurred to Aru that she always wore the locket with the charm which Aldrei had given her. *"As long as you have this around your neck, Aru, anyone but the rightful owner can see the dragon."*

Blackbuck set the Warden back on a more careful and oppressive duty, causing Aru to have to slip a healthy amount of laudanum into her mushroom liqueur the following evening so she and Nureek could meet the others in the garden.

They met at the old well in the bottom of the periwinkle garden just before midnight, in the thick of darkness. Because the sky was dense and overcast, lanterns and fireflies supplied the only light. Everyone had to step cautiously, as many lizards were in the garden. As Aru and Nureek approached the well, they saw a great swarming cloud of butterflies, dark shapes cascading and ascending, fluttering like leaves in a blustery wind. Aldrei held in his arms a thick branch covered completely with their sleepily fanning forms, but hundreds more swirled in the air around him.

Only one guard oversaw these gardens to the north of the house, and he and Lekki had been pals for years. Still, they went carefully and met with whispers. Aranieda was there also—she was using a cane now—and the Jerboa had come. Aeon hadn't joined them. The Jerboa said Aldrei wouldn't allow it. He was home, writing his memoirs.

"Aeon questioned markedly why he couldn't comma," said Aldrei.

"But he colon join us, period," added the Jerboa solemnly.

"The whole thing could be a huge apostrophe," said Aldrei, and then he squealed, "and our friend is far too great an ass to risk!"

They both laughed. Despite much shushing they, as usual, went on louder and quite a bit longer than one would think was necessary.

Aru held Nureek's hand while they stood amidst the fluttering butterflies, looking down over the rim of the well and into the basket that waited to descend into darkness. Aranieda had placed some potted four o'clock flowers in the basket, that the scent might encourage her. After Aru climbed into the basket, she handed her a candle.

"Near the bottom of the well you'll find the doorway. You must use this key," she said. Aru's hand shook, but she pocketed the key. Aldrei and the Jerboa placed the branch of butterflies in the basket with her.

"I've bestowed a favor upon you, Aru," said the Jerboa. "The lovely gift of befuddlement. You'll have the power to surround the hound in a cloud of confusion, allowing a chance against him. Something I borrowed from a stoat. You'll succeed in your bargaining."

Aru thanked him as she mustered all her courage, both real and feigned. She just hoped to return at all. Meanwhile, the well was crawling with lizards. A bell hanging down from the basket would warn them, but she had to be wary that none were crushed as she travelled down. *Lekki never could have done this,* she thought. At her signal, Nureek began cranking the basket down.

The basket creaked and waggled as it moved downward by slow degrees, scraping side to side against the damp stone lining the well, lurching now and then. Aru would have been much more frightened of it falling if she hadn't been so terrified of the monster waiting below.

At first she could see the faces of her friends peering down at her but after a while she was alone in a small world defined by the walls of the well and her candlelight. She had plenty of time as she went down to look around her and to consider one last time what she would say to Grmhrel. Perhaps she should begin with, "Please don't squash me!" Aru knew from her evening in the library that Grmhrel was notorious as a beast of rage. Rage is what took his humanity away from him, centuries ago. He had a history of killing others who could have been useful to him. But she did have a plan.

The basket stopped with a jerk, just above the waterline. At first Aru didn't see anything, then she found the outline of a small and slimy wooden door. She had no trouble opening it, other than having to contend with the shakiness of her hands. The key wasn't necessary, as the door wasn't locked. Taking up the candle and the big branch of butterflies, hoisting up her skirts, and with the canvas bag around her neck, she scrambled up and through the opening.

Moving in the non-reality of fear, Aru stood up as much as the tunnel allowed and she made her way down the slope toward the opening she could see below. Aru stumbled on something. A bone. Scattered all along the passageway, and in heaps here and there, were dry bones, cracked and chewed on. What type of bones she did not know.

She paused at the entrance to the cavern, clutching the branch and the dripping candle. Trembles and fear engulfed her. And it was muggy down there. Aru peered through the swarm of butterflies into the glittery dusk. The butterflies flitted around her, fluttering in her face, mobbing her, crowding around the branch. Spots of light, fireflies flew all about, up high, just enough to hint at the crystal beauty of the cavern walls. Aru couldn't quite discern the size of the cavern, but it was filled with a lake; a thick, mineral water that looked almost as if one could walk right across it. There was a small island, bare and flat.

With a jolt of her heart she realized he was standing right by her. She smelled his putrid breath, he stood that close. How had she not noticed him? Aru feared the sight of his mane of snakes, somehow afraid she'd turn to stone. But she stood fast and made herself look at him; the big dog creature. Impassable, morbid, nasty, bloody eyes. His scummy teeth were too big to fit in his mouth, his tongue was long and dripping.

Their conversation took place without use of air or the lips.

—*Ah, my supper has arrived,* said the monster, in his gurgling voice, without any hint of surprise.

—*My name is Aru. I've brought light for your crystal caverns.* Aru's hands were clenched as she held on to the butterfly bough. She spoke for a few minutes, while he only listened. This wasn't like she had imagined. Aru talked in circles, relying completely on the Jerboa's magic rather than any ideas because none would come. Her mind had gone empty; fear had driven out every single bud of a thought. Befuddlement was surely the only thing that kept him from eating her right there and then.

—*I brought you the darkness you require,* she said, finally.

—*You give me little flutterflies,* he said. *Yet you are the girl with the sight. I know who you are. Why should you bring me little flies? You could have stayed in your world and stayed alive.*

For a moment, Aru couldn't find her voice.

—*I carry the light to give you shadows forever more,* she said at last.

—*Give it to me, then.*

—*I will,* she said, but she didn't.

He growled so that the rocks shook. Without words at all, he shouted, *I'd have devoured you already if I didn't want to hear you tell me what's in the bag!*

Aru responded in a firm manner, *I can make your shadows return.*

—*Do it now.*

—*I'll light up your cavern once again, but you must give me something.*

—*I will simply kill you now, useless mortal,* he growled, and was gathering himself to do so when Aru took a step toward him.

—*Old Fool!* she cried. *I am no mortal. I am not the daughter of Wuurue the woodswoman, as people say. I am your own daughter, and you know it, the result of your interlude with Eda the Tiruuvan. How did you think I received the ability to see the underworld lizards? I have dwelt in the western woods all these passing years, and you too blind to know. You'll not kill me, your own daughter, and you'll not kill me, carrier of lézarvoyance whom you could never destroy! No, you'll listen to me, monster, because I and I alone am the key to your achievement of your former magic, your shadow puppets. Your little servants. Or make boredom the only state in the province of your abiding tomb forevermore!*

Aru hadn't been sure she'd be able to look him right in his horrifying face and tell a blatant lie. But the words came out with force and she enjoyed saying them. The satisfaction of coming up with this strategy, the pride in her boldness, it made her feel more real, more alive!

Grmhrel sat back on his haunches. He sneered. *What's in the bag?*

—I want free passage for any and all aboveworlders who wish to come and go through your caverns. There won't be many to venture down this way, but you must let all of my country dwellers who wish to enter do so.

—I'll play along, said Grmhrel. *No one but you may pass.*

Within minutes they had agreed that only those bearing the medicine would be allowed, but they would also have a safe return. It was the quickest bargain Aru had ever seen made. Perhaps because he already knew what she was thinking. Had he ever been confused at all?

The light that splashed out of the bag as Aru opened it lit up all the crystal nearby. Breathtaking. But it was nothing like when the butterflies came to hover, each picking up their piece of diamond, flying to light the entire cavern, the brilliance increasing steadily. Aru set down the bag and more butterflies continued to dip down into it and one by one the diamonds took to the air. Bright and sparkling in crystal light, the cavern was huge and splashed with millions of colors. Overwhelming. Long stalactites in a drapery from the ceiling cast sharp and flickery shadows on the walls.

—Now you take this branch and bag to the island for me, said Grmhrel.

Butterflies continued to collect the diamonds. Aru didn't argue. Triumph filled her with exhilaration. She had overcome tremendous fear. She had saved the day for countless people! Grabbing up the butterfly branch and the sack once again, she loaded them into one of several rowboats waiting on the shore, and with great effort rowed across the thick white water to the island, enjoying a strength of heart she hadn't known she possessed. Butterflies trailed her across the lake.

As she stepped out onto the tiny island with the big branch in her arms, she heard Grmhrel again, *You are not my daughter, Aru. Even so, your doggedness amuses me. Away you drove the little attendant I sent you. Eh! I've not known my influences broken with such a small effort. And you made your way here to the coast regardless, although not as speedily as you might have done with the assistance.*

Eepe! thought Aru. But she didn't have time to react.

Hideous howl-like laughter filled the cave, and then the foulest of odors, as dozens of dogs came, wretched, dark and greasy, slavering and panting, to stand along the shores of the lake, staring at Aru as if they hadn't eaten in weeks. Some of the hounds sat down, distracted, to scratch hard at fleas, and the solid rock shook as they did so. Aru covered her head. Seven of the dogs jumped into the lake and swam to join her on the island, growling and baring their teeth all the while.

They started to tear into her, rip her flesh apart. Aru slid into dumbfounded shock. Her spirit left her eyes vacant and staring. Was there pain? She couldn't have told you. Yes, mortal pain, unbelievable pain.

The sound of tearing flesh and cracking bone, the smell of her own blood as a dog ripped open her chest and pulled out her heart, blood vessels rent apart as the dog jerked his snout high, holding up his prize, ready to gulp, the heart wrapped in his long tongue, squeezed like a sponge. The heart fought hard, beating against his toothy grip, but to no avail. There it went, she watched it go, as he dug a hole with his front paws and buried it right there on the island.

The second dog took her head, gnawing it off with razor teeth, snapping the neck with a sickening crunch, clasping the head in gruesome jaws as she plunged into the lake and swam to the far end. Each stroke of the dog's paddle was a deliberate, emotionless thing, the head scarcely impairing the beast's progress up the lake. Clambering with slippery paws and outstretched claws onto the rock at the far end, the bitch stood up on her hind legs to reach up and with great force impale the head on a salt stalagmite. The eyes and mouth were still open wide, useless now, staring into nothing at all.

Two more dogs took Aru's arms, yanking them away in a game of tug and then swimming off to set them in the bottoms of the wells of the lower worlds. Aru's legs, the same. Torn from their place by rough black dogs and taken to the wells. The wells of Grmhrel's realm! From the histories Aru knew that those who rise up inside these shafts from the underworld come out in worlds still deeper below. Now, Aru's flesh left to rot in the passages to these wells, her bones left to lie there.

Not much was left of her body now. The seventh dog snatched up the remainder. Her vulva, her body's magic ring, her gateway to becoming—it was there. The hound placed this as the passage out—an ogee arch which Aru somehow squeezed her way through. When she arrived on the other side she found herself safe in Nureek's arms.

Grmhrel's voice drifted up from the well, *I never said I wouldn't cause you to remember.*

Aru, panting, looked up at Nureek and whispered; all she could say was, "There's more to the world than it seems."

The sun shone high above. Aru had been gone for hours and those waiting at the well had such relief to see her so alive. There had been a mild quake; had she felt it down there? Did he make the bargain?

Some of the lizards were already returning down the well. "The lizards are returning to their master. Will they all go?" Aru whispered to Aldrei.

"Unlikely, but many of them will." He sounded almost solemn.

The realization spread from Aru to Nureek and then to Aranieda. They'd done it! They'd made the pact with Grmhrel. The serum could now be brought to the lower worlds.

The exhausted friends hugged one another and laughed with joy. Nureek teased Aru about her dirty face as he kissed her forehead and cheeks. She felt too weak to stand and she trembled greatly, as if from the cold, but she kept laughing also. Aldrei and the Jerboa weren't celebrating as much as the others. A strange thing, for those who so much loved to laugh. Nureek was the first to notice this. "Is something amiss, you two?" he asked.

A couple of butterflies fluttered up out of the well. Aru gasped. They looked as if they'd been burnt, their color was gone. Their lower wings were all ragged, their antennae frazzled. The pair had dropped their diamonds. They flew aimlessly around the top of the well for a moment and then headed off toward the sun.

Aru and her friends stood silent as several more grey butterflies came up the well. Then a lot more of them appeared, some without diamonds, others dropping theirs on the grass before teetering away. More and more came up; they kept coming until certainly it was all of them. It must have been every one. Several of them died right there on the grass beside the well.

A grey butterfly buzzed around the Jerboa's ears and handed over its diamond before it, too, flew away. After it had gone the Jerboa looked around for a moment and then said, "Many butterflies remain below, but not enough to light the caverns to Grmhrel's satisfaction. Most of the fairies find the lack of sky and sunlight too vexing for their little spirits. The brilliance of the crystal reflections wasn't enough. They say they'll never again go below, but from this day forward will ever seek the light."

Nureek leaned over and stared morosely down the well. How could they have such success, only to have it fly away? Aru didn't know what to do. Disbelief filled her. Then from inside she drew some strength: *We'll figure this out. We'll find a way.*

Aldrei snorted and laughed loudly. The Jerboa smiled as Aldrei went on, but the others were not amused. How could he laugh at a time like this? How can he find humor in dismay? The deaths of fairies, the failure of their desperate plan . . . Aldrei, never to be fully trusted, such a cold heart he could show—

"A couple of senseless old farts we are, after all, Jerboa," said Aldrei. "With all the long ears between us, we've overlooked the obvious. Dragonfays. That's who we'll send. The dragons love caverns."

The Jerboa laughed also, and right away called the meadow mice to gather the diamonds. Dozens of them came. The little animals chattered and squeaked and within minutes had gathered all the diamonds from the lawn and the well. One or two of the stones may have been cheeked, but the rest overfilled the huge beer stein from Aldrei's picnic basket.

"I suppose all the ones which must have fallen into the lake are gone," said Aru. "The water there is thick with minerals, thick as barley gruel."

There was a moment of silence.

"Tilapia fish," replied Aranieda, "we'll simply enlist some tilapia fish to gather the diamonds to send back to into flight with dragonflies."

"Well, all right, then," said Aru. "Fish and dragonflies it is. Such a shame about the butterflies we lost. But dragons do sound like the sort of fairy who could thrive in a cave." She received the stein of glowing diamonds from Aldrei.

"Let's all go now and get some sleep!" said Aranieda.

Over the next week the news was promising about Sheeki. Then, finally, Aru and Nureek were relieved to meet with Lekki and hear that the baby was strong and had regained his health. Other news, however, caused them great distress.

The tests of the serum had been completed. The medicine had proven itself beyond expectations. But fairy dust, a key ingredient, was in short supply, so only one large lot of the serum could be made at this time. This much was thought to be enough to help the most vulnerable; it could be distributed among the worlds to help babies and elders, but it'd be some time before another batch could be made.

Blackbuck had convinced Mr. Variegat that the serum was rightfully his (which of course it wasn't) and had directed Mr. Variegat to sell the entire lot to an overseas company. Lekki had pleaded with this corporation, but they liked their deal and would not sell the serum back. It was to be shipped out within the week.

"I can't believe Mr. Variegat would betray you so," said Aru.

"Well, you know, the fact of the matter is that Mr. Variegat is a chameleon, Aru," replied Lekki. "I should have realized this might happen. He is only acting as chameleons do. Their loyalty belongs to whomever they are with at the time. It is their nature. You know the old saying—"

"I know," sighed Aru. *"It takes a million chameleons to know a chameleon."*

And there was something else. Blackbuck had been seen bathing at the steam baths in a nearby mountain village. He hadn't been wearing the silver belt. Lekki, through friends, learned that his father had gone to the shrimp witches to have the silversmith's curse broken. These old witches, Bubbles and Clah, lived far away on an island in the sea but everyone knew of them. With their friend, the bearded monkey, they were responsible for much of the trouble in the known world. They were feisty, powerful little women and Bubbles always carried a pistol. So that was that. Blackbuck had his power back.

At Anemone the grounds just southeast of the house rose up to form an embankment, a natural hill shaped like a curving levee, and from the top of it one could see the ocean. Toward the end of this ridge was an old stone tower. Aru had never been up there, but thought it must have an amazing view from the small unglazed window at the top.

When Aru and Nureek received an urgent message to meet Aranieda at the tower, they had no idea what it was about, but they hurried over without their breakfast. Lekki and Aranieda were sitting under a crabapple tree up on the embankment, not far from the tower, drinking whiskey from a bottle and laughing a lot. They stood up to greet them.

"Whatever is going on?" asked Aru. Lekki took Aru by the shoulder and pointed her toward the window up in the old tower. His breath smelled like the whiskey. Was he intoxicated? Someone's face appeared at the window and then moved away again. Was that Blackbuck? "Is that—?"

"Yes. It is." Lekki excused himself to sneeze.

"Upon my grizzled whiskers!" whispered Nureek. Then he laughed. "What sort of game is afoot here?"

Aranieda smiled and handed Aru the bottle. "We're celebrating," she said.

Aru told her no thank you, but Nureek took a swig, just for the fun of it. "Celebrating?" he asked.

"When we heard that Blackbuck had freed himself from his silver girdle, Lekki and I decided it was time to act. And so we did."

"Easiest act of high treason I have ever committed!" snorted Lekki, sitting back down. "Aranieda and I both knew my father kept the old east tower stocked with supplies for our family in case of some sort of disaster. For as long as I can remember it has been an occupation of his, he keeps enough food and household goods in there to keep several people for many years.

"Almost as if he has been hoping for adversity, in some way. He has been rather obsessed with catastrophes. I do not think the reality of such a disaster, should one actually take place, has ever fully occurred to him. Has he considered what life would be like in such circumstances? These plans for his own survival along with everyone else's demise, perhaps they are a result of some morbid fear, or perhaps this makes him feel clever. I do not know.

"And so all these years he has kept this place ready," Lekki had a gulp of whiskey, "and Aranieda and I were thinking that perhaps the time has come that his complacency about the disease be linked with his desire to be the chosen one, the survivor."

Aranieda agreed, "As loathsome as all this sounds, I don't believe the Blackbuck is fully aware of his own behavior. He lives in his own world, and is able to convince himself that he is a great king, loved by all. But I am concerned that, yes, this grandiose survivor insanity has come to be his motivation in life."

"And so," said Lekki with a sad and rather drunken smile, "the two of us decided to help my father achieve his special dream."

"We," added Aranieda, taking the bottle, "enlisted the aid of several of Lekki's friends from around the palace. You see, it happened like this: a young mother brought her two children up the north wing walkway, calling for a doctor, two days ago while Blackbuck was having his coffee on his bedroom balcony. She was carrying one of her little boys, who looked awful sickly and was covered with a spotted rash.

"Yesterday, the handmaid who brought Blackbuck his tea was dismissed to the dormitory by the matron after she noticed an open rash on the girl's wrist.

"After Blackbuck happened upon Eaks, the old gardener, coughing up blood behind the patio hedgery, and his face all covered with spots, Blackbuck began to worry. This rash and fever, all these things are symptoms of the disease introduced by his local hypogeous snails." She broke out laughing.

Lekki continued for her, "In panic, my father locked himself inside the old tower. He thought he had a couple of faithful servants with him, but the pair ducked out at the last moment and bolted the door from the outside, with our cheerful supervision! My father never anticipated that someone would reinforce his seclusion by locking him in!

"Meanwhile, the mother washed the spots off her precious child at the garden pump, the handmaiden miraculously recovered from her fever, and old Eaks, well, he simply spat a wad of his fine blackberry leather into his kerchief just after my father went away. I gave Eaks a lovely new hankie for his trouble."

"So now, here he is," said Aranieda, waving to the face in the window. "Quite safe on his own property with the store of goods he has hoarded away. And the rest of us are safe from him. Everyone's safe."

Aru had taken her inbreath in order to respond, but a wild, rushing noise came from up in the tower. The friends stared at the window openings, startled. Aru recognised that noise. And soon the views of a passing antler and the sound of a gale made the situation quite clear.

"He'll destroy that place inside!" exclaimed Nureek.

"His prerogative." That was Aldrei, who had just appeared over the hill. Aeon, in donkey form, accompanied him. "True congratulations on your exquisite stupidity, Avariceo!" called out Aldrei in a high and resounding voice, probably audible even above the racket. He waved up at Blackbuck and his noises, and he wholly meant it, laughing and cackling and jumping up and down. He so loved a good fool, and human animals seemed to run a never ending supply of them.

"He really is going to destroy inside there," said Aru.

Then they learned, during all the wild gale, that Aldrei could hear something else. It sounded like a scratching. Scraping. Aldrei listened with his long ear and told the others that the news was not good. Blackbuck was using his antler to cut into the wall of the tower. He had already made some progress in carving a hole that would soon be through the wall. He was probably enlarging the window and it wouldn't take long for him to create an area large enough to fit through.

"How is this possible?" asked Aranieda.

"He can carve right through stone?" added Aru.

"Oh, rabid daughters of a swamp gnome!" Lekki cried, holding his head. "But it is not solid stone. The tower is an ancient water tower, built of wood in the primitive ages but reinforced later with soapstone for insulation. In his rage, with his magic, he may carve right through to freedom before our eyes." Lekki sneezed violently, several times.

The others politely wished him health, except Aldrei, who shouted, "Hey! Contain yourself!" and cackled.

They all looked back at the tower. Aeon gazed fixedly at Aldrei and waggled his head, flapping his ears. Aldrei laughed and said, "All righty, old friend, I suppose I could. Just to make you happy."

As Aldrei—without apparent effort—began to call up a distant force, Aru sensed that she was about to witness a display of the grandest magic she had ever experienced. Beside the sound of the wind another noise could soon be heard. The voices of children laughing and chattering grew louder and louder as a long dark cloud, a stream, appeared in the southern sky near the horizon and in no time flew right overhead. These weren't children, those voices. Birds. A swirl of bright tropical birds had arrived, a river of flamboyance to encircle the tower, rushing and screaming together. Tighter and tighter drew the horde of birds in their flight around the little stronghold as Aldrei hopped up and down and began to sing. With Aldrei's song and the whirlwind of birds acting as a turbine, the stormwinds of Blackbuck's fury were drawn out of the window and made to encircle the tower, a rush of wind so strong as to be utterly impassable.

But the birds couldn't fly there, circling, forever. So what might be Aldrei's plan? Did he have one? Aru wondered how the stolen wind could possibly be kept.

All this went on for a long time. The birds circled and the wind whirled, for twenty minutes or more. And then, Aeon began to sing. Aeon, the unassuming donkey who had always accompanied Aldrei like a faithful puppy, began to sing.

Sometimes a work of genius in art will move a person to tears, or a piece of music can do the same. The song of Aeon was like that, only a hundredfold. Everyone who could hear it, everyone from the mountains to the shore, stopped what they were doing and began to wail, just from the beauty of the sound. The pure tone of his voice came as real and as sublimely transcendent as the most magical, beautiful accordion masterpiece. The ants came out of their holes in the ground, and they shed their little tears. The worms came out of the crabapples in the tree, and they sobbed. Aru and Nureek, Lekki and Aranieda, they all fell to the ground and cried with the whole of their hearts.

Although nobody saw, Blackbuck himself lay on the floor in the tower, weeping from the sheer beauty of Aeon's honest melody. Eventually, with a slowing of the music, the birds began to rise into the sky. They circled several times, then performed a quick migration back to their homes many leagues to the south. As Aeon's song began to ebb, and then came to its gentle conclusion, the fierce wind continued. A tornado of horrible strength, but only surrounding the stone walls of the tower. The integrity of all those tears caused by Aeon's song, a magic far more potent than Blackbuck's own, would keep the tower enclosed by wind forever, or until donkeys came to end it.

It was done.

"But what now?" said Nureek after a few minutes. "We can't keep him confined until he rots. His powers will remain, no matter how long he waits there. He'll need rehabilitation."

"Arranged for," smiled Aranieda, and she pointed. "There is a vent in the roof," she said, "and we have one of the best therapists in the land scheduled to visit him daily."

A large parrot peeked out from between the crabapple leaves, wiping her eyes. With a nod and a shriek she flew high above the tornado and spiraled down towards the tower roof.

"It is in reality more than he deserves," said Lekki.

"No worries about a rescue," laughed Aranieda, "because nobody likes him."

It ought to have been time to celebrate, but the problem of the misappropriated serum remained. The way to deliver the medicine had been opened, and now without Blackbuck's meddling the welfare of the people would again be paramount. Snail disease, as it was known in the villages, was under control along the coast. All this felt glorious, but the fact remained that in some of the lower worlds there existed a state of emergency. Because of the temporary shortage of fairy dust, due to the difficulty of procuring it, no fresh serum could be made. The old duck who represented the corporation which now owned the manufactured product would not be bothered to listen to reason. Appeals to his humanity fell on deaf ears. The serum would soon be on its way to a distant land to be included, at great profit, in a recipe for a cold remedy and laxative.

Lekki was now King Arven Lekkchaos Chymynroddion the Blackbuck, Master at Anemone, titled both by blood and by popular consensus. He invited his friends for a visit to his beach home in Amryliw. They had plans to make. They had a serum to steal.

Dressed as workers, Aranieda and Aru and Nureek walked right into the Upper Liwiych dockyards through the main gate. Nureek pushed a wheelbarrow in order to mask his infirmity. Lekki hadn't come along, for the simple reason that there was too great a chance of someone recognizing him. He knew so many people.

With a copy of the bill of lading in hand, it should have been relatively easy for the three to locate the serum in Warehouse B as it sat waiting at the docks. It wasn't. They hadn't known that a four-masted schooner would be at the wharf that afternoon, with the dockyard a complete madhouse, crawling with laborers and overstuffed with crates.

It smelled good in the warehouse. At one end were stacks and stacks of bulging cotton and burlap sacks newly unloaded from the big schooner. Already they took up much of the space and more were coming. Aru read the print on the bags as she walked past: *cacao beans, vanilla beans, allspice, cardamom, galangal, cinnamon bark, cumin, nutmeg, dried rhizomes of turmeric, ginger root, whole cloves.* "I'm hungry," she said.

"Look!" said Aranieda. "Saffron!"

At the other end of the building, local farm wagons offloaded bales of tobacco and cotton, crocks of sauerkraut, and chili peppers, dried tomatoes, and mustard. These would be going on board the vessel.

There were also tons of crates and barrels of miscellaneous content, stacked high and waiting. In this mess of commodities somewhere would be that small box of serum. An inventory system was clearly in place but apparently it wasn't being followed by the lumpers.

It didn't take much time to determine that all the cargo in the warehouse carried tags with the name of the schooner. This was terrible news. It meant that the serum would already be out on the wharf in the loading area. A watchkeeper patrolled the docks out there.

The SS Frolicsome was a tramp steamer. She rested in her berth just in front of the much longer schooner. She was a splendid thing, painted in vivid colors and with gilded carving from prow to stern. A bulge halfway up the freeboard continued all along to the stern, and above this point the hull was varnished teak. She had several masts. Her cargo was stacked in neat rows on the dock, all types of crates and boxes and barrels. There were a lot of wine barrels.

Aranieda hadn't recovered enough from her spraying that she should be doing any transforming, but she insisted. Only she could search through the steamer's cargo under the attentive eye of the green heron watchman stationed out on the wharf.

It took Aranieda all afternoon and well into the evening to examine everything. In spider form she carefully checked every single crate and parcel. The serum was not there. When she returned to meet Aru and Nureek, who were waiting quietly, she told them this could only mean one thing. The serum was already aboard the Frolicsome. Not only that, workers were loading the ship even though darkness had arrived. There had been a last-minute change to her itinerary. She was to be launched at daybreak!

They decided to hide until the loading was done, then sneak up the gangway and search the ship. In the meantime, they had a few hours to figure out how to evade the guards. First, though, they must leave the warehouse, as it would soon be locked up. A few buildings away was a ropewalk. Certainly that would be empty at night. A small unlocked door in the back gave them entry.

High windows let in enough moonlight that the friends could see well enough not to trip over things. They followed the rail tracks along the walk, hoping to come to an office or some place where they could sit comfortably. It smelled of hemp and pine tar. They walked on and on. Such a remarkably long building! Coils of rope lay everywhere. Aru saw rope as thick as she was tall. How could anyone need cordage that heavy? They passed two carriages on the different sets of rails.

Both held lines of partially twisted rope extending until it was out of sight down the ropewalk into darkness. Giving up on a sofa, or even chairs, Aru and Nureek arranged a sitting area out of bobbins and spools of hemp yarn.

Aranieda had exhausted herself searching the cargo for the serum, so during the next while Nureek took it upon himself to make a few stealthy trips back over to the loading area to keep an eye on the situation there. And just their luck, it seemed, there had been a stowaway recently on an outbound clipper. As a result, all ladders had been stowed and two guards stood on duty at night. But, just as the friends sat in the ropery and worried over their options the answer to their problem walked right in.

"Oh, it's a rat!" shrieked Aru, holding up her skirts as she clambered onto a rope coil.

"It's minding its own business," said Aranieda.

The thing went right past them, bold as brass, and then disappeared underneath some hemp bundles. Shortly, it reappeared in the form of a woman with beady eyes. She wore a drab greyish-brown coat. Nureek jumped up, wary and defensive.

"I've word from your friend Lekki!" screaked the woman, throwing up her hands. "A young chipmunk pal of mine, cheeky thing, woke me up early, said a chimney swift told him you folks needed this message right away." She stood looking at them, twiddling her fingers.

Without waiting for a response, the woman went on to recite, not very well, this message:

> Hello. My friends, it appears you have met some sort of hurdle. In order to assist your efforts I have made it a point to stumble into a meeting of the Liwiych Tree Hollow Society, of which both this evening's dockyard watchkeepers are dedicated members. I invited the whole crew to a late supper at Lolly's Peck and Gnaw, and made quite sure the vodka flowed freely. You will find your guards well overfed and a bit tipsy and, if you are patient, they will be dead to the world, as I also tampered with their escargot. Please be gentle in your dealings with them, as they are going to be terribly ill in the morning.

They thanked the lady for her kindness in bringing them the information, Nureek tipped her, and she left. However, as happy an end as this was to one problem, they soon found the stifling how-do-you-do of another. On Nureek's next excursion to the dockside, he saw that although the laborers were finished with loading the ship, the gangway, for some bizarre reason, had been withdrawn. They had no way aboard. The hull reached as high as the warehouse walls.

At this point it was out of the question for Aranieda to transform, and even a cougar couldn't leap that high. Aru sat gripping her head as if she could squeeze an idea out of it. If they couldn't come up with something quickly the medicine would be gone.

As they wasted precious time rejecting a string of unworthy ideas, several of their colorless butterflies appeared from somewhere in order to mob the old carriage lamp the friends were using for light. Aranieda sadly mentioned that the Jerboa's magic barrage of confusion had affected the butterflies down in the cave. Those who had come up the well in tatters hadn't recovered from their smothering experience underground. Recalling the dimness of the caverns, they flew in the evening and night, yet spent their time looking for the diamond light.

Just when the depression surrounding the three friends had become nearly thick enough to perceive with the eyes, Aranieda noticed a coil of insulated wire. This gave her inspiration. She shared her idea. Both her partners looked sceptical. Nureek started to protest, but Aranieda interrupted him with, "We need to find some horseshoes and a wooden pole, a long one. Hurry."

Late that night they stood in the shadows, peering at the wharf. The only sounds were the lapping of the water and the creaking of ships against the dock, the chains clanking against the Frolicsome's iron hull. Staring through the dim night, they spotted both the watchkeepers. One was perched on the railing of the dockside and the other sat on a sack of grain, blinking his big round eyes in an effort to stay awake. Both sentries looked completely stuffed and not a little drunken. The one on the rail hopped down and stumbled over to speak to the other.

"Who would have thought," she declared, "that You-Know-Who would get us boiled as albatrosses on such costly hooch."

"Who knew?" said the other. "But, no matter who reprimands us, we'll jush ask them who they think they are to be acc-using us of such hooliganism. We'll inshist the real problem is we are the ones whoose lives aren't worth half a hoot to any supedvisnor. Soopervishre."

"To who?"

The woman plopped down onto the ground next to the other guard's feet. With several tugs of effort, she pulled a rifle out of the scabbard on her back and set it down beside her.

"They're armed!" whispered Aru.

"It's all right, those are only pellet guns," said Nureek.

As the three nervous burglars watched from the shadows, the guard who was seated on the ground, followed soon by the other, fell into deep, loudly snoring sleep. It proved a relatively simple matter to load them both into the wheelbarrow and take them to the rear of the ropewalk. There, locked snugly in a storeroom, the sleepers dozed in as much comfort as could be managed. The pair didn't seem likely to wake any time soon, but a lot of noise was about to be made and the friends couldn't be too careful.

They returned to the wharf, where Aru looked up at the steamer. Oh! That thing was tall.

"You don't need to do this if you don't want to," said Nureek. "We'll find another way."

"I'll be all right," Aru reassured him, as convincingly as she could.

Moving as silently as possible, and sticking to the shadows, they positioned themselves in the dark area next to the eel boxes.

The city of Liwiych was famous for its eel pies, eel jelly, and smoked eel. The secret to the fine flavor was the rinsing of the live electric eels. These were kept in cages in the sea with fresh water pouring over them as a way of getting rid of any muddy flavor. One of these big cages was tied up just behind the Frolicsome, all processed and full of clean eels waiting to be harvested. This was opportune timing because the eels had endured quite enough of this treatment and were definitely agitated. Angry eels were a key element in Aranieda's plan.

Aru and Aranieda had carefully wrapped four horseshoes with the insulated wire they had found in the old ropery. Nureek had nailed dowels to the horseshoes and worked out a way to strap them securely onto Aru's hands and feet. Aranieda had supervised the whole process carefully, because an error in judgement through any part of this plan could cost Aru or someone else their life. Now they sat quietly by the eels, waiting for the right time.

There were about sixty large eels in the cage, by Aranieda's calculations. The plan was relatively simple: the horseshoes were attached to two lengths of wire. The end of the one wire was stripped and then affixed to the steel cage, the end of the other was attached to bare wire that had been wrapped around the middle of the long wooden pole. With Aru wearing the horseshoes, the lower end of the pole would be held down into the water of the eel box by Nureek. He and Aranieda would then agitate the eels, provoking them to jump up and attack the shiny wire-wrapped middle of the pole. This would electrify the horseshoes with an erratic pulse current, turning them into magnets. Using these, Aru could go right up the side of the ship.

They were nearly ready. Aranieda looked at her pocket watch. "It's almost time," she said.

Aru had stripped down to her chemise and bloomers and was balancing on top of the railing, ready to climb the ship's hull. She wore the horseshoes on her hands and feet. The way the hull bulged outward made the climb a particularly scary idea. She'd be practically on her back while she made it over the protruding section. Not only that, Aru had been warned that she would need to make the top before the magnets became too hot to bear.

Aranieda stared at her watch. "Get ready, Aru!" she called, as she motioned for Nureek to stick the end of the pole into the water. Aranieda and he began waving at the eels, insulting them, and throwing little rusty bolts at them. Nureek wiggled the pole to attract them to the shiny wire. It worked. The eels were infuriated and began jumping up out of the water to attack the pole with their electricity.

"Now, Aru!" called Aranieda, and Aru leaped from the wharf railing to the side of the ship. Clang! The timing was perfect. Yes, the impact of the magnets on the steel hull was loud, but Aru had eleven more chances to mask the sound as the town clock finished striking midnight. She had to move each hand and foot one at a time, as far as she could manage. Clang! Her left hand. Clang! A foot. Clang! Her other foot. As she crawled over the bulge she missed a clock chime entirely. Clang! Her hand. Right on time. Then, clang! Her timing was off a bit. It went on like this, and yet it was over quickly. When the clock stopped striking, Aru froze on the hull of the ship. Unable to move, she clung there. She hadn't quite made the top. And now she was up high, paralyzed with fear of falling. Even through her leather gloves, the magnets were getting hot.

"Keep going!" she heard Nureek shout. He sounded terrified.

"Aru! You've got to keep moving!" Aranieda called.

The horseshoes were burning Aru's hands.

She was almost there. She must keep going, there was no choice. Aru lifted her right foot. Clang! Oh, that was loud! With huge effort and another loud clang Aru reached the top. Hoisting herself over the rail, she pulled the horseshoes off her hands and let them drop into the water below. She removed the ones from her feet. Then she waved to her partners and crept off to find her way to the hold. She hoped beyond hope there was no one aboard. She'd never explain what she was doing up there in her underwear.

Aru located a hatchway and went down into the darkness. She found a lantern in the corridor of the first level below. She lit it. She saw rows of cabins. It occurred to her that there might be passengers sleeping aboard. Aru held her breath as she found a route down two more levels, then she was in the hold. She had no way to know if this was the correct section of the ship. So many crates and barrels, and all jammed in tight together! She nearly sat down and cried. How would she ever possibly search through this?

After some more investigation, Aru realized that the goods were well organized, compartment by compartment. It would help her a great deal if she could only locate the right section. She searched, and the hours went by. Her mind went blurry from looking at package after package, and then she wasn't sure if she'd gone through this area already. At last Aru found a compartment somewhere amidships on the steerage deck. It contained the more fragile and miscellaneous cargo. She just knew the serum would be in this compartment somewhere. The goods were packed several containers deep on shelves, so at first it was a matter of checking the visible packages. Then, she had to remove items from the shelves to see behind them. She wasn't finding it. In her despair, Aru remembered the fairy stone given to her by the Steelhead Queen. There was fairy dust in the serum! She clutched at the ring of stone on her necklace. Just maybe . . .

Well, the package number wasn't quite right, but the case was clearly labeled: *Mulberry Harbor Medicinals*. That was the name of the company that manufactured the serum. Aru pried it open and peeked inside. There must have been a hundred tiny bottles, each not bigger than a hummingbird's breast, and fitted with a filigree brass stopper.

The egg-shaped bottles were of pressed marble glass. Aru picked one up and examined it for a moment in the lantern light. Deep midnight-blue glass enriched with lighter hues and whites and wrinkly embedded foil. The pattern reminded Aru of churning, choppy waves. She found the packing slip. This was the serum.

Aru heard a sneeze. Not close by, but still she froze. Then mustering her best stealth despite lugging the package, she made her way back to the upper deck. After hunting around in the grey predawn she found a coil of thin rope for her descent. She happened to glance down at the eel box, and saw that it was empty. Completely empty. The eels, having lunged in anger at the wired pole, had realized they could jump out of the cage. Every one had gone. As Aru stared down at the vacant eel box, she noticed a lantern at the main gate of the dockyard. It was the morning watchkeeper, coming to relieve the others!

In panic she attached the line to the case of bottles so she could lower it over the side. Despite her efforts, it knocked against the hull of the ship several times on the way down. Then Aru followed the instructions Aranieda had given her for her own descent. She looped the middle of the rope around an anchor point and threw the ends over the side. She then straddled the ropes and wrapped them as one around her hip and up across her chest, then around behind her neck. Holding on to the ropes in both directions for dear life, she stepped backward over the rail and, letting the rope play out, she descended quickly, the friction against her body keeping her from sliding too fast. She tumbled into Nureek and Aranieda's arms as they caught her. Then the three of them, with the precious package in their wheelbarrow, hightailed it along the wharf and down the path beside the malthouse to be lost in the shadows before anyone saw them.

A few days later, after the dust of all their activity had settled, Aru and Nureek took an afternoon with Aldrei and Aeon to climb the forested ridge overlooking Anemone. At the top they sat chatting and laughing together as they enjoyed the view of the palace and lands, and the ocean beyond. Behind them the sun slowly descended above the rugged hills.

Eventually, it was time to go. The four friends stood up and gazed off into the glowing sky as it prepared to fill with color. "It's an odd thing," mentioned Aru, "but I can't help but feel the sun ought to set over the ocean. The ocean belongs in the west, you see."

This statement led to such a long and involved discussion about personal perspective and attitude and the meaning of life that the friends found themselves on the hilltop later than they had intended. Still rapt in conversation, they finished descending the trail in darkness. The stars shone brightly. The universe seemed so big. Aru's heart pounded and her head was spinning from thinking too deeply.

"Are we real?" she whispered.

"What do you mean?" Nureek replied. "Of course we're real, we exist. That makes us real, doesn't it."

"Thanks to H. A. Byrd," said Aldrei.

Aru stared. "A jaybird? What jaybird?"

I wish to acknowledge those
who helped me through the publishing process of this book:

First, my family, in particular my husband Kevin. And thank you most especially to my son Keziah who contributed in countless ways throughout the entire project. He gave me ideas and encouragement, tons of technological help—he did all the formatting—and all the beautiful waves are his.

Also, my editor Anita Holladay, who gave so many hours
of expert scrutiny and truly helped to birth this book.

My beta readers: Lisa Personius, Larry Taylor, Tania Forest, Keziah Wesley, Margaret Bartley, Laurel Boucher, Ellen Elizabeth Mae

Others who encouraged me are Molly Clark, Averey Hocker, Matt Hocker, Dani Cutler, Linda Nielsen, Anita Feng, Michael Jaross, Marc Watson, Thea Swanson, Phoebe Morryce, and Jackie Dierksen.

And certainly, the loving support of the Arlington Fiction Writers:
Traci and Peter Harrett, Betsy Diedrick, Brandy Morgan-Davis, Lisa Personius, John Reinier, Keziah Wesley, Larry Taylor, and Franklin Vincenzi.

Love to all of you truly thoughtful people. Your help to me is invaluable
and my thanks are a hundredfold.